TRACKS *of* *our* TEARS

A Family Saga

TRACKS OF OUR
TEARS TRILOGY II

JAMES ALLEN

 FriesenPress

One Printers Way
Altona, MB RoG oBo
Canada

www.friesenpress.com

Copyright © 2024 by Words To Build Upon Holdings Limited
First Edition — 2024

ISBN
978-1-03-915632-6 (Hardcover)
978-1-03-915631-9 (Paperback)
978-1-03-915633-3 (eBook)

1. FICTION, HISTORICAL, WORLD WAR II

Distributed to the trade by The Ingram Book Company

A Dedication

This incredible trilogy that began with *From Promise to Peril* could not have been conceived nor written without the strength and influence of my dearly departed wife, Regina, who has been the love of my life since we first met. We were just seventeen years old in our final year of high school. Sadly, she was taken from us after more than fifty wonderful years together.

Without her silent inspiration guiding me day by day, the journey to tell this story would never have been taken.

On every page, Regina guided my fingers across the keyboard as surely as if she was standing at my shoulder, nudging me on when I had little understanding or knowledge of exactly where I was heading. I am forever grateful to have found Regina and that she chose to share her life with me.

TABLE OF CONTENTS

PREFACE

PREVIOUSLY IN BOOK ONE, *FROM PROMISE TO PERIL - A FAMILY Saga*, the upwardly mobile Landesburg family sells off their modest German dairy farm to seek financial success in late 19th century Berlin, where their son Sigmund eventually graduates from a prestigious medical school. Sigmund's medical practice thrives and together with his wife Marissa, the great granddaughter of Otto von Bismarck, they rise to social prominence.

As a dramatic symbol of his love, Sigmund gifts Marissa with a beautiful, uniquely crafted diamond and sapphire ring, to be passed down through following generations. As their daughter Anna grows up, she is recognized as an intellectual prodigy and is privately tutored with another gifted child, Marta. Together, their deep bond of friendship provides a firm foundation to sustain them throughout their incredible lifetimes.

Marta becomes a world-renowned violin virtuoso with the Berlin Philharmonic Orchestra and graces numerous magnificent stages throughout Nazi occupied Europe and also in America. She and the maestro of the BPO become so influential and popular throughout the world, they are appointed Germany's cultural ambassadors for the state, financed and controlled by Joseph Goebbels and Adolf Hitler.

Following the rise of Nazism throughout the 1930s, the Jewish Anna and gentile Marta find themselves and their families swept into the riptide of history. Nevertheless, Anna and Marta's friendship strengthens their resolve to flourish, despite their vastly different perspectives leading to war in Nazi Germany.

This gripping story traces the Landesburgs through overwhelming obstacles as they face escalating persecution and must struggle to protect their aristocratic family from the tyranny and violence beginning to surround them. Years later when Anna's daughter Pietra is born, Anna's mother, Marissa, passes the amazing ring to Anna, as was always intended.

After the tragic loss of her father and mother, and with the unwavering support and influence of Marta's military family, Anna perseveres to drastic lengths to ensure the long-term safety of her teenaged daughter, Pietra, also a gifted violinist who, under the inspiration given her by her Aunt Marta, is offered safe haven from Juilliard School of Music in New York City, far from the reach of Nazi persecution.

Soon after, the Gestapo begin to brutally enforce the Nazi decrees as part of their *Final Solution* and arrest Jewish professors and students under the charge of insurrection against the state. These prestigious captives include Anna's husband Jacob, a professor of theology at the university. They are sent to Buchenwald Concentration Camp, where Jacob is executed.

As the threat to Anna's family escalates, her son Dietrich who remains in Berlin, is protectively and deviously adopted by Marta and her supportive husband, Klaus, using false documentation to hide Dietrich's Jewish ancestry. Klaus, a high ranking Lieutenant Major and his father, General von Brauchitsch, conspire together to recruit the brilliant and well-qualified Anna into Abwehr, the German Counterintelligence Agency, reporting directly to the general and eventually to Adolf Hitler.

This effective ruse places Anna deep within Abwehr shortly before the outbreak of WWll under a cleverly contrived new identity. Her analytical mind and mathematical skillset, together with her mastery of several foreign languages, make her a valuable and trusted asset of the Third Reich.

During this time, Anna's unique and distinguished talents are soon recognized by her immediate superiors, who have ensured her dedication and allegiance to the Reich by controlling access to her son Dietrich, initially using their protection and secured custody of him as potential leverage against Anna to guarantee her compliance. Her steadfast contributions are profoundly effective, working her way up the chain of command into the inner sanctum of Germany's High Command.

There, with the incredible support of Admiral Canaris and General von Brauchitsch, Anna finds the perfect platform to creatively seize unique opportunities to utilize her divided loyalties, eventually holding the keys to penetrate Hitler's Inner Circle. Using her innate brilliance and significant subversive influence, she navigates perilous waters to seek redemption, to alter the outcome of the war in ways she could never have imagined.

I
BATTLELINES ARE DEFINED

IT WAS LATE AUGUST 1939. NATURE'S GLORIOUS COLORS HAD begun to gradually alter Europe's picturesque landscape. For those graced with a window to peer through and the quiet personal moments to savor them, the peaceful serenity of autumn was time for many to pause for reflective introspection. Anna was not one of those fortunate few.

In less predictable fashion, Hitler was about to change the landscape too, in unimaginable ways that would defy the comprehension of the watching world. It was only days before the German invasion of Poland and much like Hitler's patience, these days were growing noticeably shorter.

Since learning of Hitler's inflexible insistence to put his magnificent war machine into motion, Anna had been thrust into the inner sanctum of Abwehr, Germany's Military Intelligence Unit. Although still adjusting to her new role, it was a position she had earned by her natural affinity for codebreaking and her profound multilingual fluency.

An equally significant asset was her seemingly unwavering loyalty to the Third Reich, however, the seeds of her apparent dedication were not nourished by impassioned belief. Quite to the contrary, her loyalty was rooted in the leverage the Reich held over her.

Anna's appointment to Abwehr by General von Brauchitsch protected her true identity and of course, her Jewish ancestry, which were known only to the general and Admiral Canaris. It was a secret so closely guarded, that if ever disclosed would have fatal consequences not only for Anna, but equally so for the general, the admiral and their families.

In the months leading up to the invasion of Poland, the initial planning of this multi-faceted attack was left mostly to Hitler's closest war-mongering advisors to haggle amongst one another. The Fuhrer was not interested in a consensus of military opinions. Playing politics with his various chiefs of staff was of no long-term interest to him. His strategy was to watch and listen to what they had to offer, and only then would he make the decision best suiting his personal objectives.

Adolf Hitler, a brilliant strategist, had no hesitation to be decisive when he needed to be.

For months the German propaganda machine had been in full gear under Goebbels' capable direction. This untrue and highly provocative propaganda was to assert to the international press the impression the Poles had been conducting a relentless and bloody cleansing against indigenous Germans residing throughout Poland.

These covert attacks would appear to be the work of Polish anti-German saboteurs, furthering the appearance of Polish aggression against Germany. The escalation of existing tensions along the Polish border would provide justification for the German invasion.

With this intent, Supreme Command was given specific orders from the Fuhrer; to delay any formal declaration of war until after launching numerous false flag attacks by Germany... against itself. The tip of the spear was targeted directly at Katowice, which was the heart of the often-disputed, resource rich province of Silesia.

As the days passed, the stakes were never higher for everyone connected to the mission, irrespective of rank. There were multitudes of moving parts requiring focused attention to intricate details. The timing of complicated logistics was critical, as the mobilization of hundreds of thousands of troops were already approaching various points along the border.

Amid these massive troop deployments, Admiral Canaris convened a brief meeting at the behest of General Halder, the Chief of the General Staff. In attendance were General von Brauchitsch, Major Groscurth and Anna.

"Agent Schindler has recently supplied our requisition for Polish uniforms of various ranks, equipment, and identification papers, consistent with Gruppenfuhrer Heidrich's orders. At precisely 06:00

hours tomorrow morning, Operation Himmler will be underway. As agreed, this will consist of seven individual incursions by Naujocks' Brandenburgers. Anna, can you confirm the coded transmission was received precisely as instructed?"

"Yes, Admiral. The draft order was received by Naujocks himself. His team is being deployed as we speak and will be fully operational by 04:00."

Admiral Canaris spoke freely in the secured confines of the boardroom to the trusted few who were within earshot of his personal trepidations.

"With so much at stake, I continue to have serious misgivings dealing with such a dubious group of radicalized misfits. My greatest reservation continues to be the operational methods of these undisciplined personnel. Despite causing general disruption of enemy logistics, they have a penchant for disobeying orders.

"I am uncomfortable with our dependence upon Naujocks' success. The failure of these operations could adversely affect the casualties of our well-trained troops, leaving their fate very much in Naujocks' devious hands. He continually operates entirely outside of our direct command."

"Sir, if I may speak candidly," responded Major Groscurth. The admiral nodded affirmatively. "Gestapo Muller has personally endorsed the involvement of the Brandenburgers for this operation. Is it wise to question his motivations at this late stage?... With all due respect, Admiral."

"That is precisely what I question Major—Naujocks' motivations to serve whom? The Fatherland or Reinhard Heydrich?"

To this point, General von Brauchitsch had remained quiet. As always, his mind was alert and in lockstep with the admiral's apprehensions.

"My advice, Sir, is that we proceed with what is already in motion," he said. "This is not the time for second guessing. It is not a luxury we have been afforded. Naujocks is just a tool of war. However, I completely agree we must continue to be mindful of both Heydrich and Mullers' mixed loyalties, to the Fuhrer, and more significantly, to each other."

*****

On August 25th, one day before Hitler's planned invasion of Poland, Benito Mussolini, the First Marshal of the Italian Empire, notified Hitler about the status of Italy's armed forces being seriously under-supplied on their southern border, a critical weakness Britain would surely exploit in the event of the outbreak of war. Il Duce needed to be forthright with the Fuhrer despite the fear of incurring his wrath, to urgently deliver the necessary arms and munitions to fortify Italy's border.

Hitler conferred only with Joachim von Ribbentrop, Hitler's Reich Foreign Minister. He had been sitting with Hitler and heard the entire conversation between Il Duce and the Fuhrer. When the call ended, von Ribbentrop took a deep breath and paused to light a cigarette. He was unflappable and the Fuhrer could read his body language. The minister had earned the respect of his Fuhrer and was allowed a moment to ponder his response.

"I can redirect the necessary armaments and transport from other operations of a less urgent nature. I will personally review the logistics to determine the required escalation of troops to put the wheels in motion."

"And the time to complete this escalation, by your estimate, Minister?" Hitler frowned in anticipation of the answer.

"Our realistic objective should be within a week, perhaps five or six days."

"Excellent… five days it is! We will postpone the invasion until August 31st."

"Let me stipulate, five days to deliver troops and armaments, Mein Fuhrer, however, full deployment would take Il Duce another few, and very long days to complete. We must expect as much."

"Agreed. Notify Minister Goebbels immediately to confirm the short delay. He can deal with Himmler's inevitable complaints personally."

*****

The battlelines for war were predictably becoming more clearly defined. Hitler's last-minute deferral of the invasion, although only a few days, had to be immediately re-orchestrated. The wide range of emotions within the offices of Abwehr, barely controlled by High

Command, were to the point of fraying as tension and anxiety mounted with each passing hour. The delay meant moving their military juggernaut into a holding position for an additional five days.

When Reichsfuhrer Heinrich Himmler was informed by Joseph Goebbels that the August 26th date of invasion would necessarily be postponed until August 31st, Himmler was beside himself with frustration.

"If you think for a moment that hundreds of thousands of ground troops could remain undetected, less than thirty miles west of the border for another five days than originally agreed upon, you are very much misinformed!" barked the Reichsfuhrer to Joseph Goebbels.

"You of all people must know this, Herr Goebbels! With every passing day we delay, we jeopardize the appearance of retaliation against the Poles. Has the Fuhrer been made aware of this delay?"

"The order to postpone came from the Fuhrer himself just minutes ago. Von Ribbentrop and I agree with his decision. As you are also aware, it appears negotiations with Stalin are about to be finalized, leaving us the opportunity to fully address Mussolini's insistent request that Italy's preparedness for war be completed prior to commencing the invasion of Poland."

"Has Admiral Raeder been informed?"

"No, Reichsfuhrer. The order to stand down has just been received from command. I suspect the Admiral will also be displeased."

"Let us be blessed with only his displeasure, as you so calmly expressed. I know he will have a major burr up his ass. He will want someone's head on a platter, particularly Il Duce's!"

The Reichsfuhrer quickly redirected his comments to General Oster, still venting his anger toward everyone in the room. "Can we contact our covert operations in time to hold their present positions? This delay is badly timed. Why was no prior notice given for Christ's sake?"

"Sir, we are confident we can communicate with most of the teams directly, but I have concerns about two of the missions already under deep cover. We can inform Naujocks, but he is the only one on the ground with the authority and the contacts to do so. He cannot risk breaking radio silence now. An extraction at this point in time is not a practical option," advised Oster.

"Very well. Do what you can... Shit! Any team not standing down will be at the mercy of the Poles and without support until after the invasion begins. I doubt there will be anything left of them by that time. The perils of war I suppose... at least their usefulness will have served our purposes. Major Groscurth, I insist you handle this matter personally with Naujocks... don't take any shit from him! Secure channels only. See to it immediately, Major!" With a snap of his heels, Major Groscurth acknowledged the order and exited the boardroom hastily.

*****

If there was tension in High Command, it was even more demonstrable on the ground. As General Oster had cautioned, two of the Brandenburger missions near Katowicz could not be notified to stand down. During these covert attacks, saboteurs burned down a house and several Germans were killed in the ensuing melee; a civilian woman and her companion were needlessly, shot to death; all these deaths to properly stage the scene.

Shortly thereafter, a railway station in Smolniki was attacked. In retaliation, Poles ransacked and destroyed the offices of a German newspaper, killing a civilian in the process. On the surface, these incidents were only minor border tensions that were to be expected at this difficult time.

Just as the midnight hour was approaching, a wireless transmission was received from Albert Naujocks informing Abwehr of the few skirmishes along the Polish border, which had by this point, already been carried out. Naujocks knew the perilous situation to which his men were now exposed. He was a calculating and frightening character, who did not balk at the precariousness of his mission. His unwavering confidence was contagious among those he commanded.

Naujocks reported stating, "Luck has been in our favor, Major. Relatively minor skirmishes are now escalating on both sides of the border. Had your orders been four hours later, we would have had a shitstorm of grief. The damage would have been irreversible; however, it was minimized. I doubt it will be given much notice by the Poles."

Despite mounting global suspicions, the Poles were duped by Germany's deceitful ruse, the scale of which was still thought by Hitler to be a guarded secret. In the face of unified global demands for Germany to stand down at the very precipice of war, German

High Command remained obstinate but refused any suggestion the secrecy of the final date of invasion may have been compromised.

*****

A few days later, the British Royal Navy requested the Polish Navy send three of its destroyers, the *Storm*, the *Lightning*, and the *Thunder* to sea, before the inevitable commencement of the invasion of the port city of Gdansk.

In anticipation of the looming German invasion against Westerplatte, which defended Gdansk, the British feared the ships would quickly succumb to the overwhelming power of the German Navy and the Luftwaffe. Sinking the ships and killing the crewmembers would be costly and unnecessarily wasteful.

The British request for Poland to harbor the ships at Edinburgh, Scotland made sense. Despite the fact Polish forces at Westerplatte would be massively overwhelmed, particularly without the support of the three destroyers currently stationed there, the Polish Navy agreed with the Royal Navy's request.

On the night of August 29th, they entered the Baltic Sea from the port of Gdansk. Their families prayed their passage would be unimpeded, as they departed the safety of the harbor under cover of darkness. Only a skeleton crew manned the ships as the *Storm* maneuvered methodically, serving as lead escort for the accompanying destroyers.

Twenty-four hours after departure, tensions were mounting when the Polish fleet cleared the Ore Sond waterway to face the open expanse of the Kattegat Strait.

In no time, the tight formation had passed just north of Grena, Denmark when a German cruiser was detected trailing the convoy from a safe, non-threatening distance heading north. The north end of Kattegat Strait separated Denmark and Sweden by a mere fifty-miles wide corridor of ice-water flowing from the north. The intended course from that point was south-west to the North Sea.

"*Komandor*, we've had that German cruiser continuing two miles south of us since they picked us up near Grena. Radar confirms it is not in pursuit but holding a steady course at thirty-five knots."

Komandor Stankiewicz knew their small fleet would attract the attention of the Germans, but the Poles were in no position to engage, nor did they have reason to; neither did the Germans. Although war was imminent, no formal declaration had yet been made. Stankiewicz was a seasoned veteran who had a reputation for keeping his poise.

"Maintain present course. When we pass Laeso Island, prepare to adjust course ten degrees north, north-east. Plot our course through Skagerrak directly toward Oslo. Let's see if those bastards tip their hand or bugger off. Maintain present speed, Lieutenant."

"I'll see to it, Sir."

Two hours passed uneventfully. Nothing changed until two German reconnaissance planes appeared within minutes of the departure of the trailing German cruiser. "As I suspected, they'll monitor our progress as long as they need to determine our destination. If we break west toward the U.K. now, the Luftwaffe will be on us before we know what hit us. We'll be dead in the water if we try to run for it."

Without deliberation, Stankiewicz ordered, "Set that course for Oslo and hope they lose interest in us. They're not stupid enough to escalate to war over this, at least not yet!"

With intent to deceive German surveillance, the three ships veered off their intended course and headed north in the direction of Norway. It was uncertain how far the reconnaissance aircraft would escort them off their intended destination, but Stankiewicz had no alternative.

In a few hours, they were almost within sight of the channel to *Oslofjorden* when the seaplanes finally took the bait and returned to the mainland. Within minutes, Komandor Stankiewicz made a difficult but immediate choice to break hard to port to re-establish his originally intended course.

"Take us to maximum speed Lieutenant. Make a run for the open sea. Now is the time for prayer!"

Maintaining a very tight formation, the ships continued successfully into the North Sea, directly to the port of Edinburg. By so doing, they avoided certain destruction or capture by the vastly superior German Navy and Air Force. They would later play an active supportive role throughout the rest of the war in support of the Royal Navy.

German command misinterpreted the departure of the destroyers from the Bay of Gdansk, further confirming to them Poland and Britain were unaware of the timing of Germany's invasion. Gdansk was obviously a high value target.

Hitler reasoned that evacuating the bulk of the Polish Navy from Gdansk was profoundly counter to mounting a capable defense of the Polish port. Hence, to his mind, the crucial secrecy of the invasion remained intact.

2

NOWHERE TO RUN

IN THE STILL OF THE NIGHT ON AUGUST 31ST, 1939, TWENTY members of Alfred Naujocks' Brandenburger squads staged an armed attack on an undefended radio station. It was located in Gleiwitz, several miles inside the German border and was regarded by the Germans as being a soft and unsuspecting target. Due to the relevance of this specific mission, Naujock's men were fully prepared had it been otherwise.

Dressed as Polish anti-German saboteurs, the attackers were unimpeded as they moved stealthily under cover of darkness to take positions in the trees and deep brush. The tree line surrounding the expanse of open field left the radio tower fully exposed against any potential threat against it. Naujocks was personally directing the staging of this attack.

"Three of us will directly approach the office; I don't expect any resistance. Only one car is parked outside. D.T. and Pascovic! Take the north flank and you two numb-nuts approach from the south. Perimeter is secured so anyone else stupid enough to join the party gets dead, understand? This should be a cakewalk... *Move out!*"

The deployment was briskly and silently carried out. There would be no resistance, but this was a radio station, and as far as Naujocks was aware, still broadcasting live. Any hint of the approach could immediately alert the occupants of the small building, raising the possibility of an immediate broadcast warning potentially jeopardizing the staging of their false flag attack.

Naujocks was followed closely by his two accomplices as they silently crept up the concrete steps leading to the main entrance.

Once in position, he forcefully slammed his heavy boot just below the locked door handle and the frame immediately gave way, sending a burst of wooden splinters into the room. The action was to intentionally leave evidence of a forced entrance.

Although fully prepared for some token resistance, the offices were surprisingly unoccupied. Perhaps the parked car and the interior office lights were intended to create the impression the station was operating through the late-night hours to discourage attempted intrusions. Nevertheless, Naujocks' team had with them several human props of their own to create the intended effect of their ruse.

It was time to signal a nondescript panel truck waiting near the tree line to approach the station entrance. Its cargo would soon be revealed. Three steady flickers of Naujocks' flashlight to the driver indicated the all-clear.

Franciszek Honiok was a Silesian German, a well-known German farmer sympathetic to the Polish cause. The Gestapo had arrested him the previous day to play an important role in this incredible ruse. Still gagged and bound, he was pulled from the back of the truck by two men. He would become the first casualty of WWII.

"Get his ass outa there! Com'on you old bastard, let's go!" Naujocks barked. "This won't take but a minute."

Dressed as a Polish saboteur, Honiok was forcibly seated at the desk and given a lethal injection, forever silencing his muffled screaming and despair. In the seconds following, one of the men shot him several times, intentionally splattering his blood about the chair, the desk, and the wall behind him.

Within seconds of the ghastly murder, Naujocks activated the microphone and in Polish, read aloud the anti-German message Anna and the Admiral had prepared. Upon completion, the team destroyed the radio equipment and ransacked the offices. "Good enough. Get the rest o' them others and position 'em where they're suppose ta be."

Them others were prisoners taken from the Dachau Concentration Camp, who were drugged to render them semi-conscious; considered easier to orchestrate their positioning before execution. With uniforms supplied by Agent Schindler, a few were dressed and equipped as Germans, and others as Polish militia, like the prior attacks of the 26th of August.

Once set into position, they were immediately slaughtered by machinegun fire, their faces disfigured to the extent identification could not be confirmed, forcing the authorities to rely on the phony identification supplied by Abwehr. It was a gruesome and horrific blood bath. In less than ten minutes of the initial attack, Naujocks' men left the site precisely as ordered.

This operation was code-named *Konserve* (canned goods) by Himmler and was used for numerous other incursions occurring that day near the border to exaggerate the aggressive mistreatment inflicted upon Germany by the Poles. These staged attacks were conducted by German forces upon themselves as a guise, to fan the flames of years of disputed territory between Poland and Germany.

Hitler seized full advantage of the false flag incidents not retracted when the main invasion was temporarily delayed, as well as those carried out by Naujocks' men on August 31st. They would serve as the final straw, being ignited for the purpose of justifying Adolf Hitler's decision to invade Poland.

Later that same day, Hitler used these premeditated and fake Polish attacks against Germany when speaking to the Reichstag to justify his decision to invade Poland. He had already confided to his staff ten days prior that German credibility was irrelevant when all is said and done. To his mind, no one will care whether the victor told the truth.

*****

Under the command of Admiral Canaris, Abwehr's role received the recognition it deserved from Reichsfuhrer Himmler. His emissary personally delivered the deserving platitudes, most of which were gratefully received by many inside Abwehr. Secretly, Admiral Canaris was not one of them.

The false-flag missions accomplished Hitler and Göring's objectives. Whether world opinion believed their reasoning or not was no longer, if ever, relevant to Hitler. The deed was done. It was assumed by High Command this great deception provided an auspicious beginning to a war the rest of Europe had done its best to avoid.

In confidence, Admiral Canaris privately addressed General von Brauchitsch, Major Groscurth, General Oster, and the recently appointed Anna. All had been struggling with the fraudulent and undignified manner in which the provocative false attacks had to be orchestrated. It was the proper time to address the ambivalence the inner circle was experiencing, an unspeakable topic outside these confined and fully secured premises.

The admiral began, "I take no pride in what we have accomplished these past few days. Our complicity in this deception deeply pains me. Now we will be painted by the same dark brush that has always tainted the Fuhrer's punitive obsessions: equally guilty, history will say of us.

"For our forces not to respond to these inflammatory attacks, Germany would appear to be weak-kneed and unwilling to retaliate against the Poles. This ruse has finally provided the dubious time to mobilize forces deep into Polish territory through multiple border crossings of high value, and undeservingly so," Admiral Canaris lamented.

"If I may, Admiral," General von Brauchitsch interjected, "I feel the need to reiterate what we have discussed many times before, Sir. We share your pain, but the beast was already out of its cage, and the chance to keep him caged has passed. I strongly believe these incidents should serve to bolster our determination to do everything in our power to affect positive change going forward. Let us proceed with rejuvenated spirit to devour the beast, one bite at a time. We are in the position to do it, as long as we choose our points of attack very selectively."

Major Groscurth also began to disclose his pragmatic insights by adding, "Present circumstances are our only priority. The incursions have given the Fuhrer what he has long desired. It is up to us to see his orders through, and with meticulous attention to their degree of importance in the current scheme of things. That is where our individual tasks should be focused until the new norm is firmly established."

In summation, General Oster tried valiantly to untangle the situation confronting them. "It seems we are in a proverbial catch-22. On the one hand, our Fuhrer's initial deceptions have been completed and now the task before us is to manage and advise on the fall-out from the attacks.

"Conversely, we all agree our long-term mandate to subvert him remains strong. This is just not the time to shift our focus from our current military obligations. We are all at cross purposes. It won't be the first time, nor will it be the last. Let's get about our business, till we meet again under a different set of circumstances."

Admiral Canaris was buoyed by his staff's lucid clarifications of their own perspectives, except for one that continued to matter. "Anna, you are a trusted and respected voice we are anxious to hear. Based upon what has transpired here today, I trust you better understand the magnitude of our constant dilemma."

"Certainly, Admiral. Gentlemen, clearly you are all under tremendous pressure to instruct the officers under your command to carry out whatever must be done through the military chain of command. It is your obligation to do so. However, I am not involved with the chain of command outside of this office. Neither do I possess your specific expertise to carry out complex military maneuvers.

"However, where I excel, is looking at the grand scheme of things from a technical and logistical perspective, seeing opportunities that miss the naked eye; ones that could serve our own common interests in the name of humanity. In the coming weeks, I will research and analyze various potential scenarios as the course of war unfolds. I am well equipped to determine the viability of assignments and to calculate applicable risk assessments.

"I assure you the process will yield interesting possibilities. There are countless missions I intend to thoroughly investigate. I will submit only the most opportunistic ones for your consideration from a military point of view.

"I am confident your time will not be unnecessarily diverted from your normal military duties, unless and until each of you decide my strategies are in line with your objectives. That will be entirely within your domain. In the meantime, the exercise will help me learn more about what you are expecting from me. Is that a workable objective for each of you?"

*****

Before daybreak on September 1st, the German invasion against Poland's borders began with the attack against Westerplatte, the armed Polish garrison at the port of Gdansk. As the Poles and the British had previously acknowledged, this was the most prized Polish seaport on the Baltic Sea; hence their hesitancy to evacuate the small protective fleet of destroyers just two days prior to the invasion. Nevertheless, the port's tactical significance to Poland could not be overstated.

The Polish Corridor, as it was named, had been a strategic objective of Germany. Their eventual control of the port of Gdansk would enable the unfettered establishment of German supply lines and military reinforcements directly into Warsaw, the very heart of Poland.

It was a massive, coordinated series of strikes designed to quickly overwhelm the drastically outnumbered Polish Army defending the Hel Peninsula. Approximately 2,800 Polish troops held the garrison against the invading German land forces, who were supported by the relentless pounding of German battleships and submarine fire from the Bay of Gdansk. It would become known as the *Battle of Hel*.

Simultaneously from the first day of the invasion, more than one and a half million German soldiers had been deployed to multiple points of attack. Major coordinated assaults stretched from the city of Szczecin at the tip of the north-western Polish border, and south to Kostrzyn, at over 150 kilometers distance.

In these moments of supreme domination, the influx of the amassing invaders completely overtook office buildings with brute force, killing unarmed office civilians and shopkeepers, with no retribution. The immediate and unprovoked act of war was intended to demonstrate intentional brutality to underscore the senselessness of resistance.

Residents and families huddled together in fear, many with hands held high to signify there was no willingness to challenge these mostly teenaged troops. Diverted looks of acceptance by the submissive civilians could not clearly identify in these young boys the adrenaline rush they must have experienced in the moments of their own inflicted terror. Direct eye contact with them could be perceived as defiance. Retaliation would be exacted with punishing results. It was an instinctive reaction.

In a matter of hours, the occupation had swollen the limits of the central business districts in both Szczecin and Kostrzyn by the sheer magnitude of troops and artillery. Critical vantage points throughout both cities were simultaneously scoped out by senior officers, with no discernable reluctance or hesitancy. The invasion had been well rehearsed and was orchestrated in every gruesome detail.

Bridge after bridge, city after city, they fell like dominos, providing German forces unfettered progress all the way to Warsaw. Progress was so rapid on this newly annexed territory, the logistics of supply lines had to be reconsidered from the premeditated plans of the Nazi war rooms. Nothing and no one were standing up to this incredibly powerful assault. Within days, the German advance was well ahead of schedule. The race to Warsaw was in top gear.

*****

Since the dawning of the first day, the focus of the German forces was to intimidate and crush any resistance they encountered. By doing so, they were able to fortify their stronghold quickly, leaving no ambiguity about their intentions. Their target had always been Warsaw.

In the wake of the German advance toward the capital city, from every direction save the east, any remaining Polish military personnel continued to retreat and reposition daily, trying desperately to focus on protecting what remained of their capital city after the aerial bombing attacks it had endured several days before. Without additional support, the city would be lost.

The German forces efficiently tightened the circle they had created around their prize. In response, Polish troops driven from the border cities and others further inland that had previously fallen, raced toward Warsaw to join the fight. It was not only the strategic foundation of the entire country, but also the most sacred symbol of Polish history and tradition.

Despite facing only minimal ongoing resistance, Hitler vindictively ordered his Commander in Chief of the Luftwaffe, Hermann Göring, to further escalate additional bombing runs, this time focusing their attacks not only upon civilian and infrastructure targets, but specifically upon the very heart and soul of Warsaw's remains: the sacred historic section of the original city within which the Warsaw Royal Castle stood.

The city had already fallen but the historical significance of Hitler's ruthless act of cruelty was only intended to further denigrate the spirit of its people. The day would come to be known as *Bloody Sunday*. It was a clear and violent message from the Germans, stinging the spirit of their captors in ways they could never have imagined.

Much like a two-fisted bully in a peaceful schoolyard, the damage this bully inflicted was far beyond black eyes and broken teeth; it was a scar on the German republic itself, forever disfiguring them throughout the pages of history. Memories of this reprehensible act of war inflicted upon the Polish people would never be erased.

Any remaining Polish forces had been completely focused on the advancing Germans from the north, from the west, and from the south. Now, the Russian forces approached from the east. The desperation and futility of many Polish civilians eventually led to mass suicides, as the drawing of one's final breath seemed to offer the only remaining hope of spiritual peace.

*****

Meanwhile 180 miles to the north, the Battle of Gdansk continued. Here on the peninsula, Polish resistance was far more resilient than German forces had originally anticipated. Nevertheless, after several weeks of relentless pounding, the valiant Polish defensive lines on the Hel Peninsula were finally breached. With no possibility of escape, the remaining Polish fighters were forced to surrender on October 15th.

The way to Warsaw was now open from the north, other than intermittent and isolated pockets of ineffective resistance. When the last fighters finally capitulated, their defeat fully exposed the soft northern underbelly of all points south of the Bay of Gdansk.

3
TOUGH CHOICES

♂

BY 1940, MOST GERMAN CIVILIANS WERE NAÏVE TO THE realities of war, particularly the deceitful politics triggering the invasion. The public widely believed what they read in the newspapers; that Germany's military intervention was justified, and even necessary to the economic and political stability of Europe. For many of these people at this early stage of the war, life carried on much as before.

Dietrich was the son of the Jewish Anna. Nevertheless, his adoption application by Klaus and Marta was unimpeded. In times of war, many orphaned children lost their family providers and needed humanitarian support from other well-meaning families. Dietrich's paperwork and supporting documentation asserted a Roman Catholic ancestry and aroused no hint of fabrication. It spoke to the power of General von Brauchitsch' influence within Abwehr.

The adoption itself was a mere formality to complete. The customary registration and fastidious investigation of racial purity however, typically required for an adolescent's admission to the Hitler Youth, could have been a much more difficult hurdle. Of course, the documentation was more than sufficient but nevertheless, due to the privileges accorded the general's reputation, the process was entirely bypassed and was thankfully given an unequivocal green light for his grandson's acceptance.

A potentially difficult task remaining for the general however, was convincing his daughter-in-law, Marta, to support Dietrich joining the rank and file of the Hitler Youth. By this point, more than ten million male children had enrolled in the movement: more than sixty percent of all German born male adolescents between fourteen and eighteen years of age.

Despite the protestations of many parents who objected strenuously to the conscription of their own sons, the penalty for noncompliance made it impossible for their sons to graduate from high school and further, denied these children the ability to attend university or find meaningful employment when high school was completed. Parents were therefore compelled to relinquish control of their sons to the state.

Most definitely, the general's adopted grandson was expected to be a more than willing applicant; to enthusiastically stand proudly one day beside the general's biological grandson, Manfred.

By this time, Manfred had matured into a confident and supremely dedicated conscript of the German military. Throughout his service in the Hitler Youth, he took his oath seriously and continued to distinguish himself through his sheer determination to serve the Fatherland. His life's dream was to be assigned to flight school to serve in the Luftwaffe.

Together, his father Klaus, and grandfather, General von Brauchitsch, considered him to be a shining example of Germany's purest Aryan heritage; a product perfectly shaped in his physical and mental conditioning. Their pride in his accomplishments at this early stage of his life exceeded the expectations of his family's military heritage. It was a new beginning in young Manfred's life that was pre-ordained.

As to be expected, Marta saw her son in a different light. Although her pride in him was effusive, and no less genuine than his influential family role models, she was plagued by where his unquestionable dedication would take him. She often experienced nightmares, replete with dark and destructive images that awaited him with open jaws of despair. These frightening images haunted Marta, often to the point of macabre obsession.

She kept her deepest personal fears very much to herself. This was not a subject she could share with the general or Klaus. Invariably, they would most certainly chastise her for seeding doubt and worry on Manfred's pathway to glory. There was no place for such negative feelings on the course of his journey forward.

Instead, she tried to focus her mind on the predicament facing Dietrich. Marta was understandably torn about this moral and religious dilemma. She considered it to be a terrible injustice inflicted upon Dietrich personally, and an insult to his Jewish heritage. The general knew Marta's serious reservations. It had been discussed between them in the past but had not been sufficiently resolved. The day had now arrived for them to do so.

The general was uncommonly tense and not his usual relaxed self with Marta on this day. He sat uncomfortably on the edge of the sofa when he confirmed to his daughter-in-law there would be no justification for Dietrich's exemption.

"I understand your conflict about this matter Marta, but his enrolment cannot be delayed without arousing unavoidable suspicions. Must I remind you that every young German of Aryan descent is expected to enroll, with or without parental consent? You already know most of this, Marta."

Gradually he shifted himself deeper into the back of the sofa, reclining briefly to take a deep breath waiting for her next retort. Without uttering a word, but showing considerable dismay, Marta rose to pour her exasperated father-in-law and herself another Scotch. It was only a minor diversion to allow them to consider their options before she responded, although there were none to ponder.

"Just to be clear Walther, you know how very much I respect and admire what you have done for Anna's family, and what it has meant to me personally. But Dietrich's participation in the movement is something we only considered in passing. Although we both knew this day would come, I agree it can no longer be avoided. Dietrich has already been asked repeatedly at school why he is not registered and is already facing ostracism from his friends for not being enrolled."

The general thoughtfully responded. "These were only relatively insignificant considerations when we contrived his adoption proceedings, but you are quite correct about delaying any longer. It would only prove counterproductive to what we have already achieved for him. Considering the situation, how do you think he will handle it?" Walther asked.

"Manfred has spoken with Dietrich about the brigade, but only tangentially. Manny is an ardent leader within his squadron. He's well respected among both his peers and his commanders. Dietrich already looks up to him and I know Manny will be a pillar of strength for him.

"Klaus, Manny, and I will handle this from here. Heaven knows you should not be investing your time with these unnecessary preoccupations. We must do what must be done. That's all there is to it, I'm afraid."

"Thank you, Marta. I appreciate your support on this sensitive issue. Frankly, I expected more pushback from you, but I'm so thankful you did not." The general stood and embraced Marta, kissing her cheek tenderly.

"I really must get back to the barracks. I have a very full day tomorrow and will not likely be able to see you for some time. I just won't have the time or focus to deal with this matter unless it becomes necessary for me to intervene.

"Richard will initiate the registration process on Dietrich's behalf with Artur Axmann's office. He is the newly appointed *Reichsjugendführer*. I was involved in his appointment, but I think it best if I do not draw his attention to any of this now. Dietrich should not be treated any differently than the others. I hope you and he will understand."

"Of course, Walther. I love you as always and thank you for all you do for us. Please stay safe, I beg you."

*****

Within days of Marta's discussion with the general, she, Klaus, and Manfred sat together over dinner with Dietrich. Manny and Marta had already prepared the groundwork with him, and Dietrich was anxious for Klaus to speak his mind directly. He held Klaus in very high esteem. It would be a knowledgeable and insightful opinion Dietrich needed to hear.

As dinner plates were being cleared, Klaus opened the subject. He had very little time for small talk, no matter how sensitive the situation.

"I understand you and the family have previously talked about your participation in the Hitler Youth. We find ourselves at a serious crossroad and understand how conflicted you must be feeling right now, Dietrich. We are sympathetic to the position in which we have placed you. However, it is time we talk about your, and our predicament, being mindful that you continue to remain safe from the persecution you would be facing without my father's intervention."

"You are not telling me anything I have not previously acknowledged to you both. I mean no disrespect, I assure you. I carefully considered this situation over the past few months, and I consider myself fortunate to remain out of harm's way because of what your family has done for mine. The issue I find most disturbing about the Hitler Youth, however, is the racism it actively promotes. That is what I am struggling with."

"That's understandable, but unfortunately it is also unavoidable. However, there is much more to the Youth Movement than its underlying racism. Although our family has our own strong opinions against that specific aspect of the movement, we cannot possibly imagine it from your family perspective.

"Without registering for enrollment, your education and prospects for the future will be sacrificed. That is an unfortunate and unavoidable fact not to be overlooked. Perhaps we should focus more upon the benefits it will provide to establish a sound future for you."

To this point Marta and Manny simply watched and listened attentively. Neither were intent on interrupting. Since Marta and Klaus' separation, Klaus visited only rarely. He related well with the boys despite his extended absences and their admiration for him had never diminished. It was a conversation both young men were eager to share.

Manny had stayed quiet, until he saw his father glance toward him, directly but discreetly, to silently suggest this was an appropriate time for him to offer his own perspective.

"You know there are many amazing things my friends and I really enjoyed since our enrolment. For me, it was the physical conditioning, the military discipline and training I needed to be granted admission to the Luftwaffe. It's what I always wanted, and this training enabled me to achieve that."

"But I have no military aspirations, Manny. I have seen too much violence in my life already," Dietrich confessed.

Klaus picked up on his son's lead. "You know, the military and fitness training the movement provides is not the whole story. It can also serve as a steppingstone to many other opportunities as well. We need analysts, mathematicians, psychologists, doctors in all areas of expertise, many professions not directly involved with violence and combat.

"You are a very intelligent young man, Dietrich, with tremendous opportunities before you. You are very much like your mother. If you set your mind to do something, you will always distinguish yourself.

"Furthermore, myself and my father have the influence to groom you for whatever career you ultimately decide to follow. These doors will open for you, of this I am certain, but they are one hundred percent dependent upon your enrolment in the Youth Brigade. What matters most however, is not what *I* think, it is what *you* think, Dietrich."

An earnest silence ensued, not to be broken by anyone other than Dietrich. Enough was already said and continuing to push harder would be unfair to him. He needed time to absorb Klaus' reassurance, knowing now the ultimate final decision would be his own.

"What you have said makes good sense and as always, you have appealed to my better judgement. You know I will do as you ask and I assure you that I will make you proud of what I intend to accomplish." Dietrich was an articulate young man, and his words confirmed he had his mother's strong resolve.

"You never disappoint our family Dietrich, and consistently manage to exceed our expectations of you. Your maturity and reasoning are most impressive."

"Thank you, Klaus. I know of no one stronger than my mother, nor more opinionated than my father, bless his soul. I see both in me, but I have learned this can be a deadly combination. The challenge for me is to temper my resolve to survive these times, by doing what I must."

Dietrich took a reflective moment to pause before continuing. "Mother once told me *compromise is not a weakness, it is a skill to be considered when other options are not reasonable.* I interpret that to mean this moment will test the true measure of my character.

"I believe it will not be dampened by the necessary compromises I must make at this time in my life; much as Mother has adapted to her circumstances. We are *cut from the same cloth,* as my papa used to say. We both have the resolve he did to remain who we once were. I will not disappoint you, nor my mother. However, I have but one request."

"Certainly, son." Klaus replied. "Anything you need."

"I need to know Mother will not be aware of this matter. Quite frankly, I don't know how she would react to my decision. But I do know I don't want to deal with it right now, or even if I ever see her again, the good Lord willing."

"I know your mother well, Dietrich, since before you were born. She and Marta became closer than sisters at a very young age and have remained so to this day. You will do well by your heritage young man."

Reassuringly Klaus placed his hand on Dietrich's shoulder. "You must remain confident, Dietrich. You will see her again soon, I promise you. I see an amazing future ahead of you and I am determined she will continue to play an important role in it. You have my word I will do everything in my power to make it happen."

4

The Mentor Finds the Protégé

It was early spring, 1940. Pietra Friedman was approaching her eighteenth birthday. She was a six-year-old child prodigy, discovered by Juilliard School of Music at the well-publicized annual *Nationals* competition in Berlin. Her much-celebrated natural gift had continued to blossom since that time until, at the tender age of thirteen, it was the perfect opportunity to be whisked away by her grandparents to America to escape the Jewish persecution in Berlin that persisted to the present day.

Her painful separation from her younger brother, Dietrich, and her mother, Anna, was the price she had to pay for her freedom and safety. Since her defection in 1934, and despite being separated from her family to be nurtured by Juilliard School and her legal guardians, her love of the violin totally consumed and fulfilled her in ways she could not have imagined.

It was a dedicated commitment she willfully embraced and although there were numerous sacrifices she had to accept, she adapted well to her growing fame and public recognition. Pietra had defined herself as more than just an unforeseen artist of growing international repute. As a young musical talent, she quickly learned to accept her rightful place among the adult contemporaries of the time. The world could no longer regard her musical gift as being *amazing... for a child*. She found this qualification very limiting and unfair.

Karen Liu was an outstanding talent as well, having left China when her parents emigrated to America. As a renowned cellist, Karen and Pietra had much more than music in common. They had been studying together for over three years and their common bond had become a sisterhood, something missing from both of their young lives; Karen because she was an only child with two professional career parents, and Pietra because of the estrangement from her family in Germany.

The daily practice regimen placed demands on every enrolled student, many of whom had been granted bursaries and various scholarships to varying degrees. Excellence was the minimum standard that would perpetuate the generosity of numerous benefactors over the long term. However, the threshold of qualification was a moving target, the bar being continuously raised with each passing year. The competition for bursaries and scholarships was fierce within the student body.

"Let's escape for a few hours, Pietra. The quartet has had a productive week and I think we all earned some fun time this weekend. What do you think, are you with us?" Karen asked excitedly.

"I don't see why not. Let's meet downstairs in the main vestibule in an hour or so. You call Lynda and I'll speak to Penny. I know she was planning to go home this weekend, but I hope she can defer her departure till tomorrow morning. I just need to freshen up a bit. See you shortly!"

Pietra climbed the stairs to the second floor. Karen was right, they had earned a break now and then. Both had made such a strong commitment to their music, and to one another. Their progress these past weeks provided a grand feeling of self-satisfaction and accomplishment, each of them inspiring the other.

As she exited the stairwell and entered the mutedly lit hallway, there, by her room was her instructor, Professor Kuzmicz, sliding something under the door. She took him quite by surprise. He was startled initially but was eager to share some wonderful news.

"Ah, Pietra. There you are! I thought I had missed you. I just assumed you had already left for your aunt and uncle's home for the weekend." A genuine smile creased his face indicating he was indeed, delighted about something.

"No, I'm not leaving until tomorrow. What's all the excitement about, Professor?" Pietra enquired.

"Rather than tell you now, I just slid the announcement under your door. I am thrilled to share it with you, though. I would enjoy seeing your reaction if I may?"

"Yes, of course. I must say you have me at a loss."

Pietra eagerly unlocked her door and ushered her still smiling friend into her sitting area. It was a modest room, as to be expected, but this old building served the students reasonably well, however everything was dimly lit, and every room was painted a light-brown color with well-worn matching floorboards. The atmosphere was often so dingy and faded, totally uninspiring to say the least. Clearly creativity and inspiration were not to be drawn from the lackluster décor; evidently, it was expected to be well ingrained in the spirit, deep within these incredibly gifted students.

The professor stooped to retrieve the letter before taking a seat. He was giddy as a young schoolboy.

"My, my Professor! I've never seen you like this before. I must say your enthusiasm has my fingers trembling with anticipation." Pietra fumbled only briefly and gently tore the edge of the envelope to reveal not so much a letter, but a beautifully gilded invitation in lavishly scripted lettering. It was the first time she had received anything so thoughtfully crafted. As impressed as she was with this marvelous presentation, the message was even more profound.

The Shubert Theater
Home of the Metropolitan Opera

225 West 44th Street
Manhattan, New York.

The New York Philharmonic Orchestra together with the Metropolitan Opera humbly request the honor of your acceptance to grace our stage as our special guest performers on the 11th day of May 1940 for the presentation of Mozart's

"Le Nozze di Figaro."

Introducing

Juilliard String Quartet
Led by Miss Pietra Friedman, First Violin

Supported by Miss Lynda Gottfried and Miss Penelope
Anderson, Violas, and Miss Karen Liu, Cello

Mozart: String Quartet no. 19 in C major (Dissonance)

*"Oh, my goodness, Professor! Is this really happening to us? Do the girls
know of this yet?"* Pietra's eyes were glistening with pure joy. It was an
incredible moment.

"I only just received this by personal delivery. I learned about the
invitation three days ago, but I was sworn to secrecy. But no, the
ladies have not been informed. I am so very proud of each of you!"

"Can we tell them together? We are all having dinner about
6:30 this evening. Perhaps you could join us and help celebrate this
accomplishment for Juilliard! What do you think, Professor?" Pietra
was beaming with excitement.

"Are you certain I wouldn't be intruding? Perhaps I could join you
for a small glass of champagne befitting the occasion."

"That would be lovely! We're gathering downstairs in about an
hour. See you there!"

When the professor departed, Pietra's mind raced at the very
thought of sharing this special moment with the young ladies of
the ensemble, and of course her family and Aunt Marta. Though
she never forgot about her mother, Aunt Emilie and Gertrude, she
understood little about where they were, or for that matter if they
would ever find each other again. The very thought of celebrating this
precious moment without them would forever be tarnished by their
mysterious circumstances.

She reflected on her last communication with her mother, the
letter informing her of her grandparents' sudden passing, and shortly
thereafter, the news of her dear father's death. Her only solace was
her assurance Dietrich was still safe from harm since his adoption by
Aunt Marta and Klaus.

How could their lives have gone so terribly awry? Had it not
been for her loving family and their dedicated support, none of these
wonderful experiences in America would have been possible. It was
a debt of gratitude continuing to push Pietra to greater heights of
musical and personal stature. Surely this invitation was one of several
important steppingstones her Aunt Marta had once told her about.

After a few moments of spiritual praise and gratitude, her recurring sadness for her family circumstances remained woefully unresolved. The guilt she often felt plagued her every day, but also strengthened her fortitude to carry on. It was why she was here in the first place, and she swore to make the most of it.

*****

It would be a significant step forward for *Juilliard* to be recognized at such a professional level. The New York Philharmonic and the Metropolitan Opera were iconic throughout America and the civilized world. Just sharing the stage with them ranked the musical institution among the best the world had to offer.

Juilliard was founded in 1910 with intent to provide a musical education comparable to established European conservatories, enabling gifted American students to remain in America to further advance their education.

This evening's gala performance was an opportunity to shine its glorious spotlight equally upon Juilliard, as well as the lovely and talented musicians of the quartet, who had worked so tirelessly to hone their craft; and deservingly so.

Within hours, Marta received a telegram from Pietra and was overcome with pride and exuberant enthusiasm for her niece's amazing accomplishment. When the reality of the wonderful news set in however, she had no concept about with whom to share the delightful announcement.

She sat alone in her home with her thoughts, accompanied as always by a few cold martinis. These moments had become reflex actions, always bringing back precious memories of Anna and Marta together. In the quiet, secluded loneliness, her alcohol consumption caused her to take pause and she began to weep silently.

It was a combination of tears of joy for Pietra, and tears of her own sorrow for being apart from her lifetime companion, Anna. She felt so terribly alone and as she often did in times like this, she removed a small pouch from her bag and sorrowfully sniffed the white powder to fortify her spirits.

Some of life's greatest accomplishments are often unsatisfying when there is no one with whom to share them. Marta vividly remembered so many similar times she had felt the pervasive loneliness, often in stark contrast to the adulation and public popularity following her concert performances; none more than on the quiet and forlorn night of introspection from her suite overlooking Times Square on that cold Christmas night in New York.

She shook her head to break through the despondence beginning to engulf her and reached for the telephone to speak with Wilhelm Furtwangler. He was not only her much-admired colleague, but he was also a very close and dear friend, through the good times and the bad.

"Hello, Wilhelm! It's Marta. I hope I'm not calling too late this evening...*wonderful!* I have some exciting news, and I simply can't wait until morning to share it with you. I just received Pietra's telegram informing me her string quartet has received an invitation from the New York Philharmonic *and* the Metropolitan Opera to perform with them in New York City this May!"

She paused only long enough to hear Maestro's delight upon hearing the news. "Yes, I agree. It was only a matter of when. The time is nigh, my dear Maestro! I'm so very proud and excited for her, of course. I only wish I could inform Anna... No, there is still no news from her, but Klaus assures me she is well, and Dietrich and I expect to hear something soon...You know I will keep you abreast of things..." Marta paused and listened patiently.

"I was not aware of that Wilhelm. Do you suppose he would do that for her?... My darling it would be incredible if you could arrange it... *Happy?* Yes, I'm ecstatic just thinking about the possibility! Thank you, Wilhelm, thank you!... Yes, I will. I promise. See you soon. Goodnight, Wilhelm."

In the weeks leading up to the concert, news of Pietra's upcoming performance was not publicized anywhere in Germany, being suppressed by the propaganda minister who, from his perspective, remained furious about Pietra's defection.

Marta's conversation with Maestro Furtwangler the night she received the telegram from Pietra, revealed the world renowned and premiere classical violinist, Jascha Heifetz would be touring in America about mid-May; coincidentally, about the same time as Pietra's concert. Maestro would do his best to engage Master Heifetz' possible cooperation in arranging something very special for the quartet.

Furtwangler had met a very young Jascha Heifetz many years prior, when the then child prodigy made his debut appearance with the Berlin Philharmonic in 1912, at the incredibly young age of just eleven. Since then, Furtwangler and Jascha maintained their professional and personal relationships throughout their lifetimes.

Maestro promised Marta he would call upon this close friendship and his influence with both Jascha and Bruno Walter, the conductor of the New York Philharmonic at the time, to extend Maestro Walter's personal invitation to Master Heifetz to attend Pietra's professional debut in New York.

Just days before the Juilliard Quartet performance, Marta was advised by Furtwangler that, at his urging, Maestro Walter had taken his request even further, by arranging a private audience with Master Heifetz and the quartet after the concert performance. All of this was unknown to Pietra and her quartet. Notably, Pietra had two role models she had always aspired to become: her Aunt Marta, justifiably so, and even more so, Master Heifetz.

*****

In the years leading up to WWII, the American economy continued to reel in the wake of the Great Depression. During this time, most Americans suffered a punishing reduction in their average standard of living of about sixty percent. Unemployment was hovering at an all-time high of twenty-five percent and bankruptcy became a common process for both individual families and numerous businesses, leaving many Americans destitute.

Women were openly discouraged from participating in the workplace in deference to the belief that American males needed the jobs more than women. The best place for a woman was the traditional practice of taking care of the home and raising children.

As the possibility of war throughout Europe began to draw America deeper into its grasp, theaters across America were struggling to survive, since most families had greater priorities at the time than attending the theater. Nevertheless, the evening performance on May 11th played out before a full house of over 1,300 admiring patrons.

The Shubert Theater was an ideal venue. Constructed in 1914, it had become a major landmark for New York's social circles. It had hosted over 600 pre-Broadway tryouts of which there were over 300 world premieres, more than twice as many as any competing theater in New York, including the major cities in the eastern United States.

The exterior facades and ornate interior décor created a magnificent setting, with two additional balcony levels overlooking the expansive main floor. While very few patrons were familiar with the Juilliard Quartet, many of the others soon would be.

When the house lights began to dim and the stage curtains majestically separated, the clamor of conversations immediately subsided. The stage lights revealed the already seated quartet. The applause was politely courteous to these four young artists, who were largely unknown to the public, and equally so among these sophisticated classical enthusiasts.

Most likely, the patrons were not here to see the quartet. They were here to enjoy the established mastery of Maestro Bruno Walter and the Metropolitan Opera's interpretations of Mozart's *Le Nozze di Figaro*.

From the gentle stirrings of the first stanzas of Mozart's Quartet No. 19, the initially slow and ominous drama gently led to a dark but beckoning place; an unfamiliar one to the astute listeners. When the joyful melodic passages came into play however, the somber mood lifted and became bright and fanciful, at which point the modest expectations of the classically enlightened audience were more than exceeded.

This brilliant ensemble was captivating. The musicians' delicate sensitivity to the gentle, slowly growing complexities of the second and third movements, fully captured the approving audience's focus, and deservingly so.

When the final crescendo ended in perfect unison, the grateful and approving patrons enthusiastically expressed their overwhelming acknowledgement, and many stood to lead the appreciative applause. Their response stood in stark contrast to their apprehensive but polite welcome, and appropriately set the stage for the featured performance.

When the curtains were closed, the respectful crowd continued to rave with other patrons about the incredible performance they had just witnessed. It is an exciting moment when an advocate of the classics discovers something new, whether it be a specific musical piece never heard before, or a wonderful new performer who suddenly appears, seemingly from out of nowhere.

The brief break allowed the stage crew the time required to reset, permitting the full orchestra a few moments to retune while the operatic performers took their respective places.

Behind stage during the brief intermission, Maestro Walter introduced the renowned owners of the Shubert Theater, brothers Lee and Jacob Shubert, who were overjoyed to personally greet Pietra, Karen, Lynda, and Penelope. They had not met prior to this gala event, and rightfully trusted the Maestro's and the programming director's wise judgement in booking the young quartet for their debut.

Over the past decade, the Shubert *"brothers had become powerful theater moguls with a nationwide presence"*. (Gale Research) For the quartet, it was a fortuitous introduction, surely one to open many more doors to fame and fortune.

In attendance as well, was the recently appointed and very proud president of Juilliard, Ernest Hutcheson, a famed concert pianist and conductor in his own right. He had seen the incredible growth and development of many of the school's students and was keenly aware of the work ethic and God-given talent possessed by each member of this popular quartet. It was, indeed, a defining moment for everyone concerned.

The young ladies were decidedly unaccustomed to their newly discovered celebrity status and maintained their professional composure, all the while suppressing their personal jubilation to appear calm and collected. They were totally unaware when Master Jascha Heifetz entered backstage.

Pietra and her troupe were so involved in discussion with the Schubert brothers, their focus was undivided. When Maestro Walter approached the group with another gentleman, no one took immediate notice of his guest, until Maestro politely interrupted. "Pietra, ladies. I have someone here who is most anxious to meet you."

The ladies and the Schubert's were surprised by the polite intrusion and their heads pivoted simultaneously to the Maestro. "Dear ladies and gentlemen, I am honored to present a very special guest to you this evening, who came a very long way to meet you."

The instant the troupe saw Master Heifetz standing before them with his trademark smile, there was stunned silence. Shock overcame them and quickly dashed what remained of their reserved demeanor.

The ladies knew the significance of this moment in meeting an icon in their specific field of endeavor. They recognized him immediately and stood awkwardly with their mouths agape.

"It appears we may have taken you by surprise, ladies. Master Heifetz, please allow me to introduce our amazing quartet; Miss Pietra Friedman on violin, Karen Siu on cello, and Lynda Gottfried and Penelope Anderson, our splendid violas."

Master Heifetz stepped closer and extended a warm handshake to each of the young performers. "Good evening, ladies. Please forgive my untimely intrusion. I was genuinely moved by your superb performance this evening and simply had to meet each of you as soon as I could."

Pietra was the first to speak, stammering a little as she gathered her thoughts. She grasped his extended hand enthusiastically and uncharacteristically shook it in a manly way, pumping his hand up and down as if she was milking a cow! Such youthful enthusiasm, he must have thought!

"It is a delight to finally meet you, Master Heifetz! I am truly honored to make your acquaintance. It has been my dream to meet you one day, I can assure you. I am…quite overcome!"

Pietra placed her hand over her heart and continued to ramble adoringly to her idol. "You cannot imagine the impact you have had on my music, and on my life. I will be forever indebted to you for the inspiration you have instilled in me. We are truly blessed by your presence and had no idea you were attending this evening."

She turned to face Bruno Walter and enquired, "Maestro, did you know about this happy coincidence?"

Master Heifetz interjected. He was never one to be timid. "Maestro contacted me at the behest of Wilhelm Furtwangler and his most esteemed violinist, who I understand is your dear Auntie."

Pietra reeled with this unexpected revelation. "*My Aunt Marta!* You and my aunt have been my two greatest inspirations, Master Heifetz!"

"Please Pietra, you are too kind. We are all professionals here. I insist you call me Jascha. Please." He raised her delicate hand to kiss it with his usual flair for impeccable taste.

"I had just returned to America from touring Central and South America for the past month when Bruno contacted me. I have watched your growing career with great interest, and I too am so pleased to finally meet you in person. You are an amazing talent,

Pietra, as are your lovely companions. You all deserve every accolade for your sensitive interpretation of Mozart's *Dissonance*. Truly amazing to behold. I congratulate each of you. Very well done."

"Jascha and ladies, please forgive me but I still have much to do. I will leave you now to permit you to become better acquainted. We will speak again tomorrow for certain."

"Of course, Maestro! You have a concert to deliver," Master Heifetz responded, and quickly returned his focus to Pietra.

"I first met your lovely Aunt on tour in Vienna several years ago. She too caught my attention on numerous occasions since our first engagement together. I admire many things about her, but none more than her zest for life. She lives it to the fullest, and always makes me smile, I must say. Her enthusiasm is quite contagious. How in the world could I not happily do as she requested?"

As the discussions continued, the other dignitaries looking on graciously excused themselves to return to their seats. The easy verbal exchange between the Master and this young up-and-coming protégé flowed so naturally between them.

It was apparent Pietra was leaving an indelible impression upon her special admirer, so much so, he offered to visit Juilliard the following morning before his afternoon rehearsal. His featured performance the next day at Carnegie Hall had become an annual event with the New York Philharmonic and explained why he had been able to attend the quartet's opening performance.

"I have a small confession to make, Pietra." As Jascha said this, he looked anxiously side to side, creating a touch of suspense to what he was about to say.

"It's a little embarrassing, I must admit. I have seen this opera so many times. Although it is one of my favorites, I would much rather take some time to become better acquainted with you. Perhaps I could invite you and your chaperone for a quiet meal this evening if you don't mind me being so forward.

"I work with numerous young and aspiring musicians to help them in any way I am able. They have a maturity about them you also appear to possess; it is a magnetic presence I don't see often in someone as young as yourself."

"You flatter me, Master…" Heifetz raised an eyebrow in a teasing and subtle way. Pietra corrected herself, "… my apologies… *Jascha*. I appreciate your kind words. In addition to our chaperone, would you mind terribly if Karen Liu, our cellist, joins us as well?"

"Wonderful! That's a fine idea! I always stay at the Plaza Hotel when I am in New York. It's only minutes from Carnegie Hall and has become my home away from home, so to speak. The dining room is marvelous!"

The ladies eagerly gathered their personal things, leaving their instruments to be delivered to the residence later in the evening. It was a cool night by this time. They retrieved their stylish jackets provided for these occasions, when Master Heifetz graciously offered, "I will have my driver take you both to your residence to allow you to dress more comfortably for dinner, if you wish. I will instruct him to wait for you downstairs until you are ready. He can return you home afterward as well."

"That would be lovely, Jascha. That's most thoughtful of you. Thank you."

Dinner was truly memorable, as Master Heifetz had assured the young ladies it would be. The chaperone sat close by but was never intended to dine with those in his charge. It was a delightful meal of roast *Duckling a l'Orange*, prepared to perfection. The young ladies were still underage to consume alcohol, and other than a tasty *Manhattan*, the Master respectfully abstained as well.

"So please tell us how you cope with your travel itinerary over such a prolific career. Does it become tiring after a while?" Pietra asked innocently.

"It does on occasion but my dear wife, Florence, is quite used to it. That alone, eases my fatigue. She and the children are always so very understanding. She had a successful movie career of her own but when we were married, she deferred her career to stay home to raise our young ones."

"How old are the children, Jascha?" Karen enquired. "Please tell us about them."

"Our eldest daughter Regina, from Florence's first marriage, just turned twelve last week, as a matter of fact. Regrettably, I missed her birthday since I was in Mexico at the time and came straight to New York for my own performance day after tomorrow. My family is most forgiving of me." He paused ever so briefly to savor the final sip of his cocktail before resuming.

"We love her dearly and have two of our own as well; Josefa who is ten and our son Robert, who is now almost eight years old. They are much like their mother...quite precocious, I must say. I love them dearly and appreciate their inquisitiveness and zest for life. I'm so very proud of them.

"But tell me ladies, do you practice together often, or are you focusing more on your individual pursuits?"

"We do enjoy our individuality but playing in the quartet increases our scope of music in profound ways, I think," Pietra offered. Karen nodded in agreement.

"Very perceptive of you... I could not agree more," said Jascha. "Please continue."

"Music is all encompassing, and learning to play supportively and patiently with other musicians is fundamental to any personal success we may experience. Were it not for our collaboration in the quartet, I'm certain we would both have missed the opportunity to play for Maestro Walter this evening," Pietra explained. "Why...nor would we have met you, Sir!"

Karen thoughtfully added, "We participate in symphonic orchestrations less frequently, but the quartet enables us to expand our repertoire to better adjust to the full symphonic experience when it is asked of us. What we do as artists is important to us."

Pietra nodded in agreement. It was clear they were usually on the same page, figuratively and literally. Pietra continued Karen's thought further. "We strongly believe we are able to connect emotionally with people. Art transcends race and language and to have such an impact is a responsibility we do not accept lightly."

"Bravo, ladies! Eloquently put if I may say so!" Jascha exclaimed with obvious delight.

It was approaching midnight. Jascha was sipping his aromatic coffee as the very pleasurable evening was winding down. "I must ask you something Jascha, but I ask you to be frank with me, please," Pietra apprehensively requested.

"My, this sounds intriguing, my dear. Of course! I will always be honest with whomever I am speaking. My honesty often gets me in trouble, but I never avoid it. I remember my dear father telling me, *if you always tell the truth, you will never have to remember what you said.* What is it you want to know, Pietra?"

"Karen and I live for our music, as do most musicians we meet. We don't have much of a life outside the practice halls, especially while we are continuing our general education subjects as well. Together... well, there are precious few moments to do much more."

"What is it you are asking, Pietra? I don't understand," Jascha responded. Pietra continued, "Some of our colleagues bemoan the fact so much dedication and practice becomes too tedious to maintain. How often at this stage of your glorious career do you typically practice? Does it ever become tedious for you?"

"What I am about to say may seem evasive, but I assure you I'm not avoiding your question. It has been many, many years since anyone has asked me this. Let me help you find your own answer."

Jascha poured a final cup of coffee and pondered his upcoming comments. *The discipline of practice every day is essential. When I do skip a day, I notice a difference in my playing. After two days, the critics notice, and after three days, so does the audience. You must preserve your enthusiasm for playing. Loss of that enthusiasm is deadly to musicianship.* (J. Heifetz) Does that answer your question?" he enquired caringly.

Pietra reflected carefully on his thoughtfully articulated answer. "Not an answer I was expecting, but your message is very impactful. It is good advice to help any serious musician clarify to whom exactly we are accountable. Thank you for your insight, my dear friend. Sharing this time together makes me wonder how very much more I could learn from you."

Jascha charged the bill to his room as the fine evening had come to a fitting close. Being the gentleman he was, he stood to assist the ladies with their coats, just as the car was pulling into the front courtyard of the hotel, right on cue.

As the young guests entered the limousine, almost as an afterthought he once again enquired, "Is it possible to take a small tour of Juilliard tomorrow morning? I haven't seen the facilities since the reconstruction several years ago. What do you think?"

In their excitement, the ladies had forgotten his initial offer and were surprised at Jascha's intriguing suggestion, knowing full well Mr. Hutcheson, the president of the school, would be thrilled at the prospect. Pietra eagerly spoke up suggesting, "Perhaps you would consider briefly addressing our class, if the opportunity arises?"

"I will take that as a definitive 'Yes.' I look forward to seeing you then. Good night, dear ladies. Thank you for keeping an old man entertained tonight. I enjoyed myself immensely."

*****

Bright and early next morning, Pietra and Karen contacted Mr. Hutcheson's secretary to inform her about Master Heifetz' kind and unexpected offer, and the urgency for a prompt response from Mr. Hutcheson. Heifetz had suggested 10:00 A.M. was best for him and hoped Juilliard could accommodate his tight schedule on such short notice.

As expected, Mr. Hutcheson was enthusiastic about the amazing opportunity before him and adjusted his otherwise busy agenda accordingly. He promptly called the Plaza Hotel just before 8:30 to leave a message to confirm everyone's availability.

"Ladies, I believe your credibility as up and coming professionals explains Master Heifetz' very high opinion of you and reflects well upon our school. Your performance last night was perfection, as we knew would be the case. Pietra, your aunt and Maestro Walter opened the door for the quartet, and each of you made the most of it. The board members and I are so very proud of the troupe's fine accomplishment.

"The original tight agenda for our facilities can certainly be adjusted to suit Master Heifetz. Depending upon his limited time with us today, hopefully he can say a few words of encouragement to a few of the faculty and some of our advanced students for a private gathering in one of the boardrooms I can make available. Unfortunately, we will not have sufficient time with him to prepare a small buffet, but I am certain he would not be expecting one today."

Pietra was quick to intervene and offered some keen insight into the man and the legend. "I agree, sir. His engaging personality and dedication to education and musical development was most striking to me personally. His enthusiasm is genuine and highly contagious. I have read a great deal about his life, but I learned so much more in the few hours he shared with us. I'm sure a few minutes with the students will be a wise investment of his time, for him…and more so for our colleagues."

"I'm optimistic he will be open to taking a few questions from the students. His reputation is so supportive of young talent and I'm certain he will oblige us, even if only for a few minutes." Mr. Hutcheson himself was a very capable musician and politician. His position dictated he had to be adept at both.

Shortly before ten o'clock, Master Heifetz' limousine arrived at the main doors. It was a beautiful sunny day in May and the gardens were already freshly groomed for the upcoming change of seasons. The small entourage of greeters naturally included Mr. Hutcheson, Pietra, and Karen. This was to be an impromptu event but an auspicious one, nevertheless.

Master Heifetz stepped into the morning sunshine bearing his customary disarming smile. He was so incredibly charismatic. Having met the prior evening, he and Mr. Hutcheson shook hands briefly. For Pietra and Karen however, he hugged them both, warmly and respectfully. He was the consummate gentleman and in his usual good humor. It helped relax everyone and set the tone for this casual gathering.

"This lovely day is so much cooler than I expected since returning to America. Your gracious hospitality, however, gives me the warmth I've been craving. I'm very grateful you could accommodate my request to drop by this morning."

The group lingered only momentarily in the main lobby, which now featured a much higher ceiling with expansive glass panels rising some fifteen feet. The beaming sunshine illuminated the tasteful cornice moldings, further flattering a colorful hand painted mural. It was an inspiring attempt to represent a scene depicting Beethoven's *Pastoral Symphony*. It was a worthy tribute indeed, now brightening the once previous, morose entranceway that once was.

"My, my! This is such an improvement on the gloomy atmosphere I still remember from years ago. Excellent work, Ernest! I approve whole-heartedly!"

Mr. Hutcheson responded appreciatively, "The parents of one of our previous students commissioned a local artist to create it for us. The feeling is consistent with what we were looking to achieve."

The conversation continued, as Mr. Hutcheson gradually ushered the small entourage through the vestibule and down the hall to a series of private practice rooms, many of which were already occupied by various performers. Despite being early in the day, it was already a veritable hive of activity.

"We are so honored you could visit us this morning, Master Heifetz. If your time permits, I want to show you more of our refurbished facilities, especially our new theatrical hall. Perhaps afterward, depending upon your time, you would indulge us by speaking briefly with some of our advanced students in our graduate studies program." Mr. Hutcheson offered.

"Of course. You read my mind, Ernest. I'm happy to do so, but I must leave no later than eleven for rehearsal. Our performance at Carnegie is scheduled for tonight."

Within fifteen minutes, the tour of the main floor was completed, and a few questions were addressed sufficiently to move to the largest of three boardrooms, where about thirty people were already assembled. Pietra was asked by Mr. Hutcheson to do a brief introduction and was delighted to oblige.

She proceeded to the main entrance near the front of the boardroom, while Mr. Hutcheson escorted Jascha to his office, enabling him to enter from the rear.

"Good morning, everyone! As you are all aware, our String Quartet made a successful debut last night at the Schubert Theater before an appreciative audience that included a very special guest. Unknown to us, Maestro Bruno Walter, and my dear Aunt Marta, whom I speak of incessantly, honored us by arranging a surprise celebrity visit."

Sounds of intermittent light conversation and pent-up excitement spread tantalizingly throughout the room. It was a suspenseful moment. Jascha, by this time, stood inconspicuously at the back of the boardroom, having entered unnoticed through the doorway from Mr. Hutcheson's private office.

"The special guest was none other than Master Jascha Heifetz." The murmuring became more audible, and heads turned in unison to gaze about the room in hopes of seeing him.

"Delightfully, he has kindly offered to visit our school this morning for a few minutes to offer some of his incredible insights to our unique professions. Please extend a warm Juilliard welcome to our esteemed guest, Master Jascha Heifetz!"

Rising as one, the attendees stood and applauded. It was the most enthusiastic welcome the boardroom had ever hosted. The buzz of excitement quickly subsided when Jascha began to speak.

"Good morning, ladies and gentlemen," said Heifetz with a smile. "Thank you so very much. It is indeed a pleasure to return to Juilliard after so many years. My sincere appreciation to Mr. Hutcheson for arranging this event on such short notice.

"I have been a very close friend of Maestro Walter for many, many years and I am also a colleague of Marta von Brauchitsch, both of whom I respect and admire immensely. It was their kind request that brought us together last evening and gave me the distinct honor of meeting the outstanding members of your String Quartet. As anticipated, they performed brilliantly.

"Over dinner, I was captivated by Pietra and Karen as I came to know more about them. They gave me cause to remember that stage of my own life and the questions and uncertainties once concerning me. I see greatness in both as they, like many of you no doubt, are standing at the edge of an invisible precipice. It is a moment each of you have strived to attain, probably since you were young children." Jascha paused to poignantly permit a moment of self-reflection for the students gathered here.

"If you can relate to what I just said, I have a rhetorical question for each of you to consider." He calmly paused, giving them a moment longer to reflect. "Will you be consumed and overcome by it... or will you spread your wings to soar in it?" He paused again to purposely allow the moment to linger, letting each student relate more deeply to his analogy.

"... For myself, I chose the latter, and I am thankful I did. As I considered what I would speak about this morning, I recalled something I have thought about many times but haven't often articulated. Since those days, and right up to the present, musicians have always been referred to as being delicate, sensitive artists." A few soft murmurs spread throughout the gathering in agreement.

"Listen to my response carefully when I tell you what I know to be true. *It takes the nerves of a bullfighter, the digestion of a peasant, the vitality of a nightclub hostess, the tact of a diplomat, and the concentration of a Tibetan monk to lead the strenuous life of a virtuoso. The great compensation, of course, is the human one.* (J. Heifetz)

"This is precisely why I am here with you today; to encourage you to remain confident and dedicated to your craft, if in fact you are so truly gifted by the Lord above. And if you are so gifted, it is your obligation to mankind to see it through. How else could you make such an impression on the world in which we live?"

It was like flipping a switch. The applause erupted spontaneously in this private and intimate setting. Heifetz' touching insight ignited such passion which, in a public venue, would have been difficult to achieve. The talent in this gathering was immeasurable, and the students desperately needed to hear the truth. No one else had earned the right to deliver it more than Heifetz.

The applause dimmed when Pietra approached the front of the room. It was her privilege to address him for a few final words of gratitude, but she wanted to say something he too would remember.

"Master Heifetz, you are revered throughout the world for many things, including what you have accomplished by your visit with us today; giving back more than you receive. Your life has created a social platform to constantly inspire others, which you have done throughout your entire career. Heaven only knows how preoccupied you must be with other passions in your life, and the many causes you support so willingly.

"From what I have read about you and have now witnessed personally, your energy and genuine dedication are extraordinary. Thank you for your graciousness to have shared a few precious moments with us. We are truly humbled by your presence. Thank you, Master Heifetz, thank you."

When final courtesies were extended and Jascha was entering his limousine, the lives of those students in attendance had been altered in powerful and immeasurable ways. As he had intended, the influence upon Pietra was especially profound.

5

A WELL DESIGNED DECEPTION

♂

THE UNIQUE STATUS OF THE BERLIN PHILHARMONIC Orchestra (BPO) as the premiere orchestra in the world was a title not in dispute in 1940. The success of the world-famous orchestra had become a much coveted and high-profile instrument of propaganda for the Nazi Party. Under the direct control of Minister Goebbels and Adolf Hitler, the BPO also had unlimited funding. Their intent was to utilize it to their strategic advantage on the world stage.

Despite the racist decree forcing four Jewish performers to flee Germany, most notably first violinist Gilbert Back, the non-Jewish orchestra members were well-provided for and were the highest paid musicians in Germany. Josef Goebbels kept his promise to Maestro Furtwangler to assure his musicians remained exempt from serving in the military. By Goebbels' estimation, the contributions of these symphonic performers to the success of the Fatherland were comparable in value to front line troops fighting in the trenches.

Since the outbreak of war, travel itineraries of the Philharmonic were confined initially to domestic venues to avoid the hazards of war outside Germany's ever-expanding borders. Culture, specifically the art of classical music, was being retooled for political purposes, to flaunt another aspect of the ubiquitous strength of Germany's superiority. To ensure the purity of the Reich's orchestra, Certificates of Ethnicity were considered mandatory for every Philharmonic performer to legitimize their revered status within the symphony orchestra.

During these tenuous times, Marta and Maestro Furtwangler continued to walk an invisible tightrope, bridging the Reich's supreme authority and control over them, and the constant struggle to maintain a reasonable degree of freedom over their musical expression. Strict limitations were imposed on composers of preferred heritage, and tighter scrutiny ensured only the purest of Germanic bloodlines would grace the same stages as the BPO.

Consistent with Goebbels' request that Marta be the orchestra's pre-eminent cultural ambassador, her solo guest appearances across Europe had consistently attracted hundreds of thousands of upper-class concert goers. They were infatuated and enticed by her prolific profiles on tabloids in every major city in which she was scheduled to appear.

The mystique preceding her, from smaller venues to major cultural centers, consistently promoted her flamboyant and colorful character. Such was the extent of her well-known flair for fashion; consistently mimicked by her adoring fans, but never quite replicated. Her inherent panache became a unique trademark, clearly a style of her own.

Soon it would become time to reassert her magnetic personality once again on stages extending outside the confines of the Fatherland on behalf of the Reich, to now include most of Nazi-occupied Europe.

It was late-April 1940 when the call came from Minister Goebbels' office summoning both Maestro Furtwangler and Marta to his office. These impromptu meetings were a regular occurrence for the maestro but did not often require Marta's attendance as well.

"Do you know what this meeting is concerning, Wilhelm? I have not been requested to appear before Minister Goebbels in quite some time. I rather prefer it remain that way."

Maestro responded, "Yes, I suspect what this is about. Minister Hinkel and I have had brief telephone conversations. In his view, this is an opportunity to explore even greater possibilities for the BPO at this critical stage of the war, specifically within Nazi controlled Europe. This will be our first such discussion with Minister Goebbels. I imagine today's meeting will address this matter more fully."

Since becoming a featured emissary of the BPO at the Fuhrer's and Goebbels' specific request, Marta continued to have reservations about the appointment. To date, her role had been primarily limited to prioritizing her scheduling availability to co-operate with their requests, and consulting with Maestro and Hans Hinkel about pro-gramming content from time to time. Hinkel had been appointed by Goebbels to act as liaison with the BPO as the commissioner for the Public Enlightenment and Propaganda Ministry.

His role was not to usurp Goebbels' role, but rather to support it, by ensuring strict adherence to numerous cultural and intellectual mandates. In short, he oversaw the enforcement of the removal of Jews from any role in cultural pursuits. It was also his responsibility to work closely with Marta and the maestro on behalf of Minister Goebbels.

Furtwangler was always forthright with his premier performer. Marta had been a reliable and trusted friend, as well as a dedicated professional who consistently spoke her mind openly to him. Their reliable collaboration wielded considerable leverage to defend and protect the artistic freedom of the Philharmonic. Together they were an incredibly influential tandem.

As their car approached the Ordenspalais, an eighteenth-century masterpiece of architecture located across the street from the Reich Chancellery, it was a setting of opulence. Together, these buildings symbolized Germany's historic splendor of the past, and the invincibility of the present.

The hallowed halls of marble and limestone with deeply coffered ceilings, were intimidatingly suspended some eighty feet above the throngs of human commotion below. The echoes of footsteps resonated from the heavy boots of numerous military personnel carrying out their daily activities, many of which were critically controlled administrative matters whose hard lined decrees were as strongly forged on paper as the walls housing the offices of those drafting them.

A magnificent staircase of dark oak beckoned the small entourage and the security detail greeting them to lead their way to the second level, where the Ministry of Propaganda was ominously located. The architectural design reflected the enduring strength of Nazi resolve; nothing about the building was ever intended to be subtle.

Once there, a fully armed and uniformed guard, replete with the customary flair for distinction one would expect for an officer of his station, did not speak a word. His demeanor remained stoic and absent any hint of personality or charm. His cold deportment was as Goebbels demanded; rigidly high standards and absolute unwillingness to yield to sociability. Clearly, the intended effect of intimidation of Goebbels' office began outside the main door.

Once inside Minister Goebbels' private office however, his effusive charm was never more evident when he displayed his pleasure at seeing Marta again. Being the sly and cunning fox he was, after the customary brief courtesies and fawning over Marta, some of which bordered on flirtatiousness, he finally engaged with Furtwangler and Minister Hinkel. It was as if they were nothing more than an unnecessary distraction from her.

"Marta and esteemed gentlemen, please be seated."

"Once again, I must ask your forgiveness for my short notice. As you can imagine, the priorities of war often dictate where my time is most urgently needed. It is not often I am afforded the pleasure of your company. Minister Hinkle and I sincerely wish you and the Philharmonic could be given more of my focus, to which you both are most deserving. We are so proud of your accomplishments and today, it is our strong desire to build upon them."

"Thank you, Minister. We value your support, and we are pleased to accommodate you to the extent we are able." Maestro stroked Goebbels' ego, despite hating to be subservient to his beck and call.

Goebbels began by saying, "As testimony to the Fuhrer's visionary leadership, the Reich's successful campaigns in Eastern Europe and Scandinavia have been successful and are now in the final process of being militarily and politically stabilized. I am pleased to inform you that just last month, Norway and Denmark have agreed to adopt a co-operative and supporting posture with the Reich; and only a few days ago we have secured the full co-operation of King Leopold of Belgium as well."

"Please accept our heartiest congratulations, Minister!" offered Maestro Furtwangler. "It would appear the war is proceeding according to plan."

"Perhaps this would be a good time to offer you a glass of brandy to help celebrate this auspicious occasion." Goebbels smiled in response. The attendant had been standing at the ready and graciously served an outstanding, aged brandy. The attendant did so in his usual unobtrusive way, while the minister continued.

"The reason we are here today is to put your minds at ease. As you understand, our intent is always to demonstrate unflagging resolve to continually establish new milestones for the finest symphony orchestra in the civilized world, the BPO."

"I'm certain I speak for Marta as well when I say you have our keen interest," Maestro offered enthusiastically.

"Yes, Minister," Marta added. "Throughout our history, especially during the darkest days of the Great War, the Philharmonic has been a steady beacon of hope that continues to prevail. We strongly believe as you do, our music provides a positive distraction from the perils of war to reassure our people our greatest institutions always remain intact, even through difficult times."

"Eloquently put, Marta! We are of the same mind, as I knew we would be." Goebbels stood and raised his glass to toast their successful union and continued to bridge the conversation to direct Minister Hinkle to outline their most recent proposal.

"Thank you, Minister Goebbels. From the outset of the war, it is essential Germany continue to showcase the BPO for what it has always been; a beacon of light, as you so aptly put it Marta, of which all Germans can be proud. It is an orchestra populated by the finest German musicians, masterfully interpreting our own German composers' works to continually reaffirm the highest standards of excellence, creating delight and pride among our people. Culturally and artistically, our orchestra is the envy of the world. To maintain our unique status, however, it is imperative we continue our efforts to feature the BPO performing on the finest stages Europe has to offer.

"Our recent conquests in Scandinavia have always been strong bastions of support for classical music. This support always starts at the top, being led by the first families, King Christian X of Denmark, and of course, King Leopold of Belgium. Both royal families' predisposition for classical music enabled the Reich to gain their full co-operation for what we are about to propose to you and the BPO."

"What is it precisely, you and Minister Goebbels are proposing?" Furtwangler enquired.

"During the war, it is our intention to not only continue concert performances for the BPO throughout our occupied territories, but to increase the frequency of them." The boldness of this unexpected proclamation left Maestro and Marta speechless. The minister continued to provide the specifics.

"In recent months, Denmark has become of potential strategic value to the Reich. In return for certain concessions, it is now a protectorate of the Fatherland. We wish to celebrate our close Danish relationship as an example of mutual co-operation between our nations, so others will understand the wisdom of potential alliances with us as well."

Pausing briefly, Hinkle subtly edged his seat closer to Maestro and Marta who were sitting across from him. For added emphasis he then leaned in ever so slightly, and placed his extended fingertips, one hand touching the other. It was a gesture to stress more clearly the importance of what he was about to say.

"We want a tour to be arranged for the BPO to include concerts in Copenhagen, Antwerp, and Brussels, each city having world renowned concert halls meeting the exacting standards our fine orchestra requires.

"To ease the pressure on the entire BPO, we are suggesting you, Maestro and Marta, perform as featured guests with the Antwerp Symphony. However, two performances, specifically in the *Ancienne Belgique* in Brussels and the *Copenhagen Theater*, must feature the entire BPO. Global press coverage would be well publicized in those prominent cities and will be promoted aggressively with the full weight of this office driving the effort."

Marta and Maestro looked at each other momentarily, both being uncertain about the reasoning behind such a tour at this time. Maestro was the first to speak up.

"Perhaps I may enquire the reason the Fuhrer is so eager to expedite this tour, especially so soon after such recent occupations of both Denmark and Belgium. You mentioned these occupations have been *militarily stabilized.* This begs the question I must ask about the safety of ourselves and the musicians accompanying us at this delicate time."

Minister Goebbels interjected in anticipation of where this discussion was likely heading. "You must know your musicians will always be assured of their personal safety, my dear Maestro. I take issue you consider our success to be so tenuous. I remind you these were not forced occupations inflicted upon our enemies of the state. In both cases, these are protectorates of the Fatherland. To my knowledge, there have never been unpleasant incidents of this nature thus far. Why such sudden concerns, Maestro?"

Maestro nodded to Marta to express her, and his own growing concerns about security issues of late. "Sir..." She paused momentarily for effect. "May I be direct with you, Herr Goebbels?" He nodded affirmatively.

"Recently we have become increasingly aware of, shall I say, rising animosity toward us, personally as well as politically. If you recall, there was an unexpected and bitter protest outside Symphony Hall in Boston. It was a frightening incident I shall not soon forget. It was a passionate protest of the persecution of Jews that drew mixed reaction from public onlookers. I remind you this was two years ago, in America; another world away from Europe. Despite the distance, it enflamed public opinion against us.

"Since that time, there has been a groundswell of support from many nations outside of the Fatherland to support that cause. As this will be our first tour outside Germany since the war began, there are many who bear resentment and hatred for the provocative actions of our state and military.

"Sirs, we mean no disrespect, however, when you speak of assurances, please remember we are musicians, first and foremost, and are unaccustomed to any hostility potentially directed against us."

"You raise a fair question, Marta. We would never expose you or any of your entourage to harm, nor would we tolerate the public embarrassment of a breach of our security. In either instance however, we cannot afford to display any sign of fear or weakness, simply because none exists."

A solemn silence hung ominously throughout the room. Goebbels casually strode toward his desk, turning his back and moving away from his guests. He meticulously removed a cigarette. It remained in his left hand, the right fidgeting with his lighter, opening and closing it repeatedly. As abruptly as it began, the shroud of quiet reflection lifted when he articulated his thoughts.

"I take your concerns seriously... and must reluctantly confess, I failed to consider this matter from your unique perspective, Marta. Henceforth, I will see security protocols are thoroughly reviewed and significantly increased to meet yours, and my own expectations for your continued safety. Agreed?"

*****

In the days and weeks ahead, travel itineraries, security protocols and scheduling of specific programming content would be decided upon and thoroughly implemented to meet the best interests of all parties. True to his word, the minister himself worked closely with Heinrich Himmler's personal deputy, Reinhard Heydrich to oversee a complete overhaul of security protocol for the individual members of the BPO musicians and support staff, especially during international appearances.

Goebbels' whole-hearted admission of having underestimated potential threats against Marta and Maestro, exposed a weakness not previously considered by him. It was a wake-up call, not only requiring Marta's boldness and courage to express, but equally so, for Goebbels' respect and humility to take affirmative action; bearing in mind humility was an attribute he seldom expressed.

Despite their own well-founded trepidations, the musicians and staff followed the lead of Maestro and Marta, overcoming their hesitation based upon Marta's previous unpleasant experience.

The struggle to maintain political and artistic freedom was a continuous balancing act between the demands of state control, and the ability to achieve some workable degree of autonomy, part of which included exceptional privileges and preferential considerations. The BPO's interactions under Nazi pressure made compromise an artform by Furtwangler. The very survival of the BPO was his only priority. His superficial co-operation with Goebbels was never about his acceptance of Nazi ideology.

*****

The *Maatschappij Concerten Orchestra* was the predecessor to the Antwerp Symphony Orchestra and was under the baton of Maestro Mortelmans. Various musical societies within Belgium and Denmark were extremely influential during this time, specifically radical Flemish Nationalists, who vehemently opposed the German occupation of Belgium.

They held great sway with a very astute public, extending well beyond the realm of classical music. The extent of their influence on public opinion was profound, whether for or against, often shaping prevailing political interests.

Hitler and Goebbels were brilliant, manipulative strategists and drew upon the cultural expertise of Commissioner Hans Hinkle to effectively counter the Flemish Nationalists' efforts. Their effective collaboration recognized the importance of allying their interests with the most influential German-friendly music societies. By feigning the Reich's support of them, together with strong financial backing, Hitler's political influence within these countries was greatly enhanced.

Through this well designed deception, the Fuhrer gained the much-needed public support he urgently required. He used this support as an influential bargaining chip to finalize Nazi negotiations with the

Danish Crown, thereby avoiding the need to invade Denmark. In return, the Danes would continue to govern themselves under the unfettered reign of King Christian.

The strategic operations and strategies of German High Command were remarkably complex, using a broad range of tactics from intimidation to seduction, as the circumstances required. Likened to moving chess pieces controlled by a grand master, it was not easy to discern truth from cleverly disguised misdirection.

The master of manipulation was Adolf Hitler. No regard was given to honesty, morality, or integrity; only limitless pursuit to satisfy Reich objectives. There was always a means to an end and the Nazis prevalent greed and insatiable self-interest knew no boundaries.

*****

The Antwerp engagement found Maestro and Marta, and their personal attendants, safely checked into the lavish and always dependable *Hotel De Witte Lelie*. Built in the late eighteenth century, this very up-scale boutique hotel featured only eleven suites, tastefully designed, and distinctively furnished.

Impeccable cuisine was catered to each suite either inside the exquisite dining area of the suite, or outside on the private terrace overlooking a well-manicured cultured garden. This was a quiet sanctuary of sublime peacefulness and a thankful respite from the preoccupations of war.

Unlike typical larger hotels, the main entrance to the *De Witte* was always securely locked and it featured a doorbell outside to summon the concierge. There was no public or paparazzi access to the interior lobby, nor anywhere inside the building. It was managed much like a private residence, for the few dignitaries who could afford it.

These details were conducive to providing the security Minister Goebbels had promised for his cultural emissaries. His personally selected security team added immeasurably to their safety in this quaint but naturally well-fortified residence. It could be locked down in an instant, if necessary.

It was mid-afternoon on a gorgeous, sunny afternoon in late May 1940, only a few blocks from the railway station in mid-town and almost walking distance to the revered Queen Elisabeth Hall, where the only rehearsal prior to the performance was scheduled for the following morning. The concert would follow later the same evening with a full house, anticipated to number about 800 attendees.

To honor and recognize the outstanding achievements of the Third Reich, an all-Beethoven program had been agreed upon. Of course, the evening featured the BPO's personal cultural ambassadors, Maestro Wilhelm Furtwangler, and his violin virtuoso, Madame von Brauchitsch.

The program opened with the powerful and controversial *Egmont Overture*. This symbolic and compelling overture was written by Beethoven to commemorate the execution of the famous Flemish martyr, Count Egmont, who defied the invading Spaniards by choosing not to flee and instead, stood resolutely by his adamant refusal to surrender his ideal of liberty.

His cause was a classic example of the plea for justice against dictatorial tyranny; one for which he would willingly sacrifice his life. It was an ironic selection to be performed by the Germans on this unique celebratory occasion, to acknowledge Denmark as a Protectorate of Germany. It would prove to be a bold slap in the face for the typically timid and submissive Danes.

This evening, the Antwerp Symphony followed the baton and interpretive command of the Third Reich's own Maestro Furtwangler, precisely as the Fuhrer had intended. As expected, the performance was delivered magnificently, but the programming choice was considered by many to be in poor taste and enflamed the passions of many Danish patrons.

During the ambivalent applause, sounds of disapproval could be heard randomly scattered throughout the theater, as many Danes vocally expressed themselves by booing the performance.

Maestro was visibly unmoved by the inappropriate behavior, but deep inside his belly he understood the Danes' justifiable contempt. It was precisely the reason the arrogance of the state was often called into question by both Marta and Furtwangler. This was an unnecessary embarrassment by the state to have imposed their cultural insensitivities upon the program, but Maestro and Marta had been helpless to prevent it.

By the conclusion of Beethoven's Violin Concerto, which was sheer perfection by Marta, the slight disruption following Egmont had gathered steam, to the point it became more concerning for the two prolific guests. In response, the members of the Antwerp Symphony displayed profound shame for the audience's reaction, interpreting it to be insulting to their honored guest performers; another reminder of why state and art should remain mutually independent.

Once curtains were closed, a group of concerned players led by the first violinist, approached Maestro and Marta.

"Please accept our humble apology on behalf of the members of the orchestra, Maestro. Your leadership this evening brought out the best in us, which our audience has now seen fit to taint so pitifully. It in no way represents our opinion of your dutiful performance. I trust you both can forgive us."

"You are so kind, Herr Janssens. These are sensitive political issues. Your audience has every right to vilify our questionable judgement in programming. Of course, it will take time for Denmark to adjust to the political landscape. You have done nothing to be ashamed of, but we very much appreciate your thoughtful gesture. We assure you it is entirely unnecessary."

By this time, the support staff had already begun to pack various equipment, leaving the celebrity guests to depart the rear doors of the auditorium to return to the Lille Hotel under the usual security detail. As they approached the exit area, Marta and Maestro were met by two armed security guards, in full military uniform.

"I ask your indulgence Sir, and Madame. We have a slight problem outside. It will be under control shortly, I assure you. Please bear with us for a few minutes while we clear the area before we safely escort you to your vehicle."

Apparently, there was a large gathering of protesters chanting obscenities, intended to further denigrate Germany's occupation of Denmark. The vocal displeasure displayed inside the theater was still festering among many attendees outside the theater as well.

"My, my. I can hear the shouting. How many of them are out there, officer?" Marta asked inquisitively.

Before he could respond, the sound of single shots of gunfire echoed from the scene. More shouting, this time indiscernible, indicating the shots had caused confusion and panic outside. Suddenly, short bursts of machine gun fire responded to the apparent threat. People could be heard screaming as chaos evidently erupted.

Maestro, usually calm and controlled, suddenly expressed his outrage. *"This is bloody bullshit!"* he hollered.

His fists were tightly clenched as he continued to shout in frustration, not at the guard, but at the entire circumstance in which they found themselves. "We should not have to deal with this shit, Marta!"

She placed her hand on his still clenched fist, consolingly and reassuringly. "We were both worried about this type of thing happening at some point Wilhelm, although I'm certain order will soon be restored. We'll be safe at the hotel shortly to relax and gather ourselves."

"You are right, of course. I apologize for my outburst, Marta, but my nerves have become a bit frayed this evening." He sighed with resignation and embarrassment. "I shall not do that again, I promise you. I just want us to get the hell out of here. It was only a matter of time, but I've had enough for one day."

In about ten minutes the clamor outside had subsided, and ambulance sirens sounded their arrival. Clearly order had been restored, the horror of machine gun fire having served its lethal purpose; not a pleasant way to close out the evening's performance.

By the time the rear doors finally opened, two ambulances had finished securing the injured and prepared to exit the scene. All that remained were several pools of spilled blood, no doubt staining more than the concrete. "This was disgusting and totally unnecessary, Wilhelm. This could have been avoided had the minister taken our concerns more seriously. Let's get back to the hotel and enjoy a fine brandy together. We've both earned it tonight."

When the limousine arrived, numerous guards had been preposted about the perimeter of the hotel; an added measure of security that calmed the frayed nerves of the two fatigued celebrities. Although some protesters had also appeared on the scene, they appeared to have no serious inclination to confront the well-armed German military having already assumed strong defensive positions.

Within minutes, Wilhelm ushered Marta to his suite. As they often did when travelling together, they would commiserate about the evening just concluded. This one was unlike any Wilhelm had experienced and to Marta's mind, Wilhelm needed some reassurance.

"Despite all that has occurred this evening, it's a perfect night to enjoy the balcony overlooking the gardens below. It is so peaceful here, *finally*," Marta exclaimed, trying intently to help Maestro process the obvious stress they had both experienced.

"I embarrassed myself in front of you tonight, Marta. Please forgive me. I don't know what came over me. It's never happened to me before."

"There's nothing to apologize for, my dear friend. How many times have you been there for me? I cannot even count. We are always there for one another."

Marta remained on the balcony savoring the lovely view, admiring the discretely positioned lighting in and about the gardens and walkways. It was an inspiring sight. Maestro prepared two well-deserved glasses of brandy. As he presented them, they gently touched their glasses together. "To dear friendships," Maestro offered.

Nothing more was said between them for a short, silent moment while Wilhelm seated himself on the lounge, seemingly exhausted. Marta remained alone at the railing, contemplatively offering some reassuring insights.

"You know, I sometimes feel that in these confusing and perilous times, we can still find comfort in the knowledge that classical music has always stood the test of time... It will continue to do so because it constantly stirs our passions to remind us of something we often forget. It is one of the greatest human achievements every great culture throughout history has left its indelible mark upon. Why do you suppose that is Wilhelm?"

Maestro sipped his brandy slowly and satisfyingly, drawing a deep breath as he tried to restoke his self-confidence. He was evidently not in a talkative mood and said nothing by way of a response. Marta simply resumed her thought vocally, trying to rationalize the incident that occurred just a brief hour or so prior.

"Very well then, I'll tell you why. So those that follow can continue dreaming of and building upon what others before them have accomplished. Despite the turmoil that surrounds us, we are leaving our mark too, perhaps as humankind has always intended, before us and on into the future. Musicians like us have persevered, despite the inevitable obstacles that will continue to confront us. Just something to think about."

Maestro was still sitting quietly on his chair when Marta bent over him and gently kissed the top of his head. "I'll excuse myself for the night. Sleep well my dear friend, sleep well."

"Good night, Marta... and thank you. Your friendship means everything to me. You sleep well also."

6

TAKE YOUR SHOVELS TO THE
FIELD, NOT YOUR RIFLE
♂

MORNING'S FIRST BEAMS OF SUNLIGHT RACED INSTANTA-
neously from treetops to the eastern side of the hand-hewed pine-
wood walls of the barn, faster than the blink of an eye. It was a miracle
of nature, the instant of daybreak, which all too often escapes our
conscious perceptions. Life moves forward with commonplace and
mundane tasks often taking precedence over these glorious moments.
It too would be forgotten as only a fleeting experience absorbed by
the passage of time.

This potato farm could be considered typical of many others
located on the western fringe of the village of Wiory, to the southwest of Warsaw. Days were growing longer as they do in April, and
the country air was still crisp, fragranced by the scent of pine trees
pregnant with aromas so pungent as to sting the nose.

Jan Szymanski was seventeen years of age, the younger of two
older brothers, Josef and Mikael. Their mother Marianna had raised
her boys alone from the time they were barely teens. Since the death
of her husband who had succumbed to heart failure several years ago,
schooling was necessarily curtailed for the boys. Life was not always
fair, but neither was it expected to be. Survival of the farm took precedence such as life was, and potatoes had to be harvested.

Information about the invasion did not come as a shock to many
of the peasant farmers. What little of world affairs they would hear

57

was sporadic at best. The attitude of many families here was acceptance, unable to do anything to stop it. Should the boys rush off to war, likely to perish in the mayhem, or mind their own business and somehow protect their farm… and each other? None of them really had any concept of the true gravity of war, but they knew enough.

News of the German advance was received by whispers of radio communications here and there, often not heard by many in the countryside in areas not already subjected to the direct ravages of the invasion. Information, regardless of its relevance, became screened and sorted by word of mouth, from neighbor to distant neighbor, with little reliability of accurate content. With each successive rumor passing from person to person, the stories became further distorted from the facts. There was no baseline of truth, nor any steady frame of reference.

Few details of the punishing defeat of their countrymen, and the indiscriminate slaughter of women and children were available, since so few survived to report it. The tragic spreading news, although sporadic, could not be questioned or challenged, and most certainly never exaggerated. It simply had to be true.

When Warsaw fell several months ago, there was no immediate impact in Wiory. Tears were shed for the capital city few of the villagers had ever seen, and for the lives lost during the Great War whose memories had long since faded. For the remaining seniors who could still remember those tragedies, many had lost family, comrades in arms, and in some cases their own limbs. What lingered to this day though was their fragile confidence and relatively innocent perspectives of life itself.

Once the harsh reality of another war set in, escaping from their home was never even considered. Harvesting continued much as before with but one certainty; their innate understanding nature's course cannot be altered by matters such as war. Despite the extent of man's destructiveness and general chaos, time did not stop, or even slow its passage.

The Szymanski boys were built like their father, of sturdy frame and lean muscle. Their daily tasks kept them that way. Never did they openly aspire for more, and why would they? Marianna ruled the farm with an iron fist, and signs of affection were not part of her makeup. Beneath her tough and often vocal exterior, *Ma* was consistent and never displayed a softer side. There simply wasn't one.

She provided far more than home cooking and handling business matters and remained steadfast to her traditions to assure everyone in Wiory she was always in total control of the family business and keeping the bills paid. It was a humble but common life, shared by so many other similar neighboring villages.

Mariana's reasoning was simple; people had to eat, with no time for fighting or soldiering. *"Bullets have no conscience"*, their mother often confided to her boys. "Take your shovel to the fields, not the rifle! The German bastards will get hungry too. They're no different than you and me. We'll be safe by staying the only course we know. They will surely need us. All in good time."

This they did, as surely as the morning sun would continue to rise above the treetops. It was futile to argue with her. She would never leave the only home she had known for the past twenty-two years.

*****

Almost two weeks later, a jeep and cargo truck threw up dusty clouds of dried clay as they approached the west side of this sleepy docile village. A soldier of slight build and fixated demeanor led this modest military convoy up the shallow grade of the dirt roadway separating scattered clusters of pine trees. He may have cast only a small shadow, but his massive ego and arrogance were immeasurable.

Jan and Josef leaned on their shovels to ease their overworked back muscles from stooping most of the day in the warm afternoon sun in May. Not a word was spoken until the cloud of dust cleared and the officer approached with three of his armed troops taking up the rear. Six other regulars established the makings of a perimeter to maintain a watchful eye down the hill they had traversed.

As he drew closer, the officer continued to scan the well-maintained farmhouse, noting no doubt the pride of ownership readily apparent in the simple edged garden beds and painted veranda.

"You there! Who else is with you here?" he barked at the boys.

"Who wants to know?" Josef asked indignantly. The officer's response was equally curt. "Me, asshole! Answer my fucking question." Josef was wise enough not to provoke him further.

"Just our mother inside and our brother in the barn," as Mikael emerged, wiping his greasy hands on a tattered hand towel to join his brothers. Duc, the family Doberman, was by his side and began to bark threateningly and ran ahead when he saw the intruders. Josef hollered, "*Duc! Stay boy. Stay!*" Duc was a protective beast, but he followed Josef's command. He stopped in his tracks and withdrew to stand beside Josef at the ready.

The Lieutenant all but ignored the dog other than to say, "You would all be well advised to be as obedient as your fucking dog. Do you think you can manage that? Get your mother out here, now!" he ordered, sending two of the armed group of three ambling toward the old house to ensure she did so.

Jan ran ahead to summon his mother, still clutching his shovel. Marianna had been napping and knew nothing of the unannounced arrival. She could be cantankerous as hell and Jan's intent was to remind her of their greater purpose. It would not be wise to antagonize these visitors, such was her custom when facing any confrontation. This was no time for her usual abrasiveness and prideful manner.

Marianna reluctantly gathered herself when Jan awakened her. She was a stocky built, tough old bird with the broad stance of a German tank. Even Rommel would think twice about confronting this intimidating woman in one of his Panzers.

A few moments later, after Jan had returned to his brothers, their mother stepped outside, covering her eyes from the blinding afternoon sun. Surprisingly, she gave the impression of cautious interest, despite the fire in her dark and defiant eyes. Thankfully, it was as warm a greeting as the boys could have anticipated from her, but it still created the distinct impression she would not be intimidated by these unwelcome intruders.

Saying nothing, she stood beside her sons and calmly deferred to whatever message the officer was here to deliver.

"This farm is now the property of the German Reich, and you are our prisoners of war. As we speak, your neighbors, your friends, and your families are receiving the same glad tidings as you miserable lot. You will obey my orders or each of you will be shot, here and now! Do you understand the sincerity of my meaning?"

Three rifles were simultaneously raised in unison and pointed at their heads, which spoke volumes about his earnest warning.

After a pause, with no forthcoming comments or change of body language having been offered by these indifferent and seemingly relaxed captives, Mikael tucked the oily rag into his back pocket and stood with his arms hanging beside him. He had an enviable physique in his tattered and soiled work shirt. The sleeves were rolled up just below his elbows. He was too powerfully built to roll them any higher.

Jan and Josef continued to lean on the shoulder-length wooden handled shovels that served them so well. It seemed it was as good a time as any to take a short break for a few well-deserved minutes. Having been given no direct orders themselves, they saw no need to move or verbally respond, and instead, began to scrutinize this small band of uniformed soldiers, deciding to keep their thoughts to themselves for the time being.

It was a bit unnerving for the young lieutenant in charge, or perhaps he was unsettled by the family's passivity, but he shifted his gaze to bark again at one of the riflemen.

"Corporal, take two of the troopers to search the house and the barn. Confirm if anyone else is in hiding and is reluctant to join us." As he was about to return his gaze to the boys, and perhaps to elicit at least a grunt of protest, he shouted, "*Be thorough, corporal! Do not leave any stone unturned!*"

This was to be expected, but the greater purpose of this forced search and invasion of home and property was to discover if weapons of any kind were hidden inside to potentially be used against them, in whatever form the Germans imagined. It was the power of the unspoken words, not the spoken ones, captivating this farming family. They were too naïve to even conceive of the imminent danger this disruption could hold in store for them.

Their innocence was genuine but was also a blessing. Awareness of fatal repercussions was not considered in their very limited reality. They had not witnessed firsthand the tragedy befalling their fellow countrymen and women who were indiscriminately killed or maimed by the preceding carnage of the Third Reich.

Sounds of shattering dishes and furnishings could be heard from inside the house. The search must be thorough and intimidating. It was a test of their resolve, both the troopers to be meticulous, and these peasant farmers to grin and bear these moments of insult and disrespect for their privacy.

After what seemed like a total waste of time, the troopers reported nothing of value or consequence could be found. The house and barn were clean of anything of questionable merit. The officer noted his satisfaction, without a hint of apology, as would be expected from someone in his position.

"Your fields are better than most others in this shit-hole territory. We have seen so many. How do you explain the difference?" He directed his question to Jan's older brothers but didn't appear to favor either one for an explanation.

"We've been farming since we were kids. Our father made us carry the bulk of the load when we were too young to say no. He busted his ass his whole life and made us do the work while he brewed his damn schnapps. If we didn't do the work, he'd bust our chops, especially when he was drunk," Mikael explained.

"So, you're telling me you just work harder than anyone else. Is that it?" the officer asked.

Josef intervened and offered another point of view. "Pretty much, but we also mix wood chips and horse manure into the fields, by hand if we have to. It's hard work but always gives us a better yield. Not too many others have three boys to do that kinda' work."

"What's your name, boy? Are you the oldest?" said the officer, referring now to Mikael.

"Mikael Szymanski... and yes, I am."

"You will come with us. We have need of strong workers for the Reich. Your brothers and your mother may stay here to take care of the harvest. You don't need all three of you to run this godforsaken place." The officer nodded to his guards to take Mikael to the truck.

They immediately stepped toward Mikael, one of them pointing his rifle at him, the other grabbing him by his dirty shirt collar in his fist, pulling him toward the waiting truck. It would take much more than a tug on his shirt to make this young man move.

Mikael immediately began to protest, as did his brothers. *"You can't just take me! What have I done? You have no right to do this!"* he hollered to the Lieutenant, as he struggled to free himself.

"Hey! Leave him alone, you bastard!" Jan shouted and stepped forward, now firmly grasping his shovel menacingly and directing it at the one holding his brother.

Duc sprinted toward the one losing his grip on Mikael and lunged at him, powerfully baring his full set of teeth. He caught the guard's forearm in his mouth, tearing at it and ripping the uniform, quickly saturating it with blood. The next instant, two shots were fired, followed by a sharp wince of pain. Duc crashed lifelessly to the dusty grass, his teeth still exposing the blood from his victim, his tongue laying extended across the corner of his mouth.

During the escalating confrontation, two more guards had quickly stepped up to protect the commanding officer. This was not a subject for negotiation and the lieutenant was not receptive to having his command questioned. Without a word, the lieutenant only had to cast his gaze in their direction and shift his eyes back to Jan. The message was clear.

One guard fixed his crosshairs on Jan's forehead, only inches from his face. "Drop the shovel now or I swear to God I'll blow your head off."

Jan froze in his tracks, knowing he was helpless to stop them from taking Mikael. The rage in his eyes subsided and they began to tear, ever so slightly. Marianna and Josef stayed out of the potential melee, whereupon the other guard swiftly delivered a solid blow to Jan's belly, knocking the wind out of him in the process. As he hunched over, another firm kick in his belly was enough to convince the family of the Germans' sincerity.

"That's enough!" Mikael shouted. "Let it be boys. Just let it be. Take good care of Ma till I come back."

"All of you shut your fucking mouths, or you will be shot. It makes little difference to me. Am I making myself clear to you assholes?" The lieutenant slowly walked to stand near the dead dog and withdrew his service revolver. Contemptuously, he shot Duc between the eyes, just for added emphasis.

Mikael was forcibly directed to the waiting truck by a rifle barrel shoved into his lower back. Cooperation was not a request. When the tarp was thrown open, exposing the darkened interior, there appeared to be others who were bound and gagged. They had also been conscripted for some other forced labor the Germans needed.

Now directing the conversation to Jan and Josef, and indirectly to Marianna, he stated emphatically, "You will continue your harvest as planned. Whatever crops you grow are the property of the Reich, which you will continue to produce and harvest in your service to the Fatherland. To do otherwise will necessitate severe reprisals... from me! Are we clear?"

He continued, "As compensation, you will be entitled to whatever remains of your production quotas, after satisfaction of the Fatherland's requirements, of course. Your newly discovered loyalty to your captors will serve you well... so much better than some of your neighbors. Of this I am certain."

With no further exchange of words, the soldiers turned in unison to return to the car, signaling the peripheral lookouts to board the truck. As they maneuvered the vehicles on the straggles of dusty green grass, the jeep slowed to a stop and the officer leaned out the window and mockingly hollered, "We will return in a few days with your assigned quota to arrange for transfer of your inventories. We look forward to doing business with you!" He nodded to the driver, and they quickly faded into the dust in the distance.

Almost prophetically, Jan mumbled out loud, "May you all fade into dust, you fuckin' bastards!" The caravan had barely descended to the bottom of the hill while the family looked on disbelievingly. The shock of losing Mikael had begun to set in and within seconds, tears were difficult to control. The boys walked away silently to grieve Mikael's arrest privately. Duc's body would remain where it was until they were ready to deal with it together.

Tears were not customary here, nor would they ever be. The family would likely never see or hear of Mikael again.

Within about ten minutes, the boys re-entered their home, and found Marianna already picking up a few items tossed about the room. For the most part, nothing of value had been removed or damaged since nothing of real value had ever been possessed by the family.

Even sentimentality was not an issue, with the single exception of the old hunting rifle lying on the floor with a smashed wooden stock that used to cradle against their father's shoulder from time to time. Singularly, this was an unnecessary indignation. It was the common remembrance the boys had shared when hunting with their father, but it was nothing worth moaning about to each other. There were far greater matters to preoccupy their minds.

"We all knew this day would come sooner or later, so let's be thankful it's already happened. We are all still alive and Mikael is strong as an ox. If anyone can survive where he's going, Mikael will," Josef said unemotionally.

"Think of how bad it could have been. I spoke with Vlad at the market just three days ago. He warned me these people are ruthless and told me we should not argue or fight back. His cousin's family in Warsaw hasn't been heard from in weeks. Maybe nothing, but his mind can only imagine the worst," offered Jan.

"These pigs need us to do what they cannot," Jan continued as he was still gathering himself, wiping a few tears and blowing his nose. "I think the worst is yet to come."

Josef, now on his knees, picking up a few broken dishes, added incredulously, "Vlad said there were so many of them in Warsaw. Is anyone left in Germany?"

"Did you see that arrogant cocksucker? I wanted to flatten his face with the back of my shovel, the smug prick! If he's the best they've got to lead a few men, any chance these Krauts have to beat us will be despite their stupidity... Ma, what are you thinking?" Jan asked. "I'm so very sorry this happened to you. Are you OK?"

"Of course, I am OK. If your father was here, he wouldn't have taken their shit... but we would all be dead to show for it. We do what we must to stay together. We need time to reckon with the situation. For now, let's clean up this mess. I have dinner to prepare... and you boys have chores to do, including taking care of Duc. Let's be thankful it wasn't one of us. Get after it and we can talk later." she snapped.

Always a woman of few words but forceful intentions, Marianna was much like her husband, except for his big mouth, especially when he drank his beloved vodka at the back of the barn. She was correct, the boys agreed among themselves. No one was about to challenge this woman of strong opinions, especially when she was right.

Pragmatism was her strong suit, and the boys looked up to her, right or wrong. These would be desperate times, whatever the future held. Among them, they all agreed to just do what Ma says and somehow they would find their way.

*****

About ten days later, a small procession of military grunts reappeared. The quotas were assigned and were very specific, based on what assessment factors no one neither knew nor understood. Word was, they had raised some hell in a few of their unscheduled visitations, roughing up those who resisted and killing one in the process.

For the most part, the farmers all had the same mindset. Co-operate as best you can. Eat your rations, be thankful for them, and fill your bellies by swallowing your pride... for the present anyway.

And so it was. Between harvesting and collecting firewood, there was no time for idle complaints. The Germans also requisitioned last fall's dried firewood, leaving only the remnants that fell off their trucks. Every two weeks or so in this peak season they would surely return, laughing and bullying the conscripted peasant farmers, each time spiritually grinding them further into the dirt than the preceding weeks.

Mocking the farmers was their habit - openly and aggressively from the Germans, but silently, behind diverted, hateful glances from their captives. For the most part no one was physically abused, as long as they toed the line and kept their irrelevant opinions to themselves.

Winter would eventually establish itself for another bout of additional hardship, as the usual routines were maintained. Its structure varied only slightly as time wore on, from farm to farm. Oddly, the farmers developed a closer kinship than they had known amongst each other in prior times.

Perhaps it was those bonds and invisible shackles they wore as perpetual evidence of the new world foisted upon them, for reasons known only to their captors. Life was still simple here and for many, it would always be so. A sense of fairness, or the obvious lack of it, was never a consideration; to what end no one could ever justify.

The boys quickly became men by working all day, every day harder than the one before. Their priority was one of survival and doing as they were instructed, without reservation. Admittedly, their work became meaningless, and they reluctantly accepted their subservience to the German intruders.

Their concerns were not as much about surviving from day to day, as it was about making their way through the oppressive and harsh winter months ahead of them. Years of living on this farm had taught the family how much they needed to store and how long they could extend themselves through the final weeks of the inevitable prolonged cold weather.

"We need to organize ourselves with some of the nearest farms to share and support one another. These regular pick-ups are wiping us out. The rations they leave behind simply aren't enough." Josef remarked.

In response Jan added, "They're all feeling like we do. Our circumstances are always the same. Problem is the Krauts don't give a shit about whether winter kills us or not. Christ, they've already cleaned us out of dried firewood. Burning damp pine this winter is going to smoke us out of the house!"

Marianna had already sat with the boys after finishing up the dishes and was within earshot of their conversation. "You boys are right about one thing. None of our friends are working any harder than they must to meet their quotas, same as us. We can all do better, but let's do it for the benefit of our own families."

"Ma makes sense. We all know a few good places in the woods where we can stash supplies, where the Krauts will never look. You've seen them, they just watch us load up their truck. Most of them are too stupid and too lazy to check out the forest. Let's take every advantage we can, without being careless."

Although the youngest of the family, Jan had an easy going and pragmatic approach to most problems the family encountered, and he was never fearful of speaking his mind. "We can talk among ourselves till hell freezes over and end up frozen to death sooner or later. I've already squirrelled away a few bags here and there. You guys didn't notice, so why should they?"

"What! You crazy little bugger!" Josef hugged his brother, both scowling at him and laughing at the same time. "Where did you put them?"

"Remember when we tried to make that shitty schnapps a few years ago?"

"I do... and it *was* shitty! That's what I remember the most. I haven't been in that smelly cave since we shut the stills down after Dad died."

"It was pretty much grown over, as I thought it might. Can't even find it unless you know exactly where it is. It's a great place to use for storing what we can."

"Great idea, but why wouldn't you tell us about it before?" Josef wondered.

"If I did, what would you have said?" Josef quickly retorted. "No way!"

"That's precisely why I decided not to!"

"That explains why we fell just short of our quotas, isn't it? I knew I hadn't miscounted! I got some serious shit from the Krauts that day.

In fact, that's how I broke my tooth. Couldn't tell you or Ma what really happened though. I adjusted the count a couple of bags when I saw we were going to be short. They were too busy shooting the shit to count themselves, but they still knew we were a little off."

Josef shifted the topic back to what mattered most. "Let's get something organized right away, but we have to be selective about who we talk to about this."

"I'll talk to Heinz and Dimitri tomorrow. We'll offer them a few bags of potatoes and beets; they'll help cover some of the shortages we have with meat and bread. They can store what they have in the cave as well. We only need the few we can trust. Let's make damn sure they keep their mouths shut to anyone else who could give us grief. Understand?"

"I agree. The fewer who know about this the better!" Jan replied.

7

A DREAM FULFILLED

AFTER THE GREAT WAR IN 1918, THE TREATY OF VERSAILLES stipulated the dismantling of what remained of the German military, specifically including the dissolution of the German air force. Since early 1935, however, in direct violation of the peace treaty, German pilots had been secretly training in the Soviet Union at Lipetsk Airforce Base.

By the time Germany invaded Poland in 1939, the Germans had already gained three years of proven battle experience fighting in the Spanish Civil War, serving as a dress rehearsal for WWII. It was an invaluable opportunity to learn and assess valuable flight capabilities of their newly designed aircraft, as well as the skills of the young pilots who commanded them.

Tremendous emphasis was also given to the development of battle tactics, including training of ground support personnel. These live training operations created a professionally seasoned and technologically advanced air force, unmatched anywhere in the world, *before* the Second World War began. The Luftwaffe, commanded by Reichsmarshall Göring, would play a significant role in support of the German war machine.

Optimism, morale and an incredibly strong sense of honor and duty to the Fatherland had been deeply entrenched in the minds and spirit of almost ten million young, idealistic German soldiers. Since their adolescence in the Hitler Youth, these young warriors had been controlled and conditioned to the extent their valiant dedication knew no bounds.

On the battlefield, thousands of eager young men quickly moved up the ranks of the military, and deservedly so. Their practical knowledge and experience were an incredible asset to thousands more who strove to emulate the same standards of military excellence.

Repeatedly, Reichsmarshall Göring passionately challenged the brave young men under his command, to be prepared to die with unwavering commitment for the Fatherland. Every young man willingly embraced this incredible aspiration.

One of those so influenced and dedicated, was Lieutenant Manfred von Brauchitsch, now barely nineteen years old. Manfred was still enrolled in the Hitler Youth during the Spanish Civil War and was too young to have participated in Russian flight training at Lipetsk, however with the timely influence of his grandfather, he was accepted into flight school at the very young age of seventeen. His bright mind, physical strength, chiseled features, and absolute dedication groomed him to become a proverbial poster boy for recruiting other adolescents too eager for battle to know better.

Manfred quickly learned to refine his skills and natural raw talent for his chosen role in the prestigious Luftwaffe. Further supported by the spirited and steady encouragement of his father Klaus, he was destined to become one day what he always dreamed of: the captain of his own fighter squadron.

*****

Following the invasion of France in May 1940, the Juvincourt Airfield in northern France was quickly overrun by German forces and became one of Germany's most strategic airfields for the Luftwaffe. It would be Manfred's first mission facing live action in the cockpit of his Messerschmitt Bf-109. He was under the command of Major von Bernegg who had been a veteran of the Great War.

The major provided a wealth of personal experience in times of war and had a reassuring manner about him, often interpreted for what it was - confidence and courage under fire, which he instilled in the minds of his talented young warriors of the air. Von Bernegg believed German pilots were highly capable and well trained. Implementing their skillset was just a matter of self-reliance based upon what they were taught. Manfred took his advice seriously.

Fighter escort for heavy bombing raids had already exacted a toll by shredding the Juvincourt Airfields. Manfred's first mission was to assist with laying supportive ground cover for the mobilized German Army as they overwhelmed the French to seize control. The continuous strafing of the airfields below required a steady hand and good judgement to better ensure the mission was accomplished without undue risk to advancing ground troops.

On this particular day under clear skies, the Luftwaffe struck quickly and scored major hits on the first bombing runs, taking out communication towers and significantly destroying or disabling many French aircraft sitting helplessly on the tarmac. It was a surprise attack, permitting only fifteen to twenty enemy aircraft to take off and gain sufficient altitude to engage the swarming Messerschmitts eagerly awaiting above.

The few French and RAF fighter planes able to join the battle over Juvincourt fought valiantly, despite being greatly outnumbered. In the ensuing dogfights, one crack RAF pilot severely damaged a Bf-109, enough to force it to leave the battle in an attempt to limp back to base. The pilot struggled to maintain altitude, but the plane soon disappeared over the tree line and exploded on impact.

Lieutenant von Brauchitsch was immediately ordered by command to replace the fallen comrade who had been flying wingman for one of the Luftwaffe's top-rated pilots, Lieutenant Colonel Gerhard Barkhorn. Manfred's new assignment was to fill in as Barkhorn's wingman.

Barkhorn was already preoccupied with not one, but two French Dewoitine fighter aircraft managing to take off. Although not expecting anything more than a routine strafing mission, Manfred remained calm and ready to engage without hesitation. Circling from above he assessed the situation, quickly dropping to lower altitude to approach the scene on the perfect trajectory to engage in the heavily contested dogfight unfolding before him.

His job was to single-mindedly engage the opposing wingman to draw his fire away from Barkhorn, leaving Lieutenant Barkhorn to focus one-on-one with his adversary. In mere seconds he achieved what he wanted.

Now, Manfred was dealing with his own dogfight. Having drawn the Frenchman's fire, and no doubt his ire, Manfred pulled back on the stick and banked steeply, knowing his plane was more maneuverable than the French plane. As predicted, the trailing plane broke away after only a few seconds, unable to maintain Manfred's speed and vertical ascent. The instant he broke away, the chase was on.

Manfred used his higher altitude to his advantage by scanning the sky and maneuvering for better position. This time he was the hunter and having identified his prey, he attempted to close on him and re-engage. In the following minutes, the two combatants raced through the open skies, each one swerving and looping to jockey for greater advantage. Anything Manfred may have lacked in experience was fully compensated by the keenness of his piloting skills and the confidence to proficiently execute them. He soon overmatched the French fighter.

Pinpointing the crosshairs of his gunsights on the wing of the Dewoitine, Manfred squeezed the trigger firing a short burst, sustaining damage to its aileron in the process. The pilot lost partial maneuverability of his aircraft but was no longer able to effectively engage. Calmly, Manfred circled back to methodically finish him off. In seconds, his first kill was confirmed.

Moments later, Flight Major Barkhorn took his man down as well and the swarming Bf-109s finished their final runs and headed back to base.

Manfred was thrilled by his accomplishment and heard supporting chatter in his headset from his air team who witnessed the kill. The victory was a small one, but one he had dreamed about since he was just a kid. The adrenalin rush of his first encounter facing live rounds was not only satisfying... it was also surprisingly addictive.

As the aircrafts touched down one by one and taxied to their designated locations, the pilots popped their canopies and heroically stepped onto the tarmac, amid cheers and laughter surrounding the young lieutenant. It was a light-hearted moment, shattering the almost imperceptible tension of the young man's successful first mission.

"Well done, kid! Did you shit your pants when the order came in? I probably would have!" said Irwin, one of Manny's close friends from his graduating class.

"No time to think about it really. I'm glad it happened that way. No time for worry or doubt... just go!" Meanwhile, Flight Major Barkhorn had joined the small but rowdy group of young pilots.

"Hell of a way to meet you, Lieutenant! I'm Gerhard Barkhorn. Thanks for coming to the rescue, young man. Truth be told, I probably would have taken care of both of those bastards if you hadn't jumped in." Barkhorn had a wry smile crease his handsome face. He paused only slightly adding, "Just bustin' yer balls, Kid. Outstanding job! Glad to help you get broken in. Welcome aboard!"

It was an auspicious beginning for Lieutenant von Brauchitsch. It wouldn't be long before he seized the spotlight again.

*****

By this time, Manfred had risen in popularity with his fellow pilots for his incredible marksmanship providing strategic air support during the German victory over France. He was no longer relegated to routine strafing runs and took advantage of every opportunity afforded him by confidently building his shining reputation as an up-and-coming pilot. In his first month alone, he was credited with seven kills and attracted the watchful eyes of Major von Bernegg, as well as Flight Major Barkhorn.

It was mid-June 1940, when Manfred was summoned by Major von Bernegg. "Come in, Lieutenant. I'm anxious to speak with you. Please have a seat."

Manfred had developed a rather high profile under the Major's care and supervision. They had a strong fondness for one another, despite the considerable difference in age and rank. The Major was well into his twilight years, having served more than twenty-five years in military command. He was a veteran of the Great War, well before the rise of Adolf Hitler.

"Your rise to prominence has attracted keen interest from Flight Major Barkhorn and, of course, your grandfather, General von Brauchitsch. His influence and high opinion of your dedication and innate skillsets were instrumental in determining where you would serve the Fatherland when you graduated from the academy. Our friendship and mutual admiration for one another were significant factors in having you assigned to my command. I'm proud to have you among our ranks, young man."

"Thank you, Sir. I consider myself fortunate to serve under you. May I enquire why I am here today, Major? How can I be of service?" Manfred respectfully enquired.

"I was recently informed I am being replaced by Major Hanns Trubenbach by months end. He's an excellent tactician and was personally recommended by Reichsmarschall Göring to take over my command. It seems my usefulness here at Juvincourt has come to an end. I agree with Göring's decision. It is time for me to step down."

"I shall miss you, Major. It was your confidence that brought out the best in me, Sir. I cannot imagine developing my skills so quickly, were it not for your positive influence. I'll never forget what you did for me, and I will be forever grateful."

The major placed his hand reassuringly on Manfred's shoulder as he spoke. "I appreciate the compliment, Lieutenant, but it had little to do with me. It is your ability, determination, and fearlessness opening those doors, not me. Always remember that Manfred. It is precisely why you will be leaving Juvincourt in the next forty-eight hours."

Manfred looked incredulously at his major, as the order had taken him totally by surprise. The Major continued, "You have been assigned to the Eastern Front. June 16th you will be joining Flight Major Barkhorn, based upon both my, and his own recommendation to JG-52 Fighter Wing, 2nd Gruppe. It is under the command of Captain von Komatzki. I don't know him well, but his Gruppe is regarded as one of the finest in Jagdgeschwader 52. Congratulations, Lieutenant!"

"Thank you! I welcome the challenge, Sir." Manfred responded, maintaining his composure despite his exuberance upon hearing the news.

"You have done well here against French and British fighters. They are formidable opponents and very well trained. They have held their ground well against us despite being outnumbered. The Russians, however, are far less intimidating. A young man with your skills will excel against them. I'll inform Flight Major Barkhorn to get you up to speed on the details.

"This is an outstanding opportunity to rub shoulders with the best pilots we have, Lieutenant. My advice is to pay close attention, not only to what they say, but to what they do. You will learn a great deal about their make-up by how they handle themselves in the skies *and* on the ground. I know you will make the most of it. Good luck, young man."

*****

OPERATION BARBAROSSA, THE EASTERN FRONT

Hundreds of Luftwaffe fighter pilots, many fresh out of the academy, were out-fitted with newly manufactured Bf-109s, as were refurbished bomber squadrons. The pilots and maintenance support service personnel congregated for reassignment to various airfields close to the German-Soviet demarcation line on the western border of Russia; an immense expanse covering almost 3,000 kilometers.

Barkhorn, Manfred and several other prominent officers were enjoying themselves in the Officers' Club to sort out the posted roster assignments for the upcoming invasion of Russia; many of them meeting for the first time.

After some final shuffling of personnel, it was confirmed Manfred and Barkhorn would serve together under Oberlieutenant Rudolf Resch on JG 52nd Fighter Wing, now based in Sobolewo in north-eastern Poland. It would become an integral part of the front line for *Operation Barbarossa,* a major offensive committed to one purpose: the siege of Moscow.

They shared a few cold beers that same evening with several of their squadron and fellow graduates from the academy. It wasn't often they had the chance to get reacquainted with anyone outside the Wing, but when they did, the conversation always led back to business: boasting, exaggerating, teasing, and laughing. It took the edge off the growing anticipation of what was to follow.

For those close to him, Gerhard was known simply as *Gerd.* He was a gregarious and popular leader who spoke supportively, based upon his respected experience under fire. Everyone looked up to him.

"I've been informed Reichsmarshall Göring himself is arriving here tomorrow to meet with the top brass. Word is he'll be giving us a brief pep-talk shortly after. Resch tells me we should expect a steady diet of four to six missions a day for each of us. Nothing we didn't already expect."

"Wow! We all wanted to see some action. I guess we're gonna get what we asked for, right quick!" Manny offered enthusiastically.

No one dared complain about the workload. It was all part of a day's work and flying was all they talked about. The familiarity and relaxed atmosphere became more apparent, until a particularly distinguished officer entered the bar and was greeted by everyone closest to the entrance. Smiles and enthusiastic handshakes were exchanged and drew everyone's attention, especially the interest of the newest young pilots in the room.

Manfred wondered aloud, "So, who's the guy everybody's fussing over? Do you know him, Gerd?"

"Oh, yeah. I've been waiting for him to get here. That's someone you gotta meet. It's Erich Hartmann. Look sharp and don't drink too much so you can pay attention to everything he says. There's no one like him. Great guy." Gerd took a final mouthful to finish his beer. "Hang back a minute, would ya, fellas?"

When Gerd stepped away from the group at the bar, Flight Major Hartmann saw him immediately. He was always smiling, but seeing Gerd, he was now beaming. Hartmann shifted his attention and broke away from his admirers, only to attract many more, but his gait quickened toward Gerd. No handshakes were offered, just a full embrace of two best friends.

"You're looking good, you son-of-a-bitch! How are you Gerd? It's been too long, my friend, too damned long."

"Right back at ya, Erich. Damn it, I missed you! How's that pretty sweetheart of yours? All good, I hope?"

"Never better. I've finally asked Ursula to marry me," Hartmann proudly boasted. "About time, Lieutenant! Did she have to think about it very long? Congratulations, man! Hey, congrats on the new stripes too! I heard you're a Flight Major now. Well done, Erich... I'm proud as hell of what you've accomplished. Let me buy you a beer and introduce you to a couple of the guys."

Small talk continued here and there, but Gerd held young Manfred's introduction until the last. Before he did so, Hartman quietly asked of Gerd, "Is that the one I've been hearing about? He's the von Brauchitsch kid, right?"

"One and the same. He's got something special; a sharp mind and he's got confidence without being too cocky. If anyone's got a chance to chase you, Erich, it's him. Take some time to get to know him. You'll be impressed, I guarandamntee you. He's got more natural talent than anyone I've ever met, next to you."

"That's high praise, coming from you. He graduated the same year I did, but from a different academy. His family contacts helped, but I didn't realize it was the same kid you told me about. I think he's got a dozen kills under his belt in just a couple of months out of Juvincourt. He's gonna feast on the fuckin' Russians."

"Two more days and we're gonna find out what he's made of. Hell... what we're *all* made of!" Gerd confided to Erich.

"Hey, Manny! Come on over here, would ya?"

Manny put down his beer on the bar, and straightened the tie that didn't require adjustment, just a natural instinct by this time.

"Lieutenant Manfred von Brauchitsch, this here is Flight Major Erich Hartmann, best friend of mine in the entire Luftwaffe."

Looking as sharp and debonair as anyone, Manny offered a slight but respectful smile and a firm handshake to match. "Good to meet you personally, Sir. I've heard a great deal about you, of course." Manny never shrank from anyone but noticed the straight-forward and confident manner in which the flight major held himself. The man exuded a natural ease that probably accompanied him into the cockpit as well. He couldn't wait to see him in action.

After an hour had passed, Gerd turned and raised another beer to the squadron members upon whom they all relied. "Let's call it a night. Time to get down to business boys!"

*****

On June 22, 1941, the first of over four million German soldiers invaded Russia. The world had never before witnessed an invasion on such a monumental scale. The Russians were largely unprepared for the overwhelming coordinated assault.

From the first day of *Operation Barbarossa*, it was an incredible opportunity for the Luftwaffe to flex its muscles, and that's precisely what they did. The Russians made no apparent effort to disperse their massive air force across multiple airfields, foolishly leaving vast numbers of aircraft, fully exposed in the open fields to extensive devastation from repeated German bombing raids.

When armed troops arrived shortly thereafter, wreckage confirmed more than two thousand destroyed Russian aircraft, compared to only thirty-five German aircraft shot down. Within only three days, Russian losses numbered more than two thousand more. It was an initial slaughter, testing the resilience and determination of the Russian forces in unimaginable ways, eventually proving the German offensive to be the biggest and most costly miscalculation Hitler would ever make.

During the assault, the dependence of the German Army upon the Luftwaffe presented the pilots with an opportunity to shine. From the opening salvo in May and during the balance of the year, the Luftwaffe established themselves as the superior air force. As predicted by Major von Bernegg, Manny's commanding officer in Juvincourt, the skies over Russia were a target-rich environment for the better trained and better equipped Germans, and they showed no restraint in exhibiting their obvious dominance.

Hitler was gleeful at the swiftness of Germany's progress. Riding on the heels of the Luftwaffe air victories, the German army advanced two hundred miles into Russian territory in the first week of combat, capturing or killing 600,000 troops in the process.

German airbases along the demarcation line were hastily buzzing with round the clock air attacks, requiring multiple missions for the tireless aircrews and support personnel. Their superior training and preparation were used to full advantage.

Manfred continued to fly wing support, alternating between Gerd and Erich, as the situation required. He further defined his own flying technique whenever the opportunity arose, often being scolded for poor positioning or the occasional reckless abandon that became part of his flying mastery. Both aces piled up the kills at an incredible pace, further establishing them as the best fighter pilots Germany had to offer. Manfred watched, listened, and learned quickly.

Sitting down to a meal, the three teammates were usually insepa-rable, and some of the open criticism carried over to the dinner table. On occasion they were joined by a few regulars, including one of the veteran aces who quietly went about his business, preferring to speak by his actions, not his words. His name was Major Gunter Rall.

Gerd was the first to notice him leaving the buffet with a full plate. These men had voracious appetites. "Hey, Gunter. Grab a seat with us, would you? Maybe you can talk some sense into this kid."

"You give that kid shit every damn day. What's he done this time?" He sat down across from Manfred and looked directly at him and winked his eye. Manny had long since developed a thick skin and took the brunt of his mates' constant critique, knowing full well he was progressing rapidly and doing them proud with his steady growth and willingness to learn.

Gerd continued, "Don't get me wrong Gunter, Manny's doin' a great job. Nuthin' but upside here. Just too quick to break away and join the fray. Don't want him to get his ass shot off... mine either!"

"I've been at this for some time, Manny. I remember my own eagerness to jump in, as if it was yesterday. Like Gerd says, *too hungry!* How long you been flying wing now?"

"Almost a year now, but I know I can do more here. I've soloed before and I can handle myself, I know it."

Erich finally took the edge off his hunger pangs and jumped into the conversation. "Manny's already been credited with a dozen kills; mostly flying bomber support out of Juvincourt. Probably another five or six against the Russians too, as a wingman, for Christ's sake! He's capable, Gunter. I think he's ready... *IF* he can keep his pants zipped and doesn't get reckless."

Gerd chimed in, offering, "Manny held his ground over Juvincourt and stood dead even with the Brits with some one-on-ones. We all know by comparison the Russian Yak-4s are obsolete and even their new MiG-3s and Focke-190s don't have properly trained pilots to fly them. Their leadership in battle is amateurish, at best. Doesn't mean we shouldn't take them seriously, but Manny could handle this. Lieutenant Major Resch says it's my call."

"Maybe it's time we get off the fence and let the boy have a go," Gerd thought out loud.

"Here's an idea. How 'bout you fly *his* wing for a few missions and see what he can do up close?" Gunter suggested matter-of-factly.

The table fell silent while Erich and Gerd sat quietly staring at one another for a few long seconds. Erich nodded his approval without uttering a word. That was all Gerd needed.

"OK, Manny. Let's do this. I'll inform Resch and we'll change it up at morning's first light. You got what you want. Gotta admit, you deserve it Manny. I'm tired of bustin' your balls anyway. Congrats!"

The following morning, a half hour before daybreak, another faint and steady rumble of menacing intent could be heard approaching Vilnius from the southeast. Yet another endless series of bombing runs designed to strip Lithuania of anything standing, and all points east on the road to Moscow.

As the sun rose behind the flying armada, it was a crisp and clear morning playing out in an amazing panorama of peaceful summer colors. Lieutenant von Brauchitsch was calm and fully alert above the glorious landscape below, poised at the ready to lead his own formation with Gerd on his wing.

The bombers, with their deadly payloads, continued their pre-established runs when dozens of Russian fighters raced to engage the German fighter escort to deter the approaching formation. Striking just one critical kill shot could take a few bombers off their course, sufficiently to save strategic targets below from the impending inferno that would ensue. German fighter support was specifically tasked to eliminate the Russian attack before any relevant damage was sustained to the heavy bombers.

"Here they come. Forty to forty-five bogies at two o'clock. Watch your six boys!" barked the squadron commander. Wingmen, stay tight, stay focused."

Manfred was in the lead group of seven charging forward full throttle behind their commander. The hunt was on to eliminate the threat, quickly and efficiently. Approaching with the sun at their backs was an advantage the gunners were about to exploit, firing short bursts of ammunition to pick apart the steady Russian formation into more easily digestible pieces.

Manny had free access to multiple targets with Gerd tight on his right wing, allowing Manny to choose his point of attack. Manny closed quickly with short but accurate bursts, disabling one Yak-4 by ripping into his right wing. The disabled plane fell back out of formation, losing altitude rapidly.

Recircling from above, Manny moved in closer to tighten formation. Several dogfights were already underway, still too far away to hear the gunfire over the roar of the bomber convoy.

"Watch your eleven, Manny. We've got company! Two Focke-190s coming right at us."

"Let's draw their attention away from the payload. We're not here to babysit. See if they take the bait and both give chase. Formation, pull tighter to cover our positions," Manny ordered.

Sure enough, the two rapidly approaching Russians broke away, tantalized by the chance to take out the German two-some. They were quickly accompanied by two more Focke-190s in support.

"Take us where you wanna go. I'm staying tight on your wing as long as I can, Kid," Gerd confirmed. "Roger that. I'm increasing altitude. Let's clear some space for the six of us to tango."

Manny pulled the throttle back, taking a steep angle of ascent. The Fockes could not maintain speed. As the distance between them increased, Manny banked sharply to become the aggressor. "Let's take these two on, face to face. I'll take the higher one, you the lower. Whether we strike them or not on approach, break away aft immediately and take the one closest to you. I'll find the other nearby. Got it, Gerd?"

"Roger that."

As they bore down on the two targeted Russians, both Bf-109s fired steady bursts at them simultaneously. It was only a small window, but both crafts despite firing back, did not have position to score hits.

"Taking my shot and prepare to break right, Boss!... Direct hit!" The debris from the explosion flashed by Manny's plane; one piece rattled when it glanced off his canopy and dropped away harmlessly. "Got the son-of-a-bitch!"

"Me too, Kid. Clipped his wing and spilled fuel. He's goin' nowhere but down. Those other two are coming fast. We're not done yet. See 'em at 9:00! Let's welcome those Fockes."

"I got 'em, Gerd. Got a couple of others south-east just breaking cloud cover but coming in fast. Looks like they're after Gunter's team," Manny shouted.

"He's good. Stay the hell out 'a there," Gerd barked. "Sorry Boss... just a suggestion! They're breaking formation. Let's pick up a few more solos!"

Immediately, Manny and Gerd closed tight behind the attacking Fockes to draw them away from their primary targets, the heavies, which had just opened the bomb bays and steadied their approach after dropping altitude. The ground flack was not as heavy as expected, but still enough to rattle the gyroscopes. Their courses were holding steady.

Manny went after the wing man first, barely missing the canopy shot, but he buried a few in the fuselage, clipping a wing joint in the process. The craft was unsteady but maintained its speed trying to break away out of desperation. "Boss, take the wingman down and rejoin me. I'm after the lead Focke."

When the damaged winger turned away, so did the abandoned leader. He went vertical to lose himself in the light of the still rising sun for only a brief moment. Manny was hot on his tail, matching his adversary with each twist and turn. *This son-of-a-bitch is good! Maybe not all these guys are pussies,* Manny thought to himself.

As the leader raced to lower cloud cover, Manny bore down to where he thought he would exit the cumulus camouflage... Wrong choice! Manny broke left, but the Focke stayed steady and circled back to efficiently line Manny up in his gunsight. Before Manny could evade him, the Russian took his shot. Anticipating the burst, Manny broke left and high. One trailer clipped his wing, but no serious damage was sustained. Hydraulics were still holding. Time to get serious with this guy.

Manny knew his 109 was more maneuverable than the Focke. He'd lost sight of Gerd and saw open skies ahead. At full throttle his 109 outpaced the chase plane and he established an elliptical flightpath with his engines screaming at full power. In seconds he re-established himself as the hunter, not the hunted. *"There you are you little bastard."*

Manny remembered Erich telling him not to fire at the enemy, fire slightly ahead of him. Short bursts only and prepare to withdraw. Carefully lining up the crosshairs, he squeezed the trigger... *Damn it!* First one missed, but not by much. The bobbing and weaving continued. Again, he reset his target... anticipating where he would be, but slightly ahead... *Got him!*

The action subsided as quickly as it began. The bombers had done their evil deed. How many died below was not something to consider for fighter support. It was the job that had to be done. It was accomplished. No sense chasing the retreating Russians. Time to regather and head to base.

In only seconds, there on Manny's tail was Gerd, feisty as ever. "Well, have a look at that, would ya! We got us another ace! Good job, young man. I'll buy you the next beer. Well done, Manny!"

It was a big test for Manny that day, but as always, he only became better. In all, twenty-two Russian aircraft were destroyed and the damage from the bombing raid received high praise from Commander Resch and Reichsmarshall Göring. It was an auspicious beginning to Operation Barbarossa.

8

FACING THE DEVIL HIMSELF

ANNA CONTINUED PRIORITIZING AND CALMLY EXECUTING the multitude of crucial tasks constantly evolving since the first day of the invasion. Efficiency and focus were two of the cornerstones High Command strove to attain. They were determined to lead by example, causing this high level of proficiency to ripple throughout the chain of command.

In theory, Anna and her immediate superiors supported these ideals; however, from a practical perspective, efficiency would soon prove to be an elusive ideal. It was a constant source of frustration for many, something very few were willing to openly address.

When Hitler reorganized Abwehr in 1938, it was instructed by his advisors to create local stations in each military district throughout Germany, of which there were many; sub-offices, so to speak. These stations were called *Abwehrstelles*, or ASTs for short. Each AST encompassed the same sub-divisions of expertise as Abwehr, namely espionage, sabotage, and counterintelligence. In the three years since the reorganization, those decisions to purposely diffuse and complicate military infrastructure were starting to take their toll.

As if this was not confusing enough, each AST could plan and strategize their various assignments, on the clear understanding the ultimate execution of their duties was consistent with Admiral Canaris' oversight. However, there was little enforcement and accountability to assure consistency with most similarly authorized ASTs.

Even the recruiting of potential agents was subcontracted to various civilian authorities having no formal affiliations with the military. The frequent abuses of these responsibilities, and the lack of practical experience were often contributing factors to the failure of many missions.

During this period, Anna was constantly vigilant about seeking ways and methods to improve numerous procedural inefficiencies. It was simply her nature to be thorough, to the point of obsession. Her responsibilities to the Admiral and General von Brauchitsch were always of paramount importance, despite her justifiable hatred of Hitler's Reich. She refused to do anything less for fear of compromising the work of her direct superior officers.

Many of the Hitler directives were difficult to implement using these antiquated systems, many sorely lacking a greater measure of streamlining and transparency. These inefficiencies inevitably imposed obvious limitations upon the cohesiveness of operations within the inner circle. It was time for Anna to speak her mind.

"Good morning, Major Groscurth. May I speak privately with you and General von Brauchitsch before our group meeting later today?" Anna's confidence had grown appreciably in her new supportive role, but this was the first time she took the initiative to speak up so proactively.

"That is precisely why you were selected to work with us," the Major stated reassuringly. Any initial apprehensions Anna may have felt quickly dissipated.

"It is a matter of some importance, but I am uncertain as to whether the others will be open to my criticism. Perhaps they may misconstrue my intentions."

"Yes, of course, Anna. I am always eager for your feedback on operations, and I appreciate you coming to me first on any matter of shall I say, a delicate nature. This is the first time you have raised your concerns, and I trust your judgment. Let me confirm the General's availability."

At the urging of the major, the general obliged the major's request, instructing his aide, Richard to rearrange his already full agenda. It was agreed a meeting in the general's private dining room would be appropriate.

Anna was encouraged by the general's effort to accommodate her at such a hectic time, but it demonstrated the relevance of her role in the department. He unhesitatingly agreed Anna had never been one to question anything she was directed to do, He admired her for erring on the conservative side and respected her discretion. A meeting of this nature was probably overdue, what with their stressful agenda of late. Some off-the-record discussions were certainly warranted.

Anna came right to the point, as was her nature. These officers had no time for social banter either.

"Sirs, we have been adhering to several procedural systems I must call into question. I do so however, in the interest of serving you both to the utmost of my capabilities and hope you take what I am about to say from this specific point of view."

"We would have it no other way Anna. You have consistently executed whatever orders we directed to you and are well equipped by now to see operational inefficiencies from a very different perspective than our own. Tell us your thoughts. We are anxious to hear them."

"Thank you, General. We have been given conflicting and often contradicting reports, which in my opinion are proving to be counter-productive to our general mandate, more specifically to the mandate of Admiral Canaris.

"From a functional viewpoint, numerous complex operations within Abwehr conflict with other unrelated missions. These operations often appear self-serving to certain division leaders, some of whom proceed with apparent indifference for one another, often compromising the positive results we are trying to cohesively achieve.

"On several specific occasions, this inefficiency has created nega-tive consequences for other covert operations. It is only a matter of time before this could cause unfavorable military consequences."

"Has something occurred causing you to come forward now?" asked Major Groscurth.

"Yes, in fact a number of times. Most recently, two agents were operating independently under deep cover within the same covert operation, neither one knowing about the participation of the other. As you can imagine, there are many moving parts of each operation, which inadvertently tend to become entangled the more deeply undercover our agents are imbedded. Simply put, Abwehr should… in fact, *must* have more direct oversight. This would facilitate retain-ing much greater administrative control over multiple operations."

General von Brauchitsch shifted his direct gaze to the major. It was apparent they were both aware there were gross inefficiencies to which Anna had not been given prior access.

In the absence of any immediate verbal response, Anna continued. "As an example, if I may be specific, a recent communication from SIS London (British Intelligence) pertaining to our military capabilities in the south of France was intercepted yesterday... and copied to an AST operating out of Antwerp. In effect, *we are spying on each other!*" Her eyes widened to better emphasize the very preposterousness of her discovery.

"How in the hell was that allowed to happen?" the general exclaimed.

"In this case the transmitted message was not accurately deciphered. The case in point is that but for the incompetence of an agent in Belgium, he was not aware of the current rolling code. The information was highly sensitive, crucial to the success of another mission. Had the agent carried out his responsibilities competently, it would have seriously compromised a covert assignment having tragic consequences for the participants.

"Only by sheer incompetence it was unable to be deciphered. It should not have been copied in the first place! This is inexcusable! Our systems have serious flaws due to our lack of accountable redundancy."

Groscurth looked intently at the general, reflecting upon Anna's critique, not responding, but rather taking a moment to sip his coffee. Clearing his throat rather awkwardly, he showed noticeable uneasiness.

"I had already suspected you would be discussing our double agent situation in Prague. However, we were not aware of this inexcusable blunder. I am not pleased to hear of this, but very thankful you discovered it. This isn't the first time this has happened is it, Anna?"

"No Sir, it is not!"

"Walther, we have seen this coming since the reorganization the Fuhrer himself instituted. I think we both agree with Anna's assessment of our network being in serious disorder. There are better systems we have been reluctant to implement, and certain obvious failings we should be prepared to rectify."

The general interrupted by asking succinctly, "But should we, Major?" He drew out a cigarette and pondered what he was about to say. "The Fuhrer made it clear to us he wanted as little *intelligence* as possible in our Intelligence Bureau, did he not? Now we are tasting yet another direct result of his own stupidity!"

Anna was speechless. This was the first time the general had spoken in such terms about the Fuhrer, at least while in her presence. Without an adjournment to confer privately, which Anna had fully anticipated, the general had already decided Anna should be brought into the loop, so to speak. It was apparent the major concurred.

"We have an interesting dilemma, Anna, and you have just touched upon it. We have had an impact on certain matters of which you are already aware, and now you understand more fully the limitations of our clandestine sympathies. We agree we could do more, but the risks are significant for us all. These inefficiencies... Hell, these stupidities are well known to us. To put it succinctly, Hitler's meddling continually weakens our cohesive military efforts.

"Comparatively speaking, there is no immediate adverse risk to us if we passively allow some of these inefficiencies to continue to play out. Getting a mandate from the Fuhrer to oversee every AST would not only be difficult to achieve, but I dare say it would be nigh on impossible. The Fuhrer must be stopped, sooner or later, one way or the other. Exercising prudent judgement provides a means to slowly accomplish that result."

Anna hesitated momentarily before responding with a question of serious consequence. "If I am not overstepping, General, would the admiral also concur with this decision?"

The general offered his thoughts, which were consistent with those of the major. In summary he added, "Yes, he is very much aware of this predicament, and I will confirm his solid support of our decision. The utmost regret is that our own men and women will continue to be placed in additional peril if this nonsense continues unabated."

"If I might make a suggestion, Sirs?" Anna enquired.

"Please do, Anna." the Major responded.

Anna continued, "The problem clearly suggests there is not only insufficient oversight on general operations throughout certain ASTs, but there are also unauthorized actions, which appear to be circumstantially suspicious. I suggest we use this knowledge very discreetly within our own investigative connections to covertly confirm or deny our misgivings; perhaps by way of setting up a ruse, if you will."

"Where are you going with this, Anna? I don't follow," the general admitted.

"I am thinking about using what we have already found to plant a series of phantom messages, unique to each AST. If one or more reach out to leak information to the Antwerp agent for example, or another we have not yet discovered, it will identify to us the ones warranting further investigation by our office."

"And by so doing, if such nefarious agents are identified through our proactive efforts, this exercise would potentially deflect similar suspicions away from ourselves," suggested the major.

"I like what I hear." The general looked contemplatively for a moment and continued, "Anna, can you prepare these phantom transmissions, but restrict the selection of ASTs only to those whose behavior patterns presently warrant closer scrutiny? The major and I will assist you in this capacity. We will not likely be able to dupe anyone the second or third time around. We have but one shot at this so we must make our selections wisely. This is good work Anna. Well done!" offered the general.

As an afterthought, he added, "Oh... see that we identify the agent who dropped the ball on the expired code... and find out to whom he reported. Keep us posted, but do so only through our secured lines, as per protocol. Let's contain this as quickly as possible. I don't want us letting our guard down, not even for a moment."

*****

During this time, the general reviewed Anna's notations with Major Groscurth and Admiral Canaris. She meticulously investigated only the most questionable infractions warranting the entrapment being proposed. There were nine such possibilities, decided upon as most likely sources of leaked information.

The contrived phantom communications were specifically drafted on potentially sensitive matters to attract the attention of any would be double agent. They were unique to each AST and were selectively trickle-fed into the customary flow of daily intelligence communications.

If Anna's suspicions and subsequent assessments were proven to be accurate, the illicit forwarding would be quickly traced to identify the sender, and ideally the identity of the specific receiver. Either one would inevitably lead to the discovery of the other through whatever means of encouragement Abwehr chose to implement. It was agreed the traps were to be set in motion.

Within hours of the decision to proceed, the first message was coded and transmitted. Tracers and wiretaps were actively monitoring from the instant the message was sent. They would continue to do so for another twenty-four hours, waiting silently, just listening. Would anyone come forward to take the bait?

Each passing hour would initiate the process again to another specific AST in question with its own signature transmission, until all nine were activated; more waiting and listening. The tension was palpable. Each passing hour put more teams into play.

Suddenly, the fourth transmission was relayed within minutes of its confirmed receipt. "Got one!" the team leader shouted to the major, who was overseeing the operation.

"Get it in play! Get it in play!" urged Groscurth to his team leader, as he enthusiastically pumped his fist in the air. He turned and winked at Anna, who had remained all night just observing and waiting to be called upon. Her preparation and thoroughness had yielded promising results.

Then came the sixth… and the ninth! Like dominoes, the traps were activated. "We have them, Sir!"

After another eight or ten minutes the technician proudly exclaimed, "We have one in the 13th District… one in Limoges, and… I regret to say, we have one from this very office, Sir. It's coming from *Appropriations*, Major."

"Show me, Lieutenant… What the hell? This cannot be accurate! *Appropriations?*"

Anna looked quizzically at the data. Without saying a word, she withdrew to her office and referenced recent work orders and project allocation records. Systematically she withdrew several file folders making further notations of dates, invoices, and command directives on which she would have to compile deeper research. Appropriations was not an answer, but it was a clue worth following. There were connections here to be tracked by cross-referencing, which would identify any questionable patterns or similarities.

Within the hour, Anna exited her office and summoned the major as she approached. "Sir, I suggest we note anyone on shift tonight having prior access to the coding and Enigma machines, as well as anyone with possible ties to Appropriations, if in fact any such connection may even exist."

"I see where you are going with this Anna." He squeezed her arm appreciatively. "I think our work here is just beginning."

*****

Over the following weeks, Anna headed a special task force to study each aspect of the cases she was building. The task force consisted of specially selected individuals she and the generals trusted, but only within strictly defined limitations. No one other than herself would be given access to the complete picture.

There was no hint of any overt assumptions about anyone's apparent guilt or innocence. To the participants, it was simply an administrative process under audit and review. As the data was compiled, the cross-referencing revealed the evidence they had been suspecting, and a great deal more.

As it turned out, some ASTs had trained and activated numerous low-level agents, who did not possess the appropriate skills to escape detection. Their techniques were unsophisticated and posed no significant threat; much as a private business would require protecting their customer lists. Their security clearances were only rudimentary.

Nevertheless, every coded transmission was duly recorded and authorized by the initials of the attending general in command, of which there were only four. It was extremely unlikely for anyone to question these initialed authorizations, as there were thousands of them. However, Anna was now able to narrow down the list of suspects and worked backward to analyze each step, irrespective of the degree of relevance.

Sure enough, the lists were soon paired down to a few hundred transmissions, making the task more manageable. Upon closer scrutiny, these transmissions bore one sporadic irregularity. In each instance it was a certain match to the phantom transmission of the night in question!

Time would reveal the AST in Limoges France employed a woman from the French Foreign Ministry, who had been secretively compromised by Abwehr. Previously unknown to Abwehr, MI-6 had discovered her treasonous behavior and compelled her reluctant co-operation on behalf of the British, to redirect false information about British troop movements and supply lines during the invasion of France. The only reason this double agent had been discovered, was Anna's ruse.

"Awareness of this security breach may benefit us greatly, Admiral, in ways we may not have originally intended," said General von Brauchitsch to Admiral Canaris.

"How so Walther? What are you proposing?"

"Sir, the knowledge of our covert intelligence trap has not been shared with anyone outside of our tight circle, nor should it be, after the fact. I propose we continue to send other selective phantom messages through the same contact in Limoges, with intent to mislead and confuse the British to our longer-term advantage. Neither the British nor the woman in the Ministry have any idea about our discovery. The rogue agent can unwittingly become our double agent once again, completely unaware of whose purpose she will now serve."

"Brilliant Walther, brilliant! Bring the others up to speed and make certain Anna continues to oversee all transmissions of this nature. She is damned good at what she does. In fact, see to it she is rewarded in some fitting way. She has served us well without asking anything of us in return. I trust your judgment about her one hundred percent!" He grasped the general's hand firmly and emphasized, "You have done well, my friend."

"I will give her your kindest regards, Admiral."

*****

The involvement of someone in the Appropriations Department led to a well-disguised and complicated trail of greater impact than the Limoges breach. It was akin to peeling back each layer of an onion. The system was discovered to be rotten to the core. This caused Admiral Canaris to re-evaluate the blatant weaknesses of security protocols.

Security clearances in Abwehr were thought to be tightly controlled at almost every level of its operations. The coordination and efficiencies from AST to AST were certainly lacking, but efforts had been made by Admiral Canaris' team to address the previous shortcomings within the Abwehr administrative offices themselves, with one notable exception… Appropriations.

This department had been inadvertently and foolishly overlooked due to the apparent innocuous nature of its mandate. The rigorous standard for operations and counterintelligence were of a less conscientious standard in Appropriations. Although originally intended to finance supply management of various routine military materiel, it now became an exposed weak link that had been compromised.

After further extensive investigation, it was revealed a cipher clerk within Abwehr had been feeding valuable intelligence to his father… who was employed in Appropriations. The father was under severe financial duress since his divorce from his wife and was receptive to lucrative financial incentives offered by certain undisclosed foreign influences.

It was about this same time in the summer of 1940, when Alexander Demyanov, a Russian secret agent working directly with the Soviet Intelligence Service (NKVD), was parachuted into a rural area in eastern Germany. His instructions from Moscow were to initiate a campaign of deception by circulating a toxic combination of authentic and false information, specifically to Abwehr. It seemed Abwehr was always eager, even sometimes over-anxious, to glean access to sensitive intelligence, irrespective of the credibility of the source.

Within months of Demyanov's foreign interference, operating under his codename *Max*, he manipulatively consorted with influential German military contacts, under the guise of being a Russian defector. In truth, he was a highly skilled, Soviet trained agent, whose capabilities were on a much superior level than those of German espionage agents typically recruited by Abwehr. His technical familiarity with Russian operations, combined with his engaging charisma, enabled Max to eventually gain the trust of Abwehr's senior command, none other than an unsuspecting Admiral Canaris.

To add credibility to his sincerity to defect, Demyanov confessed his involvement with the now exposed leak in Appropriations. He gambled his confession to Abwehr would not result in his execution; thinking he could serve a greater purpose to appear willing to work with German intelligence against the Russians. He was in fact, the formerly *undisclosed foreign influence!* His daring gamble worked. Abwehr promptly vetted and recruited him to serve as their very capable double agent. Little did they realize, he already was.

What was unknown to Abwehr, was that Demyanov continued to feed valuable information to the Russians, eventually costing the lives of dozens of German undercover field agents. Most of his disclosures to Abwehr were misleading and outright false, but some were genuine to maintain the illusion he was working against the Russians.

This intricate deception was another of the internal leaks Anna's ingenuity helped to uncover. Despite Anna's mixed loyalties, rooting out the security breach in Appropriations and Abwehr's eagerness for retribution against the Russians, were productive and exciting accomplishments. She owed her life and the survival of her remaining family to General von Brauchitsch, and this priority of allegiance to him instilled within her a strong sense of personal satisfaction. The more she could contribute positively to his success, the more meaningful was her very existence, and all the more protected were her children.

The turning of Demyanov was perceived by many to mark the beginning of a new era in German intelligence. Nevertheless, his guise was so effective that sometime later, Demyanov would be awarded the German Iron Cross for his service to the Empire. The successful exposure of the treason had no doubt clouded their better judgement about Demyanov's trustworthiness.

Although Demyanov was never caught, he continued to serve Soviet interests throughout the remainder of the war, however under the watchful eyes of Anna and the astute oversight she had implemented, the leak from inside Abwehr was permanently closed. Within its walls, Anna was lauded for her creative and unquestioned service, although knowledge of this accomplishment was strictly confined within her small circle of command.

*****

The breach of Appropriations had also posed an even greater threat to certain services and financial infrastructure, specifically for the accounting and coordination with the Reich Chancellery to access *Konto 5*, which was under their questionable jurisdiction.

This bank account was initially established for the exclusive use of the Fuhrer. How he chose to use it was subject to his own personal discretion. Hitler routinely accessed Konto 5 to compensate his various generals, and others in German High Command, for the purpose of personally incentivizing them; in effect, bribing them to remain loyal to him. He strongly believed they would remain unwilling to bite the hand that fed them so generously.

Some of his most notable payments were to Herman Göring, Eric Raeder, Erwin Rommel, and Reinhard Heydrich, and of particularly curious note, Walther von Brauchitsch. Although Hitler's system was not technically illegal, funds nevertheless were secretly dispensed in the manner and to the extent he chose, mostly without any documentation.

When the Fuhrer was informed of Anna's outstanding accomplishments, he felt compelled to speak with her personally. Despite her significant contribution, Hitler seldom met with anyone outside of High Command. The Fuhrer emphasized to General von Brauchitsch that only he should accompany Anna to her audience with him.

Upon receiving the call from the Fuhrer's office, General von Brauchitsch summoned Anna to his office. He knew this request from von Ribbentrop on behalf of the Fuhrer, would most definitely unnerve her. As soon as she was announced, the general rose to personally greet her.

"Good morning, Anna. I trust you slept well?" he enquired.

"Why, yes General, I did. Thank you for asking." It was not like him to ask such an irrelevant question. Despite the general having developed a close working relationship with Anna, the superficial formalities applying elsewhere were typically dispensed with, in the interest of time and efficiency.

The general closed the door behind him, as was normal for most of his personal dialogue with his staff. He assumed his customary position perching on the corner of his desk, arms crossed.

"How can I be of help this morning, General?" Anna enquired as she continued to stand for the moment, anticipating incorrectly her discussion with the general today would be brief.

"I have been speaking this morning with the Minister of Foreign Affairs, Joachim von Ribbentrop. As you are aware, he sits at the right hand of the Fuhrer and advises him on more than the usual complex matters of state. His role has also become that of a personal advisor."

Anna continued to pay close attention but failed to see how she could be of relevance to any conversation with von Ribbentrop.

"I thought it best to deliver this news to you personally, and I have been asked to do so for reasons about to become obvious." He raised his right arm to casually direct Anna to be more comfortable.

"Please, have a seat, Anna." With some anxious trepidation, the general cleared his throat and with some apparent forethought, paused a little longer to sip his coffee.

"The Fuhrer and the Minister are most impressed with your outstanding contribution to the Reich... and have requested you attend a private audience with them." He purposely continued speaking to allow Anna a moment to reconcile the situation before she reacted spontaneously. She appeared to be in shock. She was.

"The request from the Fuhrer is to be treated extremely confidentially. Except for myself, and the admiral, knowledge of this meeting is to remain outside our chain of command."

"General, this is something I am not prepared to do! I despise the man!" Anna began to tremble, and her lips were quivering perceptibly. She stopped speaking while she absorbed the full impact of the Fuhrer's request.

By now, she had collapsed into the chair in front of the general, who did his level best to be detached from his personal feelings for her. He was unsure what to say and as he was composing himself in the intervening seconds, Anna asked the general to please repeat what he had just said.

"I stated this secret audience must be kept strictly between ourselves and will not be shared with anyone in our chain of command."

Only now did Anna process what the general had originally said and immediately began thinking to herself it was a highly irregular qualification. Her mind was racing, and this news had taken her completely by surprise. Was this explicit restriction a possible indication her immediate superiors were somehow the subject of Hitler's lack of trust in them? Why were they being excluded from anything Anna was ordered to do?

The general resumed by clarifying. "The meeting has been scheduled ten days from now, when the *Fuhrersonderzug* will be in northern Berlin." Anna once again, was speechless. The general paused awkwardly to adjust his stiffly starched collar, as if having difficulty breathing. He recognized her inner turmoil and very much felt his own.

"Are you well, Anna? Please say something, for Christ's sake." She shook her head briefly and responded out of courtesy to the man who had risked everything for her safety and began to stammer, "Yes... yes, I am fine, General. Just a bit... I am somewhat overwhelmed right now. Please forgive me... but... I'm very confused."

To the general's mind, it was much more than confusion. Anna was visibly shaken by anguish and the general was naturally concerned for her. He had expected a strong reaction but thought it wise not to console her at this time. Orders were meant to be followed, and for Anna there would be no exception; nor would she ask for one. Since working inside Abwehr, she had always appeared unflappable, and handled pressure situations with apparent ease. Now, she was showing her fallible side; she was human after all.

"Let's address this matter when you feel up to the task, perhaps over the next few days. I think you need some time to adjust to this circumstance. My door is always open for you, Anna."

"Thank you, General. As always, you are most thoughtful." She rose from her seat and had turned toward the door to leave, when the general picked up her notepad from the table stating, "Please pardon me, Anna... you seem to have forgotten this."

*****

When the day of the meeting finally arrived, Anna was sitting beside the general behind the lead car of his motorcade. Totally out of character, she had felt unwell since learning of Hitler's request and had begged off a subsequent meeting with the general. She simply stated she would do whatever was asked of her. Her apprehensions, however, were still taking a serious toll on her normally calm demeanor.

"Just relax as best you can, Anna. This is not something you could expect to fully prepare for, and I totally understand." The general was mindful not to state the obvious; she would never be loyal, nor pretend to be, to the very incarnation of evil she was about to face. He wisely chose not to refer to her fully justified hatred of the man.

Anna was verbally non-responsive and nervously preoccupied with her thoughts. After several awkward moments, the general tried again to engage with her. "You understand the Fuhrer only wishes to meet with you to acknowledge his appreciation for what you have accomplished in Abwehr, Anna. I cannot imagine the stress you are under, however under a very different set of circumstances, this would be a proud moment for anyone under his ultimate command.

"I expect this recognition will be sincere, as well as brief. You will get through this… We will get through it together," he assured her. Again, only silence.

After an anxious pause, Anna responded, "General, I do not want to appear cold toward you and I apologize if I appear to be so. Since I was made aware of this meeting, I have felt unwell, and I cannot sleep; I cannot rest. I am not eating, and I tremble without provocation. I do not know how I am going to manage what is about to take place. It has brought my mind back to the terrible things I have tried so hard to reconcile, but never will."

The general carefully reflected to himself and cautiously decided to share more with her than he had been prepared to discuss.

"Perhaps this will ease your pain somewhat. Although it was not my intention to speak of this now, it is perhaps the best time after all. A few weeks ago, Admiral Canaris personally recommended I find some way to reward you for all you have accomplished. We both know what matters most to you, and I gave you my assurances I would deliver on my promise. It is time I do so."

Anna's focus changed from one of despair to hopefulness. He saw the exuberant expression of anticipation in her face. "Yes, Anna! Klaus and I are arranging for you to see Dietrich and Marta within the next few weeks. The details are not yet worked out, but the admiral has given his blessings to see it is done."

Anna was overjoyed and began to weep openly. In a state of shock, she held her hand to cover her mouth. The news took her breath away. It was as if the last few anxious weeks were melting away, even though the meeting she dreaded was only an hour away.

"Thank you, General, you cannot imagine how pleased and relieved I am!" He quickly interjected, "No need for me to imagine, I am seeing it with my own eyes."

"Now, first things first. You must regain your focus for what lies ahead. We will be boarding a separate car from where we are meeting the Fuhrer. You will have an opportunity to do what you must to fix your make-up and the things women must do. You of all people know how to do it. This won't be the first time I've seen you transform yourself."

The private train housing Hitler's mobile headquarters sat ominously at the Zossen station. It was unlike any train Anna had seen. Layered in heavy armor, the dark gray, imposing shell was not designed to please the eye. Even the wheels were layered over with protective reinforced plates giving it a much sleeker appearance, seeming to be something out of the future. Doubtless, what it lacked in stylish design, it gained in functionality.

When Anna emerged from the third car to enter Hitler's private residence, General von Brauchitsch immediately rose to greet her. Despite being slightly red-eyed, she looked lovely; business-like, and reasonably fashionable, as would befit her respected station. Sitting behind his massive desk was the Fuhrer, who she immediately recognized. Opposite him was his closest aide, the Minister of Foreign Affairs, Joachim von Ribbentrop, to whom she was presently being introduced.

"And now it is my honor to introduce you to our Fuhrer. Mein Fuhrer, Madame Anna Pavlova." Hitler was in his full regalia and very much matched the description given by Marta several years before. Anna politely curtsied and extended her hand as he offered his own.

She decided earlier to remain silent and permit him to speak first, and as the general had advised, the meeting was not expected to take more than a few minutes of the Fuhrer's time. "Anna it is a delight to meet you," said Hitler. "Your stellar reputation precedes you, which bodes well for your future in the Reich we all serve."

She graciously accepted the compliment. "I was intrigued to have received your order to attend today. You are too kind, Mein Fuhrer." Hitler inadvertently lightened the moment with a genuine laugh, which surprised everyone, including von Ribbentrop.

"No, no. You have been completely misinformed Anna. Let me clarify, it was an *invitation* for you to attend. I dare not say you could have denied my order, as you put it. Certainly, one would presume you could have denied my invitation..." he waved his hand nonchalantly, "had you declined either, I would have been most disappointed."

"Please be seated, Anna. May we offer you a glass of wine, or a cup of fine tea perhaps?" She decided in advance to accept any offer of a beverage. She feared her throat would be too dry to function without something to drink, and she believed the tea might possibly calm her tattered nerves. She was still trembling and struggled to control it. "Why, some tea would be most welcome. I thank you."

"My staff have informed me of your most recent success in sourcing not only some gross incompetence in our field offices, but more importantly some nefarious matters that came to light, as a direct result of your creativity and diligent persistence. I consider it more important to meet with you in person than to send an emissary on my behalf. I wanted to commend you personally. Very well-done, Anna. Very well indeed!" He lifted his glass in her honor.

It was a flattering gesture, eliciting an understated but forced smile from her lips. From the corner of her eye, she could see the corkscrew within arm's reach on the adjacent bureau, and briefly fantasized about how very much she wanted to jam it directly into his heart, assuming the first strike would find its fateful mark. One can only dream, she thought.

"There is not much of consequence escaping my attention, Anna. I am told you have an amazing affinity for mathematics and coding analysis. You have proven to be a most impressive woman, demonstrating integrity and dedication to the Reich. In view of your abilities and my recognition for your insightful intelligence work, I want to task you with a responsibility that would make me terribly indebted to you. Does this sound... how did you put it... Ahh, yes; does this sound *intriguing* to you as well?"

"You have my undivided attention, Sir." At this point, Anna maintained direct eye contact with the Fuhrer. Doing this to the Fuhrer was unheard of; perhaps something more was intended.

She was careful not to display open disrespect, but she refused to show any fear of him. She would not allow herself to be intimidated and steadfastly refused to figuratively kneel before him. To masochistic bullies and sexual sociopaths, both of which she considered him to be, they use their power to exploit the weak.

Formidable women who held their own ground would force them to keep their penis in their pants, symbolically speaking. Sexual tension could be emasculating, and she used it to her subtle but effective advantage. It was something Marta had told her years ago that helped her get through intimidating moments with powerful men.

He continued with his train of thought and momentarily diverted his attention back to the general. "The glaring omission of adequate security in Appropriations continues to concern me. For now, that will be a private matter for further discussion with Admiral Canaris. However, this serious breach Anna discovered, has caused me to rethink the flawed wisdom of having my banking matters under Abwehr's supervision.

"My Chief of the Reich Chancellery is Hans Lammers of the SS. He presently handles all matters concerning account disbursements for Konto 5. He has been answerable to no one except myself, and increasingly I find I have insufficient time and attention for such matters to keep him in check. Too much temptation plants the seeds of greed. I need someone I trust to ensure accurate accountability of various transactions.

"For these reasons, it is my decision Anna be given exclusive administrative oversight on my behalf for cypher encoding my private payments and other potentially sensitive expenses. This responsibility, however, will not be supported enthusiastically by Chief Lammers. Be that as it may, my personal enthusiasm is all that matters on this issue. Am I making myself clear, General?"

"Most certainly, Mein Fuhrer. My only concern is Anna's additional workload. You can see for yourself the extent to which Abwehr has come to rely on her intuition and expertise. She has become a vital component of our complex operational team. I worry these added responsibilities may distract her from our intended purpose."

Hitler slowly returned his gaze to Anna, simply ignoring the general's concerns. "Do you have anything to add at this time Anna? I should clarify to you this is no longer an invitation to assist me." He smiled cunningly like a serpent toying with its prey. It was also the first time she was asked for her thoughts on the matter.

"I am flattered by your confidence in me, Sirs. I have always enjoyed a challenge and will continue to serve in whatever capacity asked of me." Anna was now addressing all the officers present, and not exclusively the Fuhrer. She tactfully shared her distracted focus from one to the other; being mindful to include Hitler, however briefly it may have appeared.

Hitler acknowledged her deftly choreographed acceptance and demonstrated his supportive enthusiasm he had spoken of earlier. "Excellent Anna! I will issue a confidential directive notifying High Command these matters will no longer be under Appropriation's mandate, with immediate effect."

Speaking directly to von Ribbentrop, he directed, "Minister, see to it you and Chief Lammers co-ordinate agendas to bring Anna current on the matters discussed today. See to this personally. I do not want your staff having knowledge of this arrangement. I insist this transition be completed with all necessary urgency."

Standing now and turning directly toward Anna, the Fuhrer closed the meeting by saying, "I am so pleased to finally meet you in person, Anna. You have exceeded even my high expectations of you. For the time being, Minister von Ribbentrop will keep me posted on your progress with Chief Lammers. I assure you he will not be an issue for you, and certainly not for myself. I look forward to seeing you again someday soon."

Once escorted to the waiting security detail, Anna and the general sat back in the rear seat, looked at one another, and deeply breathed a visible sigh of relief. The so-called brief meeting had taken about an hour. It had been a nerve-wracking one for both.

*****

It was apparent Hitler's decision was a direct result of his lack of trust in many of his officers to facilitate his intricate system of bribery and other financial indulgences. With each payment Lammers disbursed, he continually stressed the confidentiality of each transaction, strongly insisting each recipient not keep written records. This left the official payments open to his own abuse and misappropriation, at least up to now.

To say the least, Lammers was infuriated about the Fuhrer's bookkeeper having oversight of his control of the account, valued at approximately $40 million Reichsmarks in cash alone, at that time. This did not include the properties and artworks confiscated from Jews and other enemies of the Reich, the values of which were unimaginable. It was several months later before the entire inventory of illiquid assets was fully disclosed to Anna. Interestingly, the Landesburg and Friedman estates were not among them.

9
TRACKS OF HER TEARS

TO CHILDREN SUCH AS JULIA CHODAKOWSKA, POBEREZE WAS the only home they had known. Its name was as simple as the people, and as fitting a name as any; the translation was *Poor Place*. The District of Stanislawow was nestled at the northern edge of the Carpathian Mountains, providing a heavily forested backdrop through which Julia and her schoolmates had wandered aimlessly during summer's longest days. Those peaceful times with nature's gifts seemed to ensure a future of innocence and peacefulness as seen through the eager and welcoming eyes of youth.

Soon, the contrasts would become stark in her new reality. Julia was only thirteen years old when the German invasion took place, and shortly thereafter, Warsaw would fall. She was far too young to have comprehended the significance of that historic event and had to this date, seen few alterations in her family's life she could specifically attribute to the direct impact of war. But for the mothers and the few remaining men in her village, their perspectives were shockingly different.

Food was always in short supply, and many fathers and older boys had long since been conscripted into the military, including her own father. Julia missed his company, in particular his funny stories making her mother always laugh. Wherever he was, whatever he was doing, she never considered the possibility he may never return. Mother did cry so much more than she used to, and often prayed for his safe return.

Julia was a hard-working young girl who toiled tirelessly with her mother to tend to her younger sister and baby brother. Both Tanya and Mikel worshipped their big sister; Mikel, being only two years of age, his worship being more a matter of total dependence and adoration of Julia. He was a handful to be certain, and while Julia and Tanya were in school, their mother often struggled to balance managing the bakery and keeping Mikel out of mischief.

School had just begun a few weeks ago and Julia was delighted to resume classes with many of her friends. She welcomed the intellectual challenges school would bring after a summer of heat in the kitchens of the local bakery helping her mother. Working with her was not always as enjoyable as Julia thought it would be. The hours were long and the cleaning up was endless, and there just never seemed to be enough time to enjoy the simple pastimes summers used to provide.

Still, the family never went to bed hungry, so there was something of benefit compared to some other families in the village who were less fortunate. If you could catch a fresh fish and share a loaf of warm bread, few things in life could match those moments.

There was a beautiful brook close to the village, and the winding shoreline meandered a little bit right and a little to the left here and there, but always guiding the constant flow of fresh water within its natural cushioned borders. Even the few well-spaced rock formations could not stop the current, rather they could only make suggestions to nudge the crisp, sparkling majesty, only slightly to wherever it naturally had to go.

Since Julia could remember she, Margit, and Katarina visited a small corner of the clearing opposite the village side of the brook, and slightly upriver. It was their play-fort they had meticulously groomed to be clear of unsightly weeds, unless they bore wildflowers of any color or design.

"Those are gifts from God no one should dare pull from their hiding places. They worked hard for the right to be here, just like us," Julia pronounced.

Margit added supportively, "They come back to blossom every year I can remember. It wouldn't be home without them." Margit was a little bit plumper than her two best friends, and it was part of her natural charm and welcoming disposition. Cute as a button, her easy-going manner endeared her to many of her school mates, but no one as much as Julia and Katarina.

When she took a liking to someone, she was loyal, and worthy of shared confidences that would never be betrayed. Her genuine smile came from her heart and never failed to light up a room.

Crossing the ten or twelve feet separating the village side of the brook from the other required a measure of challenge to balance oneself from rocks to fallen tree trunk without soaking yourself. Despite their best efforts, falling off the slippery stepping-stones had already happened once or twice. They would all laugh at one another and considered it to be an initiation of sorts; just awkward enough to safely reach the far side to keep many unwanted visitors away from their private recluse.

"Oh look! There's Sasha with his father." Katarina waved and shouted to the far side of the brook. "Hello Sasha! Are you going to catch a big one for us too?"

"Katarina, shush! You're embarrassing us. You know how much I like him. Oh, why you do these things, I'll never understand." For many of the families, fishing for dinner wasn't to relax, it was a good way to catch a fresh and tasty dinner that within the hour would be sizzling on someone's plate.

Sasha was looking up at his father and spoke quietly with him for a brief minute. Mr. Petrovski waved back and shouted to the girls. "I'll tell you what we'll do. If we catch more than one, we're happy to share whatever we catch, OK?" The girls nodded and called out to acknowledge the offer. This was a favorite place for many villagers to frequent, especially when the fish were biting.

"My father told me there is a good fishing season, so I guess there's a bad one too. But since the river is always open, isn't that as good a time as any?" Margit pondered. Julia responded, being the wiser of the three. "I don't really know, but it has something to do with how cold the water is, whether it's better at night or first thing early morning. Too complicated for me, but I do know this. It's so much easier for someone else to catch them for us."

The girls shared a few snickers and totally agreed. This was as restful a place as any on earth, as the girls continued languishing a bit while they were entertained by the small commotion when a fish struck the bait from the opposite shore.

This was a good day, it turned out. The girls clapped and shouted their encouragement of the fine effort, as one by one the brook yielded three trout, all a decent size for this peacefully winding river-bed. "Well done, Sasha! Very well done indeed!"

Within a few minutes, the girls began to gather their few items, and in single file they successfully negotiated their way back across to the village side of the river.

"Here you go girls… the biggest one is for you!" Sasha's father declared.

"Wait a minute Pa," Sasha exclaimed. "First let me clean it for you, Julia. It's the dirty part so I'm happy to do it for you. It won't take me long, and I'll bring it to your house as soon as I finish. Would that be alright?"

Julia and her friends beamed with appreciation for such a gentlemanly gesture. It was not something they had expected. "Oh, that's so very thoughtful," said Julia. "Thank you both so very much. I know my family will really enjoy this tonight!"

As the girls giggled and followed the pathway home, the conversation was solely reserved for the breakthrough that had occurred. It was exactly what Julia had silently hoped for, but was afraid to suggest, even to her closest friends. Sasha really liked her, and the girls agreed. They laughingly teased her about her conquest all the way home.

"So, did Sasha's father just *give* the fish to you? You didn't ask him to, did you?" Julia's mother inquired.

"No, not exactly. It was just a joke, Mother, but we didn't think he would do it. Besides, we already knew Sasha and his father. He's one of the carpenters who works at the church."

"Is he the one who lost his leg?" Mother asked.

"That's him! I think that's why he's still in the village. I feel sorry for him but he's such a kind man… and so is Sasha, just like his father. I really like him, and I think he likes me too!"

Over the following weeks, Julia's friendship with Sasha continued to develop, although every moment they shared always included Margit and Katarina as well. The four friends were almost inseparable at school, at church and not reluctantly, even at the girls' play-fort on occasion.

Sasha, however, spent most hours after school, working with his father to learn the trade. Although his father seldom made excuses for his handicap, his son's willingness to help was invaluable. Over the past few years, working together had created a strong bond between father and son.

One glorious Sunday afternoon in October 1940, the four companions were lost in their fantasies, discussing among other things their aspirations for the future, and entertaining one another with questions about what existed in the world beyond the village. Julia was always the inquisitive one who usually said anything of common interest, or so it sometimes seemed.

"Well, hardly anyone shops in the bakery we don't already know, but sometimes a lady from another city comes to visit her sister who has twin boys here in Pobereze. She's very nice and always says hello to me and my mother. Yesterday I overheard them talking about some terrible things happening not far from where she lives."

"What kind of things was she talking about? What did you hear?" asked a concerned Katarina.

"I didn't hear very much because she and mother started speaking softly, probably so I wouldn't hear."

"So, what *did* you hear for heaven's sake? It must have been something secret," implored Sasha.

Julia continued hesitatingly. "Some men came into their village. No one had seen them before. They were looking into every store and pushing people out of their way to see what was inside. Margit, they were carrying rifles and they said bad words even Mother wouldn't speak of. They frightened everyone and the villagers didn't know why they treated them so badly."

"Where did they come from? Where they German soldiers? Oh, I pray they were not!" Margit blurted out anxiously.

"Mother asked the same question, but the lady didn't think so. She didn't recognize the uniforms, but thinks they were Ukrainians, looking to cause some trouble. Whatever they were looking for, they didn't seem to find it."

"Julia, did the lady think they would come here too?" Sasha asked with a very concerned look on his face.

"Not really. Whatever they wanted they're not likely to find it here."

"You're probably right. There's nothing here anyone would want, except maybe baked bread and decent fishing!"

"I couldn't hear much more than what I told you, but I will speak to my mother and ask a few questions to see what else she can tell me, OK?"

On that note of mild reassurance, Katarina and Margit caught sight of two loons coming into view. The girls had seen the birds before, but for them to be so close to the tree-fort was a rarity, and the girls were not about to miss them. Margit quietly summoned Julia and Sasha to join them, but instead the young couple continued to sit next to each other talking quietly.

Sasha readjusted himself just a little, to move closer to rest his hand on Julia's, ever so slightly. It was his first sign of affection toward her. Julia was moved by the gesture and pretended not to notice. She had no idea what to do, so she left her hand right where it was. They were both at an apparent loss for words.

Without breaking the silence, they both raised their heads to look inquisitively into the other's eyes. Sasha leaned forward sensitively and softly touched his lips to hers. Neither had ever kissed anyone like this before and Julia, staring into Sasha's exciting, deep blue eyes, backed away ever so imperceptibly.

Her face was flushed, making her even more desirable. This time however, it was Julia who wanted more, and she kissed him again. It was a tender moment they would cherish for the first, and sadly, the last time.

*****

A few days later, Julia was returning home with an armload of kindling, which was her custom after school. Not surprisingly, she was still savoring the magical moment of Sasha's affection when her happy gait was shaken by sudden sounds of intermittent gunfire… and screaming people. Standing starkly alone, she froze in the shadows of the forest, clutching the spoils of her task tightly to provide protection from the reality of the moment now unfolding. The gunfire was continuous now and unrelenting.

Julia dropped her bundle, moving gingerly and uncertainly to the forest's edge, lying closely to the ground as her parents had taught her. She was horrified to see the sight of thirty or more armed and uniformed soldiers firing their guns repeatedly into the houses and businesses lining the street.

Instantly, Julia's happy and contented eyes erupted with tears of panic for her mother and her sister Tanya, and her beloved brother Mikel. The soldiers were spread up and down the main road, firing at will into the scrambling villagers. The gunfire continued to chatter incessantly. Dozens of her neighbors collapsed to the ground, in the middle of the street or from where they stood on the wooded walkways of the town, many clutching their young ones to shield them from harm.

Among them she saw what appeared to be her mother, already felled by the onslaught of the merciless gunfire. Amid the screaming, Julia heard the sporadic wails of young children, some of them no doubt being that of her sister and baby brother. That lurid realization gripped her very core; helplessly, she sank to her wobbling knees.

Her peripheral vision suddenly darkened and appeared to recede farther away from the horrific panorama now unfolding. The trees, now seemingly swirling around her more rapidly, sucked the very ground from where she kneeled. Julia collapsed face forward in a heavy heap of sullen despair.

The carnage continued until the echoes of misery were silenced, and finally became shrouded by the gathering smoke and burning smell of gunfire. Julia, having reawakened from her brief blackout, instinctively and quietly crawled backward, away from the pathway into the cover of heavy brush and fallen leaves, helpless to do anything more.

She was numb with fear, having no concept of how long the genocide continued. Neither did she know the meaning of the word, simply who and what had been taken from her, with no concept of the *why*. In an instant, she would experience the passing glimpses of a life she once knew. Still in shock, Julia trembled profoundly; an innocent young child with no understanding or explanation for what evil had befallen her world.

Darkness soon settled upon the village and hovered, slowly engulfing her, as if consuming her in a state of abject hopelessness... perhaps augmented in large part to the arrival of the dampening coldness and the frightful stench of the dank night air. She was wearing nothing more than her school dress and a light woolen tunic.

By this time, her thoughts raced from moment to moment. Why did this happen to her family? There was no more screaming, nor even sobbing. Was everyone dead? Where were Margit and Katarina... and dear God, where was Sasha? How she missed Margit's beaming smile and Katarina's silly questions; and yes, what of Sasha's lovely kisses? Did they or anyone else survive?

Whether Julia slept or not, she was not certain. It was more a combination of suspended withdrawal, emotional exhaustion, and fear so pervasive it was like nothing she had ever experienced.

As dawn broke and loosened the death grip of the shroud of dark despair, she slowly regained consciousness and in so doing was thrust once again into her horrific reality. Her heart instantly and mercilessly pounded from deep within her weary chest. The nightmares had been real!

She started to stir, and nature's needs defined her first priorities. Her immediate thoughts oscillated between weeping uncontrollably as the child within, and alternatively trying to reconcile what possible action she must take. In these first few hours Julia reluctantly began to realize her very survival may well be determined by the decisions she was about to make.

It was imperative she discover within her, the ability to think as the self-reliant young woman she would eventually be forced to become. Profound sadness and overwhelming grief were understandable, but any feelings of helplessness must be quashed from existence from this point forward. She pledged this to herself.

As she composed herself through sheer determination, she was certain the savage troopers would soon return to reap the spoils of their rampage. For the time being though, the wave of destruction had progressed farther southwest into the faintly beating heart of the more distant parts of the village. If she was to salvage anything useful from her childhood, or use her resourcefulness to collect some warmer clothing, now was the time to do so. It was the last time to take brief pause.

Shuffling on her hands and knees to get closer to the scene of devastation, Julia could not yet see any posted soldiers, presumably Ukrainian, but she knew her time was short. She also knew this forest well and worked her familiarity to her advantage. Staying within its protective cover, she carefully circled the house from behind where she could stay out of the open. Once there, she scanned the back yards nearest her house and quickly darted to the broken rear door.

As she apprehensively entered, not knowing what she would find inside, she was relieved none of her family had been there when the slaughter occurred. Thankfully, they were not.' Had they been, the scene would have been even more emotionally torturous for her. It was dreadfully painful as it was, but she struggled to achieve at least a small degree of objectivity.

It was no longer home, she told herself. Her thinking was to regard it as nothing more than an old empty house, devoid of the warmth, comfort and nurturing she always associated with it.

Julia drew deep, intermittent breaths and clenched her strong fists to maintain her resolve. Struggling to think rationally, not emotionally, she only took items of necessity. She grabbed a few items of heavier clothing and, yes, her hiking boots! Her frilly favorites were few and far between but served her no purpose any longer. There was no time for sentimentality.

In her parent's bedroom was her mother's non-stylish, but oh so practical leather bag, which had always served as moneybag, medical kit and wall-safe for anything of the remotest value. Two apples and a banana on the kitchen pantry would stave off her soon to arrive aching belly cramps. She would be thankful she took them.

Completing her final scan of the house, there on the window ledge was her wooden, hand-me-down flute she had been learning to play, without much progress she thought. Grasping it as an afterthought, she tucked it into the bag and cautiously peered out to the yard from which she had emerged the forest.

She hesitated briefly, torn with emotion as she ached to see her family again… but those images she would immediately suppress from her consciousness, perhaps for the remainder of what her new life would provide. Finding their disfigured bodies in the carnage would tear her to pieces and likely lead to her capture, or worse.

Almost cold-bloodedly, she vowed she would not try to locate the remains of her slaughtered family. The horrifying sight would haunt her forever, destroying her in the process and exposing her to even more grief and despair. She wiped her tears in frustration with trembling fingers. *Enough of this! What's done is done!* Taking a deep breath, she checked from side to side, and quickly bolted back into the welcoming natural camouflage to reconnoiter where her next steps would take her.

*****

What villagers had thought about their quaint and nondescript village in the southern District of Stanislawow were not only thoughts of fondness, but more so, familiarity. Otherwise, it was not known for much and was generally underdeveloped. The only thing abundant was the general state of poverty. It was a simple life which in looking back, was far better than most.

Even farming here was difficult considering the soil was often infertile. Every nutrient had been squeezed from it through generation after generation of agricultural abuse. Like the people who farmed it, there was no respite for the soil either. People only lived in this place because no one else wanted to.

Since her early youth, Julia had a quick and inquisitive mind and was always asking endless questions of her parents and teachers, often to the point of irritation. Always thirsty for more, she carried herself well and behaved as a child of many more than her now fourteen years. She would need this maturity to continue to develop more quickly than before.

There were no sounds coming from the village, but the silence was not tranquil, it was mournful and morose. Needing some time to think, even if only for a few minutes of calmness, Julia moved away from the pathways to sit near a dense cluster of trees and shrubs. Taking one of the apples from her bag, she savored its freshness, and welcomed its sweet juices, while vaguely recalling a trip up-river with her father, to a busy and much larger city than her own. *"What should I do, Father? What would you do?"* She softly whispered to herself.

Julia took a quick mental inventory of her skillsets. It was something she felt compelled to do. Was it her father's guiding hand? This exercise seemed to restore confidence and reassurance within her. If ever she needed it, now was the time.

She knew for example, how to track the sun to ascertain direction on that trip, since her father used such skills to find his own way from time to time. How little we realize the significance of such things as children. *"Pay attention and learn."* She could still hear those words of her father.

It was an attitude Julia had developed since as long as she could remember. At the time, she had no awareness of the useful habits her father had instilled in her; it had just become a large part of who she was; inquisitive about everything.

Included in this mental exercise was her good physical health, her sharp mental acuity, her often endless resourcefulness, and yes, the unfamiliar feeling growing inside her; determination and unwillingness to ever give up... *ever!*

She recognized the soldiers' uniforms as being Russian or Ukrainian and even spoke some of their language. They were not totally unfamiliar to her. Perhaps this too could be used to her ultimate advantage.

She wisely rationalized heading east was only entering the firestorm of destruction, since the Russians had evidently expanded their already swollen borders to now include her village. The flow of humanity from other villages would only be driven in one direction; to the west. What could be worse, being overrun by the butchering Ukrainians, or confronting the invading Germans?

She reasoned heading north and west could provide her best chance of escape. She would adapt along the way, she thought, and use the natural routes provided by the Caspian Mountains and the network of rivers as best she could. Julia was confident she could wiggle through any obstacles as inconspicuously as her creativity could allow. She was too naïve to properly understand the challenges she would have to face. It was probably better that way.

Absurd as it may appear, this was the thought process of an adolescent child still in her fourteenth year, but it was her choice not to be a desperate one. Acceptance of desperation could become her worst enemy, potentially leading her to eventual defeat. She must maintain control of herself, and in so doing maintain what little of it she had, shaping her destiny as best as circumstances would allow. She wasn't going down without a fight.

The edge of the River Rzadza was only a few kilometers to the north; as good a starting point as any. Julia was aware the area was sparsely populated between here and there, and surmised it had little value for the invading forces. She was correct in her assumption but had no practical knowledge to support it. Yes, she decided! She must follow the river's course toward the larger city she remembered from two years prior with Father.

She progressed on a parallel route to the familiar pathways, however she wisely reasoned using the pathways themselves presented risks she could not afford to take. The wooded areas had already lost much of its foliage, save for the pine trees which softened and muted her footsteps. Inevitably, she reasoned, any surviving families and desperate loners would be simply guided by the natural flow of the well-trodden pathways and sooner or later, they would walk into potential waiting ambushes. To Julia's mind, it was an obvious trap just waiting to happen.

Sure enough, early the first day she heard a few stragglers on the pathway running parallel to her silent route. Her first impulse was to run to join them, but she quickly and correctly decided against it. There *were* ambushes set up by the unscrupulous invaders! The chatter of machine gun fire once again rattled her to the core. The instinctive reaction had more meaning now after witnessing its deadly result in the village.

Helplessly, Julia watched them fall where they had stood, desperately hugging each other to their final breaths. One young mother, screaming with fear, clutched her young child and turned back to run away. It was futile and only delayed the inevitable. In mere seconds she took several fatal shots to her back. The baby dropped to the ground like a limp doll while the mother's body twisted and contorted from the powerful impact of the lethal burst of gunfire.

This brutal and indiscriminate act of violence, although horrific to Julia, was already less shocking to her tender fragility as the decimation of her family, which she noted about herself.

Julia thought of the fallen child, and whether it had survived the fall. She felt deeply about the baby but coldly rationalized its loss was of no consequence any longer. It was an adjustment of perception already starting to deaden her senses. This was just the beginning. Who or what would she have to become to find her journey's end?

Now, even more determined to stay safely away from the pathway, Julia remained deeper in the heavy forest, reaching the river just before dusk of the first day. It was early enough to regain her bearings and reconnoiter the viability of further progress. Her energy level was good, all things considered, and the walking did not exhaust her as much as her acceptance of her new realities. Finding sleep would recharge her with fresh perspective to face another day.

This was to be found about three hundred meters to the east side of the deadly pathway. There was a hollowed-out dip in the ground at the base of a fallen tree, half filled with pine needles and freshly fallen leaves. Thankfully, there had been no rain for some time, so she burrowed herself into the dry pit and covered herself from view, all the while tucking her mother's bag close to her belly. In complete exhaustion, she drifted away in minutes seeking the mercy of a deep sleep.

*****

The heap of fallen bodies, continued to twitch and flail from the impact of the continuing gunfire, long after life had been taken from them. Many were clawing the dirt with broken nails and gnarled fingers, dragging themselves inch by painstaking inch to escape the horror inflicted upon them. Julia herself clawed her way forward from the few souls about to grasp her extended leg to drag her into the morass of inhumanity painfully engulfing them.

As she stumbled forward, the cadavers were almost upon her, tearing away at her aching feet and ripping away her bedraggled clothing. Some even tried to leap on top of her to be carried by her surging adrenalin and her strong instinctive spirit driving her forward.

The farther she ran, the greater the number of souls in hot pursuit of her rapidly tiring body. Slowed by the dead weight, she was losing ground and slipped into a deep hollow hidden by the fallen leaves. Down she fell! The horrific swarms of the dead had finally made their capture. She screamed and swung her arms with flailing fists to defend herself, kicking her legs violently to shake them off ......

"*Off me! Get off me! Let me go!!*" Julia awoke panic stricken, sweating profusely in the coldness of early dawn. As she regained her senses, the nightmare slowly evaporated, however, her head was still spinning out of control. She wrapped her arms around her chest and shoulders trying to console herself and wept uncontrollably and silently on the earthen floor.

*****

From a safe distance, Julia followed the course of the river, developing the habit of pivoting her head frequently from side to side, and less frequently fully turning her torso to face behind her route of progress, all the while listening intently for potential disturbances. She was not running. She convinced herself caution was her greatest consideration, not the impulsiveness and carelessness of haste.

The razing of her world was permeated with panic and reckless abandon. As such, she thoughtfully considered if she maintained some objectivity, and did not become foolish herself, she could continue moving forward, beyond the incursion surely gripping the main cities and well-travelled roadways.

Unknown to her was the fact the Germans were far too preoccupied with fortifying their control of France, Belgium, and the Netherlands than to worry about engaging the Russians from the east. Their focus was no longer on defending the prize of Warsaw, it was to hold fast to their foothold in Western Europe.

They were stretched too thinly to cover all flanks. This was the price they would pay for their relative ease of conquest over the under-manned Polish forces. By contrast, the Russian focus was only directed toward Warsaw, and this reward could be theirs for the taking.

*****

Julia's earlier suspicions were correct. By sheer chance there were a few slivers of openings through which she could pass. Following her own intuition, she was determined to stay with the river as far as she could, wherever it led her to eventually make a crossing to the north.

The comfort and familiarity of the river's shoreline eventually emptied peacefully into an intersection point she barely remembered. It was the River Wista, which had split mostly to the west and more slightly to the direct north, farther away from the capital city of Warsaw. She knew the Wista led to a city of which she knew nothing more than would be expected of a youngster of her age. At least she was heading in the correct general direction. It couldn't be much farther now, she thought, but the main roads were battered and broken, some areas in total disrepair.

By the end of day, Julia realized she could not continue using the shoreline to guide her. The trees and forests could no longer hide her presence as she approached the outskirts of the city. Nervously, she realized hiding in plain sight would become necessary. God willing, no one would notice or care about the goings on of a simple peasant girl minding her own business. She was no prize and had nothing to offer. She prayed it would remain so.

Within hours and shaking to the bone from the cold, Julia pulled her heavy coat collar closer to her numb, haggard features and pressed back into the thinning forest. She prayed she could bear just one more night sleeping like a stray animal. As the darkness closed in upon her, only her sorrowful eyes could be seen peering from under her makeshift toque. She was stiff and cold but so exhausted from the perilous journey the dropping temperature was the least of her problems, as she fell fast asleep.

By daybreak, the matter of finding something to eat was now her greatest priority. She knew a thing or two about foraging. Another skill she had never considered! This time of year, there was always life beneath the fallen foliage, and she knew it might be her last chance to feast on nature's bounty for some time... mushrooms!

Her mother had taught her well and the last autumn nights of the season could still feed a family, if you knew what you were looking for. It wasn't long before she sought out small clusters of these edible delights, always concealed from view but in predictable spaces. It wouldn't be the first time she rinsed them at the water's edge and savored them raw, tender, and succulent. In the remaining few evenings before winter's frost, these hidden treasures would store well in her pockets to sustain her in the days ahead.

She pressed on, and within the hour she came upon a sign indicating the direction and distance of two more kilometers before she would reach Pultusk. The name was vaguely familiar to her... *Yes! She remembered!* It was the city in which her uncle and aunt had been living since before she was born. Surely this would be a safer haven! The very thought of them rejuvenated her spirit as she optimistically maintained her course further north.

She was unaffected by the tedium of her travel route and in no time, she was just another vagabond blending in with others, randomly coming and going. With each step forward, however, her initial hopefulness of finding family quickly dissipated. Walking further into the city, its sparse remains totally devoured her. It was one levelled building followed by another, occasionally interspersed with barren crater shells and small hillsides of broken rubble, leaving no identifiable trace of what once existed there.

The streets she vaguely remembered, once teeming with cars and trucks from the perspective of a very young child, were now almost vacant. People were no longer cramming sidewalks and bustling through intersections. Civilians were replaced by uniformed soldiers, who were significantly more apparent than her memories recorded, but these were not the same as the Russians back home. No, these must be Germans!

To this point, no one paid attention to the poor schoolgirl wandering the streets aimlessly. She did her best to stay off the main streets whenever possible, but there was a price to pay for this decision. There were others scavenging for whatever they could find of value or even basic sustenance to survive a few more days. Julia became just another one among them.

In so doing, she encountered more obstacles of destruction, evidence of lives torn apart. Most of these areas showed few signs of clearing and some still entombed human remains; clearly not considered to be a priority for anyone other than the vanquished, or what remained of them.

Her thoughts inevitably flashed back to her own family, every day but less frequently. Her focus had to remain steadfast, hence she consistently suppressed in her mind, the etched scars that would inevitably plague her forever. There would be another time for memories and sentimentality. This was certainly not one of them. She could not afford such unproductive diversions.

The farther north she travelled, troop movements became sparse and less frequent. The evidence of their previous workmanship was everywhere. It would be recorded that more than eighty-five percent of the once beautiful and historic city of Pultusk was decimated. Only rubble remained to leave a dead skyline of ash and fallen brick. Were it not for the signage, now several kilometers behind her, Julia would not have known this was what became of the city she had been seeking.

It had long since lost any sense of familiarity by the time she arrived. Nothing was recognizable and she had no frame of reference. Finding her aunt and uncle among the remains of the scorched cadavers, once a home to tens of thousands, was impossible. It was the second time in her young life she felt so very alone, and her pace had been reduced to little more than a crawl.

She was surviving on precious pools of rainwater and littered garbage. It was difficult and tedious to supplement the stash in her pockets, now only partially filled with mushrooms. Decimated buildings once serving as tributes to their designers and craftsmen left numerous coves, niches, and passageways, becoming temporary homes to many who suffered their own atrocities.

Helplessly and in some ways illogically to Julia, the few scattered survivors seemed content to reshape suitable hovels for themselves out of the chaos. Julia had no ties to these places and chose to keep moving to the north and west, slowly and methodically. Oddly enough, having no one in this world full of strangers was perhaps an advantage for this not so helpless child of war.

Forward progress here had become painfully slow. The fallen debris and rubble had to be carefully negotiated and every misstep, sometimes through broken glass windows and occasional live electrical wiring could trigger more shifting concrete and falling timber.

It was a perilous process, keeping her head up to maintain her sense of direction and avoidance of others, while at the same time looking down to seek something solid to provide sure footing. Her feet and legs ached. Her boots were never intended for this sort of punishing treatment. The blisters and constant abuse burned her feet with searing pain.

In her half-conscious state of mental and physical exhaustion, she had inevitably let her guard down as nightfall approached, and visibility had become so terribly difficult. Unwittingly, Julia stumbled down yet another almost unsurpassable mound of a building's remains, creating a small but unavoidable landslide of loose debris dropping her to her rear end.

She was forced to tumble down the steep, ten-foot avalanche among the shifting, sliding cascade spilling out to the solid surface below. It was a painful ordeal squeezing tears from her eyes, more of mental anguish than the pain of physical cuts and bruises. When her crude, rough ride was ended, she was sitting dejectedly, almost face to face at the bottom, in front of a mother and father and a young boy.

The four victims said nothing for a brief moment, and everyone simply stared at one another through the small billows of dust created by her helpless descent. No one among them uttered a word or gestured in any way, neither did Julia readjust herself from where she had landed on her bottom. After the brief moment, Julia broke the tongue-tied silence between them.

"Hello... my name is Julia," was awkwardly all that came to her mind. Her eyes were still moist from the few sniffles she had just shed, which by now had traced irregular tracks of her tears through the concrete dust and dirt along the length of her emaciated cheekbones. Her relentless spirit prevailed and quickly redefined her circumstances as Julia commenced to giggle, raising her war weary arms to extend them as she declared laughingly, "Here I am!"

It was the oddest spontaneous introduction, and it was perfectly appropriate as the young family somehow found the courage to smile and chuckle back at their unannounced guest.

"Oh my! Are you hurt? That must have been a painful tumble," the young woman offered. Julia was slightly dazed from her head over heels entrance.

"Forgive me, I am Gilda. This is my husband Paul... and our brave young man here is Karl," as she proudly wrapped her arm around him. They exchanged genuine nods of welcome to one another and commenced to chat away with the usual questions and concerns for their common predicaments.

Paul had worked in the customs office, the one that *used to be*. He had not yet left for work the morning the air strike hit their modest building, blowing it away from under them. Regrettably, their oldest boy perished. He was only seven, and they could not find his remains. They had nothing left to save apart from their lives, but despite everything they praised the Lord for their survival.

Julia thought to herself how fortunate she was in comparison to what she was hearing from this broken and destitute family. It was difficult enough to be dreadfully alone, but to have lost a son and to be desperate to save their youngest one, and each other in these horrific conditions must have been unbearable.

This fortuitous meeting reassured Julia how truly blessed she was to be alive, to be relatively unhurt, to be strong and resourceful, and never broken of spirit. She had no one to worry about other than herself. This was indeed an invigorating experience for her. It was all about perspective she thought, and until she found this loving family, hers had been slipping steadily downward.

"You must be hungry, Julia. Here. Have some bread. It's stale, but it's all we have I'm afraid."

"You are so kind, but please, save it for your son. I can share what's left of an apple I found today... and here, I have some mushrooms too! Take some of these boy... have something! Go on now, you will like them." The boy, who was probably three or four years of age, looked pleadingly at his mother and hesitatingly devoured a few mushrooms and the remains of the already half-eaten apple.

After sharing their scavenged and odd assortment of food, the friends managed to build a small fire for warmth, and Julia gratefully accepted their invitation to stay the night near the fire. Such remarkable hospitality from these fine young people! Julia was grateful to have met them.

The next morning, they bid farewell to each other, Paul and Gilda maintaining their conviction they were better off staying amidst the remaining walls and occasional roofs the city had to offer, clinging to the hope of finding whatever shelter these provided against the ravages of the coming winter months. Surely help would find its way to them, in whatever form it provided.

Julia, although famished and filthy dirty, pressed on with her journey. Her mother's leather bag, representing all her worldly possessions, remained securely attached to her hip. This old leather bag was all the security she would need, for reasons she could not fully understand or appreciate.

*****

On this gloomy, overcast day, she was so thankful to have shared the warm fire and vividly recalled the heat on her face as she tried to seek sleep the previous night. At some point she must have rolled over to expose her back to the fire, predictably warming her spine to her very core.

The comforting heat no doubt enabled her to relax and must have been when she thankfully drifted off. In the relative absence of food, perhaps it was the warmth that sustained her; the warmth and what remained of her rapidly thinning veils of body fat.

The roadways were travelled by very few once she had crossed the outskirts of Pultusk. Its remaining broken shell would not support many of those who were continuing to be comforted by its memory, among them Paul, Gilda, and their beautiful and innocent little boy. Julia was not optimistic their city's remains would sustain them for long.

The consequences of war, death being foremost among them, are not always immediate or merciful, but rather more as a consequence of the infliction of prolonged pain and suffering. The human loss of family providers and the subsequent abandonment of the frail and elderly, the thousands upon thousands of children, and their broken hearts, minds, hopes and spirits; these are the deferred catastrophic ravages of war. May God rest their beautiful souls, Julia thought.

The immediate future would redefine Julia's world and profoundly harden her character in ways better suited for much worse days to follow. By late autumn 1940, Julia's newly evolving toughness and determination would be taken to the limits of her still innocent young body and spirit.

10
WAS IT A WITCHES' COVEN?

♂

THE FREEZING COLD WAS NUMBING HER TO THE CORE. THERE was no getting used to it, however her raging hunger took even greater precedence. Was this what life would now become? Her priorities oscillated from the frightful need to find warmth, replaced by the urgent need for food, replaced by dire need for sleep! The cycle seemed endless. Amid these rural and inhospitably barren roadways, Julia had no workable strategy to survive, other than keeping her immediate focus to keep placing one foot ahead of the other.

Time passed at its own pace, but the pervasively grey skies subdued the light, sufficiently disguising any hints of suitable reference. Whatever thoughts she had, whether good or bad, whether positive or negative, contributed their influence on the ultimate result of her life. This much she knew to be true. Her mind was powerful and was the source of everything - if she could just master how best to guide it. *"Trust in God. Trust in God"*, she mumbled to herself.

As if by divine direction, for she no longer had any specific direction in her own mind, she simply followed the road. Totally exhausted now, darkness had shrouded her semi-comatose state, but slowly began to yield to her gradual regaining of consciousness. For an instant, she thought she must have been hallucinating until she identified an almost imperceptible wisp of smoke.

Her eyes were barely able to see through the tiny slits of her half-closed eyelids. She kept them almost closed intentionally, as if opening them fully would sap the last reserves of her gradually dissipating energy. Her nose was still working she thought. The scent was becoming slightly more distinct, meat... *it was the smell of smoking meat she could recognize!*

Julia's mind began to slowly reawaken, encouraging her body to follow suit. Her fading energy and diminishing resolve gradually re-ignited, one feeding off the other. Her resilience enabled her to increase her tedious pace. Hope, though faint, was the catalyst re-emerging within her, to once again flow through her famished veins.

As she followed the winding road, a small grove of trees almost barren of foliage stood out starkly against a glowing light, summoning her to draw closer. She rounded the curve to see an orange hue in the distance. Drawing closer still, Julia discovered a robust and glimmering fire pit featuring a roasting pig rotating slowly above it. Sparks of burning ash encircled the pit that snapped and crackled from the melting fat rolling around and around this mirage of visual delight.

About the pit were about twenty-five people, maybe more, some huddled near the bases of a few barren deciduous trees. Behind them, a backdrop of evergreens lined a thick pine forest's edge. Their faces were glowing from the reflected orange and reddish hue of the fire before them.

Was it a witch's coven? Who else could thrive in this foreboding place other than pure evil? Evidently, Julia had not yet been seen through the darkness of night, as the spectators were unable to see her approach against the blackened setting behind the blazing spectacle.

Before they could notice her image, Julia stood very still before approaching any closer to assess the situation, specifically the people, all the while desperate to join them but trying to establish it was safe enough for her to do so. They appeared to be crudely dressed and bundled haphazardly, more for practicality as would be expected amid this lonely, impoverished setting.

They all wore a dark assortment of makeshift headwear pulled down securely below their ears to keep the night frost at bay. These were not military, whether German or Russian. They were likely no different than her friends she left behind in Pultusk. God willing, they would be as hospitable as Gilda and her family.

Julia had spent so much time purposely avoiding contact with anyone, perhaps her mistrust of others was simply rooted in her growing paranoia. In her present physical state, she decided she had no alternative other than to pray they would permit her to join them.

With the decision made, she drew a deep breath to bolster her confidence and proceeded toward whatever awaited her.

Tentatively but now committed, she drew closer to the eerie light and at some point, came into their unsuspecting collective view. Their initial reaction was mixed, as the timid among them withdrew a step or two, while the confrontational protectors of the flock quickly became evident.

"Stay right where you are! Are you alone?" as Julia stared down the barrel of an old hunting rifle like the one her father once held. The voice was barking aggressively in Polish, for which Julia was somewhat relieved to hear.

"I am alone, and I come as a friend. I'm cold and starving, and… and I smelled smoke from your fire. My name is Julia and I travelled here from Pobereze."

A man identified himself as Pavel and lowered his rifle, but not his guard. "You are just a child." Pavel paused a moment, suspicious of this frail intruder and intently scanned the black void behind her looking for others. "You are a long way from home, Julia. How did you travel this far? Most of the roads are blocked or destroyed."

"As nature provided, I suppose… I walked."

"Does anyone else know where you are?"

"I would pray someone did, but I assure you I am very much alone."

"All the more pitiful, but even more courageous. Come and join us." He lowered his rifle now hanging by his side. "You're among friends now and are welcome to feast with us."

His wife Manal, their young daughter Mariam, as well as Petrov, Kristian, Lionel, and others whose names she could not remember, accompanied Pavel. These few friendly people were more approachable than the others among them and enabled Julia to lower her own guard somewhat. Meanwhile, the two named Kristian and Lionel, used hand crafted wooden staffs to adeptly remove the heavy spit supporting the crisp, succulent pig.

It continued to crackle, tantalizing everyone when it was reverently laid out on an old tree stump, serving as a primitive but very functional cutting block. The longest twenty minutes of everyone's lives was waiting for the prize to cool a bit, to permit a full bearded butcher who stepped out of the darkness to carry out his skillful and welcome task.

To supplement this unexpected and gluttonous event, boiled potatoes and ladles of borscht soup were carefully distributed and were appreciatively savored by everyone. The only four or five tin cups among them were passed from one gaping mouth to another, as if it was an offering of the holy Eucharist in the sanctity of the peaceful darkness.

It only took moments of kindness to change her initial perceptions of the frightening and foreboding place Julia first imagined. Her impression was now one of warmth and friendship in a comforting wilderness. How often do our personal expectations become jaded when our circumstances reflect the depths of despair?

Many praises of thanks from everyone were spoken to Manal and Mariam for their tasty and innovative cooking skills. What they created out of freshly pulled potatoes and beets was truly magnificent.

The men began to gorge their bellies as if there was no tomorrow. The melting fat and dripping grease had saturated their unkempt beards, shimmering all the way up to their shining cheekbones now reflecting the orange light of the still glowing fire.

Showing little deference to the men, Julia sought the company of Manal and Mariam, along with the remaining three women among the group. It seemed the women sitting closest to the ravenous men, perhaps feared one of them losing a finger in the process.

Here in the company of her new-found companions, Julia heard brief snippets of their stories of hardship and devastating losses and decided the less she shared with them of her own tragedies, the better. There was nothing, and certainly no words capable of ever bringing her family back. Julia did not want to relive it again and decided to keep her own story brief and uninteresting, choosing instead to listen and let them talk.

There would be a time ahead for such discussions when she better ascertained with who best to share her confidences. She sought to learn some things that someday might prove helpful to her, based upon the advice of her mother who always said, *"Pay attention to details. It is wiser to learn from other's mistakes, than from your own."*

Manal and Mariam were quick to approach Julia. It was a comforting gesture signifying she may become more than just a dinner guest. "I've never even heard of Pobereze, but Pavel says its somewhere near the Russian border. If I may ask, where is your family,

Julia? You can't be much older than Mariam. It's far too young to be alone in this place."

"It's just a small village with little to offer, but it's where I grew up, so I had nothing to compare it to. To me it was home, but sadly no longer." Offering no further detail, Julia returned to the sweetness of the thick, juicy chunk of pork and quickly became as greasy as the others. No matter, she thought. The pain in her aching belly started to subside almost immediately. It was very satisfying.

Eager to talk with someone new, especially being a young girl, Mariam opened her confidences to Julia as they continued to attack their meal. Having been deprived for so long, it was hard to understand one another since their mouths were constantly over filled. It was almost comical with all the spitting, splashing, and dribbling going on. This pig had not been sacrificed in vain.

Manal was very sociable, in a natural way. "Some of us are friends and neighbors with each other, at least we used to be. It seemed only natural to stay together on the road to nowhere. It was painful to leave our homes, especially when we had to run away so quickly. We grabbed what we could, but we don't dare go back. The soldiers burned down everything and killed most of the villagers choosing to stay. My mother was among them."

Manal tried to choke back her tears. "It was the hardest thing we ever had to do. If we took... if we took her with us... we would all be caught and killed." She sobbed openly as her nose was running now and she started to choke. Her coughing and gasping forced her to awkwardly spit out some meat just to get her breath again. "Augh... I'm so sorry."

By this time Mariam had also broken into tears and wrapped her arms round her mother's shoulders to comfort her. Julia hesitated to express her sympathies, not knowing if it was her place to do so. She was so dehydrated she had no tears to offer. It was an awkward circumstance, so she just placed a greasy hand gently on Mariam's.

When Manal regained some composure, she continued as best she could. "We're just farmers mostly. We don't know how to fight. We never had to do it before."

Julia did her best to offer some comfort to this now openly grieving family by saying, "Your husband seems such a kind man. I suspect he's a good protector and although I don't know him at all, he will surely take care of you both."

Pavel had just finished allocating a few tasks for the clean-up of the inevitable mess following the feast. The fire was subdued to a safer extent to provide his tribe some necessary warmth and to keep potential predators away through the night: not just the four-legged ones. A few reliable sentries pledged to stay awake in shifts to secure the campsite from unwelcome intruders.

"Julia, of course you're welcome to stay with us if you wish." Julia smiled and nodded her thankful acceptance. "I suggest you take a spot near my family, as you now appear to be better acquainted."

"Thank you, Pavel. You are most kind," she replied.

The night air had become noticeably colder, especially after having withdrawn farther from the fire. It was only a short time before everyone settled in for the night. It was serenely quiet, except for the intermittent sounds of continuous belching and farting. No one cared about nature's symphony. Sleep was all that mattered.

*****

Except for young Mariam, Julia was the youngest of this band of *The Forgotten*. Most of the group were farmers, led primarily by Pavel, but there was the butcher Tevia, Kristian and Lionel were both carpenters, while the quiet one, Werner, was a mechanic and general tradesman. Pavel later confirmed nothing remained of their village. It used to be a mere stone's throw from the northwest district of Pultusk. It was likely wiped out with the rest of the city simply because of its proximity.

Trust the Germans to be indiscriminate and always thorough. Julia remembered seeing the remains of what was likely their village, and had walked right through it only a couple of days prior. She thought it best to not speak of it.

Pavel and Kristian were the definitive leaders of the pack; with the intelligence and gut instinct their leadership would demand of them. Despite their better judgment there were also a few who were neither selected nor preferred to be among them, but just happened to tag along.

Pavel and Kristian were extremely mindful of potential problems arising from three brothers, all of whom appeared decidedly more cunning and self-serving than Pavel would have liked. These three had a reputation for being manipulative toward that end. In the beginning, Pavel had felt their boldness and aggressiveness would be a strength the group may require, also knowing full well there could be a day of reckoning against them, as the group sought to find their new *Garden of Eden.*

The hap-hazard plan was to find an abandoned village somewhere north and west, as far away from here as possible, to live mostly alone and self-sufficiently, passing the rest of the war in relative peace to rebuild the lives already having been ripped away from them. Whether practical or not only time would tell, but it was a noble and bonding objective that, at the very least, provided a rational and reasonable means to provide what they needed most... continued hope.

Julia weighed her options carefully, though there were precious few of them. She evaluated to herself the wisdom of staying with these decent people. It appeared they would take her on the same general route she had been following on her own. The group could provide her with the comfort of knowing she had some protection against whatever could befall her in the weeks ahead. Maybe they would even locate their Garden of Eden.

Food was still aplenty, provided by the roasted pig. Tevia had estimated the tasty pork would feed them well for several more days if they were judicious. Overeating the night before was a celebration of sorts they all desperately needed, so there was no guilt from anyone for having been so gluttonous. The feast would provide future memories they would not soon forget.

They had no wagons or oxen, mostly just the clothes on their backs, a few bags of extra clothing and some pots and pans for use during better times. During their march, quiet conversations and friendships were forged which served them well to keep their minds focused on other matters than fighting the dropping temperatures and the relentless physical abuse of their endless journey.

Julia pretty much stayed with Pavel's family and those of Kristian, whose wife Elisabeth was just three months into her first pregnancy. Bless her heart, *Lizzy* kept pace with the others and was always the first one to offer help wherever it was needed. The goal was to find a suitable place to call home within a few months before the pregnancy would make travel more difficult for her.

"What are you hoping for Lizzy, boy or girl?" asked Julia.

"It isn't something I've thought about much, and being an only child, I have no experience with either. Kristian, however, is determined it will be a boy. Since before we married, he has wanted a son. He and his brother Lionel are anxious to teach the boy how to be a fine carpenter and together the three of them will build us a beautiful home, somewhere peaceful… and safe from all this madness."

"It's good for you both to have dreams for the future, especially when two young people are so much in love." Manal offered thoughtfully.

Julia, always inquisitive added, "It intrigues me that despite these terrible times, we still find a way to discover new love. I wonder, is it love that gives us hope, or is it through hope we find love?"

Having no answers to such a question the friends walked on, choosing perhaps to ponder quietly and introspectively, or to simply dismiss any semblance of deep thought and let their minds slip back into the drudgery of their monotonous journey.

As sunset approached, another suitable campsite was selected for its remote location, and the modest shelter the forests provided. These were locations of little to no value to the Germans. There was nothing to plunder nor was it even suitable for farming, precisely what Pavel and Kristian had sought for the approaching night.

Three small fires were prepared, each of a much less prolific nature than the night before. These were strictly for warmth and boiling water for something black and nasty, serving as makeshift coffee. The pork, however, was savored by everyone and was cool and tasty to everyone's appreciative palate.

A home brew distilled from potatoes delighted a few of the men who became increasingly intoxicated, until a few of the leaders terminated their boisterous behaviors, much to the dismay of one or two of them.

Noticeable among them was the youngest brother of the family Pavel had previous concerns about. Andrew was getting increasingly bold and confrontational, probably too young and inexperienced to handle his liquor. When he staggered to sit close to Julia, his stench and stinking breath were offensive to her. She knew she was no prize either, but this boy was a pig.

When he tried to pull her closer to him, Pavel noted Julia's obvious discomfort but before he could intervene, Andrew's older brother restrained the younger one, while pulling him to his feet to escort him away from making a scene they would all regret. The boy grimaced and scowled at Julia for her justified rebuke and mumbled menacingly to her saying, "I'll see you again soon, you pretty little thing!"

*****

Morning came as a distant rooster announced the beginning of the day. It was a boastful and natural thing for a full-breasted bird, but to the resourceful few it wasn't long before the bird was located, captured, and restrained for future consumption. These people didn't miss a trick.

In no time, everyone was repacked and fully mobile in very short order, as the day promised to be as glorious as any nature could provide. "Pavel, you are being awfully quiet this morning. You seem preoccupied about something." Manal enquired.

"I'm just keeping my eyes open. We cannot afford unwanted surprises. Manal, can you tell Julia that Kristian and I wish to speak with her? And can you keep the others back some, so we can talk privately please?" Manal needed no further explanation and always respected Pavel's sound judgment.

Within a matter of minutes, Julia moved ahead to accompany both men, and did not appear to notice the procession falling slightly behind their leaders to create some privacy.

"Good morning, Pavel... Kristian." She acknowledged them with a nod. "You wanted to speak with me?" The weather continued to clear, as the midday sun split the remaining cloud cover momentarily, then fading and reappearing until it was apparent clear skies were forthcoming. The sunshine completely altered the damp and dismal mood of the previous day.

"Yes, thank you Julia. We're both intrigued and somewhat amazed by you, well... for someone of your age, to have survived such a long and difficult journey to bring you safely to our camp. You have already earned our respect, Julia."

"Thank you both, but I am alright, and I believe I always will be, so long as I remain cautious and mindful of the dangers surrounding me... surrounding us all."

"You have a maturity well beyond your years, but we need to know what you saw and what you may have learned about Russian troop activity near and about east Poland. There have been rumors of course, but you have seen things personally on your long journey, have you not? What you may know can help us on the road ahead, Julia."

Despite Julia's initial decision to keep details of her experiences mostly to herself, these people had graciously taken her in, at a desperate time in her tender life. It was an act of kindness not only sustaining her physical needs, but also restoring her faith and fervent belief that kindness and compassion still existed in her world.

"I'll help in any way I am able, of course Pavel. What do you need to know?"

The conversation was free flowing among the three of them. Julia had already proven to herself she inherently understood what factors she thought relevant to her safety. Her intelligence quickly became apparent and added immeasurably to their growing admiration of her. She described somewhat painfully, but also as objectively as possible, some of her ordeal, emphasizing the abject ruthlessness to which she had been exposed.

"Whoever they were, Russians I suspect, they were ruthless butchers. They showed neither hesitation nor remorse toward our people, very few of whom were Jews. Their clear intent was to exterminate us, as if we were nothing more than mindless rats; but it was also the enthusiastic way they carried out their mission against us.

"Mostly we were just women and kids. Some of them laughed and shouted encouragement to the others. Some even urged a few victims to run, particularly those on the forest pathway so they could make a game of their task. They were evil."

As she recounted the horror, Julia trembled uncontrollably, and her eyes became misty again as she summed up her story. "Whatever the rumors say, whatever your worst imaginings, do not ever underestimate the magnitude of their inhumanity."

Reliving her story had left her emotionally drained. Julia recounted those terrifying memories she had tried so hard to suppress. Out of respect for her ordeal, which was so terribly difficult to articulate, and the haunting brutality of that fateful day, the two men guided her reassuringly to sit on a fallen tree to compose herself.

Both Pavel and Kristian were mature men in their late twenties and were now veterans of war. How they had escaped conscription she did not know, nor was she asking. Nevertheless, they were visibly shaken by Julia's account of the massacre, and after hearing her story, even more so for the horrific risks to which their wives and beloved children may be exposed.

The trailing entourage had no concept of what was happening up ahead, but no one spoke up to enquire about the moment. For Pavel in particular, this was an endearing experience after which he committed himself to protect Julia from further pain and suffering to his last breath, as if he were protecting one of his own.

It was as fitting a spot as any to take a break. It was late season, and there were mostly half rotten apples lying about, among which some were still quite tasty. They all needed the sweet sugar and indulged themselves before moving on. The jolt of energy gave added incentive for them to make good haste while the weather remained clear.

*****

Ten days passed, and each one was uneventful, thankfully. There were a few refugees who formed their own collaborative groups, sometimes heading south toward Pultusk in the same direction from which Pavel's group had left, each one seeking refuge where none likely existed. Julia asked herself, "What were they leaving behind them for us to find. It was most certainly not *Eden*."

The exchange of information by each successive group was much the same as the ones before, but sometimes proved to be helpful. Tragedy was all around them. Word was the Germans had completed construction of concentration camps to the north, in the city of Dzialdowo.

In the region of Lotzen near to Olsztyn, which was the general course Pavel's group was presently taking, the Wehrmacht established a military headquarters serving the entire region as far south as Ciechanow. It was becoming apparent the safest haven for them could be where they were already standing, and the walls of paralyzing fear were inexorably closing in upon them.

Most of these peasant farmers had few worthy opinions to speak of, on any matters of relevance. Their lives were simple and as such they had no impressions of their own to offer, content to remain totally dependent upon the guidance offered by Pavel, Kristian, and very few others. Fortunately, Julia and Manal were included within the inner circle.

Conversations around the evening fires were gradually becoming more tense, as the journey offered too few choices of eventual escape. Military roadblocks had been reported as the cities were becoming increasingly militarized, forcing travelers to seek refuge even deeper into the harsh but protective forests. Decisions about where to go were slow to develop, and the pressure was placing additional strain on everyone.

At the end of day, when a new campsite was agreed upon, the task of searching through the heavily forested terrain often found Julia and others foraging alone for kindling to keep themselves productive. She was always one to do her fair share and confidently relied upon her natural bearings to locate her way back to the campsite, even as darkness was beginning to fall.

One such late afternoon, just as dusk was approaching, she was returning with her bundle of wood close to the camp's perimeter, when she heard the distinct sound of a cracking twig.

She instinctively froze motionless and kept her senses finely tuned to the sounds around her, based upon her previous practical experience. Muffled sounds of distant conversation continued from the area of the camp, just as before. That much remained consistent. But whatever, or whomever had entered the gathering darkness close to her was not venturing to assist her with her load. Surely it was someone from the camp with ulterior motives.

Julia told herself not to panic, but nevertheless she knew what she had heard. Someone was close, just watching… and waiting. She shuffled and readjusted her heavy load as best she could, and calmly fumbled to grasp one of the heavier branches in her right hand, squeezing it so tightly she could feel her fingers pulsating. Julia was prepared to defend herself with a vengeance if need be.

She proceeded cautiously, turning her head from right to left, again and again, looking for any sign of motion and briefly considered to herself, was this just another example of her growing paranoia?

No, it was not! The mysterious and now shadowy creature jumped her from behind, much too quickly for her to identify. She grappled with him, all the while continuing to hold fast to the solid and sturdy weapon she was relying upon and with her free hand, dug her mostly broken nails into the hairy arms restraining her. As she struggled, and inhaled a deep breath, she smelled a familiar stinking reek of body odour and the sour stench of his rancid breath. *It was Andrew!*

Without thinking, Julia leaped as high as she could while still being held tightly in his strong grasp and in the same motion managed to raise her legs even higher. She was able to partially extend them outward. By doing so, her reaction caught him totally off guard. He was unprepared for the shift of weight and was unexpectedly off balance, as they both crashed to the ground.

He was still restraining her when she slid her grip slightly further up the shaft of the sturdy branch exposing about six inches of it, and forcefully jammed the stump into his ribs behind her. His grip relaxed as he grimaced in pain, while Julia broke free long enough to stand and turn to face the dirty bastard.

He gathered himself and grinned menacingly at this feisty young woman. "I'll give you that one you little bitch! Now you're mine!"

"You want me? Come get me you ugly fucking pig!" Despite her slight, emaciated body of probably not even a hundred pounds, Julia's never-quit attitude demonstrated the valiant determination of a mighty warrior. She swung her weapon repeatedly, as hard and as quickly as she could, trying again to catch him not fully prepared for her formidable defense. He raised his arm defensively to deflect the first blow, and she scored another painful strike across his forearm.

He moaned with the impact and became enraged. He charged straight toward her, with his blackened teeth tightly clenched and his arms fully extended, driving his shoulder into her chest to force her backwards, crushing her against a massive tree, knocking the wind out of her. She fell to the ground, stunned and clearly shaken by the violent impact.

Images swirled around her through disoriented waves of darkness. She was stunned momentarily and shook her head trying unsuccessfully to regain her faculties. She had lost sense of what was happening, or for that matter where she was. The sudden impact made it painful just to breathe.

As her senses gradually began to clear, her assailant had already pulled off her boots and pants and was frantically trying to tear her sweater off as well. Julia desperately summoned whatever control she could muster and feigned prolonged unconsciousness for a brief fraction of time.

She laid spread eagled on the ground half naked, while the animal anxiously dropped his pants. She waited... and she waited a mere second more... it was interminable... but as he was ready to mount her... *NOW!* In an instant she drove her right knee directly into his crotch.

His raging eyes looked as if they would explode in agony as he collapsed on top of her, writhing in pain. The unsuspected blow immediately changed his demeanor from one of lustfulness to blind hateful rage. He no longer wanted to rape her, now he wanted to choke the very life out of her!

He slapped her face with his clenched fist and wrapped his gnarled laborer's hands around her tiny neck. His chokehold was more than she could bear, as she struggled desperately, kicking her legs convulsively but was unable to gasp for air. His idiotic glare was the last thing she would see, as she again fell into deep and irrepressible unconsciousness. Julia was for all intent and purposes leaving this earth, and on the virtual edge of oblivion.

Unknown to her was the intervening presence of Andrew's oldest brother Martin, who upon seeing what his brother had done, sprung on top of him, pulling him off Julia's beaten and helpless body. He aggressively threw Andrew off to the side... and instead of reviving Julia, he took his brother's place and started to prepare himself to ravage her unconscious or even dead corpse, for all he knew.

Martin grabbed Julia's ankles and forcibly elevated her legs to fully expose her. Julia was unaware of this, nor did she hear the hollering and the general commotion as Pavel came running with his rifle in hand, not expecting to find Julia being sexually assaulted.

What he saw was enough for Pavel. As if to give in to his own raging frustration with the evils of life, Pavel recoiled the butt of his shotgun as far behind him as he possibly could and swung it violently, striking the side of Martin's skull. The direct hit from his mighty swing undeniably crushed the side of his head. In so doing, the blow lifted Martin's limp body in brutal fashion from his innocent victim.

Pavel staggered back to draw a deep breath and slowly turned to face Andrew sitting against the base of another tree. Seeing his pants still gathered around his ankles, Pavel more fully understood the gravity of the brothers' intent. Still in a blind rage, he slowly and premeditatively raised the shotgun and pointed it at Andrew's bare chest... and simply, with finality, blew him away.

He threw his discharged weapon onto the ground and shouted to the camp for help, hugging Julia's limpness close to his chest, sobbing uncontrollably like a young child. She was non-responsive, but still breathing.

*****

Over the next twenty-four hours, Julia slept soundly, never moving and completely unconscious. Late the following day, she mumbled repeatedly and appeared to gradually regain consciousness, but only intermittently, falling back asleep to relive the attack again and again in the nightmares continuing to plague her. As the days passed, she muttered incomprehensibly, tossing and turning in a confused haze of alternating anguish and relief.

She had no memories of the retribution Pavel had served upon her assailants. These matters were better left unsaid by anyone in the camp, including Dustin, the one remaining brother. He did not dare to confront Pavel, nor did he speak with anyone. After the bodies were buried in an unmarked grave, he drifted even further from the group through his own self-imposed solitude.

*****

"Julia... Julia! Wake up now. You need to eat some soup." It was the soft soothing voice of Manal. The pungent but sweet aroma of the beet soup near her nose did the trick, as Julia started to stir again. She was gaining strength with each passing day and had seemed less confused, finally.

Manal helped Julia sit up and after Julia slowly devoured a cup of hot soup, Manal commenced to tenderly wash her with some warm water. The cuts were presumed to be superficial but extensive bruising about her back and neck was as black as night, with purple discoloration surrounding the injured tissue.

Even from the gentle caring touch of an experienced mother Julia winced, and very half-heartedly tried to attend to her own care. She had great difficulty moving but did so with searing pain from torn and stretched muscles running the length of her battered back. Perhaps several days of additional rest were what she needed most.

It was three more days before Julia could walk again without being disoriented. In the absence of a wagon, the group had fashioned a stretcher to transport Julia and the entire camp with her, deeper into the forest. With Julia they were no longer as mobile as before the assault, but Pavel and Manal were determined they were not leaving without her. No one protested; not a soul, perhaps because no other option was viable.

During this down time, Kristian and Lionel agreed to go on alone to scout the best route they should resume when Julia was sufficiently recovered. Everyone needed the break from the drudgery of forced marching. Tevia and others stayed fully occupied trapping rabbits and pigeons and even tracked a deer, which eventually eluded capture. Maybe farming and carpentry were more their specialty, they mused to themselves through their frustrated efforts.

It became evident Julia had been concussed by the direct impact of her head hitting hard against the tree. She was unable to speak in more than a hoarse whisper due to the extensive swelling about her throat. These things would heal relatively quickly, but it was the emotional scars of the overwhelming physical assault continuing to haunt her. The image of Andrew's taunting and derisive expressions of facial fury were still burned into her psyche. This, more than anything, was triggering her perpetual nocturnal visions.

Two days after they left camp, Kristian and Lionel returned, looking considerably more ashen than when they had departed. They recounted how they happened upon five young Polish laborers who had evacuated from the east at the first sign of trouble. Russian troops had inflicted such brutality and indiscriminate destruction, there was nothing left of home to return.

Their village was torched and totally consumed by fire. As they described their horrific experience, Kristian saw the consistency with everything Julia had shared with Pavel and himself. As Julia had already told them... *"whatever your worst imaginings"*. This had now become too real for them to bear.

They went on to describe, "German military activity has secured all roads heading north and west. From the safety of the treeline, we saw another group of nine or ten migrants, who were quickly intercepted and taken into captivity. We fear we will suffer the same fate Pavel! The only question is how deep into the forest should we go before continuing northwest. South and east are out of the question!"

"Sit down boys. Drink something. You both look like shit," said Pavel, trying to calm them as best he could. Manal brought hot soup and fresh water, which they devoured immediately. Kristian wiped his mouth against the sleeve of his filthy sweater, and then resumed. "The Russians aren't *coming* Pavel. They're *already here!*"

Lionel was still slurping his soup and remained nonresponsive. He seemed content to let Kristian finish his report. He knew he would not be able to stay composed well enough to make sense of things.

"Where is my wife? I must see her. And how is Julia? We have to move from here Pavel; much deeper into the trees... *and we must do it now!*"

"Julia is recovering nicely Kristian. Go see your wife, of course. Both are well, but please, I ask you to keep the matters we discussed to yourself. We don't want everyone to panic. Do you understand me, my friend?"

He placed his arm around them both and they agreed to clean up and resume their debriefing after they had eaten. Pavel just turned to stand beside Manal, saying nothing, and watched dejectedly as the two men slipped into the darkness. Their message as expected, was less than reassuring.

*****

Julia and Manal were asked to join the five leaders for a discussion about the limited options before them. None of which was without pain and sacrifice, but it was agreed there was one offering a slim possibility of survival.

Migration to the north was certain to take them to the Grodno region, in and around the city of Slonim. It was known as the *Land of a Thousand Lakes* and covered vast areas where nature had prevailed well against the onslaught of humanity.

It offered nothing of military value, and little of strategic value. Pavel believed the wrath and scarring of this pointless war could leave this area largely unaffected, in the hands of nature where it belonged. Since the roads north were still not viable, the way would have to be negotiated by finding natural pathways through heavily forested lands to stay as undetected as their circumstances would allow.

Pavel was candid with his leaders and to his credit, explained the situation honestly. "Our original plan to locate an abandoned village, or even a farmhouse in such wilderness will be highly unlikely. The benefit of this route will depend upon our ability to elude both the Germans and the Russians. While it may not be probable, it is still possible.

"Our greatest enemy, however, will not be the Germans, or the Russians. Our biggest challenge in my opinion, will be learning how to survive by living on the land through the coming winter. Our fore-fathers did it a long time ago, why couldn't we?"

Pavel took pause to let the group contemplate their predicament while pouring another cup of putrid coffee. "I'll tell you why. It's already so late in the season. We've lost the ability to stock up on suitable rations to keep our bellies full and our families warm. Even if we had supplies, we have no oxen or wagons. I have no doubt this would be our greatest challenge. How our ancestors survived must have been even more difficult, but even for them, winter was not a good time to start. Right now, I simply don't have an answer."

Julia remained uncommonly quiet and offered little by way of her participation in these discussions. Pavel and Manal noted her relative passivity but considering her ordeal, and the physical difficulty she had speaking, it came as no surprise. In truth, she did not like the chances of hiding in the forest, for that is precisely what was being offered as their salvation. Their hope to settle somewhere was no longer a realistic proposition, but hiding in the wilderness was even less so.

The more Julia struggled with these thoughts the more she became convinced her chances of survival were better if she was alone. They already saw what had happened to larger groups of migrants. Easier for one to be overlooked, but ten or more… twenty-five in this case? Sooner or later, they would surely be found, probably close to starving or worse, already frozen to death.

It was approaching late November; another reason to make her decision quickly. The days had grown short, and the nights were sub-zero more often than not. She was determined if she was to die, it would not be at the hands of the Russians, hence heading north or east with Pavel's people was out of the question.

*****

At dawn's first light she found Pavel tending to the last glowing embers of the evening fire, which he had carefully reduced just enough to heat morning coffee for those still willing to swallow this pigswill mash. She could see his breath in the remnants of the cold night air. "You are awake early Julia. Are you feeling better?"

"Yes, very much so Pavel. I am finally feeling more myself again. Thank you so much for all you and your family have done for me. I would not be here were it not for your kindness and thoughtful care."

Pavel was crouched close to the ground, tending to what remained of the small fire, looking up toward her still standing so apprehensively. "It sounds as if you are saying goodbye, Julia."

He continued to poke around the glowing embers and spread dirt around the gradually reducing perimeter.

"I knew the day was approaching, sooner or later... and you seemed uncommonly quiet last night," as he lifted his head and made eye contact with her again. "I can't say I'm surprised."

With resignation, he pushed himself up from the ground to stand closer to Julia and leaned closer still. He whispered softly to her in a very hushed tone. "Between you and me... I don't like our chances either."

"You leave me speechless Pavel. You read my very thoughts. I don't want to appear I am abandoning you... but... well, I think any chances I have to survive this winter will be better on my own. I brought myself this far, and I don't attract any unwanted attention. If I need the help of strangers... again, I have a better chance someone may take me in if I am travelling alone.

"I'm planning to cross the River Sona, back a small piece where it partially splits the meadow. I don't know whether I will have another opportunity to cross to the other side if I go farther north with you, but I am determined I must eventually head west."

"We will miss you, Julia. Anything we can give you; you only have to ask."

"Your kindness knows no bounds my dear friend, but no thank you. Manal and Mariam are fortunate to have you protecting them." As Pavel looked at her so dejectedly, Julia stepped between his extended arms and kissed him softly on his cheek.

"Before you go…" He fumbled with his heavy coat for a moment. "Here! Take my knife. It may help to feed you and protect you. Something to remember us by as well."

"But I cannot! It is a fine instrument… but your father gave it to you as a boy, did he not?" she queried.

"You remembered! Yes, he did, but if he had ever met you, I know he would approve. I have similar ones I retrieved from the forest. They will be suitable for me." He was alluding to those once belonging to the two brothers. They would no longer be needing them.

Tears welled up in her already moistened eyes. "Please give my love to Manal and Mariam. Your family will always be in my prayers."

Not one for long goodbyes, Julia gathered her few things and looked sheepishly into Pavel's eyes. "I must leave now, as the wind is picking up from the north. I fear a storm is in the making and I don't want anyone to follow me. I hope you understand Pavel. Be well, and may God find you safe haven, my dear friend."

Julia adjusted her precious bag onto her hip inside her still serviceable and reliable winter coat and secured the sheath of Pavel's noble gift to her leather belt. She walked briskly into the shards of piercing light just beginning to filter through the dense tree branches.

Pavel could discern the wisps of her warm breath dissipating into the cold morning air and watched and waited for her to bid a final farewell wave. She never looked back again and was quickly consumed by the refuge of the forest.

11
A PROFOUND REJUVENATION

♂

JULIA FELT IN COMMAND AGAIN FROM THE MOMENT OF HER
tearful goodbye. Once again, her mind was her strongest asset against
whatever might befall her. The weather indicated there was more
than a hint of change coming, and within the hour the wind began to
escalate noticeably. The forest was dense with the pungent aroma of
pine, which combined with the heavy mustiness emanating from the
fallen leaves from the mixture of deciduous trees scattered throughout the landscape. It was intoxicating.

Remembering Kristian's report to Pavel, access to any nearby
bridge would surely be well secured by the Germans and therefore
too dangerous to attempt. Crossing the river by foot would be dangerous too, but to Julia's mind, it was the lesser of two evils.

It was several hours later when she approached the quaint
meadow she clearly remembered. It was divided haphazardly by a
small tributary feeding the main river. The sun, once so welcoming
earlier in the morning, was now hiding elusively behind the gathering billows of cloud. From the clearing of the meadow, she could
see the distant overcast skies intending to soon swallow whatever
sporadic sunshine remained.

A little farther west, Julia continued to walk through the high
grass of the open forest, maintaining her vigilance by keeping a brisk
pace, but not so quickly to be unable to detect anyone else's presence.
There was much to fear being alone here, but thankfully her defensive
habits had become more finely honed, becoming second nature to her
already finely attuned senses. They had served her well in the past.
She relied upon them to continue to do so.

Within a few hours, the mostly tall weeds were interspersed with a few scattered rocks leading her way. It had been a mostly dry autumn season and with the approach of winter, the distant sounds of the customary crackling and slashing of rushing water were no longer distinct, indicating a less forceful water flow.

This bode well for Julia since a crossing could be less arduous than she was anticipating. Combined with the whirling sounds of the winds high above and the occasional stiff breezes blowing across the open expanses, it was a calming reminder life and nature were still thriving.

She pressed on until she could see in the near distance by the edge of the meadow what appeared to be a broad depression in the landscape, creating a semicircle around where she stood. As she eagerly approached, there it was! This had to be the River Sona! She drew closer, now hearing the not-so-distant sounds of flowing water, still splashing and dancing along its way to naturally follow the path of least resistance.

It was a peaceful place in nature, here in the middle of nowhere. As she looked over the bank, however, the river appeared too deep and too broad to risk a crossing. Julia continued to follow the shoreline for about twenty minutes, carefully scrutinizing her situation to locate the narrowest and most shallow point available, all the while considering the precarious footing she may encounter.

She knew the water would be freezing but nevertheless, she had to risk a crossing. It wasn't going to get any warmer than it was now. One misplaced step could be disastrous if she became soaked from head to toe and was washed down river by the still powerful current. There was much more to consider here than crossing the lazy brook back home to access her play-fort.

Julia estimated the depth of the river at this point to be about waist high, which would be perilous enough. In preparation, she removed her heavy coat and bundled it as tightly as she was able, careful to wrap it around her leather bag which she repositioned around her neck.

As she was about to proceed, she stopped suddenly and thought to herself, *Wait! Think about when you reach the other side, you fool! I only have one pair of boots and one pair of heavy pants. I will surely need them to be dry for the other side!*

Having never attempted the crossing of a deep river, especially one flowing this swiftly, Julia reached this insightful conclusion of the not so obvious. In preparation, she unraveled the bundle and rewrapped it to now include her pants, undershirt and sweater as well.

She also removed her heavy boots and worn out socks, thoughtfully tying the laces together firmly, double knotting them, and slung them flamboyantly around her neck to hang against her back. Now she was properly prepared!

Protecting the bundle from the water was critical for her survival, assuming she was successful getting to the opposite shore. She gingerly negotiated the first few rocks leading to the water's edge and stepped slowly into the sinking mud below the sparkling surface of the frigid water.

Thankfully there was firm ground just below the mud, but the water was frightfully colder than she had anticipated. Despite being only ankle deep, the shock sent an instant jab of abhorrent coldness she immediately felt up to her knee.

The next step could not be a hesitant one she thought. She submerged her right foot deeper than the first, until it separated the soft and shifting mud below. The same rush of ice water engulfed her leg in an instant, sending the now familiar jolt of anguish higher up her leg. She could not see through the rushing water, so focused her view only on the opposite shoreline she had estimated was no more than sixteen to eighteen feet across.

Another cautious step, followed by another, and another. *My God this is painful!* In only seconds, the icy demon had consumed her waistline. Her lower body, already losing feeling from the numbness of the rushing water, was threateningly close to being dragged further away from the opposite shore.

Julia had to keep moving... and trust she could maintain her already precarious footing. She struggled against the pressure of the water as nature did its best to force her downriver. She would not yield. She... would... not... yield! Push... push... *"I can do this!"*

As the water became deeper, Julia was forced to stand still for a moment to remove her precious bundle from across her chest. Struggling to maintain her perilous balance with a broader stance, she raised it above her head in the event she encountered deeper water yet.

She held on for dear life, but the boots about her neck were becoming wet in the process. She felt even more exposed to the cold with her arms held high and could not use them to protectively shelter her bare chest and ribs against the relentless and bitter assault of the river.

Only a few more steps, as dreadful numbness engulfed her... she carefully placed her left foot... almost stumbling until she realized the water was becoming slightly shallower again. Unable to feel anything below the freezing coldness which had anaesthetized her body up to her chest, Julia staggered to push herself the rest of the way beyond the middle of the river closer to the opposite shore.

No longer sensing anything in her lower extremities, she feared she would surely stumble, losing her battle against nature's freezing fury. My God, she thought! If her grip fails to hold the bag and it slips away to be washed down river, she might as well follow it to her painful death. She could never survive without it!

Five or six more feet... four... *"God help me"*... three... As she rose higher above the still rapid torrent of water, Julia broke free from the death grip of the river, hurling herself to the ground, at the same time throwing her precious bundle further away from the river's edge. *"I've done it! Thanks be to God!"*

Involuntarily, she held her arms tightly to her chest struggling to regain her breath... shaking, uncontrollably as she lay on the cold grass in the fetal position. She knew it must be warmer here than the deadly ice-water, but she could feel nothing below her shoulders!

Involuntarily, her tears began to seep from the corner of her eyes and streamed across her half-frozen face. As they flowed toward her ear, she sensed the comfort of the warm wetness crossing the freezing cold skin of her face. *There was no time to lay here like this! There is still warmth within my body, and I desperately must preserve it.*

Shaking and trembling like a half inebriated drunk, Julia awkwardly stripped her soaked underpants from her naked body and unraveled her bundled coat. Her hands and fingers were useless stumps. Frantically, she grabbed another shirt from her bag to wipe away any excess water from her trembling body. The water now consisted of small ice droplets clinging to her exposed skin. She rubbed and brushed the beads off as quickly as possible but was unable to reach her back.

Julia's teeth were noisily clattering but as quickly as she could move, she hooked her stubby, almost nonresponsive fingers into the openings of her sweater to pull it over her head. Then, trying to hold her pants securely enough to step into them, she could not keep her balance and crashed to the ground.

Falling was a miracle from God, she thought. He had pushed her over to save her! This was the only way to put her pants on! Although the impact of her fall was painful, Julia was excited to just feel it, and was buoyed by feeling *something* in her lower extremities again. Her faint hope was restored within her.

Anxiously, she struggled to her knees but even fumbling to secure her belt was a challenging process. Her fingers were still like claws. Regaining her footing now, she staggered and wrapped the coat tightly to her emaciated and half-frozen body, snuggling inside as an innocent frightened child. She was entitled to feel this way... she actually *was* a frightened child!

Dropping onto her backside, she fumbled with her old haggard wool socks, forcing her frozen feet deeper into them, feeling nothing in either foot. She anxiously began to untie the knotted shoelaces on her boots. *Damn it!*

It was an arduous, almost impossible task with her trembling hands, which were now, like her toes, *burning* with cold. Despite her growing frustration she persisted, after blowing several warm breaths into her cupped hands. The swollen knots would not loosen... *Oh, damn! Why had I tightened them so much?* Frantic now, she began using her teeth to bite into them and finally, mercifully, the laces began to separate. Gratefully, she jammed her feet into the blessed boots. Thankfully, the insides were still dry.

Totally exhausted, Julia rolled up to huddle against the base of a tree but quickly realized this was not controlling her hyperthermia. Although almost totally spent, she struggled to her aching feet again and proceeded to swing her arms and twist her torso from side to side. Then she switched her focus to her legs, doing squats, then lifting each one from a standing position, bending her knees alternately like a marching soldier.

Squatting, stretching, and grimacing, Julia sapped every ounce of her remaining physicality in a desperate attempt to increase her heart rate to restore sufficient body heat, until several grueling minutes later, the trembling began to finally subside. Her heart was racing, pumping as hard as it could to distribute her welcoming warm blood to her nearly expired extremities. It was a gratified feeling of accomplishment she shared with only herself.

As she had done before, Julia sought out a hollowed pocket of refuge near a fallen tree. She positioned herself on the leeward side so the tree would provide some shelter from the blowing night winds that would surely follow, and then gathered a plentiful supply of fallen leaves and branches to nestle among them. Her tasks completed, she thankfully drew her heavy coat collar tightly to her neck and pulled her toque as low down on her scruffy head as it would allow, exposing almost nothing to the probable bitter night frost.

Out of sheer exhaustion, Julia slept soundly without any regard for maintaining further vigilance. There comes a time when the body prioritizes what it needs to sustain itself. This was such a time.

*****

Sometime the next morning, Julia finally began to stir and struggled to open her once sleep deprived eyes. Frighteningly at first, she suddenly realized they were now crusted over with icy tears. Ever so carefully, she rubbed her eyes to crack, and then carefully dislodge the thin layers of frozen tears still sealing her eyelids. As she peeked silently about her, she was astounded at the brightness of the vision before her.

The panoramic scene was a wonderland of striking yet serene tranquility; completely undisturbed, untouched and virginal in its scope… the things dreams are made of. Everything was cloaked in an exquisite shroud of freshly fallen snow! The glorious blanket had left her totally undetectable to any inquisitive wildlife, human or otherwise. She mused how much more difficult her river crossing had been than she ever could have imagined, and was thankful she had been so naïve, or she may not have even tried.

In these quiet moments of reflection and peaceful solitude, Julia took a moment to pray, finding herself strangely comfortable and warm. She had no immediate desire to even adjust her position. She prayed, not to ask God for help, but rather to be grateful for having survived her most recent ordeal.

It is impossible to feel hopelessness when you are grateful, she thought. And feelings of hopelessness are never conducive to seeking pragmatic solutions. With renewed determination, Julia eventually rose somewhat reluctantly from the soft, white pocket of her massive cocoon, sensing a profound rejuvenation of spirit.

She knew full well she could not withstand this pattern of survival indefinitely and became alert to finding a better source of refuge than her present God-given accommodations. Good fortune had shone upon her, but she understood it was a providential happenchance. Although famished, she was at least much warmer than before, as the gently falling snow had embraced her with the gift of natural protection from the bitterly cold winds.

The first snowfall of the season was a gentle one, having arrived almost unannounced were it not for yesterday's cloud patterns and subsequent overcast, usually preceding this wondrous display of nature's winter glory.

It was an awe-inspiring moment in which she found comfort, but only temporarily. The winds definitively began to pick up speed and could be heard howling menacingly through the trees as another weather front took control; this one perhaps far more intense than the evening before. As it gained in intensity, it gathered much of the fresh fallen powder, making it blow horizontally from west to east.

Staying in the forest without food would no longer sustain her. The biting cold was certain to follow shortly and would surely prove to be far less forgiving as the previous night. She must find proper shelter, food, and warmth, and she must do so soon.

After gathering her few possessions, she once again forced herself to keep trudging west. It was laborious work, lifting each leg higher and higher, step by step through the ever-deepening snow. As the hours of walking in total solitude against the bitter winds passed, she heard the unmistakable sound of a passing car or truck in the distance. It was the first indication in days she was not completely alone in this part of the world.

As she saw the clearing spreading the dimming light of day before her, Julia reached what must have been a gravel roadway, now almost undetectable. Her only course of action was to cautiously follow the tire tracks to wherever they led before the swirling winds erased them.

Within the hour, the vantage of her forested domain no longer defined the boundaries of the roadway which now led her through wide open landscapes, probably now barren farmers' fields. The trees had thinned out noticeably on both sides of the road, exposing an entirely open vista through which she could barely see some gently rolling hills dressed in effervescent sparkling white diamonds and shining silver crystals; amazingly beautiful, but menacingly deadly.

After a short time, the intensity of the snow became blinding, making it more difficult to see much of anything in the distance, however between occasional breaks of the gusting winds, she could barely distinguish the stark silhouettes of some devastated farmhouses. What few she could see must have been maliciously torched and were not at all habitable, due to the apparent firestorm of destruction that must have engulfed them.

Now well outside the confines of the forest, the wild winds became more forceful, bringing with them a bitter cold front piercing the small openings of her trusty old coat.

The abuse of neglect was profound on the remains of the few blurred houses creeping into her quickly narrowing view. These had once been someone's homes, but within these now desolate skeletons of stone and timber, any hint of faded memories had been torn from their feeble embrace. These were inhospitable remains offering nothing more than a porous windbreak at best.

Julia was running out of time. The ice crystals picked up by the ferocity of the wind tore into her, piercing tiny crevices in her parka and toque, some even penetrating these miniscule cracks in her makeshift armor; biting, stinging, and tearing away at her briefly exposed and long since neglected pretty, young face.

Out of nothing more than desperation, and perhaps due only to willful thinking, she came upon the remnants of what must have once been a small barn. The remaining wood in this disheveled place showed no signs of having been burned and therefore appeared to have withstood the pounding of Mother Nature much better than the structures she saw throughout her perilous day. As with the others though, none of the roof remained here either.

Traces of oil and gas were still barely apparent to her keen sense of smell, even after years of absorption into the once saturated earthen floor. Perhaps an old machine shop, she wondered? It likely housed equipment which had probably been confiscated, as everything else had been stripped clean. The crumbled structure itself had eventually succumbed to the ravages of whatever violence it had sustained and evidently became too fragile to withstand exposure to further months of nature's abuses.

Over time, wind and weather had cleared the ground, save for a small niche, barely visible behind a few empty fuel containers buried within the rubble. The heavily falling snow continued blowing in from the west, leaving one side of the barn floor relatively clear of significant accumulation.

Julia, now half-heartedly, was becoming discouraged, turning over a few scattered pieces of timber, looking for who knows what, when suddenly she made a discovery. Her prize was a large bundle of straw still hidden against the base of the partially remaining wall! It must have been inadvertently covered by a large piece of the crumbling roof.

She approached the bale inquisitively and as she drew closer, her sense of smell although muted, was still able to recognize rotted horse manure and traces of rodent droppings. Despite the stench, it could still adequately serve some good purpose, but it would be of little use to her out here in the open air.

Julia remembered seeing an adjacent broken-down shed close to a small cluster of trees, a few of which still stood defiantly. The shed was partially enclosed with three walls still vertical, barely enough to support what remained of a metal roof. She felt the all too familiar shaking of her core, reminding her again how horribly close she had been to the death grip she had endured when crossing the Sona. She was not confident she could withstand another deep chill and was forced to act quickly.

With trembling frozen hands inside her tattered gloves, she grasped the bindings of the bale but could not lift it, probably being more than half her body weight. Though she applied force against it, the bale seemed immoveable. In a mounting rage of frustration, Julia realized the bale was frozen to the ground below.

Repeatedly, she angrily attacked the bale, kicking and pounding the bundle forcefully, more out of anger than any specific reason. In so doing, her violent assault loosened the bale's firm hold of the ground beneath... and the bundle's frozen bonds cracked! Encouraged by the slight shifting of the bale, she continued to kick it. Mercifully, the bale broke free!

Julia summoned what little strength remained and valiantly attempted to drag it out from under the fallen timber, no doubt having kept her prize sheltered from the ravages of summer's heat and stormy winter weather. Physically exhausted to the point of collapse, Julia knew she must get away from the unremitting bitter winds. There comes a time when a body succumbs to the relentlessness of the blistering cold, and her physical tolerance had long since been diminishing.

With nothing more than sheer determination, she struggled to haul the bale the necessary forty feet or so to the partially roofed shed, afraid to stop for fear of not being able to resume this incredible challenge. The muscles in her thighs and back were cramping and she screamed with agony. A few feet more... *a few feet more! Don't stop to look! Keep moving!* Failing to do so would signify her dismal collapse, likely resulting in her certain death on this very spot!

Her heart was pounding to the point of exploding within her chest. She did not care... *she could not care!* Pulling and now pushing, she gradually approached the corner of her sanctuary, as close to the inside corner of the shed as possible. Desperately climbing over it, Julia collapsed to the ground behind her prize and wrestled to burrow her exhausted frame even closer.

Her chest was heaving now, the freezing air burning her lungs with each successive gasp. No matter, her head was light from oxygen deprivation. Her body fought for what it needed most. The winds continued to pick up with such ferocity the tin roof rattled loudly, as if being finally removed from its moorings. It continued to hold!

Panting heavily, Julia immediately commenced breaking off several manageable clumps of straw with the steel knife Pavel had given her, ripping them apart to cover the ground beneath her and covering her already numb feet and legs. For all she knew, this could be her final resting place. Though stiff with aching muscles, what few she still had, she was not yet aware her shaking and trembling from the cold had passed.

The exertion of her task had pushed her stamina and her pulse to maximum capacity. Without knowing it, this determined last gasp to survive would sustain her just enough to restore her own body heat, to be absorbed once more in her new cocoon till morning. She would sleep soundly for the next day and a half until her shrunken belly screamed for food to signal the beginning of yet another day.

*****

Weather's fury had subsided to softer gusts of winter's winds by the time Julia regained consciousness. Again, the swirling winds of the night had softly deposited layers of its majestic embrace in and about Julia's tiny remnants of shelter. For the first time in her life, she was saddened to wake, preferring at this defining moment to have simply escaped additional suffering and continual torment, to find a more peaceful and everlasting place.

The sadness of her reality evoked fresh morning tears, the warmth of which somehow soothed her spirit and reawakened within her the desire to find her way back from the very precipice of the infinite summoning abyss.

Surprisingly, the shed had withstood the storm's vengeance and now featured glorious sculptures of magnificent cascading drifts gently caressing the fragile walls defiantly supporting it. She rose awkwardly to get to her knees. Her strained muscles were deservingly reluctant to function again.

This not-so-fragile young warrior kept battling to get to her knees, and after several minutes, was finally able to do so... but standing erect was another matter. Gradually and very tearfully, she eased herself from all fours, to the point where she could support herself by resting first her elbows, and then her hands on her knees. In another minute or so, she courageously tried to stand fully erect, groaning loudly as she did so.

"Augh!! Oh, my word!" She cried out. "Oh, shit! ... There we go. Nothing to it!" she exclaimed with proud satisfaction and a hefty dollop of sarcasm. In the total absence of sound, no breeze could be heard, no gentle rustling of fallen leaves, no chirp of a lonely bird... nothing except her involuntary grunting and groaning to crudely break the solemn silence.

Despite her life force being almost extinguished just a few hours ago, Julia had clung to a final shred of good humor she still held in reserve, even if only for her own entertainment.

Now, if she could just get her hips and legs to co-operate, she thought. As she started to move ever so tentatively, in a hesitant and awkward manner, her stomach groaned and squealed for attention. "I know. I know. I'll find us something soon!" as if to speak within herself, from mind to body, from bone to joint, organ to organ.

Her tired and stiffened joints gradually loosened enough to regain some usefulness. Although very wobbly at first, her balance steadied, and aside from being short choppy strides, she began to walk again. It was a start.

Grimacing through the pain in her shoulders and back, and severe stiffness in her thighs and hips, she knew if she carefully persisted, they too would loosen in time. She learned the importance of genuinely listening to what her body was telling her; it spoke to her in ways strangely comforting to her, as if she was having internal conversations and was no longer completely alone.

At the start of every new day, Julia knew she was on borrowed time; now more than ever. Resuming her self-imposed march this day however, simply had to yield nourishment; and not just a rotted cabbage or frozen potatoes buried in a sheet of ice, assuming she could even find some. *She desperately needed real food!* Her extreme hunger was no less urgent than her need for warmth and rest the previous day, which she found. But devouring some decent food could not be delayed another day, if she had any chance of survival.

The cycle was indeed still turning. Not knowing where the road would take her, she maintained a continual and unbreakable thread of hope, with the fervent belief God would not have provided for her, only to have her eventually succumb to imminent failure because she willfully decided to quit.

It would probably be Christmas sometime soon, she suddenly realized. She had lost track of time and was tired of the freezing cold. Fortunately, the blanketing impressions freshly falling snow provides, soothed, albeit ever so slightly, the abject ugliness of her world.

However, even harsher weather would prove an overwhelming challenge, one she might not be able to overcome. Self-doubt was beginning to take hold of her. Eventually the weather would break her, one way or the other, and stop her quest to move forward at some point.

Sooner or later, she knew her circumstances must be altered. Heat and occasional hot food were more vital now than ever. Her immediate future had to be rethought through a more pragmatic approach.

It was then she determined it was time to drastically change her demeanor from the driven, independent adult trapped in a child's emaciated body, to that of a poor, helpless orphan seeking refuge at this special time of goodwill toward men.

12
DISCOVERING SACRED DOCUMENTS

CONDITIONS HAD BEEN IMPROVING THE FARTHER NORTH-west Julia travelled. The entire civilized world had evidently not been blown into oblivion, which she had come to expect as the normal state of things. It was still frigidly cold, but peaceful here, made so by fresh and silently falling snow, masking the scars of destruction buried beneath it.

The road wound its way through open land with very few mature trees, mostly broad fields once bearing harvests of corn, barley, and potatoes. *Would today be any different,* she thought? Although barren and desolate, there was not a mark of disturbance in the hardening crusts of snow, as far as she could see up to and over the crest of the surrounding hillsides. The serenity of the open vista was peaceful and appeared untouched by human hands.

It had been hours, but her pace remained steady and determined. With the passage of time, however, she was becoming disoriented by dehydration and had no frame of reference in the white, unblemished world in which she found herself. The extreme hunger gnawed deep inside her belly, constantly demanding her attention.

She had not eaten since her final meal of borsht soup and boiled potatoes with Manal and Pavel. How long ago she could not even recall. Her stomach now ached repeatedly, insisting one final time it could no longer function without something nourishing to eat.

Once again, the subdued glare of the diminishing sun was barely enough to penetrate the gently falling snow, forcing her to squint through watery eyes. Julia struggled to focus them, burning now as the snow had begun to freeze on her frosted eyelids. There was nothing in reserve to serve her body's demands.

Unknowingly, she staggered near the completely hidden edge of the invisible road. As she did so, her foot slipped and collapsed uncontrollably when her wobbling left leg took her down a shallow embankment. Painfully, the right leg reluctantly obliged the lead of her left, and she thumped to her bottom rolling slowly, and somewhat thankfully to her new resting place.

The unexpected thud of her fall wasn't so much painful as it was stimulating. The fall jolted Julia to her senses. Just lying there on her back for a moment, she carefully wiped the fresh snow away from her eyelids and frostbitten cheeks. She raised herself to a sitting position while still slumped on the slight grade, having so rudely summoned her. The faintly perceptible winds had shifted now, and Julia rearranged her heavy collar and her toque, both of which had become askew from her sudden and involuntary tumble.

Amid these distractions, the stomach pains had become more controllable, so she rolled to her knees and pushed herself awkwardly to assume a broader stance than she was normally accustomed, to steady herself more assuredly than before.

She set one foot ahead of the other and covered no more than a hundred or so meters when her persistence paid off. Julia could detect faint aromas of what she imagined were baked biscuits! A far cry from the stenches to which she had become accustomed, she thought. Eagerly and inquisitively, she pressed on with renewed enthusiasm, trying to overcome her growing sense of desperation.

The road led to a simple but what appeared to be occupied farmhouse, as indicated by the smoke rising from the stone chimney and the dimly lit interior light. The source of the biscuits no doubt! Her belly churned in her emptiness inside, as if reignited by the very possibility of food. Was it Christmas she wondered?

Approaching steadily, she followed a direct line to the wooden porch, since any pathway possibly existing was lost to the snowy world above it. Although a little dilapidated and in some need of repair, she was thankful nonetheless by the prospects hidden behind the humble front doorway. Without hesitation she tapped on the door. Her heart was in her mouth when the handle turned to release the squeaking door.

A man in his early fifties with a graying beard and suspicious bearing appeared before her as he asked bluntly, "Who are you and what do you want? I have nothing I can give a dirty beggar," he stated as a matter of fact. He was not aggressive in his tone, and thankfully not confrontational.

Julia strained to speak and struggled to clear her dried throat. "Please sir, my name is Julia. I am without any family, and I am doing my best just to survive. I have been walking for days since leaving the River Sona. Can you give me something… anything to eat? I mean you no harm, but I fear I am about to die without food."

"How long have you been walking, Julia? Are you a Jew? Do not lie to me, girl!"

"I swear I am not. I have been running from the Russians since they invaded us. They killed my family with all the others and destroyed our village in Pobereze. I had nowhere to go but away. I have no one left, *please sir.*" Her sincerity and the genuineness of her despairing appeal became even more convincing as seen in the moistness of her pleading eyes.

"You stink like a filthy pig…but I suppose I can help you as best I can. You must clean yourself before you can sit at my table." The door opened more widely and without further exchange or trepidation, Julia entered his home. It was the first such time she had experienced the inside of a house in the almost three months since her travels began. *Thank you, dear God, thank you!* she silently prayed.

It was a basic but cozy home offering a small taste of paradise, although she knew not what that entailed. There was a fireplace crackling and the smell of the biscuits she could now almost taste in the warm inviting air within. She was too exhausted to notice much but there was a single sofa chair near to the fireplace and the kitchen featured a modest but functional table and four wooden chairs. There appeared to be a room in the back and a bathroom. *Oh, for a bathroom… with a tub!* she thought.

"Thank you for your kindness, sir. I am so sorry if I am intruding. I have nowhere to go, and I was afraid the coldness would take me, if hunger didn't take me first." Again, her blue eyes watered, and dimly glistened. She forced herself to keep her head up to use eye contact to convey her desperation. This simple gesture was unnatural for her now after slogging through forests, broken concrete and rubble, swamps, marshes, and half frozen riverbeds. Her hunched over posture and bowed head had become the new norm.

"Yes, yes. I already opened my door to you! Come with me but take those smelly boots off first. I will fill the bathtub. It's not much, but it's all I have. You don't appear too fancy for it, huh?" It was the first indication of a wry smile from this stranger, and it felt wonderful.

"Wash up a bit at the sink and I'll run some water. It's not hot, but I'll boil more for your bath. Just give me a few minutes." He directed her to the washroom and resumed the brief conversation.

"There are some towels in there to wrap yourself in until the water is ready. I'll fetch you a biscuit to hold you till dinner. It won't take long I assure you." He exited and closed the door behind him, a gesture of respect Julia could not help but notice.

After peeling off her putrid clothing, she wrapped one towel around her hips, and another hung about her shoulders covering her breasts while she sat patiently on the edge of the tub. She basked in the warmth of the bathroom and was engulfed in a renewed flood of sustaining hopefulness.

The man did not knock but announced himself on the other side of the still closed door. As he entered, he placed a biscuit on the countertop and struggled with a pot of steaming water. It sloshed sloppily into the waiting tub. "Let me fetch two more pots Julia. It will be well worth the wait."

As he closed the door again behind him, Julia immediately broke the warm biscuit in half and consumed it in mere seconds. She removed her towels and stepped into the shallow but welcoming water, choosing not to wait any longer. It had been so very long. This was no time for modesty. It was the least of her concerns.

Henry said nothing when he returned a few minutes later but was visibly taken aback at the vision of this beaten young child, sitting unabashedly naked in his half-filled tub of water. He respectfully poured the contents of the bucket carefully, close to her half-extended legs and feet.

After the final bucket was poured, and Henry closed the door behind him, Julia was able to slide her torso fully beneath the water and just soak. It was delightful to feel alive again, albeit ever so slightly. She laid there for a time, flat on her back with only her knees and head exposed above the soothing warmth surrounding her.

Not realizing she had dozed off, she was startled by the tapping on the bathroom door. "Julia, are you alright?" Julia twitched suddenly and her arms flailed somewhat. The splashing water indicated to Henry what had taken so long. Julia briefly choked on a mouthful of water, coughing as she did so. "Yes… yes, I'm fine. I'll be just a moment."

"May I open the door? I have some clean clothes for you."

"Please just give me a minute," she responded.

"I'll just leave these on the floor for you. Take your time."

Henry kindly provided some suitable clean clothes, in a tidy bundle folded so nicely, making Julia feel as if she was to be swaddled in royal attire. She had no need to fumble through her leather bag for another ragged piece of worn-out clothing. Her bag was likely still sitting at the foot of the chair by the fireplace, probably the same spot she had inadvertently dropped it. She had no immediate recollection. The biscuit Henry provided stimulated her now angry, growling stomach and now it demanded more.

Julia finished dressing herself and simply towel dried her tangled and unkempt excuse for hair. Its length was excessively long and roughly tousled with many large knots, still containing some difficult to remove debris. She effortlessly wrapped a small towel around her head in the amazing way women have; men never quite able to master. As she hesitatingly entered the main room, Henry encouraged her to take a seat at the very inviting table he had thoughtfully set before them.

"Please, sit down, girl, no need to be shy with me. Eat as much as you want."

Julia ashamedly kept her head lowered and only raised it to clumsily sneak an occasional peek at her host. She felt too embarrassed to look him directly in the eye.

Little was said initially between the two strangers as Julia could simply not contain herself any longer. She devoured a large bowl of steaming barley soup, and then another, along with a half dozen baked biscuits, with generous applications of creamy butter leaking onto her eager fingers.

When she started licking and sucking her fingers to savor every ounce of the melted butter, Henry started to smile, not just from the sight of this young and thankful urchin, but more from the feeling of genuine satisfaction he felt from being able to extend his thoughtful hospitality to a child of such evident deserving need.

"Well, you were indeed a hungry young lady, weren't you," Henry exclaimed.

"I'm so sorry, I hope I didn't eat too much. I just couldn't help myself," she stated apologetically.

Henry responded and helped put her mind at ease. "No, no, not at all. I'm thankful you enjoyed the food and for your company." While she was finishing her meal, Henry placed a few blankets on the sofa chair with an extra pillow from his bed.

"You must be exhausted Julia." She acknowledged his statement of the obvious with a weary nod. It was evident she was struggling to keep her eyelids open. "You can sleep on the chair as long as you like… whenever you are ready. We can talk some more tomorrow if you want."

*****

It was midday before Julia started to stir. It was a sound safe sleep; something eluding her since leaving the relatively safe confines of Pavel's makeshift camp. It was also the first time in months she woke up not stinking like a wild animal. The smell of perked coffee nudged her welcomingly back to consciousness.

When her eyelids finally lifted, she could see Henry working quietly at the kitchen sink with his back toward her. She just continued to sit silently, thoughtfully considering for a moment who, or what could have awaited her on the interior side of his door. The scene before her could have been entirely different and not dissimilar to her worst expectations. She had been truly blessed to find this kind old man.

Julia stretched her arms upright and extended her legs beyond the warmth of the woolen blanket and sighed to alert him she was awake. "Good morning, Henry. What time is it?" It was such an irrelevant question. More relevant might be, what day is it?

Showing his teasing demeanor, Henry responded, "Morning has long since left us, Julia. It's almost two o'clock, *in the afternoon!* You slept well, I assume?"

"Yes, thank you for asking. I think I needed that more than I knew."

"Come, have some coffee while I make us some eggs. It won't take but a minute."

"You are too kind, Henry."

Perhaps because Henry hadn't spoken to anyone in quite some time, he fumbled a bit searching for a way to break the impersonal awkwardness between them. Julia remained mostly silent too, fearing her idle words would intrude on this man's quiet life. It was the last thing she wanted to do, being more interested in staying here as long as he could bear.

Out of the blue, Henry spoke up, just to fill the vacant air space it seemed.

"If you feel well enough today, I could sure use a hand with something. It's not very much work but it's something I haven't done for a long time. Would that be alright?" he asked hesitatingly.

"Why, yes. Of course, I will. Whatever I can do, I'll be happy to help." Julia eagerly replied.

"Christmas is day after tomorrow. I wasn't going to bother for just myself, but I have an idea we should do this afternoon after we eat… if… if you feel up to it." Henry cracked a few eggs, and a pot of hot porridge was already steaming on the stove.

"I thought maybe you would want me to leave today. I would understand if you did. It's already later than I expected. I don't want to overstay my welcome."

"Nonsense, leave if you must, but you could probably use some time to rest and find your strength again. Why don't we just take it one day at a time? That's good with me."

"May I set the table for us?" Julia asked. "I'm not used to sitting while someone else does the work."

"Plates are in the cupboard and the forks and knives are in the drawer below. Oh, and don't forget the spoons too," he replied.

During their meal, tentative and bashful conversation left many things unsaid. They were still strangers after all, but gradually they both persevered and the flow of conversation between them became more natural.

"I was thinking we could find a small pine tree together. I hadn't thought about doing it since my dear wife passed almost ten years ago. Now that you're here, maybe it's a good time to put one up. What do you think?"

Julia wasn't up to a long walk, for reasons too obvious to mention. She thought to herself she would walk all day if she had to, just to stay in his house one more day, but within a very short time they found the perfect tree just inside a small grove of trees not far behind the house. During the short walk, they continued with some small talk to help pass the time.

"So, did you and your wife have any children?"

"We had a son. Archie was a good boy but was conscripted into the army in 1938. He was killed in the siege of Warsaw, so now there's nobody left but me," he sadly confessed.

"I have a brother and his family living somewhere in Germany, but I sure wasn't going there. I decided to stay in Poland. I just want a simple life. I don't need very much."

The conversation flowed more naturally between them, but Julia noticed there were many comfortable moments of silence between them as well. The awkwardness had suddenly disappeared.

Before the sun had fully set, the tree was dressed in a few traditional decorations. It was a modest and happy diversion, bringing the two friends another step closer to one another. To Julia, it was the first task she completed in a long while, simply for the sheer enjoyment of it. This would become one of the most pleasant times in her recent memory.

*****

In very short order, Julia and Henry enjoyed the company of each other. It was agreed some arrangement could develop between them to satisfy each other's longer-term objectives, although none existed for either one at the present time. As he already said to her, "one day at a time".

In the months ahead, Henry would speak of his wife and son infrequently. It was evident he had spent too much time alone; he very much needed the company Julia provided. Although apparently quietly reserved by nature, he gradually shared a few reminiscences of his personal life. Julia was happy to hear whatever popped into his mind but paid little attention to it, thinking it was probably good therapy for Henry to remember his happy times from the past.

For Julia, she repaid her undying gratitude for the kindness he had shown her by remaining patient with his stories, which on occasion ran on too long for her liking. She preferred to keep most details of her own horrific story behind her. As she recovered, weeks became months and Julia gained some much-needed weight. She filled out and looked more like a maturing woman than the frail morsel of a child Henry had once met.

As the year progressed, the thankfulness she felt to God, more than to Henry bless his soul, restored her fading religious faith. Since shortly after she knocked on his door, Julia made a habit of frequently reading Henry's Bible to him after her daily regimen of chores.

When he took the wagon into a tiny village nearby about once a week to pick up a few supplies, she encouraged him to return with the local newspaper, which soon became a new priority in the order of things. She would read the paper to him, sometimes for hours at a time after each trip to town. Although severely restricted in its content by the Reich, it was her only contact with anything beyond the old farmhouse she now called home.

Henry's eyesight had degraded significantly, especially without eyeglasses which was a luxury he could not afford. Surprisingly, Henry was extremely helpful teaching her new words and concepts to significantly expand her vocabulary. He was an excellent tutor, and Julia was blessed with a bright mind. Together, the process enabled her to keep current on relevant information as well.

One morning in early April 1942, the two friends relaxed on the porch and used the time for idle conversation. As their relationship developed, Henry spoke openly to Julia about his lonely circumstances and explained how his small farm had somehow escaped being torched like many others nearby.

"I remember the day German troops came, setting fire to all the farmhouses around here. When they were coming closer, I had nowhere else to go, so I just stayed put. About the same time, two military trucks pulled up out front and somebody shouted at them in German. As they were coming up the walkway to my door, all of a sudden they just simply stopped in their tracks and ran back to climb onto the trucks. Maybe they were being sent somewhere else, I dunno. But a few of them tossed their flaming torches toward my front porch."

"What did you do? Why didn't you run away? They could have shot you!" Julia asked excitedly.

"Until that very moment, I only assumed the worst, and I thought my farm was lost. Truth be told, I didn't even care about my life anymore either. When the trucks both pulled away, I remember thinking, *What the hell?* I might as well get off my ass to grab my old pail. I fetched a few buckets of water from the well to dowse the flames. They only partially burned the far side of the porch." Henry turned in his seat and pointed behind where he was sitting.

"You can see the damage it caused right there. Why my house was spared, I have no idea. It had rained a lot just a few days before, so maybe the wood was still damp inside. Some things I don't question anymore." His own good fortune defied his imagination to the present day.

The small farmhouse was on a remote side road, rarely used. It was likely assumed nothing of significance remained, hence no reason for anyone to travel here. It was as if the war was moving steadily away from his peaceful refuge, forgetting what might have been.

After sitting quietly for a while, Henry must have been still reflecting on those fortuitous days when his home was saved from certain destruction.

"You know what, Julia? Since that day, you're the only person to knock on my door. It's been over a year and a half now since the Germans drove away."

Julia listened attentively, finding some of his stories to be highly entertaining and informative. She learned the closest village was five miles to the north, near to the outer edges of the larger city of Ciechanow.

These times together were satisfyingly pleasant. Julia had long since ceased to question herself about the *whys* and *why nots* of the course of her life. Somehow her willpower and belief in almighty God had provided everything she truly needed, and certainly not a great deal more.

Her personal experiences now had more clarity, no longer being blurred by the constant trauma and fear which had been so mentally preoccupying. Through her more recent perspectives, she was reminded how much better off she was in comparison to literally everyone she had met. It was profound to think that despite her hardships, she had never met anyone with whom she would willingly trade places, and her life was truly sacred to her.

It was a wonderful diversion to accompany Henry to the south side of Ciechanow on occasion. He was initially reluctant to take her with him, based upon the belief someone might take offense to him sharing his home with such a young woman. What did it really matter when he hardly knew anyone in the city? Julia preferred it that way, though.

Eventually Henry overcame his silly shyness, and he would encourage her to wear a dress from his wife's closet, something prettier than the customary work pants and sweater she often wore about the house and gardens. It took a while, but he once said, "I'm very proud to be seen with you Julia. I don't give a damn what anyone thinks of me anymore. Thank you for coming with me today. You make me feel young again."

Julia did nothing to dissuade such compliments. They made her feel better about herself and in response, she would nestle her arm under his to assure him she felt something similar toward him too. Julia was very grateful for his kindnesses but knew her genuine love for him would not transcend to anything more than appreciative affection.

*****

About a month later on a fine spring day, a glorious sunrise beckoned. It was May 1942. The soothing sounds of singing birds reminded Henry of times thought to be long lost. Since the earth had been rocked so violently from the brutal wave of German destruction, it wasn't solely the people who were cowering for distant cover, so too were the foxes, wolves, rabbits, and birds. The wildlife had somehow instinctively hidden or had left, distancing itself in the pursuit of quieter places.

The two friends were sharing a fresh pot of coffee on the front porch when Henry began to reminisce again. Out of nowhere, he said, "As I look back, I don't remember hearing whistling birds since that time."

"What time are you talking about, Henry?" Julia asked.

"The birds... they've come back. I'm amazed they even bothered to try, but I'm so thankful they did."

"As am I. It's funny how the things we all take for granted aren't noticed until they're gone. The sounds of spring are soothing aren't they?" Julia continued sipping her morning coffee in a moment of peaceful reflection. "What are you thinking, Henry? Is everything with us alright?"

"Oh, quite so, Julia. My life, such as it was, has changed for the better since you came here. I don't tell you this often enough, but I'm so much happier with you living here, Julia."

"As am I to be here. I can't imagine how I would have survived if..."

Henry held a finger to his mouth to quickly shush her.

"No need to even go there, that's not why I brought up the topic. However, it does occur to me that everyone has a birthday, albeit just one every year. In what... the fifteen or sixteen months we've been together, we must have missed a birthday or two, don't you think?" Henry focused his gaze to force the issue, expecting an answer.

Julia smiled inquisitively at the absurdity of his question, and coyly responded. "Yes, perhaps there was one. Yes, I do recall now. Just one though."

"Ah ha!" Henry exclaimed. "Why didn't you ever say anything to me? Sometimes talking with you is like pulling teeth, Julia. When was it? Please tell me."

"April 11ᵗʰ, if you must know."

"Why, that was only a few weeks ago. Why didn't you tell me?" he repeated.

"That's so kind of you to care but whatever would we do differently? It really wouldn't matter. Would we throw a party for all the neighbors?" she laughingly suggested. Henry began to chuckle.

"Obviously not, but at the very least we could have had a fancy meal, something special we could cook together. The only problem is, I can't cook much of anything, so maybe you could help me out... just a little? What do you think?"

"Ahh, so now you are proposing I cook you a special meal to celebrate my own birthday. Is that about right?" Julia teased as she continued.

"I'll tell you what. If you can find us a find us a nice, plump chicken tomorrow, I'll roast it and make some *patyczki*, just like my mother made for the family on holidays. I've never done it myself, but I helped her prepare it many times. You know, why not? Let's do this Henry!"

"Wonderful! We'll go to the village tomorrow morning and get whatever you think we need. This will be fun for us, Julia."

*****

Although it was a rarity, sometimes Julia decided not to join Henry on his trips to the city. This was one of those days, and Henry was visibly disheartened.

"I thought you would enjoy the trip today. The weather couldn't be better, my dear. I'm so disappointed. Are you sure you are alright?"

"Oh yes, I'm just fine Henry, but I think I need some quiet time. You are right, the day is perfect but if you don't mind, today I would just like to spend a pleasant afternoon sitting on the porch in the shade." Julia confided. Henry never argued or protested, despite his occasional disappointment. He knew when to let her enjoy some private time too. He never seemed to realize Julia had wisely decided to slowly redevelop some independence from him.

"Enjoy your day, Henry."

Henry frowned, but only briefly and pulled himself onto the wagon using the spokes of a wheel to support his climb. He grabbed the reins, tipping his hat to her as was his habit. He turned to smile at her and waved a brief farewell.

Finally, she thought, a private moment. Julia had longed to do something she had considered for months but couldn't quite bring herself to do. It seemed to her the more time passed, she became more reluctant, or even incapable of examining the contents of her mother's old leather bag.

In all this time, she had protected it without having carefully inspected the contents. Other than removing the fruit she stole away with almost two years ago, there seemed no fitting time for her to allow a moment of reminiscence and unnecessary sorrow. The bag was unobtrusive to her and proved to be no inconvenience, but it had also become sacred to her in some strange way. Over time, it had just become part of her and represented the only remaining substance of her past.

Sitting on the porch, soothed by the light of the morning sun, Julia unfastened the leather bindings she had tied so tightly long ago. It was as fitting a time as any to examine its contents, specifically the private and symbolic confidences cherished by her mother.

The exterior of the bag, although well worn, had been dampened by snow and soaked by rain repeatedly, yet other than a few small cracks, it never yielded a leak to the naked eye. The usual items, all of which bore some relevance to her mother came as no surprise to her.

Her flute was in the center pouch, the reason for its inclusion by Julia still not readily apparent. However, rolled inside some sturdy parchment, tied with a string were what appeared to be official documents of some obvious importance. As the roll was finally being unraveled, Julia discovered the birth certificates of her brother, her sister and herself, sacred documents she did not know even existed until this very moment.

Good keepsakes she thought, so out of respect for what must have been valuable to her mother, she rerolled them back into the parchment but did so more tightly than they were, to fit them inside the protective tube of her flute. It seemed like a more secure place befitting their apparent importance.

Despite the sanctity of the moment, she did not ponder her casual indifference to her discovery. In fact, she remained somewhat detached from any emotion, as had become her custom. Why would she feel any differently now? It was the continued development of this detachment that would serve to protect and insulate her throughout her adulthood. It would serve as a defense mechanism she would be unable to easily shed.

As she retied the straps of her trusty bag and placed it safely out of the way, she left the bittersweet memories of her mysterious discovery behind for the moment and tried to refocus on the sheer glory of the day.

By the time Henry returned, the sun had already begun to set. As Julia stood up from her chair to greet him, a beautiful panorama of orange and red provided a magnificent backdrop for his arrival, enveloping the silhouette of Henry on his horse and wagon in the foreground.

Henry raised his hand to wave to her, no doubt satisfied with the accomplishments of the journey. "My, my, Henry. Someone seems to have got too much sun. Your cheekbones and the back of your neck are glowing."

"Perhaps so, my dear. These things happen in early spring... always will I suppose," Henry replied, just waving off a bit of a burn. "I hope you had a restful day."

"That I did, Julia replied. "Here, let me help you with that," as she took a bag of groceries.

"Please be careful, there's a nice bottle of wine in there somewhere. We don't want it broken," Henry cautioned. "Something special for tomorrow I thought you might enjoy. I'll be with you shortly after I tend to the horse."

"That's fine, Henry, but let's hurry along. Dinner is almost ready." Shortly thereafter, the succulent scent of a simmering rabbit stew summoned Julia to return to the kitchen and Henry soon followed closely behind.

*****

By the following afternoon, the house was filled with the magical aromas of Julia and Henry's collaboration in the kitchen together. Henry's bottle of red wine was a thoughtful gesture Julia appreciated.

"I was told by the shop keeper it's a very good one, and he staked his reputation on it; probably exaggerated since it was the *only* wine he had. Either way, it's the perfect treat to make our dinner even better," Henry boastfully explained.

"Thank you, Henry. This is so thoughtful of you. I've never tasted wine before, but I'm sure I will enjoy it," Julia acknowledged.

As decided between them, the dinner featured a fine feast of homemade patyczki - chicken on a stick, basted in butter and baked in breadcrumbs. An assortment of potatoes and beans supplemented the chicken so nicely. Their joint efforts provided pleasant memories between them, as they often did. Sometimes the simple pleasures of life are there for the taking, only requiring sufficient effort and occasional inspiration to carve them out from the day-to-day tedium of life.

When they finally seated themselves and offered their thankfulness, Henry carefully poured Julia a small portion of wine, remembering it would be her first taste of wine that wasn't handheld by a priest offering the sacramental cup. Confidently she raised her glass and downed it like a glass of water. Henry was mortified!

In seconds, Julia's face turned beet red, her eyes watered profusely, and she began to cough and sputter, likened to an old car leaking oil.

"My goodness, Julia. We're in no rush here," as Henry was both concerned as much as amused by her reaction. "Wine is to be savored throughout the meal. I want you to enjoy it, but you must pace yourself too! Are you alright?"

"... Some wa... some water, please." Julia coughed to clear her throat and offered her empty glass to him.

"Of course, my dear." As he took her empty glass to fetch the water, he sarcastically asked, "So, did you enjoy the wine?"

They both commenced to laugh and giggle, and Henry quickly returned to his damsel in distress, who by this time was wiping red wine splatters from her blouse, her skirt, and her place setting. When Julia drank the cool water, her blushed face had already begun to restore its natural color and she became more composed again.

"My, my... that was very good. I think I'll just stick with water for a while though, don't you think that's best?"

"Yes, it might just be." Henry assured her.

Another hidden pleasure would gradually develop over time as well, when several months later, Henry and Julia began to routinely sleep together, but rarely sharing physical affections. Julia was now sixteen and was no longer a little girl. There was but one bed. When he eventually initiated something more, she responded with the genuine affection she felt for him, and absent any feelings of commitment, she reluctantly acquiesced. Thanks to Pavel's past intervention, it was the only close physical experience she had with a man.

Julia rarely accommodated these thoughts, in large part because of those prior circumstances, but also because the opportunity and desire had not presented itself. She had far greater priorities to be concerned about in her life but now, despite her initial reluctance, Henry made her feel something new and exciting she had never even imagined before.

It was much more than simply providing a service her landlord had meekly sought. Although a kind and gentle man, she always knew she would leave him when the appropriate timing presented itself. She took no personal offense from his rare advances and found unexpected pleasure from the experience.

*****

By this time, Julia had been to the city several times with Henry and began to do so more frequently. The persecution of the Jews in Ciechanow had been particularly vicious. It was an area in which over thirty percent of its population, some three thousands of them, had made their home. The Germans had succeeded in completely eradicating the Jewish presence shortly after the outbreak of the war, during which time the Reich had replaced them through their process of Germanization.

During the occupation, the remaining non-Jewish Polish population had been reintegrated with the German *superior race*; but only those Germans with the purest Aryan bloodlines were given the formerly Jewish owned properties. Only modest housing was distributed to preselected Poles, depending upon their predetermined placement on the German People's List by the Nazis.

This new status quo provided whatever social structure was deemed to be acceptable to the Master Race. For whatever reason, Henry was one of only a few Poles who appeared unhampered and was left alone to come and go as he chose. Despite that freedom, he chose not to go anywhere else.

Since the invasion two years ago, and because of the strategic location of Ciechanow, the railway system had been significantly redeveloped, having suffered extensive damage from heavy German bombing attacks during the occupation. These lines were a priority to the military invasion and were laboriously restored by the Germans to proper function by using forced Polish slave labor.

This was not the Ciechanow Julia remembered. Despite imagining the horror this city must have faced during the initial stages of the German invasion, no doubt similar to her own tragic experiences, she accepted the face of the city as being consistent with any expectations she may have had. Air raid bombing had taken its deadly toll, but not to the extent suffered by Pultusk where she tried to find her aunt and uncle.

The destruction throughout the city didn't seem to affect Julia to a significant extent. She had seen much worse and was hardened to it, often to the point of indifference. There was abject poverty and many, many street people were begging for handouts. Julia considered herself to be blessed to have simply knocked on Henry's front door.

Propaganda was predominant throughout the press and served to continue bolstering German confidence, both within the military and the remaining civilians back home. Simultaneously, the lies and distorted truths served to further denigrate the subservient Poles, all of which was carefully orchestrated under the watchful and intrusive mind of the Minister of Propaganda, Joseph Goebbels.

*****

To Julia, her restlessness had been growing with each passing day. She was no longer willing to surrender her growing spirit to this simple life any longer, even if it meant dealing with profound feelings of guilt about leaving Henry. Gradually, she started to envision grander objectives from the previously humble limits of her past imaginings.

She could not afford to overstay her time here, if she had not already done so. She was convinced her affection and thankfulness for all Henry had given her would never fade. Life had proven to be replete with difficult and sometimes regrettable choices. This was surely not going to be one of them.

As the weeks turned to months, Julia had been squirrelling away what few zlotys she could, little by little as Henry's trust in her increased. In so doing, he had become more dependent upon her resourcefulness and obvious intellect. While not well schooled, she had always possessed a sharp mind. It was time to use it again. She abhorred the thought of stealing from him, but she had no other alternative to affect her departure.

After several weeks and despite her confusion and uncertainty, Julia calculated she had enough cash to buy a train ticket in Ciechanow to travel as far as Kutno, which was a place she knew nothing about, save for the location being as far west as she dared. She could not face another incursion by the Russians as they were still moving eastward, and Julia was aware the Germans were continuing to focus on repelling any potential future invasion of Europe. Again, for Julia it was better to confront the German backs than the Russian faces.

Julia could easily make the walk to Ciechanow. Considering the incredible ordeals over which she always triumphed, her stamina and determination would never be in question. She knew the route well, and as the day approached to finally depart, she bundled a few clothes belonging to Henry's wife, together with a few necessary items, and, of course, grabbed her leather bag.

She was not comfortable with tearful goodbyes. Henry would sleep at least until sunrise, as was his habit. She doubted he would chase after her, but he had to know this day was approaching. With deep gratitude, absent any regrets, Julia closed the door gently for the last time and walked in silence as she sought the next chapter in her life.

13
A MISSION OF MERCY

BY MIDDAY, JULIA APPROACHED CIECHANOW ALONE, THE first and only time she had ever done so. To this point, she was comfortable in her familiar solitude. It had become natural for her to depend upon her own intuition. Above all else, her instincts had taken her to where she was today, far better off than any alternative option she had encountered or could possibly conceive.

When Julia approached the edge of the city, it bore the ill effects of a brutal war. Whatever had caused the damages left no doubt to Julia it was violent and punitive.

Rubble continued to be scattered about the mostly obliterated sections of sparse sidewalks still remaining, and the buildings near the city center were a haphazard mixture of sites of abject destruction, intermingled with very imposing but fully functioning buildings; many with German swastikas flagrantly perched ominously above the doorways. Gone were the familiar scenes of pedestrian traffic going about their daily business. Now, for those few, they groveled it seemed, for remnants of anything to sustain a hungry stomach.

There was something unpleasantly stale in the air; for such an inviting day, the stench of death burned the nose, to suggest you should be fearful just for inhaling it. A nauseated feeling settled in Julia's belly as she quickened her pace, but only slightly to avoid attracting the gaze of the uniformed Germans who abounded everywhere. Although the city had the appearance of a lawful place, it was a rigidly enforced form of order, without compromise. It was an intimidating perspective.

She was undeterred locating the central station, which was not difficult for her to find. She walked as if she belonged and felt reassured by the guiding hand of God when the station first appeared before her. It was much as she faintly remembered.

A small crowd had gathered at the ticket booth, which was to be expected. The dilemma, however, was one she was not at all prepared for. There were German officers checking everyone's destinations and identification papers. They were asking questions in an aggressive tone of voice.

The menacing manner caused her heart to pound. Julia could feel her pulse striking her temple. Unpreparedness gripped her to the depths of her being. Instinctively, she drew a long deep breath to calm her increasingly frazzled nerves.

Julia's mind raced to seek a rational course of action when she realized that among her mother's papers, were her birth certificate and family documents. Although they could confirm she was not Jewish, she was increasingly anxious about sharing any of those personal papers with anyone, let alone a Nazi official. *Thank you, Mother!*

Were it not for those papers, she knew she could never convince any inquiring officer she was not Jewish. She also realized any reluctance to offer her papers would indicate probable guilt. She would certainly not be given any benefit of the doubt.

Furthermore, was there something else they might require? She was unfamiliar with the procedure and had never considered the situation before this moment. Henry would have taken care of these matters for her; and her father before him, now seeming so very long ago.

Without thinking, she nonchalantly assumed a position at the back of the line, but only momentarily. She had been watching the processing of other commuters with great intent but could not hear the nature of the questioning. What was she to do? The longer she stayed in line, the more conspicuous she would become by leaving it. She must break off now to avoid undue suspicion.

There was a newspaper rack not more than thirty feet away at the far end of the ticket booth. With an air of disciplined calmness, she opened her bag and for a few brief seconds proceeded to fumble inside it, seemingly haven forgotten something. Picking up Henry's bedraggled suitcase, Julia casually stepped away from the back of the line and leisurely walked to the rack of newspapers.

She dared not appear too hurried, so she placed the case on the ground beside the stand, allowing her to offhandedly begin flipping through a few pages, as if looking for something specific. Then she placed the paper back on the rack, retrieved her case and gradually stepped away to blend in with the scant pedestrian flow, following the sidewalk to wherever it led.

With pounding heart, and without further premeditation, Julia simply followed along the main road, alone with her thoughts. She had always considered it a miracle to travel so far from Pobereze without a single identity checkpoint; knowing it would be required at some point was only a matter of time.

She felt overwhelmed with uncertainty and was thankful she had decided to back away.

"How very precious these papers have become", she reconciled to herself. Did she avert disaster by not producing her papers, or did she simply lose her nerve and prolong the uncertainty of finding her destiny? Life offered many choices, but not many happy ones from her perspective. She could not cast her fate to the winds of chance; certainly not now.

The sidewalk ended some time ago, at a point escaping her awareness. Her focus was elsewhere. She estimated it was no more than three or four hours outside the city when a sign indicated her arrival in the village of Opinogora Gorna, which as it turned out was about ten kilometers northeast of Ciechanow.

She had no specific recollection of how far, or which direction she had taken since she departed the train station. It seemed no more than moments had passed and, although she was somewhat aimless on her journey, there seemed nothing to pose a threat to her in this peaceful place.

Not far into the quiet village, Julia noticed a steeple coming into view, over a small ridge of trees. She pressed on inquisitively and was relieved no one in uniform was present in this serene setting.

The church came into full view, and she realized how very long it had been since she had set foot in one. As a child she attended the Catholic Church in Pobereze with her mother, while the younger ones stayed with their father. It was an innocent part of her childhood she missed, but there were too many pieces of it she preferred not to reflect upon. Another time perhaps.

This was the *Kosciol Zygmunta* Catholic Church, and she felt drawn to it somehow. With no concept of what day of the week it was, she approached the front steps and ascended them to the main doors. To no surprise at this hour, they were still locked.

With barely a shrug, Julia cast a glance upward to contemplate her options, perhaps seeking comfort in divine intervention. Reluctantly, she descended the steps to where she began, never realizing just how fatigued she had become until this very moment. She had been walking the entire day since leaving Henry's home and ached from carrying the suitcase. Her back and shoulders were not accustomed to the weight.

Strolling aimlessly along her way, she passed numerous small cottages, some of which remained in relatively good condition. The devastation Julia had seen first-hand was not as apparent here, but many scars of violence remained, no doubt exactly as they had been left.

Several small shops valiantly tried to continue serving their community. Most of the civilians, many of which were Jewish, had likely been conscripted, killed, or simply evacuated from the area. Julia had read about the severe persecution of the Jews in Ciechanow. For the villagers left behind, there was nowhere else to go. The absence of viable alternatives, rest assured, indicated the basic needs of the remaining villagers were still somehow being provided for.

It was harvest time and life was carrying on, as it must. Julia felt the coins in her sweater pocket, the zwote intended to buy her train fare. She was reassured just by knowing they were there. It was getting late in the day and one of the few shops still open was selling what little remained of some bruised fruit, one dried out cabbage, a loaf of baked bread and surprisingly, two small pieces of roasted chicken.

The prime pickings were long since sold. She was famished and was not at all fussy about the limited choices spread out before her. At least she was now in the position to make her purchases and thankfully satisfy her cravings.

With her sack replenished, Julia didn't hesitate to retreat to the already familiar grounds of the church, clutching the bag filled with her bounty. In anticipation of her meal and the faint aroma of the barely warm chicken parts, she hastened her pace. With added purpose, she quickly sought out a cozy wooden bench behind the church nestled under the trees.

Only now did she realize how truly famished she had become. She eagerly jammed her hand into the bag, seized a dried piece of chicken and voraciously bit into it... and feasted. "Oh, my goodness, this is so damned delicious!"

Like a starving dog with a bone, Julia barely finished gnawing on the first piece, and dug in for the other. Tearing away at the small loaf of bread, she ripped a large chunk from it and stuffed it into her now gaping mouth. It had been a long time since she had a meal. It was a faint reminder of the times before she found dear Henry.

She was comforted by her thoughts of him now, who by this time would be dealing with her departure with powerlessness and lingering disappointment, but nonetheless his thankfulness for having known her. Julia prayed that over time, he would surely come to accept her decision, even though he might not fully understand it.

The days were getting noticeably shorter, and the sinking sun had long since started to set, stretching the shadows across the yard before her like pulling a soft grey blanket around her shoulders before finding restful sleep. The season was approaching full autumn. Above the church, the upper tree line dressed the village in an amber and orange hue reflecting off the richly colored foliage.

The heat of day was gradually dissipating. It was cooling but dry, leaving Julia confident she would regain her strength in the coming days. The peacefulness of the moment was only fleeting as she slipped into involuntary sleep.

*****

Julia was only slightly aware of the gentle, rustling sounds of the leaves, bending resiliently against the soothing warm breezes of a new day. Thinking she was still dreaming, she was shaken awake by the gentle nudging of an elderly man who was now leaning over her. He had white hair and a scruffy beard but had a notable tenderness about him she found comforting.

"Wake up girl, wake up. What are you doing here? Where are you from?" He sensed this young girl was still dazed with sleep, so without giving her time to answer, he continued, "We get vagabonds sleeping here sometimes, but we feed them and move them along. You don't look like one of them. What is your name?"

"My name is Julia," she offered as she struggled to right herself and gather her thoughts. She had clearly forgotten where in the world she was and was trying to make sense through her groggy awkwardness. Fighting off an urge to yawn, she stretched herself somewhat rudely when she arched her stiffened back. A bit embarrassed, Julia expressed her apology and briefly explained she had lost track of time and must have fallen into a deeper sleep than intended.

She was no longer the impoverished, filthy orphan she had once been. Her clothing while modest, was not tattered and soiled. She was no longer emaciated, and in the past year she had taken on a youthful but more mature appearance.

"I must ask you... are you a Jew? We cannot help you in any way if you are, I am so very sorry to say." Julia could see genuine empathy in his greying eyes.

"No, no I am not... I'm a Catholic girl." Enthusiastically, she quickly blurted out, "I even have papers to prove it!" She tried to untie the laces of her bag until the man eased her obvious concern.

"No, not necessary right now. Are you just passing through? What brings you here, Julia?"

"The war took my family from me. I was alone and had nowhere specific to go. The journey led me here, I suppose."

The elderly gentleman was Stanley, and he had been doing general maintenance here since his home had been destroyed during the occupation. He had a small room at the back of the church he now called home. "Come with me, Julia. I will take you to Mother Helena. She is a wonderful woman who will want to meet you."

Julia gathered her belongings and Stanley graciously took hold of the suitcase to assist her while gently guiding her to the rear entrance of the old church. Despite her usual skepticism, she felt Stanley's genuine compassion immediately and followed his lead past the meagre flowerbeds bearing no more than a few wilted bushes.

They stood defiantly against the slowly advancing weeds from the stark surrounding grass. The signs of wither were evident, no doubt having endured the end of a stifling hot summer, but at least they had been recently trimmed, so someone must still care.

These were definitive signs of deprivation, and nature's endless struggle against it for balance and survival. It is often said the strongest weed in the ground is the one growing between the cracks of the concrete; that applied to people as well.

Stanley pressed the latch and pulled against the heavy weight of the door to the service entrance, politely holding it open for Julia to pass. She thought silently about the simple act, not remembering anyone ever extending such a courteous gesture toward her. Once inside, the slight odor of the old church was familiar, reminding Julia again of times long lost.

When the heavy latch had firmly closed, it sent an echo throughout the main chamber of the church, boldly announcing Stanley and Julia's arrival. Surprised Stanley was not alone, a Sister turned enquiringly to face this pretty young woman who had been following Stanley's lead so attentively. Before uttering a word, she revealed a glowing smile of welcome, quite unreservedly Julia thought.

Sister Helena had been overseeing the Altar Guild preparation for services scheduled for the weekend. As it happens, it was Saturday today, so the church was looking especially grand with a few modest bundles of fresh cut flowers strategically placed about the altar. It created a particularly welcoming atmosphere.

"Well, Stanley, who have you found at the Lord's door this morning? How very lovely you are my dear!"

"Sister Helena, may I present Julia? She was temporarily resting herself in the back garden. As a practicing Catholic, she was simply waiting for our doors to open and must have dozed off for a short time. Julia, Sister Helena," Stanley proudly announced.

"So nice to meet you, Julia." She extended her hand warmly and stated, "A Roman Catholic is not someone we take for granted here in Opinogora. I am certain you must have papers to support your entitlement to share our place of worship, Julia?"

"Yes, Sister, yes of course!" Julia eagerly rummaged inside her trusty leather bag to retrieve her wooden flute. It took but a moment to carefully remove the papers and proudly unroll them for presentation. Again, she was only starting to comprehend the significance and good fortune she would enjoy by her mother's wisdom and sound judgment in keeping them safe from harm. Julia could not imagine how very difficult things could have been without having possession of them.

The sister adjusted her glasses and examined the documents carefully. After a short pause, she was satisfied Julia was truthful about her claims. During these few tense moments for Julia, she looked about the church in appreciation of its warm hospitable atmosphere.

"The church is so lovely, Sister. I can see how very well you and Stanley must care for it."

"It is lovely, isn't it?" Sister Helena agreed.

"It has been some time since the members of the congregation have been able to shift their daily priorities to now include adorning their place of worship with lovely examples of nature's boundless beauty. It saddens us not having been able to enjoy them as often these days, but these have been difficult times for everyone. We do our best. Through the perils of war, the church has continued to provide a peaceful respite for those seeking comfort and reassurance from its unwavering presence."

Stanley graciously explained what Julia had told him, but only briefly, to permit Julia to speak for herself, which she did over a hot cup of tea and a few biscuits. Sister explained, very apologetically, the Nazis' habit to frequent the churches in suburban areas looking for Jews seeking refuge.

"Under Father Breitkopf's guidance and wisdom, the church regrettably could not support such things for fear of serious reprisals. We have seen many friends suffer the consequences for showing their sympathies to our former Jewish neighbors. It brings back many painful memories we shall not soon forget. Let me see if Father is available for a few brief minutes to meet you and say *Hello*. I will be back momentarily."

Stanley politely excused himself to resume his daily tasks, leaving Julia alone in the quaint tranquility of the church chamber. The morning sunshine shone beautifully through the colored glass windows and reflected multicolored beams of light scattering across the wooden pews. It was a simple but magical experience. She became entranced by the vision, to the extent she was initially startled when Sister Helena returned to lead the way to the parish office.

Father Breitkopf rose from his understated wooden desk to greet Julia when Sister introduced her young guest to him.

"It is always a pleasure to welcome someone of common faith to our midst. Welcome, Julia. I am Father Breitkopf." Julia was taken by his pleasant demeanor and bright smile. He was a diminutive elderly man with a balding head and spectacles, giving him an intellectual appearance. He had long, lean fingers with neatly trimmed fingernails that spoke to his attention to detail. He spoke as eloquently as his manner.

"I understand you have travelled a considerable distance to be with us today, under some difficult conditions. It appears God has looked favorably upon you to guide your way; and at such a very young age, I might add."

Julia was impressed by the attention she was receiving. Were these people in the habit of impressing newcomers with such acts of boundless kindness, or were there simply so few others who came their way?

"I strongly believe the Lord was watching over me during my travels and helped me to make wise choices along the way; all of which led me to your door, Father. I am grateful to meet you, Sister Helena, and of course, Stanley. You are all so gracious."

"I am hopeful you find a home here in our village. Perhaps you will attend our service tomorrow morning and we will come to know you better in the days ahead. For the moment, however, please forgive my rudeness but I must return to my paperwork. I look forward to speaking with you again soon, Julia."

Sister Helena took Julia's elbow and escorted her back to the tea table. She was pleased Father Breitkopf could spare a few minutes to meet this wandering young soul.

"I believe Father approves of you Julia. His kindness knows no bounds; however, the best interests of this church are always his priority. If you are interested, I will speak with him to see if we can find a place for you here." Julia's bond with Sister Helena was immediate, and from their first sip of tea it was apparent they each fulfilled what may have been absent for so long from each of their lives.

And so it was that Julia was welcomed by the warmth of Sister Helena and her genuine and heartfelt embrace. Hope is eternal, and a mere glimmer of it had brought them together.

*****

Over the ensuing weeks, and following Sister Helena's lead, Julia was extended offers of kindness from several of the parishioners who kept her in their prayers. Some gave her used clothing, a book here and there she was eager to read but most importantly, they offered their friendship. Julia felt blessed to have been just tired enough to choose the church bench, fortunate enough to have been guided to the Sister, and wise enough to accept it.

The days grew shorter, and temperatures were dropping as autumn passed from its glorious splendor to a windy mass of swirling leaves. Guided by Father Breitkopf, Sister Helena's discreet feelers of enquiry supportively aligned Julia's well-being within the mandate of the church.

So much tragedy had befallen this village and its family's experiences, no doubt permeating throughout so many distant corners of Poland. Julia provided a reminder that no matter what horrors may have occurred here, there were still those for whom good fortune could be found within reach.

Julia was never comfortable being dependent upon other people, nor would her fighting and determined spirit be permitted to fade. She always paid her dues working hard with cleaning and tending to the everyday chores of the church, all of which she was quite adept.

Between Stanley's gardening and general maintenance of the church and those occasional times Sister Helena's administrative matters needed assistance, there was always justification to keep Julia productively occupied. She was comfortable sleeping on a two-seated lumpy old couch in the Deacon's office, well-worn with age, but after a full day of hard work it was as comforting as a luxurious featherbed to Julia's grateful frame.

One afternoon much like any other, a small detail of German officers entered the unlocked rear door of the church, not noisily or threatening in any way but with specific intent, nonetheless. The lead officer was already acquainted with Sister Helena and was greeted by her with the customary politeness she extended to him.

"Hello Lieutenant. We haven't seen you in some time. What can we do to be of service today?" she enquired.

As she spoke, three junior troopers simply walked through the service area without saying a word, nor acknowledging Sister's presence. Their weapons in hand, one took the basement stairs while the other two proceeded into the front of the church. These inspections had become rather routine from time to time, and Sister knew enough to be gracious to them. For Julia, it would be her first such encounter.

"May I offer you some hot coffee Lieutenant? I just brewed it twenty minutes ago."

"Not necessary, Sister. I understand you have a young woman working here who I am anxious to meet. Where is this woman now?"

"I think she is working with Stanley out back. She has been of good support since she knocked on our door several weeks ago. Come. I will take you to her." Very obligingly, Helena co-operated fully, with no fear or hesitation.

One trooper had just returned from his cursory inspection of the small cold cellar below, and having discovered nothing of consequence, joined the senior officer. As they rounded the rear of the church, Julia could be seen gathering leaves and twigs in and about the various headstones of the old cemetery. She had already been informed these inspections were random events, and there should be nothing to fear.

"Julia!" shouted Sister Helena across the short expanse of the sacred grounds.

Julia paused to raise her head and stood erect with her hand shielding the sun from her eyes, still holding her rake while Stanley could be seen observing the scene before him not more than thirty or forty feet away.

It was a break they both could use, but there was anxiousness in Julia's demeanor as she acknowledged the presence of the lieutenant and walked briskly toward him. It was understandable to have such feelings, but any hint of visible nervousness could indicate suspicion of wrongdoing. She quickly gathered herself, wiping her brow with her shirt's sleeve.

"This is Lieutenant von Siefel, and he would like…"

"Show me your papers young lady, if you even possess them," the officer interrupted with his usual disdain.

"Certainly, Officer." Julia looked to Sister Helena for assurance and asked, "I suppose they are still where you put them for safe-keeping, Sister?" Sister Helena offered only a slight nod of her head to confirm.

"Go fetch them. This man will accompany you," ordered the officer.

In only moments Julia returned to the yard, walking briskly to appear more eager to be forthright with the officer. He accepted the rolled document and scanned its content. "You are a long way from home… Julia. How did you find your way here? Who were you with?"

Julia, without showing reluctance, briefly explained her circumstances having travelled alone, being consistent with what Sister

Helena had probably already told the officer. There was no need for many details. The truth was the truth. What was sufficient was the birth certificate confirming her baptism in the holy Catholic Church in Pobereze.

When her brief interrogation was concluded to the satisfaction of the officer, he re-joined his escort and left unceremoniously, as promptly as they had arrived, absent any courtesies or apologies.

They had barely left the church property when Sister Helena immediately praised her young friend. "Well done, Julia. I can imagine how distressing that may have been for you personally, but I'm proud of you for staying calm. It is imperative we do not appear deceptive or uncooperative with them."

"It was the first time I had to show my papers to a German. I may have appeared calm to you, but I assure you I was not. The officer was very intimidating, but you prepared me well, Sister. I suppose over time I will become accustomed to their arrogant intrusions. I must confess my feelings of hatred toward them."

"You will get used to it. Consider this visit a stark reminder we have no rights to privacy, we have no freedom of speech, we do not own our property, in our own country! They can do whatever they want to us if you so much as look at them the wrong way. They are unaccountable for any actions they may take. Always remember though, the less said with these people, the better off we will be."

The inspections were repeated every two to six weeks, but never in a predictably reliable way. The random patterns were intended to keep people off-guard in the never-ending search for Jews hiding anywhere among the villagers, whether sympathetic or naïve enough to try to help them. For most of the villagers, and the Jews already taken away, helplessness and hopelessness eventually sapped their spirit to the point of abject despair.

As winter approached, the focus of yard work changed to one of gathering enough wood to keep the fireplaces operating at full efficiency. The far side of the cemetery was near to the north side of church property, a spot where large expanses of both deciduous and coniferous trees used to thrive.

In years past, it was rare for Stanley having to cut any more than nature had shed naturally, but since the war the forest here was indeed dwindling, as the villagers' requirements and those of the military were taking their deadly toll.

It was certain to be a lean and bitter winter, and extra effort Stanley and Julia invested this fall season preparing for winter, would yield its weight in gold by March and April. Sister Helena performed miracles finding economical but nutritious meals for the small staff of the church, but always found enough for those unfortunates who simply could not support themselves in the village.

The weather gradually turned, and the oppressive freezing cold held the village in its deadly grasp. The warm hospitality of the church was never more evident. Steaming hot potato and barley soup was devoured with eager enthusiasm, especially on those rare occasions when scarce remnants of meat and bone marrow on a cleanly cut bone added more depth, no matter how faint the hint of flavor. In these leanest of times the church took great pride in feeding the stomach, as much as the spirit. Especially in winter, the meals sometimes became an active focal point of the community.

By this time, there were only occasional military inspections, none of which produced anything. The Germans finally appeared to have more productive tasks on their minds and eventually left Father Breitkopf and Sister Helena to the business of nurturing the poor.

Julia's proactive devotion to helping the Catholic Church care for their flock was tireless, and her dedication did not go unnoticed. She became a valuable ambassador of the church as the congregation began to grow again, in part as an expression of gratitude many had felt for the genuine interest Julia had shown for their well-being on behalf of the church.

With the blessings of Father Breitkopf and Sister Helena, Julia helped to organize a small co-operative food sharing arrangement among the villagers. This barter system provided various goods and services, stimulating greater interdependence among them. It was about each person doing what they could to give and to share, but in a much more centralized and organized fashion than they had done before.

It was not cash dependent, as there was so little of it available. These creative gestures of support stimulated something thought to have been lost, not just for the villagers, but within Julia herself. It was about having trust and faith in others again; a nourishing wholesomeness extending beyond spiritual faith.

*****

In the days following, and very much unknown to Julia, Stanley had been secretly scheming with the Sister by keeping busy with a project mostly of his own doing. Although Julia was aware he was repairing something, she had no idea what it was. He was constantly tinkering and keeping the premises in good repair.

Within three or four days, unknown to Julia, Stanley had completely dismantled and reconstructed an old storage room to better serve as a small but functional room he had converted. It was to become Julia's private bedroom.

It was a project Stanley was particularly proud of. He meticulously saved every possible piece of timber to make do with what little he had available. All it required was the inspiration, and the innovation to implement it. The Sister contributed a folding bed, tucked away for occasional use from time to time. Previously there had been nowhere to set it up. Every inch of the church had been fully utilized, or so they had thought. But now with a bit of ingenuity, sufficient space for the cot and an old side table would serve Julia well.

When the room was about to be unveiled, the collaborators dismissively asked Julia to fetch a bench from storage to access the top kitchen cupboards. Unsuspectingly, she walked to the closed storage room, opened the door, and fumbled in the dark to locate the familiar light switch she discovered was no longer there. The room had no other source of light than from the adjacent kitchen.

As Julia's eyes adjusted to the dimness of the room, she turned inquisitively to Sister and Stanley, both of whom were now standing behind her with beaming smiles. Stanley guided her hand to the newly positioned switch and revealed the new room to Julia's disbelieving eyes.

"No! Is it possible?" She turned to face them in a flood of tearful acknowledgment, holding both hands against her cheeks in disbelief.

"It's not much my dear, but we always do what we can." Sister Helena gave her a warm embrace and immediately gave credit where the credit was due. "This was Stanley's idea. It is him you should be thanking."

Julia lunged at him and wrapped her arms around him enthusiastically, kissing his weathered cheek. Stanley looked at her sheepishly, and proudly for having accomplished his noble gesture of thoughtfulness. "We thought it was time we made you one of our family, Julia. Consider it an early Christmas present."

*****

Julia distinguished herself in ways not overlooked by Sister Helena. One morning she walked into the vestry to find Julia engaged in conversation with Walter, a mechanic who was a widowed father of two young children. "Sister, may we speak with you for a moment?" Julia asked. "Of course, dear. Good day to you Walter. How are you and the children?"

"It's good to see you again. They are both well, Sister. Thank you for asking. They are still adjusting to losing their dear mother, but we do our best," Walter responded dejectedly.

Julia quickly interjected to tell Helena the predicament he was facing.

Julia did not know the extent of their prior relationship and began to explain Walter's circumstances.

"It has been most difficult for the children since Katarina passed. Walter must go to Konopki tomorrow and will not return for several days. It's far too dangerous to take the children with him and there is no one to watch over them while he's away.

"Sister, they have become fond of me these last few months. I could tend to them if we can let them stay here until his return. I will keep my chores in good order and perhaps with Stanley's help, we will find ways to keep them busy during the day."

Calmly, Sister Helena turned her attention directly to Walter, "May I ask when you plan to return from Konopki, Walter?"

"Of course, Sister. As you know, I am a very good mechanic, but there's not enough to keep me busy here. The only way to make more money is to take my work to other towns and villages. I don't know what else I can do. The weather is far too cold to take the children."

"I understand… but you *will return* within a few days. Can we agree?"

Turning her attention back to Julia, the Sister looked almost scoldingly into her eyes. "You know how hard it has become making these difficult decisions Julia, but as I think more about it, we are here to serve our flock. The most important among them are our children.

They represent the future, for all of us. We can all share this responsibility by working together. It's safe to say they will surely bring more life to our quiet house of worship."

With one final glare of admonition, Sister Helena remarked very sternly, "We look forward to seeing you by the end of the week, Walter."

Over the next few days Julia, as usual, took to her tasks in earnest. She had always given her best effort and attention to her duties, which consistently defined her dedicated work ethic. It was next to impossible to be even more efficient than she already was to find enough extra time to tend to the children. Stanley was immensely helpful in this regard and took some time reading to the boys and encouraging them to play outside while he fetched firewood or shoveled the walkway from the soft dusting of freshly fallen snow from the previous night.

They played well together for the most part and seemed to understand Julia's time for them was limited. David, the eldest, was almost five years old, and did his best to keep his three-year-old brother well occupied.

It was fascinating for Julia to watch the boys, to make certain their mutual companionship remained on solid ground. In an instant, the relationship between siblings at this age could suddenly sour, often for reasons appearing trivial to an adult; not so for young ones such as these.

Julia was determined there would be only minimal inconvenience to Sister Helena, however she was admittedly unnerved by Sister's aggressive manner toward Walter. For such a gentle and loving person, she had every right to be blunt with Walter to ensure she did not overextend the obligations of the church. It must have been difficult for her to feel as she did, to always keep a steady hand on the helm. It often fell on her shoulders to be answerable for the conduct of the church.

The first uneventful two days of the boy's stay wound down to a close. After a short prayer, and hugs and kisses, the little ones happily settled into Julia's previous lumpy couch for the night.

Although quite spent, Julia and Sister shared a relaxing pot of tea at the table while Stanley was reading in his room in the back. It provided some private time together they had both come to cherish.

This evening however, there was one topic of discussion needing to be addressed. It was as appropriate a time as any.

"Sister, you know how much I appreciate you taking the boys in for a few days, but I also sense you were not very happy with me for suggesting it. Just so you know, Walter never asked me to take them in. It was my idea, and I should have asked you privately to avoid placing you in an awkward situation. I sincerely apologize for doing so."

"You are a kind-hearted young girl Julia, but yes, I was a bit upset; not by you, as much as by the circumstances in which we find ourselves." Sister sipped her steeped tea and languished in a moment of reflection, as if to suggest there was more to this story she had not disclosed. Julia could not help but notice her apprehensions.

"Is there something I am missing Sister? You and I have always been direct with one another; unless perhaps I should mind my own business," she stated dismissively.

The silence from Helena was unexpected. Julia said no more and started to rise from her seat to finish her tea elsewhere… except there was nowhere else to go other than her own room. Doing so could offend Sister Helena. The children were already fast asleep on the lumpy couch. *My, this is awkward,* Julia thought.

Sister stood quickly and extended her hand, placing it on Julia's forearm. "Wait Julia, please stay. I do indeed have something I must tell you. Please, sit with me a while longer. It is an important matter I need to share with you."

Julia was uncertain as to what to do, other than comply with Sister's reluctant request. "Is everything alright, Sister? If it's something I have done, or not done, please tell me. I will do anything you ask of me to correct it; you must know that." Julia sat adjacent to Sister and remained quiet.

"Walter is not just a mechanic looking for work. He has much more on his plate than you may expect. What I am about to speak of must remain between the two of us for the present. My hope and expectation will convey my faith in you to help you understand what is happening here."

Julia could read Sister's facial gestures, revealing her obvious apprehension and evasiveness she was evidently feeling. Placing her hand on her forehead just momentarily, she sighed and whispered to herself, but audible enough so Julia could still hear. "Oh, where do I begin?" Julia remained mute to allow Sister to take the conversation in whatever direction she chose.

"Stanley and I see how you gravitate so naturally to the children in our parish here at Zygmunta Church. Your affection and concern go well beyond David and little Ernst. We can see those feelings are genuine. It is for this reason I have decided to tell you what I must.

"It has been two years since the Germans took Ciechanow. Despite very little resistance, they were brutally effective. It was a city they wanted badly for its railway lines and the concentration of Jews living there. Only a few days later they entered Opinogora. We have no railway line, but we had Jews. They wreaked havoc when they forcibly loaded entire Jewish families onto their trucks; mothers, fathers, and children. They were callously indiscriminate. These were our friends... many of us grew up together."

Sister Helena's emotional side became evident as she recalled the horror of those days. She dabbed her eyes with a handkerchief to maintain her composure and continued.

"None of us were told where they were taken, or why. A few of the men in the village tried to stand up to them, but it was hopeless. They were shot on the spot and their bodies were left on the street as a lesson for us to back away. We found out sometime later our Jewish friends were taken to a concentration camp in Treblinka. We can only imagine what happened to them.

"Since that time over the past year, the world has become aware of the gravity of Nazi oppression and the killing of innocent Polish and Jewish children in the Warsaw Ghetto. The response from the rest of the world to these horrors has only been vocal, but negligible. About the time you, me and Stanley found each other last September, these unspeakable crimes have caused many Catholic activists to stand up to protect young children from the tyranny of Germany."

Sister stopped speaking and stood up suddenly to fetch something. "Wait here for a moment Julia, I have something I want you to read."

Julia's mind was racing with confusion as to what was happening, and she did what she was told. Within a few anxious minutes, Sister returned with some papers she was eager to share.

"This is an article written by Zofia Kossak, a prominent Polish journalist; a piece she calls *Protest*. It calls upon people everywhere, led by Polish Catholics, to secretly support an underground Catholic organization named *Zegota*. Its founder is Irena Sendler, whose purpose is to save thousands of Jewish women and children from the Nazi genocide. Walter, Stanley, and I are proud to be an active part of it. This movement now provides a system of support we did not have before. We are no longer helpless to act.

"Before I tell you more, though, is it possible, just possible, you would consider joining us in this worthy but dangerous task? I would understand if you decline, but you must understand if our work here is discovered, you would be naturally implicated, as would Father Breitkopf. We would surely be put to death and the church would be burned to the ground. What I am saying to you is that it would not be possible for you to stay here if you remain passive about what we do."

Julia was stunned. "I don't know what to say, Sister... except, please trust me and tell me more. I want very much to be involved."

Sister Helena extended both hands and firmly grasped Julia's hand in her own. "Thank you, Julia! I am so very proud of you... Very well then; let me begin. Walter's business in Konopki is not about machinist work. He is working in support of Zegota.

"It is fraught with danger, Julia, which is why I was so insistent he return safely in three days. His passions run deep since his wife died so suddenly. He has a kind heart but frankly, her death has affected his objectivity, and if truth be told, it has also affected mine. While we are thankful for his enthusiasm and passion for our cause, I was merely urging him to make careful decisions going forward.

"If his assignment is discovered and he is captured by the Germans, he would be tortured to disclose the names of those who are with us. It has already happened with others before. This is the price we pay for protecting young ones who cannot defend themselves.

"Like many of us, Walter has his own priorities and obligations here in Opinogora. Our church is not an orphanage, and the Lord knows we already have more of them to help than we can manage. His own children should not be subrogated to the dire needs of those Zegota strives to protect."

Julia searched deep within herself, uncertain about the potential peril she could encounter, but she was definite about one thing; she was passionate about the chance to contribute in some meaningful way. She looked closely into Sister Helena's trusting eyes and knew her answer immediately.

"Sister, I want desperately to stand with you. I am too young to have children of my own and I have no ailing parents to watch out for. There is no one who depends on me. You have my word I will support this cause in any way asked of me. Just tell me what I must do."

Sister Helena breathed a deep sigh of relief. She was confident Julia would support the cause but until she heard it from Julia's lips, there was always a possibility she would decline. Julia was too young to attract suspicion but had maturity beyond her years. With the proper knowledge and patience, she could become an incredible and unsuspected asset to this cause.

*****

It was nearing dusk on Friday afternoon, when winter's final exhausted breath expired across the open plains and rolling hills of Golina. Walter's wagon rolled up to the rear of the Kosciol Zygmunta Catholic Church. It had been four arduous days during which Walter had taken two young Jewish boys posing as his own, from a Polish couple living outside of Mlawa.

Shortly after the German occupation, these boys had been living under the floorboards of a horse stable. It had been a temporary hiding place for the children since their parents were imprisoned at the Soldau Concentration Camp, along with many former Jewish families during the purge of the small town.

The elderly owners of the small farm did their best to keep the boys fed and sheltered but could not chance sharing the main house with them for fear of being discovered by roving German patrols. However, the boys would likely perish if they weren't removed from the foreboding cold of the barn to find a more suitable home.

When word of the boys' existence was disclosed to *Zegota*, another Polish family in Konopki offered to provide a permanent foster home for them, on the clear condition proper documentation be provided to protect the adoptive family.

Most of Zegota's work was concentrated upon the aftershock of the German purging of the Warsaw Ghetto, to safely relocate Jewish refugee women and children. Hundreds of sets of false identities were provided to Zegota by the Exiled Polish Government working out of London, England; two of them had been reserved for the family in Konopki.

These two young boys, now in Walter's care, were among the last to be found anywhere close to the hotbed of Mlawa. The rescue of these children from the Mlawa area made it tragically apparent to Irena Sendler that Zegota's mission had to be expanded across most of occupied Poland as well. Sendler's personal authorization was necessary to sanction Walter's rescue of the young boys.

When Walter stepped down from the wagon and was reunited with his own boys, he dropped to his bone-weary knees on the still frozen ground, crying like a baby in their comforting embraces. Sister Helena and Julia were moved to tears as well. This was Walter's first rescue mission. It would not be his last. His merciful act of bravery reinforced Julia's already growing passion and further justified its noble cause.

Walter stood and stretched his legs and back as he scuffled the boys' hair playfully and outstretched his arms to Sister Helena, who received his gesture warmly.

"Hello Sister. Please forgive me for returning late. It could not be helped." He continued to arch his back, grimacing as he did so. "Hello Julia. It is good to see you again."

"We are all so thankful you arrived safely. The boys missed you, but we managed to keep them busy while you were gone. They were most helpful." Julia assured him.

Sister Helena beckoned him inside to the warmth of the kitchen. "Come now. You must be exhausted and hungry after such a long trip. Julia, would you please tend to the children while I serve some dinner to Walter?"

"Of course, Sister. Boys! Let's help Stanley tend to the horse. David, please fetch the bag of oats in the shed behind the door. Careful not to spill them. We must keep the horse fed too! Then we can gather more firewood before dinner." They both ran to Julia, and each took a hand to escort her out of view to the back of the church.

"Please sit Walter. Can I make some tea for you, or possibly something much stronger perhaps? It must have been a longer journey than expected."

"A shot of whiskey would be wonderful, just to warm my insides. It was far too long to be sitting in the open. The boys stayed in the back the entire way under the straw and a couple of blankets, but we made it!"

"… A job well done, Walter. I suspected you might need an extra day or so. It's a very long way to Mlawa, especially in the biting cold. I can't imagine. We can catch up in the next few days. Right now, you just need to eat and rest up. All in due course."

*****

Months of harsh winter's fury passed, and spring thankfully arrived. As the seasons changed it was another time for fresh beginnings. This was true for Julia as well. She and Sister Helena worked tirelessly with Zegota, trying discreetly to locate abandoned children who were hidden away. Many were so well hidden from the Germans, the task of finding them was extremely difficult. If they remained well concealed from the Germans, that was equally true for Zegota.

Gradually, as trust was developed and word was carried secretively through established personal contacts, small clusters of mothers and young children would come to be relocated. They were typically scattered randomly outside the cities, mostly in rural farm areas within thirty kilometers of Ciechanow.

None of these Jewish families would ever come near the doors of the church and contact with them was only through word of mouth. Julia and Sister arranged documentation, details of which were sourced through Zegota. The church itself was never exposed to danger. Father Breitkopf wisely insisted upon it.

It was fulfilling work, but eventually fewer and fewer refugees were able to be located. Through the course of the war, Irena Sendler's children's section in Warsaw placed 2,500 Jewish children with foster homes and various orphanages; of these, sixty-five mothers and children were safely relocated by Helena and Julia. Together, they had indeed made a positive contribution.

14

An Ominous Coincidence?

♂

THE FIRST ORDER OF BUSINESS NOW, WAS GENERAL VON Brauchitsch' fulfillment of his pledge to Anna several weeks ago. Admiral Canaris' specific authorization had enabled the general to effectively implement it. In early December 1941, it was a perfect time to arrange a private reunion in Anna's honor befitting her dedication and loyalty to both her profession and more importantly, her family.

In advance, Klaus ordered the chefs to prepare a proper dining experience for only a select few of the inner circle, and two guests who would remain unnamed. There would be no pomp and circumstance, since what mattered this day was not recognition and celebration, as much as heartfelt and genuine respect for an amazing woman silently suffering from devastating personal loss. It was time to restore faith and sentiment where it mattered most.

It was a day like any other when Anna was bid to attend the general's office without any explanation or advance notice. When she entered reception, the general's door remained closed as it typically was, when Elisabeth announced Anna's arrival. In only a minute the door opened, and the general summoned her to enter. Anna was fully prepared for another assignment or status updates on present operations, all the while clutching her notes and dictation pad, such was her custom.

Not a word was spoken, as no suitable ones were required for a moment such as this. Standing in front of the general's desk were none other than Marta and Dietrich, already shaking with pent up anticipation and flowing tears of joy from the instant Anna entered the room. She was thunderstruck with emotion.

Dropping her notepad awkwardly to the floor, Anna wept uncontrollably, covering her mouth with cupped hands. As Dietrich eagerly approached and wrapped his comforting arms around her heaving chest, Anna staggered, almost falling, and her son quickly supported her weight until her light-headedness passed. She embraced her once lost loving son, his own tears of happiness streaming down his beautiful full cheeks. For Dietrich, it was to witness the very resurrection of Christ.

It had been two lingering years, seeming an eternity since they had parted; from a point in time when they could not even grieve together for the tragic loss of Dietrich's devoted father Jacob, taken so suddenly, so irretrievably from them. Their shared intense grief was inextricably wound in indissoluble bonds of love, concern, and compassion for each other's well-being. Some forms of love never fade nor disappear; rather they continue to grow, being nourished in a period of absence by the hope sustaining it.

Anna kissed her beautiful young son repeatedly. She was lost in the moment until she opened her weeping eyes to see her dearest lifelong friend, Marta, wiping her own tears. Thoughtfully, Marta patiently held herself back to not distract Anna from her son's embrace for an instant longer.

Anna kept her arm around Dietrich's shoulder and gestured to Marta with the raising of her other, gathering her closely to cling to them together. Still not a word had been exchanged among them. The only sound was the uncontrollable sobbing. Their heartfelt reactions to this reunion were already conveying more than any words could possibly express.

"Oh, how I have missed you Mother! I prayed for you every day and never gave up hope we would be together again. I kept believing because Marta promised me you would always be safe with the general here to protect you. She and Lena have cared and comforted me every day we have been apart."

Anna turned her head, still holding Marta and Dietrich tightly and kissed Marta's cheek affectionately. "Thank you, Marta. I knew he would always be safe with you and Klaus."

"Hello Sweetheart! You look well my darling, doesn't she Dietrich? We danced together when Klaus told us the wonderful news! We tried to convince Walther to let you come home, but he said…"

"Shhh!" Anna intervened. "Not now… all is well, and I want to enjoy the moment. Please don't blame the general. He has done so much for our family… and now this! … as he had promised me Marta. He is a good and kind man!"

"We sent word to you through Klaus but never asked Walther for his blessing to do so. He would have forbidden it. What harm could it do? I just had to let you know you were always in our thoughts and prayers."

"Yes, my dear. I remember that day vividly. His message picked up my spirits and restored my fading confidence, at a time I so desperately needed it. Klaus' message kept me going so I could better focus on my responsibilities here."

Anna reached out again to Dietrich and cuddled him to her breast adding, "… and look at what you and Klaus have done. You have turned my young boy into a handsome young man! … a worthy young brother of Manny. Klaus is so very proud of you both. Is Manny happy and well?"

"He is Mother," interjected Dietrich. "We have become best friends. He comes to my soccer games, and we have truly become brothers, very close ones, I might add."

"Yes", Marta confirmed. "With Klaus being away so much, Manny has become a supportive role model for Dietrich. It's like having another man in the house." She stroked his forehead affectionately to guide his hair away from his eyes, as any mother would do. The simple spontaneous gesture spoke volumes to Anna, confirming Marta's love for Dietrich was genuine.

The reminiscing continued but not before they realized the general was now noticeably absent, having left them alone for some private time together. He was very thoughtful that way.

When there was finally an appropriate pause, Marta informed Elisabeth they were ready to proceed to the dining room and Klaus was notified it was time to join them with the general. An exquisite meal had been prepared to take a much-needed break from the matters of war. These were the moments that knew no politics, nor religions.

There were endless topics of discussion, and none of them concerned national security, or code breaking, or subterfuge... just personal joy and happy memories of times past. It was readily apparent the close bond between Anna and Marta had only become more strongly forged during their forced exile from one another. As they remembered their tearful parting, they became intensely aware matters could have been far worse than they were now able to comprehend. It was indeed a time for rejoicing.

This extraordinary act of graciousness by Walther and Admiral Canaris for Anna's well-being was acknowledged privately and genuinely by Anna. It reinforced in the general, that Anna's undying loyalty to him was indeed unwavering.

Also of great personal impact were the heartfelt demonstrations of love and respect Marta had discovered for her father-in-law. It was what Walther had wanted from her since the day she married Klaus. Who could have foreseen the direction their relationship would take over the last twenty years?

Marta's obstinate and self-indulgent tendencies had crossed paths with her equally stubborn and demanding father-in-law numerous times, and seldom was there a victor. Now, as a direct result of one great deed, providing for the long-term safety of Anna's family, there was genuine compassion for one another to an extent it had never existed before. The general's pride in her was effusive.

*****

In the preceding months, the stress of war on the eastern front had taken its toll when the general's heart condition once again began to deteriorate. It had been almost nine years since Sigmund had performed his life saving surgical procedure. Walther understood his energy and vitality were significantly beginning to fade again.

Only Marta and Klaus had knowledge of his prior condition, as he had always insisted, but now they both agreed it could no longer remain that way. Reluctantly, the general agreed with their decision and sadly, was soon diagnosed with coronary artery disease. His condition was advanced and incurable.

Anna and many others within the circle of Abwehr Command were not made aware of the general's diagnosis, however when his availability became more restricted to them, many simply suspected it was a result of exhaustion and battle fatigue related to his involvement with Operation Barbarossa.

Perhaps it was for these reasons visits were permitted between Anna and Marta, with noticeably less scrutiny from security. The general's reasoning was that the trust Anna had earned with him was deserving on its own merits, however on a personal note, one could argue General von Brauchitsch used his influence to provide more latitude to Anna and Marta. It was the general's way of balancing the scales of retribution in their favor; driven by his guilt for the travesty the Landesburg family had been forced to endure.

In fact, security became so lax, only a single security escort was assigned when the ladies were graciously permitted to see one another outside the Abwehr facility, and arrangements were agreed upon allowing Anna to stay overnight at Marta and Klaus' home on Cuvrystrasse. Their home was already a well secured location, as was common for families related to those in high command. It was a perfect fit for Abwehr's requirements.

When Anna heard the news, she was understandably ecstatic. Matters of war were never a topic of discussion between she and Marta for security reasons, but their conversations abounded with all things social and personal. Marta openly discussed anything on her mind with Anna; she always had done so, and now being together again, conversation flowed freely between them.

Conversely, Anna could not be as forthright, remaining steadfast to her commitment to Abwehr concerning matters of business never being disclosed to anyone, including Marta. Anna stressed about this from time to time and found it particularly challenging not to disclose details of her private audience with Hitler, as Marta had shared with her four years prior.

For the two friends it was likened to reliving their childhoods together. Despite troubled times, interspersed with personal tragedy and continual bouts of remorse, these reunions were welcome personal indulgences. Once again, it put the turbulent events of the past few years into a more meaningful perspective. Each of Anna's ensuing visits rejuvenated her, helping to better suppress her occasional somber reflections.

On this weekend visit, as often happened, a fresh, icy bottle of vodka was cracked open. Their absorbing conversation flowed naturally and meandered down whatever course the vodka took them.

"Marta, who would have thought this was possible three years ago? Dietrich and you have come into my life again, and every time we meet, my spirit is recharged. Each visit sustains me till the next one. I am so very relieved and grateful to be able to do this again."

She sipped her well-deserved cocktail, setting it on the side table while adjusting herself by placing her elbows on her knees to lean forward ever so slightly. These cherished moments with her dearest friend always created rich, fond memories she often relived many times over. "So, tell me more about your life now. How are things between you and Klaus these days?"

"The touring certainly takes its toll on me, but I wouldn't have it any other way. It's all I know Anna, and I'm fortunate to live the life I adore. The boys appear to stay out of trouble, and their schooling continues as it should. I'm so very proud of them."

Marta paused to enjoy another sip of her martini before addressing Anna's perceptive, but never intrusive question. "Although Klaus and I are still married, he's not here anymore and consequently, he has drifted even further from Manny. It sometimes feels as if Klaus has already passed. I will always love him, but the sadness I feel most deeply, is that I don't miss him as much anymore."

"Oh Marta. It's terrible to hear you say that. The war is taking its toll on everyone, and in ways we could never have imagined."

"You know what saddens me as well, perhaps more than I should admit?" Marta sighed despondently.

"You mean there's more? My goodness, my dear lady. What else has happened? Are Manny and Dietrich alright?" Anna pressed Marta with obvious concern.

"Oh, yes! They're both continuing to do well. They are a positive balance in my life that often steadies me."

"What is it, Marta? It's something you seem reluctant to tell me. I'm quite concerned," Anna repeated for emphasis.

Marta stood to prepare yet another cocktail. "Are you sure you don't want another, Sweetheart?"

"No, I really think I've had enough for now. Perhaps you should be mindful about your own consumption. I grow more concerned every time we are together. Please tell me what's going on with you. It's not like you to keep holding back. Have you lost confidence in me?" Anna protested.

"No, never, Anna! It's just so embarrassing and I find myself becoming more confused."

"Well, there's no time like the present. Get on with it. Whatever it is you always have my support. Now, please."

"Do you remember what came between Klaus and me and tore us apart in the first place?" Marta asked between sips.

"Why, yes. It was your unfaithfulness in Boston, wasn't it?" Anna's mind always remained sharp about even the slightest detail, especially on this matter being such a significant indiscretion.

"Yes, with Manuel Rosenthal." Anna appeared to have Marta opening up to her again, and she wisely chose to just let her speak.

"Since my American tour in late 1938, Manuel and I continued our courtship as best we could by way of telegrams and long-distance telephone calls. Not a satisfying way to keep our love alive, as you can only imagine. Over time though, our messages were becoming less frequent. The affection between us was always genuine, but with the attention to my career obligations in Europe, it was demanding enough without personal illicit entanglements to worry about.

"On the other side of the vast ocean between us, Manuel's professional obligations were also rightfully focused upon his assistant conductor responsibilities with the Boston Symphony Orchestra under his dear friend, the resident conductor Serge Koussevitzky.

"It had been months since our last correspondence, when Manuel sadly disclosed the news that after our scandalous indiscretions, the well-publicized affair eventually forced him to step away from the Boston Symphony in the summer of 1939. Subsequently, his close friendship with Maestro Koussevitzky was regrettably terminated."

"Oh. It's so sad to hear that, Marta. I do recall he and the maestro had some difficult times after news of the scandal became public," Anna stated sympathetically.

"Well, following Manuel's resignation, amazing opportunities with both the *Orchestre National* and the *Orchestral Philharmonique* were offered to him, to bolster an already incredible cast of musicians. The objective was to provide quality musical entertainment to expand radio broadcasting performances during the war.

"To entice top performers throughout Europe to join them, they were offering exorbitant wages. It was an outstanding moment for popular music celebrities to take advantage of the situation, despite Nazi intervention to regulate the musical content.

"I was stunned when Manuel declined several generous offers. Conducting was his life's passion, but as I would soon discover, that passion was only exceeded by his unwavering patriotism to his beloved France."

"Really, how could he serve France in the music business? I'm intrigued," Anna asked.

Marta continued. Whatever she was trying to say was obviously troubling her.

"After weighing his options, he followed his heart and unhesitatingly volunteered to enter the French military just prior to Germany's declaration of war on Poland. Since receiving Manuel's telegram shortly thereafter, I've tried repeatedly to communicate with him, not to discourage his decision, but to offer my steadfast support of him. Disappointingly, none of my messages were ever returned, leaving me to only imagine the worst of possibilities."

"Oh no, Marta! You must be heart-broken with worry." Anna reached out to take Marta's hand, just as she was about to refill another glass. She did not let go. "Please, Marta. Can we just talk before you fix another one?"

Ashamedly, or so it appeared, Marta stayed put and lit a cigarette instead. "Sorry, dear. I need something to steady my nerves. I hope you don't mind."

What Marta didn't know was that when war between Germany and France became inevitable, Manuel became a medical corporal stationed in Alsace with the 300th Infantry Regiment. Unknown to Marta during this time, Manuel's battalion fought valiantly but would eventually succumb to the military juggernaut that was the German Wehrmacht. While serving on the frontline in the Vosges, Manuel and his surviving French comrades would be captured by the Germans. He would spend nine months as a prisoner of war.

Marta resumed. "Worrying about Manny's safety day by day served no positive purpose for me, other than to sustain my fading hope we would find each other again, if destiny would permit. Reconciling his probable loss, was a slow but progressive process; much like the loss of you from the everyday life we had always enjoyed together."

Anna leaned forward to look deeply into Marta's eyes, as she often did when startling disclosures were shared between them. "And how are you coming to grips with his probable loss now, Sweetheart? How long has it been since you last heard from him?"

"Over two years; long enough to accept the reality of what has happened. I still think of him and continue to cherish our brief time together." With that, the tears and sniffles began to commence. Anna was quick to find a box of tissues. There was always one on hand for their deeper discussions.

As she wiped her final tears, she confessed her current mental challenges. "Sometimes, these dreadful situations make me feel as if I'm in a careening car, racing out of control to some unknown misfortune, not entirely of my own making; helplessness, without the direction or the power to change it."

"Oh my. I had no idea what you were going through. I am so sorry for your pain Sweetheart. I only wish I could have been more accessible for you."

"But now, that is in the past. When I have moments of uncertain introspection and personal despair, which I still do, I turn to my music to feed my passionate desires. It's the rock steadying my way forward and it continues to be invaluable in helping to restore the normal order of things."

"Well done, Marta. I'm so very proud of your proactive courage and determination. Let's pray we never have to be apart again for a very long time," Anna softly encouraged.

"Now, with or without your consent, I really must have another! I'm so sick of this depressing bullshit, aren't you?"

"It wasn't bullshit to me but, I admit your point is well taken. I'll have another too, please. And while you are pouring us another, I must use the washroom. Be right back, dear."

*****

When the ladies had resettled, Marta continued in another direction. "On a happier note, I continue to be in demand with the press and am often approached by new designers, just not as much as in my younger years. I think as I age, as gracefully as I am able, so too does my fan base. Perhaps it's what sustains my popularity because they can relate to me in a familiar way."

Marta raised her now half-filled glass and downed it with a flourish. "My that's tasty! I think my cocktails always taste better when we're together. I'm getting another. Come, I'll pour you another one too."

"No, Marta, now I really have had enough. Try slowing yourself down a little, for your own sake, I beg of you."

"Yes, yes. You're always the strong one, so serious. I'll try to do better with this, I promise; just not right now, OK?"

Anna stood to follow Marta to the bar to refresh yet another glass. The sound of the martini being shaken noisily over ice had become all too familiar during these happy but still uncertain times.

The chatter continued for quite some time. They returned to the parlor to briefly stand by the expansive window, taking in the glorious view overlooking a very busy Cuvreystrasse below. It was the beginning of the winter season and snow had begun to fall heavily.

"My goodness, Marta. I had almost forgotten how truly beautiful it is to take in this glorious view. We must never take these moments for granted."

They both sighed and withdrew from the peaceful scene, having enjoyed the tranquil pause. Now sitting beside one another, they continued reminiscing and enjoying a few laughs; perhaps the alcohol had begun catching up with them.

"You know, since rejuvenating our relationship, Walther often invites me to accompany him to various prestigious events, even to this day. He really enjoys me holding his arm by my side. He told me I make him feel younger again. What man doesn't want a beautiful, sexy lady at his side... even if I am his daughter-in-law? It's good for his public profile... and for my career too!

"There are no false pretenses here though. Our relationship has really blossomed. We have both earned each other's respect. It only took us decades to achieve it."

"You never miss a trick, do you, Sweetheart!" Anna teased.

"You know me well, Anna. I always do my best not to!" They both began to giggle about the silly things they could say to one another. As the hours passed, the ladies continued to relax in the parlor and sat comfortably in the cozy, high-backed chairs.

"So, tell me, what's happening with the symphony and specifically your life under the microscope? I think about you often and imagine all the places you tour and the interesting people you must meet. Please tell me more, Marta." Anna eagerly inquired.

"You are right, Anna. I meet some truly amazing people at these functions… Which reminds me…" She placed her cocktail glass on the table and lit another cigarette. Marta took a long, satisfying draw, exhaling slowly as she thoughtfully directed the smoke away from Anna.

"Remember when I first met Coco Chanel, before Manny was born?"

"Yes, of course! How could I forget such a thing?"

"Well, just recently we have become reacquainted with each other again, but only from time to time. In fact, do you recall me attending the summer fashion show in Paris last July?"

"Look who you're talking to Marta. Do you think I would know anything about those matters? … Really?"

"Sorry honey, I simply forget sometimes. It was the annual fashion gala at the Hotel Ritz in Paris. All the fashion moguls attend every year. Anyway, who do I run into but none other than Coco! I have continued to wear her gowns from time to time, but lately we have started to grow closer than we had ever been. She's still quite lovely, despite the passing years. She has become more mature, as we all have, but also more self-assured.

"She forever remains the flamboyant character always defining her; one of many reasons I very much admire her. She sought me out when she learned I would be attending the event. We have met a few times since, and she is starting to confide personal matters to me, very personal ones, I might add. She has even invited me to her villa!"

"Oh, please tell me about it. I can only imagine how lovely it must be," Anna encouraged.

The two friends began to banter at great length about Madame Chanel's lavish lifestyle, something Marta herself had been known for, as her own celebrity status continued to grow. However, Madame Chanel was on a very different plateau. The world had by this time, distinguished her as the wealthiest woman on earth.

"She calls it *La Pausa*. It is truly a one-of-a-kind mansion located on the French Riviera, close to Monte Carlo. It was featured a few years ago in *American Vogue* magazine, for heaven's sake! The view is breathtaking, overlooking the Mediterranean Sea. It truly inspired me, not for its incredible value, but more for her attention to fine detail. She views *La Pausa* as being an important part of her legacy; something she can leave behind; something far more personal than her business fortune."

"I had no idea Coco was such a sentimentalist," Anna opined, "so different from the cold and manipulative businesswoman she is known to be. What inspired her to name it *La Pausa*?"

"That's part of the theme of her creation, well... her legacy one could say. It touched me so deeply. It means *The Pause*. It was originally constructed where Mary Magdalene rested under the olive trees, when walking from Jerusalem after Jesus was crucified, or so the legend is told. Coco planted rows and rows of olive trees and entire groves of orange trees. There's so much wild lavender flowing down the hillsides with magnificent clusters of vibrant roses. It is a true spectacle of nature I shall never forget."

"It sounds lovely Marta. Does she live there year-round? I just assumed she lived in Paris." Anna enquired.

"Believe it or not, for all its grandeur, she uses it mostly as a summer home, and entertains many famous celebrities when she's there."

Anna quickly interjected... "Such as yourself, Marta!"

"No, not at all, but thank you Anna. Her circle extends far beyond the likes of me, my dear. She's not a name dropper by any means, but I learned she's socialized there with many artists, poets, and world class musicians. Why, when I was there for a few days, the poet Pierre Reverdy was *living there* as her guest, for God's sake... not as her lover, heavens no; that esteemed privilege was always reserved for the Duke of Westminster, for several years in fact.

"Some of her gala events included so many guests whose names I recognized, such as Igor Stravinsky, Pablo Picasso, Salvador Dali, to name a few... I can't remember them all. Oh, I do recall an interesting one though, Lucino Visconti.

"I recall his name because he had the audacity to bring along a couple of his friends. Who would do that to such a prestigious event? His guests were none other than Giacomo Puccini and Arturo Toscanini! My friend Manuel, who conducted when I was in Boston, is a dear friend of Arturo; that's probably why I remember him so vividly."

"Marta, this is amazing! You rub shoulders with so many socialites - many you may not have met personally, but I promise you, the people you have named most likely are among your own admirers. You are a good fit for them, I assure you. Do you intend to see her again? Maybe there's another contract in the offing?" she said facetiously.

"That's always a possibility, I suppose, but I'm delighted just to be counted among her friends. I never know where our conversations may take us. Sometimes, Coco keeps me on the edge of my seat."

"Much as you do for me!" Anna added.

Although no one else was sharing the luxurious parlor, in very hushed tones, Marta excitedly leaned closer to Anna to push the limits of her confidentiality with Coco and whispered softly, "There is no one I can speak to about this, other than you of course, but in a moment of confidence, she told me her current lover is Baron Hans Gunther von Dincklage!"

Anna's eyes widened with astonishment at this very intimate disclosure. She was prompted to instinctively turn her head ever so slightly, as if to expect someone overhearing them. Softly Anna responded, "Is that the same General von Dincklage working with your father-in-law? Could it possibly be?"

"All I heard is he knows Walther... perhaps it is so. I know little else of his business, but I can tell you a great deal about his sexual proclivities, if you understand my meaning..."

"That's the last news I am anxious to hear... well... at the very least right now!" Much like the school children they once were, they both giggled again, more mischievously than before.

As the conversation moved on to other lighter matters, Anna's mind continued to return to Coco's intentions with Marta. She did not want to draw more attention to this connection with Marta at this specific time, however Anna could not help but consider carefully to herself the wisdom of speaking with the general about this matter. Perhaps it was simply co-incidental? Or could there be more to this than meets the eye?

It was Saturday night, December 6th, 1941. The weekend with Marta was an important respite for Anna, always exceeding her highest expectations. All good things must come to an end however, and when Sunday evening approached, she readied herself for the return to her exile.

It was no longer a place she hated, nor was she intimidated by it anymore. Abwehr had now become so familiar. She simply returned dutifully, and precisely as she was instructed. She was mindful to never abuse her new privileges.

When the security detail arrived at Marta's door, there was no hesitation from Anna to be swiftly returned to her private on-site suite. At the time, she had no concept of how the world had changed so irreversibly earlier that same Sunday morning.

15
BALANCING DIVIDED LOYALTIES

ON DECEMBER 7, 1941, THE STARK REALITIES OF WAR CAP-
tured global headlines when Japan launched a massive air attack
against the American naval fleet stationed in Pearl Harbor. Inside
German High Command, many greeted news of the unprovoked
attack with uneasy expressions of trepidation, however Hitler's spirit
was visibly buoyed by the tragic event. He was said to have been
delighted by the news.

Behind closed doors, Abwehr commanders were disturbed by
the Fuhrer's biased exuberance upon learning of the Japanese attack.
Admiral Canaris, General von Brauchitsch, Major Groscurth, Major
Oster, and of course Anna, were reporting on their communications
with several of Hitler's advisors since his open declaration of war
against the Americans, just one day after the attack. He had already
ordered German U-boats to attack American supply ships on site,
likely destined for Great Britain.

Admiral Canaris opened the meeting with his candid perspectives.
"In my discussions with von Ribbentrop this morning, he strongly
supports the Fuhrer's view the attack has come at an opportune time
for Germany. He believes the United States would have declared war
on us in a matter of weeks, even without Japan's unprovoked aggression. Whether he is correct in this assumption, we may never know.

"In the past several months, Operation Barbarossa has come to
a standstill, finding our troops presently bogged down in one of the
worst Russian winters in recent memory. Public opinion has turned
against us, as surely as the weather, supporting compelling arguments

in the global press we have over-extended our ability to supply our border troops.

"Despite these negative realities, the Fuhrer considers the attack on Pearl Harbor to be beneficial to German interests, as Japan will now bear the brunt of American retaliation. Similarly, the British will now be forced to divide their defense to protect their significant Asian interests as well."

"Admiral, if I may..." the admiral nodded to General von Brauchitsch who rose from his seat.

"Thank you, Sir. I also spoke briefly with Minister von Ribbentrop and Reichsfuhrer Himmler. They confided to me that while the attention and focus of the Allies will now be divided, so too shall our own. The American presence in the Pacific will be rebuilt. It will take time, to be sure; a year to eighteen months by their estimate.

"However, their manufacturing capabilities cannot be underestimated. They will become a worthy antagonist of the Fatherland, potentially strong enough to turn the course of this war. We may well regret this upcoming feud between the Fuhrer and the American president. There is so much bad blood between them already."

Some stirring of random disgruntled remarks, consisting mostly of grimacing and private dissentions among the other officers were somewhat muffled by the reshuffling of seats. The general stress and unsettling confusion of these private disclosures signified there were no immediate resolutions about to be tabled by them. Anna spoke up when their quiet pause presented the opportunity for her to do so.

"Sirs, may I suggest a discussion may be helpful with Minister Goebbels. It is my understanding the Fuhrer is proposing to address the Reichstag, the day after tomorrow."

"Yes, that is our understanding as well. What do you have in mind, Anna?" the admiral asked.

"Although I have my own strong misgivings about the Fuhrer, there is no doubt he is a captivating and most persuasive speaker. Perhaps, Admiral, you could advise the minister to use his considerable influence with the Fuhrer to temper his usual flair, to tone down his reckless impulse for which he is also well known, before he addresses the Reichstag to further antagonize the Americans.

"Whether this is the appropriate time for controlling his tempestuous nature, or conversely provoking his outrage for questioning his tone, either way the minister should best advise him. For what it is worth, I believe making the effort to rationalize with the Fuhrer may pay serious dividends to long term German interests.

"General, as an added point, your daughter and Maestro Furtwangler know the minister well. While they do not support his political views, they consider him to be not only brilliant in his capacity as Propaganda Minister, but equally as manipulative and cunning as the Fuhrer. For these reasons, Minister Goebbels is the most likely person to have significant influence with him. I would trust his judgement at this critical time more than the Fuhrer's."

The room fell silent as the admiral and the general pondered Anna's recommendation.

"Your suggestion has merit, Anna. We dare not challenge the Fuhrer's military decisions. We have seen situations where others have foolishly done so. It is notable they only attempt it once."

The admiral paused to collect his thoughts and resumed his line of thinking. "We understand von Ribbentrop would never challenge the Fuhrer, whether he agrees or disagrees with his military or political decisions, however, Hitler often defers to Goebbels' judgement for his unique point of view. He respects Goebbels' astute opinions concerning his ability to shape, and to even alter domestic and international responses to the Fuhrer's provocative actions."

The admiral added thoughtfully, "There is nothing to lose here, in my opinion. Good suggestion, Anna. What do you think, Walther?"

"Sir, if Goebbels has a talent, it is his ability to deflect blame. No one understands world opinion more than he, and never has it been so important to the Reich than now. I agree we should approach Goebbels and reasonably engage him to use his own judgement as to how he will address the matter with the Fuhrer."

On the advice of von Ribbentrop, Hitler agreed to review various approaches and potential modifications to his Reichstag address. It was Goebbels he had heavily relied upon at the Beer Hall Putsch in Munich, the Fire Decree leading to the resignation of Hindenburg, the false flag attacks just prior to the invasion of Poland, and the profound influence of the BPO to garner credibility and support for the Nazi Party from German aristocracy and business icons. Without even considering Hitler's military achievements, the list of Goebbels' accomplishments alone was endless.

The Fuhrer was enthusiastic about his propaganda minister's constructive commentary, but only to the extent it supported Hitler's original motivations. Despite Goebbels' advice, Hitler did not diminish his contempt for the American President Roosevelt. In fact, he became even more emboldened by the Propaganda Minister's support, delivering a scathing verbal attack, specifically directed against the president.

On December 11th, Hitler delivered his justifications for war against America in a convincing and forceful manner, thereby further bolstering German support of Hitler and the Nazi Party. He accusingly asserted it was the failure of FDR's New Deal that was responsible for American provocations against Germany.

The Reichstag building shook with loud applause while the members stood in unison to convey their overwhelming support of their duly elected leader. Hitler's declaration of war was his only course of action and reaffirmed the will of the people. There was no blame placed on his shoulders by the German people for an action considered to be fully justified.

Just one week later, on December 19th, Hitler's enflamed aggressiveness resulted in his sudden dismissal of General von Brauchitsch from his strategic military responsibilities pertaining to Operation Barbarossa; Hitler's opinion being there was no time for weakness and self-doubting among his commanding officers when facing the mounting obstacles inside Russian borders. The general continued to be retained, however only as a minor consulting advisor. His days of influence had ended abruptly.

*****

Abwehr closely monitored numerous global military events to provide constant updated reports to High Command. Their expansive networks of ASTs forwarded secret communications in real time, which were now overseen and relayed by Abwehr in priority of urgency and confirmation of content. Anna was an integral advocate of this process she had been so insistent to implement.

It was early February 1942 when Anna contacted Elisabeth to determine the whereabouts of General von Brauchitsch and informed her of the urgency of communicating with him. "I'm afraid the general will not be returning today as he is feeling unwell recently. I will try to connect with him, but he will be difficult to reach."

"No… this cannot wait." Without hesitation, Anna redirected her request. "Connect me with the Admiral. It is a matter of some urgency I speak with him, preferably in person."

Within minutes Admiral Canaris' office confirmed his availability and he adjourned his meeting early to accommodate her request. Accompanying the admiral was General Oster. To Anna's mind, this was more supporting evidence of her value, placing her infrequent requests among Admiral Canaris' priorities.

"Good morning, Admiral, General Oster. Thank you for meeting with me on short notice. The general is unavailable, hence my urgent interruption of your meetings today. I chose not to discuss this matter over internal lines."

The admiral just waved off any inconvenience it may have caused and acknowledged the probable wisdom of her decision. He then added, "I called upon Major Groscurth to also join us in the general's absence. Please proceed, Anna."

Anna continued, "We have received notification of a convoy ostensibly being directed to run a British blockade in the Channel. High Command is determined to reposition a support squadron for the *Scharnhorst*, the *Gneisenau*, and the *Prinz Eugen* out of Brest. The decision has been made to reposition the ships to the port of Wilhelmshaven to counter a possible British invasion of Norway.

"The British are aware the refurbishing and preparedness of these ships are nearing completion and will be expecting the convoy to be navigating around the Island. They will no doubt maneuver their battleships to intercept our vessels there. Fog and heavy seas are anticipated tonight, making conditions favorable to make a direct run north through the channel, taking the British completely by surprise. It is a calculated risk but will save valuable time and resources, compared to an outside run around the British Isles."

Anna had already prepared an overlay of the proposed route for the admiral's cursory inspection. "Sir, the command came directly from the office of Admiral Gunter Lutjens. I believe you are familiar with him, Sir?"

"Yes, of course. He has been responsible for a successful run of commerce raids against American convoys. In the last two months alone, those battleships have taken twenty or more British and American cargo ships to the bottom of the Atlantic; just incredible what they have accomplished."

"Sir, this order was also signed off by Admiral Raeder, who had been in opposition to such a tactic unless the Fuhrer himself supports the order, which he has now agreed to do. The intent of the operation can only be presumed to be a *full go*. We know the British are already decrypting our Enigma transmissions, thanks to the Poles. They must know by now this repositioning has been under consideration since the Fuhrer's Directive in January."

Anna concluded by saying, "They just don't know precisely when; nor do they suspect we have the audacity to challenge them in the channel."

"I agree with your evaluation. We know the British are carefully monitoring our repairs to these ships, having caused so much havoc for American merchant shipping and supply lines. If we can tactfully enlighten MI-6 to prepare for this engagement in the few hours remaining, it could set back German success in the straits."

The admiral straightened his bent back and took a long, deep breath, pausing with his own deliberate risk assessment, as was his habit on matters of duplicitous deception. It was always a measured and well-considered evaluation of potential consequences, particularly on timely decisions being made without the endorsement of the general, who normally oversaw these operations.

After a momentary pause, he added, "Anna, in the absence of General von Brauchitsch, you and General Oster will handle all aspects of the encoded transmissions. Trust no one other than yourselves. I will inform the general personally upon his return. You were correct to come to us directly Anna. Your analysis is timely. Had you waited another day, this information would have been irrelevant."

Britain routinely monitored German communications that had been Enigma coded and while not always reliable on its own merits, when combined with RAF air reconnaissance, reliability was often visually confirmed to determine authenticity. This night was predicted to be heavily overcast, which would significantly hinder visible confirmation.

As further backup, an extensive underground network of British agents operating in France as part of M-16, would often be called upon to support the reliability of these coded transmissions before repositioning existing British naval forces. The Germans knew these agents were watching, but their identities and precise whereabouts were almost impossible to trace. The British ground efforts to closely monitor German ship movements, progress on dry dock repairs, and reporting of bombing damage upon targeted strikes, were invaluable to planning and logistics for strategic operations.

This mission was well conceived by Admirals Reader and Lutgens. Determining the time of departure was sensibly considered to coincide with the completion of final British flyovers for the day, and maximum tide levels in the channel. However, the key element to German success on the *Channel Dash* was the element of surprise.

Behind closed doors, the admiral outlined the situation, acknowledging the brief window of opportunity before them. He began in earnest to summarize his dilemma by weighing his alternatives. It was the afternoon of February 11, 1942. The admiral began.

"The squadron is scheduled to be launched at 21:14 hours under cover of darkness, further enhanced by a combination of fog and snow obstructing whatever slivers of moonlight may remain. Conditions should be optimal for a stealthy and direct voyage north.

"Gentlemen, Anna, these are the precise decisions at such critical moments that hold so many lives in the balance, for both sides of the conflict. On the one hand, if this fully operational fleet arrives safely in Wilhelmshaven, it would significantly discourage any British attack from the sea to liberate Norway. By our estimation, such an offensive mission would prove too costly for the Royal Navy, in both time and expediency.

"Alternatively, without these battleships securely positioned off the southern coast of Norway, our land-based defenses are too weak to hold off a British assault. My best bet says the British would be foolish to diminish their bulwark defense of the English Channel against our potential assault from France. Maintaining an impenetrable defensive wall will always remain of greater importance to them."

"I think I speak for all of us Admiral, including General von Brauchitsch, by stating the obvious." General Oster was a man of few words, but when he spoke, his words were chosen carefully.

"We are not in a position to deliberate this further, as time is short. I agree we cannot lose this opportunity to slow down the war machine we have created. We are struggling to cope with our overwhelming successes and have spread ourselves too thinly across multiple fronts. We cannot break the British. It would consume too much of our attention and limit our resources across the fronts we are now scrambling to defend."

He paused thoughtfully over what he was considering. "What we are about to do is treasonous, at the highest level. But it is the price we must pay to change our focus from the British and instead, fortify the German strongholds we presently occupy. Many of the Fuhrer's personal advisors speak of this behind closed doors, afraid to speak out against him. *Why would they?* The Fuhrer refuses to listen to reason.

"To be clear to each of us, if the British do their jobs and seize the opportunity before them, the resulting loss of our battleships in the channel will force the Fuhrer to reconsider his aggressive posture toward Britain. Despite a heavy heart... let's feed them to the Royal Navy."

The admiral paused reflectively, scanning the eyes of those present, inviting any dissenting views. None were offered. "Then we all agree."

Within the hour, an encrypted message was sent by Anna and General Oster, both knowing full well it would be decoded by British Admiralty. The impact of this transmission, if taken seriously, would heavily shift the advantage to the British, however, there was insufficient supporting data to confirm the legitimacy of the transmission.

Weather conditions and the jamming of radio signals by German command made it futile for British attempts to accurately monitor the course of the squadron upon leaving Brest. These circumstances were clearly outside the control of Abwehr and very much left to chance.

Once the convoy's departure was confirmed heading south out of Brest, as per British expectations, the squadron was lost in the murky shadows of night and their subsequent course alteration to the north was never confirmed. The direction of their true course north would not be determined by the British until the fleet was approaching the Straits of Dover, more than twelve hours later.

The British chose not to act upon the unconfirmed coded message from Abwehr, thinking perhaps it was a trap. Was Germany using the battleships as bait to draw the British in against additional superior forces? The British relied heavily upon strict protocol, as they should have without further supportive confirmation, and erred on the side of caution.

Vice Admiral Otto Ciliax was in direct command and through the night, he skillfully maneuvered his hidden convoy through hundreds of mines German minesweepers had previously catalogued with skillful accuracy. The high tides had also lifted the naval squadron out of reach of most of the mines, as the Germans had also calculated.

Despite this, the *Sharnhorst* suffered serious damage from a single mine, significantly restricting its ability to maintain maximum speed. When the heavy fog dissipated and the driving rain subsided, the RAF realized the Royal Navy had been duped by the Germans. The decoded message was not a ruse! RAF fighter planes sprang into action to attack the disabled *Sharnhorst*, a weakness the RAF tried to use to their advantage.

Were it not for the overwhelming support of the swarming Luftwaffe, the wounded flagship would likely have perished. The *Sharnhorst* survived the air attacks sufficiently and rejoined the squadron. Support from her southern flanks from the menacing Luftwaffe allowed the severely damaged vessel to limp its way to safe harbor. Mission accomplished.

The belated British attack put the Royal Navy at a major disadvantage, not easily overcome. It was considered a stunning upset to the British Admiralty. When Admiral Ciliax, the German commander of the operation, sent a wire to Admiral Saalwachter in Paris confirming *Operation Cerebus* had been successfully completed, the *Times* reported on February 14th, *"Nothing more mortifying to the pride of our sea-power has happened since the seventeenth century. It spelled the end of the Royal Navy legend that in wartime no enemy battle fleet could pass through what we proudly call the English Channel."* (The Times, 1942)

*****

Admiral Canaris' previous attempt to tactfully enlighten the British about the *Channel Dash* had been too subtle, in view of the inability of Britain to corroborate the information. The abject failure had cost Abwehr dearly in achieving a German setback. As a direct result, this turning point necessitated that Abwehr become more emboldened in their subsequent communication flow to SIS in London.

It was time to utilize their double agent in Limoges, the woman working in the French Foreign Ministry. Abwehr had purposely never confronted nor challenged her complicity with British Intelligence, nor was it known to her AST superiors.

Anna was instructed to communicate directly with her Abwehr handler to review the specifics of her work, all of which had been meticulously scrutinized in accordance with Anna's prior direction. After subsequent discussion with the admiral and General von Brauchitsch, it was agreed this channel of communication should be more actively engaged than originally anticipated.

This link to British Intelligence was slowly and methodically reactivated to forward data concerning specific military capabilities and mobilization strategies. In the months following, and in a most glaring affront to the German war effort, even *Luftwaffe* battle orders were now trickle fed through the link, proving to be invaluable to British Intelligence.

Using the data being fed by Admiral Canaris, General Oster and Anna, the RAF could now determine where the majority of Luftwaffe aircraft were deployed at any given time. This highly valued information was vital to better enable British Intelligence to initiate a series of RAF air attacks. By adjusting the timing and locations of their bombing runs to cities less well defended, the attrition suffered by RAF bombing squadrons was noticeably reduced.

It was a continual balancing act requiring tedious hours of deception. The damage inflicted upon their own countrymen could not be measured quantitatively, but clearly helped to level the playing field for the Allied forces in an attempt to keep Hitler in check.

These treasonous actions by Abwehr's leadership dramatically escalated their risk of exposure to deadly reprisals from the Reich, often finding them questioning their mixed loyalties. By contrast, Anna felt no inner conflict and was secretly gratified to surreptitiously defy the Fuhrer in any manner she was able.

16
NO TURNING BACK

♂

OPINOGORA, POLAND

BY THE TIME AUTUMN ARRIVED IN 1942, JULIA HAD PROVEN
what Helena already knew to be true. She was capable of handling
greater responsibilities someday, in more significant ways; ones
to possibly take her away from this once quaint village and the
friendships she would leave behind. The future of Opinogora was
considered irrelevant to the needs of the German invaders and as
time passed, little of anything changed. The small village was lost
somewhere in time.

It was late autumn when Julia's opportunity came. About mid-
morning, she was informed by Stanley to join Sister Helena and
Father Breitkopf in his office. The day was a splendid one with typically seasonable breezes, scattering nature's colors about the outside
of the church; into the corners at one instant, and splaying them the
next, up and across the windows above. The cool of night still lingered and felt refreshing until the morning sun chased it away with
autumn's final wafts of soothing warmth. Mother Nature's benevo-
lence seemed in perfect balance.

Father broke off his conversation with Sister and rose amicably as
Julia approached to tap the inside of the already open door. "Good
morning, Julia. I hope this glorious day finds you well. Please sit, my
dear. I'll be with you in just a moment."

Father finished shuffling some paperwork into one neat pile of
documents. He was always so fastidious, assuring himself everything
was in perfect order before moving on to the next.

"Now then... Sister and I have been discussing how very supportive you have been during your time with us. From the day you arrived, your welcoming nature and warm heart have drawn so many to our humble doors."

Julia was visibly humbled by his effusive but genuine praise.

Sister Helena smiled proudly upon hearing Father's heartfelt commendations for their young companion. "It's true Julia. Your contributions have been most noteworthy, which have given us cause to have mixed feelings about what we must tell you. Please Father, I think it best if you begin."

Julia reacted immediately, naturally being quite mystified. "My word, Sister! Whatever you are about to say, I'm quite uncertain. Have I done anything to disappoint you both? I pray that isn't the case."

Father interjected, "Heaven's no, most certainly not, Julia. It's quite to the contrary. I received a telegram recently from Father Francis, who serves his parish west of Kutno in Konin. He has been a very close and trusted friend since we met at the seminary over twenty-five years ago. He's a wonderful and dedicated man I am proud to call my friend, and my brother in Christ." Julia looked attentively, as if waiting for a shoe to drop.

"Sadly, his brother was killed in the invasion. Although I barely knew him, I did have occasion to meet his wife a few years ago when I was passing through the city. The telegram from Francis informed me of her sudden and regrettable passing. Although she was unwell for some time, she now leaves behind her three young children."

"Oh, I am very sorry to hear that, Father." Julia's look of dismay became apparent as Father continued.

"The reason we are sharing this terrible circumstance is because Father Francis enquired if I could suggest someone to assist him as a custodian of the children. The last thing we want to do is separate the children from one another and the orphanages are already overflowing.

"It's a much larger parish than ours and there is a rectory attached to the church where the children lived with their parents. It's a fine home and there is a kindly housekeeper who takes care of cooking and cleaning and so forth. She is an elderly woman who is quite capable of doing her present chores as the matron of the house, but she cannot do much more. Looking after the children and taking care of the house on her own is simply too much for her to manage.

"You have a gentle and caring way about you Julia, especially your manner with young children. You are also an incredibly intelligent woman, something Father Francis is seeking. Sister and I immediately thought of you possibly becoming the caregiver of the three children. You would receive appropriate wages of course, but make no mistake, it will be a significant responsibility. In my opinion, this is a noble task worthy of your consideration. However, it is a decision only you can make."

Julia had been listening attentively and pondered the offer carefully. She wanted to help however, a yearning had developed inside her, ignited by her work on the Zegota project. It was most gratifying while it lasted but doing their job well had thankfully achieved the desired outcome; there were no longer any abandoned Jewish children in the diocese.

The experience stimulated her appetite temporarily but left her craving something more challenging, far greater than attending to mundane chores about the church and assisting with occasional childcare.

"I want to help of course, Father. I must admit though, when Sister Helena and I finished our work with Irena Sendler, I developed an appetite for greater possibilities for myself, or so I had hoped."

Julia dropped her gaze almost ashamedly, ever so briefly. After a few deliberate seconds of quiet thought, she looked directly into Father Breitkopf's eyes and resumed speaking.

"I want to be totally honest with you. As I expressed to you some time ago, I know I am capable of contributing much more." Julia saw concern on Father Breitkopf's face. It was not disappointment, but something of a more complex nature Julia could not accurately assess.

"I'm not saying *no*, but I hope you understand my initial hesitation." Again, she dropped her gaze only slightly, feeling she had disappointed Father with her own selfish ambitions.

Father reached out to gently take her hand and comfortingly offered, "I completely understand your dilemma. Sister and I feel the same way. There's more I must tell you, Julia, not to persuade you to do something you don't want to do, but to help you find the right fit. It is the reason we told Father Francis about you in the first place."

Julia's eyes were riveted to Father's in anticipation of what he was about to tell her. As he settled back into his chair, Father continued with some relevant and intriguing information.

"Two of the children are attending school during the day, so only the youngest one would require your supervision initially. Father Francis' housekeeper has graciously offered to occasionally assist with the children to free up some of your time should Father require more from you. It should provide you with ample time to assist in other ways to satisfy what you are looking for as well.

"I'm not at liberty to provide details because I pledged I would not do so. In all candor, I know very little, but my faith and confidence in Father Francis is enough to know the details are best deferred to him, if he decides you prove to be approachable for what he has in mind. I trust his good judgement will find the qualities in you we have discovered too... because of your specific accomplishments with Irena and Sister Helena, I might add."

Julia's ears perked up in an instant by Father's clarification that her involvement with Irena Sendler was a specific factor in his and Sister Helena's recommendation to Father Francis. To say Julia was inquisitive would be a serious understatement. It was notable that Father Breitkopf was intriguingly evasive about the details, but it was enough to suggest there could be so much more behind this offer than she had first thought.

Julia knew this day was bound to arrive, sooner or later. After only a moment of quiet consideration, she made a bold decision. "Yes, Father. I am willing to move on, especially to serve such an urgent need. I am delighted to be able to help. My only misgiving is leaving Opinogora. You have all been so kind and supportive of me since the day we met. I will be forever grateful for all you have done for me."

"It has been our pleasure to have known you, Julia. You have opened your caring heart and commendable passion for life to us, the very ideals our church has striven to achieve. You will not be soon forgotten. With your permission, I will contact Father Francis. I know he will be delighted to hear the news!"

In the coming days, Stanley took the news of Julia's departure the hardest. He was a sensitive man who often struggled to control his emotions. Despite knowing her decision to move on was best for her, it was heart-breaking for him personally.

"Before I found you sleeping on the bench in the garden, the past few years had left an emptiness inside of me you helped to heal, Julia."

He wiped his sleeve across his watering eyes and struggled to continue. "You are making the right decision Julia, and it was your strong spirit you awakened in me that will help me carry on. I'm very proud to have known you, young lady."

"Oh, Stanley... You always say the nicest things. I will miss you terribly."

Sister Helena quickly soothed Julia's concerns by stating, "We all have the same reluctance to see you leave us. You have been a gift from God since you walked through our door. It is time for us to share your gift with others who have more urgent needs than our own. You will do well there Julia. I know you will."

Although a tearful parting was inevitable, everyone understood Julia could give back so much more, especially to such a very deserving family. Father Breitkopf prepared his personal letter of reference and confirmed her sponsorship from the parish and Sister Helena. This time Julia understood the value of proper identification, which now included her handwritten letter of employment. Her safe passage to Konin should be well assured.

*****

Kutno served as a major hub for many train connections throughout the region and normally offered easy access directly to Konin. Currently however, the connecting line to Konin was still in considerable disrepair due to the extensive German bombardment during the invasion. Father Francis had graciously offered to meet Julia in Kutno upon her arrival to personally drive her the rest of the way to his parish.

The journey offered an entirely new perspective for Julia on what appeared to be a new world order. It would be only her second direct encounter with German authority, so logically she was still anxious. This time, however, she felt much more prepared. She was determined to cross this formerly impassable mental bridge still festering in her mind since Ciechanow, now almost two years ago. There would be no turning back this time, so she drew a deep breath, averted her gaze, and smiled ever so slightly.

Only a few words were exchanged between her and the officer and immediately after, she had no clear recollection of what they were! She realized that together with her faith and her complete set of documentation, she arose no suspicions throughout the process.

Julia's papers were in good order and passing through the Nazi security check was uneventful. Thankfully, the former dreaded moment was no longer of consequence. It was a clear indication of her preparedness and increasingly developing maturity.

Were it not for the graciousness of others, specifically Mother Helena, Father Breitkopf, Stanley and yes, Henry, she believed she would have still been foraging for food and shelter in the forest... or worse. She shuddered at the very thought.

The train ticket provided a comfortable tour covering about 140 kilometers of a badly wounded Poland, but what remained of it served as an enduring framework not fully broken. These moments were no longer an ordeal she had to endure, inch by painstaking inch, to which she had become accustomed since her escape from Pobereze. This was a taste of civility she enjoyed immensely and did not take lightly. It was an opening through new doors, leading to her still uncertain future.

Alone with her private thoughts, Julia had learned first-hand, the twists and turns fortune afforded her. Were the days of despair finally behind her? She thought it best to savor these moments while she could, not certain if they might suddenly be ripped away because of strange circumstances, totally outside of her own control. The answers were not to be found here and would continue to elude her.

The passengers in her railway car appeared to be mostly business-people. They were nicely attired and although there was only subdued, leisurely conversation among a few, there was a restfulness surrounding them, with no immediate presence of danger. The tension she and others may have initially shared at the boarding station subsided considerably, having gradually become a more natural state of normality. Julia soaked up this experience with a mixture of growing independence, and overwhelming gratitude.

The train meandered steadily through mostly desolate farm fields once yielding plentiful crops, now showing few signs of life as the season grew short. They provided soothing solace to Julia's tired eyes. The adrenalin rush of her emotional morning departure and the anxiety of passing through security were finally taking their toll. When combined with the steady rumble of the tracks below her, humming with consistent regularity and a gentle almost imperceptible rocking, Julia peacefully nodded off to restful sleep.

The journey continued through several cities she had never known to exist, including Glinojeck and Bielsk, and the train was now approaching the city of Plock. At each brief stop, a few fellow passengers exchanged places with other travellers whose reasons for this trip would never be known to her. The majority carried on, presumably heading for the city of Kutno, as was Julia. It was a common junction point leading to numerous places primarily to the south and southwest.

The train slowed on its approach to Plock, which was known to have been home to a disproportionally high percentage of Jews when the war began. Julia had only scant knowledge of this circumstance. Nor was she aware these people had been essentially wiped out since 1939 by the particularly thorough methods of the Gestapo.

This area was now one of the Nazi strongholds, and it was controlled with an iron fist. Even if she possessed such awareness, it would not likely have deferred her travel plans this day. The stop here would be no different than the others, or so she thought.

Julia was seated near the front of the train, on the south side of the car from which passengers disembarked, and she was close enough to observe the sparsely gathered groups of people scattered from one end of the station to the other. It was entertaining to her as she fantasized briefly about who these people were, and what their stories could tell in this place and time in history. Closer to full stop, she ceased fantasizing; the moment she saw the German military presence awaiting them.

These were fully armed troopers lined up on both sides of the passenger cars. Among them were several rigid looking officers of some much higher ranking, judging by their caps, and colorful insignias of apparent rank... and of course, the prominently placed Nazi swastikas on the shoulders of their uniforms. Julia's pulse instinctively quickened to pound deep within her chest. Her stomach muscles tightened as the stress began to mount.

When the train slowed to a brief crawl and came to a full stop, armed troopers mounted the steps in unison, blocking the attempts of any passenger trying to exit. What was happening was unexpected and unnerving, but it was futile to prevent. *"Don't make direct eye contact, don't give them attitude, and most importantly do not panic,"* she told herself.

One of the officers, no doubt Gestapo, mounted the stairs and climbed into Julia's car. He was the first to intrude upon the unsuspecting travelers. He stood silently, almost stoically as he closely scrutinized the scene in front of him.

"You will produce your papers and open your luggage for inspection… immediately! Do as I say, or you will remain here in Plock for longer than you can imagine!" The car was about half full so there was ample space for unimpeded cooperation, which was exactly what everyone did. Through the muffled sounds of subdued mumbling and the shuffling of baggage, a voice spoke out.

"May I ask what is happening, Sir? How long will this take? Forgive me officer, but I must be in Kutno this afternoon on business matters of some importance," enquired a middle aged, and well-dressed man.

"That is none of your fucking business!" The officer paused momentarily as he bent over slightly to glare frighteningly into the man's nervous and shifting eyes, as if to stare deeply into the man's already disturbed soul.

"Take this one outside!" he instructed two of the troopers. Immediately they forcefully seized the man, who did not resist in any way, and they threw him out the door to the concrete platform below. As he tumbled, his glasses fell to the ground and skittered away from him. The officer followed his men outside, walking slowly toward him and in so doing, crushed the man's glasses under his heavy black boot.

The officer said nothing and only nodded to the two troopers. Without a word they both stepped forward pulling the passenger to his feet. They repeatedly punched the unsuspecting gentleman in the stomach, forcing him to collapse again to the concrete platform. He was dazed and bloody as the officer approached, and the two assailants hauled the man very roughly to his feet. Julia and others on board could easily see the disheveled man from their vantage point.

With no remorse or explanation, the officer calmly enquired of him, "Now, where are your papers?"

The staggering passenger was spitting blood and he fumbled through his coat pocket awkwardly as the officer, politely it seemed, calmly extended his gloved hand to receive the identification he requested.

"Ahh, you are a banker. Just what the world needs, another bean counter! And your purpose in Kutno?"

"I am... I'm a senior Vice President of the Central Bank." He was grimacing with pain and out of breath after the beating, spitting blood as he tried to speak. "My duties often take me from city to city... I meant no disrespect, Sir."

"Perhaps the next time, you will learn to simply keep your mouth shut until asked to open it!"

"Next!" he hollered in the direction of the doorway of the car nearest him. The troopers dragged the assaulted passenger and unceremoniously threw him near the foot of the rear door of the same car.

In groups of five, each passenger stood before one of three Gestapo officers, exiting the door in the front and re-entering at the rear. The interrogations were concise and moved briskly without further incident. Thankfully, Julia's encounter was brief and uneventful as well. Their point had been made clear.

The process continued from car to car as the gang of bullies repeated the process farther down the line, leaving a few troopers standing guard beside the lead car.

Perhaps some thirty minutes later, Julia could clearly hear shouting from some commotion several cars down the line. Evidently, someone had panicked, perhaps someone without papers, or some contraband yet to be discovered. Within seconds there were more commands shouted, and a man could be seen running from the confrontation back toward the more weakly fortified lead car of the train.

Julia and the passengers were all absorbed in what was happening, when the panicked man suddenly began to slow his pace. Some short distance in front of the man's intended path, the adjacent guards by Julia's car had raised their rifles. They aimed and fired several times.

Julia, and no doubt many others, jumped involuntarily as the echoes of the gunfire reverberated off the concrete platform. How very loud was the sudden and unexpected sound striking fear into the hearts of everyone. The sharp crack and recoil of the rifles were significantly amplified between the station walls and the length of the train. Julia's entire frame tightened.

The shots proved to be lethal, and the man collapsed at the feet of these henchmen. His eyes were still open, and pools of blood immediately oozed onto the concrete around his upper torso. No one even bothered to move his crumpled body from where it lay. The terror, intrusively thrust upon everyone in Julia's car, was beyond control and composure became impossible to maintain, as evidenced by the now sobbing and weeping passengers who bore witness. It no doubt extended throughout the cars behind them as well.

It was less than an hour, when as suddenly as this ordeal began, it ended, without explanation, without provocation, and with nothing accomplished but for the harsh reminder of the reality of war. Within ten minutes, Julia could again hear the rumbling of the tracks and felt the gentle rocking of the car, as if nothing of any consequence had happened that cold November day.

*****

Kutno was strategically located almost precisely in the geographic center of Poland. Situated less than fifty kilometers southwest from Plock, it had survived the *Battle of Bzura* in 1939. As a direct result of the heroic defense of the Polish military, the Germans were forced to re-think their strategy before eventually overpowering the Polish resistance.

This major battle was a significant stand by the overmatched Poles, effectively delaying the inevitable fall of Warsaw, albeit for only a few weeks of time. This bloody and hard-fought battle resulted in the deaths of 8,000 Germans and almost 20,000 Polish forces.

Julia did not know the extent of the violence preceding her arrival in Kutno. She was just thankful to be here safely, having no idea what might have transpired in the past. It was well past dark when the train began to slow again. The interior car lamps were dimly lit. Julia strained to see but it was impossible to identify anything outside in the pitch black. After a very long journey, the train gradually began to crawl as before, edging inch by inch before it came to a full stop.

Her memories of the extensive devastation of Pultusk were especially vivid and still haunted her from time to time; those of Ciechanow far less so. She didn't know quite what to expect in Kutno, but it felt very satisfying to stand and stretch a little before she gathered her luggage. She exited the train with the passengers she had shared so much with but had never met. It was only a short walk east to the *Hotel of the Inner City*. The signage reassured her of the proper direction and several other passengers were heading the same way.

She was originally instructed to wait for Father Francis' arrival inside the hotel. He insisted to Father Breitkopf this would be much safer for a young woman travelling alone, than to leave her waiting at the station under the watchful eyes of the Reich.

While the area appeared in good order, there were several job sites still teeming with laborers of every sort. It was well after dark but the movement of heavy machinery and the coming and going of trucks continued to create considerable commotion, causing stale-smelling, sooty clouds of heavy construction dust reflecting through the bright floodlights. Even at night, the military presence was highly visible as they appeared to be randomly checking documents to keep the final passengers of the day from lingering.

It was only a short walk to the hotel and due to her delayed arrival, Father Francis had already settled into a chair by the fire adjacent to the lobby. It was a simple task to find him. He was sitting alone with his priest's collar visibly exposed. He was sipping tea while reading the local paper.

By this time, a few other passengers began to enter the hotel lobby, mostly young couples and a few elderly gentlemen. Julia was easy to identify when she entered the main doors, being the only single young woman of the few people gathered there.

Upon entering, Julia scanned the lobby, catching the eye of Father Francis right away. When their eyes met, he stood to greet her.

"Good evening, young lady. I presume you must be Julia?" He tucked the folded newspaper under his arm and extended the other. "Father Francis, at your service. So very nice to meet you!"

"Thank you, Father, as I am to meet you. How considerate it is for you to meet me here. I became concerned about our delay, but it couldn't be helped. I apologize for the inconvenience it may have caused."

He was an engaging and rather plump fellow, and she felt trustful of him, particularly as he was so highly regarded by Father Breitkopf. Father Francis' gesture of courtesy toward her would be a good foundation for Julia to build upon she thought, and from the outset, she was grateful to have been referred to him.

Once settled in the car, casual conversation flowed freely between them and in a short while, Julia felt increasingly reassured by his pleasant company. Father confided to Julia the story of what had transpired to the parents of the orphans she was about to meet. She had no trepidations about helping this family whatsoever and now that she was exchanging kindnesses with Father Francis, she could only imagine the joy of meeting the young ones.

Their father was Father Francis' deceased brother who had lived with his wife and family in the Rectory. After his death, Father Francis had pledged to help their mother in any way he could, as if they were his own. They were, after all, his two twin nieces and his young nephew, and he loved them dearly.

"I am not accustomed to seeing so many German troops in the city and about the station. Opinogora has become a forgotten place that mustn't interest them any longer." Julia casually commented.

"Perhaps so, but here the story is starkly different." Father Francis explained. "The rail lines were severely damaged during the German invasion, but the strategic importance of the railway caused the Germans to use forced laborers to affect the necessary rebuilding. As you could see when you arrived, the shift work carries on twenty-four hours of every day, even through the night."

Father stopped speaking for a few minutes while he navigated the city roads to locate the main highway to Poznan.

"Sorry Julia, there are always roadblocks and endless detours because of the extensive construction. I must pay close attention because detours can change from day to day." Julia obliged him by remaining quiet to allow him to focus his attention. He resumed speaking when the task was completed.

"Between Kutno and Konin, the Polish underground has recently coordinated the sabotage of railway tunnels, hundreds of kilometers of rail lines, and compromised oil supplies and repair facilities with reckless abandon: the bloody fools. There are no trains running west of Kutno, nor will there be, until control is fully restored by the Germans. The hunt for saboteurs is always ongoing."

Julia intervened to explain her lateness. "There were soldiers and Gestapo officers who delayed our departure from Plock, which is why we were so late arriving. It was most disturbing. We were roughly treated and forced off the train. Why, they even shot one of the passengers before our very eyes!"

Father continued, explaining, "They probably weren't looking for Jews since they previously herded out every last one they could find in Plock. The search was likely more about finding possible saboteurs. Our parish is far enough from here, so other than a few random visits here and there, they leave us pretty much alone."

Julia was surprised Father Francis had his own car. She didn't intend to be intrusive, but she was intrigued. "You must be fortunate to have kept your car, Father."

"Yes. From time to time, I am given some privileges others are not. Terrible things have happened to the Catholic Church which disturb me greatly, but I always do my utmost to cooperate with whatever the Germans ask of me. I'm just one of a few priests continuing to provide religious services in occupied Poland.

"I am told more than eighty percent of our parishes have been shut down in the German sector. Most of the clergy were taken into custody and have just disappeared. Many of them are acquaintances of mine. It's been quite frightful, I must say."

Julia was surprised, and even disturbed, Father Francis seemed so glib about his cooperation with the Germans. She understood his precarious circumstances, but it was his general air of indifference about doing so; it was almost as if he was proud of having earned their favoritism. He had apparently been granted the consideration of the Reich permitting him to continue using his own car, for reasons he chose not to explain further.

It was always an awkward topic of discussion to turn Jews away, Father explained, as it was with Sister Helena. It was incongruent for the Catholic Church to do so, but the very survival of the church could not be taken for granted in these unique and troubling times. Co-operation with the German captors was often coerced, and as it turned out, inevitable.

The roads outside the city were in decent repair and within less than two hours, they accessed the property of *Our Lady of the Scapular*, on the outskirts of what remained of the main city. It was located on the shore of the Warta River about eighty kilometers west of Kutno. It was a beautiful property, and the fine old church was perched near the top of a gradually rising stretch of ground. The relatively large parking area caught Julia's immediate attention.

"I've never seen so much parking space beside any church I have attended. How many of the congregation could possibly afford the luxury of having their own car, I wonder?" she asked inquisitively.

"You would be surprised, Julia. Before the invasion, this church was always well attended. The local parishioners simply walked or used their wagons or carriages, but now we have numerous people of financial means coming here from miles around, many of them relocated Germans. It is their generous support keeping our coffers full."

Father Francis sighed with fatigue after the long drive, and he parked his car close to the side entrance of his residence. "Now then, let me help you with your bags and show you to your room. Bronia will introduce you to the children and give you the full tour in the morning."

The vestry was to the left and rear side of the church. It over-looked an open elevation facing the river's edge, not easily seen in the blackness of night through the single row of cedar trees bordering the eastern edge of the old cemetery. The gentle breeze was negligible and almost imperceptible this night, and smoke slowly streamed undisturbed from the stone chimney. The church and vestry, although in modest disrepair, possessed a very inviting feel.

"This is the entrance to my office and my personal residence, which I use often for business and parochial matters. Just follow me this way to the entrance of the main house." Julia thought it odd that Father distinguished between *business and parochial* matters. What other business could he have other than parochial ones?

As they entered, the warm glow of the interior revealed a soft and inviting hue of comfort. It would be a fine reprieve for both weary new friends and was a pleasurable feeling Julia would always remember. The coziness of the setting was akin to coming home again, one she could only imagine, given the fact she had never known such a fine home as this.

Before saying good night, Father directed Julia to a small room and washroom of her own, situated next to the children's rooms, and he excused himself for the evening. Although it had been a long journey and she was anxious to sleep, she could not wait till morning to meet them; Louisa and Katia, twin girls who were then seven years old, and Paul who had just turned three.

After Father Francis retired for the night, no doubt exhausted by the day's travel, Julia impatiently but quietly, opened the door to peek into the children's room.

She had not seen the sight of sleeping children, cuddled peacefully under their heavy bedding as they were, since her brother and sister did so in what seemed so very long ago. Julia's eyes glistened at the memory, however, as was her habit she quickly righted herself and shut out the warmth of her own childhood moments. She remained incapable of overcoming her deepest feelings of unease her painful memories evoked.

It had been a very long day, as she lay stretched out upon the welcoming fresh smelling bedsheets. She stared aimlessly at the barren ceiling to reflect upon the events of her day, thankful she had arrived safely. The blissful peacefulness was broken only by the steady *tick tock* of the mantle clock. It was only moments before sleep overcame her.

*****

By early morning, Julia arose to the sound of a teapot whistling in the kitchen, announcing the beginning of the new day. Feeling embarrassed for fear of oversleeping she quickly washed and dressed, fussing with her hair only briefly. Not looking her best, she opened her door to see an elderly woman who had started preparing the morning breakfast.

"A very good morning to you, my dear! My name is Bronia. Welcome to Father Francis' home. You must be Julia."

"Yes, I am. Father Francis spoke so highly of you on our way from Kutno. It's wonderful to meet you, Bronia." Julia extended her hand. Thoughtfully, Bronia paused momentarily to dry her hands on her apron and in the same motion pulled Julia toward her to offer an affectionate embrace.

"I'm certain of that!" she giggled sarcastically. "We'll have time for chit-chat later but do go wake the children and get them ready for eats, and then it's off to school for them."

"May I go in and wake them now?" Julia asked uncertainly.

"If you don't go into their room, you will have no chance of waking them. Now... Go!" Bronia shooed her away as she turned back to tending the stove. She was very blunt, but certainly not in a mean way.

Julia gently tapped on the door and apprehensively entered the room, noting the children appeared not to have moved an inch all night. The bedding was barely disturbed. Oh, to be young again, and to savor the sleep of an innocent child one more time, she thought.

After a gentle nudging, the children quickly became alert at the sight of a fully-grown stranger in their room and were momentarily startled. "Where is Uncle and... and who are you? ... Are you our new Nanny? Please say yes!" exclaimed either Katia or Louisa, as Julia knew neither. A broad, beaming smile creased Julia's face at this heartwarming greeting. These little ones were so delighted to meet her and were evidently eagerly anticipating her arrival.

It became evident over breakfast the girls were equally precocious and full of questions exuding a natural sense of enthusiasm for life. "How old are you? Do you still go to school? Where are you from? Where is your family?" and on and on. Julia felt a new sense of celebrity she found refreshing. She told them what she could but promised them right after school there would be more time to play *twenty questions*. She had many to ask of them as well.

Her first task was to walk the girls to school less than a kilometer away. *"It is easy to find,"* and *"You will really like it,"* they assured her. Young Peter was just three years old, and he clung tightly to Julia's hand during the entire walk to school and back, not saying much at all, as the girls were intent to keep the conversation flowing among the three of them.

Louisa and Katia were both seven and a half years of age, in their third grade of school. The best part was recess, and their *"friends were not as many as we had last year because so many of them had to move away."* Only later would Julia learn that about a third of the population had been Jewish and had been removed forcibly when the Germans arrived.

It was the beginning of a beautiful friendship between Julia and the children, and it developed more fully in only a few days. They evidently adored their uncle, but the passing of their mother was not so very long ago in their short lifetimes. Little Peter had no memory of her whatsoever. It was sad, but perhaps better than to mourn the death of a loved one at such tender ages. Julia was determined to help bridge the unfortunate gap as best she could.

In the weeks following, routines were established, and Julia's focus was demanded every minute of every day, or so it seemed. She was very happy to be so absorbed and involved in all aspects of the children's lives. It was fulfilling. Father Francis was completely occupied with his daily regimen of responsibilities pertaining to the needs of his parishioners and distanced himself from the children, or so it seemed.

His personal area in the vestry was a much grander one than Julia had seen in her experience. It featured the separate entrance to his office, next to his private rooms. Other than requiring routine cleaning, these rooms were completely off-limits to the children and the hired help. Respecting his privacy was a matter never to be questioned.

Julia further noted Father Francis had frequent private meetings with some questionable characters, many of whom were German officers. It was not uncommon for four or five vehicles to be parked outside the church at the same time, some of which were military ones.

It was difficult to miss seeing them through the windows of the main house and loud voices were frequently heard laughing or shouting through the common walls adjoining that section of the vestry. These matters were well beyond Julia's purview and frankly, were none of her concern. It was intriguing to her though.

When the twins were at school, Julia played incessantly with Peter and puttered about with Bronia assisting her in maintaining the family home. Julia had always been a hard worker and was easily adaptable to new situations. Never one to sit idly by, she was a seemingly perfect fit for what was expected of her. Julia was confident she was in a good place at this stage of her life.

*****

As the weather became colder, so too did Julia's feelings toward Father Francis. They were founded upon her initial suspicions about his privileged status, as further evidenced by his growing familiarity with the Germans. His comfort level with Julia, however, gradually became more trusting when she was occasionally called upon to make cocktails and serve pastries to his special guests. At first, her services were required only when Bronia was otherwise pre-occupied, but over time Julia's youthful frame and pretty features evidently pleased the leering men.

It was not a role she welcomed, but the occasional flirtations she simply interpreted as being harmless distractions. Although sexist in nature, they fell well short of being offensive to her. Father Francis, to his credit, very rarely found it necessary to tactfully intervene.

One afternoon when young Paul was napping, Father Francis summoned Julia to his office. For Julia and Bronia, discussions in his office were very infrequent, so the request fed Julia's growing curiosity.

"How may I help you Father... a cup of tea perhaps?" Julia offered as she entered his open door.

"No, no... that won't be necessary, but I do need to discuss something of importance with you. Please sit, Julia. Make yourself comfortable."

He gestured her to the seat in front of his antique and strikingly beautiful mahogany desk. Leather trim had been tastefully inlaid on the border of the top, carefully detailed to highlight the natural fine grain of the shimmering lacquered finish. It was lovely indeed, and Father cherished it. He was particularly pleased to have it available for his private use and proudly stated it was a gift from one of his German acquaintances, as further evidence of their gratitude.

"We don't often have the time to speak together, but I want you to know how very happy I am with what you have accomplished with the children, first and foremost. They and Bronia are delighted having you in our home. I too, am so pleased you are here, Julia. You have taken such loving care of the children and by doing so, you have taken the burden of their care off my tired shoulders. Thank you, young lady."

It was the first time in her three months here that he ever referred to her in such personal and familiar terms. She took note of his more sensitive manner toward her.

"I have recently communicated with Father Breitkopf about your accomplishments with the children and with other minor tasks about our diocese. He has reassured me of your proven trustworthiness at his church and is confident you are perfectly suited to assist me with greater challenges needing to be dealt with by my office from time to time. This would include your recent work as my hostess for certain high-profile guests.

"Your unquestioning co-operation in that capacity was not intended to be part of your area of responsibility, yet you did as I asked, without complaint. Your valuable contribution to making my guests comfortable means a great deal to me. They are as impressed with you as I am. I thank you for your consistent demonstration of your loyalty to me, Julia."

"Father, I do not mind if my responsibilities sometimes overlap those of Bronia, nor does she. It is best we keep working together as a family, for the best interests of the children. They are important to me, to be sure, and I have grown very fond of them. I am happy here and will always do as you and Bronia ask of me."

"That's precisely the attitude I am looking for, Julia, and as an expression of my sincere appreciation, this is for you." Quite unexpectedly, Father took an envelope from his desk drawer, and simply slid it within Julia's reach.

"What is this, Father?" Julia enquired.

"A little something extra for your dedication and support. You deserve it."

Julia timidly reached for the mysterious package, which was unsealed and without removing anything, she peered inside. Shocked, Julia gasped at the significant bundle of Reichsmarks inside. "Father, this is a thoughtful gesture, but I assure you it is not necessary. This is... this is too much!"

"Nonsense. I insist that *it is necessary*... and well deserved. I only ask that you keep this just between us. Would that be alright, Julia?"

Julia nodded appreciatively, not certain as to what more she could say. This appeared to be more money than her entire monthly wages!

"I want you to continue impressing my guests, just as you have always done. You add immeasurably to what I have striven to accomplish with these people. They take very good care of me, so I want to take good care of you as well. I have assured them your German is far from fluent, and except for only one or two of the senior officers, including Colonel Claus von Stauffenberg, none of them speak Polish very well, some not at all.

"They feel more comfortable because of your apparent inability to speak German. Due to the nature of our discussions, they must be kept to the strict confines of my office. Our church provides a haven for each of them since our agenda is often unsuitable for a military office environment. Much safer to address these matters off site, away from prying eyes and tape-recorded conversations. Do you understand what I am saying Julia?"

"I do, Father. However, I must remind you my German has significantly improved. Other than many technical military terms, I understand most of their conversations." Julia clarified.

"Yes, I am aware of that fact, Julia, however they are not. I have noticed when certain graphic topics are revealed in our discussions with them, you do not flinch or cast disparaging glances. You appear indifferent and remain solely focused on the menial tasks you are given. You appear unaffected by some shocking revelations that come to light now and then. Your steady composure impresses me, Julia."

"What is discussed in these meetings is none of my affair. I assumed my apparent indifference would serve you better. The less I appear to understand suits all of us."

"There is one more matter I want to suggest to you which I trust you will not misconstrue." Julia's brow was raised for a split second. Father continued, "You are a pretty young lady, and I want you to always look your best for these occasions. Please help yourself to the dresses that belonged to my sister-in-law. She always looked particularly beautiful in them. I have no doubt they will serve you well too.

"Anita was about your size and Bronia is an excellent seamstress to help with any alterations they may require. I want to create a very positive and comfortable atmosphere for my guests to speak freely and openly, and your appearance will help to disarm them."

"How so, Father?"

"I know a thing or two about powerful men. They tend to speak more openly and aggressively in front of a beautiful woman. I think their underlying intention is to impress a desirable woman by doing so. I should know… I've heard thousands of their private confessions."

*****

In the months following, the Church of Our Lady of The Scapular continued hosting numerous meetings for Father Francis, Colonel von Stauffenberg, and the usual group of attendees. Only on rare occasions were the doors opened to others of various rank, who no doubt had a unique skillset or specific influence serving the general objective.

Keeping the Catholic Church protected from the unflagging determination of the Fuhrer to eradicate it, was thought to be the original premise, in Julia's mind. As noble as this cause was, Julia had come to the realization there was far more about the nature of these meetings than she had first imagined; something much more sinister.

Since the invasion began, the Catholic Church vehemently opposed any form of foreign domination and became progressively more proactive in defending Polish nationalism. In response to this opposition, about eighty percent of Catholic clergy had been imprisoned by the Nazis in the Dachau Concentration Camp, many of whom were tortured and executed. It was a ruthless extermination motivated to stop the growing resistance of the Catholic Church to Nazi decrees. Of even greater consequence was the Nazis' brutal attempt to denigrate and suppress Roman Catholicism entirely.

The Archbishop of Krakow, Adam Sapieha, was the head of the Polish Church at the time and spoke openly about the shame of the Nazi reign of terror. His resistance efforts were influential when he established a secretive seminary to serve as an act of cultural resistance. As history would reveal, one of his seminarians was Karol Wojtyla, who several years later would become known to the world as Pope John Paul II.

Largely due to Sapieha's efforts, the Polish Underground Home Army and the Catholic Church were fundamentally interlinked for the entire duration of the war. As an independence activist, he worked arm in arm with the Polish government-in-exile to oppose Nazi brutality and threats against the Catholic Church. From as early as 1936 up to late 1942, the widely unpopular dismantling of Roman Catholicism by Hitler met with profound and growing opposition from within his own ranks.

As a direct result, there had been numerous futile attempts on the Fuhrer's life, but as the war progressed, these attempts became more ominous and extremely well organized by high-ranking military and political conspiracies to overthrow the Reich.

Many assassination attempts becoming known to the Reich were thwarted and dealt with ruthlessly, but numerous others continued to silently proliferate to achieve their deadly objectives. When the Fuhrer was informed of the growing numbers of nefarious plots against him, he was forced to reconsider the wisdom of his maltreatment and religious persecution of Roman Catholicism which had no doubt, inspired many of his domestic and internal party enemies.

A compromise of sorts provided a way for the Fuhrer to save face by discreetly acquiescing to growing pressure against him. On the clear condition the church ceased all political interference, Hitler decreed Catholic Churches would be allowed to survive and would henceforth no longer suffer Nazi oppression.

Although very strict limitations were imposed as to where, when, and by what means church functions would be permitted, the intent to further decimate the church relented. Persecution of the Jews, however, continued unabated and despite many religious leaders continuing to use their platforms to speak out against Jewish persecution, a significant percentage of Catholics and clergy incredibly began to vocally declare Jewish persecution by the Reich was justified. Many believed if Roman Catholics supported anti-Semitism, the church would have a better chance of avoiding Hitler's wrath.

To this end, as the Christmas season of 1942 approached, Nazi tolerance of the Catholic Church gradually became less radical and provocative. In its place, there was a degree of cautious optimism by the church for the re-emerging co-existence of limited religious freedom for Catholics, albeit to continue under the watchful scrutiny of the Third Reich.

17
SUSPICIONS ARE CONFIRMED

♂

WIORY, KONIN DISTRICT OF POLAND

IT HAD BEEN ALMOST TWO WEEKS SINCE THE FIRST DAY OF Advent. At the request of Father Francis, Julia had been taking on a few additional responsibilities in the church itself, working with him more closely than originally intended. Julia's familiarity with the congregation also developed, particularly during the recent weeks leading up to Christmas.

Before every Sunday service, the children would attend Sunday school, a central aspect of their education. During this time, Julia would customarily assist Father Francis with the meet-and-greet tradition each week at the doors of the church, picking up where she had left off in Opinogora. It was a tradition to welcome not only the regulars, but also to meet those newcomers whose lives had cause to drift; many seeking to find their way to God again.

The ensuing weeks were extremely busy to the extent the matters of war seemed to be left behind. Even the frequency of Colonel von Stauffenberg's meetings had been curtailed, or so it would seem, until the holiday season had passed peacefully. Other than very superficial searches of the church premises by the Reich, basically just going through the motions to seek out Jewish refugees, the presence of any German military who were not involved in Father's meetings became less frequent. These unannounced visits no longer intimidated anyone and for the most part, the village was left undisturbed.

Early each morning, before the children were awake, Julia kept abreast of political and global events by reading various newspapers.

Her understanding of world issues, despite being heavily biased by Nazi propaganda, often encouraged further discussion with Father Francis during the rare occasions he was available. He would frequently speak of the occupation with Julia, and through his firsthand discussions with his military contacts, his personal opinions were always insightful and provided another biased view of German perspectives as well.

The more Julia learned about the war, she became increasingly determined to stay as far west as she was able, even though almost fifty percent of Poland was already occupied by the Germans. The Russians controlled everything from the east.

"I see you often spend what little time you have to relax by reading my newspapers. I encourage you to keep doing so, but may I also suggest you browse through my books as well. It is a wonderful collection I am very proud to own. It seems such a waste not to share them with you."

"Why, thank you, Father! I only see them when I'm dusting the shelves and tidying up. I think they would be too difficult for me to read, but I would like to try, with your permission."

"Of course, Julia. They will likely push your limits, but that's the only way to learn. You have a sharp mind. I have no doubt you will enjoy reading them. If you like, I can even help you from time to time with your comprehension of these absorbing stories. It's not often I can discuss these books with anyone. I can recommend a few of my favorites to get you started if you wish."

"Thank you, Father. That would be wonderful, and you know I will be very careful with them!" Julia responded excitedly.

Over time, in combination with reading the Scriptures and local newspapers, Father Francis' encouragement for Julia to read more challenging books had a profound effect on her command of Polish and German. Her comprehension and articulate expressions would continue to become increasingly more refined, much faster in fact, than Father had anticipated. Although it was a struggle for her initially, she was doggedly persistent and not surprisingly, her self-confidence continued to steadily blossom as well.

She became Father's only learned audience of one, since others in the village approached him about matters mostly pertaining to God. Many of them simply lacked the mental capacity to consider the politics of war, most of which were beyond their immediate priorities about how best to ensure their family's survival. For the time being Julia was satisfied, and thankful she and the children could be in the safe confines of the Father's care.

The genuine fondness she felt for these people, particularly for the children, was something to which she was growing more accustomed, especially as her attachment to them was maturing within her. These thoughts were becoming more difficult for Julia to resist and were yet another indication of her continual inner conflicts.

Sentiment was a characteristic she had been able to avoid, as much by circumstance, as personal choice. Notwithstanding these strong yet unfamiliar feelings, Julia's vigilant habits remained deeply ingrained throughout her adolescence. In the recesses of her mind, she consistently vowed to herself she would need these habits again at some point, when she resumed pushing west toward the Allies.

*****

It was ten days until Christmas, and Julia's more proactive interactions with the congregation, both Polish and German had been noted by Father Francis. She had a certain magnetism about her that drew others in. Over her time here, she was slowly becoming more self-confident and was an integral part of what this parish had been sorely lacking. She was approachable, not only to the members of the parish, but also to Father Francis and particularly the patrons who contributed so generously to the church.

"Julia, I need your opinion on some changes I am considering regarding the Christmas services this year. Would you be so kind to bring us both some coffee and join me in the office to discuss things? It shouldn't take more than a few minutes. I'm sure Bronia can manage the children for you."

"Of course, Father. I'll meet you there." Julia obliged as she always tried to do.

It was a quiet and peaceful December day. Although cold, the air outside was calm, leaving the dormant trees and surrounding shrubs still as a painting, nestled peacefully among the shallow snow drifts from a few days ago. Every now and then, the crusty surfaces brilliantly reflected the sparkling morning sunshine, so bright it was painful to the naked eye.

Julia found Father Francis already deeply ensconced in some financial documents, which must have fully absorbed his interest as he was startled by her prompt return. Julia's sudden appearance surprised him briefly when she entered the room without knocking. She was still holding the silver tray replete with cream, sugar, and a few baked biscuits. It required both hands to safely carry her delightful bounty. She stopped in her tracks with embarrassment.

"I'm so sorry if I am disturbing you, Father. My hands were full. Is this still a good time? Perhaps I could return later if you prefer?"

"No, no. I was so immersed in some reports I prepared for the colonel. I just lost myself in the details. But do come in, please. Everything is fine." He walked out from behind his desk to join her in his sitting area next to the coffee table by the fire.

"I'm looking forward to my coffee. I missed my first one this morning, for some reason or other. Please, help yourself, Julia."

"So, you wanted to speak with me. How may I help you today?"

"Yes, very much so. Finally, the Christmas services are upon us and although I am delighted, we have a logistics problem to solve, and I need your input. During my financial reviews, our efforts to build a firm financial foundation for the church have not only been met, but they have also significantly surpassed our expectations. To the benefit of everyone in our parish, a large part of the excess is due to the generosity of our German military connections." He paused momentarily to sip his coffee.

"Why, that's wonderful news, Father! There are so many worthy causes we are better able to support within the parish, I'm certain. This is all due to your tireless work, Father. You should be very proud of your accomplishments."

"Thank you, Julia, however, here is our current dilemma. Few Catholic Churches continue to remain open to provide the Holy Communion even at this sacred time, however our parish is one of them. Since the occupation, we have always been well supported, both spiritually and financially by the people we serve, especially the Germans.

"Despite this, the local Poles are entitled to enjoy this holy occasion too, especially since we have missed two years of Christmas services celebrating the eve of our Lord's birth. But... there is not enough room available, even with two separate services on Christmas Eve.

"How would you feel if we reserve that specific holy night for the Germans, who have supported us so richly? It would mean our Polish parishioners would celebrate the night before. We could even expand the services to include a full buffet dinner to mark the occasion. What do you think? You know our congregation as well as me, maybe more so."

Julia sat quietly for a moment before responding. Father waited silently, but restlessly, and somewhat anxiously, shifting in his chair and repeatedly sipped his coffee to relax his nerves. "I see our predicament. Clearly you must consider the Germans, especially so for Colonel von Stauffenberg. Without his efforts the church itself would possibly not continue to exist. He is the only one you must consider, to my mind. The rest is simply politics and hurt feelings... Yes... we Poles shall overcome."

Father stammered a bit with the clarity of Julia's thinking. She was quite correct about the colonel, but Father never expressed his own feelings about the matter quite so succinctly.

"Well, how shall I say this, I... I'm a bit flabbergasted, Julia. Perhaps it is you who should be wearing this collar, not me!" he suggested sarcastically. "With your growing influence, I needed to know where you would stand on this issue. Do you think our Polish friends will be satisfied as clearly as yourself?"

"Perhaps *satisfied* is the best word to describe them. We have all been so downtrodden for far too long. Let's all just be content to enjoy the season and our good fortune because the colonel has found us. Everything will be fine. I'm sure of it. And I particularly like the idea of a wonderful banquet following the late afternoon service too. An excellent act of spiritual diplomacy, Father!" Julia and Father both enjoyed a good laugh together.

*****

Tomorrow was the day before Christmas Eve, not normally a significant event in Julia's life these past few years, but the season was slowly evolving again into something much more. Of course, it brought back her thoughts of Henry, less often now, but she still kept him in her heart with special reverence for all he had done for her.

Thousands of Germans had been relocated and settled in this area as part of the Germanization of Poland. Additionally, a large percentage of German military were no longer as apprehensive about being practicing Catholics. They were now demonstratively supportive of their faith again since the Fuhrer had granted leniency toward the church. In particular, the Church of the Lady of the Scapular stood as a bulwark against previous German persecution, due largely to the influence of Colonel von Stauffenberg, who had shouldered most of the responsibility for its survival.

It was agreed that to accommodate German civilians and various officers of the Catholic faith, their services for Mass were reserved for Christmas Eve. As agreed by Julia and Father Francis, this priority treatment meant Polish service would only be available the day prior. It was a small sacrifice readily accepted by the usual Polish congregation. They were just thankful to have a Christmas service, something sacred to them that was painfully absent since 1938.

For the Polish villagers, there was much to be done. The church was also reinstating its former tradition of hosting the community dinner, which was being supported by everyone in the village. Because of the war, it had been years since this annual event had been possible, and it was a delightful gesture to which local vendors contributed whatever they could to this total community effort.

Deliveries of late harvested fruit preserves, vegetables, home baked bread, and cookies for the children were creating a steady flow of generosity at the rear doors. The season brought out the best in these generally impoverished people. This kept Julia totally preoccupied, as she took the lead in assisting Bronia, who had become somewhat overwhelmed with the stress this event placed upon her still broad shoulders. This day however, she had become quite visibly flushed and appeared unsteady on her feet.

"I'll be just fine dear... I just need to sit for a moment; a little lightheaded, I'm sure that's all it is."

"As you wish Bronia, but I still think I should do the heavy lifting, don't you agree?" Never one to tell this hard-working poor soul of a woman anything she didn't already know; she would work until she dropped if Julia hadn't stepped up to assist her.

Julia had just managed to clear some space, and was a bit flushed herself from the physical exertion when another pounding was heard from the rear doors. Wiping her sweating forehead, she shoved the heavy door open to come face to face with a burly farmer with his hat askew, bearing the full weight of a huge sack of potatoes on his sturdy shoulders. He appeared to be taken aback somehow, as he had expected Bronia behind the door, but it was apparent this was indeed a wonderful and quite unexpected surprise for him.

"Hello... do I maybe have the wrong door?" he joked. "I am Jan, the potato man from Wiory. I spoke to Bronia last week about bringing my potatoes. They're for tomorrow's supper," he proudly exclaimed.

"Oh yes, please do come in. We were expecting you. Bronia told me you were coming sometime today," she explained while wiping her wet hands on her apron. "Thank you so much. My name is Julia," as she extended her still partially wet hand.

Her hair was tossed in disarray and clung to her already beaded forehead. Perspiration dripped from the tip of her nose as Jan placed the heavy load under the shelving near the double sink and proceeded to the wagon to get another one. *Two bags,* she thought! *This is wonderful!*

"You are most generous, Jan. This will fill many hungry bellies, no doubt. You are very kind." Jan's face reddened, as well it should, since he could not wipe the broad grin from his face from the moment he saw Julia. She could not help but notice. She locked eyes with him and responded somewhat flirtingly, "Do you always smile so at every woman you meet?"

"For this one, I think I always will!" as another blush covered his face. Without pausing, Jan placed the second bag beside the first.

"Are you toying with me, *Jan the Potato Man*?" It was evident Jan was awestruck with Julia, as she was equally interested in him. Now, even his ears were glowing!

All the while, Bronia had been watching this exchange and found it quite entertaining, to say the least. It was apparent this was a new experience for both young ones and Bronia was enjoying every minute. By now, she had regained her breath and waddled over to greet Jan personally with her customary warm hug.

Looking about the kitchen and seeing the second heavy bag lying obtrusively on the floor in front of the sink she loudly exclaimed, "Well for heaven's sake, that makes no sense at all. Where are we supposed to stand, or should we just sit on the extra bag in front of the sink?"

"Oops, sorry, Bronia. I guess I wasn't thinking," Jan confessed.

Always quick to admonish him, but in a harmless way, she responded sarcastically, "Oh, you're always thinking, Jan, but I think today your mind is focused elsewhere." Patting him on the shoulder she gave him a wink of the eye to let him know she was only teasing. "Perhaps just move the boxes of brine to the cupboard and put both bags beside the sink."

As he did so, Bronia kindly offered, "Will you stay for a hot cup of tea, Jan? It won't take but a minute."

"Don't hurry for me Bronia. I'm in no rush today." he replied, still grinning ear to ear, although more sheepishly now as he continued to be fixated on Julia.

"I suppose you will be joining us for dinner tomorrow too?" Bronia continued. "You always work so hard. You and your brother must be sure to bring Marianna for dinner as well. We don't see the family as often as we should. Father Francis notices these things you know, and so do I," as she shook her stubby finger at him somewhat tauntingly.

"Maybe now that you've met Julia, you might visit us more often? What do you think?" She and Jan shared a friendly chuckle.

"You *will* be coming for our feast tomorrow, won't you, Jan?" Julia cheerfully enquired. "Many friends of the church will be here, so you should be here as well. Isn't that right Bronia?"

Julia gazed engagingly into Jan's receptive eyes and understood his silent response. Having never experienced these strange but delightful waves of unfamiliar feelings, she was compelled to test the water with him and let her sensations take her where they might.

Without a word other than a hesitant stammer from Jan, Bronia exclaimed, "Very well, Jan! I'll accept that as a definitive *Yes*. Enjoy your tea but be here early tomorrow because there will be more work to do setting up the tables and so on. Now, I have much to do before my day ends. Julia, please lock up after Jan finishes his tea. I bid you both a good night, and God bless."

So, for the first time in Julia's life she took a moment for herself to enjoy the companionship of a handsome young man, with no agenda in mind except to follow the process to wherever it led… except neither knew where to begin. Julia sat silently watching Jan sip his tea. In the fleeting seconds of silence, time stood still while she briefly recalled previous times, terrible and frightening ones, when desperation had guided her way forward.

The willingness to simply move ahead through such perilous times was founded upon her trust in God's capable guiding hands. Fear of the unknown had never stopped her journey then. Perhaps this part of it was her destiny too. She inhaled anxiously... and exhaled calmly. There was nothing to fear here, so she began.

"Jan, I have opened many doors in my life not knowing what was on the other side." She calmly nodded in the direction of the rear door of the kitchen and said "I'm so very happy I opened this one tonight and found you on the other side. I feel..." Julia corrected herself... "I *know* I have found a friend in you. Who knows where our friendship will take us? I'm so very pleased to meet you."

Julia extended her hand to shake his own, almost in a joking manner, but Jan did not accept it that way. He held her hand gently in his, as sensitively as he knew how, having never been faced with such a moment, and kissed it ever so tenderly.

"I'm very happy to know you too, Julia. There is so much I want to say, but I don't know how to say it. I have no experience with these things. Will you help me find the words to make you happy?"

"Maybe we can find them together, would that be alright, Jan?" The conversation did not continue much beyond those first moments, but both were confident it would. The gentle and tender moment was broken, but only until tomorrow, Julia mused.

Jan headed back home after saying goodnight... and he was truthful to Bronia when he said he was in no hurry to do so. The two young ones were quite taken with each other, that much was obvious. He pondered about what had just happened to him and just looked to the heavens to thank God for helping him grow potatoes.

*****

When Julia and Bronia met the following day, they resumed organizing the preparation and workstations for the evening's event. It wasn't long before the conversation between them quickly returned to the pleasant exchange between Julia and Jan.

"You seem to know him well, Bronia. Please tell me a little more about him. He fumbles a bit and seems so shy, but he's so very pleasant to talk to."

"I don't see the family as often as I used to. Since the boys' father died three or four years back, Jan and his older brothers worked the family farm with their mother, Marianna. The Germans took her oldest boy, Mikael. She was devastated to lose him and continues to be. It's just so sad. She and I were close for a few years but the pressure of keeping up the farm without her husband and now without Mikael, has kept them all pre-occupied, I suppose. They're a good Christian family, there's no doubt."

"I don't suppose Jan is married, is he?" Julia started to redden in the face a little. "I'm sorry, Bronia. I don't mean to be so forward, but I really felt a connection with him. This is all so new to me, and I didn't even think about whether he was married until now."

"Come now, no need to fuss about it; no, he's not married." Bronia rested her comforting hand on Julia's still wet hands as she had just finished rinsing the sink. It was a tender moment of reassurance between them that Julia needed right now.

"Don't dither about it, my dear. It's a part of growing up you must deal with someday, part of becoming an adult. He's a good, kind-hearted young man who's not afraid of hard work. Let's just see where all this may go, shall we?"

By late afternoon, preparations were well underway when Jan entered the already open rear door. He found the kitchen bustling with activity. Between the heat of the baking oven and the boiling vegetables on the stove, it had become intolerably hot inside, and the cold air from the open door made the heat more manageable.

Snow had fallen most of the afternoon and there was a bite of frost still in the air. The oppressive heat of the busy kitchen was heavy with comforting aromas of fragrant baked bread and of course, roasted turkey and baked ham. This would indeed be a feast long overdue.

Jan was clean shaven and as well dressed as the Christmas turkey, but he rolled up his sleeves and joined some other villagers already setting up tables and chairs, coffee, and buffet stations. Despite not knowing anyone well, he stepped up and engaged himself with whatever task was at hand, all the while scanning the width and depth of the festively trimmed banquet room looking for Julia, trying not to be too obvious.

Meanwhile, Julia was in the vestry, tending to the children. She was fastidiously fussing to prepare them for this happy day, intending to proudly display these beautiful little people for all to see, none more important than their Uncle Francis. She took great pride tending to their everyday needs, but it was indeed a rare occasion when she could fuss so caringly.

This was a much-deserved holiday after all, and some additional measure of pampering was well warranted. Only when this pleasurable task was complete, did Julia finally realize it was time for some self-indulgence on her part too.

As before, Father Francis had generously suggested she choose one of his sister-in-law's best dresses for herself, surely a close enough fit. Bronia, being a woman of so many talents had made the necessary alterations in her genuine attempt to fashion Julia to be the *Belle of the Ball*.

Having already accepted Bronia's thoughtful assistance to dress her hair more fashionably, practicality was not the impression Julia sought today. She trusted herself to Bronia's capable care and when completed, barely recognized herself in the hallway mirror.

Her loose curls caressed her shoulders ever so slightly, while still exposing the graceful curves of her youthful neck. It was the first occasion Julia would reveal a modest cleavage and she gazed at herself proudly. In her mind, she was many things, but she never realized until this moment, beautiful was one of them.

She was very pleased, but there was only one more thing she would try to improve upon. For too long Julia was unable to display a confident smile, certainly not a natural one since the innocence of her childhood.

Still gazing in the mirror, in her own simple way she thought, *I have good teeth, so why not show them off?* Tonight, she would do so without the normal hesitation and uncertainty customarily causing her to purse her lips ashamedly. Could she really become attractive to a man? Could she step out from behind the protective exterior shaping her every gesture for so long? Perhaps it was time to find out. Julia was on unfamiliar ground now, but she knew she was already off to a good start.

She gathered herself one last time and reflexively twisted a final curl, stepping out of the vestry and into the narthex of the church. The only exit led her directly to the front left side of the church where the congregation had already started to fill the pews.

The organist, Richard, was softly playing familiar Christmas hymns to set the stage for the gathering patrons. The timing was entirely coincidental but served to wordlessly announce Julia's memorable grand entrance.

It was the first time she had worn makeup of any kind. It was modestly and tastefully applied by Bronia and highlighted Julia's brilliant blue eyes. The perfect amount of blush on her cheeks served to remind those present of her youthful budding womanhood. Julia was indeed a blossoming young lady, whose stunning introduction had been long overdue.

As if on cue, a silent hush spread throughout the gathering, and faces turned in unison. Time was moving in slow motion. There in the second pew sat Jan, with gaping mouth and widening eyes. It wasn't a look of which he would have been proud. It was a natural reaction, but not a flattering one; nonetheless, it was genuine.

Within a few brief seconds, he regained his composure and his familiar smile returned, shining bigger and brighter than before, as his eyes reduced to prideful creases reflecting absolute delight.

Julia blushed with embarrassment, which only enhanced her loveliness. It was nature's makeup enveloping her from head to toe. Jan stood immediately, which was a proclamation Julia was his, and only his.

Without hesitation, Jan approached this young woman he hardly knew and reached out for her hand, which she offered to him willingly. The silent agreement had been forged between them as irrevocably as the passing of night into daybreak.

Not only did Jan's family come for dinner that memorable night, but Jan also came to services every week from that day forward. For Jan and Julia, it was the beginning of a very loving relationship, and the ultimate prize was each other.

*****

The next day, on Christmas Eve, Colonel von Stauffenberg, his lovely wife, Magdalena and their two eldest children attended Father Francis' midnight Mass, along with many officers who were mostly unknown to Father and Julia. Introductions were not even considered, as the colonel maintained strict military protocol deemed most appropriate during these still tenuous times for the Catholic

Church. The only exception was to introduce Father Francis and Julia to his family.

"Good evening, Father Francis, and hello Julia. Please allow me to introduce my dear wife, Magdalena and our sons Michael and David."

Magdalena was a classic beauty and her bright eyes shone with unpretentious delight at meeting them. Her dress was simple but elegant and tasteful, accentuated by her endearing smile. Together, the Stauffenbergs made a very handsome couple.

"Hello Father, Julia. So nice to meet you both. May I say your dress is quite fetching, Julia. You look lovely this evening."

Julia was flattered to have been considered worthy of an introduction, which under the circumstances, was exceptionally kind of the colonel. It was a small courtesy further enhancing her respect for him.

It was apparent the colonel was highly regarded by his peers. It was Christmas after all, and his entourage were mostly light-hearted and more mellow than he, but the line of informality was only slightly blurred by their steadfast respect and abundantly clear admiration for him.

The beautiful service was fondly received by congregants, many of whom had formerly been prohibited from participating in such a sacred demonstration of faith. It was indeed a restoration of tradition, knowing no divide nor distinction between nations. Would this someday become a reality again? If and when it ever happened, assuredly it would not come to pass so quickly.

This year, Father Francis' sermon was not his traditional one, having long since decided to avoid any potential rebuke antagonizing or exceeding Hitler's clear guidelines of acceptability. It was still a very fragile situation for the church and anyone supporting it. At least the road to co-existence was still an open one, for now. Father Francis was determined not to jeopardize the opportunity, and not just because of the longevity of the church; there were other matters of even greater consequence to consider as well.

*****

With the Christmas celebration now behind them, many would suppose some restful family time and personal introspection would be in order in contemplation of the beckoning new year. However, it would soon be evident these were only fleeting thoughts for Father Francis. Over the up-coming weeks, his plate was full and required demanding preparation for the tasks he was about to help co-ordinate.

One fine morning, he instructed Bronia to tend to the children for a while to address some important matters with Julia directly. When Julia entered his office, Father rose from behind his desk and shifted his position to sit more comfortably in the chair located closest to Julia's. By his change of posture and the softened tone of his voice, Julia sensed something of great importance lay ahead.

Cautiously and a little tentatively, he began. "Before our meetings resume again in this early New Year, I want to build on what we discussed a few months ago. I thought it wise to do so sooner than later since there are several important matters to address that should become known to you. I want you to be prepared for what is about to happen. Clearly, these are sensitive matters, and as such, I do not want any undue surprises, neither for me, nor for you."

"You have my undivided attention, Father. You know you can always be candid with me," Julia assured him.

"There are some things I want to explain to you about the colonel to provide you some much needed context about him. He is an outstanding individual who is descended from one of the most distinguished aristocratic families in Germany. He is the Count of Stauffenberg, a nobleman who is very close to the Fuhrer for reasons continually confounding to me, other than the prestige of his family's reputation and their influence Hitler needs to further enhance the domestic and international credibility of The Reich.

"You should understand the colonel is not, nor ever has been, an official Nazi party member, and he remains a staunch practicing Catholic; as far as the Nazis are concerned, these are two very relevant inconsistencies between the colonel and almost any other German within Hitler's High Command. Yet despite these ideological differences, his direct relationship with Hitler continues to thrive.

"As much as the colonel respects the Fuhrer's outstanding military accomplishments, he abhors his deranged persecution of Jews and his aggressive suppression of the Catholic Church. The violent attacks against the Catholic clergy in the past two years have caused serious dissention from many under Hitler's direct command.

"Colonel von Stauffenberg and many others, consider the Fuhrer's actions to be unjust and blatantly immoral. Julia, the purpose of our meetings here these past several months is to develop a plan to forcibly put an end to this disgusting tyranny, by any means possible."

Father took a large mouthful of cold water before proceeding and shifted his chair even closer to Julia than before. Julia's mind was racing, not understanding where this conversation was heading.

He spoke quietly. "I want you to be mindful as well, some of our guests are not as gentlemanly as they may first appear. Some among them are downright vile people who will be required to carry out some despicable acts, potentially including treason, and possibly even murder.

"You must understand these acts are not inspired by hatred or vindictiveness; quite to the contrary. They are inspired by honor and patriotism, and by unflagging dedication not just to Germany, but to our very humanity."

In response, Julia's facial expression was one of disbelief, but as always, her eyes did not break contact with Father's own.

"Although we are living in dangerous and harrowing times, I do not intend to place you at risk any more than I already have, but your very association with us may inadvertently do just that, simply by helping us to courier documents or attend our secretive meetings, for example, you will appear to be complicit. You asked me to be candid with you, Julia. Is that candid enough?" Once again, Father paused for more water, indicating he expected a response from Julia.

"This is not something I was expecting to hear from you, Father. I suspected something of a sinister nature was happening behind closed doors, and when you opened them to me my suspicions were eventually confirmed." Julia paused thoughtfully for a moment to sip her coffee to consider these startling revelations, and more particularly, her next comments.

"Father, I have survived many horrific situations in my very short lifetime. In fact, too many for a long lifetime. You just said something resonating with me; *we are living in dangerous and harrowing times*. Unfortunately, that is the only life I truly know. Nothing shocks me anymore."

"It saddens me to hear you say that Julia. But be that as it may, this is another reason I wanted you to be compensated accordingly. It is vital you have confidence and trust in what we are trying to accomplish."

Having completed his lengthy and illuminating conversation with Julia, Father Francis simply stopped talking and set himself deeper into the back of his chair. He knew it was a great deal for Julia to absorb.

"Pardon me for being so blunt, Father. Would it be accurate for me to say that essentially my extra compensation is to buy my trust, as well as my silence, if I may be so direct?" Julia stated her position as boldly as she could. The statement took Father Francis by surprise. He stammered a little and was clearly taken aback.

"Will that be a problem for you?" he asked.

Julia did not even hesitate. "Absolutely not, Father. It was never about the money. I believe there is more to me than being charged with the care of the children. I care about them deeply, you already know that, but I very much want to do my part in this war, no matter how small a part I may play.

"This war took everything I held dear to me - my family, my home, my innocence, and my self-confidence. But my spirit and my faith in God remain firm. Thank you for being open with me, as I will always be with you."

"I am relieved to hear that, Julia. And, based upon my recent discussion with Father Breitkopf, he further confirms your trustworthiness for what I am about to confide to you. I believe our relationship will become even more fruitful and productive than it already has become; of this I am certain."

*****

As the New Year progressed, icy winds raced bitterly and mercilessly across the frozen landscape. It was a harsh winter, the worst in history, and as unforgiving as the atrocities preceding it. Despite the frigid conditions, however, normal everyday activities remained as before.

This particular morning, a young mother outside the church braced herself against the wind to protectively carry her baby bundled closely in her arms. She leaned into the howling wind to make her way carefully across the street, passing five or six young children playing a makeshift soccer game in the frozen church parking lot.

It seemed the youngsters were more indifferent to the frigid conditions than the German soldiers being pounded by nature's fury on the outskirts of Leningrad. In stark contrast, this was a quiet peaceful scene, but for the occasional shouting of friendly encouragement from some of the children, urging their teammates on.

Not long after, two military cars came into view over the gradual rise approaching the driveway to the church. One of them was Colonel von Stauffenberg's vehicle, followed closely by the second. They slowed to a crawl and cautiously edged up the slippery entrance to the parking area close to where the children were playing.

The colonel and his adjutant were the first to exit their car and two other officers from the second followed behind them toward Father Francis' side entrance to his office. The colonel exchanged no pleasantries with the others and was strictly business as usual. His associate banged the brass knocker loudly and Father Francis, who was expecting them, promptly responded to welcome them inside.

"Good morning, Colonel, gentlemen. Please come in. I have been expecting you this fine and frosty day. Welcome." Puffs of frozen condensation from their breath indicated just how frigid it was this bitter January morning.

True to form, von Stauffenberg offered only minimal greetings, with no carry over of a personal nature from the pleasant exchanges at the Christmas Mass just weeks before. He had fully resumed his businesslike and focused demeanor, befitting his rapidly growing reputation.

This time, the two officers accompanying the colonel were unknown to Father Francis, which was the reason this meeting had been convened. New contacts were few and far between and often slow to develop. The necessary vetting process was a tedious one but was essential to protect the anonymity and safety of everyone potentially involved. The degree of due diligence could never be compromised by carelessness and foolish haste. There was simply too much at stake to do otherwise.

The colonel greeted Julia warmly and she was prompt to offer to take their coats, winter hats, and gloves as Father had instructed. She was not introduced to anyone since her relevance at this point was unimportant to the newcomers.

Father Francis directed the small group of gentlemen to his office. "Please, make yourselves comfortable. It is a particularly cold morning.

Thank you all for coming." Turning to Julia, he asked, "Perhaps you could prepare some hot tea and coffee for our guests this morning?"

"Of course, Father," she replied. As expeditiously as possible, Julia exited to prepare some piping hot beverages and closed the office door softly behind her.

Father Francis was eager to finally meet the new contacts, based upon information about them the colonel had shared with him previously. The fact they were here this morning confirmed the strict vetting had evidently been to the complete satisfaction of Colonel von Stauffenberg's demanding standards.

The middle-aged officer was introduced as General Henning von Tresckow, Chief of Staff of the 2nd Army. His personal and trusted aide-de-camp was a lieutenant named Victor. Together, they brought significantly more military expertise to the table than any of the current collaborators to date, including Colonel von Stauffenberg.

The general was, by all appearances, a middle aged and dignified looking man, more so after he removed his cap to reveal his balding head. His gaze was steely eyed, and the setting of his jaw indicated confidence, with not so much as a hint of a smile. This was a solemn gentleman who was to be taken seriously.

Colonel von Stauffenberg opened the dialogue with a brief reference to the general's efficient role in coordinating the invasion of France. The general was held in high esteem by the Fuhrer for his strategic military planning and strict enforcement of it.

In only a moment or two, the general indicated his impatience with the colonel's platitudes, deserving or otherwise, and had no time to dawdle with accolades about his past. He pressed on to address more urgent and relevant matters.

"Father, I am told your close relationship with Adam Sapieha has been extremely helpful in co-ordinating many aspects of our collaboration with the colonel. We appreciate his and your support. I was encouraged when I was approached by the colonel to inform me of his long-term intentions. They resonated perfectly with my own."

"As with each of us, General. The Archbishop and I are thankful for your expertise for what we are about to achieve. Your involvement with us has provided a critical missing link that is vital to our success." Father Francis stated succinctly.

The general continued, "Recently, there have been rumblings of unrest within the military and across the political landscape, much of which has been precipitated by the Fuhrer's violent attacks against the Catholic Church. In the beginning, his military accomplishments earned my loyalty and support. However, the means by which it has been achieved has no place in history other than one of disgrace, for Germany and all mankind. The time has arrived for us to come together to reconcile this travesty."

He turned to look directly into Stauffenberg's eyes and stated categorically, "If we do not put an end to the madness we are experiencing from the Fuhrer, *the German people will be burdened with a guilt the world will not forget in a hundred years. This guilt will fall not only on Hitler, Himmler, Göring, and their comrades but on you and me, your wife and mine, your children and mine…*" (Von Tresckow)

He raised his right arm to point to the window and continued… *"that woman crossing the street this morning, and those children playing ball"* … (Von Tresckow) He paused to let his comments sink in more fully… "They are no different than my family or yours. What possible threat is an innocent child to the power of the Reich? It is time to act for the sake of the future of humanity."

There was an intense moment of silence, broken only by a brief tap on the door as Julia entered the awkward setting to see the five men staring silently at one another, grasping for the appropriate response to the general's impassioned words.

She could only assume they had reached an impasse, or some other turning point in the short time she was absent. She froze in her tracks with hesitant unease as to how to proceed. Father saw her indecisiveness and forgivingly ushered her in to continue with her task.

"Please, Julia. Come." He turned to General Tresckow apologetically, "Please forgive the interruption. You may speak freely here. Julia has been thoroughly vetted. She has become invaluable to me and has proven her loyalty many times over. Please continue, Sir."

"Very well. The Fuhrer's disgusting conduct has dishonored our nation. I am convinced bringing an end to National Socialism will save Germany and all of Europe from the inhuman barbarism we are witnessing, which has but one inevitable result: the destruction of the German people. There is nothing short of his assassination that can change our destiny from one of death and despair. It is my intent to make this happen."

Colonel von Stauffenberg spoke supportively of Tresckow's passionate admissions. "General, I speak for many among the ranks of the Wehrmacht who are convinced this is our only course of action. We must develop a plan of action to establish an independent government whose immediate purpose is to negotiate Germany's position going forward to prevent an inevitable Russian invasion of the Fatherland.

"It is now time that something was done. But the man who has the courage to do something must do it in the knowledge that he will go down in German history as a traitor. If he does not do it, however, he will be a traitor to his own conscience." (Von Stauffenberg)

18
THEY CAME OUT OF NOWHERE

♂

JANUARY 30TH, 1943, WAS THE TENTH ANNIVERSARY OF Hitler's appointment to lead the Third Reich, proffered by former Reich president, Field Marshal von Hindenburg. It was a significant accomplishment Hitler and Goebbels intended to proudly celebrate with the citizens of Berlin. After a series of recent air defeats in both Europe and North Africa, German public confidence was waning. This memorable milestone could not have come at a better time.

Throughout Berlin, several venues had been carefully orchestrated to honor the achievements of the Reich, and to re-affirm to the nation Hitler's leadership was limitless. Berlin was selected to be the obvious choice to host these well publicized events.

The anniversary of Hitler's ascension to power in Nazi Germany was a day on which he would glorify the accomplishments of his military leaders, with the entire world listening. The national holiday featured a grand parade through the central city. Streets along the route were lined with hundreds of thousands of supportive spectators, their eager enthusiasm being demanded of them. It was an opportunity very similar to his parade procession entering the Olympic stadium in 1936.

Reichsmarschall Göring was scheduled to deliver his address outside the Air Ministry building at precisely 11:00 AM that morning. Propaganda Minister Goebbels would speak at another massive rally at 4:00 PM. Both speeches would be broadcast live on radio.

In honor of the Fuhrer's proud accomplishments, most of the factories were closed for the dayshift to ensure the parade route

260

was overflowing to capacity with his dedicated subjects. Among the crowds lining the parade route on this grey and overcast day, were Anna's sister Emilie, and her now eighteen-year-old daughter Gertrude, the granddaughter of Sigmund and Marissa.

After Sigmund's death, General von Brauchitsch provided the necessary paperwork indicating Emilie was a distant niece of the general, whose family had been killed in the early days of the war. As the general's staff had insisted, the documentation identified the mother and daughter as being Roman Catholics, with the express purpose of keeping them safe from Jewish persecution.

Emilie and her daughter were seamstresses, living and working in the factories in the Siemensstadt District in western Berlin, alongside thousands of young women working tirelessly six days a week to maintain the supply of uniforms for the unending number of young German warriors who wore them. It was backbreaking and unsatisfying labor on tedious assembly lines, in steamy and poorly ventilated factories.

"Mother, I understand the Fuhrer himself might be here today. This is the first time the factory has closed to allow us to see him. Our supervisor insisted everyone be here or we will not be paid. It feels good to enjoy the fresh air while we can. Thankfully, it's a rather pleasant day and not too frightfully cold."

Almost indifferently, Emilie commented, "I'm pleased the factory is closed today as well but I was hoping we could enjoy some much-needed sunshine. Such a shame it's so overcast. If only there was more fresh air. My Lord, the air still bears the stench of bleach and oil from the factory. Can we ever escape from it?"

As best she could, Gertrude scanned about the area. Not heeding her mother's constant negativity but continuing with her own thoughts, she offered, "Armed soldiers are everywhere. You can see them on the balconies and rooftops too! Why in the world is that even necessary, I wonder? I do hope we can see the Fuhrer pass by from here. Do you think we will, Mother?"

"I suppose so dear, although I am not keen to even see the man. Why would you even ask me?"

"I had hoped we could enjoy our day together. When was the last time we had the chance? Can we not just do that, Mother? I'm sorry, but I don't want anything to spoil it, certainly not thoughts about where we work night and day. This is still refreshing, so do your best to stop being so grumpy, please!"

For young Gertrude, this was her young life, though not one of her choosing. She had labored continuously since her early teens. Despite this difficult experience, she always maintained her natural sunny disposition through the circumstances in which she found herself. Her mother, however, still bore the bitterness from having their lives being torn away, including the loss of her and Gertrude's own identities.

The Third Reich, whether directly or indirectly, had killed Emilie's mother and father and taken their comfortable life away from them with the seizure of their home and possessions. Were it not for General von Brauchitsch coming to their aid, as Jews they would have been thrown on the streets, or suffered considerably worse.

Emilie did her best to simply do what she was told, for the relative safety of her only daughter. She knew of no other Jews toiling day and night in the factories, so she kept her head down and her mouth shut, pledging she would never reveal her story to anyone, including young Gertrude, in the interests of protecting their benefactor. There was no one in her life she could trust with her secretive past.

Hours passed so slowly. Crowds had been gathering since before dawn, up and down the parade route leading to the front of the Air Ministry building where the massing of thousands were packed inside the heavily barricaded perimeter. Inside the grand hall, hundreds of dignitaries were pre-assigned seats near as possible to the podium at stage center. Göring's speech would commence at 11:00 AM sharp.

Outside the building, hundreds of thousands of inquisitive spectators had been physically forced by armed military to follow the parade. As it passed through the streets nearer the ministry, the pressure on the already tightly compacted crowd became intense.

Every exit from this part of the city had been cordoned off and would remain so until the speeches had been completed and broadcast to the already frustrated and impatient crowds. They had been standing since before daybreak. Although it was a cold but pleasant winter day, standing for four or five hours without washroom facilities was taking its toll on everyone. For many, it was still better than working, or so it was presumed.

Two massive screens provided a feeble attempt for the crowd to witness the speeches in real time. "Oh, look Mother! Who is it that just sat down?" Struggling for a better vantage point was impossible and the video feed was too grainy to see much detail. "He's too fat to be the Fuhrer. Can you see anything Mother?"

Gertrude was standing tip toed, trying anxiously to crane her neck and gain a sharper view of the entourage of military men entering the stage with the chests of their uniforms covered conspicuously by many medals and ribbons *making them appear more important than they actually were*, according to Emilie.

"It's difficult to know for certain from here… but it appears to be Herr Göring, I think." Emilie shushed her daughter, as did numerous others throughout the tightly crowded gathering when he approached the lectern. "Quiet now, I want to hear what he has to say."

The crowd became hushed when the microphone was connected, and the shrill electrical screeching caught the attention of the waiting throngs. Göring grasped the microphone, doing his typical best to appear intimidating and arrogant, as was befitting of his general pompous manner.

Within mere seconds of Göring commencing his speech, a squadron of three RAF Mosquito bombers broke through the low cloud cover. The sudden howling and roaring thunder sent frightening shock waves through the massive crowds, shaking the ground below. The explosive impact of their deadly rounds of gunfire into the unsuspecting people in the streets caused immediate pandemonium. Negligible ground flack was the best the unsuspecting Germans could offer in retaliation.

The pitch of the screaming Merlin engines at full throttle was deafening and at four hundred miles per hour, the attack was skillfully and perilously close to the surrounding buildings across the main intersection. This bold daylight air attack was the first to ever strike Berlin. It came out of nowhere, completely undetected since they flew into the city at high rates of speed, well below the altitude any radar required to detect them.

The Abwehr team under Admiral Canaris, had agreed to leak the detailed timing and specific locations of the speeches to British operatives two days before the scheduled celebration. This was never intended to be a significant military strike, rather its sole purpose was to boldly embarrass Germany's top brass in front of the entire world.

The first and only pass had strafed the defenseless crowd, leaving behind a small swath of destruction, not significant militarily but from the perspective of shattering German morale, the message was delivered powerfully; especially so because Göring, at the beginning of the war, had personally assured Germany that Berlin would never be bombed.

British Intelligence was also aware the state broadcasting company was located a few miles from the Air Ministry Building, only forty seconds of flight time for the speeding flyby.

Upon approach, the continued gunfire splayed the broadcast studio, causing another state of confusion while still recording. In a few mere seconds, the microphones were frantically disconnected, however the initial cacophony of gunfire was clearly broadcast for the entire world to hear.

The RAF had delivered a message to the Germans. It was an intended statement of undeniable payback, as small retribution for German air attacks on civilian homes in London during the Battle of Britain.

Unable to run for cover, the deadly nightmare became a massive sea of humanity trapped in the open city squares with no viable hope of escape. Panic-stricken amongst debris and shattered glass, and tending to the injured and the fallen, it was absolute bedlam. Screaming, shouting, and crying ensued; there was nowhere to find cover. No one knew what to expect next. Would more attacks soon follow?

In only seconds, the roaring of the British fighter planes had reverberated through the streets, echoing from building to building until it dissolved in the wake of the exhaust as quickly as it had begun. The resulting panic in the streets of Berlin was traumatizing and emotionally draining. Over the next ten to fifteen minutes, the chaos was steadily diminished by the pervasive sounds of crying and sobbing.

In the commotion, hundreds trying to escape had aggressively pushed through others in their way, creating sporadic waves of panic. Emilie was one of those who stumbled, instantly causing her to fall to the ground. Gertrude immediately crouched on her knees to cradle her mother from further harm and fought to protect her from dozens of others struggling with futility to escape from another more devastating air attack.

Weeping and sniffling, Gertrude held her ground by covering her mother protectively as best she could. People were stomping and falling on top of anyone injured after the first pass, unable to stop the ripple effect of those shoving behind them, causing more to trip and fall as well. It was a living nightmare.

"Are you alright Mommy? What is happening to us?" Remarkably, a stranger saw what had happened and quickly helped Gertrude pull Emilie to her feet, saving both from being trampled to death. He disappeared seconds later and was forcibly swept into the mayhem.

Within twenty minutes or so, military personnel scrambled to evacuate the relatively few dead and injured from the scene, but heavy security refused to permit anyone else from leaving.

"Why don't they let us go, Mother? I'm too afraid to stay, and... and I think I messed myself!" Gertrude confided embarrassingly in Emilie's attentive ear. "Don't be concerned dear. There must be many with the same problem, but they seem determined not to let any of us leave until the speeches are finished. Just be patient and we will get through this, my child."

It was an hour and three minutes before Göring finally resumed his speech again. He was the Supreme Commander of the German Luftwaffe. He and he alone was responsible for this military ineptitude. Now, shaking with embarrassment and fury, he tried valiantly to restore the confidence and reassurance he had intended to originally impart to the nervous spectators. The crowd's focus, however, was elsewhere.

There were no spontaneous rounds of applause when the Reichsmarschall reappeared. There was constant mumbling throughout the terrifying scene, and the people were justifiably unable to settle. Göring interpreted this as being disrespectful and offensive to him personally and became even more unnerved.

For the balance of his speech, it was apparent the crowd's attention was now shared equally between his address, and their constant scanning of the skies above. Not at all what Nazi leadership was expecting to achieve.

When Göring's angry tirade finally subsided, the thousands of onlookers were mercifully permitted to leave the square. The celebration was an unmitigated disaster... but it was not over.

*****

Later in the day, at four o'clock sharp, the Minister of Propaganda Joseph Goebbels took center stage inside Berlin's largest indoor stadium. Every seat was occupied for the event.

For the second time that day, another Mosquito squadron No. 139, timed another brazen attack to coincide with Goebbels' opening remarks. The effect was the same as the first, and its deadly impact outside the stadium was felt inside the confines of the arena as well.

The minister appeared undaunted and after only a momentary pause, he continued speaking. This time, the numerous audio technicians nervously stayed the course. They feared Goebbels' scorn more than the death and destruction outside the building.

Goebbels' defiant indignation was apparent. The welcoming crowd, by his estimation, was not appreciative enough to satisfy him, as it was clearly less than enthusiastic. His rhetoric was as bold and captivating as he had ever delivered, fueled no doubt by the embarrassing humiliation inflicted by the RAF fighter planes earlier that day.

In his arrogance, not a word was said about the dead and the wounded. It was just his contempt for the British and his personal dignity mattering most to him.

This time the angry and determined crowds burst through the security gates amid the sounds of other gunshots being fired into the air to control the impulsive and desperate attempts to flee. Steel barriers were pushed aside, and armed soldiers were trampled if they dared to obstruct the overflowing mob.

Utter chaos won the day. The side streets and adjacent buildings were trashed amid shards of broken glass. The groundswell of confused and terrorized people was quickly absorbed into the network of numerous side streets and alleyways, wherever they found the freedom of space in their harried escape.

It was a major embarrassment for Nazi leadership and discomforting and traumatizing to the thousands of attendees who were forced to scatter for their very lives. The previous unwillingness of German High Command to alert the public about the truth concerning the growing threat against their safety was now undeniably announced; the strafing of the Mosquito squadrons having delivered this awareness most effectively. Within weeks of the British air attacks, Germany finally began what should have been done months ago, the evacuation of women and children from Berlin.

Only one aircraft was brought down about fifty miles south of Berlin that day. The young captain and crew all perished but the indelible mark they left had proven to Germany that the Allies had the capability to strike the heart of Germany at will. The United Press described the daring raid as a major success.

For added emphasis, a similar surprise attack was repeated several months later to specifically desecrate Hitler's 54th birthday celebration. These aerial ambushes were very similar to the U.S. air attack against Japan led by Jimmy Doolittle, intended to tap into, and drain the civilian and military morale of the enemy.

While there was no immediate evidence German morale was adversely affected in the long term, these raids confirmed the people of Berlin could expect more of the same in the coming months ahead. As it happened, Hitler chose not to attend his day of adulation and instead, passed the day brooding with his astrologer at his Bavarian retreat. Hitler was not a person who endured embarrassment lightly, particularly when it completely tarnished his personal celebration.

*****

The company *Parfums Chanel* employed more than four thousand people. The vast majority were women in Coco Chanel's exclusive fashion boutique stores throughout France. When the war began in late 1939, she decided to close the doors of her successful business empire stating it was *"not a time for fashion"*. (C. Chanel)

Her decision resulted in thousands of women losing their jobs at a time when they needed them most. Many people speculated Madame Chanel's decision was a spiteful one, directed against her employees who had once forced the closure of her business due to a labor rights issue at the time.

During her self-imposed retirement, Madame Chanel directed her energy and talents to political matters, proving herself to be supportive of, and complicit with those of France's occupying enemy, Germany. As a famous French fashion designer, her personal collaborations with German leadership and other political and business contacts were too numerous to mention.

About this time, one of her notable business distractions was her strong insistence to lawfully reacquire full ownership of her perfume empire. She had previously sold fifty percent of the ownership to the Wertheimers, a very wealthy Jewish family. This transaction enabled her to significantly expand the scale of her already successful business by providing whatever funds she required to do so.

Driven by her well documented loathing of Jews, Madame Chanel manipulated her Aryan rights to justify the reacquisition of her company shares from the Wertheimer family by using her influence with the Reich to seize all Jewish owned properties and businesses.

In her letter to the German government, she argued *"Parfums Chanel is still the property of Jews... and has been legally abandoned by the owners. I have an undisputable right of priority. The profits I have received from my creations since the foundation of this business... are disproportionate."* (C. Chanel)

Despite her impassioned plea, Chanel was not able to wrest her company away from the Wertheimers, because the control of the company had been legitimately transferred to a non-Jewish Frenchman named Felix Amiot, who subsequently fled to the United States. It was noteworthy that despite being unsuccessful in her attempt to seize control of her company, she still made enormous personal profits, making her one of the richest women in the world at the time.

*****

ABWEHR OFFICE OF GENERAL VON SCHELLENBERG

About this time, Coco Chanel's long-term intimate relationship with Baron von Dinklage had become well known and was respected by those in High Command. The couple would socialize frequently and interact with these influential military leaders concerning sensitive political matters.

In short, her opinions were taken seriously, to the extent the Baron suggested General Schellenberg consider using Chanel's diplomatic contacts to extract or communicate useful information potentially beneficial to the Reich. Schellenberg was intrigued by the prospect and a meeting with him was expeditiously arranged to explore her potential willingness to do so.

Already an acquaintance of Madame Chanel through the Baron's relationship with her, General Schellenberg dispensed with the usual social banter and addressed Coco directly.

"Madame Chanel, your fervent support of the Reich has caught our attention and is greatly valued by the Fuhrer and me. For someone of your high esteem and global presence, a commitment between us could become formalized, if you would be receptive to such a possibility."

"Yes, the Baron and I have addressed this matter between us and as I indicated to him, I would be very receptive to whatever is asked of me to serve the Reich, in any capacity you may require. My support of you and the Fuhrer is absolute," Chanel replied.

"The Baron is, no doubt, less than objective about his opinion of you, which is quite understandable in view of your personal relationship with him. However, the respect for your quick mind and your obvious diplomatic skills are also shared by many of my colleagues who have come to know you better day by day over these past few years. They too hold you in high esteem, which is further validation for me."

"You are too kind, General. If I may be so bold, Sir, I believe my reputation precedes me." True to form, Chanel did not seek idle flattery. Her formidability was world renowned, and she enjoyed flaunting the positive attributes others saw in her.

The general continued, "Our consensus is we have need of your unique diplomatic skillsets to communicate some delicate information to a few of your powerful colleagues and close friends. Many of them hold positions of significant influence. I am informed, for example, you have close personal ties with the Duke of Westminster and the British Prime Minister as well, do you not?"

"That is correct. My friendships and business associations are typically of a long-term nature, totally by choice, General, I assure you; it attests to my genuine affection for many of them, and they sense that about me too."

"You must understand, what we require from you is not technical expertise, Madame Chanel. Rather we need your influence to open doors as our emissary, with intent to pass along sensitive and secretive information on our behalf from time to time.

"This ability would enable private communication between myself, and our European and British adversaries. Too often in times of war, direct communication between adversaries is nigh impossible to achieve. It can cost the lives of thousands in its absence."

The general by this time, stood up slowly from behind his desk and sat casually on the corner, facing Madame Chanel with a pensive look, drawing notice from the other attendees. Not a word was spoken between them, and no one was willing to break the silence until the general chose to do so. It was evident he had something very specific in mind, indicating he had decided to solicit her direct support.

"I understand you have closed your business operations temporarily during this dreadful war. I applaud your shrewd business acumen, Madame. You don't strike me as someone eager to retire though." The comment was intended to break the slight tension in the room. It was unexpected, and the general's humorous sarcasm was appreciated. However, no one knew for certain where he was heading.

"It is evident to me you may be seeking a different and more challenging direction at this time in your life."

Madame Chanel quietly and subtly nodded her head in agreement and instinctively raised an eyebrow for emphasis of the obvious. The general continued, "If you are receptive, I am prepared to formally ink a deal with you."

He turned to von Dinklage. "Baron, please inform Dorota to bring me the necessary documentation for Madame." As the Baron exited the room, General Schellenberg turned to face Chanel directly.

"I suggest you study our contract thoroughly, Madame. Take whatever time you require but I don't recommend you take much of it. If you agree with our terms, we have an assignment we must discuss further with you that I personally consider very time sensitive. I know you will serve the Reich capably and professionally and I very much look forward to working with you in the years ahead."

19
The True Depth of the Conspiracy

♂

ANNA AND MARTA BOTH AGREED THE SUCCESSFUL BUSINESS relationship between Coco Chanel and Marta had blossomed into a much closer personal friendship, at least on the surface. Coco was well recognized as a highly intelligent businesswoman, who was an undisputed visionary within the fashion aristocracy of the time. Much like Marta, she had a penchant for skillfully manipulating others, especially if she wanted something from someone.

So deftly skilled was she, her prey often succumbed to her charming ways without resistance. It was these very wiles leading her to rub shoulders with not only other fashion icons, but also with Europe's political and military leaders, among whom were such notables as Winston Churchill, and the Duke of Westminster Grosvenor; not to mention many prominent leaders of the Third Reich, including of course Walter Schellenberg, Minister Goebbels and Adolf Hitler.

Anna met privately with General von Brauchitsch, who had by this time gradually resumed many of his Abwehr duties. She described Coco's influential talents and suspicious interest in personally meeting with him. The general was not disturbed or apprehensive about Chanel's interest in him, but he was intrigued, to say the least.

He fully agreed with Anna that Madame Chanel's intent should be immediately and tactfully scrutinized. It was a response Anna had expected from him.

"Thank you for your discretion in coming to me first, Anna. I agree this is a matter to be discussed with Admiral Canaris and I insist on complete candor with him, wherever this may lead. Let's give this the priority it deserves and arrange another meeting later in the day, if possible."

It was late the same afternoon before agendas were adjusted to accommodate Anna's request. The potential seriousness of these circumstances had to be dealt with swiftly, but cautiously.

Anna began, "Admiral, you are aware of my close friendship with Marta von Brauchitsch, the General's daughter-in-law. And you know my sincere appreciation for your decision to permit me to finally reconnect with her again, do you not?"

"Yes, of course. The general and I agree you have proven your loyalty to our cause repeatedly and our faith in you is absolute, Anna."

Anna repeated her conversation, consistent with her earlier discussion between the general and herself, specifically pertaining to Coco Chanel's increasingly close relationship with Marta.

"Sir, I have discreetly discovered certain details that… how shall I say, are of a very personal nature concerning Madame Chanel. It appears shortly after the Nazis occupied Paris, Chanel met and subsequently became intimately involved with Baron von Dinklage of the SS, who was at the time senior military advisor to Deputy Fuhrer General Schellenberg.

"Sirs, as you are both aware, the Ritz Hotel serves as headquarters for the Reich. The Ritz is known to cater to the needs of numerous upper-echelon military staff. There is no doubt the romantic relationship between von Dinklage and Madame Chanel was a key factor facilitating Madame Chanel to conveniently take up permanent residence at the Ritz as well."

"I was aware there was a long-term relationship between them," the general confirmed. "I have met the lady at the Ritz from time to time with the Baron. What else do you have?"

"Well Sir, it is my understanding Madame Chanel recently became an agent of Abwehr at the behest of the Baron and General Schellenberg, in return for another Director of Abwehr, who shall remain nameless for the moment, who used his influence to secure the release of Chanel's nephew, Andre Palasse, from prison."

The admiral was previously aware of this information, as Anna had suspected, but he remained purposely silent so not to lead the conversation in any way. The admiral waited patiently, to permit

Anna's thorough and somewhat delicate descriptions of the unfolding series of events leading to Marta.

"I must say, your top-secret clearances have served you well, Anna. However, I fail to see the relevance of your findings. I assume you are leading me somewhere?"

"Agent *Westminster*, Madame Chanel's code name, has been registered as Agent F-7124. It may be nothing, but since her appointment a few months ago, she has been proactively seeking to establish a much closer relationship with Marta, specifically expressing a strong inquisitiveness toward her father-in-law, General von Brauchitsch."

The admiral remained patiently quiet, watching and listening intently to Anna's intriguing interpretation of events. Her insightful and refreshing perspectives never ceased to fascinate him.

"My concern, Admiral, is whether this interest is based upon more than Madame Chanel's genuine friendship and past business relationship with Marta... or is it motivated by something far more sinister?... Perhaps an assignment given her by Joseph Goebbels and General Schellenberg to investigate General von Brauchitsch?"

A long pause ensued. Both the general and the admiral drew deep breaths to carefully consider Anna's well-founded suspicions. The admiral shook his head from side to side as he stood up and began to pace about the room. The tension was evident, and well outside his normal calm bearing.

"This is extremely perceptive of you, Anna. We know there are those of the SS, particularly within the Nazi Party, infiltrating Abwehr for their own nefarious purposes. Himmler and Schellenberg are two of the more subversive in their determination to protect the Fuhrer. In fact, High Command is of the belief there are numerous conspirators within the military plotting to overthrow the Fuhrer.

"There is a growing conspiracy attracting their scrutiny of late. It is derisively known as the *Schwarze Kapelle* (Black Orchestra). I don't believe we are currently among the names of potential conspirators; however, a number of senior Wehrmacht officers most certainly are."

General von Brauchitsch finally broke his silence and offered his thoughts on the matter.

"There is much more to their suspicions than unfounded paranoia, Admiral. Himmler and Schellenberg are not to be considered lightly. I sense as the war has shifted momentum in favor of the Allies, the Fuhrer is suspecting everyone in his path.

"Sir, I cannot be less than candid about this but," the general paused…
"my own relationship with the Fuhrer has grown more distant of late. I
am certain I am included among his newfound preoccupations."

After a brief pause, the general continued, "I believe we should appear
to embrace their plot to investigate us, if that indeed is Madame Chanel's
intent. We must be prepared for this possibility and take no overt action
to dissuade them. Discouraging Chanel's interest in Marta and myself
could be taken by some to be indications of guilt. We must address this
head on, so to speak, in my humble opinion, Sir."

"I agree Walther. Let's do as you suggest but remain mindful of
their possible motives. Anna, is there anything to be potentially concerned about with Marta?"

"No Sir. Marta and I do not discuss matters concerning my work
here. You have my personal assurances, Admiral."

"I would expect no less from you. However, I advise you behave
normally in her presence to not discourage her relationship with
Chanel. I want to be clear with you that I am not casting any negative
aspersions directed at Marta."

The admiral took brief pause to tread carefully, assuring there
were no misunderstandings… "It has been said we should keep our
friends close, but our enemies closer. Please understand, it is not
about deceiving Marta or Marta deceiving us; it is simply about not
disclosing our motives, enabling the situation to play out absent our
proactive influence. She will not be exposed to any danger from our
end, I assure you."

*****

By April 1943, the momentum of the war had clearly shifted to
the Allies favor; however, German leadership remained on course,
loyal for the most part, despite Hitler's fading popularity within his
own military ranks. To do otherwise within High Command would
have been futile and would assuredly result in brutal retaliation from
the Reich upon not only the collaborators themselves, but their families as well. Nevertheless, rumblings of dissension within the upper
echelon continued to worsen in the months following.

At this time, there were growing numbers within Hitler's close
circle who had lost faith in fighting a war of this magnitude on

multiple fronts. The Eastern Front in Russia had taken a tremendous toll on the German military in both manpower and resources, worsened by extremely bitter winter weather, stopping the German advance in its tracks.

Since the end of 1941, Russia had been steadily pushing the Germans farther back from the outskirts of Moscow in merciless fashion, killing almost 800,000 German troops in the process. This casualty count did not include the hundreds of thousands of souls frozen or starved to death. Clearly, Mother Nature was a major factor taking its own toll.

It was a pivotal time in the war, magnifying the inability of Germany to supply its war weary troops with necessary clothing and food to endure Russia's harsh conditions. General von Brauchitsch had warned the Fuhrer about the monumental task of invading Russia. While his apprehensions were well-founded, the Fuhrer interpreted the general's remarks to be counter-productive, to the extent it negatively affected their past relationship.

Operation Barbarossa was an abysmal failure, even before the Russians mounted a successful winter counter-offensive against Germany. When von Brauchitsch' prophesy became reality, the fierce consternation from the Fuhrer toward the general was overwhelming; a major factor leading to the general's anxiety attacks aggravating his fragile heart condition.

Similarly, on the Western Front, the British were proving to be more daunting than German Command had anticipated. Their unbending resilience gave cause for German leadership to reassess the wisdom of continuing to challenge the well prepared and militarily capable British armed forces.

*****

Within only weeks of Chanel's collaboration with Schellenberg, her first assignment was a highly relevant one. Typically, an agent of Abwehr received several months or even years of training. However, in Chanel's case, there was insufficient time, and her specific talents would have to be exploited hastily.

What was sought by High Command were Chanel's God given natural talents, among them her amazing charisma. To General Schellenberg, it was simply a matter of implementing them to their greatest advantage.

At the behest of the general, Chanel was sent to Madrid. Having numerous influential friends in high places, Sir Samuel Hoare, the British Ambassador to Spain was counted among them. Chanel's mission was to convey a message from Hitler's Foreign Intelligence office clearly stating that if Germany's defeat ever became imminent, Germany was prepared to come to terms with the British.

The ambassador was a close and trusted friend of Winston Churchill and as such he, together with Chanel, could verify the fact that many among Third Reich leadership wanted peace.

When Chanel and Baron von Dinklage returned to the RSHA headquarters in Berlin shortly thereafter, Chanel offered her assistance to Schellenberg to personally convince Churchill to negotiate with Germany. These events caused General Schellenberg among others, to become strong advocates of initiating such a proposal, supported by Hitler, to consider a separate peace negotiation directly with Great Britain.

Numerous influential and high-ranking Nazi leaders believed if Germany and Britain could agree, the war between the two countries would potentially cease. There was one significant stipulation: Germany would control all of Europe and in return, would provide assurances the United Kingdom would no longer be subjected to further German aggression.

With this objective in mind, Schellenberg selected several of Hitler's personal advisors, including Colonel von Stauffenberg, who also supported the strategy and together, as absurd as it may appear, they relied upon Madame Chanel to act on their behalf as an intermediary. Her well-established personal connections within British aristocracy, specifically her past intimate relationship with the Duke of Westminster, were considered extremely relevant assets.

It was thought that British Prime Minister Winston Churchill, who had remained a close and trusted friend of Madame Chanel, could provide additional credibility to this proposal. The intent of Chanel's mission was to directly inform the British that many senior SS officers were actively seeking an end to the bloodshed. Through her connections, a meeting was sought with the British. The operation was codenamed *"Operation Modellhut"* (Model Hat).

A top-secret meeting was hastily arranged in Berlin to include General Schellenberg, Gunther von Dinklage, Coco Chanel, and two other SS officers including Colonel von Stauffenberg, whose aristocratic and highly influential family brought additional credibility to the proposal. Although not in attendance, Heinrich Himmler was also supportive of the operation, as he too had been desperately searching for a viable solution to stop the war.

Were it not for the untimely serious illness of Churchill, his significant influence was not offered to Chanel and her co-conspirator, Vera Lombardi, to potentially consummate a peace negotiation. Furthermore, British security later identified Ms. Lombardi as a German spy, who turned on Chanel.

Under severe pressure, Lombardi was coerced to disclose their role, mistakenly interpreted to be an attempt to overthrow Hitler. Fearing for his own life, Schellenberg intervened and severed all further contact with Madame Chanel.

Although a peace agreement was highly unlikely, Churchill's positive influence could have been enough to tip the scales in favor of commencing secretive peace negotiations. It was a topic that would remain open to discussion by historians for years to come.

Although Vera Lombardi was returned to prison once again on charges of espionage, Chanel was not. Despite Lombardi's arrest, Madame Chanel was released from any charges of espionage due to insufficient evidence against her. She was subsequently permitted to return safely to Paris and suffered abject disappointment about the failure of her assignment, remaining discouraged for many years thereafter.

When her secret agent status was necessarily revoked by Schellenberg's office, there was no further investigation of General von Brauchitsch, at least by way of the relationship through Marta. Chanel was never proven to have been a collaborator in treason; not only because there was insufficient evidence but also, largely due to Churchill's later intervention, and von Dinklage and Schellenberg's ability to destroy incriminating documentation which could have been used to likely incarcerate her.

These actions were a testament to Chanel's amazing influence and support from friends in high places. However, she would no longer be politically active and spent the rest of her later years in self-imposed exile in Switzerland.

*****

THE FRAU SOLF TEA PARTY—HEIDELBERG

Dr. Wilhelm Solf was the product of a wealthy and very liberal minded family in Berlin, who became a career diplomat serving as an ambassador to Japan during the Great War. He and his wife Hanna were financially and intellectually well-connected. Both were politically open-minded, which was not surprising based upon Herr Solf's proven aptitude for diplomacy.

Shortly after Dr. Solf's death, his wife continued her husband's legacy by hosting several philanthropic activities in their private home in an affluent and historic district of Heidelberg. These functions provided a wonderful and relaxed venue for aristocratic intellectuals and prominent socialites to gather. Over time, however, their private agenda attracted the attention of influential political moderates, many of whom were fervent anti-Nazis.

These attendees were people of significant influence, whose opinions had tremendous relevance in German high society. Over time, invitations were thoughtfully and discreetly extended to other like-minded individuals. To be on the guest list was an affirmation of one's social status and was regarded by many to be a distinct privilege originally intended to provide solidarity against the oppression of Jews and any other ethnicities being degraded by the Nazi regime.

Solf social affairs were the epitome of sophistication for German aristocracy, and as such, their credibility and reputation were undeniable. Often included on the guest lists were elite people such as a senior official from the Foreign Office named Otto Kiep, his close personal friend, Erich Vermehrens who was a senior agent of Abwehr, the Countess Hannah von Bredlow who was the granddaughter of Otto von Bismarck, Count Albrecht von Bernstorff and his nephew, who was the former German ambassador to the United States, State Secretary Arthur Zarden and his daughter, and numerous others of similar prestigious status.

On September 10, 1943, there was an innocuous birthday party of very little apparent significance. It was intended to be a simple tea party hosted by Elisabeth von Thadden, a close friend of Hanna Solf and her daughter Lagi. Unknown to Hanna Solf, Von Thadden had a history of passive anti-Nazi activity and unfortunately, the necessity for discreet but thorough screening of her guests was, on occasion, treated too casually by her. These get-togethers were long suspected by Nazi authorities to include prominent Jewish sympathizers.

On this occasion, through a series of referrals, Elisabeth von Thadden had extended an invitation to a handsome Swiss physician named Paul Reckzeh, purportedly with tenure at the Charité Hospital in Berlin; co-incidentally the same hospital in which Dr. Sigmund Landesburg practiced and lectured years before.

The young, charismatic doctor was unusually open and candid about his anti-Nazi persuasions, as it was the prevailing opinion of many Swiss, and he quickly caught the attention and support of both Otto Kiep and Count Bernstorff, in particular.

As the evening progressed, several customary attendees were drawn to Dr. Reckzeh and welcomed his charming and likeable presence among them. His appearance was striking, and he exuded a pleasant self-confidence when he offered keen insights, refreshing to many of the guests who began to gravitate toward him. He was extremely refined and purposely asked many open-ended questions to encourage more expanded conversation.

Within a few hours, after several cocktails were consumed, various guests became increasingly self-assured to converse more openly with Reckzeh, particularly in view of their confidence and trust in Hanna Solf's customary and capable screening of guests.

Discussions often addressed common issues concerning the war, including sympathetic opinions against Jewish persecution. However, over time, alcohol consumption loosened lips as it often does, and many guests predictably lowered their guard too quickly.

A few of them expressed a more aggressive posture, inevitably escalating to the matters of hiding Jews and furnishing them false documentation to provide safe passage out of Germany. These casual disclosures were serious and defiant breaches of Nazi mandates and would prove to be the biggest mistake of Madame von Thadden's life, as well as Hanna Solf's for trusting in her.

Inviting the charming young doctor to her party was a fatal mistake. No one in attendance suspected Dr. Reckzeh's strategic seduction of numerous guests in his capacity as a spy, working undercover for the Gestapo under Heinrich Himmler.

A few days after the event, Reckzeh submitted his confidential report to the Gestapo, replete with incriminating evidence which would be immediately investigated and soon confirmed. In the ensuing four months, the Nazis remained mute about many of their discoveries of treason and patiently used their time to carefully deploy a wider net to determine the true depth of the conspiracy. As leads were being further explored, the full scope of the treason was still largely unknown.

*****

Abwehr was naturally proactively involved with Himmler's investigation of various leads on his behalf. Himmler at this point remained largely unaware of any direct Abwehr involvement. However, Admiral Canaris knew immediately the investigation would inevitably lead to himself and his trusted accomplices, including General von Brauchitsch, Major Hans Oster, Major Groscurth, and most definitely, Anna. These revelations would drastically impact the future of Abwehr itself.

The shockwave of reality swiftly set upon Admiral Canaris' inner circle. Behind closed doors, a brief meeting was convened for Admiral Canaris' main collaborators to assess damage control. The admiral began slowly and calmly as he addressed the small group who had the most to lose from Reichsfuhrer Himmler's devastating disclosures.

"Thankfully, Abwehr leadership has not yet come under serious suspicion by the investigative scrutiny of Himmler. Since the startling revelations from the Solf party, his obsession to find the roots of the *Black Orchestra* have been all consuming and will eventually bear the fruit of his labor: the complicity of Abwehr's inner circle.

"Until now, he has had nothing more than a few unvalidated suspicions Abwehr may have been compromised to some minor degree but does not realize the main perpetrators are right under his own nose.

"One of our agents, Erich Vermehrens, attended the tea party and will be implicated by his close association with Otto Kiep from the Foreign Office. Kiep's arrest is highly likely, which will of course connect Vermehrens, leading Himmler directly back to our office."

General von Brauchitsch politely interjected. "Admiral, it is my understanding Kiep is already suspected to have direct ties of a personal nature to the US Consulate. He is likely to be the easiest target for aggressive interrogation. They will torture him for high treason;

there is no end to what he could reveal. I am particularly concerned about his knowledge of the July 20th plot to assassinate the Fuhrer. That information will place General von Tresckow's operation in serious jeopardy, Sir."

"If I may ask, Sirs," Anna enquired. "We understand it is only a matter of time before the truth is fully disclosed. Please forgive my self-serving question but... what can we do to protect our outside interests and how much time do you think we have before it is too late to act?"

"Good question, Anna. They still don't know the extent of where the investigation may lead. I am in agreement with the general that Kiep will break soon after his arrest. It is Erich Vermehrens who holds the key. We will not survive his interrogation. He knows our operation all too well."

The admiral turned his attention back to the general. "Walther, determine where Erich is presently. If he is outside of Berlin, God willing outside of Germany, let's tip him off to delay his return and evade his inevitable capture, at least long enough to get him and his family out of harm's way. British Secret Intelligence understand he would be an incredible asset. It should not be difficult for them to turn him."

"Anna, transcribe a coded message of the highest priority to the British Prime Minister. If we can engage the help of the British on this matter, it will be our best chance to spare us additional time. However, in response to your question, I assure you this matter will only delay the inevitable for a short time, perhaps an additional week or ten days, at most.

"In the meantime, Major, you and Anna start shredding whatever sensitive documents and wire transmissions we may be holding; anything exposing our misdeeds. We're not looking for just the obvious, in fact, I will handle anything pertaining to myself directly. I will be found guilty as hell of all charges, and deservedly so. Nothing can change the situation, so I must deal with it.

"But those *Zossen Files* must be removed from the site and preserved. We took years to compile them so history will know the truth about the Reich. We worked too hard and too long to let them be destroyed.

"Please know I am proud of all of you for your tireless devotion. We will discuss progress when it becomes relevant, but in the meantime, cover your own asses as best you can and may God speed."

20

WE ARE BOTH IN GOD'S HANDS NOW

♂

THE DISCOVERY OF THE MEMBERSHIP OF THE *BLACK ORCHESTRA* was inevitable and it was the first indication causing Anna to carefully consider taking personal, drastic measures for her own safety. Himmler's thorough investigation was an eventuality even Admiral Canaris was helpless to prevent. When the conspirators would be discovered, Anna was well aware of her probable fate; it was unthinkably horrific.

Based upon her experience as an impartial translator, she had passively participated in numerous Abwehr interrogations. She knew the brutality of their methods and the lengths to which they would go to extract information. There was nothing she could imagine she had not already witnessed.

Anna thanked the Lord above that Admiral Canaris had been so forthright in confiding the gravity of the situation so unhesitatingly to his small group of trusted collaborators. Having been given the courtesy of early notice, she knew the admiral well and their days were clearly numbered. She was determined not to waste a day of it.

It was imperative the normal daily patterns remained constant; however, this was far from a normal work environment. Crisis after crisis was always the order of the day and planning her potential escape in advance was extremely difficult at best.

Thankfully, Anna had long since been given more latitude planning her own agenda, without approval from her superior officers. The responsibility the Fuhrer had assigned to her to provide oversight for the *Konto 5* Account over two years ago, had been handled meticulously by Anna, much to the dismay of Chief Lammers of the Reich Chancellery.

He had been a vile enemy of Anna's since the day of her appointment and had used any and every opportunity to denigrate her to the Fuhrer and his Chief of Staff. Lammers was rebuffed by them at every failed attempt to remove her. The level of trust and moderate independence she had attained since the meeting with Hitler, would now better serve her to use any extended leeway she required to devise the means of her escape.

It was time for another visit with Marta. This time however, it would not be a social one.

*****

It was an early Saturday morning when Anna departed the confines of the Abwehr facilities and instructed her usual driver accordingly. Nothing was abnormal this day, with the only exception being the turmoil beginning to churn deep within her belly. She had very little sleep last night and her mind had worked overtime, reflecting upon various hypothetical scenarios for possible consideration, ruling out one plan after another.

Having long since accepted the danger she would face one day, and knowing the limited timeline before her, Anna was too mentally exhausted by days end to dwell on contriving an effective plan of escape. Her options were few, but attention to practical details required a clear head and fastidious attention to detail, which mental fatigue did not fully accommodate. The grinding schedule she faced with each new day afforded her neither the time nor focus she needed to develop a pragmatic course of action. Urgency, previously lacking, was now driving her to get the job done.

This task was a lifesaving challenge requiring outside support. In this regard, Marta was the only person who comprehended many of Anna's unique circumstances. The two friends together, were a formidable team with boundless creativity and perseverance. Their unbreakable bond grounded Anna against her growing angst.

Within an hour of departing Zossen, Anna's driver and the security escort slowly entered the round-about continuing east on Stauffenbergstrasse, in the district of Tiergarten in Berlin. She fixed her gaze when passing the government buildings known as *The Bendlerblock*. It housed the Abwehr offices in which Klaus was working.

His father, the general, commuted frequently between his Zossen office and Berlin. She feared for Klaus, since learning the current situation would no doubt include him as a suspected co-conspirator as well. He had been conspicuously absent from Admiral Canaris' briefing.

Anna was torn as to whether she should advise Marta, but thought better of the idea, realizing Klaus' father would deliver the news directly to his son at some point. The general could disclose whatever he wished to convey to Marta and Klaus about the probable implications about to befall both he and his son, but those matters were well outside Anna's limited purview.

Within minutes, the car pulled up to the front of the stately von Brauchitsch mansion and the driver courteously opened the rear door for Anna to exit. He reached for her overnight bag and closed the door firmly as he escorted her through the iron gate leading to the main door.

"Thank you, Officer. You are most kind," Anna offered.

When Marta greeted Anna, naturally excited about her arrival, she was immediately taken aback. Despite Anna's attempt to remain calm and collected, Marta recognized the look of anxious despair on Anna's abnormally distraught face, knowing something had gone terribly awry. It was evident from the moment she opened her door.

"It's always grand to see you again, Anna, but you look a bit off your game. What has happened, Sweetheart? Is everything alright?" she asked.

"Yes, and no, Marta. I'm fine, but I'm now under a great deal of pressure. It must be more evident than I thought… Oh, it's so good to see you, my dear friend. I need you now more than ever."

Marta's spontaneous reaction was one of serious concern, imagining the worst of possibilities. Anna drew a very concerned Marta toward her embrace, *almost as if to console her!*

"There is much we must discuss today. Please, let's fetch some tea and get us both settled down. We can accomplish anything when we stand together."

In times of extreme distress, it was often Anna who was the calmest. Marta took Anna's wrap and summoned her housekeeper, Lena, who by this time was already coming into the foyer to greet Anna herself. "Miss Anna. How very happy I am to see you!"

"You're so kind. Thank you, Lena." Anna replied. "I trust you are well also?" Lena was always so engaging but never crossed the line of familiarity unless specifically asked to do so. "Yes, very much so. Thank you for asking."

Marta quickly added, "Perhaps a few fresh scones, with some tea would be lovely, Lena."

"Of course, Miss Marta. I won't be but a few minutes." Lena was always fastidious to a fault and was almost in lockstep with whatever the household required. Originally, young Manfred had been her primary responsibility but had left home a few years ago and was living his dreams in the service of his country with the Luftwaffe.

Dietrich filled the void for Lena, so to speak. She was instrumental in tending to his every need after his adoption. She thought of both boys like her own sons and was dutifully invaluable to Marta since their calls to duty; Manfred in flight school and Dietrich in the Hitler Youth, the latter still never disclosed to Anna.

"I imagine Dietrich is still at the Academy this weekend. I trust he is well and living up to Klaus' expectations of him. As much as I miss him terribly, I am not here to speak with him today, but please tell him how very much I love and miss him. I am so thankful he is under your constant care, Marta. I hope one day he will be better able to understand some of the reasons I have been unable to be with him."

In only a few minutes, both ladies briefly caught up with the customary pleasantries to defer the main issue of the day until Lena had delivered the tea and exited the parlor to allow the privacy Anna required. Despite being anxious to address her new circumstance, Anna did her best to feign calmness.

She was careful to maintain her poise and her pledge of confidentiality to her superior officers, most specifically those affecting the general and Klaus, and only divulged brief scants of her new reality to Marta.

"You were very astute about my apparent stress this morning, Marta. You read me like a book. But enough of my theatrics, let me begin."

Anna took another sip of tea and steadied her thoughts. "Certain information crossed my desk recently, which most certainly was not meant for me to see. You know much of what has happened I cannot discuss with you, so please forgive me. What I *can* tell you is I am in grave danger..." Anna paused briefly, "... as are my superior officers." She was perilously close to an invisible line she dared not cross.

Marta stared directly and disbelievingly into Anna's eyes with a sixth sense something terrible was about to happen. Anna tried to keep calm despite all she had endured. Of significance here was not only Marta's concerns for Anna, but also for Walther and Klaus, who were among Anna's superior officers. In response to this realization, Marta began trembling with growing anxiety, looking to Anna for some reassurance that was not to be found.

Anna remained speechless for a moment and despite her trepidations, she nodded affirmatively to Marta's unasked question.

Marta's mouth was now agape as Anna continued. "It is imperative you do not disclose any of this to either of them. They are as aware as I am of our common circumstances, but they will surely tell you more about it when they deem it necessary. This revelation must not come from me. Do you understand me, Marta?"

The silent pause of acknowledgement was both stark and deafening. "It is time for me to attempt my escape from Abwehr... and from Berlin. We all knew this day would come; I just didn't anticipate it to be so sudden and unexpected."

"Oh, dear God!" Marta gasped, as she placed both hands upon her cheeks in disbelief. "Will you be safe? Where will you go?" As she asked her question, she placed her hands on Anna's.

"That depends very much on what decisions I make in the next very few days, which is why I came here today. You are the only soul on this earth I can speak to about these matters. I cannot plan an appropriate course of action without your help, Marta. Forgive me, but there is one burning question I must ask you. Please tell me you still have the ring safely hidden?"

"Yes, of course Anna! I did exactly..."

"Thank you, Lord!" Anna interjected. "I have considered my limited options over the last several weeks and shamefully, I don't have much to work with. Although a bit threadbare, I continue to believe none of my discreet inquiries have been discovered. Either way, I have no alternative than to continue to believe my ingenuity will provide.

"My first of many priorities is to find cash, hence my interest in the ring. My pay is very modest since most of what I require is fully provided. However, without additional cash even fewer options are available to me." Anna sipped her tea as she contemplated how best to direct her conversation with a very attentive Marta.

"Listen to me very carefully. It is impossible for me to do myself what I am about to ask of you, for reasons that will become obvious. I need you to instruct your jeweler to remove the blue sapphire from the mantle of the ring. I know it was the best possible quality, so whatever its present value, my father must have paid a pretty penny for it.

"I don't need much money, but whatever cash you can obtain for the stone will help me immensely for travel expenses I cannot possibly cover on my own. If possible though, please keep the remaining skeleton of the ring intact for me… till sometime in the future, when we meet again."

"Anna, there is no reason to sell anything. I can give you whatever money you may need. You should already know that…"

"I do know that Marta, but I do not want any possible trace of a connection between you and Klaus and my escape. I simply could not expose you to such unnecessary risk. It is also why I cannot tell you anything of my plans. Perhaps I am just being paranoid but attribute it to my background in intelligence; always suspicious and covering my trail so to speak. It is far better this way, trust me."

"I will do as you ask, and right away! It won't take but a few days. Our jeweler has always been fair with us. He will surely offer me a reasonable value. I'll tell him it's to purchase something as a surprise for Klaus."

"Thank you, Marta. My timeframe is rather uncertain, but I was directly advised I should prepare for serious repercussions within the next two weeks, otherwise I may lose the element of surprise. I have personal knowledge placing me in imminent danger from very powerful people. I will only have one chance, at best, to get myself away from here."

"You are frightening me, Anna! I cannot imagine Walther could not help you in some way." No sooner had Marta said the words when she realized Anna could not count on the general's support any longer. He was probably in similar danger. Other than Marta, and without Walther, Anna was truly facing this grave predicament alone.

"I have many things I must tend to before I return to base. I will need a few hours on my own but I'll contact my driver later today so he can return to meet me here as usual. I don't want to attract any unwarranted attention based upon any significant change of habits. I promise I will get back to you by the end of the coming week. Fair enough?"

Marta wanted to do whatever she could to help but resisted any arguments with Anna when Anna simply said, "I hope you understand," and looked pleadingly into Marta's eyes to just do as Anna instructed.

The same evening, the two friends bid their farewells and kept the visit shorter than usual. Anna would tell her security escort she had been taken with a bad headache and thought it best to return a day earlier than usual to the base.

*****

It would be the longest week of Anna's Abwehr career. She resumed her work at a feverish pace, but nothing could help pass the time fast enough. There was still much thought to be given to her tenuous plans for escape. Anything requiring prearranged timing and logistics were ready to be set in motion, but there was still so much she could not control to potentially go wrong.

By the following weekend, there were thankfully no matters of significant urgency necessitating Anna remain on the base. She had no manner in which to contact Marta to confirm the sale of the blue sapphire, and she specifically did not want to message Marta through Klaus for fear of implicating them both. No, the best decision was to arrive at Marta's home as she normally would, with the expectation the funds would be available to her.

If the transaction had been for any reason delayed and the funds were not available, she planned to enjoy her time with the family as best she could, considering the circumstances. She would return to the base one final time and defer her escape one additional week. With or without the money, she was determined there could be no further delays. There were not many opportunities remaining until

Himmler's net would inevitably entrap her to face the same fate as her superiors would no doubt have to endure. Again, she could only imagine the worst.

Anna was comforted knowing she had been extremely fastidious with any files of a sensitive nature, specifically those pertaining to *Black Orchestra* operations, no matter how oblique the references. Even the admiral, General von Brauchitsch, and General Oster had no direct knowledge of how Anna disguised, manipulated, and encoded her way through clandestine record keeping, nor any knowledge whatsoever about her trusted and encrypted bookkeeping for Hitler's *Konto 5* Account.

They knew Anna would handle the task with her usual and customary proficiency. There was nothing of significance remaining from her end which could potentially incriminate her superior officers who had become among her most revered relationships.

With specific regard to her work within Abwehr, very little Anna would inevitably discover in the course of her work escaped the eyes of the admiral. For most of their time working together, particularly after Anna was entrusted to be complicit as a Jewish sympathizer, the admiral gave her free rein to discover her own instinctive revelations. There was no need to confide additional sensitive information potentially exposing her to even more risk than necessary at this point. In these past several weeks, he would deftly guide her well-founded suspicions to wherever they ultimately took her. He was a master at his craft, and she learned a great deal from his tactful and persuasive manner.

Since Dr. Reckzeh's report on the Solf party revelations, the admiral and the general took Anna's best interests to heart, a sentiment typically never applying in this line of work. In an almost casual manner, they informed Anna her usual two-man security detail would be absent for the next month or so, as they were temporarily reassigned to other duties. She was advised only a single individual would be escorting her for the next few weeks until the regulars returned.

"I suggest you take advantage of this driver's services, Anna. You have never abused the very limited privileges we have tried to provide for you, but perhaps it is time for you to take things a step further. You have my personal authorization to use his services as you would your personal chauffeur. He will take you safely wherever you may wish to go. He can drop you and return at the time and place of your choosing."

There was a very decisive and poignant pause as the admiral awaited her response.

"Admiral, you leave me speechless. I thank you for your kindness but… I don't think…" She fumbled for words, not something she often did. Her eyes met the admiral's and remained focused upon them. He squeezed her hand tightly and for the first time in the three years of their close relationship, his eyes began to momentarily tear. Despite a touch of possible embarrassment, he made no attempt to break eye contact with her.

"I have already discussed this possibility with Generals Oster and von Brauchitsch. They whole-heartedly agree with my decision." Without expressing the words specifically, only now was Anna fully comprehending his meaning. He was telling her not to return!

Anna lowered her head submissively for only a moment, thinking to herself some definitive confirmation had to be made by her to accurately confirm her interpretation was correct. In the softest of tones, Anna regained her focus and stated very quietly as she struggled to stop a tear running down the contour of her cheek, "I shall miss you, Admiral."

"As I will you, Anna. If you leave on a Friday afternoon, I feel confident no one will notice your absence for two or three days. How and where you go, I must not know, but there is something I must give you to assist you on your journey." The admiral rose from his seat to approach the wall safe in his office. There he withdrew a small, sealed envelope bearing no identifiable markings of any kind.

"The general and I want you to have this, Anna. Lord knows you have earned it."

Anna quizzically looked at his kindly aged face, which was now even more so from the stress and anxiety he was personally enduring, and she accepted the small envelope from his hand. Inside was not one, but two passports: one Swiss and one Belgian, in the names of Ester Elisabeth Keller and Linette Vivian Etienne. Both passports bore Anna's photo with a much lighter shade of brown, almost blonde hair. In addition, there was a money clip containing more than she was willing to count at this awkward moment.

"You are always a step ahead of me, Admiral. I am deeply moved by your gesture. You will always be in my prayers, which I trust you already know."

"They will be looking for you, of that you can be assured. If you are caught, I can do nothing to protect you from whatever madness Himmler may resort. You simply must not allow that to happen. Do you understand my meaning, Anna?" The admiral paused purposely for Anna to fully comprehend the words he dared not speak. He was instructing Anna to kill herself rather than be caught. "There is a cyanide capsule in the envelope too."

"You have knowledge of potentially damaging consequences, for and against both sides of these conflicts. I pray you have learned enough from your work here to carry you through whatever may confront you. Of importance though I must add, you are an intelligent and capable woman who is quick to adapt. Your insights and natural instinct will serve you well.

"Your driver will dispose of the car so it will never be discovered. It will be the last time you or I will ever see him again. You know you will be in our thoughts and prayers."

Those were the last words the admiral would say to her.

*****

The next day Anna gathered a few personal items she would typically take on her usual visits to Marta, being careful to leave many personal items, such as most of her clothing and one or two old photos of her children when they were just babies. She hated to leave the photos, of course. They were all she had to remind her of them, but it was necessary to indicate her apparent intent to return.

This decision alone could buy her an extra day or so before suspicions were aroused. Without any fanfare or sentimental goodbyes, she walked away from Abwehr as she would on any other day, but this time she was turning the page to another new beginning.

The newly assigned driver seemed a pleasant sort and he was certainly not talkative at all, typical of many of her past security details. Other than *"Yes, Madame."* and *"Good day, Madame,"* the silence in the car was as expected.

Anna could not help but wonder what would become of this man, and whether he was placing himself in some danger by accepting this rather unique assignment. The admiral was emphatic stating *"neither Anna nor himself would ever see this man again"*. The very thought caused Anna to shudder.

She decided in this quiet time, as the danger ahead of her was becoming more ominous, she would instruct the driver to wait for her at the back of the Grand Hostel Hotel. Cars of similar markings had used the alleyway in the past, all the way back to her father's times when he used to meet with General von Brauchitsch. Nothing should appear out of the ordinary and the car was too conspicuous to remain on the street in front of Marta's home.

Anna found herself staring into the rear-view mirror and saw the middle-aged driver's steely grey eyes, as if to see into the depths of his soul. Not that he would ever understand the reason for her prolonged eye contact, nor would he have cause to mention it; neither did Anna. She simply found herself overcome with dread that something sinister would happen to him, perhaps something intended for her. Was she making too much of things, she wondered? She diverted her mind away from the thought and focused on other more crucial matters still within her control.

Anna calculated she would need two hours to conclude her visit with Marta. Cash, or no cash, was not a concern for her now, after the admiral's thoughtful generosity. The driver slowed his approach to the main gates of the residence and turned the engine off to exit the car and escort Anna to the main door. As he took hold of her overnight bags, Anna imparted a slight change of plans, standing to face him for the first time.

"Since the hotel is only about a fifteen minute walk from here, I will meet you at the rear of the hotel at precisely 2:00 o'clock. I have a few errands to run in the area taking me close to the hotel about that time. However, if for any reason I am more than thirty minutes late, I want you to immediately leave the hotel without me and follow whatever instructions you were given by your commander. I will take another car to get back to Abwehr from there."

Before she could say another word, the driver immediately protested, albeit very politely. "Madame, I have no urgency to return to Abwehr without you. Any time suiting you better, it is my pleasure to accommodate you. I am not comfortable leaving you in the care of a public taxi driver. I'm dreadfully sorry, Madame, but your safety is my only priority."

"I fully understand, Officer. I appreciate your concern, but I must insist. You were instructed to obey my wishes, no matter when or where I may tell you to take me. Is my understanding correct?"

Sheepishly, the gentleman looked pleadingly into her eyes, which were staring straight back at his own. His discomfort was evident, but Anna was not backing down. "Do I make myself clear, Officer?"

"Yes, Madame. Of course. I wish you a safe return."

"Then I shall see you again before 2:30. I look forward to seeing you then. Have a pleasant afternoon, Sir."

*****

From the instant Marta opened the imposing front door, their shared greetings were awkwardly emotional. They were both as prepared as they could be in the current situation, neither one knowing with any degree of certainty when, or if they would ever see one another again. Oddly, this was not the first time this had happened.

In the ensuing two hours the friends tried bravely to enjoy a cup of coffee, savoring their conversation more than the coffee. It was tremendously difficult to sit facing each other, stumbling through such emotional discourse. Throughout their entire friendship they never had cause to speak so haltingly to one another.

"You know Marta, as I look back at our situation after Jacob was taken, neither of us had any expectations about what might happen to us. I was so despondent and confused. You were the only reason I could move forward, or back for that matter. It was your faith in me that gave me the strength to persevere. I was in no condition to make any decisions for myself, yet somehow, I survived, as did Dietrich and your family. Despite the terrible times we faced, those worrisome circumstances eventually dissolved over time."

"I purposely try to forget those memories, but you are right, Anna. I think we just placed one foot ahead of the other and simply refused to give up."

"I firmly believe I am in a much stronger position today, both mentally and physically, than I was at that time. I have a clear head and feel prepared to conduct myself intelligently and prudently. I am now asking you to continue to trust in me, and more importantly, to trust in yourself."

"I will... and I do, with every fiber of my being. Once again, we are both in God's hands... and oh... I have something for you."

Marta turned and slid the bureau drawer open to retrieve a money clip securing a bundle of currency notes. "I have 1,400 Reichsmarks in exchange for the sapphire..." She placed it into Anna's hand. "This should sustain you for a while, as you requested... and this will sustain you even longer."

It was another 600 Reichsmarks. "It will not be missed Anna. I always keep some cash on hand even Klaus knows nothing about. We will be fine without it. Just don't argue with me, please just accept it."

"Thank you, Marta! Thank you."

"Despite the jeweler's initial protestations to remove it from such a beautiful setting, he did in fact, do as I asked. He offered to purchase the ring outright, but we quickly resolved such a transaction would not be possible. He did not press me any further on the matter."

Marta held out the palm of her hand and slowly opened it to Anna's view. The skeleton of the ring was nestled in her palm and was hesitatingly accepted by Anna, although her original intention had been for it to remain in Marta's possession. There was no time for further discussion, as time was becoming an issue. Anna tucked the ring into a small pocket inside her leather attaché case for the time being. The exquisite silver case remained with Marta.

Before departing, Anna tied her hair into a young and sassy pony-tail, a style she never wore. A pair of Marta's sunglasses would suit the moment and were perched upon her head with apparent casual indifference. The day was clouding over but leaving the glasses in place for the afternoon's final blinding rays seemed appropriate and superbly fashionable. Marta quietly looked on, feeling the tension growing again and worried for Anna's safety.

Within Anna's limited timeframe, an all too brief farewell could never be sufficient, but a final reassuring embrace and the exchanges of "*I love you!*" were all that truly needed to be said. Marta sobbed heavily, no longer containing herself despite her best efforts to do so.

Suddenly, from what sounded to be only a short distance away, there was a massive, earth-shaking explosion, catching everyone in the house completely off guard!

It shook the very foundations of the house and rattled the windows, causing Anna and Marta to cower instinctively. Lena was returning to the parlor to freshen the tea, and she stumbled from the tremors, falling hard upon the unforgiving marble floor; the china teapot shattering on impact. The explosion from the blast was deafening, still causing their ears to ring.

All three struggled to regain their balance, clinging to each other's wobbling frames. The finely displayed china shifted, some rattled and fell from the shelving. The sounds of dishware smashing on the floor could be heard from the kitchen.

"Are you alright Lena?" Marta shouted. "Yes Miss Marta. I'm fine."

"Is it another air raid?" Marta exclaimed. "It sounded awfully close!"

"I don't think so. I don't hear any sirens or the drone of bombers. Everything here seems as it was," Anna reassured her.

They gathered at the front door and timidly opened it. Along the normally busy street, children were crying as they clung to their mothers, seeking reassurance while other passers-by hunkered down to their knees, some even laying down on the grass across the street. Other neighbors were also peeking apprehensively from their homes wondering no doubt what had happened.

"There!... A few blocks away! Do you see the smoke starting to rise over the rooftops?" Anna was pointing in the general direction she would be heading. Sooner or later, she would discover what had happened, she thought.

"Yes, I do now! My goodness, do you think anyone was hurt? It shook the house... I ... I've never felt anything quite like it before!"

"It appears to be only one explosion, probably an accidental one. I'm certain the authorities will soon restore control. Let's hope no one was badly hurt.

"I'm very sorry but I really must rush away, Marta. I'm behind schedule already and don't want to be too late meeting my driver. Stay safely inside no matter what, and stay close to the radio and the telephone. Klaus will know what is best for you and the boys. Stop your tears and gather yourself. I've never seen you quite so shaken, Sweetheart."

"It's not the damned explosion Anna... it's you having to leave us this way! I'm very concerned for your safety." Marta dabbed the corner of her eyes, which again had become puffy from the strain of the moment.

Anna just ignored Marta's sorrowful tears. "My undying love to Manny and Dietrich, as always! I don't know when, but you know I will contact you whenever it is safe to do so. At the very least I will get a message to you confirming my well-being. All will be well soon enough. Just be patient with me, do you understand?"

Anna refused to give in to the emotions of the moment, and after a final hug of reassurance, she closed the door securely behind her. She had her own serious apprehensions but decided they were not Marta's concerns. She walked purposefully and maintained her steady resolve walking toward her scheduled rendezvous at the Grand Hostel. She was already fifteen minutes late.

People were by now beginning to resume their normal activities as it was becoming clear whatever happened was indeed a single event. She gradually increased her pace to make up for lost time and had no intention of missing her ride to somewhere outside the city limits.

As Anna rounded the city block some ten minutes later, she could see the Hostel Hotel, large plumes of dust and smoke still rising ominously above it. She decided to approach from the opposite side of the street. She drew closer now and saw several police cars with lights flashing, and whining sirens adding to the chaotic scene. It was quite a commotion. A large crowd had gathered to get a better view of what had occurred. This was not at all what she had been anticipating!

Tentatively, Anna attempted to lose herself in the crowd, mingling with the impromptu spectators, trying to overhear something to explain the general goings on. Her first thought was one of uncertainty and although the extended deadline to meet her driver was fast approaching, she thought it unwise to try in any way to advance through the police barriers already being put into place. By avoiding them altogether she would not become even remotely involved in any potential altercation.

She reasoned if she missed her rendezvous, it was a matter of relatively little concern. While she certainly had no time to waste, her curiosity got the better of her. She had no apprehensions about catching a taxicab to exit the city, so she stayed a little longer to investigate, without drawing any undue attention.

Within minutes the newspaper press arrived at the scene, and two ambulances appeared, causing the attending police to restrain and separate the agitated and quickly growing crowd of onlookers to allow closer access for emergency services.

The powerful explosion momentarily stunning Anna and Marta, had apparently destroyed the entire back wall of the hotel, partially collapsing the interior floors. Unknown to Anna, the rear of the bank facing the loading docks that served both buildings where the military vehicle was parked, also withstood significant structural damage.

Were it not for the additional steel and iron reinforced walls of the bank, the impact of the blast would have been much more devastating. As it was, every window and numerous other exterior features were totally blown out from the rear of the hotel onto the side streets as a result of the powerful percussive affect. No doubt many lives had been lost.

The rumor was spreading there had been multiple gunshots fired in the alleyway likely causing fatalities. It was a prophetic moment when Anna heard someone shout, "The shooting involved a military vehicle parked at the rear of the hotel!"

A terrifying thought just occurred to Anna when she involuntarily asked herself, "*Was this incident related in some way to me*, she thought?... *Was the explosion intended to kill me?*"

Her heart started to pound uncontrollably, and her head began to spin out of control, causing her to stagger momentarily. There was a park bench only a few feet from where she was standing. Awkwardly, she steadied herself to sit for a moment, slowly gathering herself again.

"*It will be the last time you or I will ever see him again.*" The words of Admiral Canaris played over and over in Anna's mind, haunting her now more than the moment they were spoken.

Anna knew she dared not return to Marta's home, irrespective of the danger she may be facing. She had seen and heard enough... it was time to calmly walk away. More importantly, she needed time to rethink her circumstances. Whatever she would ultimately decide to do, returning to Abwehr was no longer an option.

She headed south in the general direction of the *Stadtbahn* train station before the police and military completely cordoned off the area. She knew she could not allow herself to be detained by the authorities, positively identifying her in their attempt to find any eyewitnesses. Certainly, Abwehr would be involved in the investigative process.

Anna's presence here would arouse unwanted suspicions against her and create tedious delays in preparing an alternate plan to escape. Another attempt would be highly unlikely. The troubling question now was whether Abwehr would be conducting the investigation in accordance with its present mandate, or more likely become the prime suspect of an investigation led by Himmler?

In the several hours following the incredible blast, newspaper and radio reports were released describing what appeared to be a self-detonated car bomb, leaving a crater four feet deep with a twenty-foot diameter where a military car had been parked. There was no remaining trace of the car, nor the driver; nothing to be used to confirm positive identification. The motive or circumstances behind such an explosion were not known.

Anna knew over the next several days and weeks everything possible would be meticulously gathered and intensively examined within the entire bomb radius. There was no doubt whatsoever her sudden absence would be tied inextricably to this perplexingly suspicious and violent occurrence. One thing was certain. From this day forward, Anna would now become a highly sought fugitive from the Reich.

*****

When news of the car bombing crossed General von Brauchitsch's desk within the hour of the shocking incident, his first visceral reaction was panic. He and Admiral Canaris were the only Abwehr officers who had collaborated to whisk Anna away, but the explosion was never meant to be part of it. Even Marta failed to consider the bomb may have had any connection to Anna. After all, she was with Anna when the explosion occurred.

The general's first call, before speaking to the admiral, was to Marta. There was already a message for him to return her call.

"Hello, Marta. I was in meetings all morning and missed your call. Is everything alright?" He decided not to show any immediate signs of worry for Anna's safety, and assumed whatever Anna was doing was no longer within his control. The less he said about the matter was safer for all concerned.

"Yes, Walther. Thank you for returning my call. I wanted to confirm I was with Anna earlier today. She was under a great deal of stress but did well to keep it under control. I am reluctant to say much more, but I'm confident she will remain well."

This was Marta's way of indirectly informing Walther about Anna's apparent state of mind that day, but she was uncertain about what else she should disclose. Her evasiveness was not founded in mistrust of her father-in-law, but rather one of fear for Anna's long-term safety.

"I'm pleased to hear that, Sweetheart." He too was reluctant to be open with her. Both sides were feeling out the situation, holding Anna's circumstances hanging precariously between them.

"There was a terrible explosion not far from home this afternoon. It shook the house and cracked a few windows, but it appeared to be somewhere near Tiergarten. Have you heard anything about it you can tell me?" Marta had shifted the topic to something other than Anna. Her interest was genuine, as was her manner with Walther at this point.

"Yes... yes it was quite a shock. I know nothing about it but the injured are being attended to and our people are already investigating. Probably nothing more than a gas leak. Are you and Lena alright? Was Dietrich at home too?"

"No, he wasn't, thankfully. It was very upsetting. But yes, everyone is well. Just a few broken dishes here and there. Nothing to worry about," she replied.

"So, Anna was with you this afternoon? What time of day was that?"

"About the time of the blast, maybe 2:30. Why do you ask?"

"She was with you when the explosion occurred?" he asked excitedly.

"Why, *yes*."

Walther silently gasped with relief, instinctively placing his hand over the telephone, but was mindful to maintain his typical calm manner. "Well, until there is more information about the explosion, I suggest you stay indoors, at least until we know more about the cause. I'm sure Klaus will be in touch soon, as will I. Take care of yourself, my dear. We will talk again soon."

When Walther hung up the phone, his mind was divided. Delighted Anna had not been in her car at the time of the blast, but equally worried about her whereabouts, and if indeed there was a connection of which he was not aware.

He grabbed his phone to ask his administrator to connect him to the admiral. Her immediate response was, "He is standing right here,

General." Walther rose to approach the door to greet the admiral. He was already about to enter.

"Admiral! I was just calling you. There are some matters we must discuss."

Walther approached the admiral, directing him to take a seat, as he addressed his administrator. "Please hold my calls, Elisabeth."

As the general closed his door, the admiral was clearly distressed. "What the hell is going on, Walther? I was just informed of the explosion. Do you suppose Anna was the intended target? And if so, who the hell is behind this? Do you know if she has been killed?" It was evident Admiral Canaris was rattled, a trait he had not expressed in the past.

"First let me just clarify Anna was not in the car at the time of the blast. She is very much alive and well. She was with Marta at the time."

"Thank heaven!" The general sighed, relieved Anna survived. He partially collapsed to sit on the side of the general's desk to support himself.

"Yes, I had the same trepidations until I spoke with Marta. I've only had mere moments since learning Anna was not involved, but whoever, or whatever triggered this event, may offer a solution for the inevitable questions about Anna's failure to return to the office today, but I must admit, I am mystified."

The admiral pondered the situation and offered, "No one else knew about Anna's family circumstances outside of Abwehr. I'm certain we have kept a tight lid on this within these walls... Who else had a score to settle with her? Himmler, Goebbels... the Fuhrer? They were the only ones with the balls to have attempted this."

"It is a short list, Admiral. However, I don't think the Fuhrer is on it. He personally recognized her contributions to Abwehr and applauded her insight in ferreting out the Limoges security leak. No, this was someone else who had something to lose by Anna's cunning expertise."

Walther sat in silence, as did Canaris, both still assessing the matter. Thinking out loud, Walther had a revelation. "Wait a minute - is it possible?"

"What is it, Walther? Where are you going with this?"

"... *Son of a bitch!*" Walther exclaimed. "Sorry, Admiral. What about Lammers? He was pissed when the Fuhrer entrusted oversight of the *Konto-5* Account to Anna. It was a serious slap in the face when he was never consulted about her appointment.

"I'll lay odds it was him, the fucking asshole! He had the balls to pull this off. He wouldn't even have to consult with Himmler. Better he didn't, or should I say, *couldn't*. Himmler would have reported it directly to Hitler. He can't stand the bastard either."

"So, this assassination attempt, if that's what it was, had nothing whatsoever to do with the Solf investigation?" the admiral clarified.

"No. Believe it or not, maybe the timing of this was just a co-incidence. The investigation is still in the early stages and hasn't gone far yet," the general added. "I'll be damned."

"Let's go with this, Walther. Anna routinely made these excur-sions to the city. It's possible someone working for Lammers could have seen a pattern. No one else would have had a motive to inves-tigate her, let alone want to eliminate her. No one here or on the outside knew anything about her. She was a mystery to everyone, and her security clearance was so high, no one dared to question it. She was an enigma."

"Best we let her remain that way. For Anna's sake, and our own, she died in the explosion. Agreed?"

"I agree, Admiral. May you rest in peace, Anna, wherever you may be."

21
THE PERFECT SCAPEGOAT

♂

THROUGH NOVEMBER 18–19ᵀᴴ 1943, 440 BRITISH LANCASTER bombers relentlessly unloaded their deadly cargo over Berlin, hour after hour over two days of terror. The attacks were repeated November 22–23, this time with even more devastating effect.

Nothing sacred was left untouched, including the Kaiser Wilhelm Memorial Church. Constructed in the 1890s, it too was levelled by the bombing, and was survived only by the original bell tower, which symbolically represented the *Heart of Berlin*. It stands to this day as a memorial to the dead during WWII.

Marissa and Sigmund's beloved Tiergarten Park was extensively damaged, as well as the city districts of Charlottenburg, Schoenberg, and Spandau, all suffering similar devastation. Aided by extraordinarily dry weather conditions, the firestorms ravaged various embassies, universities, the Berlin Zoo, and numerous military administrative buildings and offices.

In subsequent massed raids, fully a quarter of Berlin's housing accommodations were rendered uninhabitable. The industrial might of Siemensstadt was severely damaged with more than 4,000 people killed, 10,000 injured, and 450,000 rendered homeless. The decimation was extremely punitive, but not complete.

In the wake of the continual infliction of pandemonium and turmoil suffered by so many civilians, and the backbreaking destruction of industry and manufacturing, the pulse of Berlin continued to beat. Civilian morale bent, but refused to break.

To the credit of the Germans, for the most part essential services continued to be maintained with relatively minor disruptions. Even war production although initially stunted, absorbed the powerful blows inflicted upon it and incredibly, started rising again.

Despite the public embarrassment of German High Command, the obvious vulnerability of Berlin to the deadly air attacks forced large-scale civilian evacuations. During this time, false propaganda continued to distort and exaggerate the strength of public confidence although its effect was largely insignificant. However, over the past few months, those surviving the bombing of their capital city personally witnessed their true reality.

*****

The aftermath of the Solf Tea Party initially resulted in the arrests of seventy-four people, including everyone in attendance at the tea party. Elisabeth von Thadden was tortured and summarily executed. Many were incarcerated in concentration camps, including Hanna Solf and her daughter Lagi. Both were subjected to brutal torture to elicit information about other treasonous collaborators. They were imprisoned to await trial, likely to be executed shortly thereafter, based upon the evidence against them.

During one of the many bombing raids by the British, fate intervened, when Senior Judge Roland Freisler, personally assigned to most of the Solf conspirators' trials, was presiding in his courtroom. The very building it housed suffered a devastating direct hit. The judge and dozens of staff were killed instantly.

Subsequently, the entire case file against the Solf's was destroyed in the resulting inferno, before the Solf case could be heard and entered into the court record. As a result of insufficient evidence, the Solf's fortuitously were not executed and spent the remaining years of their lives in England and later in Bavaria until their deaths several years later.

Based primarily upon the coerced admissions of Kiep, however, and other supporting confessions from conspirators as far away as Turkey, the repercussions of these arrests and tortures provided more than sufficient proof of the complicity of Abwehr in potential deceitful and treasonous anti-Nazi activities.

Erich Vermehren, the Abwehr agent who attended the Solf party, and his wife, Countess von Plettenberg, had returned to Istanbul where they had been formerly stationed, the day after Hanna Solf's get-together. Within days, they were ordered to return to Berlin for questioning by the Gestapo.

Admiral Canaris and General Oster knew the Vermehrens were key conspirators and would surely face ruthless interrogation by the Gestapo. It was time to proactively buy more time before Abwehr's treasonous activity was fully exposed.

"General Oster, if Erich Vermehren returns to Berlin, it is the last time we will ever hear of he and his wife again. Erich has much to tell, and Himmler will extract everything they know before killing them. It is time to approach MI-5 in London through our direct channels to confirm British receptivity to the Vermehren defections," the admiral directed. "Oh, be certain any contact between Abwehr and MI-6 is handled directly by you, is that clear?"

"Perfectly, Admiral. I will confirm the order with you prior to dispatch. And Admiral... this is the right thing to do, for everyone involved."

At General Oster's urging, the Vermehrens both wisely surrendered their passports to British authorities, purportedly taking with them the security codes for the *Zossen Files* which were never found.

Vermehren had no access to the missing codes, nor did he have the necessary security clearances. However, he was the perfect scapegoat to hedge Abwehr against the political and military blow-back that would likely have ensued. Without the Vermehren confession, which would certainly have been conducted under extreme duress, Canaris and Oster were not implicated at this time. The Vermehren defection, however, was the last straw for the Fuhrer.

As the puzzle continued to be slowly unravelled, Himmler's suspicion Abwehr was a hotbed of anti-Nazi activity was growing, but not yet proven. Nevertheless, Hitler and Himmler had enough circumstantial evidence to do what had always seemed to elude them; justifiable cause to abolish Abwehr.

On February 18th, 1944, Hitler signed a decree to finally do so, transferring all remaining functions formally under its authority to the supervision of Himmler. Many more conspiracies stemming from the Solf arrests were later confirmed when Himmler's net was cast progressively wider and wider with each passing month. Among them, several failed assassination attempts were revealed, although not always disclosed to Hitler.

When Hitler was made aware of the shocking information of these multiple attempts against his life, it fed his growing paranoia for his safety and accordingly, he exacted extreme retribution on anyone he even remotely suspected of wrongdoing. In all, close to three thousand perceived conspirators within the Nazi Party met their maker by Hitler's broad sweeping actions, a fate often extended to the families of those suspected as well.

Several suspects were arrested and convicted of assisting Jews to escape from Germany. Many of those *loose lips* in attendance at the Solf event discussed this secret underground openly, in the presence of Dr. Paul Reckzeh. Again, these interrogations could only imply Admiral Canaris and General Oster may have had knowledge of Jewish sympathizers operating within Abwehr, but nothing was verifiable and by this time, blame had logically shifted directly to the Vermehren defection.

Anna had done her job proficiently, leaving no trace of supporting documentation potentially being used against them. Out of frustration, however, the admiral was summarily dismissed by the Fuhrer and posted to another assignment as a *persona non grata*. Sufficient evidentiary proof did not support the claim against him personally, however, the investigation into the extent of his potential complicity would continue.

As days passed, it became painfully apparent Anna was the one holding the keys, and most surely would have been included among the incarcerated. Certainly, her sudden disappearance substantially increased the focus of Himmler's suspicions to Anna. This loose end was an incredible source of continual frustration for Himmler and Chief Lammers of the Reich Chancellery, albeit for drastically different reasons.

Chief Lammers recognized Anna held his fate in her hands, because of his egregious abuse of Hitler's trust in him. For years, he had been given free rein to manipulate the incredible assets and cash reserves of Konto 5 placed under his control - until Anna was given full clearance to provide oversight of his various transactions, many of which were blatantly self-serving.

Initially, his constant criticism of her to the Fuhrer had worn thin with Hitler, and Lammers eventually had to succumb to her higher authority absent any further protests. Hence his total disdain for her. Since her disappearance, he prayed she would never be found, however if she was, his own investigation into her background and current whereabouts would come up empty, as would Himmler's rigorous search for her.

During his thorough investigation, Himmler was made increasingly aware of Anna's role and the extent to which she held everything together. Hitler recognized her talents early and wisely appointed her to the highest security clearance available. Anna was regarded as being someone who was uniquely talented. She had no life outside Abwehr and was totally committed to the Reich, living on base under lock and key, absent any apparent family ties.

In Hitler's eyes, these circumstances established her to be a woman possessing a brilliant mind with extraordinary capabilities, who was totally subservient to his will… and equally disposable. It was an arrogant underestimation.

When Himmler began to slowly peel back the onion, layer by meticulous layer, he was astounded at the gross negligence of Hitler, and Admiral Canaris. Himmler was shocked when he learned both the admiral and General von Brauchitsch were specifically ordered by Hitler to leave Anna to her own devices in service of the Fuhrer's commands. Interestingly, the documentation of these directives was made easily available to Himmler which exonerated both military commanders.

This revelation totally disarmed Himmler because of the Fuhrer's insistence Anna was to answer to no one other than himself. It was difficult, if not impossible to attack Canaris or von Brauchitsch for doing precisely what the Fuhrer had ordered.

As the Fuhrer became more absorbed in his campaign of terror, and fighting the war on multiple fronts, he failed to oversee Anna's work, effectively leaving her answerable to no one. She and she alone held the keys to the codes and was masterful in keeping them undetected.

Her personal files were now nowhere to be found since any background checks and security clearances had been irretrievably imbedded by Anna herself. There were no apparent loose ends as to who this Anna Pavlova woman was, and where she came from.

Her current whereabouts were unknown, and her driver was killed in the car explosion. Due to the intensity of the blast, his remains were unidentifiable. Perhaps Anna was dead as well, but proof was not definitive. These factors stymied Himmler's investigation at every turn and caused Anna to be among the most wanted fugitives of the

Nazi Party. Her intimate knowledge of central intelligence operations, and the potential threat of her delivering the critical codes to the Allies made her a major flight risk.

Domestically, her detailed accounting and familiarity with the guarded transactions of Konto 5 could expose many nefarious and secretive relationships confirming payoffs and the prevalence of bribery throughout German High Command. These illicit payoffs often had political and personal overtones; many would prove disastrous to the legacy of the Reich.

Himmler immediately appointed his trusted colleague, Brigadier General of Police Walter Schellenberg, to fill the Canaris vacancy to conduct the day-to-day operations of Germany's intelligence agency under the subsequent control of the SS.

This impulsive decision by Himmler essentially gave him complete control of the military, by placing German security and intelligence matters in the hands of those who had no prior experience. This weakness would prove to be yet another costly error by German leadership, as they lost another vital component of their war machine against the Allies.

22
THE PASSING OF AN ICON

SINCE THE OCCUPATION OF FRANCE, ALLIED BOMBING RAIDS continued to take a devastating toll impacting the world below. Culture and the arts were not exempt from the perils of war when the *Orchestre National* had been necessarily disbanded. In the new year of 1944, however, the orchestra valiantly began to rebuild, using the Opera House as its temporary new home and despite having lost many of the original artists to the labors of war. Many would never return.

This musically revived assemblage once again began to re-establish its previous role as a symbolic cultural ambassador representing France, promoting famous guest performers and occasionally guest conductors.

Later that year in April, Marta was scheduled to perform as a much revered and familiar featured artist. As a German violinist in the city of Paris, she was particularly receptive to the controversial opportunity to ply her distinctive craft to French impressionist music. It was a challenge she sought to embrace, despite the protective advice of her colleagues for her to decline the offer.

True to form, Marta embraced this potentially provocative and precarious opportunity, both politically and artistically. She was naïve enough to unhesitatingly dismiss the danger she may encounter as a German artist, openly performing with intent to regain the customary adoration from her already broad base of appreciative French patrons. There was nothing timid about this formidable woman, and she was determined by her very nature to accomplish the daunting task with her customary confidence and poise.

Her habitual routines had become unalterable over the years, as they tended to be for most virtuosos throughout the course of their prolific careers. As she was readying herself for rehearsal shortly after recharging her creative juices with a mid-afternoon nap, the telephone unwelcomingly intruded upon her restful quiet moments.

Her anger immediately flared, having previously instructed hotel reception to hold any calls, irrespective of urgency. To her mind, there was nothing of greater priority than focusing on calm and introspective concert preparation.

She aggressively snatched the telephone from its cradle cursing silently to herself. "I specifically instructed I was not to be disturbed!" she hollered into the telephone.

Sheepishly, the voice of the hotel operator clarified the urgency of the interruption and confirmed to whom she was speaking. "Yes, this is she... Please connect me with him directly."

It was Major Groscurth from Abwehr. In the few seconds it required to forward his call, it was enough for her to feel apprehensive about the potentially serious nature of the call.

"Hello Major Groscurth. I am delighted to hear from you but... your call surprises me... Is everything well?"

"I very much regret disturbing you at this time, Madame von Brauchitsch, but I have just been informed... the Berlin Abwehr offices, they..." His voice trailed off in confusion and shock.

"During the heavy bombing... How can I say this?... The Abwehr offices have been destroyed, Madame. Lieutenant von Brauchitsch, I apologize, Klaus... your Klaus has regrettably been... He has been killed in the attack."

"No... No! It is not possible! Oh, please tell me it is not so!... not Klaus!"

"I am so sorry for your loss, Madame. I thought it best to inform you quickly rather than have you learn this over the radio. You are on file as next of kin."

Her voice became weak and trailed off in apparent confusion. Her lips commenced to tremble uncontrollably. "Surely, there must be some mistake?"

"I pray it were so. The entire city block is gone... There were only a few survivors. Forgive me for having to inform you of this tragic news, and again I remain so very sorry for your terrible loss, Madame."

Marta collapsed to the floor, leaning against her bedside, the telephone dropping uncontrollably from her hand. The devastating news had sucked the oxygen out of her room, crushing her spirit in ways she could not comprehend.

She had never known the depth of such abject sorrow. By what method of madness was this happening? She tried in vain to fully grasp what had happened; her breath became shallow, and her pulse began to race. Her head was spinning now, very much out of control. What could she do? ... She must call Anna. How must Anna have dealt with...

Unable to get up from the floor, Marta simply passed out involuntarily, escaping the numbness of her loss. Meanwhile, Major Groscurth was calling her name repeatedly to hear her voice again, in a futile attempt to confirm she was still in control of herself. There was no response, but the line was still connected. *"Hello! Madame von Brauchitsch! Are you there, Marta? Please say something!"*

Out of concern for Marta's wellbeing, the major again contacted hotel reception; always the consummate gentleman fulfilling his professional duties with thoughtfulness and courtesy. On his authority, the hotel staff quickly entered Marta's private suite to find her lying on the carpet where she fell next to the bed. The room was deathly still and disturbingly quiet, other than the telephone still chirping to indicate the call had been disconnected.

Tending to an unconscious Marta as best they could, quickly and respectfully, the hotel nurse checked her vital signs. Her pulse was weak; her breath remained shallow, but otherwise her condition appeared stable.

"Call the ambulance and let's get her safely back on the bed. I'll notify the gentleman who called, to confirm she has passed out but appears well. He was extremely concerned for her welfare but at this time we have no idea what has happened to her," the nurse instructed.

Minutes later, word of her situation was conveyed to Maestro Furtwangler, who was also staying in the hotel. Upon hearing Marta had a medical condition, he rushed downstairs to the hotel lobby just as the ambulance was arriving. He was frantic seeing Marta in such a helpless situation and his face was white as a ghost. He still had no idea what had occurred in her room.

Maestro addressed one of the attending paramedics. "She seemed well just a few hours ago when we shared breakfast together. I must accompany her to the hospital, please! This woman is Marta von Brauchitsch, the famous violinist. I am her next of kin. She is scheduled to perform at the Opera House tomorrow."

"You can follow us from behind, but I don't believe she will be in any condition to perform anytime soon. We'll know more after we run a few tests." Maestro felt foolish about his apparent misplaced priorities, but in fairness, he too was unprepared for anything like this.

In the hours following, Maestro connected with the major and learned about Klaus' fate. He was profoundly shaken by the news of Klaus' sudden death. It would mark the first time in Marta's distinguished career she would be unable to perform.

*****

During the Luftwaffe's continued defence of the Battle of Berlin on April 16, 1944, the RAF fighter escorts outnumbered the Germans by a margin of almost 2:1. Not only were these highly proficient German pilots defending their own soil, they were also fighting to their final gasp to protect their beloved capital city. It was these moments when each squadron leader would push the limits of his aircraft, his squadron, and himself. Lieutenant Manfred von Brauchitsch was one of them.

He was a military man through and through, like his father, and his grandfather before him. He emulated his mother with keen perceptions and confident demeanor. He was also blessed with the instinctual qualities which, when combined with the strong physical attributes of his father made him appear larger than life, oozing bravado from every pore of his being.

Manfred had become the consummate leader and a true warrior of the skies. The men under his command knew what was expected from them: "Just keep up with me... That's all I ask. Our fighters are faster. Our determination is greater. Stay calm and do what we've all been trained to do! Good luck gentlemen."

Pre-flight was not dissimilar to hundreds of prior such missions, with one significant difference: the state of mind of these pilots in preparation for perhaps their final battle above Berlin. Unwavering dedication of purpose and tenacious resolve best defined the necessary mental focus to maintain unbroken self-discipline to guide these pilots to their ultimate destiny... one they faced without visible hesitation.

Well into the battle, the Luftwaffe fought valiantly. It was certainly a target-rich environment the Germans had not seen since Operation Barbarossa, but this time, the opposition's skillful piloting forced the Luftwaffe to succumb to the overwhelming numbers of the attacking RAF fighters.

Already having five confirmed kills on the day, Manfred's Messerschmitt Bf-109 continued to maneuver brilliantly. His squadron was taking a beating. Although Manfred was performing at such an incredible level of efficiency, the fight became so heated he was forced to violate Erich Hartmann's first rule of engagement.

Manfred recalled it distinctly: *observe the enemy, decide how to proceed with the attack, make the attack, and then disengage to re-evaluate the situation.* This time, there were too many swarming bogies to cover. Having finished off his last target, Manfred knew he was unable to retreat fast enough to re-assess the situation and in the confusion lost momentary sight of a British Spitfire he had not accounted for.

He had just begun his ascent to withdraw from his previous kill, knowing instinctively he had no other option. He sensed it was only a matter of time before someone nailed his ass. As the thought flashed through his mind, it happened. His craft was strafed by a Spitfire's volley of gunfire. His windscreen was shattered by the volley and tore his left shoulder apart in the process.

Involuntarily, Manfred squinted his eyes, grimacing from the immediate searing pain. It was unlike anything he had experienced before. Trying to control his focus, he scanned his instrument panel, struggling to assess the damage to his aircraft. It was a more urgent priority than his shoulder. The machine gun fire had ripped across his fuselage creating serious damage, now causing hydraulic fuel to spew from the engine, noticeably limiting his flight control...

It was hot, blinding pain. His precious blood was splattered against what remained of his windscreen and his throttle became too slippery with blood for him to properly maintain his grip. He struggled to maintain altitude for just a fleeting moment longer while his craft was beginning to lose propulsion, leaving him with minimal control. There would be no retreat from his final attack.

His engine coughed and sputtered, expiring its final gasp, taking Lieutenant von Brauchitsch to the apex of his final ascent. Now without propulsion, he used only gravity to push the stick down and forward, speeding into the midst of the battle below. This fighter plane was never designed to be a dive-bomber, but that was what it must now become.

Knowing he had but one last pass remaining, he guided the shaking and rattling remains of his disabled aircraft toward the center of the closest Lancaster bomber in his line of flight, directly into the teeth of the tail gunner's defensive line of fire.

Manfred committed himself masterfully to his task, rapidly closing distance when another round of artillery fire ripped through the canopy. The horrific salvo of gunfire killed him instantly, but not before the badly damaged corpse of his aircraft catastrophically clipped the Lancaster's tail assembly. Small amounts of residual debris from Manfred's plane shattered on impact and simply dissolved into the fiery hell below. Rest in peace, young man.

The exploding Messerschmitt took out the stern of the fatally wounded bomber. Now forced from its former pre-assigned course on final approach to its intended target, the craft fell away chaotically from the bombing run remaining fully armed and rapidly descended, spinning uncontrollably away from the formation.

*****

Days later Marta awoke, warmly covered in cotton bed sheets and a heavy blanket, with an intravenous drip inserted into her left arm above her wrist. Still bleary-eyed from the sedatives she had received, she had no recollection of what had brought her to this strange setting when the attending nurse entered her room.

"Good morning, Madame von Brauchitsch. Welcome back. How are we feeling today? We were becoming concerned for your recovery."

"Where the hell am I? ... What has... what has happened to me?" Marta mumbled with slurred speech.

"You are our guest in the American Hospital of Paris, in Neuilly-sur-Siene."

"Please tell me... why... why am I in this fuckin' place?"

Consistent with typical medical protocol, the nurse lifted Marta's limp hand and confirmed her weak but steady pulse. "We have had difficulty contacting your next of kin, Madame. I believe your son

Dietrich will be here later today. For the moment, I suggest you get some additional rest. We will awaken you when your son arrives, I promise you."

Before the nurse briefly explained that Marta had blacked out, Marta drifted back into deep sleep in her confused state of mind, having no apparent recollection of the events she had suffered.

She did not become coherent until the following morning, when she awoke to find Dietrich sitting at her bedside. Avoiding the subject of what had happened to Klaus was no longer an option for Dietrich and Marta's worst trepidations were realized when Dietrich sadly confirmed Klaus' death. She became deeply disconsolate, and again dissolved into an even more profound and pervasive despair, so overwrought with grief and frustration she became unable, or unwilling to communicate with anyone, including Dietrich.

The next week, Marta and Dietrich were escorted home on a private plane provided by the BPO to her own personal physician's care. Shortly thereafter she was taken from the hospital to her private residence, where a full-time nurse was temporarily assigned to oversee her recovery. Marta took comfort in Dietrich's embrace when he affectionately cradled her in his arms several times a day. She remained mute but seemed to respond positively to his care with her own speechless affection.

In the weeks ahead, Marta gradually became more verbally responsive and appeared to be turning a corner when thankfully, she became more lucid. Dietrich's and Lena's concerted efforts, together with the homecare nursing, did their best to satisfy her every need, except for two.

Maintaining vigilance over her past dependencies upon alcohol and cocaine were exasperating and in the weeks ahead became much more difficult for Dietrich to address, sometimes resulting in Marta's violent outbursts of frustration and anger.

One morning Marta sat up in bed and began to holler loudly at Lena. Dietrich heard the commotion and came running to her room. "I want to see Anna today, and where the hell is Klaus? Manny is coming home this weekend and he will want to see his father, dammit!... Well don't just stand there, get me a drink... and make it a stiff one for Christ's sake! My God, what do I have to do to get you people to bloody well listen to me?"

*****

"Hello, Dr. Meuller. Thank you for calling back so quickly... Yes, she seemed better, but only briefly. Shortly after you left yesterday, she must have been hallucinating and broke into a heavy sweat... No Sir, she was white as a ghost, but still hot and feverish..."

"She started shaking more violently than before and with her escalating temper, I'm afraid she will get out of bed again. I found her sleeping on the floor, probably where she fell this morning before I awakened. I'm just so damned tired and couldn't wait until Lena relieved me. I just feel terrible that I fell asleep," Dietrich explained remorsefully.

Dietrich was beside himself about what, if anything, he and Lena could do. "Is it possible you could come by later today, or at least let's get the nurse back here? I think we still need her full time, doctor," Dietrich suggested.

Later the same day, Dr. Meuller thankfully arrived. Sedatives he prescribed eased Marta's discomfort to manageable proportions, but in short time, had to be carefully increased in the interests of her own safety, and regrettably of those tending to her continued care. All this remedial treatment begged the burning question, *How long and to what extent had these dependencies developed and more importantly, why had her withdrawal symptoms become even more prevalent?*

The answer was to be found shortly after Dr. Meuller's visit. He addressed both Dietrich and Lena directly. "Dietrich, Lena, we are approaching a serious crossroad with Miss Marta's treatment. Despite our careful monitoring of her medications, I'm afraid to say she is regressing week by week. We are missing something. I am certain of it."

"This is not what we expected to hear Doctor, but we are living with this every day. Perhaps we are not seeing the broad picture here. Her recovery has been slow but, what you are saying is unfathomable. What are you suggesting, Sir?" Dietrich anxiously enquired.

"To account for the trauma she has suffered from the loss of Klaus, together with her inability to communicate with his father, the general, and... I suspect to an even greater degree, no longer having contact with Anna, she has been left emotionally bankrupt," the doctor explained.

Dietrich added, "All the losses and heartbreak." He shook his head dismayingly... "And she doesn't yet know about Manfred's demise. I know we have all suffered from his tragic death, but we must continue protecting her from learning of this terrible tragedy. My fear is that news of Manny's death would break whatever hope and spirit she continues to cling to.

"It pains us to keep this from her but living this lie day after day at least keeps her fading hope for him alive. We feel so helpless that despite our best intentions, life becomes so damned complicated. What can we do, Doctor?" Dietrich rose to fetch some tissues for he and Lena. Inevitably the stress was taking a serious toll on everyone.

Awkwardly, Dr. Meuller needed to address a very intrusive matter. "I apologize in advance for asking this, however there is no viable alternative. Dietrich, will you grant me permission to check Marta's night table to try and determine the extent and nature of her suspected cocaine dependency?"

"Certainly, Doctor. We already checked her room thoroughly, and we found nothing. If you want us to check again, then we must. In fact, Lena have you unpacked Miss Marta's night bag? Has it been returned yet? I don't recall seeing it on the flight from the hospital in Paris," Dietrich enquired.

"It did arrive a few days after you and she returned, but I just placed it in her closet until she returned to home care. She always insisted she unpack her bags personally. I thought nothing more about it, but as I think about it now, I don't imagine she ever unpacked it, what with her condition," Lena replied.

"If you could please retrieve it, who knows what we could find, but I am certain we're missing a piece of this puzzle. I'm sorry to say, but her personal privacy is no longer the most important issue," Doctor Meuller stressed.

It was a difficult task intruding upon the sanctity of Marta's personal world, however, sure enough, there in her luggage were several vials of white powder. This discovery confirmed what the doctor suspected. What wasn't expected though, was the quantity of cocaine she kept inside a shoebox in her bedroom closet.

"Oh, my good Lord!" exclaimed Dietrich upon its discovery. Dr. Meuller raced to Dietrich's side. Inside the shoebox, of which there were always several, was a slightly smaller box of waxed cardboard, sealed with a leather strap; small, but significant considering its content.

"Her body is fighting her physical dependency to what I presume is in this box," the doctor explained. "It appears to be cocaine. If in fact it is, she's continuing to consume it to cope through her withdrawal and even worse, she is probably increasing her prescribed drugs more than we had realized. She must have been supplementing her meds from her previous supply since her initial disorientation and repeated blackouts began. This is far more serious than I had imagined.

"We must get her back to the hospital right away. Marta needs more specific and specialized care than I can offer, but it must be done. She evidently requires more than could be provided from the confines of home."

From the instant the inevitable decision was made to re-admit Marta, and the ambulance arrived to take her safely to the hospital, Dietrich breathed a regretful but deep sigh of relief, founded upon the hope Marta's recovery could be restored.

During the past few weeks, Dietrich was also under incredible pressure to return to his work at the Ministry of Health. The war had taken a heavy toll on every public office and what little infrastructure remained was operating on a shoestring budget. The endless lines of the sick and injured represented those who were turned away from the few hospitals still in operation.

Lena, of course, remained by Marta's side in her private hospital room to tend to Marta's personal needs, bathing and feeding her. As had become the pattern, attempts at conversation were only one-sided.

Faithfully, Lena was persistent in her adoration of Miss Marta. Maestro had telephoned repeatedly and tried to visit on a few occasions. When Marta finally agreed to see him, she spoke very little and was only able to force a brief smile. Her only continual preoccupation was the whereabouts of Manfred and Anna. It was apparent they were the only ones who could make a positive difference in her agonizingly slow recovery.

As Marta became occasionally more lucid, her questions and concern for Manfred remained persistent and over time, it was increasingly frustrating for her not to have received correspondence from the military about her son's welfare; nor news of his possible death, God forbid. She continued to pray for him, never once doubting the possibility he was still alive and well.

Further compounding her self-perceived isolation, and no longer having the customary and steadfast support and encouragement of Anna in these worst of Marta's times, she continued to feel desolate, abandoned and alone, never understanding Anna's inability to communicate with Marta during Anna's mysterious forced exile. Throughout her initial period of abandonment, Marta's strong dependence on cocaine had done serious damage and her excessive abuse of prescribed dosages of sedatives exacerbated her increasing depression.

In her own mind, Marta's very full life had suddenly become futile, a realization she herself would never have imagined. The extent of her addictions had destroyed her physical control. The combination of her excessive prescribed medications pushed her over the fragile precipice she had recklessly flirted with so frivolously in the past.

This once formidable woman was inadequately prepared to reconcile her grievous losses any longer. After numerous suicide attempts, Marta was forced to withdraw from the life she had known and drifted into oblivion in the secured confines of a mental health care facility outside of Berlin.

*****

Linette Etienne occupied a small furnished flat on the second floor of an apartment block in the eastern suburbs of Berlin. She lived quietly and inconspicuously, and very much alone since the car bomb changed her life so drastically, several months ago. It was now mid-January 1944. Gone from her life were her family, her home, and all the very foundations of familiarity. She had become a recluse, whose only purpose each day was to begin another one tomorrow.

Ernst and Edith Hoffman were a hard-working elderly couple living in a flat above their small grocery business facing the street below. They had built the business for almost forty years and their moderate success and perseverance enabled them to proudly raise their son. He was a good student in high school and quite adept playing his piano, until the day he was enrolled in the Hitler Youth.

His destiny, like millions of others, found him unceremoniously conscripted into the military. Since the war began, he had been given just one furlough to see his parents, and then nothing - a lifelong investment of love, nurturing and guidance, only to be taken to serve in a war not of his own making. It was a common story.

When Linette first met this family, she took on the appearance of a withdrawn, soft-spoken patron of their shop. Over time, she and Edith exchanged brief smiles to open the door of distant civility just a crack, but enough to allow a few brief pleasantries to develop between them.

As their modest relationship developed during those months following, Ernst decided to speak up in confidence to Linette. He did so despite Edith's initial protestations. "Linette, we need some help here, someone trustworthy and hard working. Since the rationing began, it has brought droves of people to our doors, hours before daybreak.

"Edith simply cannot keep working these long hours. She's not sleeping well, and her arthritis pain is crippling her from doing what must be done to keep our shop open. We desperately need help to stock the shelves, but anyone we hire would likely steal us blind."

In response, Linette sympathized with the Hoffmans. "The long hours are taking a toll on you, Edith. I can see how exhausted you are, and I know you are in a great deal of pain." Linette turned her focus to look directly at Ernst. "What is it you want me to do?" she asked.

"It's a simple job, but I must warn you it may become dangerous from time to time. The people are more desperate with every passing day, and food stamps are simply not enough. We've had break-ins at night, and even during the day, some people threaten us if we don't give them more than they are allotted. It can be frightening sometimes.

"When I go to the bank to redeem our coupons, because it's too dangerous for Edith to go herself, I have to leave her here alone when I'm gone. We're losing too much to theft. Sometimes I think we are on the brink of being beaten by hoodlums to take everything we have here. Our shelves would be empty in minutes if others joined them to take what they could. It has become a living nightmare for us, Linette."

"I don't know how you have both managed as well as you have, but of course, I'm willing to help." Linette assured him.

There was more to Linette's thought process than being a helpful Samaritan. The small grocery store was only a ten-minute walk from her flat. She paid her rent on the first day of every month, without fail, and always in cash. She already had enough money to get by and her small wages at the store would be modest.

Of greater significance, the job offered the one thing she had to have that wages alone could not reliably ensure: access to food *without* ration cards. Her growing paranoia about keeping her identification documents private, now jeopardized her ability to get access to food.

"If I work stocking shelves, can I start late into the night before the lines start to form? When you leave for the bank every morning,

I'll stay with Edith until you return. I prefer not to deal directly with the customers, if possible. I'm just not comfortable with the idea. Does that sound like a plan we can all live with?" Linette proposed.

Ernst and Edith both agreed and were delighted to have Linette's support. In this relatively impoverished side of the city, the Germans had more on their minds just maintaining order among their own ranks than tending to the constant petty thefts and violence once pre-occupying them earlier in the war. Of greater relevance to Linette was the fact their new priorities certainly no longer included their once determined search for Anna.

*****

Linette's duties at the grocery shop continued, much as she had planned, and no one paid attention to her as she remained out of the public eye. During the occasional break periods, she enjoyed reading the local newspapers the shop provided once every short while. It seemed no one had the money to buy them, but Ernst insisted they keep a few now and then, more for their own use than any of their customers.

When her shift was almost over, Linette picked up a copy of the morning delivery with intent to scan the major happenings. The Germans no longer controlled the still valiantly struggling press, hence there were always a few independents fighting to serve their communities with remnants of global and domestic stories of interest.

As she poured her coffee and opened the weekly paper, she was smitten by the headline. She collapsed onto the wooden crate she often sat upon and uncontrollably dropped her coffee cup, as well as the newspaper. Placing both hands in shock to cover her face, she sat in stunned silence and commenced to shake and sob uncontrollably.

The headline of the day had nothing to do with the war, nothing to do with the Russian invasion, nothing to do with the fall of the Third Reich... It simply read, *The Passing of An Icon: Marta von Brauchitsch Is Dead.*

23
REMEMBER THE PATRIOTS
WHO CAME BEFORE US

CHURCH OF OUR LADY OF THE
SCAPULAR, KONIN DISTRICT

IT MARKED A TURNING POINT WHEN GENERAL VON TRESCKOW collaborated with Colonel von Stauffenberg. Tresckow, along with his closest colleague, General Friedrich Olbricht, had previously developed a plan to assassinate the Fuhrer. It was developed initially by the Fuhrer's staff in late 1942 in the event of an insurrection against the Reich.

With a few adaptations, and finding one important missing component, it was tailor made for a coup d'état. General Tresckow's capable military expertise became quickly evident as he began implementing the specifics of the attempt.

From as early as March 1943, urgency continued to grow. General Hans Oster, Admiral Canaris, and General Tresckow, all of whom had originally collaborated in planning the *Oster Conspiracy* five years prior, were now reunited to attempt another well-organized and coordinated approach to achieve the nefarious deed.

It was April 1944 when the key players assembled once again in Father Francis' parish. As always, they had pledged their unwavering loyalty and were screened thoroughly by von Stauffenberg's security team.

The missing component from previous meetings was General Friedrich Fromm. As Commander of the Reserve Army, his troops were loyal to him. His control of the Reserve was crucial to seizing temporary control of Hitler's officers in High Command when the assassination was accomplished.

In return for his vital contribution, Fromm stipulated he be given a top command post in the new government under Field Marshall Erwin von Witzleben, who was to become Commander-in-Chief following a successful coup. Fromm threatened to expose the plan if the assassins did not agree to his terms.

Reluctantly, this condition was agreed upon and used as bait to assure his support. The only alternatives were to accede to his condition or neutralize him and find other means to lock down Hitler's surviving commanders. It would have been a chaotic situation and could have jeopardized the involvement of Witzleben, who's role was vital to the leadership of the new order. At this late stage, the gravity of secrecy was never more critical than now.

Colonel von Stauffenberg presided over this very consequential meeting when he addressed eight members of the assassination team. By this time, these meetings routinely included Julia, for more than simple hospitality responsibilities.

"The events of the past year should not be remembered for our many failed attempts to achieve our ultimate goal and the mistakes of others who operated independently. What these efforts have taught us, however, is where we misjudged the soundness of our plans.

"The multitude of these failures has placed the Fuhrer's security teams on a much higher level of preparedness than we were accustomed to seeing. We must learn from our mistakes because our mission simply cannot fail again. We are running out of time as the Allies, particularly America, continues to prepare for a landing in Europe that, if successful, will most certainly overwhelm our forces. General Tresckow, perhaps you will enlighten our associates."

"Certainly, Colonel. The momentum of war has clearly swung to the Allies, and if their landing is as massive and multifaceted as we expect, this advantage will become even greater. Gentlemen, our defeat will be imminent, and the results, punitive. Germany will not be in a position to negotiate, as we have already seen in the Treaty of Versailles after the Great War. *Harsh* and *punitive* cannot begin to describe the cost of our defeat.

"I am convinced the only course before us is to assume new leadership of the Reich. By so doing, we will stop this insanity before we are all inevitably crushed under the Allies' boots. Our new government has agreed to negotiate reasonably with the Allies in the interest of maintaining any semblance of victory.

"Gentleman, we have changed the world irrevocably for the worst, and retribution for our deeds will be served, I can assure you.

"As the colonel has already expressed, our efforts in the past year began in March when we tried to strike at the Fuhrer on his flight to Smolensk. The timing of his arrival was changed and forced us to defer that effort. Later that month, a frozen detonator failed to trigger an explosion mid-flight. We were fortunate to be able to defuse it upon landing and barely escaped detection. A few weeks later, a suicide bomber was unable to carry out the act when the Fuhrer departed ten minutes earlier than planned. "

"We have attempted using close range pistols, but the Fuhrer now wears a protective vest; poisoning his meals is impossible, as every meal is tested for that eventuality. Am I making my point, gentlemen?"

On cue, the colonel rose to take over where the general was leading. "It is our belief the best remaining chance to kill the Fuhrer is to trigger a time bomb, at ground level, deep inside the security net, inside the Wolf's Lair. To do this requires someone we trust absolutely, to deliver and detonate within close approximation of the target. I have volunteered to complete such a mission."

The tone of the colonel's commitment was more evident than before. His determination and decisiveness were never more apparent.

"Effective July 1st, General Fromm has agreed to appoint me his Chief of Staff of the Reserve Army. Although the general will not be proactively involved with our plot, he has nevertheless, agreed to look the other way, so to speak. This posting will provide me with close and unfettered access to the Fuhrer on a regular basis, with ample opportunities to carry out our mission at a time of our choosing."

Father Francis began to speak when Stauffenberg had finished on such a positive and determined note. "Our imbedded informers have learned heightened security is now tapping into all incoming and outgoing telephone communications, whether business or personal. Himmler's staff know the growing discontent with the Fuhrer will not likely be dissuaded and they are preparing for any eventuality.

"Hence, in the weeks ahead, myself and Julia will be making routine courier drops to predesignated locations for each of you. We have devised a system which is flexible to allow for changing circumstances, totally avoiding communication via wiretapped lines.

"Julia has wisely established different routines over the past six weeks taking her throughout various parts of the city in close proximity to your offices. Under the guise of fundraising for Catholic orphanages, she will be couriering coded messages to and from reliable drop off points we have already established.

"Many of you and other officers within the Reich offices, have supported our diocese for the past year. It is only natural the church maintains proactive contact with our congregants on behalf of this noble cause. To this end, Julia will continue to follow her newly established routines to deliver and retrieve relevant messages that on surface, appear mundane, should any of them be intercepted. We will advise each of you on the procedural details prior to your departures today."

Colonel von Stauffenberg closed out his portion of the meeting before turning it back to Father Francis and Julia to outline specifics of their communications strategy.

"Many of our patriots, including all of us within this room, are already aware the Valkyries symbolize Germany's historic perceptions of war, death, and destiny, which are inextricably intertwined.

"Yes, they are dark and horrific, as is our current patriotic mission, however these perceptions are also glorious. We are calling this mission, *Operation Valkyrie,* to honor and remember the patriots who came before us. (Von Stauffenberg) May the memories of ourselves be counted among those so honored."

*****

On June 5th, the night before the Normandy invasion, the RAF was assigned the incredible task of sortieing more than a thousand bombers responsible for dropping 5,000 tons of heavy munitions across countless miles of German gun batteries located on the beaches of Normandy, including Utah Beach, Omaha Beach, Gold, Juno, and Sword beaches.

Preparation for the largest amphibious military operation in the history of the world was meticulously orchestrated and completed in a timely and secretive fashion. By day's end more than 155,000 Allied troops would set foot on the beaches of Normandy.

*****

In the weeks following the Allied landings, organizational meetings continued at the church at random intervals. Due to the prominence of the main leadership of Operation Valkyrie, small quorums were necessary to avoid creating suspicion and detection, to better enable vital decision making.

Logistically it was impossible to gather everyone at any single location and specific time. The high profiles of senior command necessitated more reliance upon the use of the church, as well as the timely coded messaging system provided by Julia and Father Francis.

Through Julia's established connections with Zegota and the Polish Underground through Sister Helena, Julia's credibility was not in question by the Underground because of her proficient work to relocate orphaned children with Zegota. The network was already in place. Julia just found another way to tap into it.

She carefully explained, in general terms only. "Various small businesses support this communications network, all the while having no knowledge of the specific purpose they are helping to achieve, mobilizing Operation Valkyrie. Many of these businesses include conveniently located bakeries, butcher shops, fish mongers, fruit stands, and even newspaper services as well.

"The network functions efficiently, in fact, much faster than the German Postal Service at this time. Messages are often delivered within a few hours of being picked up. It is reliable, totally innocuous, and can be shut down instantly if suspicions arise. A simple solution to a complex problem if I may say so."

"Thank you, Julia," Father Francis stated proudly.

"Yes, Julia. I see why Father has such confidence in you from the beginning. Father Brietkopf sends his best regards also," the colonel disclosed.

The sudden disclosure shocked Julia, as it took her totally by surprise. Reassuring her, Colonel von Stauffenberg was quick to react. "Please don't be alarmed, Julia. Father Francis shared Father Brietkopf's letter of reference with me. He was comfortable speaking with my aide about you. The intrusion was necessary as part of our protocol. There are no exceptions. I hope you understand."

Julia, somewhat less flushed now, became more visibly in control. "Of course, Colonel. I know it was necessary, but it did take me by surprise." With that, Julia cast her eyes toward Father Francis somewhat disparagingly, but said nothing more of the matter. In response, Father apologetically acknowledged her embarrassment.

In his new capacity as Chief of Staff of the Reserve Army, Stauffenberg was, as expected, required to attend daily briefings at the Wolf's Lair. A plan was agreed upon to arm two explosive devices contained in his valise, capable of killing any group of people within an eight-to-ten-foot radius of the blast. His usual spot was only a few feet away from the Fuhrer and the intent was to kill Himmler and Göring at the same instant. Their deaths would better assure the successful transition to the new government.

The plan required Stauffenberg to excuse himself to make a phone call after he triggered the time delay inside his briefcase. If he could not exit the conference room without undue suspicion, he was willing to die from the ensuing explosion. The Colonel was totally committed to the task.

July 14th was the date of the attempt. Stauffenberg left his home that morning, kissed his five young children goodbye and hugged his darling wife, Magdalena. She had no knowledge of what was about to transpire.

The colonel maintained his customary duties in his usual calm and controlled manner and arrived on schedule at the Wolf's Lair. He joked familiarly with the security detail and as normal, was admitted without any undue suspicion.

As the attendees gathered, small talk ensued while everyone prepared their coffees and proceeded to take their usual seats. Moments later, when the Fuhrer and Göring entered from the adjoining office to commence briefings, Himmler was conspicuously absent.

Outwardly, Stauffenberg remained calm; however his stomach was churning with anxiety, his mind immediately racing as he assessed and reassessed the scenario before him. *Hitler's life can be extinguished within minutes; it is within my grasp. But Himmler is also a prime target.*

Stauffenberg continued to reason that even if this assassination was successful, Himmler's survival meant he would retain significant power to maintain stability within the Reich. He would sway the shattered confidences of Reich leadership in his favor, denying any hope of instituting the new government.

No, the only choice was to defer this opportunity until the entire objective could be achieved. His heart was pounding now, and he was sweating profusely. Time to take a breath and steady himself. Try this again at a better time to ensure getting it right.

*****

Having spoken to General Tresckow and Field Marshall von Witzleben, the three agreed the urgency to kill Hitler was far greater than eliminating Himmler. Whether he was in attendance or not, the plan would proceed the following day. The colonel again flew to Hitler's Lair and repeated the same process as the day prior.

For the second day in a row, Stauffenberg, more drained emotionally now than yesterday, faced his family without the slightest gesture to indicate anything of concern, particularly to his supportive wife. Suppressing his torn emotions, he struggled to keep his farewell brief. He would agonize about this decision on his short flight to *Wolfsschanze*.

The day provided the perfect opportunity to strike the lethal blow to the Reich. Both Himmler and Göring were present. Stauffenberg's timebomb was already triggered to detonate ten minutes after being set. Stauffenberg would not have to leave the room. It was a decision he wrestled with; whether to self-destruct, or to create possible suspicion by leaving the room with his valise left under the conference table.

Suddenly, the Fuhrer was interrupted to take an urgent call on his office line. Not excusing himself, he simply turned the meeting over to Fieldmarshall Göring for the daily briefing! Fully, six minutes remained before detonation! *Not possible! Why was this elusive dog spared again?* The most hated human on earth had been given another reprieve from certain death!

Stauffenberg began to cough, softly at first, then more deeply, feigning his urgency to exit with his valise secured only by his three remaining fingers on his left hand; the others having been lost after a bombing incident while serving in North Africa in 1943. The injury also took his left eye and right hand.

Despite his disabilities, he only had minutes remaining to defuse the lethal contents of his valise. Continuing to cough but being careful to not appear to need help from anyone, he entered the washroom, locking the door behind him. Ninety-three seconds to prevent disaster, and ultimate failure to the cause.

*****

Days passed when a very fatigued Stauffenberg learned the Gestapo might already suspect another imminent conspiracy to kill the Fuhrer. While it was an unfounded rumor, it was unnerving just the same, and it fueled the realization suspicions were increasing among Gestapo officials. The collaborators could sense a net slowly and steadily closing around them. One last chance may be all they could expect to accomplish their deadly task.

The morning of July 20, 1944 was much as any other. Stauffenberg and his accomplices knew this was their final opportunity. Hitler, Göring, and Himmler were all present at the *Wolfsschanze* briefing, which was scheduled to begin at 12:30.

A few minutes beforehand, Stauffenberg was behind bathroom doors to ostensibly change his sweat-soaked dress shirt. It had been an intensely hot and humid July day, and his nerves were understandably on edge.

The privacy of the small room barely provided adequate space for him to activate the bomb. Trembling now, he carefully inserted the pencil detonator into a sizable block of plastic explosive, setting a time delay of ten minutes.

An unexpected tap on the door immediately broke his concentration.

"Colonel, the meeting is about to begin. Are you feeling unwell, Sir?" the adjutant enquired.

"No... no not at all. Thank you for asking," he calmly responded. He whispered softly to himself, *"Shit!"*

"Very well then. I will inform them, as the Fuhrer is anxious to begin."

Fumbling with what remained of his left hand as best he could, von Stauffenberg was only able to arm one of the two detonators, choosing to consume less time than absolutely necessary to avoid arousing suspicions concerning his delayed attendance. Despite changing into a fresh clean shirt, he continued to sweat profusely. His pulse was pounding now, and his mind was racing. This was no time to lose his composure.

Upon entering the conference room, Stauffenberg sat well within the calculated bomb radius at his usual seat, calmly chatting nonchalantly with Colonel Heinz Brant, who was at the corner of the table between Hitler and himself. Stauffenberg indifferently placed his briefcase on the floor to his left, just outside the solid wooden leg of the heavy boardroom table nearest to Hitler. He continued speaking with Brant as he did so.

The bomb had been set to detonate at precisely 12:42. As was previously arranged, an aide apologetically interrupted the meeting to indicate the colonel had an urgent telephone call in Wilhelm Keitel's office where the colonel could speak privately. Himmler and Göring were both displeased with the colonel's tedious interruptions.

"Colonel, this is most bizarre. You would be wise to reassess your military priorities," Himmler stated indignantly. Göring and the Fuhrer visibly irritated as well but chose not to speak.

"My sincere apologies, gentlemen. General Fromm is calling. It's a matter of some importance, I presume. I will be right back. Please continue."

Unknown to Stauffenberg, when he rose to exit the room, Colonel Brant nonchalantly adjusted the briefcase with his foot to the side of the table leg nearest the colonel's unoccupied chair. By so doing, he inadvertently protected the Fuhrer from the direct blast. Only a minute later, the bomb detonated; the table leg deflecting and absorbing the direct force of the explosion.

The powerful blast caused the thick billows of smoke and debris to blur the scene for several minutes. When the choking grey and sooty smoke cleared, the force of the blast had blown several bodies through shattered windows and a doorway. The scene was one of mass confusion and bedlam, as staff raced to their fallen leader.

Stauffenberg's heart was racing even more now. Amid the ensuing chaos, he could only assume his mission had been accomplished. Not waiting for confirmation, he boarded his staff car to exit the *Wolfsschanze* facility, easily convincing several security stations to let him pass. The drive to the Rastenburg airport was swift and his liftoff was unimpeded.

Confusion and disorder emanated from Hitler's Lair, sending immediate shockwaves throughout the Reich. Upon landing in Berlin, Stauffenberg urgently telephoned General Olbricht to report Hitler had been assassinated. The general followed the agreed upon procedures and ordered the full mobilization of Operation Valkyrie, as he had been directed.

In their exuberance to implement Operation Valkyrie, which necessitated extreme urgency, many of the conspirators exposed their complicity by methodically ushering in the strategic stages of the coup d'état. During this brief time, however, General Fromm had already been advised by High Command the Fuhrer was very much alive. His injuries, though serious, were not fatal.

General Fromm, always wavering in his mixed loyalties, knew he would be quickly implicated in the conspiracy, since Stauffenberg answered directly to Fromm. Goebbels moved expeditiously to clarify the stability of the Reich under Hitler's absolute command. He was unwavering in his support of his Fuhrer.

Goebbels immediately rescinded General Olbricht's orders and numerous arrests were quickly underway to suppress any attempt to overthrow German leadership. The Fuhrer's explicit instructions, however, were to keep the conspirators alive for torturous interrogation to determine the full magnitude of the attempted coup.

Fromm was unnerved by the order, knowing he would most certainly be convicted of treason and punished accordingly. Immediately, in hope of saving himself from such a fate, and to ostensibly demonstrate his fanatical support of the Fuhrer, he set up a kangaroo court to quickly convict Stauffenberg, Olbricht, and two others who could implicate him in the conspiracy. They were executed by firing squad within hours of their so-called convictions.

On July 21st, the day after the assassination failed, General Treskcow shot himself in the head.

Despite Fromm's best efforts, the Fuhrer prevailed in his thorough extermination of those disloyal to him. Of the 7,000 arrests, almost 5,000 were executed, including General Franz Halder, Colonel Erwin von Lahousen... and of course, General Fromm.

*****

In the tumultuous days and weeks following the failed assassination, Julia continued with her responsibilities toward the children. She assisted Father Francis to whatever extent he required, trying desperately to resume some sense of normality, knowing each passing day could be their last.

Horrific shockwaves of retribution against suspected conspirators permeated throughout Germany. The broad scope of these actions had an unnerving and profound affect upon both Father Francis and Julia. Colonel von Stauffenberg's hasty execution, a steep price he knew he would pay for failure, and the suicide of General Treskcow, inadvertently assured the complicity of the church would not be revealed.

Fleeing the area at this time for either was out of the question for fear of inviting suspicion, however, there wasn't a day, nor an hour, when fear and dread did not run through their veins in frightful anticipation of military trucks descending upon the grounds of the church. Their nerves were constantly on edge.

One morning, Julia finished preparing the morning coffee for herself and Father. As she entered his office, there was a sudden... *BANG!*

Julia jumped instinctively, dropping the silver tea service from her grasp onto the hardwood floor. It clanged loudly amid the sounds of shattering china and the rattling of silver flatware, no doubt waking the entire household, smashing everything it held.

She immediately collapsed to the floor, shaking uncontrollably and began to sob heavily. Father leapt from his chair, fretfully looking out his window, fearing the worst about the unexpected bang from the kitchen setting off a chain reaction of distressing chaos. "Julia, are you alright?"

Bronia by this time was rushing to see what happened in the office, not realizing it was a reaction to her metal ironing board having dislodged from its hook in the pantry. "*Oh, please forgive me Father! It was my fault. I'm so sorry for frightening you both. I've never seen you so jumpy.*"

She helped Julia to her feet and apologetically led her to the armchair next to Father's desk. "Relax my dear. We can always replace the broken teapot."

It was not just paranoia. It was the stressful reality that should Hitler ever learn about the direct involvement of the church and the Polish Underground, Father Francis and Julia would be brutally tortured to reveal others who were in any way duplicitous in the attack against the Fuhrer. The church itself, would be burned to the ground, legitimizing Hitler's complete indignation of Christianity. God only knew what fate would befall the children and Bronia.

Shockingly but thankfully, the caravan of military vehicles never appeared. The involvement of the Church of The Lady of The Scapular was not tied even remotely to Operation Valkyrie. It was passively perceived by many as simply an occasional meeting place for matters pertaining to fund-raising for some ardent Roman Catholic German officers. The topic was never raised. Hence, neither was the complicity of the Polish Underground passing secretive information linked to the Valkyrie conspiracy.

24
PRAY FOR THE POUNDING
FOOTSTEPS TO GO AWAY

As THE TIDE OF WAR CONTINUED TO DRAMATICALLY SHIFT
against Germany, numerous events compounded the groundswell
of Allied and Russian triumphs. The not to be forgotten and always
resilient Poles rose to face the German army in the *Lwow Uprising*
on July 23, just days after the July 20th Valkyrie Plot eventually failed.

By this time, almost two and a half million Allied troops had
landed in northern France, of which more than 124,000 suffered
casualties. The liberation of France began in earnest in the late
summer months following D-Day, forcing the Germans to begin
their hasty withdrawal. By September 1944, most of occupied France
had been liberated amidst the death, destruction... and some joy, for
those blessed with the strength and circumstances to have survived
the ordeal.

As the Allied offensive gathered momentum, relentlessly pushing
from the west, so too was the ravaging punishment of the Russians
applying pressure on the Germans from the east. By early 1945,
Russian forces liberated Warsaw and Krakow. Only months later, on
April 13th, they took Vienna and subsequently began delivering the
inevitable deathblow to Germany by encircling Berlin.

Hitler's desperation became more evident when he received
reports of the almost unimpeded Russian progress toward Berlin.
Even as he became more deranged and unstable, he finally seemed
to understand the end was near, despite never expressing it to his
generals. A sure sign of his mental state of mind was evidenced by his

direct orders to implement a scorched earth policy. It became known as *Hitler's Nero Decree*.

All but two major bridges throughout the city had been rigged for demolition as part of his worst-case scenario. The ominous day was now upon him. Without hesitation, he directed his generals to detonate the bridges about the city, as well as the emergency pumping stations controlling the potential overflow of the River Spree and its tributaries.

Within hours, subway stations began to flood, forcing untold thousands of tunnel dwellers to scramble to the surface like drowning vermin. Although some workers did what little they could to sabotage a few munition connections to save some of the bridges, most of the electric power grids were shut down and pumping stations were inoperable, paralyzing much of Berlin by the extensive flooding.

Between the invading Allies from the west to the Russian invasion from the east, their unimpeded progress became a massive land grab.

For the Russians, this was never intended to be a liberation; this was their opportunity to exact ruthless retribution for the previous horrors Germany inflicted on the Russian people during Operation Barbarossa. If these objectives could be efficiently achieved, the capture of Adolf Hitler and the retrieval of Germany's dormant nuclear weapons program remained a distinct possibility.

It took but three days to breech the once formidable *Gates to Berlin*, leaving only desperate pockets of scrambling German troops backed by the *Volkssturm*, which was comprised of mostly police, re-conscripted elderly veterans of the first world war, and the courageous bravado of the Hitler Youth.

Their last gasps were taken when defending what remained of the short road to Berlin. They were no match for the overwhelming attack. The amassing Russian tanks now had the once formidable city within the gunsights of its short-range artillery. By now, the end of the Reich was inevitable, even to Hitler, who by this time was berating his generals and issuing orders verifiably confirming his lost grasp of reality.

In his mind, Germany was defeated because of the abject failure of his commanding officers. Defiantly, Hitler chose to remain in Berlin within his fortified bunker with his wife, Eva Braun. On April 30th, 1945, Hitler and Eva, took cyanide pills just before Hitler fatally shot her with his pistol, and then turned it upon himself. The world would draw a collective breath of relief.

On May 7, 1945, Germany surrendered unconditionally to the Allies. The Third Reich had finally met its demise.

*****

Berlin was quickly overrun by the Russians and was efficiently secured under their control. Unknown to the public at this time was the unleashing of rear echelon units directed to viciously search, seize, and destroy anything they desired in the door-to-door search for any remnant of German humanity.

For the residents of Berlin, the decision to escape was very much out of the question at this late stage. Roads and sidewalks were sealed off, systematically shutting down vehicular traffic throughout the city. Heavy restrictions were imposed to prevent pedestrians from occupying the streets, each one crawling with Russian troops and mercenaries with but one objective, the complete denigration and vengeful destruction of German dignity and self-respect.

Russian checkpoints were at every significant intersection, the intended result being to forcefully restrict civilians inside what remained of their decimated homes. No one dared to challenge the Russians.

The rage and butchery of the Russians had never been seen in the history of modern warfare. The advancing army infiltrated every residence and hiding place to be found. Wherever residents lived, worked, or hid, they would ultimately be found and dealt with in any manner of indignation the invaders chose to impose.

Even the widespread savage rapes of hundreds of thousands of women and children could not seemingly satisfy the hatred and retribution sought by the Russian invaders. So gruesome and inhuman were these indignations, many hundreds of scattered and desperate German troops struggled to their deaths to escape to the west to surrender to the Allies, rather than face certain death and humiliation by the Russians.

Not all Russian officers and the countless thousands of private militias behaved like crazed animals, but many of the young and virile among them had not been with a woman through four years of war. Even the moral and humane ones often gave in to the addictive insanity, to be swept into the mass hysteria of brutal mentality not typical of their normal behavior.

To restore control over sex deprived and often drunken troops, all of whom were fully armed with machine guns, was not an envious task for any commanding officer, even one with compassionate and sound moral judgement. The atrocities were impossible to control.

During the first three days, estimates ranged from hundreds of thousands, to as high as two million such indignities being inflicted on German and Polish women and children. It was described by historians as *"the greatest phenomenon of mass rape in history"*. (A. J. Beevor) The well-known author and Russian dissident, Aleksandr Solzhenitsyn, served in WWII as a commander in the Red Army. He personally witnessed and wrote about many war crimes against humanity inflicted by the Russians upon German civilians to avenge Germany's savage brutality against the Russian people.

*****

It seemed the bright sunlight would never again announce the dawning of another day. The skies were eerie and grey, the air dank and heavy, making it difficult to see, to breathe, to keep going. Battle-weary troops grew accustomed to these conditions of endless days of battle, but the residents of Berlin were certainly not. It was disturbingly depressing. For the German military, it was becoming futile to continue fighting an enemy devouring them whole from every possible direction.

For the millions of homeless civilians, heavy black smoke, soot, and concrete dust, constantly shrouded their beloved Berlin to an extent they had never before experienced. What happened to the sanctity and safety of their capital city; the one Göring had promised would never be bombed?

Helplessly cowering for two horrific days in her small flat, Linette endured the bombing from the RAF air raids pounding Berlin into submission to soften the way for the Russians descending upon it. Manufacturing areas were always attacked first, but by this time in the war, non-military civilian targets were also frequently targeted.

Berlin was totally defenseless to the extended final attacks. Linette's building had been damaged just days before, but half of it continued to stand. Electrical power and water were already knocked out making the building almost uninhabitable.

When Linette cautiously peered out her shattered window shortly after midnight, it was pure darkness, the moonlight not able to filter through the suspended dust and soot in the blackened night air. There wasn't a light to be seen on the entire city block.

Gradually, the bombing had ceased. But for the sounds of creaking buildings, and the occasional crumbling of falling beams, the silence was mostly unbroken. Most disturbing however, were the agonizing pleas for help from people still alive but trapped under the dense debris.

It was shortly after 4:00 in the morning when Linette hesitantly opened her door to peer into the barren hallway with nothing more than a burning candlestick to guide her way. The route was difficult to negotiate as she carefully worked her way down the severely damaged staircases. Although most of the fires were burned out, some continued to smolder.

The smoke seeped its way across the lower floors and had by now accumulated inside the stairwells. It was difficult to breathe and even more difficult to keep her burning eyes open to see through the increasingly dense smoke and dust. Only a few others attempted to leave the building. For most people living here, whether they stayed or decided to leave, no one had anywhere else to go.

Linette was barely a block away from the partially damaged building when a small flurry of explosives fell from a lone bomber, probably emptying the last remnants of its deadly payload on its way home. By chance, it delivered a final direct hit, demolishing what remained of her humble home, taking with it the lives of any remaining tenants.

With a final shrug and a shake of her head, Linette turned in the direction of the explosion to offer a brief prayer for those who undoubtedly perished. She could easily have been among them.

She tread carefully through the darkened silence, stumbling as she went. Tears welled up inside her. There was no sign of life here. It seemed the entire world had been annihilated. When she turned the corner of the street, itself being difficult to distinguish in the rubble, she was relieved to see some of the distant buildings still standing. Perhaps Ernst's shop would be one of them.

Not only had a couple of shops survived the raids, including the grocery store, but there were also a few people already gathered outside where the sidewalk used to be, each of them probably clutching a few remaining food stamps. It was the last thing she expected to see. By this point, all she wanted was a place with a roof over her head. Not wanting to engage with them on the street, she entered from the abandoned alleyway behind the shop.

There wasn't much inventory left in stock because the delivery trucks could not pass through the Russian roadblocks. No one was willing to challenge the security troops. Even if they had, it would have been impossible to navigate through the debris littering the city streets. To make matters worse, the half-flooded roads made it even more perilous to pass.

All the shops had closed for the past few days because of the intensity of the air raids. Most likely many of them would never re-open.

About 6:30 AM, just a few hours later, Ernst came downstairs to the shop as was his habit. Not sure if any customers would dare venture out, but many probably starving by this time, he didn't know what to expect. His arrival was primarily to check any damages that may have occurred from either the bombing or from smash-and-grab theft which had become a more frequent occurrence; desperate people would take anything they could salvage.

The glass windows had been smashed months ago and replaced with solid wooden panels from heavy crates Ernst salvaged. Since then, people had tried to remove the wood to use for firewood to cook and keep warm. It was a never-ending struggle to survive, every single day. People still needed to eat and take care of their families by any means possible. Just a few days ago, some women were washing clothing on the street in the gushing water from where the hydrant used to be. Life carried on somehow.

"*Linette!* I'm so thankful to see you here today. We were so worried about you." Ernst was always so gracious, and in these times, nothing could be taken for granted.

"I think God smiled on me early this morning." Linette responded. "I barely got out of my building when it suffered a direct hit. Everything is gone now, but I got out with my life, such as it is." She held up her old scruffy bag. "All I have is this. What more do I need?"

"Good heavens, Linette! Thank God you are alright." Ernst wrapped his arms around her and hugged her comfortingly. "A few days ago, I took Edith to her sister's home, just a short distance outside the city. We walked some of the way to meet them, so they didn't have to drive too far into the city to get her, just about the time the air attacks began. I was fortunate to get her out when I did. We didn't know the roadblocks would be set up so quickly at every intersection. I feel much better knowing she's safer now.

"I've come to the reluctant conclusion I must join her soon. Staying here every day is not worth the risk anymore. I hope you understand."

"Of course, Ernst. You have enough on your mind already. Don't worry about me. Although I must ask, would it be alright if I stay here for a few days until I sort things out for myself? I have nowhere to call home now."

"Yes, of course, but I doubt power will be restored anytime soon. I only wish I could do more for you. It's bound to be dangerous here alone, Linette. I hope you can find somewhere safer but stay here as long as you need."

Linette was relieved for the time being but thought it best to turn their minds to clearing out whatever inventory remained. There were still people depending on them to eat. "Whatever we don't sell today, perhaps we should just give to anyone needing it, don't you agree?"

"Yes, good idea Linette, but keep whatever you may need for yourself too, understood?"

The next two hours or so passed quickly. By now the new day was dawning and much of the smoke and dust continued to slowly dissipate. Enough remained suspended in the air to continue casting a gloomy and foreboding feeling about the streets, which remained generally quiet and hushed, but for the casual conversation outside the store entrance.

The roads were generally impassable, meaning neither work crews nor ambulances could hastily access the host of emergency situations. Nor were there any cars or pedestrians to speak of, just a pervasively unsettled eeriness, making even their familiar surroundings become lost within the foreboding grip of death and destruction.

Just as Ernst and Linette were clearing the empty cartons down to the basement and setting up the cash register, there was a disturbance outside the store. People in line began shouting to one another to run, and they quickly dispersed down the south end of the street.

Ernst ran to the door and saw the commotion, seeing what appeared to be small groups of vandals approaching from the north end of the street. As they moved closer, he realized they were not Germans; they were much worse. They were Russians!

"Linette, you must get out of here! People are running away. Russian soldiers are making their way toward this end of the street!" As Ernst spoke, the sound of gunfire echoed down the empty street intrusively shattering the silence. Linette quickly looked outside for herself and realized if she began to run now, she would likely be shot in the back, or something far worse.

"It's too late to run now. Our chances are better if we hide in the basement among the boxes," she exclaimed.

"No. You go down there and stay put," as he followed her halfway down the wooden staircase. "There! Hide yourself as best you can, even inside the crate if you can. I'll pile some cartons on top of it and come back up here." Linette looked at Ernst, not wanting him to stay and face whatever would befall him on his own. He saw her concern for him. "We must do this now, my dear," he sternly directed. "I'll be alright. Don't worry about me."

The next moments seemed like hours. Linette huddled herself inside the potato crate Ernst often used as a table and for storing perishables inside. The empty boxes on top provided Linette with little defense she feared could not adequately prevent their discovery of her. All she could do was crouch there quietly, praying she and Ernst would survive this threatening encounter.

She had heard rumors about the brutality of the Red Army striking fear into the hearts and minds of the innocent people involved, often resulting in mass suicides of entire families. People became cave dwellers, choosing to hide in the blackened basements of their homes, if they still had one. Alone, or in groups, they huddled in dark and dirty blown out buildings, surrounded by debris and scavenging rats, just praying for their personal safety.

Now Linette was one of those rats. This was her worst moment of paralyzing fear. It was no longer an imagined story; it could very well become her reality. She could hear the main door being kicked in, followed by the heart-pounding sounds of heavy footsteps. She heard the harsh and accusatory insults being directed at Ernst. Shelving was being smashed and ripped from the walls; the piercing chill of shattered glass followed. She understood the Russian profanities. She spoke the language well.

Ernst began to cry out helplessly. "*No! Please dear God, no!*" There was a loud slamming sound she could only half imagine was inflicted upon Ernst. His groans were distinct and torturous, and sadly to say, they were all too familiar to Linette's experienced ear. She could feel his agony from whatever had just happened. Then, a single gunshot and there was a sudden thump on the floor above, followed by yet another gunshot.

One final filthy slur was directed at Ernst's dead body. The subsequent derisive laughter of the executioners had a shocking and characteristic shrill to it.

Waiting helplessly, Linette prayed for the pounding footsteps to go away, holding her breath, until they began to descend the staircase to the pitch-black basement below. They were loud, crude, and boisterous as they directed the penetrating beams of their flashlights into every darkened corner of the concrete bunker, looking for the spoils of their pillage. Linette could clearly detect the darting bright flickers of light through the seams between the cartons piled above and beside her.

"Nothing much down here... but check those boxes... make sure there's nothin' worth taking," someone shouted to another. Opening the first carton, and then checking the second, the soldier yelled, "They're all fuckin' empty."

As he said the words, he must have swept his arm or his rifle across the pile and they fell away to reveal their trembling prize.

"*There we go! Look what I found boys!*" Linette remained hunched over with one hand covering her mouth, like a stuffed animal squeezed into a box one size too small. Her heart sank.

"This is the best way to start our day! *Get outta' there, you little whore!*" Linette could not move, until one of the men grabbed her by both feet and dragged her onto the concrete floor.

"Stand up, you stupid bitch!" the leader shouted, as one of the men roughly pulled her to her feet.

Linette slowly struggled to steady herself, raising her hands to shield her eyes from the blinding darts of light pointed directly into her face. Standing in front of the leader of the pack, she couldn't see their faces in the dark, her eyes still adjusting and trying to avoid the beaming flashlights still shining into her now only partially dilated eyes. "Well look at you. You *are* a pretty thing, aren't you? Take off her coat. Let's have a good look at our prize."

One of the others grabbed the collar of her coat and pulled it aggressively from her shoulders. The leader turned to the private and ordered, "Take her upstairs where there's more light. I wanna' see what I'm doin' with this one."

The two subordinates grabbed Linette's hands and forcefully dragged her up the staircase behind the leader of the pack. She stumbled along the way, wincing from the strength of their grip and the painful wrenching of her shoulder.

When they reached the main floor, her squinting eyes were barely coming into focus when she gasped at the sight of Ernst's crushed skull and the two bullet holes in his chest. The pool of blood spread out around his corpse and shimmered in the subdued ambient light. There was no mistaking Ernst suffered a painful but quick death. The poor man, she thought. Was she about to join him in the afterlife?

"What's your name, you dirty little slut?" demanded the senior officer. Linette did not respond and looked sheepishly away. She kept her usual defiance in close check. There was no need to provoke any of them with direct eye contact.

"Doesn't matter a good goddamn. Take your fuckin' clothes off!" He stared directly into her now weeping eyes. Although she spoke perfect Russian, Linette looked helplessly at him indicating she did not understand what he said. One of the men pulled up on the sweater she wore showing her what she was told. Linette did as they wanted and when they pointed, she reluctantly removed her boots and long pants as well.

Now standing in front of the five of them, they were staring at her half-naked body. She was wearing nothing but her underwear and brassiere, shivering in the cold as they were joking among themselves at her frightened expense with increasingly disgusting crudeness.

"Ok, gimme the rest of the show. Come on! You're among friends here," he stated sarcastically as he winked at one of the men.

Linette recoiled at the thought and did not respond to his order. He removed his pistol from the holster and pressed it hard against her temple, forcing her to stumble backwards. That much was clearly conveyed.

He approached more closely with his black stubble and broken teeth, so close she could smell his putrid breath. "Your choice, bitch… either you do it, or we'll do it for ya." He cocked his gun as he spoke.

Her worst imaginings had now become real. In these fleeting moments, it was as if time refused to pass. After all she had endured in the past, she now believed humankind was capable of being more evil than the wildest animal. The unique difference was humans were given the innate wisdom to know the difference between good and evil. Some of them simply choose not to care.

Humiliation was the least of Linette's concerns right now. The degradation of what was about to happen would be so traumatic, she would struggle to forget for the rest of her life… if she still had one. With resignation, she reached behind her back to unclasp her brassiere while her captors fell silent with frightening anticipation.

Linette was now visibly trembling and began to sob uncontrollably, pulling it away from her breasts. In unison, the animals let out a collective celebrative cheer, likening it to a sickening game. One of them squeezed and fondled her breasts from behind. When he stepped closer, she could feel the icy cold barrel of his rifle touching her between her thighs. She cringed as it did so.

Slowly, he ran his filthy, grimy hands down her sides, no doubt savoring the humiliation he was about to inflict upon her. Her heart was pounding rapidly now, and she shook from head to toe. When he tucked his coarse fingers and broken nails inside her pants and commenced to remove them, Linette uncontrollably urinated on the floor.

She became faint; her stance wobbling from the light-headedness. Her mind raced, trying desperately to disengage from the swirling savagery undoubtedly awaiting her. She dropped uncontrollably to her knees and succumbed so completely she was unable to extend her arm to break her fall forward. Thumping headfirst onto the filthy floor, she was lying prostrate with both legs now fully extended and thankfully, she passed out. She heard nothing more.

Suddenly, in the midst of the men's laughter, there was a loud crashing sound. The broken door of the shop, still partially ajar, was kicked fully open noisily and abruptly, breaking the ravenous anticipation of the moment for Linette's shameless captors. There in the doorway was their commanding officer, livid upon seeing what his men were about to do.

"*What the fuck is going on here!*" the officer bellowed.

Catching the men off guard, they stood totally stupefied before him, with this naked woman lying unconscious at their feet. One of the men was rapidly trying to pull up his trousers, having dropped to his ankles when the general continued to shout at them. Groggy and shaken by her grievous circumstances, Linette slowly began to stir, having no immediate presence of mind as to where she was.

As she fought to regain her awareness, she reflexively drew her arms and hands in front of her breasts and sat up, still frozen with fear and uncertainty.

The senior officer gestured to his aide, who continued to stand beside him, to assist the lady getting to her feet. The aide took her gently by her arm and softly told Linette in Russian to move away and get herself properly dressed. One of the offending rapists appeared shocked that Linette understood Russian. She awkwardly staggered off to the washroom, almost ashamedly, with her bundle of clothing held tightly to her chest. The officer, a general, then readdressed his soldiers and continued to berate them.

"You men represent the Russian Army, serving justice for your homeland. This is war, not a drunken fraternity party. I will not tolerate any more of this unprofessional behavior from the men I command. You discredit our country! For that alone, I should put all of you before a firing squad."

With that, he ripped his strapped holster open and brandished his handgun, not pointing it at them directly, but slowly gesturing toward them with intimidating intent. Through clenched teeth, his rage continued to boil over.

"Better still, I should shoot you assholes in the head myself. You men disgust me! Take your sorry asses outside and give your I.D.s to the captain. Get out of my sight before I change my mind. This isn't over for you bastards… believe me!"

When the shouting subsided, Linette hesitatingly exited the washroom and sheepishly approached the officer, the others having already left the shop. She was sniffling now, overwrought about what could have happened had he not intervened. Still under extreme duress, she had difficulty searching for words. In perfect Russian she said "I… I don't know what to say… I'm… I am in your debt." She leaned forward and gently rested her head on his chest whispering, "I thank God for sending you to me."

Ever so discreetly, the general told his aide to escort Linette away from this tormenting place, where Ernst's mutilated body still lay. "Take her to my flat and speak only to Elena on my behalf. Tell her to take care of this woman and give her the help and kindness she requires until I return. I will address the matter with her later. Now please, take her to my car and go."

The general did not return to his home the day of Linette's assault, feeling uncertain about the wisdom of his decision to assist this helpless woman in the manner he had chosen. He did not think of Linette as a captive, but others most certainly would. He was a Belarussian, raised as a faithful Roman Catholic. It would test the strength of his resolve to do what he could to help this desperate woman, for no other reason than to be a good Christian. He hoped she would soon sense that quality in him.

25
REDEMPTION BEFORE GOD

BERLIN, SEPTEMBER 1945

DURING THE RUSSIAN SIEGE, NOW JUST A FEW MONTHS AGO, RAF bombing raids had dropped more than 45,000 *tons* of bombs inside the city of Berlin in just three days. The Americans dropped another 23,000 tons in the final days as well. These relentless attacks were directed at civilian targets, forcing forty percent of Germans to flee from their homes in the city. More than 600,000 apartment blocks were no longer habitable, many being completely levelled.

Postwar Berlin was a living hell for the almost two and a half million Germans continuing to live there; this represented about half of the original population. Millions of people were herded into boxcars by the Red Army to be sent east, many to be taken to hard labor camps, some to secret police prisons, none to be heard from again.

The manufacturing district of Siemensstadt had been rebuilt after the British bombing raids of 1943 but could not withstand the total obliteration of the 1945 raid. Entire city blocks of this sector were flattened, killing thousands of workers.

Anna's sister Emilie and her daughter Gertrude had worked in those factories since Sigmund and Marissa's deaths in November 1938. Without Sigmund's protection, and General von Brauchitsch' subsequent provision of new identities for them, they would undoubtedly have faced horrific persecution and probable death. Now, even the general's once vast influence could not have protected them, as he now sat in a jail cell awaiting his own execution for his involvement in the Valkyrie attempt. Both Emilie and Gertrude's whereabouts were unknown.

Most high-rise buildings were totally gutted across the city, leaving their empty shells wide open to the skies above, the roofs having been completely burned or blown away weeks before. The interior walls were often still standing through entire swaths of roofless neighborhoods. When seen from above, these hollowed out structures had the appearance of hundreds of rows of open and hollow egg cartons.

Many of the civilian survivors continuing to remain throughout Berlin, scurried like vermin to darkened basements seeking shelter, trying to protectively hold together what remained of their families. Other than a few soup kitchens, there was no organized food supply. Electrical power, fresh water and sewage control were largely unavailable, with no timeline to be restored.

Women routinely foraged through city blocks of rubble, frantically looking for food and precious coal to burn. Entire families often picked through pools of leaking slag heaps with their bare hands to find hidden treasures proving somehow to be of use.

Food supplies such as potatoes and turnips were brought by farmers into the city and were quickly depleted by overwhelming numbers of the starving masses. Amazingly, these impoverished civilians maintained good order, standing patiently in line.

Remarkably, many of the upper-class German women continued to dress in proper attire, wearing fashionable dresses, often adorned with tasteful hats and high-heeled shoes, despite the debris and devastation around them. Appearing quite stylish and dignified was so ingrained in them, they clung steadfastly to who they always were. It was a matter of personal pride.

In stark contrast, just across the same street, beggars were everywhere pleading for morsels of food. In one of the once quiet and nearby side streets, there was an emaciated dead horse lying by the side of the road. Several men were cutting the carcass into steaks to feed their families. In only a matter of hours, the entire carcass was gone.

Women were washing clothing wherever gushing water-mains offered it, precious water from the overflowing River Spree, whose pumping stations had been deliberately crippled by the Fuhrer's vindictive orders just prior to his suicide.

Again, it was common to see the poor, who could be seen picking through piles of concrete and debris to scavenge bricks to be reused to repair what was left of their broken homes. These people were referred to as *hamsters*, digging meticulously for another nugget of useable garbage. Among them were also several middle-class women, who were still smartly dressed, doing the same filthy task, having been reduced to the same common level of subsistence.

Even the Russians could not help but notice the orderly way German civilians went about their business trying to maintain a semblance of normality. The Russian author Vasily Grossman commented upon how they cleaned and removed debris from the streets as if they were tidying the rooms of their houses.

Shortly after the war ended, in a once lovely, upscale district of the city's east side, a luxury apartment on the third floor, was surrounded by destruction for several blocks around, in every direction. Perhaps fate had saved it. The building stood defiantly against the odds with an exterior wall half blown out, the roof still partially intact. The final traces of concrete dust were still lingering in the soothing summer air.

An explosion had left a gaping hole in the exterior brick wall about twelve feet wide from the floor to where a ceiling used to be, now exposing the lovely and spacious interior through the opening to passers-by on the street below. The maid could be seen clearly, setting the dining room table for dinner with apparent indifference to the violent disruption of the war. These conditioned responses by many in the upper-class, demonstrated their resiliency and the proud way they continued to live. For these relative few, they appeared unflappable.

In a similar manner, the poor and the homeless showed indomitable strength of character as well; toiling endlessly, not so much for dignity, which had long since been sapped from their veins, but simply to stay alive to care for their children.

The scattered remains of the beautiful and inspiring Tiergarten Park, was located near the infamous Reichstag building, itself now blackened and shrapnel scarred. The sprawling and once manicured park of Berlin was now crawling with hundreds of impoverished and desperate laborers. Tediously they chipped away at the once mighty but now fallen oak trees and slowly over time, piece by piece, entire trees were consumed to feed the vagrants' fires for warmth and to cook whatever scraps they might find to sustain them.

The roving Russian predators continued to brutalize thousands of German women and children at a terrorizing pace. This forced many women to remain hidden in the evenings, especially during the hunting hours, as they were referred to, tentatively exiting their hovels that once were homes, often before sunrise when the rapists were still sleeping. In many cases, the only viable alternative for women was to become friendly with the occupying forces who were well supplied to provide for their needs.

To consort with men of the armed forces in this way, whether Russian or American, would have been outrageous and undignified before the war. Now, the reality was simple; food and protection came before morals and self-esteem, as more than one woman openly confessed.

Of necessity, Linette also became one of these women who put practicality and survival before all else. Through the numerous tragedies in her life, a list of which was too long to remember, the most frightening and disturbing was the day she was on the very precipice of being gang raped by the Russian soldiers.

She was helpless, with nowhere to run and no way to defend herself. For the first time in her life, there was an instant her spirit abandoned her, having dissociated from her physical body; perhaps already withdrawn to the sanctuary of the Lord himself. In the profound blink of an eyelash that piercing moment changed her life forever.

Was it the Lord who guided her back from the edge of despair, or was it through His messenger, General Nikolai Semenov, who intervened that fateful day? Linette did not understand, but the general's empathy for her was remarkable and did not appear to be self-serving. He was a fine example confirming not all Russians participated in or condoned the personal denigration and mass rapes being inflicted.

By contrast, General Semenov was one of numerous others who were idealistic Communists, genuinely disgusted by such inappropriate and abusive conduct. The very thought of it repulsed him because it brought shame to the uniform and the country the offenders served. In his mind, the perpetrators of these war crimes were a blight on humanity.

Nikolai Semenov returned to his flat two days after stopping Linette's sexual assault. Unknown to her, he thoughtfully spent the previous night elsewhere to provide more adequate time for Linette's emotional recovery, as well as to decide how best to handle her situation. His maid had been advised to tend to her needs until the general was comfortable about returning.

Linette had been sitting by the window of his flat overlooking the heavily damaged hotel strip. She was informed by the maid she was not under arrest and was apparently free to leave at her own discretion. Having nowhere else to go, and wanting to speak directly with the gallant officer, she chose to stay until his return.

Most of this area continued to provide essential services, sufficient to accommodate several commanding officers of the Red Army. Any German residing there after the siege had already been hastily forced from whatever lodging they had occupied. For the time being, Linette rightly decided to stay where she was, unless she was explicitly told to leave.

As she was sipping a relaxing cup of tea, she was reminded of her special moments with Marta they had often shared at Marta's home overlooking Cuvreystrasse. How she longed to be with her again.

Linette was deep in her own thoughts when she heard keys rattling against the outer door and she promptly readjusted herself by covering her partially exposed legs with her housecoat. When the door opened, she barely recognized the officer; it was more by his uniform than her blurred memory of his features.

Linette's heart was suddenly racing again, the stress of anxious uncertainty quickly mounting within her.

"Good afternoon, Madame," he said in slightly accented German. "Are you feeling better, I trust?" He had already removed his cap and had placed it under his arm, standing almost apologetically for his unannounced intrusion.

Linette placed her cup and saucer on the side table and rose to address him, not certain how or what to say. Her apprehensive posture indicated her general uncertain demeanor.

The officer continued. "Let me properly introduce myself. I am General Nikolai Semenov of the Russian Red Army."

Linette, now feeling somewhat disarmed, slowly approached him, extending her hand to him. "I am Linette Etienne. I am so pleased to see you again, Sir... and yes, I am much better now, thanks to your kindness."

"I'm so pleased, Linette. May I call you that?" he asked respectfully.

"Yes... yes most certainly, please do," she responded more welcomingly.

"I trust Elena has taken good care of you these past few days and you are feeling more like yourself again?"

"Yes, she has been most kind. I... we haven't spoken very much. I was sleeping, for how long I cannot say. I'm still very much shaken by what has happened." Still searching for words, Linette continued standing and shook her head slightly as if to clear her thoughts, "I am so very sorry... perhaps, umm, maybe I should gather my things and uh... and be on my way, if that's alright."

As she spoke, she gestured to the room where she had been sleeping. "I am very sorry for any inconvenience I have caused you, Sir."

The general realized his stiffened posture may have become intimidating to her and he placed his cap on the chair close to the entrance.

He set his valise on the floor, near to his desk on the far wall and proceeded to remove his leather dress gloves as he spoke. "Please relax, Linette. You have nothing to fear from me. My intentions are strictly honorable, I assure you. Perhaps inappropriate, I must admit, but honorable, nonetheless. Please sit where you were and enjoy the sunshine."

By this time Elana had entered from the kitchen, reluctant to intrude on the awkwardness of the moment between them.

"Ahh, Elana," he said. "Would you be so kind to make another pot of tea? I must admit, I am quite famished as well. Perhaps some bread and liverwurst, just something to take the edge off my appetite. Would you care to join me, Linette?"

"... If that would be alright. Perhaps you would prefer to eat alone? If so, I completely understand."

"Nonsense, you must be hungry too, after all you have been through. I would appreciate your company. I promise, I would not have asked you, if indeed I wanted to eat alone."

"Then I shall. That would be lovely, General."

Before they sat, the general excused himself to use the guest washroom and wash up. Upon his return he loosened the collar of his tunic, offering a sigh of satisfaction after doing so. By this time, Elana had already set the small meal at his usual place. "Ahh, this looks wonderful, Elana. Thank you."

"You are most welcome, Sir. May I pour your tea?" she graciously offered. "For you as well, Miss Linette?"

"Yes, thank you, Elana."

Gradually the conversation began to flow more naturally between them, and inevitably the anxiousness originally existing between them began to dissipate somewhat. Nikolai preferred not to engage in any specifics about the frightening episode Linette had endured, but when she asked directly why he offered shelter and care to her, he opened up to her more than she had expected. Leaving her alone that day was not an option for him, for reasons soon to be made clear.

"German women are being hunted down as if merely sport. Disgustingly, some officers among us encourage their troops to do so. It was only a matter of time before others would surely find you again, and the same thing could have been repeated.

"You were disoriented and frightened. For many reasons, I vowed to myself not to turn my back on you." He sipped his hot tea, clearing his throat before he commenced speaking again. Linette simply remained quiet, not certain what to say. She thought it best to remain silent to permit him to continue.

"From the first words you spoke to me, I realized you were a Christian woman. In many ways, you reminded me of my deceased wife, who herself was intelligent, articulate, and spiritual. These qualities in you resonated with me. This admission may sound insane to you, but it was my thought process at the time."

The general calmly stirred his tea, perhaps a little embarrassed about his admissions. Nevertheless, he continued, a little more tentatively than before. "I lost my family very early in the war. On just the second day of the German invasion, my dear wife and our young daughter were killed by Luftwaffe air strikes over the city of Brest, in south-western Belarus. They were the only family I knew and could remember; my parents having been taken when I was barely an adolescent."

He broke off the discussion temporarily, focusing upon his enjoyment of the liverwurst Elana had prepared. "Elana!" he shouted to the kitchen. "This is most delicious, and the bread, did my aide deliver it to you this morning as I had instructed?"

"Yes, Herr Semenov. It was still warm when he arrived."

"Wonderful! Please Linette, help yourself. You must be hungry as well." He graciously slid the plate of liverwurst and bread closer to her as he returned to their conversation. He raised his napkin to touch his lips before resuming, and took another sip of tea.

"Linette, I have been a professional military man for most of my life and while carrying out my duties, it has been necessary to do some terrible things. If anyone has justification to exact revenge on the German people, it is me. Being a dedicated Christian myself, my faith remains strong to this very day, despite all I have lost. As I think more about your question, finding you and deciding not to abandon you, was a chance for my redemption before God. Most people are never given the opportunity to do so, but I did not intend to lose mine."

He shuffled awkwardly before he resumed. "Whether God forgives me for my misdeeds is out of my hands... but know this about me. If I had not helped you as I did, I would never have forgiven myself."

Linette cautiously placed her hand on his after hearing his solemn confessions, which may have been more appropriate before his priest. She knew full well he did not need to explain himself to her. She now better understood his motivation for rescuing her that day. Indifferently kicking her to the street curb would have been unconscionable for him.

"You may stay as long as you require, Linette; I should clarify... for as long as I am able to stay here. There are no strings attached to my offer. I only need the place for a few hours at night, and even then, it is only rarely I am here." Linette was stunned by his offer, blessing herself and lifting her now moistened eyes toward the Lord above.

"This should provide you some time to decide where you may eventually need to go. If you require anything during my absence, Elana is here to assist you. For your continued safety, all I ask is you try to stay inside as much as possible, at least until the situation here stabilizes. Do you understand?"

Right or wrong, under the circumstances she felt strongly compelled to accept his offer, no matter how short-lived it may be; no matter what he might someday expect from her.

*****

WIORY, POLAND 1946

Jan and Julia's budding relationship initially provided a small measure of happiness for others in their quaint village. Both were shy and introverted, except when they were in each other's company, and for many of the parishioners, this newfound relationship reminded them that indeed, life and love could be rebuilt and eventually prevail.

There was no doubt about Jan and Julia's strong affection for one another and the optimism they shared for their future together. Perhaps this passionate belief was a factor binding them so closely together.

Matters of the heart, however, soon gave way to the more urgent circumstances in which they found themselves. In the wake of the German defeat, the tattered ruins of Poland were left behind. Discussions among the villagers about resettlement became more prevalent day by day, which by this time had become strained, repetitive, and exhausting, often without satisfactory resolution.

The widespread and generally disorganized evacuation, however, took its toll on the school by drastically reducing the number of both students and teachers. At this stage, continuing education was no longer a relevant priority. When the school was inevitably closed, Julia tutored the three children in the well-intentioned but futile attempt to provide some continuity in their still very young lives.

The church was not exempt from the general attrition suffered by the village. Not only had the peasant villagers started to evacuate, but the church also suffered financially when the German officers and families once stationed in the area had been forced to attempt escape, or alternatively surrendered to the Allies. Desperation, violence, and lawlessness were driven by starvation which exacted its toll on anyone foolish enough to remain in the village long term.

Father Francis knew this sacred place would not be spared from the ravages already beginning, with more of the same to surely follow. It was time to evacuate the children, Bronia, and himself from the lives they once knew.

It was months after Germany's surrender when the first Allied troops escorted vast caravans of trucks loaded with relief packages consisting of food, medical equipment, paper products, and blankets. Tens of dozens of cargo trucks heavily loaded with wooden pallets of food and water were all primarily intended for delivery to Warsaw.

Opinogora was only one of numerous impoverished villages along their route. The American and British soldiers offered friendly waves to those too timid to approach them. As quickly as supplies were off-loaded, the hungry emaciated scavengers quickly descended upon the scene with nothing more to offer in return than their heartfelt thanks and prayers.

It could be months before the Allies properly restored order this far from the capital city, but a small number of troops stayed behind, just for a few days, to at least establish their presence to provide medical care wherever it was required.

Before Father Francis finalized his decision to leave Opinogora, he asked Jan and Julia to consider accompanying them on their uncertain journey. They reluctantly declined, choosing instead to stay behind with Marianna and Josef. It was a difficult decision to make, but Father knew the answer before he asked, hoping against hope Julia would help him with the children she loved so dearly.

In the last few weeks before their departure, Father Francis had made an almost impossible attempt to stockpile some extra gasoline for the trip. It would prove to be a more challenging task than he had anticipated due to severe shortages of fuel. Within only a few days, fuel and other necessities were no longer being delivered. His plan was to head as far west as the car would take them. From there, he planned to board a train in search of longer-term safety with distant relatives already living in Belgium.

He could not endure the overwhelming concerns he had for the children but, much as most others, he had no alternative. By his own admission, he no longer possessed the youthfulness and physical stamina he would need to work the coalmines below Belgian soil. The priesthood was all he knew, and he relied upon the strength of his passion to follow God's calling. There was always a need for a pastor, he thought; at least this was his desperate belief.

On the day of their parting, Julia and Jan helped Father finish packing the car. His worldly possessions were left behind, including his book collections and his prized mahogany desk, no longer having relevant value. As they were finishing loading the trunk, Father Francis placed the final carton, a rather heavy one, at Julia's feet.

"Julia, I have personally selected this box of books as my gift to you. They are some of my well-read favorites and I cannot think of anyone more deserving to have them to remember us by. I would be honored for you to accept them."

"Why, thank you Father! That's very kind of you. I know how much they mean to you. I will read every one of them, I promise," Julia replied.

It was a tearful farewell evoking such painful emotions, especially for the children. Katia sobbed through tears, desperately pleading with Julia to come with them. Julia's only consolation to the sweet child was to assure her she would meet them again, as soon as she possibly could, knowing full well it wouldn't be during this earthly life. As the fully loaded car descended the sloping driveway for the final time, Julia was heart-broken, helplessly watching them leave, sobbing uncontrollably in Jan's comforting arms.

The church fell into disuse shortly thereafter. Father simply closed the door without locking it. With reverence, he rightfully entrusted it back to God's care and custody.

*****

After the church was abandoned, Julia worked tirelessly beside Jan and his brother Josef, carrying on working the potato farm to support their mother as they had promised to do. The nobility of hard work and the best of intentions found the family toiling even more than the Germans had demanded of them before Julia arrived.

The viral desperation of others had infected them as well, despite expanding their crops to include beets and barley. Too few paying customers remained in Golina and Wiory, and bartering was no longer a viable solution.

As winter set in, there were plenty of vegetables to eat after harvest and wildlife, though sparse, still provided an occasional feast after checking the traps they set every morning. There was a constant source of fresh water from the river and ice-fishing always proved to be worth the effort; the fish were as hungry as the fishermen, if you were patient enough to endure the cold winds howling across the open expanse of the mostly frozen river.

Several weeks at a time would pass without seeing anyone familiar. The only passers-by were unkempt strangers, and when they did, the family had to remain suspiciously vigilant. Desperate times often led to desperate measures to protect home and family. The few neighbors still remaining on the small farms stayed pretty much to themselves, but it was still reassuring to know not everyone had left Wiory behind.

When chores were done, there remained plenty of time for Julia to indulge in Father Francis' wonderful books. They were difficult to read but in hindsight, his most valuable gift was tutoring her so generously, both in conversation and in nurturing her thirst for knowledge.

During this time, Julia's appetite for reading had become ravenous and she devoured the books one by one, continuing to progress in leaps and bounds. Her reading would not have continued to develop were it not for the idle hours the winter weather had provided for her to sit by the fireplace. It was the first time in her life she could treat herself on a consistent basis to such a pleasurable experience.

Winter's short days passed peacefully and quietly for Julia, and she became an integral part of the Szymanski family. Even Marianna's stern manner softened over time to accommodate the loving daughter she never had.

*****

Through the wicked winter months, the Red Army continued to secure their vast but largely destroyed sector east of Berlin, while the western allies did the same in the west. There was an invisible line between the two sectors that was respected by the liberators and little cause was necessary to strictly enforce it. The division of Germany gradually developed a stable but still tenuous coexistence among the victors.

Similarly, Linette and General Semenov contentedly carried on with the remaining shreds of their complicated lives and over several months, each respected the privacy of the other. The shared accommodations were more than ample, considering the horrific circumstances of the multitudes struggling to survive outside their hotel doors.

There were, however, brief periods in which they would continue to commiserate with one another, often providing a more personal and comforting atmosphere for both.

"Tell me Linette, in the past several months since we have been sharing this suite, you must be getting anxious to step outside from time to time. You have done well remaining safely inside, but it must become tedious for you I'm sure," the general enquired.

"To be candid, I try not to be impatient about such things. Your overwhelming graciousness sates my restlessness so completely. I must say though, I'm not comfortable seeking other accommodations just yet, but I must do so at some point," Linette confided. "I can't imagine even trying to exist in the midst of the chaos outside."

Walking to the liquor cabinet near to the kitchen, the general retrieved two brandy glasses before he returned. "I'm in the mood for some fine brandy. Care to join me? You just raised an important point I wish to speak to you about if you don't mind."

"Yes, thank you, General. I would be very grateful to try some. I must ask, are you about to break some bad news? Perhaps you think the alcohol will help sustain me against what you are about to say." Although she smiled at his light-hearted laugh at her suggestion, Linette was naturally becoming concerned.

"Heavens no. It's not often we are able to share some time together. I appreciate the privacy you afford me with my military matters. It does not go unnoticed, I assure you. No, there is some news I am anxious to share with you. In fact, I need your opinion on something that concerns us both. It's good news, so please relax," he reassured her.

Handing Linette her glass of brandy, he lifted his own to toast the moment together. "Cheers Linette!"

The first sip of brandy was very satisfying to Linette's palate. She savored the moment and silently prepared to brace herself for the news he was about to deliver.

"I am being offered more suitable accommodations at the Hotel Adlon. I'm inclined to accept. Are you familiar with it?"

"Yes, but only in passing. Too rich for my budget I'm afraid, but I heard it is indeed lovely. It's very near to the Brandenburg Gate, isn't it?" Linette enquired.

"Yes, that's the one. I haven't seen it myself, however many of the senior staff intend to take more permanent residence there. The streets have been sufficiently cleared and some normalcy and order have been better established; much more civilized than here. It is well secured and will afford us both the opportunity to venture outside from time to time. You are most welcome to accompany Elana and me. There is plenty of room and more privacy and privileges for you as my guest."

The general stopped speaking to elicit Linette's response while he downed his brandy and poured another. "More brandy, Linette?"

"Oh, no... no I think one is enough for me. I'm very much enjoying what I have. Thank you, General."

"Just one more request to consider though. You must stop referring to me as *General*, please Linette. Nikolai is much more appropriate. I'm not your commanding officer, for heaven's sake. I have behaved as a gentleman, and I will always continue to do so. It's just who I am, and I believe you know me well enough by now to trust my honesty with you. One could even say we have developed a friendship of sorts."

Nikolai grinned somewhat coyly. "So, what do you think? Do you need more time to decide the merits of my offer?"

Linette was visibly moved by such an unexpected but thoughtful gesture. "Nikolai, I am delighted you would suggest the idea. I would be a fool to reject it, but I must reconfirm my ultimate intention is to find my own way at some point. As long as you understand the uncertainty of my future, and are willing to live with that, then certainly I am pleased to accept. I am most grateful for your kindnesses."

"Wonderful! That wasn't so painful, was it, my dear lady?"

"Perhaps I will have another brandy." Linette's smile was glowing. It was more than the brandy. She was continuing to lower her initial apprehensions about him.

26

AN INVIGORATING FEELING

♂

BY THE TIME SPRING ARRIVED, NATURE BEGAN TO EXPRESS itself once again. What a miracle it was to hear the river's waters splash over and between the rocks and swell across the occasional fallen tree limb; to smell the reawakening of the dank and once frozen earth sleeping so deeply and inconspicuously, never once violating the peaceful serenity above it. It was a time of rejuvenation for the land and the humanity toiling upon it.

Times for such reflections were short-lived when farming for a living rudely intrudes, and this season would be like no other. The world at large was forced to adapt to new limitations. Although it was finally over, everyone was struggling with the reluctance to readjust to the fallout of war, many still wondering why their lives could not simply return to what they were before the war.

Throughout the spring and summer, small groups of despondent hopefuls continued to pass routinely through Wiory to evacuate north. Some of them travelled by foot from the outskirts of Warsaw's remains and others still, from as far away as Katowice. Numerous factors beyond their control had shaped their common destinies, and heartbreak and crippling uncertainty were among them.

For only a fortunate few with horse drawn wagons, they were loaded to capacity to begin their trek northward with their neighbors to relocate outside the city of Torun, about 120 kilometers north of Wiory. The Allies had established temporary gathering stations throughout several regions in eastern Europe to organize and assist any refugees physically capable to make the journey. Torun was just one of several, but it was the closest one to Konin.

361

These were people first and foremost, entire families of people, who were ripped from the lives they once led by the oppressive and unforgiving mechanisms of war. They were considered by many to be collateral damage, the human debris of war. They were not comprised of soldiers and military personnel; they were neither the victors nor the vanquished; they were victims of circumstance from which there was no escape.

Jan and Julia often spoke to their countrymen and women passing through their village. There wasn't easy access to radio or newspaper accounts of the happenings outside their almost irrelevant, secluded lives in Wiory. Word had spread, however, about an organization called the United Nations Relief and Rehabilitation Administration, known as UNRRA, which had been assigned an almost impossible task: organizing, directing, and gathering the more than ten million homeless refugees scattered across most of Europe to relocate them elsewhere.

One summer evening over dinner, Jan was outspoken about what he had learned.

"The very idea is something I could not have imagined," he stated emphatically to the family. "I'm told the world has changed in many ways I don't understand. But western Europe is where the war was fought, not here in Wiory! Taking Mikael from us was unforgivable and I will always hate the Germans for that, but now they're gone. Why can't we just rebuild our village here? It could still become what it always was if the people come back." He thumped his fist firmly on the table for emphasis. "*This*, is where our home is."

"I don't think it's that simple, Jan," said Julia. "From what I overheard from Father Francis and the German officers in Father's office, Europe is a much more complicated problem than we know about in Wiory.

"I think international relationships are what drove the world to war. To my mind, the Allies are the only ones who have a realistic understanding of what it will take to change it for the better, in ways we cannot even imagine. Do you understand what I'm saying, Jan?"

Julia paused, being careful not to suppress Jan's thoughts and feelings. No doubt he was confused and frightened, although he had not admitted it until now. In the absence of his own solutions, he continued to ask more questions. This was his way of thinking things through.

"How do we know if our lives will be better there, than if we stay here? This is all we know." He scratched the back of his head, more out of frustration than an itchy scalp.

"We don't, Jan," Julia responded. "But staying here just trying to survive, I think the world will just leave us behind, until someday, someone smarter and stronger will come and take what we have built away from us... and we won't be able to do anything about it."

Julia stood to fix a pot of tea, and like the tea, she just let things steep a bit, saying nothing until someone else broke the silence. It would not be Josef or Marianna, by Julia's calculation. It was a few minutes of silence and quiet introspection; everyone it seemed, wanting Julia to decide.

Julia wisely shifted the conversation to engage Josef and Marianna as well. She ruled the family and Julia had no intention of casually disregarding her interests. "Marianna, whatever decision we make in the days ahead affects you and Josef too. What are your thoughts about possibly leaving the farm? It's what you've worked so hard to keep for much of your life."

"I just don't know what to do. The world has changed too fast for me." For the first time, Marianna's voice began to tremble. "I think about Mikael all the time from first light to the end of the day. I miss him and worry if he's getting enough to eat, where he is and how we could ever find him."

Josef spoke up but had no idea how to console his mother. In his entire life he never had to, even when his father died. She didn't say much at that time or even openly shed a tear. "Mom, we all worry about him. We're a strong, tough family and none of us are as strong and bull headed as Mikael... but it's been almost five years and we've heard nothing from him."

"If we leave here and he comes back, how would he find us?" Marianna protested. "The farm isn't as important to me as he is. I'm afraid that if we leave here... we leave Mikael wherever he is, God rest his soul. I don't think I'll ever see him again."

Jan stepped up but like his brother, had no familiarity with handling his mother's grief, let alone his own. "I'm not saying we should give up hope that he'll come back, but too much has happened and too much time has passed. I think if we stay so he can maybe find us again, we take any hope away for our futures too. Sorry Ma, but I don't think that's best for us anymore."

Finally, Jan said, "So, what do you think we should do, Julia?' He knew what Julia had just done. She deferred to Jan, and he handed the reins right back to her.

"Why don't we look into this UNNRA thing a bit more? If it wasn't for the Allies, Hitler could have won the war. Why shouldn't we trust them on this too?"

In the coming days and weeks, the family reconfirmed the huge camps set up by UNRRA had already been accepting refugees scattered across Europe. This massive project was backed by the President of the United States, *and* the Prime Minister of Great Britain. They supported the concept... with money from their own countries! They promised to restore law and order and provide shelter for refugees until it was safe to return and resettle in their own countries of origin.

*****

Since last Fall, the family had been witnessing the slow but steady evacuation of the village in which Jan and Josef were raised. The same was true of other villages in the region, all of them showing signs of similar neglect.

Staying to the bitter end in their quiet but soon to become desolate outpost, had not yet attracted the attention of the Americans who would be proactively rounding up as many remaining families as possible for relocation to the American Zone in West Germany. Knowing when that time would arrive was uncertain. However, anyone choosing to stay after those efforts, would be left to their own devices and surely be abandoned.

Jan and Julia spent several days discussing the details with their few remaining neighbors, mostly farmers and others who, like the Szymanski family, had been clinging to the past. In the process, Jan and Julia became stronger proponents for the evacuation and gradually came to be regarded as the most knowledgeable about what the Allied plan was offering.

The more the family learned about this concept, the more determined they were to get Marianna's support. The difficulty was to do it without pressuring her. Julia and Jan wanted to offer some hope to Marianna. Nothing had been resolved between them, since their previous discussion, but this time, Josef was determined to go. Jan raised the topic with his mother a few days later as his confidence in the relocation project became more clearly understood.

"Ma, the more we learn about this UNRRA thing, the more hope I have about Mikael. If he's still alive, he'll probably be rounded up by the Americans too. Lots of families have lost contact with each other. This plan is to reunite families, not tear them apart. Maybe we find each other in the American camp. I dunno but, it's still a chance."

"Maybe so, but that's not likely to happen, probably just bullshit. One thing for sure though, I don't wanna lose all of you if I stay behind. We all go, or no one goes. Agreed?" Marianna had spoken, and to everyone's mind, it was the right decision.

It was as close to unanimous as it would ever be, and by accepting Marianna's ultimatum, it was time to act. It was best this way, as it had the appearance of being Marianna's decision.

*****

For those who committed to join Jan's caravan, a big factor not in dispute was safety in numbers; that point was comforting, because the opposite was also true. Being abandoned to survive alone in the village was perilous at best and equally uncertain. Since the first groups departed in early summer, it had been painful to watch the once thriving and orderly community of well-maintained homes become slowly reduced to empty shells.

Through the summer, nature still thrived, as pathways and gardens became overgrown, inevitably showing the neglect of indifference. It was the fall 1946, and the fields were mostly barren, only some having been stripped clean in the final days of harvest. There was no point preparing them for another season.

The agreed upon day of departure found the Szymanski family wagon fully packed, hitched to their still reliable delivery horse. They were joined by seven families having also decided relocation was the best option. Looking forward to the once promising future everyone anticipated after the war had become illusive, and was temporarily blurred. Their faith in God and each other, sustained them. Despite their uncertain circumstances, still very much undefined, these families realized there was now at least hope, where very little had existed not long before.

It was mid-morning when the cool fresh breezes wafted peacefully through the hollow and sleepy remains of Wiory. No longer would the gentle winds carry the familiar scent of cooking cabbage and fragrant roasts of succulent pork, to be lifted and quickly diffused like fond but distant recollections of vastly different times.

The entourage lingered, standing together in prayer, and looked back upon the familiar shoreline of the Warta River for the very last time. Nervous, fretful tears of deep sorrow streaked their faces until, like their memories, they were wiped away. Their long journey forward was about to begin.

The small procession of thirty-one men, women and children proceeded at a comfortable pace, having placed the elders among them into the few seats the wagons could provide. Marianna drove the lead wagon, and the other folks fell in behind.

The first few miles of terrain were fondly familiar to the travelers and inevitably evoked lingering emotions of all but forgotten childhoods long passed. In place of free-flowing conversations, there were only stifled sniffles and wiping of tears, between occasional rounds of sobbing. It was an anxious and unhappy time, but as more of it passed, emotions were finally brought under control. It was a breakthrough of sorts, each head of the family knowing the toughest step of a long journey is always the first.

It was a clear day weather wise and there wasn't much to distract them. Jan, Josef, and Julia were joined by two of the neighbors, Alexsander and Karl. Together the group informally represented everyone's best interests.

"As we had hoped, we weren't too late getting started today," Jan opened things, "and the weather is in our favor. If we can make it to Morzyslaw before nightfall, we know a few places just inside the village where we can set up camp. Josef and I were there a week ago and there's a couple of empty houses, so maybe we can spend the first night inside. Just like us, the people left most of the furniture behind. Who knows, some of us might even sleep in a bed tonight."

In support of Jan's comment, Alexsander offered, "By the time we arrive, most of us won't even care where we sleep, we'll all be easy about it. Couple of us will have to take shifts through the night though, just to keep us all safe. There's bound to be a prowler or two... always are."

"Let's set a good pace and make sure everyone keeps up. Better we get there with some extra time to spare," Karl was quick to offer. "We gotta get on our way earlier tomorrow."

"Yes, I agree," Jan stated. "The good weather should hold for a few days, but we'll just have to adjust to what nature gives us. I'm glad we got out of Wiory when we did. We're gonna need our tents before this journey is over. Another few weeks would've been too late for us all."

There was less than an hour of daylight remaining when they came upon the beaten and weather worn sign for Morzyslaw. There was nothing here that hadn't already been stepped on, trampled, or taken by vagrants for something to burn. How this old wooden post had survived was an oddity. "Less than a kilometer more. We cut our timing pretty close."

Jan was right about the abandoned village. Most of the houses had already been vacated, several of them vandalized, even some front doors had been left askew. Julia, always so pragmatic lamented, "It amazes me these houses were just torn apart so senselessly. What I fail to understand is why desperate people who can't make the journey don't just live there and take care of the place? Especially with winter coming in the next few weeks, where else do they have to go offering a better chance of survival?"

"They're probably doing the same thing to our place," Jan added. "Just imagining it, makes me mad as hell. I don't even want to think about it."

Within the hour, two relatively intact houses were selected for the women and children, and some of the elderly as well. The men slept outside, close to a bonfire they built to cook some potatoes and beans. Karl and Josef agreed to take the first watch, Jan and Alex would take over shortly after midnight. In no time, everyone except those standing guard were already sound asleep. It had been a tiring day, but a productive one.

Neither Karl nor Alex knew much about security patrol, but they circled the small perimeter of the camp several times, idly chatting together. Alex was correct about being exhausted as he struggled to stay awake. "I feel good about Jan and Josef taking charge of things. I wouldn't know how to do it, that's for sure."

"They probably don't know either, but they'll learn as they go, and so will we by backing them up. Let's just do our best to follow their decisions. It's because of them we have a good chance of making it outta here."

By morning, the men had reheated the large pot of beans and Karl's wife stoked a stove with some remaining kindling still piled beside the back door. The smell of warm biscuits had stirred everyone's juices earlier than usual. The sun had barely risen, but the growling stomachs took precedence over the need for more sleep. Beans and fresh, hot biscuits; a good way to begin the day!

"Let's break camp as soon as we can. The gusty winds are starting to pick up a little this morning, bringing more humidity with it." Jan predicted. "Make sure the loads are still secure."

It wasn't long before the caravan reassembled, in much the same order as the prior day. There were a few expected grunts and groans from tired backs and weary legs, but there was no grumbling among them. No one had the time or patience for idle complaints, and certainly no willingness to listen.

The goal was to reach the small hamlet of Lichen Stary, situated another ten kilometers north. Jan advised the leaders about what lay ahead. "I understand it's right on the edge of a small lake, so we can top off our barrels while we're there. The map shows it's going to be a long stretch before we get to the next fresh water source, so let's make sure we take advantage to be fully prepared."

The day was mostly uneventful, and quiet conversation provided a temporary but pleasant distraction. By midday, the brisk winds had pushed the grey cloud cover farther south, now revealing a mixture of silver streaks and intermittent sunshine. It gradually crept through the breaking clouds to reveal the distant open fields. For whatever reason, they had not been farmed in recent years. Instead, they were resting peacefully, cloaked in a carpet of wild grasses now reflecting a golden-brown hue to mark another season's end.

Sporadic forests of mostly deciduous trees would soon expose their stripped frames, standing in stark contrast to the occasional clusters of deep green coniferous trees scattered among them. "I've never travelled anywhere near these places, Jan. The forests and rolling hills remind me of Pobereze when I was a young child," Julia observed.

"Do you miss those times, Julia? Since then, you've travelled much farther than me and my brothers ever did. We spent our entire lives with our ma 'n' pa in Wiory. Other than a few square miles from the farm, I haven't been anywhere else until now. This is all new to me too."

"I've tried so long to block out those days after what happened to my family; it's as if it never really happened, like a fading nightmare. I've tried hard to suppress it, but most of my happy memories have faded too. I'm not sure if that's a good thing or a bad one anymore." Jan remained quiet and continued to listen carefully when Julia opened to him about her personal past. She didn't do it often, but when she did, he was always attentive.

"Only time will tell what's ahead for us but I'm eager to start making some good memories together, wherever we eventually go. I'm sure about one thing though." Julia reached for his hand and squeezed it tightly to her chest. She turned to face him and said, "Whatever lies ahead, the war is finally over, and I want to spend the rest of my life with you by my side. I love you very much, Janic."

Even now, Jan's beaming smile always comforted her. He drew her hand to his face and kissed it tenderly. Both were so content together, there was no need to say more. They continued on for several hours, mostly in silence, when Josef suddenly exclaimed, "I smell smoke up ahead! I wondered when we might find other signs of life!"

They followed the gradually bending road, sneaking brief glimpses of the lake that lie ahead. The dirt road followed the shoreline and as they rounded the curve of the bay, the setting sun reflected shards of glistening orange and yellow light, dancing in and out of the trees surrounding it. The route led directly to a startled group of people gathered around a bonfire; no doubt the source of the smoke Josef first detected.

Still at a short distance, Jan waved his hand and shouted a friendly greeting. "*Dzien dobry!*" He couldn't discern if they were friend or foe. Neither could they tell anything about Jan and friends, for that matter. The gesture was received as intended when two of the men raised their arms to return the wave. Inquisitively, they began to approach, each holding a rifle hanging reassuringly from their right hand.

"We're heading north from Wiory," Jan offered as he turned and pointed south. "...You?"

"We left Orzorko, probably about the same time you did." He shuffled his rifle to the other hand and extended his right hand to Jan and Josef. "I'm David, and this is my son, Sal. Where are you headed?" Josef introduced himself and answered the question himself, to not be left out of the conversation. "North to Torun. There's an Allied forces camp there... for refugees. Do you know about it?"

"Same place we're going. Don't know much about it, but I have friends who went there a couple a months ago. Said it all checked out, and one came all the way back just to tell us. We didn't know what to think about it until he returned. His news was encouraging and convinced us to make a run to Torun before the colder weather sets in."

"That must be a good friend. It's a damned long way," Jan stated.

"He's a damned good friend, I'll tell you that," David replied. The men all chuckled. The ice was broken between them, and everyone was visibly more relaxed.

"We just arrived about two hours ago. You people must be exhausted; we sure were! Come. Bring your friends. We could use some friendly company."

The first impression of Lichen Stary was quiet and quaint, nestled very naturally around the southwestern corner of the lake. It was idyllic and peaceful to the naked eye but nonetheless, it too had died a lonely death by attrition. There was nothing of value here except the purity of it, something unspoiled, of no practical use for transient passers-by. It appeared mostly untouched by the war.

There evidently wasn't much commerce here, the original community was probably too small to support it. A few fishing boats had been hauled out of the lake and were turned over on the beach resting between two cabins. Other than the peaceful air about it, the village was unremarkable, offering just a short run of small cottages overlooking the tiny bay of the lake.

David and Sal led a group of twelve who, like Jan and Josef were a mixture of men, women, and children, the oldest one being David's son. He looked to be about seventeen or eighteen years old. "There's still a few more cabins we aren't using, so help yourselves. There's no one living in any of them anymore... and the rents are cheap," he joked.

Jan responded with his own dry humor, "That's good. It's about all we can afford!"

When everyone was settled in for the night after enjoying a good meal, the men quickly saw the wisdom of collaborating with each other. There was strength in numbers, so long as everyone could keep up with those in the lead. "Our plan is to get to Skulsk in maybe six or seven days, depending on how the weather holds up," Jan said. The others agreed. "Let's split the night patrols and we'll talk again at first light."

The next day began uneventfully and quickly established the morning routines in preparation for the day's journey. The group maintained a good pace covering rural farm areas prevalent in the Greater Poland Voivodeship. While they had to maintain vigilance against the unknown, there was nothing of a challenging nature interfering with the flow of conversation among the leaders.

It was as good a time as any to learn more about each other. Their shared circumstances provided common ground between them, and their developing friendship was becoming rapidly apparent.

Eight or nine hours later, most of the scattered farmhouses they passed were long since abandoned, so again, accommodation was found easily. Jan addressed the matter of selecting a few of the houses. "These places will work well for us overnight. Some of you check this one and see how many of us can sleep there. We'll walk ahead to find another. I can see a couple further up the road. It's no time to be fussy but try and use one with a decent fireplace. No telling how long until we can find such luxuries, right?"

David added, "Make sure someone stands guard through the night. Prowlers on two legs could be as bad as those with four, if you get me. One thing they'll have in common is hunger, so stay alert."

A couple of families broke off from the main group consisting of about ten people. David rejoined the main caravan and turned back to those approaching the first farmhouse. "We leave at first light. You join us at dawn by the clearing up ahead. We'll be ready for you so don't keep us waiting. Understand?"

*****

Overnight, the temperature had dropped some. This was typical in late October. The gusting winds, however, were an ominous warning something more was on its way. For the time being, the light rain was barely an inconvenience, greeting everyone with a cold and soggy beginning to a new day. The warmth and inspiration of yesterday's sunshine was now replaced by a somber cast of grey gloominess promising to make the journey increasingly arduous.

The steady drizzle soon became unpleasant, but they pressed on. By mid-afternoon, the rain began to pick up in earnest and within the next hour, the heavier rainfall commenced with a fury. Fighting against the wind was difficult enough, but the driving rain stung their faces, continually and painfully.

Jokingly, David shouted to Josef, purposely loud enough so Jan and Julia could still hear him, "I thought your brother said we have a dry stretch ahead of us. I think he said we should bring lots of water." He laughingly held his hand out to feel the rain. "Is this enough for him?"

As they peeked out from under their hoods with rain dripping from their nose and chins, Jan's smile was infectious, and they all enjoyed a good laugh at his expense. It was moments like these forming the basis of a potentially lasting friendship between them.

The service roads between the cities were only paved part of the way, and what was paved had been broken apart by military trucks and heavy artillery the Germans had been forced to reposition during the later stages of the war. It had left its toll on the roads never built to withstand the weight, leaving several long stretches with nothing more than a combination of gravel and hardened clay.

These surfaces were fine in dry or freezing weather but soon became clogged with mud during the several hours of heavy downpour. Maneuvering the heavy-laden wagons was almost impossible and the strength of the horses became sapped to the point of abuse, something none of the caravan members would ever allow.

Jan hollered over the din of the wind and rain, "Enough of this bullshit, men. This is taking too much energy for too little in return. Until this weather system clears, we have to break out the tents to give our families some shelter."

It was unanimously agreed they would abandon the journey for the time being. No one argued otherwise. Perhaps they were all thinking the same thing but were uncertain whether to speak up, considering many of the group were still quite timid. It only took minutes to see no one was objecting.

There were several tents stored in the wagons for just such an occasion. Everyone was grateful for Jan and David's foresight. Putting them up in these conditions, however, was a challenging and frustrating experience. Soldiers were accustomed to the task, but civilian farmers were not.

The relentless rain and deep, sloppy mud seemed as though the elements were working in tandem to eventually consume them. "Everywhere I look, the ground is too soft and muddy to put up tents," shouted Josef. "The ground off the road is too waterlogged. We'll be swamped before we begin."

Julia had lived in the wild for months on end when she left Pobereze. It was time to offer her ingenuity and natural adaptiveness. She had been through much worse times than these, often struggling against the elements when she was alone as a young teenager.

The loud rushing of the wind and rain still made it difficult to be heard. Julia shouted above the noise howling through the trees. "We must move farther into the heavier forest, where the trees are much taller. Leave the wagons if we must. We can get them after the storm passes. Look for groves of mature pine trees with enough clearance at the bases to set up tents closely below them."

"Why would we do that for Christ's sake? What difference does it make? Everywhere we look is soaking wet," Sal hollered back, pointing into the wooded surroundings. "It'll be just as bad in there as it is close to the road, won't it? Why waste the time and effort?"

"The heavy accumulation of pine needles around the base of the trees won't be dry but will be deep enough to allow most of the rainwater to drain through. This way the mud won't be an issue for us so we can set the tents on the pine needle base on top of the mud below. Under these conditions, this *will* work. It's the best we can do in this weather. Trust me! The water won't accumulate and will simply drain away from the base of the tents. We'll be fine, so start looking!"

Grudgingly, some of the men did as Julia directed. Even in a dense forest, Julia knew fallen pine needles were highly acidic, keeping the base of the trees clear of crowding from deciduous trees and undergrowth. Within about ten minutes, the forest offered a couple of open areas suiting their needs nicely.

The tents were quickly unpacked and spread out, and the clearance below the bottom branches was sufficient to fully extend the tent poles. It was a simple task to reinforce the poles and to stake the outer perimeter of the tents after they were in place. The ground was holding firm, just as Julia said it would.

"Good job, Julia. Where in the world do you learn these things? I don't know if we could have figured out what to do without you today. I'm so proud of you, Julia," Jan praised. "David feels the same and apologized for Sal's first reaction. He was a bit embarrassed about Sal's attitude."

Julia never dwelled on such things. "What other people may think is none of my business. I wasn't offended by him." As they continued working on the stakes, she thought for a moment and said, "Remember last winter when I was reading by the fire every day? Some of the books Father Francis gave me were adventure stories; I found them very educational too." She kept tightening the guy wires as she spoke.

"I always try to find ways to use what I learn in a practical way. It's not always possible to do, but as I think more about it, it's become one of the greatest pleasures of my life, when it works." Once again, Julia's intelligence and practical experience shone through, often at the strangest of times.

Several men went back to the wagons to get the wives and children who had remained huddled together in the rain. Everyone grabbed whatever they might need for the long hours ahead. Soaking wet and shivering, many filed into the musty tents and drew the heavy tarps across the open doors. Now all they could do was wait out the storm and pray they didn't lose anyone to exposure.

One haggard young man named Richard was taking care of his parents. His mother was severely arthritic. She had been heavy set through most of her life, but by this time the starvation and stresses of the war had reduced her to less than eighty pounds. Her frame was hunched over, making walking almost impossible for her.

She sat in a small two-wheeled wagon Richard had pulled since joining the caravan before the rains came almost a week ago. It was backbreaking for him, but he never once complained, walking every day encouraging his father by his side, every painful step of the way.

Jan knew there were not enough tents for everyone. Richard's family were among them. Jan was visibly moved by his helplessness, having left them hunched underneath their small wooden wagon. They were only covered by an already soaked woolen blanket. When the Szymanski family were entering their own tent, Jan just stood resolutely against the falling rain.

Having left Richard's family under their wagon as the rain fell upon them, Jan's compassion overcame him when his apparent indifference of the moment began to drain from him, the rain trickling from his nose and chin, seemingly cleansing his spirit.

Julia walked back outside the tent and approached closely toward him, taking his hand to urge him to get inside. He just stood there, solemnly looking at Richard trying to find somewhere better for his parents than under the wagon.

"I know what you're thinking, Jan." She paused… "Maybe we can take his parents inside with us. We'll find enough room somehow. If you and Josef take alternate shifts on security, it will leave room for his mother. It will be tight but his father…" Julia hesitated again only briefly, "I don't know… we can manage somehow."

"Are you sure, Julia?" Jan wiped his hand across his weathered face.

"If we don't help them, they could be dead by morning," Julia replied.

*****

It was another day before the persistence of the rain finally relented, Mother Nature appearing to realize these travelers had proven the strength of their resolve. By so doing, they had earned her respect. The rain had finally stopped, and the winds began to settle.

Several hours later, people were beginning to stir from inside the tents and their groaning stomachs angrily growled for something hot that didn't come in a can. After huddling closely hour after hour in such close quarters, shared body heat appeared to have sustained everyone to varying degrees. People began peering outside and one by one, they disentangled themselves to exit their cramped quarters, eager to stand upright to stretch.

As if on cue, the heavy flaps of the tents were thrown open, allowing refreshing waves of colder air to quickly engulf the interior of the smelly confines of the tents. The fresh air quickly cleansed the stale stench within. It was an invigorating feeling, to be sure.

A few minutes later, Sal hastily left the group heading toward the wagons still perched on the perilous edge of the rutted roadside. After a bit of rummaging, he retrieved a can of kerosine and some dry kindling he had carefully set aside and proudly ambled back to the camp site.

"Here… we're gonna need this to get a fire started. We're all overdue for some warmth so we don't catch our death of colds." David and his son were leaving to find some larger pieces of fallen tree limbs, reassuring the others as they departed, "It'll be soaked but should still catch after the kindling ignites." Some others joined them in the task as well.

Before he joined his father, however, Sal approached Julia, who was helping Jan readjust the tension on the guy wires. "Morning, Julia... Jan." Sheepishly but genuinely he offered, "Sorry for being such an asshole yesterday. I would never have thought of your idea. You did well Julia, and we're all grateful you're here with us."

"Thanks, Sal. Just glad I could help." Julia responded. Jan winked at her as Sal joined the others stating, "Well, look at that, would ya'!"

The strong winds had lost some of their power but, within hours, they were enough to dry up much of the excess surface water, sufficiently to resume the journey. Time was lost, but lives were spared from a potentially cold and wet grave. Without shelter the harsh elements would likely have taken some of them. Little did they know it would prove to be only a brief reprieve.

*****

Over the next two days, they picked up their pace to make up for some lost time. Jan, Julia, and Josef relied on each other to a great extent, but David and his son's input were invaluable too. They often strategized together while keeping their steady pace.

"Setting up the tents every night and repacking them again every morning has taken much more time than I had expected," Jan confided to David. "For the stragglers who joined us, like Richard and his parents, most of them don't even have tents. They just aren't well enough prepared."

David added, "Those who don't have shelter for themselves at night aren't going to make it, in my opinion. The only saving grace is the American troops will be coming to round up anyone left behind, but no one seems to know when it will happen."

"I'm told some have already spoken among themselves about it," Josef said regrettably. "The young ones will have a chance, but the older ones... it's just a matter of time before they drop out. It's going to be tough on them, but it won't be easy on the families leaving them behind either."

Jan added, "In this God forsaken mess, I have no idea how the families will find one another again. Other than first names, *we* don't even know who these people are."

"Each family has to make their own choices. The hard part will be living with their decisions," Julia continued. "Sometimes I think the main reason I survived, was because I was alone. I wouldn't have made it if I had to compromise my decisions worrying about other people..." Julia paused and thought about what she was about to say, before resuming.

"This may sound bad, but we cannot afford to get close to these people, and their fragile situations. It will affect our objectivity. It's survival of the fittest, plain and simple."

"I agree with you, Julia," David said. "Each of us has to pull our own weight. We all agreed others could join our caravan, but we made it clear in the beginning we are not here to support them, or to feed and shelter them. We are simply here to lead them. I think we should stand by what we told them, as difficult as it may be."

"So, we all agree then," Jan verified his position. "As of tomorrow, we'll start our day earlier, an hour before sunup. We can take down the tents in the dark and leave camp by daybreak. It will give us an extra hour to travel each day. Over just one week, it will save us a full day of travel. That could make a big difference to us, especially on the last half of our journey. What do you think?"

In support, David suggested, "Let's pass the word all the way down the line, but we should do it personally. There's bound to be disappointment, maybe even anger against us. It's important we watch each other's backs... This won't be an easy task, I'm afraid."

It was an anguishing two hours that followed. Sixty-seven people had sixty-seven reasons they should not be left behind. Richard and his father took the news the hardest, knowing full well, culling the caravan would most certainly include them. Richard's parents were already at the breaking point, not even having the strength to speak anymore. They were near the end, but Richard knew he could never leave them alone.

Later the same night, it was about an hour after everyone but the guard patrol had fallen into a deep sleep, exhausted by the events of the day, and more so by the tough decisions having to be made. In all, seven would be left behind, including Richard's family. He would stay behind too, having promised to never leave their side.

A short time later, out of nowhere, two sudden gun shots pierced the still of night, shattering the restful peace and quiet of anyone within earshot. Seconds later, *BANG!* Another loud blast followed. The various heads of the families raced from their tents, searching for some indication of what had happened, many of them clutching their rifles. The guards came running to the scene as well. "What the hell was that?" Jan hollered to them. "Are you alright Francis? Was anyone shot? Where's Ivan?"

Francis shouted and pointed to the rear of the caravan. "Sounded like it was down farther, close to the rear. I was near the front when I heard it. Oh no! I hope Ivan's OK!"

Jan and the others broke into a full run. Ivan's silence had everyone expecting the worst for him. Their hearts pounded as one. This was the first sign of violence since their departure less than two weeks ago.

As they approached the rear, Francis shouted, "There he is! I can see him now! Thank God he's alright!"

Ivan just stood eerily, holding his rifle down by his side. He appeared to be in shock. Speechless, he raised his left hand and pointed further into the dark. The group walked hesitatingly forward to where he was pointing. The torches had illuminated a short distance ahead of them when Jan saw it first.

"Everyone, please stay back. You don't want to see this," Jan exclaimed.

Richard's wagon was parked adjacent to a small grove of trees. Jan's heart raced as he drew nearer, only now realizing what must have happened. Richard's body was laying in front of the wagon, the back of his head blown off. Under the wagon, his parents were lying motionless.

It was evident Richard had killed his parents to finally grant them peace and end the agony their lives had become. He must have reloaded his rifle and turned it upon himself, fulfilling his promise to never leave them. Jan dropped to the ground, kneeling beside Richard's lifeless body, and wept.

27
IT'S A MIRACLE THEY
LASTED SO LONG

AFTER BURYING THE FAMILY NEAR THE SPOT WHERE THEY died, conversations were strained and hushed in quiet whispers, out of respect and sorrow for what had occurred. Although these desperate situations were prevalent during these times, this would mark the first time this group lost a member of their band of brothers.

The farther north they travelled toward Skulsk, the more attention they attracted. Day by day, word of mouth carried news in advance of the caravan's progress and the numbers continued to multiply. Some simply joined ranks from behind, gradually adding to their significance as similar families assumed their place in the journey north. There would be time for introductions at day's end, or so it was assumed. Like a giant magnet gathering polarized dust, the caravan attracted the living carnage into its midst.

Passing several villages and small towns, the extent of damage became visibly worse than in the south, resulting in greater numbers of desperate refugees. They were mostly simple folk, typically general laborers, and many skilled tradesmen. Several more were former businesspeople, shop keepers, teachers, and even doctors and the occasional lawyer. Everyone brought skills of potential value, no doubt becoming useful whenever they reached their eventual destination.

At the end of each day, another camp was set up for the night. Without fail, members of the rear caravan summoned Jan and the other leaders to meet with those who had approached them about where they were heading and if they could follow along.

It was the only time of day Jan, and a few others, customarily walked the length of their caravan, which by this point could no longer be referred to as small. Every inspection involved checking the integrity of the wagons, now numbering eleven, and making certain the horses were well attended by the owners.

Every day without fail, the group grew and now included dozens more, left homeless and not understanding what options were available to them. The leaders would reliably walk the line all the way to the back at the end of day; those already at the rear would introduce the new people to Jan, Julia, Josef, and David.

When the leaders gradually came into view toting their lanterns, one of the people in the rear eagerly exclaimed, "Ahh, that must be them. Here they come now!"

Jan turned to David exclaiming, "My God, David. I can't see many of them in the dark, but I can tell this is another beaten group."

As they approached, idle conversations among the gathering quickly subsided. Jan raised his lantern to better assess the situation, squinting into the blackness surrounding them. It was a rag tag group of beaten souls for certain, many with the look of abject hopelessness. Jan tried to be upbeat as he asked, "Who do we have here, Jorge?"

Introductions of the most relevant ones were made by first names only, simply because surnames were too much to remember. This day attracted several families and two single sisters, finding themselves in the same predicament.

"Hello, my name is Jan; this is Julia, David, and my brother Josef. We are in charge here at the moment. I see there are two wagons among you. Are your horses sturdy enough for travel?" They all nodded they were.

"Good! Your priority is to keep them well fed. Your very lives may depend on them.

"We're heading north to Torun to join the Americans. They have food and transport to take us somewhere west. We estimate it will be at least another two weeks to get there… if we're lucky. You are welcome to follow us, but you must keep up. We can't afford to lose time to those who can't. I'm sorry, but that's just the way it is."

"Yes… yes, we can keep up, I'm sure of it," assured one of the spokespeople for the new group. The others all nodded affirmatively. Right now, Jan would accept them at their word although they didn't say much. Time would bear out the truth.

"We keep moving every day unless the weather becomes our enemy. Just so you understand, we don't take votes on these things, but we all agree to do whatever the leaders decide if you continue to stay with us. We try hard to do what's good for everyone. You may not agree, but it's the best we can offer. You take care of your own food and shelter, of course. We have barely enough for ourselves." Jan paused as he always did since the tragic incident several days before.

"If you cannot keep up with us, we have no choice than to leave you behind. The journey is more difficult than you probably imagine. It is important you understand this. If you are disabled or in bad health, you should consider stepping aside to return to where you came from. I am truly sorry having to be so blunt with you.

"If you cause trouble among us, we will not hesitate to leave you where you stand. Better you know this before we begin. We must be in Torun at the refugee camp as soon as possible. As I said, we expect to be there within the next two to three weeks. Any questions?"

Jan casually surveyed the small gathering, who simply stared back at him without any response. Either this was a pack of deaf mutes, or they were too tired and confused to say much.

"OK then. If you think of one, you will find us at the front of the line. Everyone understand?" There were no objections, just nodding heads. It didn't mean they all agreed. More likely, no one was willing to openly disagree.

"We repack our wagons about an hour before sunup. The earlier we get underway, the more bad weather we avoid, so I suggest you get some rest, you're going to need it."

Sarcastically, Jan concluded by saying, "Nice talking to you."

David and Sal returned from inspecting the horses and wagons by this time and turned away to rejoin Jan, Julia, and Josef setting up the tents again. Since leaving Lichen Stary almost a week ago, there weren't any homes or buildings to accommodate anyone.

"What's our head count tonight, Sal?" Jan asked. "I count seventy-five, and twelve wagons," he replied.

"Shit! I expected a few stragglers to join us along the way, but I didn't expect this many," Jan cautioned. "Hope this doesn't get out of hand on us."

David interjected, "Don't worry Jan, it already is. They probably think we know what we're doing. I sure as hell don't... do you?"

Jan looked back with a smile and shook his head from side to side. The two of them began to chuckle. "I think the sooner we accept it, the better."

Julia spoke up and stated, "You did well, Janic, to lay down some ground rules like you did. Better to be firm with any newcomers. There are bound to be more. Let's see how many we have when we move on from Skulsk before we reassess the situation."

"God only knows, Julia, and He's not tellin'. But you're right, we'll probably know more tomorrow."

*****

Since morning's first light, the air had become progressively colder and even more unwelcoming. It was difficult to ignore but they pressed forward. By mid-afternoon, other matters pre-occupied their thoughts.

They were only a short distance from the city and were eager to find a few places to clean up and find some relief from the nipping cold, which had become increasingly difficult to tolerate; anywhere to get away from the damned chilling wind. Undaunted, the tired and shivering group proved their merit once again when they achieved their goal by ascending a small crest of a hill overlooking the city of Skulsk.

As if on cue, the leaders sighed a collective gasp, some immediately being reduced to tears. Many raised their hands to cover their mouths to hide their immediate shock. Several turned away to look skyward when they identified the silhouettes of five people ominously hanging from two withered tree limbs; two of the victims were children.

It was a natural reaction to their emotional response, driven no doubt, by a mixture of compassion for those slaughtered in this place, and the deep-seated disappointment they all felt knowing there was nothing here but more death and destruction.

"Is there no end to this chaos? It's nothing but rubble." Josef shook his head in dismay. The decimation could be seen from their vantage point because there weren't any buildings left standing to obstruct the view. The roads inside the city were unidentifiable, essentially impassable because of the widespread debris. "Look! Over there, down to your left. My God, there are still people living there!"

"Get the two doctors to come down with us if they want. I'll respect their decision either way. These people need more help than we can possibly give. I think this is one of those times we can only turn our backs and keep walking," Jan quietly instructed.

"There's no point for anyone else to enter the city with us. Let's keep the others below this rise as far away as possible. We'll stay on the outskirts."

Suddenly, a slight shift of wind changed direction unexpectedly. Jan reflexively raised his arm to cover his mouth and nose. "My God! I can smell the reek of death from here!"

Supporting evidence of the cancer of profound abuse was everywhere. The ruthless brutality preceding the weary travelers, once again intruded upon their familiar world with the sickening smell, that was barely perceptible when they arrived at the crest of the hill. The wind shift sucked the oxygen from the air; so repulsive now, it was difficult to breathe. Josef began to gag, vomiting uncontrollably at his feet.

He wiped his face with a small rag from his pocket, still crouched over, leaning on his knees. "Augh... Sorry you guys. Never smelled anything like that before... Don't want to either."

David wisely acknowledged Jan's instructions adding, "Keep your faces covered at all times. None of us can afford to get sick from the stench. The bloody winds can't even blow it away yet."

Julia was already familiar with the panorama of bloodied mayhem from her own experience in Pultusk and Ciechanow earlier in the war, however, it was a gut-wrenching shock to Jan and his family. It was their first time to personally witness the abject travesty of the German assault on their beloved country. Although they never saw the historic grandeur of what once was, the scourge and terror Poland had suffered was beyond their worst expectations.

In what had once been a quiet and tolerant city, the Jews living here represented the majority of the Skulsk population. Their forced removal by the Germans during the early days of the occupation had taken the beating heart of Skulsk with them.

Their extermination from the early days of the war left behind the permanent scars of painful and incomprehensible acts of inhumanity. A once thriving and unobtrusive village had its very traditional soul wiped from the earth. Jan knew Julia's story resonated with what had happened in Skulsk. He recognized his family had nothing to complain about, compared to what had occurred here.

When Jan and a few others returned from the rubble near the edge of the city, still covered in scattered skeletal remains among the ruins, his comments were concise and deliberate.

"There's nothing we can do for any of them. When the freezing weather sets in, they will all be done. It's a miracle they've lasted so long. Death is their only salvation, I'm afraid to say."

The city was located on the mouth of the Notec River, where it divided to the west and continued winding its way north, all the way to Torun. Sooner or later the river had to be crossed. To be able to do so at Skulsk would save an extra week of difficult travel.

David's friend, who scouted the area for him, advised that when the Allies took control of the area, they had repaired the main bridge sufficiently to allow refugees from the south to gain access to the Torun facility. Jan assumed those roads had been cleared of debris to gain access. He was correct. For miles upriver, Skulsk was the only bridge in descent repair.

The north bank on the far side of the river proved to be a suitable resting point as day's light was fading fast, and just as quickly the temperature continued to drop. Everyone agreed it was time to light some fires, eat what they could, and rest till morning's first light.

*****

HOTEL ADLON, RUSSIAN OCCUPIED BERLIN

The late October air was always so refreshing after the final humid days of September passed, but this year it was exceptionally colder than most autumn days. Linette and General Semenov had by this time settled into the Adlon Hotel, the transition being an expeditious one both found to be most satisfying.

By this time, the local streets in this exclusive area had been cleared and a new semblance of order and safety was reassuring to the quaint neighborhood, partially walled by the Brandenburg Gate. It provided an auspicious backdrop to this mostly rejuvenated sector of Berlin.

The security within this relatively small zone of the city, in addition to the continued reassurance provided by General Semenov for Linette's personal safety, were cornerstones for her to build upon. It was the perfect haven upon which no German would ever intrude. Hence, Nikolai had unknowingly insulated her from anyone seeking to find her, including Abwehr.

"Miss Linette, I understand you have accepted the general's invitation to attend the dinner party this weekend. He has asked me to help you find something appropriate to wear for the occasion," Elana offered supportively. "He thinks so highly of you and is eager to have you at his side for the event. I'm so pleased you agreed to join him."

"Yes, our friendship has developed nicely. I was surprised by his offer, but he has asked nothing of me until now. I feel safe here and decided his offer to accompany him is the least I can do for all he has done for me," Linette candidly explained, even though no explanation was needed.

"I know these events are very infrequent but I'm certain you will make him proud to have you on his arm for this one, Miss Linette."

Within a few days, the ladies made the most of a limited selection of suitable evening wear, not something easily found so soon after the allied occupation. When Nikolai returned home, he was eager to see what they had decided upon.

"I am not accustomed to attending events such as this, however I served directly under Field Marshal Rokossovsky when Berlin fell. I was flattered by his gesture to invite me and a guest. I dared not decline. I thought this would be a fine time to show you off, so to speak, and your Russian is impeccable, Linette. You are a perfect fit for the occasion," Nicholai stated enthusiastically.

"May I see the dress you selected? I trust you are happy with it. Several were brought in for the lady friends of the officers. I rather suspect everyone will try to impress the others," he explained.

"Let me fetch it for you Miss Linette, if I may," Elana offered.

"Yes, please do so, Elana."

As Elana left the room momentarily, Nikolai thoughtfully acknowledged, "Thank you for doing this, Linette. It has been years since I could even dream of such a thing. My dear wife was so very lovely and enjoyed attending these events from time to time before the war. It will bring back memories of happier times for me... perhaps for you as well."

"I'm certain it will, Nikolai. It was kind of you to think of me. I'm very much looking forward to it," Linette replied.

By this time Elana had re-entered the living room and proudly carried the dress with both arms extended. The pleats of the beautiful piece hung softly in precise formation, the light reflecting the glorious sheen of midnight blue satin.

"Why, this is quite stunning ladies. You have done well!" Nikolai praised.

"We tried to find something quite refined in an understated way, but also elegant in its simple design. I do hope you approve," Linette commented inquisitively. "And we found appropriate shoes to complement the outfit. I regret I had nothing to contribute myself," she lamented.

"Nonsense, Linette. What you are contributing is your lovely self. You are what will bring its beauty to life. It's not about the dress as much as it is about the woman wearing it, don't you agree?"

*****

About mid-afternoon the following day, Linette took a hot bath to relax herself and as she languished in the soapy warm water, she reflected upon her distant memories of family events with Jacob and her father. It had been several years since such an opportunity had presented itself again. She wanted to savor the exciting moment.

Linette was now in her mid-forties, and despite her age and the continual stress she had endured in recent years, she considered herself to continue to be an attractive woman. Her dress was distinctive and sure to enhance her slight but well-proportioned figure. Her intent was to do herself and Nikolai proud by using her best assets and womanly maturity to maximum advantage.

"Elana let's pull my hair tightly into a small bun, and in the absence of jewelry, we can leave two gentle curls hanging unobtrusively to my bare shoulders. If Nikolai wants to show me off, let's do our best to achieve the desired effect, shall we?"

Once Linette's hair met with her satisfaction, the dress was snuggly fitted to accentuate her slim and willowy body. The front of the dress rose to form a tasteful and elegantly designed collar, supported by a single strap tied at the base of her neck; a classic appearance leaving both shoulders and her bare back fully exposed. Without jewelry, the intent was to draw attention to her natural and still very beautiful face. Matching high-heeled shoes and a small clutch accentuated the outfit perfectly.

Linette remained in her room when Nikolai returned home to have a quick shower and ready himself for the reception, now just ninety minutes away. Once he was properly dressed in his full military regalia, he respectfully tapped on Linette's door. It was time for her to display her and Elana's achievements.

Drawing a deep breath, and without saying a word, Linette cautiously opened her door and stepped forward to perfectly announce herself. She was a vision of loveliness.

General Nikolai Semenov, the mighty Russian conqueror, could only stammer awkwardly, totally disarmed and clearly smitten at the sight of this beautiful woman in the doorway. Linette pirouetted gracefully, casting the luxurious pleats about his field of vision to display the seductive curves of her naked back. Demurely she teasingly offered, "Will this be satisfactory for your special evening, Officer?"

Still grappling for words, Nikolai stammered while he collected himself. "Miss Linette, I... I think that... oh my, you look so ravishing, Linette. You have indeed taken my breath away."

In response, a broad smile of satisfaction from Linette only served to make her even more profoundly seductive. Nikolai gathered his cap and offered his arm to proudly escort his beautiful companion to the waiting car outside the hotel.

It was only a short drive to the reception, and upon their arrival, to no one's surprise, Linette created quite a stir from the leering men, and no doubt from many envious women. It is amazing what effect a natural beauty can elicit when combined with impeccable good taste and the opportunity to confidently flaunt it.

Never being one to attract so much attention to herself, it was always Marta who stole the limelight. It was an experience to which Linette would naturally learn to adapt.

Inside the dining room, there were many attractive and mostly younger women in attendance that evening. Most of them were paid escorts, anxious to please and to impress the older officers accompanying them. Many of these women were German and Polish, speaking little to no Russian.

Over cocktails, and later at dinner, these women became overtly one dimensional. They were never meant to stimulate intelligent conversation. However, Linette distinguished herself very naturally as being a woman of numerous attributes: appropriate bearing, eloquence, humor, discretion, and well-placed flattery - qualities and sensuality the other women apparently lacked.

"Let me introduce you to my commanding officer, Field Marshal Konstantin Rokossovsky. Sir, I am pleased to present to you Miss Linette Etienne," Nikolai proudly stated.

Linette extended her hand. "A pleasure to meet you, Sir. General Semenov speaks very highly of you and your accomplishments. He is a great admirer of yours."

"Thank you for your kind words. The pleasure is all mine, Madame. I am so pleased you could attend this evening. Etienne... that's French is it not?" the Field Marshal enquired.

"Yes, it is. I was born and raised in Belgium," Linette responded.

"In Belgium? How in the world did you learn such impeccable Russian, dear lady?"

"My father travelled a great deal when I was a child. Often I would stay behind attending private schools studying languages. I had a natural affinity for it, something I had a flair for, I suppose. I taught Russian and French at the university here in Berlin before the war," Linette explained.

"How very divergent are the roads we all travelled to find ourselves together here," the Field Marshal stated thoughtfully.

By this time, one of the aides approached to excuse himself for interrupting. "Sir, Komandor Stanislov requests a moment of your time. I am told it is a matter requiring your attention."

"Tell him I will be right there."

Turning back to face Nikolai and Linette, the field marshal graciously excused himself stating, "Please enjoy yourself Miss Linette, General Semenov. Perhaps we can speak again another time, dear lady."

"I would welcome the opportunity. Perhaps we shall." It was incredibly obvious Linette had left a very positive first impression on the field marshal, which no doubt further enhanced his impression of Nikolai as well.

*****

It was after midnight when Nikolai and Linette returned to their suite. The alcohol and the newfound glamor of the evening were playing out in the typical relaxed and silly ways that were, more than not, subtly intended. Both had held hands and flirted with one another as the late hours of overindulgence continued to play out.

Latching the door behind him, Nikolai was determined to enjoy one last cocktail to put the finishing touches on a very satisfying evening. "Care to join me for one more, Linette?"

She gazed demurely at him and softly cooed, "If you continue to ply me with more alcohol, there's no telling what I might do. I urge us both to think wisely, Nikolai," Linette teasingly warned.

"I would never do such a thing for as fine a lady as you, my dear. Perhaps you are confusing me with someone else." Nikolai winked at her in his own playful way. He was evidently feeling light-hearted as well and blushed slightly as he did so.

"You have always been a perfect gentleman since coming into my life, Nikolai. But you leave me wondering something." Linette purred softly.

She walked slowly forward and stood closely before him, stopping just a few inches away. Fixing her gaze on him, she slowly raised her arms to wrap them around his neck, staring up temptingly into his own inviting gaze.

"In fact, you have been such a gentleman, I fear you may think badly of me if I..." She hesitated intentionally, as if questioning herself one final time.

"If you what, Linette? Please tell me what you are afraid to ask." He did not break his wanting look and waited patiently for her reply. He was determined not to make the first move to what he sensed was about to happen.

"... If I do this." With that, she reached behind her neck and pulled gently on the delicate string supporting her top. It harmlessly dropped away from her breasts. She looked longingly at Nikolai, saying what every man wants a beautiful woman to say to him. "Please make love to me."

*****

The following morning when Linette awakened, now alone in her bed, she found herself still groggy from fatigue, even more so because she had consumed too much alcohol, which was not her habit. As her mind cleared, she vividly remembered seducing Nikolai, something else she had not done to any man other than her dear Jacob.

It was not a new beginning she sought through her actions, as she briefly wrestled with scandalous thoughts of her behavior. No, she decided it was the beginning of the end, albeit a very satisfying one. She sat up on the bedside, her hair no longer in a tight bun, and ran her hands through her curls as she shook her head from side to side to loosen them more fully.

Grasping her housecoat, she opened her bedroom door and found Elana already busy in the kitchen. Linette shuffled her slippers softly across the floor to greet her.

"A very good morning, Elana. Are you well?" she stated unabashedly.

"I am, Miss Linette. I trust you enjoyed your evening with the general?" Elana enquired.

"Yes, very much so. Did you see him this morning? I was surprised I slept so very well." Linette looked at the wall clock and exclaimed, "My goodness, it's almost 11:00!"

"You must have needed the sleep, dear. I noticed the general left an envelope on his desk for you though. Did you see it?"

"No, I didn't. Just give me a moment to get it. Please be a dear and make us a pot of coffee this morning. I rather think I need more than one cup today." Linette proceeded to the parlor, tearing the envelope open to retrieve a brief handwritten message from Nikolai. Intrigued, she sat by the window while the coffee began to perk.

Dear Linette,

Thank you for such a lovely evening. I enjoyed your company immensely. The evening was much more than I had intended, but I am thankful for the wonderful time we shared together. I pray you do not have any regrets about sharing our intimacies. I sincerely apologize if it seems I took advantage of you, but it was certainly not my intention.

*Regrettably, I had to attend to business matters early
this morning, but I plan to be home late afternoon. I
think we should address what happened between us so
neither of us have any disillusions. I respect and admire
you Linette and will always continue to do so.*

*It would be my honor to share dinner with you to discuss
last evening. Enjoy your day.*

Respectfully,

Nikolai

When Linette read and reread the thoughtful message from
Nikolai, it only reinforced her respect and affection for his noble
character. He was not someone to take undue advantage of anyone,
nor was Linette inclined to do so either. Under very different circumstances, who knew what the future might have held for them?

Linette's resolve was growing, and even her deep affection for
Nikolai would not stand in her way. She felt similar conviction and
strength of resolve when she decided to escape from Abwehr. It had
been a turning point in her life she had to firmly address. So too was
this one.

As anticipated, Nikolai arrived just a few hours later. It wasn't a
matter either wanted to defer any longer than necessary. When he
entered the suite, Linette promptly rose to greet him and gave him a
peck on the cheek to break the potential awkwardness of the moment.

After the usual pleasantries during dinner, caringly provided by
Elana, Nikolai sat with Linette near the window. Thoughtfully, and
as instructed by Nikolai, Elana excused herself for the evening. There
was no need to linger longer than necessary, and she had no intent to
intrude any further on their privacy.

It was a peaceful view of the central plaza, now totally devoid of
any military presence. The scene comforted them as the city continued to embrace the restoration of civilian life. Nikolai deferred his
usual cocktail, as did Linette, neither wishing to muddy the pleasant
mood of this important discussion.

"Thank you for coming home early today, Nikolai, and for your
very considerate letter. You are, and always have been a consummate

gentleman. My memories of you could never be tarnished. You fulfilled a need in me that I am pleased to have shared with you and I want you to be assured of that," Linette carefully articulated.

She placed her hand on his, confiding, "I have no regrets."

"So, you are not disappointed with my actions? They have preoccupied my thoughts since I woke this morning. I am relieved you feel as you do, Linette, but something tells me you are about to say goodbye. Am I reading you correctly?" Nikolai took a few anxious sips of his coffee to calm his probable disappointment.

"Yes, you are correct, but I want you to understand I am leaving despite my deep fondness for you. Do you remember when I told you I must leave one day soon?" He silently nodded submissively, likened to a young boy being reprimanded by his mother.

"It is time to resume my journey to locate my family in America. I have recently read about the Americans relocating European refugees until safety and order can be restored. It has been a privilege to stay here with you, but the peacefulness and order within these walls is not representative of the country outside these confines. You understand that more than me."

Nikolai had concern written all over his face. His anguish was painfully evident. "But how will you get there? My understanding is the closest transition station is near Magdeburg. That's about 160 kilometers west of here. It's too far for a woman travelling alone, Linette. In good conscience I cannot expose you to the imminent danger you would be facing, my dear. There must be another way."

"That is my greatest concern, but one I must accept. I would have to go sooner or later when you are transferred elsewhere, a day which will surely come. At least leaving now is a decision of my own choosing," Linette explained.

Nikolai sat silently, looking blankly at a painting on the far wall for a quiet moment while he considered their dilemma. It was truly *their dilemma,* not solely Anna's. He wanted her to be assured of this point of fact.

"What if I drive you to Magdeburg myself? I can obtain diplomatic papers to allow me to accompany you. I know Field Marshal Rokosskovsky was quite taken with you. I'm confident my influence, together with his own, would be of significant assistance in helping to arrange the details. It's certainly worth a try."

"Do you think you could do that, Nikolai? My word, I never considered such a possibility. Thank you, Nikolai. Thank you!" Linette reached across to him and clasped her hands on his own.

"Let's not get ahead of ourselves just yet. This will not be a simple task, I assure you."

After some initial reluctance, the field marshal pulled some powerful strings and called in a few favors to arrange the necessary paperwork. Nikolai was correct about it not being a simple task, but with the appropriate papers and the strength of the request, the deed was quickly arranged. Linette possessed her own set of clean documents and drew no suspicion. There was no requirement for German scrutiny and if there ever was, her identity was iron clad. No nefarious complications about Linette's circumstances ever arose.

When the day of departure arrived less than a week later, the car was packed with what few things Linette had, and regrettably her strapless blue gown was not among them. It would remain in Nikolai's closet as a symbol of an impetuous love affair, ending as suddenly as it began. Three days later, outside the gates of the collection camp in Magdeburg, it was predictably a tearful goodbye to a friendship born among the ruins, but never to be forgotten.

*****

BANK OF THE NOTEC RIVER, JUST NORTH OF SKULSK

Leaving Skulsk the next morning, found everyone quiet and anxious to leave this place far behind them. When they arrived here, they had very little, but when they left, they did so with something of significant value - even more determination to keep going. With each passing day, it reinforced their belief the decision to leave Konin was the right one, no matter how grueling the journey.

They covered about six or seven kilometers north, nearing the end of another productive day. Along the route several small groups had appeared in the wooded areas adjacent to the road. More and more, people stepped forward to ask where the caravan was going and why they refused to stop and speak with them. Jan ignored most of them and just kept moving forward.

More than one man asked, "Why can't you just stop and talk to us? We don't know what to do. All we want is a few minutes of your time."

When Jan did speak, his response was always the same. "We have no time to talk. Follow us from behind and we'll speak with you when we stop. It won't be much longer now."

Campsite after campsite along the way, most people quietly stared at the procession that refused to slow down. Other than a raised hand of greeting here and there, not much of anything was shared between them.

Before dusk finished completely casting its blackened canopy, a suitably large enough area was finally found. It had been a long day, intended to put Skulsk far behind them; not just physical distance, but making its horrific memory a distant one too.

While tents were being erected, and dinners were prepared, it was time to take another head count and address the usual questions from the newcomers. Tonight, Josef headed to the rear with Jan and Julia while David checked the wagons. They all understood how much Jan struggled to be painfully blunt with anyone, even strangers. It was taking a toll on him. Josef took it upon himself to reassure his younger brother.

"You know Jan, I see how difficult it can be to ignore questions from strangers until end of day, but they simply don't understand our situation. Peter and I were just saying this morning how we are in a race against time. The nights are getting much colder now, and you know what? If anyone can't join the back for a few hours to keep up with us before they get answers, it's not our problem. If they aren't strong enough to do that, we shouldn't take them with us anyway, don't you think?"

"I agree, big brother. Pa used to call it *tough love*. Remember? It doesn't come naturally to me like it did for him." Jan and Josef enjoyed a small laugh together. "No, now that I think longer about it, I still believe he was just too lazy or too drunk. He never thought that far ahead, bless his tired old soul."

Their father was always a sour topic between the boys, filled with conflicted feelings toward him. "Let's get down the line and get this over with. I'm tired as hell tonight."

"Me too. Let's get this done." Jan turned to look for David, who was already approaching them. By this point, Jan needed his moral support. A group of about twenty or so new people had already assembled at the rear to meet Jan and the others. The numbers of new people never failed to baffle Jan and Julia, having once believed they were part of the very few who had stuck it out so long before leaving home. Every day proved them more wrong.

After repeating a similar speech each previous day, Jan took a moment to explain his initial rebuff to those he flippantly sent to the back earlier in the day. Some of them cursed at him for not stopping and on occasion, some even spit on his boots with frustration. He understood their anger and frustration and tried not to take the insults personally.

"My name is Jan, and these few of us have been leading this group for almost three weeks now, heading for the American camp in Torun. It's my responsibility to get us there before the cold weather arrives. Sorry I didn't answer your questions today. They're always the same ones everyone asks me, and I refuse to keep telling one person at a time the same thing over and over. But I'm here now to answer them.

"As our numbers keep growing, so do our responsibilities to each other. If you want to join with us, understand we can't promise to keep your families safe, since this is the first caravan we have ever led. We don't often know what lies ahead. But for all our sakes, we must keep up a good pace if we are to beat the bitter cold weather ahead of us."

Everyone's eyes were fixed on Jan, but they remained calm and quiet to let him speak. It was what they were waiting for. Why would they interrupt? Several of the families who joined the caravan in previous days and weeks also began to assemble behind and around the newcomers. It had become a daily update they all wanted to hear.

"We will do our best to keep all of us as safe as we can, but if you join us, we need your help to do it. We post guards every night to stand watch over each other. As our numbers grow, we need more guards who know how to use a rifle and aren't afraid to use it. How many of you are willing to do this for us?"

Several men raised their hands, some nervously looking around the group to see how many others were volunteering. One older man shouted, "I can do it too, but I have no bullets left. Can anyone give me some? I'm old but I can still shoot my damn gun!"

"Good for you. We'll take care of that old timer, don't worry." Jan looked about and added, "OK, get yourselves set up for some food and settle in for the night. For those of you volunteering, please stay behind so we can talk more about what needs to be done."

After some guidance and the usual *do's and don'ts* from Jan and David, those with rifles who had raised their hands were posted around the perimeter of the camp, growing substantially larger with each passing day. The experienced refugees who had already taken multiple security shifts were paired with one of the new volunteers. In due course, they would soon learn the routine as well.

These pairings also helped the group to know one another better. Bonding always strengthened the resolve of the group as a whole. It would be an important factor in the weeks and months ahead as this brotherhood continued to develop.

Desperate and hungry thieves were no doubt hidden by the blackness of night. The armed vigilance of the locked and loaded farmers and townspeople appeared to have dissuaded the bandits for the time being and motivated the guards to be serious about the potential threats surrounding them all.

As always, wagonloads were readjusted and condensed as much as possible to accommodate the elderly, and the pregnant young woman who was now part of the group. There was no complaining, but only acceptance and cooperation as these resilient families had already started adapting to new and challenging circumstances... yet another time. Despite the fact their futures were being restructured, their memories of times past would never be fully extinguished. Those memories would help to sustain them.

Daybreak delivered an overcast sky, which appeared charged with moisture, ominous but not unexpected at this time of year. The eventual objective was to follow the river to Kruszwica, at which point it would signify two-thirds of their journey north would be complete. Over the next several days they intended to break away from the river to link up with a pathway running parallel to the rail line leading directly to the American post in Torun.

During this time as the days wore on, Marianna still sat in the wagon up front, controlling their course, much as she had done throughout her family's lifetimes. Julia never had a problem keeping up with the men on foot, despite her sizable backpack. She was strong as an ox and never asked for special treatment, nor did she receive any.

The stream of refugees trekked steadily forward and with growing purpose. Men, women, and children of all ages carrying what few items they could manage, leaving everything else they once possessed behind in the ruins of a place they used to call home. Anything non-essential was left behind.

Newcomers sharing similar tragedies still joined others along the way as the gathering procession moved northeast to a new home. There were no other viable alternatives. Everyone was shrouded in a veil of blind acceptance. It provided a feeling of purpose when there seemed no other.

Miles of dampness became crusted with morning frost reinforcing the rutted clay passageways once winding peacefully through farm fields and patches of forest. At some point everyone's focus shifted inevitably to the task at hand... following the one's in front and leading the one's behind.

It took most of their limited concentration just to walk between the desolate criss-crossing road ruts which had frozen solid overnight. They would remain that way, at least until the rising temperature exceeded the freezing point to soften the crusty and perilous footing.

For the same reason, travel by night was not viable since the footing would refreeze with the sinking sun and the road such as it was, could be unforgiving. The last thing anyone could afford was a twisted or broken ankle. Such misfortune would be disastrous, and no one could be burdened more than they had already become, hauling their own body weight mile after mile for eight or ten hours a day. To add the dead weight of another would be overbearing to a point beyond breaking, irrespective of friendship, pity, or even love's best intentions or obligations.

The common threads of conversation among these travelers were muted and infrequent at first, but inevitably the invisible bonds tying them became not much more than shared body heat when sleep overcame them. Content with little more than cold, often raw potatoes, they would be sustained for yet another day. The hungry children had stopped complaining, so why should their parents do anything less?

Jan was one of four self-appointed leaders overseeing the mostly orderly procession from Konin. With every passing day, his role had been justifiably reaffirmed. The larger the group became, the greater the responsibility to make difficult and sometimes unpopular decisions as well. Among these was the constant realization minimal standards of physical ability had to be enforced among the ranks, despite the ensuing heartbreak.

It was imperative the pace had to be steadily maintained. Stragglers, whether elderly, disabled or physically unfit, would have to stay behind in whichever city or village they came upon for the benefit of the greater good. No one wanted to revisit the same tragedy befalling Richard's family.

In one case, the father and mother separated, the adult son deciding to stay with his elderly and frail mother, while his father and the son's wife carried on with their children. It was terribly sorrowful, but these few dependent people were jeopardizing the future safety and survival of everyone else.

Nor was there time for proper funerals. If anyone lost a loved one, which was inevitable along the way, a few would always step forward out of respect for the surviving family. They dug a shallow grave in the half-frozen surface or piled strewn bricks and debris to protect the corpse from gravediggers and the occasional roving pack of wolves.

Many in the constantly growing caravan however, still remained reluctant about conversation with these outsiders who would over time, become their brothers and sisters. It seemed strange but through the tedium and exertion, more of them eventually developed a growing reassurance knowing their common circumstances were not much different.

With each passing day, those keeping pace silently welcomed newcomers sharing the same fate as those before them. As expected, when fatigue set in, few acknowledgements of welcome were offered by the regulars, usually signified by nothing more than a nod or a grimace of exhausted indifference.

The first days of winter would soon be upon them. They had been prepared for this silent obstacle as well as could be expected, but the collective sighs of relief were evident among their ranks when they drew closer to their objective, the makeshift transition camp in Torun.

American flags were snapping noisily in the gusting winds, blowing relentlessly into the refugees' exposed faces. After a full day trudging into the teeth of the wind, their faces were numbed by the cold. It was near impossible to smile, their facial muscles no longer willing to respond. At the very least though, they were now glowing with a healthier reddened hue than the ashen pallor all too evident at their point of departure several weeks ago.

28
TOO WEAK TO CRY

ALLIED TRANSITION CAMP, TORUN

THE LARGE ENTOURAGE APPROACHED THE FORMERLY ABAN-
doned gateway to the future, now occupied by American troops.
These friendly but war weary saviors would soon be tasked with
processing and screening the almost two hundred migrants in Jan's
group alone seeking a far and distant place, intentionally not appearing on any map.

Since leaving Konin, Jan and Julia, Josef and David had provided
vital leadership for their comrades, and no one sought to dispute it.
As the darkness of night fell upon them again, they drew closer to
their destination, now penetrating the outskirts of Torun. Signage
along the main road directed their way past numerous American
troops, some of whom were strangely applauding their safe arrival.

"I never had anyone clap for me before. Why would they do that?"
Jan wondered out loud to Julia.

"I'm sure I don't know what to think either," she replied. "These
Americans are so different from what I imagined."

As they approached a slight curve in the road, two soldiers
stepped from the roadside, extending their arms to shake their
hands. "Welcome to the Torun camp. You've all come along way.
Congratulations! We're so happy you made it. Well done!"

Another sentry pointed forward and placed his other hand on
Jan's shoulder saying, "Just follow the lights up ahead, my friend." He
encouragingly patted Jan's shoulder.

When Jan raised his head, a yellow hue became faintly apparent above the trees. As they gradually moved closer, the light danced within the dense tree line and by the time the camp came into full view, the entire sky was glowing. "Is this our salvation, Jula?"

It was an emotional moment for Jan and countless others who were taken aback by such a reassuring welcome. It felt good to see order was well underway to being restored. It was the first time in several years for many of these people to feel welcomed anywhere.

Within minutes, two more soldiers stepped from the side and led the procession in the direction of a wooden administration building very much alive with the hustle and bustle of more military troops. High intensity flood lights mounted on twenty-five-foot light standards brightly illuminated the entire facility. It was brighter than a sunny summers day. The weary band of travelers couldn't help but squint to shade their eyes from the blinding glare.

Twelve-foot-high chain-link fencing lined both sides of a makeshift gravel pathway and within a very short distance, the way narrowed appreciably, forcing those entering into a much narrower lineup just wide enough for horse drawn wagons to pass. By this point, heavy wire netting covered the top of the enclosure as well.

Several armed guards were stationed outside the full length of the screens to reinforce the unspoken words, clearly suggesting any resistance would not be tolerated. Announcements in Polish were broadcast on loudspeakers, authoritatively informing the approaching refugees that American soldiers would be confiscating any weapons the refugees possessed, with assurances they would be returned in due course.

As the funnel of reinforced screens narrowed, it accessed another area with a well secured wooden porch extending some sixty feet across the main double doorway of an administration building. The entire process was intimidating, but the Americans themselves were welcoming and non-threatening, in glaring contrast to the brutal German captors to which these people had become so accustomed.

Two soldiers wearing sidearms approached the leaders of the caravan, one of whom spoke Polish fluently. "Do you people speak for this group?" the Polish interpreter asked.

"*Tak,*" Jan responded.

"Good. You four follow me then," he said in Polish. "I'll take you inside. Tell the others to wait here until they're called."

David walked back to those behind him to convey what was said and those within earshot nodded in agreement. There was no alternative option given. He then quickly returned to join Jan, Julia, and Josef, who were already stepping inside. A sentry obligingly reopened the door for him.

The front desk inside the main building was alive with the shuffling of paperwork and the strange new sounds of English. A heavy set and clean-shaven senior officer rose from his chair to introduce himself as Lieutenant Colson. He extended his large, thick-fingered vice-grip for a hand. Jan grasped it as firmly as Colson grasped his own.

"I'm Jan Szymanski. This is my brother Josef, Julia and this man is David who helped the three of us bring everyone here. By our last count, there are almost two hundred of us, mostly Poles."

The interpreter repeated everything Jan said. Colson understood as much Polish as Jan did English. Everything following from this point was a three-way conversation. Colson finished scanning and making notes on a worksheet attached to a clip board. Offering a slight smile, he immediately said, "We were expecting you people. We've been tracking you guys since you crossed the river in Skulsk."

These Americans were evidently well informed, well prepared, and hopefully well supplied, Jan thought to himself.

"So, tell me, you have any trouble along the way? You covered some hellish dangerous territory!" Colson emphasized.

Jan seemed surprised, thinking the journey was pretty much as he expected. He didn't think much about the danger involved. "Since the invasion, we're all used to being afraid. When the war ended, it got so much worse, so we just had to get away. We had nothing more to lose and everyone felt the same. Maybe it was better we didn't know."

"What you did was outstanding in my books, Jan. You made our job so much easier. You people must be hungry as hell. There's plenty of food inside and shit houses are outside for everybody. We're gonna keep you all together till we see your papers and figure out who every one of you sons 'o bitches are… OK? We'll start with the four of you."

The interpreter used his own professional discretion and toned down the lieutenant's course language. Colson never meant for it to sound as crude as it was. It was just his gruff manner over the years of military service.

Though he didn't have to, Colson explained the need for screening everyone's identification. "We gotta make certain there aren't German or Russian defectors infiltrating the camps. We can't afford to let any potential saboteurs inside the gates. Otherwise, it doesn't matter if you're a Czech, a Pole, Yugoslav, Croat, Serbian, Lithuanian." The list went on and on, but security and processing identification were the orders of the day.

"Better to screen and sort right away," he advised. "No point moving anymore DP's than necessary across half of eastern Europe. Any questionable cases will be processed in more detail when you arrive in western Germany."

"West Germany? Is that where you are taking us?" Jan enquired.

"Yep. Once your country gets reorganized and law and order is restored you will be brought back to wherever you came from, or at least close to it. That's the plan anyway. I got nothin' to do with any of that though. By the looks of your friends, they could sure use some medical help and good hot food to eat. It's a wonder they were able to get here. I'm amazed at what you could get out of them."

Whatever was required to gain entry, Colson was assured of receiving Jan's full cooperation and those he brought with him. Never before had Jan experienced such a mantle of responsibility, but it was one Jan was content to relinquish, having a sound mind, good intention, and respect for the new authority of the Americans.

He filled a void unchallenged by his group. Built upon his general good nature, and his determination to take care of his people, he was a good fit for Colson and a handful of others under his authority.

Returning to their ranks, Jan and Josef updated a handful of other self-appointed group leaders who had been standing outside patiently, despite the drop in temperature and the obvious hunger deep inside their growling bellies.

"Tell your families we will be OK. It's warm inside and they have food and rooms for all of us! They're gonna check our papers as fast as they can but they don't want any bullshit from anyone. These are our friends. Do you understand? Families with kids and old folks go first!"

Jan watched as his instructions filtered throughout the group, still lined up before him inside the wired fencing. Julia gave Jan a rare public embrace of support. "You're a good boss, Jan. We're all proud of you!" she exclaimed.

People offered whatever documents they had; those with nothing were admitted if others could verify their story. The screening was rudimentary at best. The camp although temporary, was heated inside and smelled of good, wholesome hot food. Dozens of guards oversaw the group and kept tight control over everyone inside the security fences.

The good food was a blessing long overdue. It had been almost twelve hours since their last meal, and their hunger was intensified by the stressful mixture of anxiety and general uncertainty of the day. For so long, they had been surviving on nothing more than a diet of potatoes, turnip, and beets. There were only so many ways to prepare potatoes, and in these circumstances, there were fewer ways still. Whether it was the hearty beef stew, or the roasted chicken, and yes, there were also potatoes, this was a meal befitting royalty. Their satiated bellies and the restoration of the deep, welcome return of their body heat made life more bearable again.

The Poles showed the signature scars of years of subsistence and deprivation, scars no longer noticed by those who bore them. Facial creases were so deep they appeared to have been well weathered over decades of maltreatment and destitution. These people had survived not one, but two waves of forcible foreign occupation. During this experience they had witnessed first-hand the deaths of loved ones, the destruction of their homelands, and the eviction of friends and families from their villages.

These resilient refugees had busted their backsides to build and maintain their homes and families, only to have them ripped from their grasp by a destiny over which they had no control, and neither sought nor deserved.

Yet here they stood still smiling, laughing, and expressing thank-fulness. Nothing would break them. They always found a way to be satisfied with what little they still possessed. At this temporary desti-nation at this specific point in time, for the first time in a long while, Jan felt the richness of his own existence.

"How far are we going, Jan? Did they tell you anything?" Julia enquired. "Do we even know where we're going? The papers said somewhere in Germany, I think." Julia's questions were never inter-preted by anyone, especially Jan, as being complaints; just enquiries to satisfy her reluctance to be dependent on anyone other than Jan.

"In three days, we leave here to head west. Colson says they have trucks and wagons to handle supplies and tents. We'll still have to walk but there won't be so much for us to carry, and we won't have to do anymore night patrols if we don't want to. Colson made it clear that's their job. These are soldiers who are trained for this work, so let's let them do it.

"When we make it to the trains in Bydgoszcz, we can get off our feet for the long haul. There are a few other camps like this one, only smaller, somewhere along the way", Jan confirmed.

"We'll find out more tomorrow. For now, let's make sure everyone has rooms and we can get some sleep too. Don't worry, Jula," which had become his pet-name for his sweetheart.

Inside the main building there were dozens of rooms with single cots already set up. They slept ten to a room with plenty of heavy blankets to go around. The only bathrooms were the ones outside. Large open showers were supplied as well, with rows of sinks for the men to shave and brush their teeth.

Men were separated from the women and young children, but aside from this, there was very little privacy. In comparison to the meagre conditions these people had endured, this was like staying at the Ritz Hotel, although none of them had any way of knowing what that was.

*****

By dawn's early light the camp was buzzing with activity. Security checks had been completed sufficiently and now enabled Jan's group to mix with others who were already settled in before them. Two smaller convoys were expected the next day, which would swell the ranks to thirteen hundred and sixty people to be departing the Torun facility two days later.

When things quieted down and the refugees rested and ate, there were a few unexpected opportunities for Jan and Julia to share a coffee or even a cup of schnapps with some of the American soldiers. Surprisingly, some of them spoke Polish, some even spoke Italian and German. America really was a diverse nation. It seemed everyone's background inevitably led back to somewhere else, Scotland, Ireland, Great Britain, the middle east, even Africa, and China.

Lieutenant Colson spent more time conversing with Jan than he typically would with anyone else. His interpreter worked for him, no matter what he wanted to speak about. The lieutenant and Jan just seemed to click.

Chuck Colson was intrigued by hearing Jan's family story from a very different perspective than his own, Julia's to a much lesser extent. She remained reluctant to share anything that wasn't necessary. What was done was done, in her mind. Colson was content to confine his idle chatter to Jan and David.

"Me and my men were one of the first battalions to hit the beach in Normandy. Wouldn't wanna do that again. I lost almost half the men I commanded that day, some of 'em never made it to the fuckin' beach. That was just over a year ago, and I still can't stop thinkin' about it." Colson swallowed another shot of schnapps and took a long drag on his cigarette. The burnt ash just dropped onto his well-worn khaki pants. He didn't even flinch to swipe it away. Evidently it wasn't the first time it happened.

"How did you feel about coming from America to fight the Germans in Europe? They didn't do anything to your people, did they?" Jan asked so naïvely.

"No, but sooner or later they probably would. The higher ups like our president, just told us where we had to go. Ain't nobody gonna ask us if we wanted to go. Just not the way it works, ya know."

"What did you do before the army? You gotta wife and kids back home?" Jan asked.

"Oh yeah. Military's all I know. I got my wife and two kids, both boys," he answered proudly.

"That must be tough for your men, I don't know how they can do that."

"It is tough, but you know what? I think what you people had to deal with is a damned sight worse. I'll lay odds you must 'a lost some of your family too," Colson added.

"Yep, my older brother. The Germans took him to a work camp in 1940, and we never heard from him again. Could still be alive somewhere, but we don't even know where to look. There isn't a day we don't miss him, especially my Ma."

"Best chance of finding him is at these camps," Colson stated. "There's about seventy of them, so if he's still alive in any of 'em, you'll find him, or he'll find you."

Jan slapped his thigh with excitement and began to tear. Colson couldn't help but notice and continued.

"See, that's the difference between here and America. At least if I go home when this shit is over, my family will still be there for me. That's the plan anyway. As I see it, it's a hell of a lot worse for you people."

Jan extended his hand to the lieutenant and said, "I never thought about it much, till now, but we're sure thankful you and the British came when you did. None of us would have a second chance if you didn't."

"We're all just doin' our jobs, but it's good to hear you say that." Colson took another long drag from his cigarette, coughing a little when he exhaled through his nose.

"Ya know what? I'm gonna be real busy tomorrow. Just in case we don't see each other again, it's been real good knowin' you, Jan."

They both stood in silence, in front of each other, eye to eye; neither spoke. It was an odd sensation, but neither knew if or when either of them would make it home again… wherever the roads may take them. They leaned in toward one another, each placing a hand on the other's shoulder. Not another word needed to be said.

*****

The first Displaced Persons (DP) camps were opened under allied military command soon after the war ended, now almost eighteen months ago. The intent was to immediately address the refugee crisis existing throughout most of Europe by providing safety, shelter, and food.

While these intentions were honorable, the facilities were woefully inadequate, and the standards of care were initially no better than prisons. Refugees were forced to live under armed guard behind barbed wire, with inadequate food. There was no physical abuse, but these makeshift camps were as frightening to the refugees as the ones thought to have been left behind.

In the spring of 1945, under the oversight of the American President Franklin Delano Roosevelt, Allied leadership attended the Yalta Conference in Crimean Russia. Their agenda was to readdress these refugee issues, which had become an international disgrace.

Under the authority of Allied command, it was agreed the United Nations Relief and Rehabilitation Administration (UNRRA) would be tasked with providing hands-on field support to house the millions of refugees in DP camps throughout the American, British, and French zones lining Germany's western border. These camps would provide a temporary home with nutritious food, professional medical care, and appropriate lodging facilities until such time as order and infrastructure could be restored in their countries of origin.

The primary objective was to repatriate the estimated seven million refugees across Europe, to be housed in seventy such camps established in almost any suitable lodging available.

*****

According to the posted reports in the administrative office, the railway line to Bydgoszcz was fully committed to military assignments. One of Colson's aides explained, "The main line has already been commandeered by the Allied military to move troops and medical supplies farther east. For the time being, rounding up more refugee stragglers as best we can, is now a secondary priority."

As a direct result of the railway being temporarily unavailable on the day of departure, the convoy would be mostly on foot, with overloaded wagons and carts, as well as ten military trucks stocked with food, tents, and medical supplies. It was a logistical miracle to even attempt such an endeavor. Once again everyone prepared for, and readily accepted yet another marathon to endure. It was just another test of their stamina, their resolve, and their will to survive. With the Americans' help, it likely wouldn't be as difficult.

This was one of the final sweeps of north Poland before the withdrawal of the military. Anyone remaining would be left unaided to deal with the devastation and chaotic violence to inevitably follow.

It took five days of steady walking before they reached Bydgoszcz. Thankfully, the frail and elderly sat in the back of several trucks under canopies. They were not heated but there was plenty of food and heavy blankets.

The Americans kept up a steady pace to which most Poles were already accustomed. The added advantage was the steady supply of hot food along the way, and medical help when it was needed.

Once in Bydgoszcz, where rail lines were finally available, additional freight trains had been re-allocated to the task of transporting the refugees across the almost eight hundred remaining kilometers of the journey. Most of the refugees had never been on a train before and had no expectation of comfort. It was just as well... there was none to be found. In the absence of passenger trains, only boxcars and cattle cars were available.

Due to the shortage of space, more restrictions were placed on baggage, and horses and wagons were being left behind. The rules were strictly enforced here. Human space was the only priority that mattered, and every available boxcar was filled to capacity.

Winter weather set in early with overnight sub-zero temperatures, so each boxcar was equipped with a wood burning, vented firebox. It added sufficient heat to make the journey survivable within cramped conditions such as these.

A few chairs were supplied for the elderly, positioned closer to the fire, and there were minimal arguments from their weary travel companions, perhaps owing in large part to the two military guards assigned to each boxcar. Standing room only was better than the alternative of staying behind. Bathroom breaks were infrequent between the very few scheduled stops and even then, only when coal and water was resupplied to feed the sooty, coal consuming behemoths hauling this human cargo.

In all, there were twenty-seven fully crammed freight cars, squealing and screeching around and through the countryside, the monotony of which was barely broken by the sight of identical grey sidings, making the remnants of each and every city appear to be one and the same. At each refilling silo, those who were able, eagerly jumped off to grab a smoke, urinate and down the distasteful concoction they self-brewed, resembling only slightly the black coffee typically sustaining them till the next stop.

Boxes of food in the form of sandwiches and fresh fruit were tossed to each carload of hungrily waving, outstretched hands and arms, while medical personnel moved quickly from car to car tending to those urgently requiring more water, diapers, laxatives and any other desperate needs.

Yet still, in the midst of this ordeal, there could be heard occasional singing and laughter from these ever so resilient people. It was progress they had sought so hard to achieve, which was fulfillment enough to sustain them through each difficult passing day.

*****

WILDFLECKEN DP CAMP, GERMANY, NOVEMBER 1946

It would take six endless days of these inhuman conditions before their destination, finally confirmed to be Wildflecken, was revealed. The singing had long since stopped. At this point they would surely have disembarked into the very gates of Hell if they had to, without hesitation. What prizes these weary, stinking and lice infected souls would be for the UNRRA staffers at Wildflecken.

The steam whistle loudly proclaimed their arrival when they rounded the final curve, as they approached the train station to be mercifully permitted to finally exit from their inhuman travel accommodations. The mass of humanity jumped down, fell down, and literally spilled from the open doors, exposing a grey sea of putrid filth, cloaked in dried vomit and defecation.

Julia and many others leaped out of the fetid railway car, sucking in the fresh, crisp air; many simply spread out on all fours to draw in deep breaths of life sustaining oxygen they had been deprived of for so very long. "Oh, my dear God. Augh!" She gasped, trying to clear her throat. "The fresh air is heaven sent."

Josef crouched beside her, echoing her gratefulness just for having survived the ordeal. "We must have lost a few souls in that overcrowded and stinking box on wheels. I recognize the smell of death from Skulsk. Augh, it's worse than I remember. How's Ma?" he asked, as his head began to clear.

Julia looked around and pointed about fifteen feet away from them. "They're over there! Jan kept her back when the pushing and shoving started. She would have been badly injured in the fracas. I don't know how we all survived, especially your mom."

They both rose to their feet, and wordlessly hugged one another in their momentary silence, knowing the family was alright. As they approached Marianna and Jan, the sounds of groaning and weeping could still be heard through the noisy release of pressurized steam clouds hissing from the train engine. It too, seemed to be sighing with relief.

"Come, Josef. Help me get Ma away from here. I think she's been sitting too long. Her muscles and joints have stiffened up. C'mon Ma, let's see if we can get you moving again."

"I'll be fine boys... once I get limbered up. Don't worry about me." Marianna assured them.

It was apparent the once beaming smiles so prevalent less than a week ago, were now replaced by faces of utter despair, lined with tears of exhaustion and overwhelming misery. Many young children were too weak to cry anymore and huddled closely beside the parents who wept for them, clutching each other's emaciated hands with whatever reassurance a parent could offer.

UNRRA staff rushed from car to car to assist pregnant women and mothers with young babies in need of diapers and cans of condensed milk. Many of these women were suffering de-hydration and were unable to provide breastmilk. It was a common problem needing immediate attention.

"Look around us Jan. We have nothing to complain about. Can you imagine if we had young kids, like them?" Julia nodded in the direction of a young mother about Julia's age. The woman rested her baby on top of a cold metal newspaper stand to change its already crusted, makeshift diaper. It was nothing more than a section of newspaper since supplies of diapers had been totally inadequate.

"The baby's bottom is raw and blistered, probably badly infected too." Julia began to break down, choking back tears of sympathy, having nowhere to wipe her own tears other than using the filthy arm sleeve of her heavy coat. "I can't bear to watch anymore."

Many infants were so dehydrated, some did not survive the journey and had to be gently pried from their mother's loving arms. There would be no more crying and suffering for them.

Each empty car displayed evidence of the dehumanizing conditions, which often revealed the cadavers of deceased loved ones, comprised mostly of the very young and the elderly, too weak to linger.

The exhausted refugees were led, and sometimes carried inside the heated buildings providing bathrooms, showers, and fresh clothes, with little or no modesty provided. Medical conditions requiring immediate attention were triaged with respectful and professional treatment and minimal segregation from the others. It was an amazingly efficient procedure which, by this time in the postwar years, had been honed to accommodate almost every possibility and unusual circumstance.

Like the transition camp in Torun, military secured areas held all new refugees until clearance had been officially granted, but here those administrative matters were deferred to the days ahead until more urgent medical assistance, water and food could be provided for everyone.

There was no discrimination here. Everyone was treated the same. These areas provided their own kitchens and sleeping quarters. Although a group of this size was one of the largest the camp had received, the adaptability and professionalism of the UNRRA staff were a sight to behold.

Jan quietly scanned the crowded room, thinking this was just one of several just like it. "Compared to many of these people, our family survived the exhausting journey well. We come from sturdy stock and thankfully we're healthy and strong enough to have endured the ordeal; better than most, it appears," Jan said to Josef, who quietly nodded in agreement.

Sadly, thirty-two souls that began the journey west, did not arrive in Wildflecken alive. Six more would die within a few days of having entered the camp as well, typically suffering from typhus and malnutrition.

After cleaning up and feeling human again, large groups of people were ushered into the kitchen halls for a meal long overdue. The newly arrived hungry masses had already learned their painful lesson from eating too much too quickly their first day in Torun. Still, it was difficult to pace themselves.

The refugees sat at tables of twelve, and within minutes of being seated, dollies with multiple racks of pre-plated hot meals rolled from the kitchen and were quickly placed in front of them. There were no choices given; everyone ate borscht soup and fresh baked bread with roasted chicken and potatoes. It was a well-organized feeding frenzy from start to finish.

Through the din of boisterous conversations and the clattering of dishes, one of the UNRRA staff tapped on his microphone to address each dining hall.

"Good evening, everyone. My name is Jacob, and I am delighted to welcome you to the Wildflecken camp. I understand you have had a long and tiring journey and we congratulate all of you for what you have accomplished by coming this far. This is your new home until you are able to return to your homeland when safe for you to do so."

There was no other reference made to the horrific journey which brought them here. There were no apologies either. It was not UNRRA's responsibility, and they were helpless to prevent it.

"During the time you will be with us, we will do everything we can to take good care of you. There is nothing to fear here. You are among friends now; friends who share the same circumstances. For the first few days, however, it is important you help us complete some important documents.

"This information will help us determine where you came from and reunite you with other members of your family who may also be here, or in other camps as well. It is important you answer a few medical questions so we can give you any necessary treatment or medicine you may require.

"This is a camp with only a small number of team members. I think there are about seventeen UNRRA staff here in Wildflecken. As we learn more about each other, our plan is to have many of you and your families work together with us to make your stay here a safe and productive one.

"Meals will be served using all the dining halls. This one will be yours for the time being until we become better organized and try to get you reunited with your families. Times will be posted for each sitting. I ask you to always be on time for your scheduled meals because there is always someone behind you who is hungry too. They cannot eat until you do."

Jacob looked around at the several hundred new faces before him, each of them staring back at him with every identifiable emotion one could imagine: heartbreak, sadness, exhaustion, remorse, thankfulness, anxiousness, and wonder, but no longer as much fear.

"Room numbers are posted for each of you on the bulletin boards at the back of the dining hall. Inside, you will find cots and clean bedding for everyone. If you cannot find your name on the list, please relax, and tell one of the UNRRA people. We try, but we are not perfect. We will clear up any confusion you may have.

"Within a few days, you will find your way around camp. New people arrive here every week. As they do, we hope you will be among those who welcome them here too."

Within hours, temporary rooms were assigned to everyone new to the camp, at least until paperwork could be properly completed. It had been a long and exhausting day. Despite being overcrowded, the small rooms served as a welcome refuge from the extreme harshness of the cold night air. The winter months in the ski country of the Bavarian hills in western Germany could be unforgiving, but here inside, no one had cause to complain.

29
WELCOME TO SKI COUNTRY!

WILDFLECKEN, MEANING *WILD PLACE*, SPANNED FIFTEEN square miles of heavily timbered wilderness in some of the deepest parts of the Bavarian Forest. For most of the camps, nature's camouflage provided excellent groundcover and their secret location never appeared on any map during the war. This ensured they were unseen by the heavy bombers of the Royal Air Force, often passing directly overhead multiple times every day. Many of these aircraft were enroute to destroy strategic munition and supply lines of military value within major cities in the heart of Nazi Germany.

The camps were originally designed and built as German officer training facilities in preparation for the war against Russia. Each camp was intended to accommodate 2,000 to 2,500 troops. Now used as refugee camps, it became necessary for them to each house up to 25,000 refugees who would call these overcrowded barracks home.

Wildflecken was typical of many such facilities. Within the camp, streets were lined with row after row of single level buildings, arranged in concentric semi-circles emanating from the centrally located cluster of administration buildings. Each radius supported multiple rows of identical blockhouses, similar to the spokes of a wheel. When these facilities were fully occupied, which happened often, the inevitable overflow of refugees made their own nests in the empty horse stables. Nothing here was left unused.

Most of the blockhouses, about sixty of them, held between 350 to 500 refugees each. These were reasonably self-contained, with bathrooms, functional kitchens, and other support services; however, every aspect of these accommodations was pushed far beyond its intended usage and capability.

One street, appropriately named Kitchen Street, extended almost a mile long and among other shops and services, featured twelve massive kitchens, each feeding about 1,700 refugees. To put this camp into proper perspective, the population of Wildflecken was greater than many American cities such as Plattsburg, N.Y., and Modesto, California. However, unlike these U.S. cities of comparable size which were populated by the residents' personal choices, the process of selection in Wildflecken was totally random. Over time, the seventy camps housed more than five million lost souls.

Within days, and sometimes weeks of their arrival, many of the refugees gradually began to reawaken within themselves the remaining dormant seeds of self-assurance. For most, however, these feelings had long since been extinguished, leaving them uncertain about trusting others; their self-confidence having been jaded by the continual oppression and trauma they had been forced to endure for so long.

The previous day to day concerns about where to find their next meal, their next overnight shelter, and how to protect their loved ones, were understandable preoccupations that on the surface, were no longer their major priorities, however, for many the crippling anxiety still lingered. Prolonged periods of corrosive stress do not quickly fade and suddenly disappear.

The continual psychological and physical scars run too deep into the core of the soul, eventually redefining the person that once was. It has been said repeatedly that time heals all wounds, but in these unique circumstances, most of the refugees believed they didn't have enough time to ever reconcile it. For those unfortunate ones, they would be haunted by their traumatic memories for the rest of their natural lives.

*****

Over a hearty breakfast of oatmeal and baked biscuits, the Szymanski family, David, and Sal were chatting among themselves, having barely begun to settle into the basic daily routines within the camp.

"It's odd for me waking up every day knowing the next meal is just outside our bedroom door. I don't think any of us really believed this was possible when we left our homes. I know I had serious doubts," Jan carefully sipped his hot coffee and said, "...Even having real coffee. I forgot how damned good it tastes."

"We're all relieved to be here, but I admit, I feel... lost somehow. Can't tell you how long it's been since I had nothing to do, certainly not in this lifetime," David commented.

"I expect they'll organize job assignments for us after finishing our paperwork. I can't believe there's only seventeen UNRRA people here to do it all. I'm sure they will post something on the board soon. There must be things we can do to help," Julia responded.

As they cleared their dishes from the table for the next sitting, a cheery fellow with a flip board and a broad smile approached. "Good morning, everyone. My name is Felix. I'm looking for Jan and Josef Szymanski... and Julia Chodakowska."

"Oh-oh, are we in some kind of trouble?" Josef nervously joked. "What did we do now?"

Jan stepped toward the young man saying, "I'm Jan Szymanski, and this is Julia and Josef. What can we do for you, Felix?" Jan said matter-of-factly.

"Nice to meet you folks. There are some people who want very much to meet you this morning in the administration building. It's only a short distance from here but it's freezing outside this morning, so grab your coats and hats. We can meet inside the main doors here as soon as you are ready."

Mystified, but without any direct questions, the three shuffled to their room to retrieve their heavy coats. "Looks like we're one of the first to meet the bosses. I'm anxious to hear what they have to say," Julia commented excitedly.

As soon as the heavy door swung open, the swirling gusts of wind caught the door, forcing Felix to brace himself. Jan and Felix both had to lean in together to seal off the invisible frozen demon. The snowdrifts Jan and Josef had shoveled before breakfast had already begun to block the door again. "Is the wind always this strong? Since we arrived, it's never let up." Julia shouted.

"Welcome to ski country!" Felix shouted sarcastically. "A lot of the colder air funnels down between the higher mountains to the southeast. The gusts of wind can last several days at a time without relenting. You'll get used to it."

It was difficult to speak and to be heard, but Felix was not to be denied trying. "This is one of the barracks where German troops were trained for alpine skiing. Hitler didn't want to leave any stone untouched. It's pleasant in the summer, but winter here can be a real bitch!" He turned and looked at Julia and grimaced. "Oops. Sorry about that! I forget myself sometimes."

"Don't worry about it. I've heard a lot worse; I promise you," she replied.

It was only a ten-minute walk, but into the teeth of the gusting wind it was still a challenge for Felix. Of course, it was nothing to which Julia and the brothers weren't already accustomed, however, the blowing snow was blinding at times, and completely masked the unfamiliar hidden pathway somewhere beneath it.

As they approached the central core of the facility, Felix described the junction area. "This is our central administration building. It's kinda like the center of town in the camp. All these other buildings handle food and supply deliveries, laundries, and quick access to Kitchen Street, which is always the busiest stretch in town." Felix continued. "Just stomp your feet on the porch so we don't take too much snow inside. It's a busy place so we don't want anyone to slip and fall, OK?"

Felix wasn't exaggerating. Inside the man entrance was a teeming mass of what appeared to be organized confusion. The steady clattering of typewriters and hundreds of people sorting and filing paperwork created a noisy backdrop. Neither Jan nor Julia had ever seen anything of the like.

"Just follow me." He turned his head slightly to be better heard as he explained over his shoulder, "I've been here almost a year now, but this is the first time I've taken any new arrivals to the Duchess' office before. You must be pretty important, or she wouldn't have asked to meet you." Jan and Julia just looked at each other and shrugged in wonder.

After winding through a few long corridors, the noise behind subsided noticeably, making it much easier to be heard. Felix directed the family to be seated while he informed the receptionist the Duchess was already expecting them.

"She's on the phone with someone now and asks that you wait a few minutes until she's free. May I offer you a cup of coffee? It's the best in Wildflecken, you really should have one."

"That's nice of you but no, we are all fine, thank you." Jan responded. The last time someone offered them a fine cup of coffee was, well... never. The decline was a natural part of who they had become. Somehow, they thought themselves to be undeserving of anyone's graciousness. It would have been embarrassing to them had they accepted.

"What do you think is happening, Jan?" Julia whispered. "Why would they want to even meet us, especially this lady who is obviously someone very important? I don't understand."

"Neither do I, Jula. I just hope we're not gonna get shit from anybody. Either way, we'll find out soon enough."

They finished their short conversation when a woman's voice could be heard on the small speaker on the secretary's desk. "Please show the Szymanski family into my office." Felix quickly jumped to his feet like a military officer had commanded his attention. He gestured for them to join him, as he tapped on the door before opening.

Upon the group entering the office, two lovely women rose from their chairs and one of them introduced herself as *The Duchess*. She greeted them speaking perfect Polish. "Good morning. Which one of you is Jan? I know you must be Julia. Good morning to you both." Turning to Josef, she said, "And you must be Josef. This dear lady is my Deputy Director of Wildflecken, Miss Kathryne Hulme. Please, have a seat and make yourselves comfortable.

"We are delighted to meet each of you," Kathryne happily stated. "As you can imagine, this camp has become a very busy place since the dreadful war thankfully ended. We know everyone here has survived many terrible experiences and I regret we must meet under such circumstances. I hope you and your friends are comfortable in the few days you have been here?" she asked with an upturned eyebrow.

"Yes, thank you, Madame. Everyone here has been so kind," Julia assured her.

"It is the responsibility of Countess and myself to ensure our UNRRA team works efficiently every day and, more times than I can count, well into the night, I might add. Although we have a heavy workload, we believe very deeply about the importance of what we do here.

"We are proud to be of service to all the refugees that come to us. Just so you know, we do not often greet our guests with the same courtesies we are extending to you today, but we are most anxious to meet each of you because of your outstanding contribution to our cause."

The family glanced briefly at one another in apparent confusion and obvious disbelief, thinking they had been mistaken for someone else. The duchess shuffled through a few documents from her desk before continuing, while the Deputy Director looked on.

"You created quite an impression with a certain..." the duchess looked carefully through her reading glasses as she confirmed the name. "... Ahh, Lieutenant Colson, I believe. He wrote some very impressive comments on your files that were meant to catch our attention."

Jan impulsively slapped his knee in uncharacteristic surprise. *That must be what this is all about,* he thought to himself. Julia sat between Jan and Josef, and firmly squeezed their knees to show her pride in both brothers' accomplishments.

"You should be proud of yourselves for what you have done. After reading the lieutenant's comments, Kathryn learned you left your home during dangerous times and gathered others needing help along the way. To safely deliver almost two hundred refugees to Torun was an amazing feat.

"It says here what you did... where was it now..." the duchess again placed her reading glasses on the bridge of her nose, scanning the document to quickly find the comment... "Ahh, here it is... *was accomplished without guidance or authority, without military escort of any form or manner; relying totally upon their own self-appointed initiative to ensure the welfare of their people.*" She placed the document back into the file and continued.

The Deputy interjected, "Those people you helped would not be in our camp today, were it not for your humanitarian efforts. Your courage and determination are commendable. We respect your initiative and the way you completed your task, and for that, we both congratulate you. It is the reason we needed to meet you right away. Simply put, we need more people like you to help us here in Wildflecken."

Jan, Julia, and Josef were stunned to hear the ladies' comments and specifically, what Lieutenant Colson wrote in their file. Jan fumbled awkwardly in response. "That's very good for you to say those nice things, but..."

The duchess took the liberty to teasingly interject before Jan finished his thought. "But what, Jan? Is Lieutenant Colson not telling us the truth?" She stared at Jan waiting for his response.

"Yes, I suppose he is, but... we just did what anyone would do... what had to be done."

"Let me clarify this, Jan. You did what had to be done, but believe me, it was certainly *NOT* what anyone else would have done. We commend you for taking charge of the situation your village was facing. You should be proud of what you and your family were able to accomplish.

"Now then, we have much to talk about, but before we begin, have you been offered anything to drink?"

"Yes... yes, we are fine thanks, Madame." Jan responded. "Nonsense! I'll not hear of it. Our coffee is the best in the camp. I personally insisted upon it! You really must try some." Duchess reached for her intercom and barked authoritatively to her assistant, "Beatrice, bring us a fresh pot of coffee and cream." This time, Jan didn't dare object.

From the moment Jan assumed leadership of his ragtag group of refugee migrants to deliver them safely to the gates of the Allied departure camp in Torun, and shook hands with Lieutenant Colson, he had distinguished himself in Colson's eyes. While Jan and Josef's resourcefulness and the deserving admiration of those they led were recognized, Julia's role was not overlooked either.

Evidently, the tough and assertive character of Colson also had a perceptive and considerate side not often seen. His was a genuinely positive reference, speaking volumes about the family's character. It immediately resonated with UNRRA.

The duchess began to explain. "Let me tell you more about what we do here, and why we were so eager to meet with you. Wildflecken is among the largest of seventy similar camps running north along the western border of Germany. The number of refugees here varies every few days, as more of them arrive from several different gathering stations throughout Europe, much like the one in Torun.

"As you can imagine, UNRRA staff itself was never intended to sustain these camp services on its own, so of necessity, many of the functions we provide rely heavily upon help from many of the refugees themselves. We find jobs here for the best qualified people, plain and simple.

"We train those refugees who have more advanced education, language, and leadership skills and, I am open to admit, those who are generally of higher intelligence. Based upon our first impressions, mainly mine and Kate's, and of course Lieutenant Colson's outstanding recommendations, it appears you three have the qualities we need here."

There was a short rap on the door and the deputy tersely directed Beatrice to enter. Felix assisted her, carrying a tray of coffee mugs, cream, and a pot of piping hot aromatic coffee. "Thank you both kindly. Just set it on the table over there. We do not wish to be disturbed. Thank you, Beatrice."

Turning attention back to her guests, she said, "Please, help yourselves. I insist." The duchess was a woman who was in firm control of those under her command. She exhibited her prowess by her every word and gesture. Julia was visibly in awe of her, and if truth be told, she was justifiably intimidated by her evident formidability.

"The tasks for which we are responsible in this department are daunting and include extensive bookkeeping; inventory control of everything from medical and food supplies to firewood, toilet paper, and diapers, as well as constant security checks and processing of documents, often in five or six different languages. We all must do our part here, and although the administrative workload is overwhelming on occasion, it's a far better alternative than other mundane manual work." The duchess rose to refill her coffee.

As she did, Jan leaned closer to Julia and whispered embarrassingly, "Do you understand what she is talking about? Too many big words for me." Julia just smiled and shushed him for the time being.

The deputy director continued to explain, "The better educated women we select to work here are exempt from the physical labor assignments such as the kitchen, the laundry and cleaning, which for some, can be backbreaking. By working in this department, our team can make productive contributions in the development of vital systematic and procedural paperwork. This paperwork is vital to ensure the continued financial support of the participating countries of the United Nations.

"Julia, your file also included an impressive letter of reference you presented in Torun from a... Father Francis from the Catholic

Church in Opinogora. Although it gave no specific details, there appears to be much more to you than one would expect. Once we learn more about your background, we are confident we will find a place for you here, one that will make a positive impact on our work here. Do you understand?"

Julia nodded her affirmation, saying what she had always done in these situations, "I'm happy to help in any way I can."

The duchess resumed with her questions, "Before I forget to ask, Julia, Polish is your mother tongue, is it not? Your fluency is much better than I expected." Julia nodded but before she could orally respond, the duchess enquired, "Do you speak any other languages? It would be a strong asset if you do."

"I wasn't able to finish school, but I learned some German along the way. It was important to me that I did so. A few friends encouraged me to read as much as I could. I started with the Bible, and many newspapers in both Polish and German. The books I read were difficult at first, but as I understood them better, they gave me more self-confidence. I even speak a little Russian, but not very well I'm afraid."

"Good for you. The refugees in these camps come from every corner of Europe. The more of them you are able to communicate with, the better off for everyone," the duchess replied.

"Jan and Josef, I suspect you have already found a few good men who can work closely with you to help oversee much of the maintenance operations the camp requires. I know you didn't come this far without learning how to delegate authority, did you now?"

"Of course, Ma'am. We already have a few good ones in mind." Jan responded.

"Excellent! I'll see that you both meet Oscar this afternoon. He is a good man you will enjoy working with. He will need your help right away. I have no doubt your team will fit very well with his own."

The duchess checked her watch. Having such a full agenda, she was always mindful of her limited time constraints. "Let's meet again over the days ahead, shall we? As always, I have so much to attend to." Duchess never had a minute to waste as she guided her guests to her office door. "Kathryn and I have enjoyed meeting each of you and I'm hopeful we can begin working together right away."

The deputy again intervened, but only briefly, "Julia, if you don't mind staying behind, I need to speak with you for a few minutes. I want to ensure Felix shows you around the office this morning. There are a several people we want you to meet today."

"Yes, I'm anxious to meet them as well." Julia replied.

*****

In the ensuing weeks, Jan and Josef were pleased to recommend David and Sal, and several others who had distinguished themselves on the journey north to Torun. The duchess was correct about Oscar being a good fit for them. He took Jan and the three men throughout the camp, deep inside the inner workings of Wildflecken, and explained some of its history along the way.

Oscar was eager to share his knowledge with these men, and they were equally enthusiastic about learning from him. He was in France before the German occupation working as a professional engineer, and had a solid understanding of electrical, heating, and mechanical matters. His expertise was critical to Wildflecken's mechanical operations.

"I understand most of you men were farmers back home, the same as many of the refugees here. Not much farming to do till spring though, not in this frozen hellhole.

"Feeding everyone is always our greatest challenge. The more we can produce for ourselves, the less we need to depend on the food shipments we receive each week. We also started receiving monthly relief rations recently. We distribute them to every registered refugee, in addition to their normal rations. It's kinda like Christmas coming every month."

"What is it that makes them so different?" Jan asked naïvely.

"They've got canned sardines, canned Spam, condensed milk, chocolate, and even a supply of cigarettes... same rations the military guys get from back home. There's always a few surprises too. Never know exactly what you're gonna get. Around here, almost anything can be had if you look hard enough.

"The people in here already started barter trading some of their relief rations for other things they want from the villagers outside the camp. The packs mostly contain high calorie and high protein food... and the American cigarettes are like gold! Everyone's got different priorities, I guess. It's become another way of life here. Your country-men are very resourceful people, Jan."

As they walked to the next building, Oscar continued to enlighten them. "Most of our refugees are tradesmen and manual laborers, and they sure as hell work hard. Not a lazy one in the group. I admire that about them. When they came here, they didn't look like much.

"You guys know better than me that it was a tough journey. Some of your people didn't survive to talk about it. It wasn't right but... desperate times, I guess. One way or the other, we had to get you here soon as we could, before you starved or froze to death. The trains were the only way to do it."

Jan and the others stayed silent about the subject. It was a grue-some ordeal, but a necessary one.

"Sometimes we get ten times the number of people in this camp than the Germans originally designed it to hold. Toss in the huge appetites of these mostly male workers; you can't imagine how much they can eat. You won't believe it but, we bake almost nine tons of bread every day in this camp alone. Of course, that includes what they sneak outside the gates to sell to the Germans.

"My focus here though, is to try to maximize the efficiency of our heating, electrical, and plumbing systems. Gotta give those krauts some credit. They always build things right the first time. The construction here is in good shape and the utilities were installed properly... but they only built these camps for about 2,500 troops. We push the limits too far here. It's my job to get this place rewired safely, keep our water lines from freezing and keep the heat on. There's always something breaking down. My biggest worry though is fire."

"How so?" David asked.

"The refugees are used to doing everything by themselves. Before the war, they didn't have much to work with, but they have just enough knowledge to be dangerous... know what I mean? If they need more electrical power, they just tap into whatever they can. They're always overloading the system.

"We blow fuses all the time and overheat the receptacles. All the buildings here are built from timber construction. It's a powder keg waiting to explode. We're too far from any organized fire crews, so if it ever happens, we only have ourselves to put it out."

"I only farmed a little back home, Oscar. I'm a pretty good electrician though, and so are a few of my friends. Some of us were trained in school, so I know we can help you do the job properly." David offered.

"Glad to have you boys here. If things work out, it will take a lot of pressure off my shoulders."

As expected, Jan, Josef, and David earned a spot among the refugee leadership. They were always among the first to get involved in any required task whether carpentry, basic electrical or plumbing work, most of which was self-taught. Under the watchful eyes of Oscar however, they learned a great deal more and did their utmost to do what was needed safely. Their organizational and leadership skills continued to increase their popularity and respect, causing their comrades to develop an even greater reliance upon them.

As the relationships continued to grow, Jan especially, possessed an expressive sense of patriotism, cooperation, and always his boundless good humor. He became a deserving role model for so many in the camp. His positive outlook and personable character were infectious. With good cause, he become a mentor to hundreds of his refugee brothers and sisters. This influence now extended well beyond those in his original caravan.

*****

At night, the cramped barracks were tight, but somehow the people managed to find just enough room to use the occasional surplus supply of raw potatoes. Rudimentary whiskey stills were easily fashioned by the versatile refugees to produce their own version of vodka. As quickly as the camp authorities could locate and dismantle one such distillery, another would suddenly pop up to satisfy the thriving underground demand. It reached the point at which small recreational stills became as frequent as a common coffee percolator. Over time, UNRRA simply learned to live with it.

The same was true of the comparatively steady food supply, even before the relief rations, which stimulated an underground of sorts with the German villagers struggling to survive outside the Wildflecken camp. Most of the German civilians survived on fewer calories than these so-called *stinking DPs*, as they were commonly referred to, and the Germans resented them for it.

When they weren't working, sleeping, or eating, the refugees were fishing. It was nothing to trim a tree branch and make a rudimentary hook of some kind. Cutting a hole in the ice to enjoy the moment to rest and talk lazily among their friends to while away some down time, enabled many to just mind their own business and stay out of trouble.

Typical of the Germans' intolerance toward the refugees, even this was met with resistance, unnecessarily making life even more difficult for the Poles. The German fishermen living in the villages near the camp, constantly patrolled the banks of the river looking for them, raising hell and making threats, demanding the Polish leave their riverbanks.

"Why don't you just go back to your precious Volga, where you all belong?" they would often holler menacingly.

Aside from fishing, these industrious people never sat idly by. For the farmers, however, many had great difficulty adjusting to their enforced idleness, especially during winter months when farming didn't preoccupy their time.

There were people here of every description; they were farmers, carpenters, bricklayers, and tradesmen, with some notable common attributes. They possessed a mighty work ethic, combined with relentless resolve and determination, never having yielded to their precarious circumstances.

30

THE VINDICTIVENESS OF THE REICH

WITHIN THIS MELTING POT OF COMMERCE AND SURVIVAL, the women also made significant contributions, primarily in the kitchens, the laundry and of course, in the duchess' administration division. Compiling and cross-checking multiple documents, filing and record keeping for each of the hundreds of thousands of processed refugees entering Wildflecken, pushed the limits of the mostly female clerical staff. The tedium of the work was constant; however, it was largely offset by the gratified feeling of accomplishment they felt, particularly when lost family members were reunited by the system.

These records would eventually survive the war to be preserved as the basis for most of the historical documentation available about this time and place in postwar Europe. Many of these select women, when given the opportunity to do so, excelled in this capacity. Among those who quickly distinguished herself was Julia.

The duchess was a truly remarkable woman who oversaw the entire Wildflecken camp. At fifty-three years of age, she spoke no fewer than five languages, most of them fluently, including impeccable French. It was very apparent she was an impressive woman of former aristocratic pretensions. Although kind-hearted and dedicated, the masses of refugees were intimidated by her strong bearing, as was Julia in the beginning.

To the contrary, Julia spoke Polish since her childhood, although now much more capable than before, she frequently defaulted to the sometimes unrefined and habitual body language and oral expressions of the poor village where she had been raised. These factors made her more approachable, and it soon became apparent the typical refugees related more naturally and openly with Julia than to the duchess and Deputy Director Hulme.

The relationship between Julia and the duchess was by no means a popularity contest. The duchess was delighted about Julia's accomplishments and the comparative ease she exhibited in carrying out her expanded duties. She quickly developed an instant fondness for Julia.

One evening as the administration building staff finally left for the day, the duchess and Kate would occasionally enjoy a few shots of whiskey to reflect upon their daily progress. Typically, it was the only chance either would have to speak uninterrupted. It was a rare opportunity to address strategic business matters few others in the camp were welcome to attend.

"Kate, since Julia has arrived in camp, I'm very pleased how well she has fit in with our staff, particularly in developing productive relationships with the refugees. Her work here has been outstanding but in far more significant ways than I had expected," the duchess observed. "I'm considering putting her talents to better use to work more closely with me as my personal assistant. What do you think of the idea?"

"I don't think you could have made a better choice. I too have noticed her accomplishments. She has an excellent work ethic and demonstrates a quick and organized mind. There's no question you need an assistant, and in my opinion, she is the best qualified for the responsibilities the position requires. I'm confident she will help to lighten your administrative load, Duchess, leaving more time and energy for you to handle the more important matters requiring your attention every day."

"Thank you, Kate. I'm delighted you agree. Oddly enough, though capable, her strengths are not in languages, but that's not where she's best suited. As you said, it's her unique organizational skills we need to better utilize. I trust her sound judgement to prioritize her tasks and quickly adapt to the constant interruptions which are an integral part of her job, don't you agree?"

"I do, Duchess. Working with her directly under your wing, I'm optimistic we can develop better communication from the refugees. They are tight lipped and untrusting souls, and for good reason; particularly relevant to what our Belgian nurse is proposing. It's a project for which Julia would be well-suited. The timing couldn't be better," Kate reassured her.

*****

Within a short period of time, Julia became an important extension of the duchess' team. Julia soon allocated many of these responsibilities to others in the department and together with another lead translator named Linette Etienne, they were successful in staving off the inevitable burn-out the duchess would suffer from time to time.

Any lengthy absence from the duchess' heavy workload would doubtless have serious negative impact for so many refugees and staff, all of whom continued to rely upon her. Without her decisive leadership, the refugees' eventual fates would have been much more uncertain.

Over the course of time, Julia and Linette gradually became more than fellow office staffers. The roads leading them to Wildflecken were as diverse as one's imaginations; Linette, from a time and place of opulence and opportunity, Julia from one of poverty and broken dreams. Between the two women, however, the broad spectrum of their individual circumstances was uncanny, but would not be disclosed between them, even as their friendship further developed.

Linette was an extraordinary person who carried out her tasks competently. Duchess immediately noted the quality of her fluency during translation sessions. Little did she or the other staffers in Wildflecken realize Linette's interpretations were expressed absent any unnecessary eloquence, thereby intentionally disguising her gift of extraordinary intelligence and refinement by the only means possible; offering nothing more than courteous but succinct responses whenever one was required, choosing to be capable, but not eloquent.

When not translating, she was a person of few words as well, creating another false impression she was introverted, insecure, or shy. Nothing could have been further from the truth.

The premeditated effort it required for Linette to continually suppress her scholarly bearing was stressful for her. Her intellectual predispositions were a powerful cornerstone of her God given talents, so natural to her from the sophisticated circles shaping a large part of her life, before and during her time with Abwehr.

There were always so many unspeakable secrets, many of which tormented her. If only she could have been comfortable within her own skin. Had she felt more at ease just being herself, she would certainly have been a formidable match for the duchess intellectually, without any intended or inadvertent pretentiousness whatsoever.

Julia knew none of this but as it was, she was in awe of Linette and could not even imagine how well she must express herself in French, her own native language according to her passport. Other than the duchess, no one was here to judge... certainly not Julia.

When Linette arrived at Wildflecken, she was determined to reveal nothing about her Jewish ancestry, nor her former social stature and horrific loss of her family. These tragic losses were commonplace for many people in the camps and yet, in Linette's circumstances, the magnitude of her secretive past forbade her to disclose anything even remotely connected to her services at Abwehr. Keeping her personal safety in mind, there was no necessity nor relevance for disclosure here.

Linette was haunted daily by the continuous, debilitating fear of being discovered by the Reich to be still alive. The vindictiveness of the Third Reich extended beyond the Fuhrer's grave. She, more than anyone, understood the legacy of retribution the Konto 5 account continued to finance against enemies of the Reich.

In every refugee camp, endless comprehensive lists of names were published and exchanged between camps to correlate family connections - a distinct advantage to anyone searching, but an equally distinct disadvantage for anyone hiding.

This single consideration alone, necessarily left Linette no opportunity to locate anyone, leaving nothing but guilt and regret about her self-imposed restricted ability to find Dietrich, Emilie, and Gertrude. The mystery of where they were and what had become of them haunted her continuously, gnawing deep within her.

Conversely, Julia's inherent intelligence and communication skills though well developed, were raw and unrefined when compared to those of her newfound companion. These skills were fully functional of course, but better suited for street-smart conversation, of a much lower class; closer to the gutter than a brass handrail. This relatability was a significant factor in making her far more approachable for most of the refugees in the camp.

As time passed, neither Julia nor Linette expended much effort to intrude on the other's privacy, revealing very little to one another about their past lives. They were both on equal footings here. Without aloofness or hesitation, they gradually accepted one another, genuinely and welcomingly.

No doubt they each correctly assumed the other had regrets and unresolved issues of their own, and both had good cause to keep quiet about it. Trust was very difficult to share, and even more difficult to earn.

What they did have in common were their quick insights and dedication to accomplishing whatever task they were assigned by the duchess. Inevitably over time, familiarity would gradually endear the two women to each other but in this instance, during their heavy daily workloads, those were considerations for other more appropriate times.

Late one evening however, after most of the staff had already retired for the day, the two ladies had a rare moment alone while clearing their dishes, when Linette initiated some casual conversation with Julia. It was only a matter of time.

"I have very much enjoyed working with you these past few months, Julia. We haven't been given much time to know more about each other outside of the office, perhaps because there is so precious little of it!"

They both smiled and chuckled a little. New ground had been broken, and Linette thoughtfully continued. "You have made my stay here a very worthwhile experience. It feels wonderful to be of some use again, and I thank you for that... truly."

"I feel the same, Linette. I was impressed with you from the moment we met. I admire your enthusiasm and your dedicated approach to everything you are assigned to do. I wanted to know more about you but thought better of asking."

"That was very considerate of you. The last thing I wanted was to become a topic of discussion. There is so much in my past I choose not to talk about."

"I completely understand. It's not my nature either. We all have our secrets, but I thought sooner or later you might open to me, whenever you were comfortable enough. I must say though, I am very much in awe of you, yet I don't know anything about you, whether you are married, have kids... nothing."

"I was married to a wonderful man but, I lost him to the war. My daughter lives in America with her cousins and there isn't a day I don't miss her terribly. My dear son, however, still resides somewhere in Berlin. I haven't seen either of them in years, but I know they were both safe and well looked after when I decided to leave Berlin. I only pray they continue to be."

Linette was not comfortable disclosing more of this topic and shifted the focus back to Julia. "But tell me about yourself, Julia. You have a husband here with you, do you not? I've heard you mention him in conversation with the duchess."

"Yes, I came here with Jan, his mother and his brother. We hope to marry someday soon and start a family once we learn when and where we will be living. Returning home to Wiory is not something we want to do. Regrettably there is nothing to return to now... but for one exception. May I...could... I'm sorry... I don't know who to ask, or how to say this." Linette sensed Julia's apprehensions about what she was trying to say and her eyes remained fixated on Julia's.

"Forgive me but, I am trying to locate Jan's oldest brother. His name is Mikael Szymanski. He was taken by the Germans in May 1940 from the family farm in Wiory. From what I'm told, he was strong as an ox and was likely sent to a hard labor camp. The family has never heard a word about what happened to him.

"I have already searched the records for Wildflecken and found nothing, but I could use your help using what little information I have to search the admittance records for the other camps under UNRRA's jurisdiction as well. In the remote chance he's still alive, or otherwise, any information concerning his whereabouts could at least help Jan's mother, Marianna, to help ease her mind. The difficulty we had about leaving Wiory was that if he did survive, he would never be able to find a trace of his family, other than finding his way to a collection center. It could be our only chance to locate him."

Linette did not hesitate to help. "Of course I will assist you, Julia!... in any way I can. It's a large part of what I do here. I must caution you though, that if I find anything in our records, the lists of refugees are always changing. If he was here and was repatriated, we won't have anything specific other than where he was taken. At the very least, you would know he was still alive."

"Thank you Linette. Your help means a great deal to us, but right now, only Jan and Josef know about this. We don't want to involve their mother, until we know something more, whether good or bad."

"You know I will keep you posted, regardless of what I find, but..." Linette cautioned, "I will need some time and I want to be thorough."

"Of course, Linette, I understand that we're all trying to make significant contributions in our time here. An even greater one for me now though, would be finding a resolution for Jan's family."

Julia continued drying her hands and closed the dish cabinets. "We had best return to our stations now. Thank you for sharing some time with me, Linette. I really enjoyed getting to know you better. I hope I didn't impose too much upon you."

The normal routines resumed, each day as full as the next. Although the work was gratifying, the endless lines of the needy and the vanquished made the work of the understaffed UNRRA team all the more remarkable to Julia and Linette, and other refugees who assisted as best they could. It was this mutual admiration driving the two friends to aspire to do even more.

*****

Ten days had passed since Julia appealed for help from Linette to locate Mikael. These were arduous days for Julia to be sure. Not wanting to pressure Linette, she trusted her judgement that it was a work in progress, yet the anxiety for news of Mikael's whereabouts continued to build. Finally, after another full day of work, Linette revealed what Julia feared the most.

"I apologize for not getting back sooner, Julia. I wanted to be thorough in my search, and when nothing was in our current system, I researched the listings of refugees that had been repatriated. I regret to say, I found no details whatsoever about Mikael specifically."

Julia, despite never having met Mikael, immediately teared up and her shoulders visibly began to slump. "This was my greatest fear... it must be difficult for you to tell me these things, Linette. Thank you for being forthright with me, as I knew you would." Julia had kept a tissue handy, knowing she would be shedding tears of joy... or tears of remorse.

Linette continued to seek closure for Julia, however painful the process. "I did not want to overlook any possible leads, hence my delay getting back to you." Linette paused a moment, trying to feel her way to find how best to reveal what she discovered. Julia was correct. It was a difficult situation for Linette.

"I learned some terrible things... if you really want to hear them." Julia nodded anxiously.

"Most of the imprisoned Poles in Torun about the middle of 1940 were teachers, farmers, and priests. They were sent to the Torun Fortress, where thousands of them were massacred or sent to Sachsenhausen and Dachau to suffer a similar fate. There were several mass graves discovered by the Allies where the Germans tried to cover evidence of their mass genocides.

"I can only assume he was lost with thousands of others. I feel terrible being the one to deliver this tragic news to you Julia, however while his death is not conclusive, I believe clinging to false hope can only prolong your pain; your family's and Marianna's."

Julia wiped her tears and after a few deep breaths, she sighed her acknowledgement of Linette's advice. She needed time to reconcile this matter, more for herself, at the very least. Telling the family was a burdensome task; one she could not face right now.

*****

As part of her daily responsibilities, Julia continued to meet with and document new arrivals, but most of her time was now spent dealing with many refugees who were not willing to be repatriated, appealing UNRRA's decision to send them home. Although the return of every refugee was within the original mandate of UNRRA, it became evident that lawlessness and humanitarian abuse in Poland were still too far out of control to risk it.

"These are life-changing decisions and by now both of you should understand these are not your decisions to make." The duchess had already been admonishing Julia and Linette of late.

"Both of you continue to be too sympathetic to our refugees. No one understands the personal experiences they have endured more than you two, having suffered them as well, but sometimes it becomes necessary to distance ourselves from them to become more objective about the grim reality in which we find ourselves. I know it is a thin line we dare not cross, but you must be determined to do it. Am I clear?"

"Yes, Duchess. Of course...we will do as you say." Hesitantly, Julia and Linette both nodded in agreement, at least for the moment.

Despite the duchess' warnings, this process was never intended to be a negotiation with the refugees, nevertheless, it was becoming more difficult to resist developing attachments to these good-natured people the longer they remained here.

One such individual was an elderly Ukrainian gentleman named Ivan. He had never married and had no children or surviving family. He was essentially a true, 71-year-old orphan of the war.

Julia was drawn to him instantly, not because of his plight, but more because of his warmth and kind nature. He was a former professor of agronomy at the Shevchenko University, in Kiev. An articulate and intelligent man, whose graciousness and helpful attitude emanated quite naturally and genuinely to the benefit of almost anyone he encountered.

"You are a welcome addition to our camp, Mr. Hudzik. My fiancé is a potato farmer from Wiory. I think you could teach him a thing or two about crop growing," Julia teased.

"Anything I can do to help. I am always available... and please, call me Ivan."

"That's so good of you, Ivan. Would you be willing to do that? I was only teasing, but as I think more about it, the idea may be a good one. I will arrange for you both to meet."

It was the beginning of a wonderful friendship. Jan made a point of taking some time to meet with Ivan, not thinking he could teach him anything about farming he didn't already know. Despite Jan's initial skepticism, however, Ivan's knowledge was profoundly interesting to Jan and Josef. Until this point, neither brother realized how much they could learn from him. Everyone had something to contribute. Ivan would certainly prove his merit, and in due course the family came to accept this very kind and likeable man into their family.

Of all the strangest things, from the time Julia had been orphaned, she tried in earnest to remain emotionally detached, especially after being reprimanded most recently by the duchess. Where was her cold objectivity she had always striven to maintain? Perhaps the difference being she was no longer solely preoccupied with basic survival, she thought.

One evening Jan, Josef, and Ivan were playing a friendly card game of *Tysiac* with Julia, Marianna, and Linette. About once a week the family would share some social time, enjoying a glass or two of schnapps with friends. Ivan had been likened to becoming their adoptive father by this time and was moved by their kindness toward him.

"Since we started working with the kitchen staff using your ideas, our crop yield has drawn the attention of the other farmers in camp. A few of them asked what we're doing they're not. I think the impact of what you taught us has proven itself, Ivan. Well done!" Jan held up his tin cup to toast him.

"If we had tried this ten years ago, we might still be farming in Wiory!" Josef sarcastically suggested.

"There's something to be said about working the earth, cultivating something nutritious from the dank smelling clay. Thank you all for believing in an old professor!" Ivan responded.

Julia thoughtfully suggested, "I just had a thought. What if we offer classes to teach others your ideas too? Many of our friends here have too much idle time... most of it is spent distilling whiskey."

"It can't hurt. In fact, farmers are in huge demand in every country offering to take in refugees. There are many people here who never farmed before. If they can pick up some experience farming in the camp, using Ivan's techniques, perhaps we could put farming skills on their immigration applications, and it will also help fill their bellies by doing it."

"I agree, Linette. Let's speak with Karl and Pierre tomorrow. I'm confident they'll approve of the idea... and who better to teach them than Ivan? What do you think, Ivan?"

"I'm excited by the idea! I've worked hard all my life, always doing something to keep myself productive. Teaching was my passion, and I would be grateful for the chance to do it again."

The following day, notices were posted, and word of mouth spread the news to every corner of the camp. By week's end, the Community Building was standing room only, as Ivan took to the task of teaching again. His basic premise was not just about doing hard work; it was more about doing smart work.

As with Jan and Josef, most farmers were skeptical at first, but became receptive to learning more. Often it seems, education opens our eyes to how much we don't know, if you have patience and the right attitude to listen. Ivan's natural manner was fatherly and humble, making people more open to his approach to new ideas.

In a short span of time, there wasn't a spare scrap of biodegradable waste that wasn't commandeered by the farming students to be mixed with manure and other specific natural vegetation; even limited amounts of wastepaper and cardboard were introduced to the compost, vastly improving aeration. Its addition increased the heat generated by the process and helped to absorb excess moisture, keeping within optimum guidelines explained by the professor.

Ivan stayed away from anything beyond the fundamentals, reminding himself many of the farming people learned their trade traditionally from their fathers, and their fathers before them. What he chose to educate them about was building upon what they had already known, by taking it to the next level.

He stressed the importance of establishing the proper correlation and best ratios of carbon, nitrogen, oxygen, and moisture to work with nature to reduce the time for natural biological activity to achieve optimum results. Many of these students had never set foot in a school before. For most, this was the only classroom they had ever known.

What made Ivan most effective was his keen desire to balance his extensive knowledge with a reasonable measure of common sense, and his students responded to him with enthusiasm. In no time the crops were showing noticeable signs of Ivan's fastidious direction and influence. For many, the exercise nourished the soul, as much as the soil. It certainly did so for Ivan.

31
THE WORLD IS WATCHING

It was a lovely and sunny April day in 1947, shortly after a lunch break, when Deputy Hulme requested Julia join her for a short walk along Kitchen Street. "We never seem to have time to get to know one another personally. I thought we could chat a bit before work totally consumes us again," she said. "The demands on us and the constant interruptions make it difficult to focus sometimes, don't you agree?"

"Yes, but you warned us it was a heavy workload, and I really enjoy what I do here, Deputy Hulme. In the beginning I felt a bit over-whelmed, but I am used to it now and it quickly passes. I don't have enough spare time to think much about it." Julia responded.

"When we are away from the others, please just call me Kate, Julia. I much prefer it."

"Thank you, Depu... I'm sorry... Kate. What is it you wish to talk to me about? Is everything alright?" Julia enquired.

"The duchess and I have been watching and listening to you as you interact with the refugees who are assigned to you." Julia became slightly on edge, and the deputy noticed her immediate apprehensions. "Relax, Julia. There is nothing wrong, and much to the contrary, we are very impressed with how well you carry out your responsibilities."

"Thank you, Ma'am... ahh, Kate." Julia fumbled, being a bit uncomfortable addressing the deputy in a more personal way.

"Over the past several months working together, we are impressed by your organizational skills and your keen ability to prioritize important aspects of your work. Your job involves many interruptions, often many that are extremely important, but I must say, Julia, you handle them well.

As the duchess told you earlier, your Polish and conversational German are among many of your assets, however, we believe your greatest asset is how well you relate so naturally with many of the refugees in camp."

"Thank you for saying so. I always try to do my best to help them."

"It's an important part of your job and you excel at it. The refugees are so accustomed to being denigrated and beaten down. Just think about it... in their experience, any documentation process they have already faced from the Germans was most likely designed to segregate them by race and religion.

"One can only imagine why they are reluctant to disclose their personal information to us. What is apparent to me though, is they appear to trust you." The deputy discreetly guided Julia by her elbow, and pointed to a small side street leading back to where they began. "Come, let's walk this way."

There were several children kicking a make-shift soccer ball between a few kiosks on the roadside and some were happily occupied rolling a bicycle tire back and forth. A bit of dust was stirred by the activity, the gentle breeze silently guiding it farther away from the peaceful scene, showing renewed evidence peace and the sounds of children's laughter could once again prevail.

As they walked on, Julia reflected for a moment about Kate's comment and resumed the conversation. "I remember how frightened I was the first time a German officer asked to see my papers. As I think back, I recall how violent the Germans were when they suspected someone of being a Jew. I've seen what they were capable of doing, Kate."

"Perhaps that's why you ask questions in such a natural and non-intimidating way. You are not reluctant to make eye contact with them and by doing these subtle things, you made the process much less threatening for them, making it more of a friendly conversation than an intimidating fact-finding interview."

Kate paused, allowing Julia to interact more openly with her. She was purposely trying to draw her out. In response, Julia hesitated thoughtfully, "I think it's because I know the pain and uncertainty they are feeling, after experiencing it first-hand myself."

Julia premeditatedly stopped herself from saying more. She had suppressed this softer side since she was orphaned, never believing it would reawaken within her. Still pausing, she was once again grappling to control her compassionate side. It was a fallible feeling she considered a weakness; one she could ill afford.

"Are you alright, Julia? Have I said something to upset you?" Kate asked anxiously. Another few seconds passed, while Julia began to re-engage.

"I'm not... I'm sorry Kate, my mind went blank for a moment. It's nothing... please continue. Where were we?"

"As I was about to say, because of the way you interact with the refugees, you have a more natural intuition about their mind set; a useful tool to better understand their most important preoccupations. It's a very good way to gain the trust they don't easily share. Because of this, I see them confide in you more naturally, even when you ask about sensitive health issues, especially the ones they're not comfortable telling us about."

By this time, the women had completed their circuitous route and were now approaching the main doors of the building. Kate stopped before stepping onto the wooden porch outside the entrance, casually nudging Julia off to the side. She spoke in a softer tone to keep other passersby from overhearing their conversation.

"Julia, there is an amazing woman working here I want you to meet. Not only is she a highly skilled medical officer, but she has also become a close friend of mine. Her name is Marie Louise Habets. With her guidance, Marie has agreed to initiate a plan the duchess and I have been considering. I would like you to become part of it as well. Rather than speak about it now, I want Marie to explain it to you herself."

"I would like that very much, although I don't understand why she would be interested in speaking to me, Kate," Julia humbly offered.

"I've also spoken to Linette about this matter too. She asked me the same question. When you both meet Marie, I think you will understand the reason for her interest in both of you. Let's talk again as soon as I can arrange a meeting, but for the time being, let's keep this conversation just among the three of us, would that be alright?"

"Of course..." Julia was taken aback somewhat, not having been previously aware Linette would also be involved, but she was delighted to hear of it. "I'm so pleased Linette will be joining us. Thank you so much for asking me to walk with you today, Kate. I really enjoyed our time together, especially on such a beautiful afternoon."

*****

Later that day, Kate informed Julia the meeting had been arranged in the duchess' office for the day after tomorrow. The timing was good for Julia since three hundred or so new arrivals needed to be processed the next day. It would be a fourteen-hour shift for many of the staff.

By the time it ended, signs of exhaustion and mental strain were written across everyone's face. As it happened, the short break with the deputy would be her only relaxing moments since the heavy workload. Neither Julia nor Linette had the time or energy to speak together before the day ended.

The following morning, after a sound and well-deserved sleep, Julia awoke and found herself reinvigorated about the exciting possibilities the day might offer. She skipped her usual breakfast with Jan, so there was only time for a few minutes of small talk with him. As soon as she finished her coffee, she briefly returned to her room to brush her hair and fastened a hairclip to keep it in place. She returned minutes later looking surprisingly attractive.

"You worked so late yesterday; we didn't have a chance to talk. I was hoping we could do so a bit this morning," Jan suggested.

"Yes, of course we can, but it will have to wait till later. So sorry, Jan."

Julia was still putting a few more bobby pins in her hair, not something she often bothered to do.

"Where are you off to in such a hurry?" he enquired, not being accustomed to her noticeable anxious manner.

"I have a meeting in the duchess' office today and I must not be late."

Jan took notice saying, "You look very pretty this morning, Jula. This must be an important meeting."

"It certainly is but I'll have to tell you about it later, I hope you understand."

Jan and Richard were still sipping coffee when Julia bent over Jan to give him a quick peck on the cheek and quickly rushed off to arrive at the administration building a few minutes early, as was her habit.

"I wonder what that's all about," Jan said rhetorically, not needing an answer from either of his friends. The men at the table appeared disinterested and just returned to quietly sip their coffees.

The dusty street was already alive with activity, and in mere seconds Julia was consumed by it. Along the way, she rode a wave of eager anticipation, mixed with a modest undercurrent of self-doubt.

She was determined to embrace the moment and not let her apprehensions wash away her slowly developing self-confidence.

Julia was greeted warmly by Beatrice who, without asking, poured a cup of the fresh coffee everyone always raved about. Only moments later, Linette rounded the corner in hopes of finding Julia already there.

"Good morning, Julia. I thought you might be here early today. We barely spoke yesterday. I hurried over thinking perhaps you might shed some light on what this meeting is about. The deputy didn't tell me very much, but I must say, she has piqued my interest." Linette was evidently as intrigued as Julia.

"Not much more than you, that's for certain, but the deputy wants to introduce us to a friend who is a doctor working closely with her on a new project being considered by UNRRA. I suppose we will both learn more about it shortly."

About five minutes passed during their brief exchange when a plainly dressed woman of slight stature but authoritative bearing approached from the main hallway. She tipped her head slightly and smiled at the ladies as she passed in front of them. She walked directly to the duchess' door as Beatrice courteously offered, "Good morning, Miss Habets. Your usual cup of tea this morning?"

"That would be lovely, Beatrice. Thank you." Whereupon she tapped firmly on the door and entered without waiting for a response, closing it behind her. This was evidently the woman Julia and Linette were about to meet. It was apparent her relationships with the duchess and her deputy were close indeed, thought Julia.

Before Julia finished her coffee, the office door reopened. It was Kate summoning Julia and Linette to join the others already inside. "Sorry to have kept you waiting, ladies. I appreciate you both being on time, especially after such a long day yesterday."

Unknown to Julia, this introduction would mark the beginning of a friendship destined to become a memorable one in her life.

None of what was to happen would have been possible, until she voluntarily took the first step to leave the safe confines of Henry's farm several years ago, to seek the unknown world somewhere on the winding pathway of her life. Were it not for her bold decision, she would not have found Father Breitkopf and Sister Helena, Father Francis and Jan, nor Lieutenant Colson, the Duchess and Kate.

Now, she and Linette were about to cross the threshold of new possibilities.

"Julia and Linette, I am pleased to introduce you to Marie Louise Habets, a dear friend and associate of Kate and myself. She is known affectionately by our staff as the *Belgian Nurse*.

Marie graciously rose and extended her hand warmly. "Julia and Linette; lovely to meet you both." Miss Habets had been a nun for several years before the war. Although no longer one, she remained extremely devout.

She took both ladies hands in hers, resting her right hand on top of both, hesitating to release them from her gentle grasp. Closing her eyes, she prayed inaudibly, reverently casting a calming air of reassurance that resonated with profound effect. It seemed she was silently inviting them to enter her world.

Without comment, everyone settled into their chairs for what would prove to be an informative and stimulating experience.

The duchess began. "When President Roosevelt appointed UNRRA to take on the burden of responsibility for the care and rehabilitation of millions of refugees, it was to rectify the mishandling of this massive undertaking by the military. In fairness, the task required skills the military were not trained to deliver in the first place – but the world has been watching.

"Now, we must demonstrate by our actions and results, that the trust the United Nations has bestowed on us is well founded. If we fail to do so, it will be extremely difficult to restore public confidence in our relief efforts, without which global funding will be impossible to obtain. As a direct consequence, our camps will be forced to close, leaving these people with nowhere to go."

Kate spoke in support of the duchess' opening comments. "We have already been forced to acknowledge repatriation has been an abysmal failure. Despite our best efforts and intentions, many of the refugees who were repatriated were treated like traitors and were imprisoned in Russian Gulags, tortured, and often killed. Many Poles were accused of supporting the Polish Underground and the Warsaw Uprising. Based upon largely unfounded suspicions, they too were arrested, and many of their families executed."

"Oh, dear Lord!" Linette exclaimed, holding her head sorrowfully in her hands, and covering her eyes in deepening anguish. Offering consolation, Julia placed her hand softly on Linette's shoulder, not uttering a word.

Kate continued after a brief pause. "Europe is simply not ready to accept these people. As more refugees continue to come to us out of sheer desperation, it has caused our camps to become even more overcrowded. I know it is unpleasant to hear these things, but unfortunately, these are the irrefutable facts."

There was a slight pause when Kate deferred to Marie to expand her perspective on the matter.

"Thank you, Kate. Ladies, every day the refugees come to us afflicted with a vast array of diseases and infections, often caused by malnutrition, sleep deprivation, over-powering stress... all of which leave them susceptible to many viruses and contagious diseases. The ones of greatest concern have been typhus, smallpox, and tuberculosis. These transmittable diseases are my specific areas of expertise. To a large extent, it is why I am here.

"There are new antibiotics, such as penicillin, to treat these diseases but unfortunately our needs are far greater than our supply. Simply put, we must do all we can to identify the symptoms quickly and efficiently to isolate those diagnosed with infections to keep the diseases from spreading. It is in the best interest of everyone in camp, both refugees as well as UNRRA workers. The severe overcrowding in such cramped quarters makes our camps breeding grounds for many contagious diseases.

"As we screen our refugees more closely, it has become increasingly apparent many are afraid to confess their various symptoms for fear of being ostracized from the others, or potentially being sent away from the camp to fend for themselves. It's not something we would ever do, but in some cases, if we don't quarantine the sick, we could quickly infect everyone here.

"Initially, typhus and tuberculosis were our biggest concerns but as we go forward, I can soon teach you what symptoms to look for. As I just said, early identification is vital to keep these infections under control.

"As Kate has already told you, our refugees have been through hell, as have both of you I understand. It is difficult enough to gain their trust and confidence about disclosing the details of their past; where they come from; who their family and friends are; what they did during the war, what is their race, religion, etcetera. Lord only knows these people have been questioned, interrogated, separated, and abused; subjected to the whims of German racial persecution.

"That information, while important to helping us reunite lost family members, is mostly confidential, hence when they answer our questions, they do so reluctantly at best. Often, they give us evasive or false information, which makes our jobs even more difficult."

"What is it you are asking us to do Marie? I'm sorry, but I am still confused," Julia asked.

"Julia and Linette, in recent months, you have both demonstrated a strong aptitude for speaking with the refugees in a way that encourages them to confide their trust in you. Although you come from different backgrounds, you have this amazing ability to relate to them on their own level, something many of the UNRRA people cannot easily achieve.

"None of our UNRRA staff are German or Polish. We are primarily from Britain, Sweden, Belgium, and France, and frankly the refugees don't think we are capable of fully understanding their predicament. Either they disrespect us, or we intimidate them."

Marie paused for a moment to allow Kate to press on, believing any questions would be answered to their satisfaction in due course, however she had some important points needing to be addressed first.

"As you both know, we have so few doctors in our camp, and we must use their time wisely. Under Marie's supervision, from this point forward, we want both of you to focus only on pre-screening health issues. Neither of you will continue doing the standard admission process. It's too time consuming and unproductive compared to what you can achieve pre-screening for contagious diseases. It is our opinion your time and talents can be put to greater advantage.

"Others will have to handle the customary workload, at least until we can monitor the spread of disease more accurately. It's the first step to bringing it under better control. It won't be easy, because sometimes even the infected people don't think their symptoms are anything more than a head cold, or the flu, until it becomes something more serious.

"The sooner you identify potential symptoms, the sooner our doctors can confirm the infections and begin necessary treatments. Let's at least catch the obvious cases quickly. I have already requisitioned the additional medications we will need, and Duchess has agreed to set up a separate quarantine building for this specific purpose."

"Marie, you said something earlier about typhus and tuberculosis. You stated they *were your greatest concerns.* Are they no longer? There must be something else you haven't told us."

Marie paused momentarily to sip her tea and gather her thoughts before proceeding further, when Duchess responded to Linette's insightful comment. "You never miss a detail, do you Linette? This is precisely why you and Julia are here." Everyone smiled to acknowledge Duchess' well-meaning compliment. "Marie, please continue."

"That is a very astute observation, Linette, and one I want to address now. I chose my words carefully and I'm pleased you caught it. It is the grave matter of the serious epidemic of venereal disease, which has now become our number one concern. For various reasons, we must tread carefully here. This is a delicate issue needing to be dealt with aggressively, but sensitively as well. Let me explain.

"Neither of you are doctors, nor can we teach you to become one. But we can teach you to look for visible symptoms of some of these conditions to help you identify the people already infected. If you continue to relate well with the refugees, they may come to confide in you about more personal problems which aren't as visibly apparent.

"With regard to VD, the issue is fraught with many complex issues. Please understand that often the shame many women feel about this disease is so debilitating they cannot disclose it to their own spouses, so why would they confide in us? The dilemma we are facing demands we prioritize the general good of the group over individual freedoms, regardless of the shame associated with it. By doing so, we will face resistance from them, to be sure."

Kate deftly added, "We believe many refugees will see this as an intimate intrusion that should be off limits to us. They will interpret our meddling as an attempt by us to regulate private sexual activity, which of course we are not... nevertheless, *that* is what they will perceive. The moral stigma associated with an infection is even more difficult to irradicate than the disease itself."

Julia, never one to hold back her insightful questions, asked, "Can you please explain in more detail what you just said? I need to know more about this to better understand what we are dealing with."

"Of course, Julia," Marie continued. "Many of the women, through no fault of their own, were raped by the Russians, or perhaps even provided sex on occasion for money to help feed their families, their sick and ailing parents, raising their children alone, without their husbands.

"Furthermore, the military are extremely concerned about the impact of troops becoming infected and, to be direct, they consider the women in the DP camps to be the primary cause of spreading the disease. Since last September, the UN is being pressured by the health division of the US refugee zone to make physical examinations of the women compulsory."

A general pall fell over the room. The silence was deafening.

At the very mention of the Russian rapes, Linette anguished visibly and shifted herself nervously in her chair, recalling her own confrontation with Russian rapists. Her mind flashed back to the moment she stood on the cusp of an horrific and brutal violation. It haunted her still.

Without understanding the basis behind Linette's sudden reaction, Marie saw her visceral response and discreetly shifted the focus of her discussion saying, "Excuse me for a moment, but I need to top up my tea. I'm really quite parched this morning."

There was a brief, but awkward pause, one Linette needed to regather herself. She righted herself as she struggled to break free from the horror of the terrible moment and prepared to mentally re-engage.

"What you... I'm sorry, ahh..." Her eyes blinked a few times in rapid succession, and she shook her head ever so slightly, trying bravely to clear her mind.

"Are you alright, Linette?" Julia asked. "Let me get you some water, dear."

"Yes, I'm so sorry... umm... please forgive me." Linette gratefully accepted the glass of water, taking a few silent sips with her eyes closed. "Thank you for your patience. Please continue, I'm... I'm fine now."

"Are you sure you are alright, dear? Perhaps we should take a short break?" Kate gently enquired.

"No... no but thank you, Kate. That's very thoughtful of you, but I really want to continue."

"Marie, if I may, why are the military only focusing on the women spreading venereal disease? What about the men? Aren't they equally responsible, if not more so?" Linette, being as direct as Julia, knew from personal experience how sensitive this subject could be.

"That's an important point, Linette. We agree with you absolutely. It presents yet another reason we don't want the military to intervene.

If screening and testing are going to be initiated here, I assure you, the men will not be exempt. We can only reduce the rate of infections by testing everyone, including the men."

"Marie, do we have to be worried for ourselves and... and the others who are working in close contact with the refugees?" Julia enquired.

"Regarding typhus and tuberculosis, we must all be alerted to keeping infections from spreading, especially among our staff. There are not enough of us working here as it is, and it will be even harder if any of us need to be quarantined," Marie responded definitively.

"This may sound obvious but, could we teach the refugees how to practice safer sexual habits? We can't simply tell them to abstain from sex, but can we provide them with condoms, for example. I'm sure that would help immensely."

"Yes, Linette. I agree. These are helpful suggestions, and they would help our people understand the seriousness of our strategy. The more pro-active we are, the sooner they will comply. The last thing we want is to have the military make the physical examinations mandatory. We believe our logic is sound.

"In the months ahead, the analysis of our study should measure the impact of our strategy to contain the spread of the infections. Our intention is to use this feedback to confirm we are moving in the right direction, and potentially serve as a model for other camps with similar problems."

"We are anxious to get started, Marie. If you can teach us what we need to know..." Julia paused to look at Linette. Now fully composed, she nodded to affirm her agreement, "... we would feel more confident we can make a positive difference within the camp, for everyone involved." Julia reasoned. "We are proud to be part of your project. Thank you for this opportunity." Julia placed her hand on Linette's as a sign of their solidarity. "We will not disappoint you."

Duchess rose as an indication she, Kate, and Marie had accomplished what needed to be done. "I'm so pleased you are ready to accept new challenges. Somehow, we all knew you would. Marie has already worked out an itinerary to get you both up to speed.

"As always, if you have any problems or reservations, you can come to us anytime. Kate will keep me posted on our progress. Now I must focus on other matters needing my attention too. Please excuse me, as I must be off to another meeting."

*****

In the ensuing days, Julia and Linette worked tirelessly with Marie, who personally tutored them on symptoms often caused by the infestation of lice, mites, and small rodents; common parasites to which the refugees were constantly exposed. Among the textbooks they shared, Marie was well equipped with photographs, not only of the typical symptoms, but more shocking, was visual evidence of the profound lethal consequences if they remained untreated.

As Julia learned more, she considered herself fortunate to have been isolated by circumstances, undoubtedly having protected her from other people during many of the lonely and desperate months of her journey before she found Henry. It occurred to her it was better she never knew the unseen dangers of living in the wild and desecrated ruins framing her life during those frantic times.

As they studied the material, Julia exclaimed, "My goodness! The symptoms of tuberculosis describe almost everyone entering our camp! People coughing and fatigued, suffering fevers and weight loss; I thought these were rites of passage," Julia remarked; to which both Linette and Marie began to giggle embarrassingly.

No one was laughing at the precariousness of the refugees, but more at the way Julia had expressed the idea. Either way, it was moments such as these that bound them together in a deeper and more personal way, reminding them they were still only human after all.

"You aren't far from the truth, Julia. If we were working in a public hospital in a civilized world, the signs of disease would be self-evident, but here, in these circumstances, it is more difficult to distinguish. You must try grouping the symptoms by discarding the ones these people all share when they arrive.

"For example, literally everyone coming here is emaciated, starving, and exhausted; but not everyone has persistent fever and chest pain, with complete loss of appetite. Do you understand what I'm trying to say?"

"Yes, I think so. Soon after we arrived here, everyone was deloused, whether we had lice or not. But no one asked us about these specific conditions. I suppose we can only identify some of the more obvious ones, is that what you're saying?"

"Precisely! After we interview twenty or thirty families together, you will start to become more adept at the process. I understand we are asking a great deal from you both, but I am confident you have the intelligence to sort this out as your experience grows."

*****

Marie was correct about her assessment of the ladies' work. They learned quickly and absorbed the material well enough to make progress with what was expected of them. Despite Marie's pleasant and understated demeanor, however, Julia and Linette both noticed they were far less intimidating to the refugees when Marie remained in the background. Working independently with the refugees let their natural communication skills shine once again, which was what had distinguished them in the first place.

Over the next six weeks, they reviewed their assessments with Marie at the end of each shift, and other staff members carefully collated the statistical information. The two doctors in the camp found a strikingly higher incidence of infections among the referred refugees than before the focused pre-screening by Julia and Linette, an indication their strategic plan was highly effective.

By September of that year, chief medical officers of the US zone convened a conference and determined "*the low incidence of V.D. among DPs is definitely and clearly proved.*" (L. Haushofer) This statistical conclusion by UNRRA, although not totally supported, was a definitive first step successfully supporting their strong belief in opposition to military directives against DP camp initiatives.

Horror stories abounded in other camps, specifically in the French zone. Several conflicts quickly got out of hand and often became unmanageable.

In an extreme case, police forcibly loaded women onto trucks destined for the hospital. When several of them refused the order, one doctor shouted aggressively at the women and accused them of turning the camp into a whorehouse by not complying with compulsory examinations and treatment. He threatened to use a machine gun to accomplish the task. Some of the women steadfastly refused to be examined against their will and fled the camp.

Many such events demonstrated the depths of passionate but conflicting positions between UNRRA staffers and the refugees in their care. Fortunately, most of these events were averted in Wildflecken.

These were turbulent times and passions ran deeply throughout the camps about the continuous abusive treatment of refugee women, specifically about the sensitive controversy concerning VD. It was an ongoing battle of wills that constantly tried to find balance between the struggle for humanitarian decency and the false perception refugees were a threat to public health.

This was not a qualification any countries offering immigration to refugees wanted to hear. The prior mishandling of this issue had significantly increased public opposition to the immigration process. As a result of establishing reliable statistical facts, false public impressions began to be rectified, and displaced persons were finally becoming recognized *"as members of an international community:* to be accorded their *"rightful claim to dignity and just treatment"*. (L. Haushofer) It was a significant first step.

*****

By 1947, the funding of the refugee relief effort had been exhausted and UNRRA was downsized again, and financially restructured into what became the International Refugee Organization (IRO).

About this time, they were still responsible for 643,000 displaced people. It would now be funded by only fifteen of the original thirty-nine supporting nations. This change was intended to be just the first phase of dissolution, which wisely retained most of the original, field tested UNRRA staff, as well as many unfunded volunteers. Among this group were Julia and Linette.

At the time of the reorganization, the Allied plan for refugee repatriation to their original homeland had to be rethought. An invisible breaking point had been reached, as fewer and fewer refugees were willing to return home. It was evident the rest of the western world would have to step up their efforts and extend their arms to these so-called *undesirables*.

32
WE ARE NOT DESPERATE HOOLIGANS!

"JULIA, PLEASE INFORM LINETTE I NEED YOU BOTH TO attend a meeting later this morning at 11:00 sharp. I have several difficult decisions to announce, and I will require strong support from the two of you."

"Certainly, Duchess. We have both been compiling the summaries of our status reports for your review. And Madame Duchess, you always have our confidence and support."

Within the next two hours, the division heads, among them Julia and Linette, assembled before the duchess. Unknown to everyone except the duchess was President Harry S. Truman's decision to send his own ambassador to witness what was about to unfold. He answered directly to the Secretary of State, General George C. Marshall.

As customary, the duchess wasted little time with unnecessary preamble and addressed the business at hand.

"The original intention of repatriating our refugees to their homes is no longer viable. This *Grand Experiment* has failed badly despite our best intentions, and our dedicated efforts to assist these people.

"It has now become a matter of grave concern for the dangerous and perilous conditions existing in post war Europe which have provided little to no chance for our refugees to re-establish the lives they had once known," explained the duchess. "Therefore, until further alternatives are announced… we will no longer force the refugees to return to their homelands."

"Yes! Thank the Lord above!" someone shouted. Another yelled support, followed by several others. The duchess displayed an approving smile she hadn't shown in far too long, and re-emphasized in no uncertain terms, "No one will be forcibly taken from our camp!"

Several people raised their arms in jubilation and hugged those close to them. Profound relief among the strong brotherhood of the IRO staff was evidenced by the mixture of smiles and compelling tears of happiness. The entire room was buzzing with scattered but indiscernible conversations.

This matter had been a major controversial issue for months on end and many in attendance collectively drew deep breaths, justifiably releasing their pent-up frustrations. Julia and Linette were as thankful as anyone, but as always, they had already done the math. There was still some serious trepidation for what was yet to be announced.

Although the positive reaction was initially one of general relief, as the moments passed, an air of anxious uncertainty began to emerge among several others preparing for another shoe to drop. The duchess knew she could not hold back the rest of her announcements and nodded to Pierre to hush the crowd so she could resume speaking.

"Tomorrow, a train will be delivering another 460 people to our gates..." She paused. "It will be the final one we can possibly admit to our camp... There will be no exceptions."

Now the pendulum had swung fully back. Her address was quickly drowned out by renewed calls of protest and more expressions of frustration. It was not the news they wanted to hear.

"This is not right!"

"Do they really expect us to leave them to the devil?"

"We must do something Duchess!"

A gasp of shock and disbelief conveyed their extreme but understandable shift of mood, now one of bleak pathos. Agitated but muffled conversations were re-ignited. UNRRA staff were logically well aware that ceasing repatriation, together with the growing financial pressure on international funding, had predetermined the entry of new refugees into the camps would be impossible to continue. Duchess allowed the disruption for only a short time, as much for her own benefit as for those she was addressing.

"Please, let me finish what I have to say! ...

The duchess paused and revisited her prepared announcement. In those few tense seconds, she decided to extemporaneously go off script. Gathering herself, she drew a deep breath. "Two years ago, just before his death, FDR prophesied that, *"As in most of the complex and difficult things in life, nations will learn to work together only by actually working together."* (K. Hulme)

"With this original intent in mind, it is no longer the time to test our resolve but rather, to make it become fully realized. Our camps were never intended to be permanent homes, and having now officially accepted the failure of repatriation, the United Nations need to find other more viable options.

"We cannot proceed alone to do what must be done. Our relief effort desperately needs strong and immediate international support. I'm not just speaking about continued funding; something much more has been missing. The IRO fully supports the efforts of the United Nations to work with the international community to open their hearts, their minds, and their doorways of genuine welcome."

The impassioned spontaneous delivery of her announcement was intended by her to touch the heart and soul of the ambassador himself. It also served to remind him, in no uncertain terms, the sometimes-forgotten awareness these were not simply numbers and statistical data... these were real families and deserving people, who simply could not be abandoned.

When the duchess had finished, the IRO directors and staff's open displays of compassion had a profound effect on President Truman's emissary, as he stepped to the microphone. "Madame Duchess, I am deeply touched by the heartfelt dedication of you and your extraordinary team of dedicated professionals. The passion you all feel toward the desperate people in your care is overwhelming.

"While the decision will not be mine alone, I can promise you I stand firmly in your corner, and I pledge to do my utmost to convey your message directly to the Secretary of State. I will aspire to do so with the same degree of empathy you have demonstrated here today.

"To all of you who have dedicated yourselves so tirelessly to this noble humanitarian effort, I thank you. The American people will not disappoint you."

Pierre did his best to rally the gathering to show their support for his pledge to convey their message directly to President Truman's executive staff. He loudly shouted, *"Here, here!"* and the room broke into another round of enthusiastic applause.

In the following weeks of uncertainty and doubt, discussions and actions among staff reconfirmed their steadfast determination to remain committed to maintaining the high degree of care which they had consistently delivered.

Their dedication was noted by the directors, but so was the fragile confidence of the refugees. It was essential the IRO maintain a steady and unaltered course each day, as they patiently awaited news from the international community, which thankfully acknowledged repatriation would no longer be enforced. This was a major breakthrough announced by the U.S. Secretary of State. Unfortunately, this decision was not fully understood by the majority of refugees.

*****

Every day the gates remained closed to more refugees appealing for help, it was gut-wrenching to turn them away. Despite these families finding their own way to Wildflecken, they were regrettably redirected to nearby Wurzburg to try and find some way of becoming self-supporting until other alternatives may become available in the impoverished depths of the German economy. Outside of this camp, who would offer a Pole a job a German needed so desperately? For many, it was an impossible prospect.

Many shunned refugees simply dropped to their knees, crying in despair, emotionally broken, and beaten by circumstances beyond their control. Others, however, became frustrated, angry, and occasionally, violent. When these incidents flared up, armed military police were called upon to maintain order and protect those inside the camp.

Delivering news of this grim reality was an unspeakably difficult task for many IRO field staffers. In confidence, many admitted that in their quiet reflective moments of privacy they would occasionally break down, emotionally sobbing with frustration after tedious, exhausting days of heartfelt rejection of entire families left outside the gates with nowhere to turn. Even Julia was one such affected staffer.

Wiping her already moistening eyes, she was noticed by Linette at the end of another trying day.

"Please help me find something positive to draw from this, Linette. It was difficult enough to have to anguish over who must go, and who may stay. I remain so very concerned about what will happen to these people... and to ourselves! There appears to be nowhere else to go."

"I agree with you, Julia. If there is any measure of common sense and compassion still remaining, none of us will be abandoned. These are decent and hardworking people who have much to contribute, if only some new doors will open for them.

"My only advice is what you once told me. Just keep working as hard as we can. We do our jobs well, and the duchess has come to depend on us. I still believe she was correct in saying what she believes and expressed herself well on behalf of us all."

"You are right, Linette. I'm sorry for taking all this so personally, but sometimes I guess I need a little reassurance."

"There is nothing to apologize for. Remember, we are only human."

Somehow, people had always found a way to survive, no matter what the circumstances. Whether by readjusting to further reductions of rationing, or squeezing a few more refugees into overcrowded rooms, it was becoming more apparent with every passing day *"that freedom was rationed too. There just wasn't enough of it to go around.* (K. Hulme)

An integral part of the duchess' management style was to welcome feedback from her front-line leaders. One of her most reliable ways to measure prevailing opinions from the refugees was through the strong influences of both Jan and his brother Josef, particularly among the men. They trusted Jan and Josef to treat them fairly and honestly and, much like Julia, they often confided in them too.

Depending upon the nature of the problem, during after-hours Jan and Josef would discuss relevant issues with Julia, the idea being to let her ultimately decide if an issue was worthy of the duchess' attention. On rare situations, they would interact directly with her. Their discretion was always found to be trustworthy.

Throughout their relationship, Jan and Julia maintained their mutual trust in one another. When it had to be called upon, Julia was always careful to limit what she could discuss with Jan, especially regarding confidential information disclosed to Julia from the duchess and Kate. To do otherwise would compromise her privileged and sometimes confidential relationships within her current office responsibilities. Her discretions had never been called into question and she fully intended to keep it that way.

The respect for one another's influence went both ways. On rare occasions, however, Jan spoke with Julia discreetly, advising her of any noteworthy discontent among the refugees, particularly so if it had the potential to become a major issue. He did so with an appropriate measure of confidentiality to maintain his trusted and valued leadership role, not only among those from his own blockhouse, but numerous others throughout the camp as well. Sometimes, it was a difficult balancing act.

*****

"Good afternoon, ladies. Is there any coffee left? I could use a strong cup about now. I'm happy I found you both alone for a moment. Do you mind if I intrude?"

"Of course not. Please sit, Duchess... let me make you a fresh cup," Julia offered.

"That would be lovely dear. I am informed there is trouble brewing among the blockhouses. It has come from a very reliable source." As she said this, she looked over the rims of her reading glasses to look directly into Julia's eyes, indicating the information had been relayed to her directly from Jan.

"Recently, there have been signs of confusion and uncertainty among some of the more outspoken refugees. It seems to stem from their perception there has been no progress by the international community to help them. We have all anticipated some tempers may boil over, but there appear to be several troublemakers with their own agenda. It appears now may be the time to clarify their misunderstandings."

"We sense it too!" confided Linette. "Very few seem willing to cooperate with the proposed Nationality screening. They interpret the process as another giant step to force them out of the camp, another step closer to the door. They are becoming frightened and angry. We fear for the worst, Duchess!"

In response, the duchess proceeded to inform the two friends, "Pierre convened a meeting of the block leaders yesterday and saw the same reaction. Four Polish liaison officers will be reporting to our camp tomorrow to begin the screening for eligibility for emigration elsewhere. These officers seem unwilling to heed our warning.

We cannot continue to ignore the anger and frustration simmering among our people. I understand it's a similar situation across all the camps."

She sipped her freshly brewed coffee appreciatively and continued in a more hushed tone, while leaning in a little closer to the table. "We anticipate some trouble tomorrow, so we must be on our toes, do you understand? Cooler heads must prevail.

"I ask you to keep this discussion just among us for the time being. I don't wish to alarm anyone, but we must not allow things to get out of control. Pierre has already warned the local constabulary to prepare themselves if the worst comes to happen. I suggest we all get a good night's sleep. We are going to need it! Good night, ladies."

Julia and Linette were speechless and stared inquisitively at each other until the duchess closed the door behind her. "I've never seen her give such an advanced warning before. Clearly, she is expecting something serious," Julia cautioned.

"I agree but as always, we should trust her judgment. I need to get to bed myself. Whatever happens tomorrow will be dealt with accordingly. Sleep well Julia."

*****

The following morning one could sense the tension permeating throughout the camp. Nervous agitation was already spreading throughout the blockhouses and groups of people were huddled nervously in secretive conversations. It prefaced the anticipated arrival of the Polish liaison officers expected to attend the Committee Building meeting.

The duchess and Kate were the lead directors trying to oversee the National screening fiasco, as the duchess aptly referred to it, which she feared could provoke serious trouble. She had not experienced any personal animosity against herself to date and believed it would not be a problem on this day either.

She was always clear and definitive about her ongoing differences with the higher authorities in defense of her refugees. This was never an issue to be questioned and as always, she demonstrated no fear for her personal safety.

The next morning as her car approached the area, the streets around the Community Building were teeming with protesters. More than a thousand people had amassed in the center of town, completely blocking the entrance to the main building. The duchess quickly instructed Pierre to park away from the crowd to permit her to walk directly through them. Despite his protestations for her safety, she insisted upon doing so, with nary a hint of hesitation.

When her car came to a full stop a short distance from the crowd, Pierre continued to implore her, "Ma'am, this is not safe for you. We've never seen this situation before, and we cannot be certain about what may happen here. If you insist upon going out there, let me walk beside you, at the very least."

"I'll be damned if the hooligans think they can intimidate me. We will not give in to them, do you understand me? I don't want to endanger you, Pierre. I'll be fine, so please don't argue with me." She proceeded to open the rear door and stepped outside. Pierre immediately stepped out as well. *"Please, Duchess!"*

"Very well then, if you must." Pierre knew how hard-headed this incredible woman could become. She was right... this was no time to argue. When she boldly stepped outside and came into view, the crowd commenced to chant encouragingly, *"Duchess! Duchess! Duchess!"*

It was an intimidating demonstration of the crowd's frustration but as she continued walking, the loyal and appreciative refugees among the crowd spontaneously shuffled tighter together to provide Duchess clear passage to the overloaded wooden porch. Pierre did not let go of her upper arm, holding his other arm in front of him to shield her protectively from goodness knows what.

The door was already fully opened and remained so because of the mass of people pressing in on the interior of the room. Two of the troublemakers made a futile attempt to block her way, espousing their communist ideals in a belligerent and derogatory manner.

Some shoving and pushing ensued but the duchess' supportive people quickly defused the confrontation, enabling this grand lady to represent them in hope of restoring and maintaining a dignified resolution on their behalf.

Predictably, however, there were several more vocal and aggressive communists among the crowd, continuing to stir up trouble. Thankfully, they were among the minority. However, when the local police arrived on the scene escorting the Polish liaison officers, the situation worsened. Thankfully, the duchess was already safely secured inside the building when all hell broke loose outside.

When the Polish liaison officers began to exit their vehicle, they were about to get a rude awakening. The issues within the camp were indeed more serious than they had anticipated. The car was immediately rushed by a solid wall of angry protesters, but this time many of them were not communists.

The increasing physicality of the communist supporters pushing and shoving everyone in their path, inflamed more outbursts of aggression and chaos. It was this moment at which the liaison officers had seen enough and began to seriously fear for their safety. This was not a situation they were prepared to endure any longer. The message had been received all too clearly now. They were not welcome here.

Only two of the four officers had begun exiting their polished black sedan bearing the golden Polish insignias. It was quickly surrounded by a wave of humanity and became jostled and violently rocked from side to side.

The officers valiantly struggled to reverse ground to get back into the car, trying fearfully to tear themselves from the grasp of the rioters. Their hats were knocked off and the badges on their decorative epaulettes were torn away. The shouting and threatening gestures were on the very edge of a full-scale riot, a critical time when something horrific could be only seconds away. Those in the car were hanging on to their comrades for dear life.

Finally, with their uniforms torn and themselves somewhat bloodied and disheveled, the doors were slammed behind them and were quickly locked. Their obvious desperation to flee encouraged the communist rioters to attack the car by smashing the windows, scattering broken glass over the passengers inside.

The driver immediately put the car into gear and stepped firmly on the accelerator to drive through anyone foolish enough to challenge the car's intended path. Within seconds, clouds of billowing dust filled the hot summer air, blinding the rioters in a cloak of confusion.

The police officers already present immediately called for back-up support and used their Billy-clubs with great affect to break apart numerous scuffles and fisticuffs throughout the still agitated crowd. Several arrests were made, most of which involved many of the communist factions who had instigated the violent outburst.

Safely inside the Community Building, the duchess and her selected staff overcame the din of concerned conversations of the refugees when a still flustered Pierre grabbed the microphone to restore order.

"Quiet down! ... Quiet down! Madame Duchess wishes to speak."

In an abnormally firm tone, she took immediate control. "You all have known me to be fair, reasonable, and most of all, honest with you... always! This nonsense outside will not be tolerated! ... I expect... no... *I demand more of you!*

"The actions of this day will only serve to hurt our cause. What you have witnessed is precisely what the international community fears the most... that we are a group of desperate hooligans with nothing to offer them. We are better than that, are we not?"

The capacity crowd inside, numbering about a hundred and forty people, buzzed with robust conversation, most of which was incomprehensible, but the raising of their fists and expressions of affirmation were predominantly evident among them. They were very much on side with the duchess' plea and visibly angry with the provocative interference of the communists outside who had initiated the disturbance. They had the loudest voices but did not speak for the vast majority.

"Please settle down... let me continue! We have repeatedly said that none of you will be repatriated to your homeland unless it is your own desire to do so. We do have a much better alternative ... *emigration!* You have my word on it!

"It is your responsibility, as well as that of my staff, to maintain order and respect for the western authorities or they may not accept you and your families. It is time to put our best foot forward, not our worst."

*****

Numerous meetings of smaller groups were immediately arranged in the days ahead to again clarify and reassure the frightened refugees the Nationality Screening was merely to validate each ethnicity, *not for repatriation, but for emigration.* It varied from one nationality to another, dependent upon the extent to which infrastructure and law and order had been restored in various parts of Europe. Poland, for example, was deemed entirely not repatriable.

News of the incident inside Wildflecken was reported in global newspapers but was mostly downplayed as nothing more than refugee discontent. The international press reported similar outbreaks in many other refugee camps as well, not serving the best interests of the refugees.

The gravity and scope of the matter, however, was accurately reported to the Secretary of State, precisely as the duchess had hoped. Her impassioned plea had significant impact, thanks in large part to the ambassador's report and in late 1947, Belgium became the first and only place of refuge offering to assist, by opening its doors for the first 20,000 immigrants.

The motivation behind this gesture was only partially driven by its humanitarian nature, but more so by the economic advantages to Belgium's coal mining operations. Only the Belgians quickly realized this was a rich resource of cheap skilled labor, and they were willing to take the prime candidates from the huge pool of applicants.

During this time, few western countries stepped up to offer more than token gestures of welcoming acceptance; certainly, no meaningful numbers of immigrants were being seriously considered by any of them. Global opinions were heavily biased against the assimilation of homeless refugees, with the apparent impression being they had little to nothing to offer in return.

The greatest fear though was the crushing uncertainty of the future of the IRO and the potential closing of more refugee camps. There were absolutely no assurances given to address the continuing state of dependency of the families left behind. Making the correct decision must have been agonizing for so many.

Despite these continuing concerns, the faces of the well-muscled young men who were ultimately selected, spoke volumes. Beaming smiles were everywhere, and not just from the proud families. The IRO staff felt their work was finally validated, and they too joined in the celebrations. Even those who were not selected, developed a deeper conviction that sooner or later, they would be selected too; their desperate and persistent prayers finally being answered.

For many of these strong and resilient young men, it would be the first meaningful employment they had ever experienced for fair wages, respectable housing, and three-square meals a day... and all this without the constant burden of brutality and fearfulness.

*****

Before daybreak, a convoy of fifteen army trucks pulled into Wildflecken camp to board the first group of heroes. Unlike the party atmosphere of the night before, the air was still, when the hushed sound of sobbing and tearful goodbyes penetrated the silent darkness. It sucked the breath from everyone.

The families gathered around when the priest's truck was moved into position near the center of the convoy to deliver his solemn blessing for a safe journey to a foreign land. For those departing, it would be the final time they heard the familiar Polish prayers spoken for a very long time. Holy water was sprinkled onto the hoods of the GMC trucks to begin the holy crusade.

Jan and Josef were driving one of the lead escort trucks. The roar of the diesel engines rattled to life, belching small clouds of sooty exhaust, rudely intruding on the momentary tranquility, at the same instant as the rising sun scattered its beckoning light.

Jan and Josef settled into their seats preparing for the two-hour drive. As they pulled away, both brothers were moved by the sight in their side mirrors. Every man in the trucks behind them was watching their women and children running behind them, tossing wildflowers all the way to the front gates, children never knowing if they would ever see their fathers again.

Did the Szymanski brothers themselves make the right decision to stay? Had they decided to, they could have been among the selected group, but instead chose to stay the course for a different fate awaiting them, one to better ensure the family bond would not be broken.

"I couldn't bear it if I saw Julia running behind our truck with the other women right now. We've come through so much to be here, Josef." Jan paused and placed his arm on his brother's leg and squeezed it reassuringly, adding, "There's something better for us. We made the right decision to stay! I'm sure of it!"

Much of the rubble of the cities on the route had been bulldozed by the Allies to clear the main roads north. The damage had been so extensive in Ludwig Station and Wurzburg, rebuilding of both cities and the railway connections had not even begun. Clear passage for troops and supplies was the absolute priority.

For many of the refugees, they could now absorb the magnitude of the power and might of the Allied forces to have completely decimated Germany so convincingly. Over the years, the stench of dampness, dirt and concrete dust had become familiar to the DPs since they moved north from Wiory. It still permeated the early Spring air in this hellish place where the world was broken, a place where even birds no longer sang.

Within hours the convoy had already been joined by three additional cargo trucks, also full of excited young laborers as they wound through the continuous decimation. Hamburg had been pounded into submission, but its strategic importance necessitated the rebuilding of the ports. Not only did the port facilitate military and relief access from the North Sea, but it also provided the deepest inland access to the transatlantic military sea transports.

Jan and Josef dropped the load of workers at the gates for departure. They parked the truck and stepped down from the cab to eat something and prepare for the drive back to camp, still in a state of confused wonder about these brave lads' futures... almost as much as their own.

33

A Solemn Tribute

♂

NUMEROUS SIMILAR CONVOYS WOULD ROUTINELY REPEAT THE same process until a total of about 22,000 prime laborers were escorted from the remaining camps to be taken by train to Belgium. In the months following, the West began to open its doors as well.

Canada's vast forests needed skilled lumbermen, while Australia chose to concentrate on hardworking unskilled workers. England, Holland, Venezuela, and France followed suit to satisfy their specific needs of industry as well. The rest of the world was watching with interest, yet the western behemoth of America remained silent and only passively involved.

Over time, the numbers of the youthful and physically fit were filtered out of the refugee population in the camps, leaving a prevalence of the elderly, the crippled, and the masses of mothers and children. Without the fathers and sons, concern for these dependents was more visibly apparent.

Administrative leaders in Europe became aware of various American magazines and periodicals, and in particular the publications of Parisian versions of New York newspapers, featuring advertisements to promote charitable donations to support Europe's refugees.

While the intent of the ads was honorable, the promotional photos depicted the helplessness of DPs, often dressed in rags with outstretched hands protruding through barbed wire fencing. This lasting image may have generated generous financial contributions to the cause, but most certainly did not serve as an encouragement for America to welcome the people to their distant shores. It begged the question, *what possible process could ever hope to include them?*

*****

Amid the controversy and the urgency of each passing day, it was common to have hundreds of files facing deadlines seemingly impossible to meet, to obtain exit visas. Working sixteen or seventeen hours of every day, the grinding pressure on the IRO staff at times became oppressive. Yet remarkably, despite the circumstances, there was always time for love.

Pregnancies proliferated throughout the camp, perhaps as a way of resuming a normal life, or just giving in to nature's glorious urges. During these postwar years, the rate of childbirths in the refugee camps was higher than the national average of any country in the world, with the single exception of China.

In July of 1948, Jan and Julia knew the signs, and proudly confided to their close circle of friends the wonderful news of Julia's pregnancy. When the announcement confirmed what Julia's dresses could no longer hide, no one beamed more than Jan's mother, Marianna. This would be her first grandchild.

"I was so concerned Marianna would be upset at this news, Jan. I am relieved she is so happy." Julia confided.

"Why would you even think she would feel otherwise? You have been part of this family since before Golina, Jula. I told you before, just be happy and stop worrying about such things."

"It's just the timing of the pregnancy that concerns me. We don't need anything, or anyone more, to worry about. I don't want us to jeopardize getting our exit visas."

"I understand, but also know Duchess and Pierre, and everyone with IRO are behind us. I feel good about our chances, and I don't care if we are rejected by America. Canada will take us for sure."

"I don't mean to be so negative, but everyone at IRO is behind Ignatz too, and just look at what he and Dorota have had to endure, again and again. One delay after the other! Five times U.S. Immigration has found another reason to delay their paperwork and force his application to expire. Now they have found dark spots on little Suzanna's lungs. The family drops off the list, and now... they have too many dependents to qualify for America! You know Ignatz will never leave her behind.

"... and remember Uwe Czuba. Their only child will never be able to walk again! Phillip told Duchess they had confirmed

Stefania's spine was too badly broken after falling from an old pine tree... she will likely never walk again. Another entire family the Americans rejected!"

"Okay Jula, enough! These are not our problems, at least not yet. We are both healthy, so our baby should be too. Just eat right, get lots of sleep, and try to relax. I've never seen you so worried, Jula." Jan wrapped her in his affectionate embrace and reassuringly spoke softly in her ear.

"Calm down. You are worried over nothing. This should be a happy time, so I suggest we make it one, OK?" Much to Jan's credit, this was the most stern conversation he ever had with Julia. Despite her initial concerns, she did her best to heed his advice and trusted his reassurances.

*****

"This morning I am helping Ivan with another group of his graduate students. It's really something to see lawyers, business owners and shop foremen learning to farm. We open another acre today that's already been cleared. School was one thing, but the hard physical work will be a very different matter for them. We'll soon find out what these people are really made of."

Jan's mischievous smile caused both Julia and he to giggle at the prospect.

Ivan was already on the site when Jan arrived. "Good morning, Jan," he said. "We commandeered a cargo truck this morning to take another prime section of compost. We have two teams to start hand bombing it as soon as it arrives, and a couple more to help turn it into the soil."

"This should be a test of their resolve, Ivan. Not as easy as it may look."

"I'm not here to judge them, Janic. Without the Farmer's Clause, these people would have no chance of getting a visa. Neither the United States nor Canada need European professionals. They want farmers."

The work was back breaking. It was mid-summer, 1948. The days were long, and the hot afternoon sun beat down with punishing intensity. Nevertheless, the work crews involved mothers and fathers and teenaged sons and daughters. Jan gave them credit though; not a soul belly-ached or complained. It was like a return to the pre-industrial era when families worked together on their private plots and found a way to enjoy simple but productive lives together.

Jan watched intently and at the end of a very long day, sat quietly with Julia, each sharing a satisfying coffee together.

"It's strange to look back on my past life, so different from this place," Jan explained. "It was hard and wholesome work to me and my brothers, taking good care of Ma. I have to admit, I think we had a pretty good life then."

After a short pause, Julia commented reassuringly, "It's good to appreciate and remember where you came from. None of us can change our past, so I'm happy for you that yours was such a good one. Those memories sustain and define who you and your family would become. Look what's happened, Janic."

"What do you mean, Jula? What are you talking about? What's happened?" Jan asked.

"I'm talking about how much you are respected here, in fact, every-where we go. Look what you've done for the people in this camp. Just getting them here was not easy for others to do. Now, with Josef and Ivan's help, you've given these people hope for their new futures, wherever they might eventually go. They look up to you because you are making a positive difference in so many of their uncertain lives.

"Once they arrive in America, just like us, they will have the possibil-ity to make a living by farming, or otherwise. It may not be their ultimate choice, but they would certainly have the blisters and calluses to prove they are willing to do whatever is needed to repay their passage fares to America. I'm so proud of you and Josef. When I tell you these things, I just want to remind you to always be proud of yourself too."

Julia leaned over to rest her head affectionately on his shoulder. There was never much privacy in their chaotic lives together, and these quiet moments offered few opportunities to express the close-ness that had developed between them. Julia's mind began racing now, as she felt compelled to speak the unspeakable... Mikael.

"Jan, there is something I must tell you, and I think now is the time." Jan suddenly stiffened with concern and shifted his weight to cause Julia to move her head away, ever so slightly so he could look at her directly. Never had Julia spoken so seriously, with such foreboding. Jan was taken aback not knowing what to expect, but he continued to keep his arm comfortingly around her shoulder.

"I spoke to Linette a few weeks ago... to help me with something," Julia paused, inhaling slowly to calm her nerves. "It's about Mikael."

Jan sat in abject silence, simply staring at Julia. Her eyes spoke volumes about what she was about to say. Jan knew immediately from Julia's slowly seeping tears, that deep sorrow had overcome her, soon followed by his own. The details were largely left unsaid, until another time when composure better provided.

*****

Throughout the farming season, hundreds of newly trained farming families produced plentiful, high-quality crops. Everyone earned their keep and felt pride in the accomplishment. By late autumn, many of them were well on the way to setting foot in America. Ivan's influence and knowledge were significant contributing factors, as was their willingness to learn and make practical use of their newfound knowledge.

With the passage of time and the beginning of another winter, the pace of document processing became much more efficient by establishing multiple Resettlement Centers, continually changing the faces of the remaining refugees. Where were the young and sturdy? With few exceptions, the filtering process had effectively removed most of them from the camp's population.

Most of the remaining refugees were the oldest, with noticeably higher percentages of the cripples and the physically frail, who had little to no chance of going anywhere soon without blood relatives to support them. It was an injustice they meekly accepted. They tried desperately to fully understand the reasons they were being left behind, but the quotas and the qualifications were stacked against them. The reasons no longer mattered.

Among the exceptions, were the Szymanski family, and of course, Linette. Their proactive positive contributions were heavily relied upon by the IRO, as they had hoped. It was now time to step in line themselves. They were shining examples of human adaptability, persistence, and the true grit required to not only survive the perils of war, but to thrive by distinguishing themselves in ways never expected of them.

They would be well suited for the new lives ahead of them. In return, the personal recommendations of the IRO assured acceptance of their visa applications. There was no longer much time for unnecessary delays, but the 't's still had to be crossed.

"Jula, we need one more piece of paper to make sure we remain together. It will be no more than any other person here would need, and you already know what it is."

"Are you finally ready to marry me, Jan?"

Jan began laughing. It was evident Julia was ready too. "It's time Jula. We want to, and now we must. Time for us to pay attention to ourselves and get this done. The baby will be here in another month or so and Ma wants us to make everything right in the eyes of the Church... and God. The others can wait... we no longer can."

"Let's get married on Christmas Day! There are only three other couples on the schedule and Duchess told me she would keep a spot open for us! I want to ask Linette to be my Maid of Honor!"

Jan never considered Julia could have said no, but it was the first time he realized the extent of her happiness about marrying him. It was always assumed, but rarely discussed. He felt good about her genuine enthusiasm and was only now seeing the sacred event in a totally new light.

Later that day, Linette was profoundly moved upon hearing the news from Julia, and more so by her gesture to ask Linette to be witness to the sanctity of their marriage. She was only too eager to accept. Until she had met Julia, Linette had not understood nor known the depths of anyone's friendship since she and Marta lost contact during the final year of the war. It was a very different life back then. For her own personal reasons, she still had not shared much of it with anyone, including Julia.

When Jan entered the administration building shortly after, he knew full well the news had preceded him. Julia and Linette were already celebrating with Kate when he appeared, grinning from ear to ear. "There he is!" Linette said excitedly. She went to greet him personally and hugged him closely. These expressions of friendship were rare in the office environment, but this was a noteworthy exception.

Beatrice saw the small commotion and curiosity got the better of her. She joined the happy moment too and was delighted by the news. As usual, others took notice and word spread quickly through the office. It was almost the end of day so for these few moments at least, their jobs were not the only priority. This was a rare occasion and spoke volumes about the significance of the event, and the fondness everyone shared for Jan and Julia.

*****

Later in the evening, after an impromptu dinner with Linette, Ivan, and Kate, several glasses of schnapps led to more good times swirling around the big event, which was scheduled for Christmas Day, the upcoming Saturday afternoon. Through the laughter though, Linette seemed to become quietly more distant, albeit for a short time, but long enough for Julia to notice she was pre-occupied with something more.

"Linette, you seem unusually quiet tonight. Is everything alright?"

"Oh, I'm sorry, Julia. Yes, everything is fine... actually, more than fine. I have an idea... May I speak privately with you both? I must ask you something... if it's not too personal."

"Of course, don't be silly. What's on your mind?" Julia was intrigued by her hesitation.

"Jan, the more I think about this, I realize it's a more suitable question for you." Now the bride *and* the groom were bristling with interest. They just stared and listened quietly, giving her their full attention.

"The wedding ring is such a solemn tribute of love and fidelity. When a man offers the ring to a woman, it is a cornerstone of the traditional wedding ceremony, binding husband to wife. This is a bit awkward but... if you don't mind, may I ask... have you given any thought to a ring for that special moment when you say your vows to one another?"

Julia paused only briefly and said, "We honestly haven't even thought about it." Jan's eyes shifted to Julia, who was staring right back at him. Neither knew where Linette was going with this. "It's just something we could never afford or hope to find; certainly not now, in camp. Don't you agree, Jan?"

Jan reacted like a deer caught in a car's headlights. He stammered and awkwardly searched for appropriate words which now eluded him... "I was um, I was going to surprise Jula with something for... for the ceremony, just... I don't wanna say." His eyes shifted nervously. It was apparent to Linette, he had in fact thought about it.

"What is it, Jan? For Heaven's sake... what could you not tell me?" Julia asked.

"I want to give you something, but... what can I buy here? You always tell me we need to keep our money for when we go to Canada. I did speak to Abraham though. He used to be a jeweler in Krakow. He's one of Ivan's farmers, but he said he can make something for me to give you at the ceremony."

Julia was taken aback at his thoughtfulness. Here she was, thinking there were no secrets between them. Tears welled up in her eyes, as she considered his kindness toward her. Linette interrupted the poignant moment and became excited about whatever it was she wanted to share with them.

"I have a wonderful idea. Let me help you with that if I may? I have something quite unique I very much want to share with you. Please, give me a few minutes. I'll be right back." Whereupon Linette stood, quickly rushing off and leaving the room.

Only a few minutes later, Linette returned to her very inquisitive friends, clutching a small bundle of cloth with a string tied securely around it. Before she opened it, she prefaced her thoughts carefully, to explain what she was about to offer. She was becoming very emotional and began hesitatingly.

"We all came here from very different backgrounds to be sure. I don't tell you much about mine, for reasons I cannot explain." Linette gently wiped a tear before it ran down her cheek. She drew a deep breath and her voice quivered as she continued.

"Since I met you both, you have taken me into your lives and made my years here more meaningful. Our friendship has filled a void existing inside of me I could not seem to satisfy. For that I will always be truly grateful."

Casting her eyes onto whatever was inside the cloth, she kept it covered from view. "This is something very sacred to me. It is the only piece of my past still remaining, and I hold it very near and dear to me. I cannot let you keep what I am about to offer you, but what I can do, is let you use this lovely symbol to represent your love for each other. It is a gift I was given by my mother and father when my daughter Pietra was born, and years before, it was given by him to my mother when I was born."

Linette untied the string, carefully taking something delicate from inside the small bundle. "It has been said many times that love rises

471

from the ashes, and always endures." The welling of her tears could no longer be suppressed, and in her trembling voice she said, "This is so very true… of this ring."

She extended her hand to Jan's and delicately placed the ring into the palm of his hand. The circle of diamonds shimmered and sparkled in the light of the bare lightbulb hanging above them. The white gold of the shank reflected even the dimmest of light. Not a word was spoken until Linette broke the stunned silence. Jan and Julia were dumbfounded and remained speechless.

"Much to my regret, I had to remove the original gemstone several years ago to buy my way to freedom. By doing so, this ring undoubtedly saved my life, and gave me the chance to keep going. Let me tell you, if it weren't for this ring, I wouldn't be here today."

"*Oh, Linette!* This is so thoughtful of you! I have never seen anything as beautiful as this. You truly honor us by sharing it with us on our wedding day."

"Jan, I'm thinking your friend Abraham may be able to find something suitable to fill the space left by the missing gemstone. What do you think? … It's a good start, yes?" Linette looked eagerly to Jan for his approval.

Neither Jan nor Julia had seen, or even imagined such a fine piece of distinctive jewelry, never minding the missing gemstone. The friends fawned over the glorious piece, sharing a mixture of excited and happy tears. This intimate defining moment would be cherished forever, not easily forgotten by the sands of time.

*****

As Christmas 1948 approached, there were many couples of all ages, not specifically seeking love and partnership, but finding it, nevertheless. Middle aged and elderly people, most of whom had suffered incredible personal loss, found companionship and dedicated affection with others in similar circumstances.

Marriages were frequent, particularly at this time of year and group ceremonies became common among the refugees. For many, including Jan and Julia, it was a necessary formalizing of their union to be accepted for immigration together, as husband and wife, to better ensure their departure to America on the same ship.

The camp had started its own Christmas tradition in 1945 for the first group of refugees in this very room. Although rudimentary, for many, the centerpiece of the camp was always the chapel. Since the first service, thousands of worshippers had walked in and out of this sanctified symbol of Christianity. It may not have been the refugees' first choice in which to be married, but for those who were unified before God within these humble walls, the memory and the blessings bestowed upon them were genuine and would last a lifetime.

The service was entrusted to Father Kazimierez Glogowski of the Roman Catholic Parochial Office in Bruckenau, West Germany. He had married countless couples and christened thousands of young children in his time here, yet he never lost his inimitable warmth and calming sense of joy at every service over which he presided.

Just before the service began, Jan leaned in closely to whisper into Julia's ear.

"You look very beautiful, Jula. I'm so proud of you for becoming my wife." In Jan's mind, Julia's appearance was reminiscent of the day she entered the front of the church in Golina when he was awestruck with pride and sheepishly overwhelmed. That was a magical moment he would always cherish. Now, this spiritual union would become another.

Each of the four couples followed Father Kazimierez' lead and recited the vows of holy matrimony. When Jan and Julia repeated those vows, Jan lovingly placed the beautiful ring on his bride's finger. Standing beside Julia was Linette, and Josef was at his brother's side.

No one other than Jan and Abraham had seen the completed ring until this moment of presentation. It was truly inspirational and achieved Jan's desired effect. Julia was overwhelmed.

Marianna sat contentedly beside Ivan and Kate, and Marie accompanied the duchess, with Pierre at her side, along with as many IRO families the chapel could hold. Not only was this a sanctified moment for each couple, but it was also the day to commemorate the birth of Christ. Hence, on this rare occasion, the Holy Communion was an integral part of the day's services, not normally included for the group wedding vows.

The highlight of the occasion without question, was the placing of the wedding ring on Julia's trembling finger. Abraham had reconstructed a lovely centerpiece from fragments of stained windows he had been fashioning for the chapel. For months he had routinely preselected the prime baubles with the beautiful hues from the unused scraps of the colored windows.

With Linette advising him, he carefully cut and reshaped a fitting representation of the original stone of midnight blue, as best he could only imagine, to sit securely on the surround of diamonds. It was a work of dedication to commemorate and honor the memories of the day for Jan and Julia. His effort and skillfulness were reflective of a truly superb creation.

The guests were in awe of Julia's auspicious wedding ring, as would be expected. Nothing of this refinement of culture, fashion, or beauty had occasion to find its way to these unpretentious surroundings, and the glory of Jan's tribute to Julia was greatly enhanced. For the safety and security of the ring, not a word was mentioned to anyone about Linette's thoughtful gesture. At her insistence, it was best to let the matter remain unspoken.

Each couple was given a brief moment to say something before Father Kazimierez' delivered the blessing of the meal. Three of them declined the offer but Jan promptly rose to address the almost full house from the head table, not wanting to lose the rare opportunity before him.

"I want to thank everyone for sharing this special time for us, and our friends sitting beside us. Julia and I congratulate each one of you on your wedding day." A round of applause and some loud whistling built upon the festive mood of the banquet room. It was the old Community Building, but it served this happy occasion perfectly.

Jan resumed with his brief comments. "I just wanna say, how proud I am to be Julia's husband. We are both so happy to share this time with our extended family." As he said this, he raised his hand and slowly extended his gaze toward and across the width of the banquet hall.

"We are thankful to have found many friends among you. As we all leave Wildflecken to travel to different places around the world, we will probably never see each other again, but I promise you, we will never forget you. Good luck and may God bless you all!"

A plentiful supply of hearty borscht soup with potato pancakes and fried chicken made for a wholesome and tasty meal to mark the occasion. All the newlyweds shared the Community Building and the remnants of the Polish band did their best to make the reception a festive one.

Within an hour of enjoying home brewed vodka shots to toast the newlyweds, the flow of drinks seemed inexhaustible. With every passing round, the partygoers became more forgiving of the make-shift band. No one seemed to notice; no one seemed to care.

Before the party revellers became too intoxicated, and as inconspicuously as possible, Josef, Ignatz, and Pierre accepted the responsibility of receiving the hand off from Jan to unobtrusively restore the ring to Linette's care and custody. Together, they safely escorted her to her room.

The ring was worth a veritable king's ransom to these refugees, so the temptation of theft had to be carefully considered. It had served its glorious purpose and its memory would not be easily erased from those in attendance.

As midnight approached, the exhausted and well hydrated guests began to retire for the night, with only a dozen or so tables still enjoying laughter and positive reflections of their times together. The band commenced to pack up their instruments after a good night's work. They had done well, and their comrades were very appreciative of their efforts.

For Jan and Julia, it would be the first night to sleep together as husband and wife. They laid in bed quietly that night, reminiscing about the happy celebration, grateful for all they had achieved, and hopeful for what was yet to come. Jan's hand was affectionately resting on Julia's plump belly as they both began to succumb to the contentment of deep sleep.

By divine timing, their soon to be born child slowly rolled and stretched. Jan's tired and half-closed eyes suddenly popped open, wide with wonder. He propped himself up on his elbow.

"Jula, I felt the baby move! I never felt that before! I think he must be a strong boy to kick you so hard. Amazing!" Lifting his head from his pillow, Jan tenderly kissed Julia's restless belly and pondered his good fortune for having met her. A tear of gratitude slowly ran from the corner of his eye and trickled onto this young unborn child, still within the womb of his dear Jula. Only now was Jan experiencing his first true grasp of fatherhood, knowing as little as any new father would of all it may entail.

34
FINAL FAREWELLS

♂

JUST A MONTH LATER ON JANUARY 27TH, 1949, A VIBRANT
and beautiful little princess was born to Jan and Julia. Regina Anna
Szymanska was healthy and alert from the day she entered her world.

Regina's birth was in the very capable hands of Marie Habets,
who by this time was the Chief of Medicine overseeing the medical
and surgical needs of several camps near and about Wurzburg and
Bruckenau. Marie's medical assistance to safely deliver Julia's baby
was her only priority on this happy day. How fittingly appropriate it
was for Marie to be the first one to bless this beautiful newborn and
place her into her mother's loving arms.

"Look how beautiful she is! Well done Julia!" Marie had delivered
thousands of babies in the course of her career, but it wasn't often she
delivered a child to a mother she knew and respected so personally.
"Such a precious gift from God. You have a family of your own now,
and I am privileged to have been here for you Julia."

Julia recovered quickly from Regina's natural childbirth. In the
months ahead and with Marianna's support, Julia naturally adapted
to caring for her lovely baby girl, perhaps owing to her experience
tending to Louisa, Katia and young Peter. It was however, her first
time to experience the magnitude of her love and nurturing affection
for her own daughter. The instinctive love she felt was far deeper than
her previous imaginings thought to be possible.

It was about a week later as they settled into bed for the night. In
that quiet moment with Jan, Julia spoke in hushed whispers when she
softly confided to him more than he would hear.

"I will always remember meeting Paul and Gilda and their young son Karl, in the ruins of Pultusk. He couldn't have been more than five years old at the time. And also, Mariam, the daughter of Pavel and Manal. Only now can I begin to grasp the strength and depth of the human spirit, and how it becomes profoundly altered by the intensity of the love motherhood provides." Julia paused, trying to get her thoughts in order.

In those quiet but fleeting seconds of reflection, she recalled brief visions of her subconscious thoughts from similar moments; not about her actual memories, because these were maternal imaginings she had never experienced before. Rather, it was her attempt to reflect upon those profound moments through the lens of her new and present perspective of motherhood; back to those times when she thought her empathy for those young parents could be understood by her.

She continued whispering to Jan with her head resting on his shoulder. Her arm was draped across his slowly heaving chest. He was breathing deeply now and likely fast asleep, but Julia continued speaking. "I distinctly remember the only way I could come to grips with my own fear and concern for those families, mostly the children, was to dismiss them from my mind. I didn't know how else to cope. How inappropriate it was now that I think back. I can't help but wonder where they are now."

Jan was snoring now, as a tear ran across her cheek, followed by another, dripping onto his nightshirt.

"I shudder at the thought," was her silent admission.

Since the beginning of time, parents could never be dismissive of tragic circumstances. It must have been a transformative moment for them, with nowhere to go but forward, all the while having no concept of what would befall them. Their reality was the touch of a clutching and adoring child, totally trusting with naïve blinding faith in the parents who would surely know what to do.

Now, as she looked back, Julia was even more thankful for having been fortuitously so very alone during those arduous years. She was absolutely reaffirmed in her original belief - it was her solitude and sole focus upon her own survival carrying her through, enabling her to eventually prevail. Although her world was different now, those were the definitive times when sentimentality was truly a weakness she could not afford.

*****

In the weeks ahead, applications for immigration visas were submitted and in no time documents for passage to Halifax, Canada were found in good order for Jan, Julia, baby Regina, Josef, and Marianna. The Szymanski family had taken all the necessary steps to ensure they remained together. Jan and Julia's decision to trust in a better future had born fruit.

In mid-March, just two weeks before the scheduled departure, the church had scheduled a group Baptism to bless the newborns of the past few months. In all, there were sixteen young ones being welcomingly embraced to the house of God. The service was simple and respectful, and committed each parent to remain mindful of their reverence for this sacred event in their young child's new life.

It was a most difficult moment when reality set in for Julia and Linette as the day for Julia's final departure was almost at hand. Although they were both thrilled for each other's probable good fortune, they were both aware they, like the others, would never see one another again. This was never discussed between them, but it was very much an unspoken reality that preoccupied their thoughts with each passing day; neither was eager to directly address it.

It was late afternoon, the day before their departure, when Linette decided she could not delay her final farewell any longer. It was becoming apparent Julia was not about to address the matter on her own volition. It was a task Linette would not address in the office, or the dining hall, or anywhere else other than in the privacy of her own room. It was time to deal with the identifiable awkwardness and unnatural anxiety preoccupying their friendship these past few days.

"Come Julia, we need to talk, and we cannot do it here." Linette extended her hand to Julia's and saw her eyes begin to tear, as if she already knew where this was leading. "Please, Julia." Linette led the way initially, pulling her along the short hallway, and other than balking briefly at the suddenness of Linette's gesture, Julia offered no protest.

Closing the door behind them, Linette directed Julia to sit on the side of the bed and took the only remaining chair to face her.

"Listen to me, my dear. I have nothing prepared so I'm just going to speak with you from my heart. We have both been tiptoeing along awkwardly with each passing day. That is not how I want to remember us, Julia." She thoughtfully took a tissue and placed a few on the bedside.

"You are only a few years older than my Pietra and Dietrich, and I think of you as my little sister. I love you dearly Julia, and I will never forget you."

Julia made a feeble attempt to respond, but Linette pressed on. "I am sorry Julia, but I have been struggling with my thoughts and I must get them off my mind. Please bear with me." Linette drew her chair closer to Julia, holding both of her hands in her own.

She continued, "You have given me friendship where I never thought I would find it... You gave me the courage to go on when I wanted to go back, and... and you made me laugh when... when I only wanted to cry. Your marriage to Jan, the birth of Regina... and her baptism before the Lord, made me a part of your family Julia, an honor I can never hope to repay."

"Oh Linette, my dear Linette. I am so emotionally confused as well... I just can't seem to bring myself to say a proper goodbye to you. You know I'm not good with these things. I have been putting this off too! If you had not come forward, I don't know that I would have done so... and I would have lived with the regret for the rest of my life."

Through their tears, both friends gathered more tissues and their conversation continued. Linette impressed upon Julia the significance her presence in the camp had upon her.

"I never shared with you much about my past ordeals, but suffice to say I was totally broken by those experiences. I spent three years hiding from everyone, and I continue to do so to this very day; nameless and faceless people; people I will never know, nor trusting anyone until I met you and Jan. Before I found my way here, every day I was living in abject fear. You confided some grave things to me about your past that resonated with how I felt. You survived a living hell, Julia... and you helped me believe I could too.

"Since I came here, and from the time we became friends, I remember finally feeling somehow reconnected again, thankful for the family life I once had and hope to have again. Without knowing it, you reassured me and helped to guide my way back from the darkest moments of my life. You inspired me to find the courage to carry on, reaffirming in me that hope can in fact be restored. For all these things I am thankful for having you in my life."

479

Julia was now crying openly as Linette struggled to remain composed. Through the tears and anguish of Linette's touching words, Julia fought to fully reconcile her disbelief and shock upon hearing such effusive praise being directed toward her, especially from such an influential and esteemed friend.

"I never had that effect on anyone, Linette. No one has said these things to me before. There are those who have inspired me to be sure, but I... I never thought it possible *I* would inspire anyone. I hadn't considered myself from any other perspective than my own.

"Despite my bitter memories, some of which continue to haunt me from time to time, I always try to remember the kindnesses I was shown from a few special people I met along the way. None of them affected me as profoundly as you... I am deeply moved Linette. Thank you! I will never forget you and will miss you always."

Both friends stood and embraced one another, as passionately as two best friends ever could, almost sobbing in unison.

"When you and Jan settle somewhere in Canada, send me a letter through my daughter so we can at least keep in contact from time to time. This is her address in New York. I am going to try to do the same thing with Dietrich, and Emilie, if I can find them again.

"Neither you nor I know where you may go in Canada. It's a very large country, so I will not be able to find you easily. Who knows where the future may take us, but we must stay in touch. Promise me you will try, Julia! Please."

"I feel better already. I don't want this to be our final goodbye either. I will write you. I promise, Linette."

*****

Amid the jubilation, there were those refugees who did their best to maintain their composure in the face of decline after decline of their emigration applications. Many of them were elderly, handicapped, or without family members to help support them. In these cases, there was nothing they could do since returning to their homeland was far too perilous, absent law and order, and without anyone to hear their desperate pleas for help.

Ivan's farming classes came to an abrupt close simply because the number of able-bodied laborers in camp were few and far between, having already emigrated to those countries still willing to reach out to qualified self-supporting families. Through Ivan's initiative, Julia estimated more than 130 refugee families were able to qualify for emigration under the Farmer's Clause. Unfortunately, Ivan was not one of them.

Being an elderly seventy-year-old man who was well educated, once having had more than sufficient financial means, was no longer relevant. The new world was more intent on selecting muscled youth than aged intelligence. Ivan's home and assets had been devoured by war, leaving him without his deceased wife and children to financially support him in these later years of his very productive life. Yet his magical manner to tend to the needs of those less fortunate than himself, with his only intent being to offer brightness to someone's day, was seeking only a shred of it for himself.

No one's absence would affect him as profoundly as Jan and his family. They represented the firmly established roots of their ancestry, having struggled for their survival and somehow managing to stay together as one. They carried with them a new and beautiful newborn child, too young to ever remember this place of her birth, but forever being shaped and destined for a gloriously better life because of it.

When his adoptive family and friends' departures were gratefully announced a few short days ago, a silent and invisible shroud inevitably began to engulf Ivan. He was delighted their approvals had been granted, however, the sparkle his eyes once conveyed had slowly drained away, leaving a mask of hollow emptiness in the vacuum that remained. The change was evident, but everyone was so busy and preoccupied, no one seemed capable or predisposed to perceive it.

On the day of the Szymanski family departure, Ivan was dressed as impeccably as he could for the celebratory send off. "You look absolutely dashing today, Ivan! I shall miss you more than you can possibly know."

"Perhaps we will meet again, even if in the next world. Take good care of Jan and your little princess. I would have enjoyed watching her grow up to into the fine woman I know she will become."

"You have much to offer my friend. Just be patient and keep your faith." As Julia offered her reassurances, she too knew Ivan's window of opportunity was gradually closing. Julia hugged him tightly while Jan looked on, as he snuggled Regina securely in his arms. So many goodbyes, intensely charged with emotion were commonplace, each one more moving than the one before. Everyone knew these farewells were their final ones.

*****

From the eastern gate, the familiar roar of the diesel engines could be heard from the approaching U.S. military trucks. Transport for over two hundred refugees from Wildflecken had been co-ordinated to link with four other prearranged military vehicles along the route to form a convoy. The closest train station at Bad Hersfeld, was about a hundred kilometers north of Wildflecken.

Since 1945, many of the main train hubs had been so badly destroyed by heavy RAF bombing, the main line from southern Bavaria to the ports of the North Sea had been effectively severed. The greatest priority for the allies was to repair the numerous secondary routes because the network of major roadways was also in total disrepair.

Luggage was stowed, each bag appearing to be a match for the others, most of them like the people, barely distinguished one from the other. Each time the refugees were relocated, repositioned, or just moved out of someone's way, more of their possessions would be necessarily cast aside. The act itself confirmed in them the only essential attachments were reserved for each other, and the shedding of their property only served to perpetuate the fading memories of their past.

Unlike the trains and transport trucks delivering the refugees to their temporary homes within these gates, there were seats for everyone, and the process was a relatively dignified one. Smiles were plentiful and hopeful faces displayed thankful enthusiasm as their latest adventure was about to unfold. Being so focused on their departure that day, neither Jan nor Julia noticed Ivan walking purposely toward the forest, still impeccably attired as he wanted to be remembered.

Two days later, some children playing in the nearby forest found Ivan hanging from a tree limb, a sad testimony for someone who was once so respected, now only fondly remembered. Sadly, it had become commonplace to witness the suicides of many others suffering similar circumstances. The system simply had no room for them. The cause of these deaths was regrettably noted in the IRO files as being... *despair*.

*****

The duchess would be departing for New York on the same ship as Linette, less than two weeks after the Szymanski's. She would carry on by train to Boston Massachusetts to reunite with her sister's daughter. They were the only remaining family she had, and although hardly knowing them, she was eager to have another chance to become part of it.

Her character and work ethic ensured her continued independence. She was adamant she would present no burden to them but was equally determined she would make a positive contribution to support the lives they were presently leading.

Having never had occasion to visit America in the past, despite her worldly skills and aristocratic privileges, she now seized the moment, having earned the right as much, and more than anyone. The experience of working with UNRRA and IRO was one she quickly embraced, but the extent of her commitments had taken its toll over time. Defiant denial to succumb to one's physical and mental limitations can eventually erode the spiritual limitations as well. She prayed her new life in America would help to restore it.

*****

Linette also had her emigration application well into process. She had entered the camp under her assumed name to be consistent with her passport. She maintained her resolve to depart Wildflecken using the same identity. No one would be the wiser, including the Szymanski family. There were no exceptions, including her own blood relatives.

For her, there were many unique considerations to be decided upon, with no one other than herself to consult. Of primary importance was her decision to continue safeguarding her own personal safety and anonymity. The long arm of the Nazi Party was still known to be vengeful and dedicated to the vindictiveness of the Fuhrer's wrath.

His whereabouts after the fall of Berlin was still largely unconfirmed, and those of his distant collaborators within the secret service remained generally unknown. Linette was not willing to do anything foolish at this late stage to potentially expose herself to additional risk.

Linette applied for sponsorship from Pietra under the guise of being the sister of her Aunt Marta. Linette reasoned that Pietra knew very well Marta did not have any siblings. In fact, Marta was not a blood relation of Pietra's family at all but had only been regarded as being her aunt in name only, owing to the closeness of her relationship with Anna since their childhood.

Linette carefully considered that using her Wildflecken identity still came with considerable risk, since her request for sponsorship could be easily rejected by Pietra. Having only one opportunity, the stakes were high. Linette reasoned it was a risk she had to take.

In the closing of her brief cover letter to the set of sponsorship documents of consent, she sent her love individually to Pietra, her husband Richard and their son Peter. The innocuous inclusion of those family names clearly indicated the applicant, this unknown person named Linette, was familiar with each of Pietra's family members.

In addition, Linette's year of birth was consistent with Anna's and there was naturally a strong similarity of handwriting. The question was, would Pietra recognize these clues and trust them to be sufficient to convince her that Linette could possibly be her mother? The contents of the letter, however, had to be discreet to avoid undue suspicion by anyone processing the documents.

Pietra had heard nothing from Anna since the letter she wrote to her in December 1938, informing Pietra of the death of her grandparents and her father. She was aware her family was in grave danger at the time, her mother having sternly warned her to stay in America. Other than a brief telegram from Marta two years later, Pietra heard nothing about her mother's whereabouts and circumstances.

A brief comment about her mother's general well-being was all Pietra was given from Marta, leaving her mother's life a complete mystery. She correctly suspected Marta had been forbidden to speak of it.

After considerable discussion with Richard, and after consulting with their personal lawyer, Richard and Pietra agreed they could not risk declining this woman's plea for sponsorship and cooperated immediately by confirming their particulars and willingness to be Linette's sponsor. If this truly was her long-lost mother, the inexplicable reasons for not communicating with her family no longer mattered.

*****

Pietra was now twenty-eight years of age with a loving husband who supported her still blossoming musical career. The love she had for her violin as a young child had never waned, and her husband's determination to respect her dedication was evident from the very beginning of their relationship.

As a young journalist attending NYU, Richard's flair for the arts proved to be the common thread connecting them. When he was granted an interview with Pietra using his press pass after a concert performance, little did he know how truly entranced with her he would become from the time of their first encounter.

Richard and Pietra had closely followed her Aunt Marta's career with enthusiastic zeal, even during the war, until the fateful day Dietrich informed her of Marta's passing, and that of Klaus and their son Manfred. Pietra and Manfred had grown up together and developed a strong bond between them until they were separated when Pietra went to America.

The war had taken a toll on everyone, but Pietra was overwhelmed with abject shock upon learning of Marta's premature death. Marta had been Pietra's personal mentor since her early childhood, the most formidable person she had known. Her sudden passing at such a relatively young age, and in such a tragic and lonely manner, was totally incomprehensible to Pietra.

Her passing had also closed another possible doorway to finding her mother, Anna. Neither Pietra nor Dietrich had heard any news of her, and although it was becoming a foregone conclusion war had somehow consumed her, they kept her in their prayers. Perhaps this was Pietra's last shred of hope, ultimately convincing her to sponsor this stranger named Linette from a DP camp somewhere in western Germany.

*****

Along the route to Hamburg, the scattered remains of devastation stretched endlessly, despite four years of repairs and reconstruction. It was depressing to comprehend the extent of the annihilation. Gazing for hours out the expansive windows of their railcar, mile after mile, hour after hour, the fully loaded train curved and weaved its way, slicing through narrow openings of rubble and debris.

Since the war ended, entire landscapes showed little evidence of reconstruction, just thousands of acres of trash, on both sides of the train tracks, still being picked through by thousands of peasant laborers with their bare hands. For many, they had nothing to work with, neither shovels, nor gloves.

Throughout Germany, fifteen million men had been lost. The women left behind, initially toiled from dawn to dusk on this thankless task, with little to eat, somehow still persevering. They were called *The Trummerfrauen*, The Rubble Women. Their work became legendary and large construction companies soon hired them, as well as the few able bodied men willing to work. They received small wages, but generous ration cards.

Inside the train, there were few conversations and no celebrations. Everyone on board began to absorb another sad perspective of reality, reinforcing within them a better understanding of why emigration was the only viable alternative. It was a constant slipstream of unimaginable images, the proportion of which only deadened the senses. Jan simply sat in contemplative stillness beside Julia, who was breast-feeding the baby.

"You're awfully quiet, Jan. What are you thinking?" Julia asked, breaking the silence of the past hour.

"Something inside me is... is different right now. I think maybe... I dunno..." He stumbled through his thoughts, trying to express an unfamiliar feeling to which he was unaccustomed. "I feel guilty maybe."

"Guilty? What do you feel guilty about? I don't understand." Julia started to press the issue.

"Maybe because I don't feel grief anymore, seeing what the Americans and the British have done to the German people here. Any sadness I feel is because it took so damned long for them to avenge us." Jan surmised. "I just don't feel sorry for these people, Jula."

"I doubt revenge was on their minds, Jan. You must live through it to fully understand it. Look at these Americans. Many of them are still just kids. They're even younger than you and me! For many they were probably still in school when the war began; now they're just doing their jobs to clean up this God-forsaken mess. The German bastards were probably the same." Black and white; Julia's perspectives remained largely objective and always pragmatic.

Jan carried his thoughts even further. "Once I thought I was a good person, although a simple one... at least my life was. I didn't know anything about the world outside of Wiory. Now, I don't even recognize who I have become. Is this making any sense to you, Jula?"

There was a break in their conversation, neither one accustomed to having deep intellectual discussions between them. Julia paused briefly as she was formulating a helpful response to Jan's misgivings about himself.

"The day my family died, I was completely horrified, frozen with fear. I had a split second to decide, but I knew I could do nothing to help them. Nothing could bring them back to me. The following day, still in shock I suppose, I was still hiding a short distance from a pathway leading away from my village, when I saw a mother with her young child, desperately alone and as frightened as me. I just sat and watched them pass by, without calling out to them. I was too afraid... not of them, but for my own life... I was afraid of the soldiers who attacked our village.

"I watched while the mother walked straight into an ambush. She turned to run back the other way, and when she did, the bastards shot her twice in the back. As she fell, her child fell to the ground too. Do you know what I did?" Jan just shook his head, not uttering a word.

"Nothing! I did *nothing* to help them! I will live with my decision until the day I die. I did not care about them, there was nothing I could do. Was the child still alive? ... I'll never know because I just did not care." Her eyes were moist now as she recounted the terrible moment to Jan.

"A big part of me died that day... I changed. I've never again felt the same as I used to be. I became a different person. I think I lost my innocence and had to adjust to a different life from that day forward. Do you understand what I am trying to explain to you?"

"Yes, I... I think so. You're telling me I changed too after the things we saw and what we had to do to stay alive." Jan looked questioningly for her reaction.

Julia did not smile, but pursed her lips as she said, "We all had to adapt to our new reality. God guided us in another direction, and saw fit to make us stronger so we could survive. Maybe the cost of our survival... was our innocence."

*****

Dusk was fast approaching when the train pulled into Hamburg to offload the refugees to the harbor entrance. There was barely enough light remaining to appreciate the incredible magnitude of two passenger ships, the likes of which the refugees had never imagined.

A steady supply of ships, many of which were US Merchant Mariners, had been running refugees on a regular basis across the Atlantic to major ports in Canada and the United States, such as Halifax, Chicago, and New York.

Their resettlement in the new world, would eventually evacuate the remaining DP camps being run by the IRO. Those many hundreds, or thousands of unsuitable immigrants, the *Ivans* of this tragedy, were left to their own devices to adapt as best they could to what remained of a broken and battle-weary circumstance. Little was known about their whereabouts.

The Szymanski family, among others, were in awe at the sheer height of the mammoth ship's hull rising some fifty feet above the waterline. The Trans-Atlantic crossing required two to three weeks of sea travel, depending upon weather conditions.

Hamburg was a major German port employing hundreds of supporting crew and dockworkers to maneuver the cranes and cargo supplies being carefully coaxed deep within the ship's cavernous hull. The panorama of activity and the sounds of shouting machine operators indicated more concern and focus for the tasks of this enormous undertaking, than for the 700 or so anxious onlookers.

"We've come a long way from our lives in Wiory. Who knew this world even existed, Ma?" said a much-bewildered Josef to his mother. They both stood watching from the second floor of the terminal along with many others, captivated by the activity below them.

Within ninety minutes, a public announcement cut ambiguously through the clamor of shouting crewmen and the groaning of forklifts and overhead cranes. As fragments of the announcement were passed from person to person, the passengers began to follow one another, shuffling themselves to the now accessible gangplank for boarding.

This was a Military Sea Transport Service customarily transporting troops and supplies. Since the end of the war, the *SS Marine Falcon* served well as one of several UNRRA repatriation ships provided by American President Lines.

It was a service necessitated by the evacuation of hundreds of thousands of homeless immigrants but was never designed for this purpose. As such, everyone carried his or her own limited baggage. What minimal amounts they had, represented all they would require. They were heading to Canada, and any apprehensions they may have felt about their new world were understandable. Their past experiences, however, gave logical cause to remain skeptical.

The ship manifest would record a total of 715 passengers seeking immigration to Canada. Not only had the refugees never seen a ship such as this up close, most had never seen the North Sea. The harbor authorities efficiently processed the inspection of relevant admission documents to match the required paperwork previously submitted by the IRO. Medical records and other pertinent information did not have to be reinspected; such was the high regard for the administrative efficiency of the IRO.

Julia would remember the instant her right foot first touched the steel gangplank. It also represented the final time her left foot would touch the blood-soaked soil of Europe. As they gratefully walked across the perilously narrow gangplank rising further above the sea below, it appeared higher than previously perceived from their now very close perspectives.

The nonstop splashing of the expelled seawater from the ship's six steam turbine engines noisily slapped the face of the languid surface of the sea below. The focus of the passengers was not on their ultimate destination, as much as it was on the first-time experiences of the moment.

The *Marine Falcon* featured few private cabins, and the expansive main decks were lined with hundreds of bunk beds to which 416 men were sent aft, and the remaining 299 women and children were allocated forward. The latter included those women with newborns who shared the private cabins with other young mothers.

These quarters were normally reserved for ship's officers. Fortunately, Julia, Marianna and baby Regina were among the few to be given shared accommodation with another young mother. It was not a ship originally intended to accommodate young families, but the ship's crew did their best to provide for the special needs of their passengers.

When the gangplank was raised and secured, the moorings were cleared and retracted for storage. Slowly and assuredly, the ship of freedom drifted away from the rubber bumpers of the concrete wharf. For most, it would be the last time these people would set foot anywhere in Europe again. What stood out at this suspended moment was the sad silence. Not a soul was present when the ship pulled away from the pier to wave a *Bon voyage* for the departing loved ones.

The banks of the Elbe River gently and inexorably guided the mighty ship toward the northern channel, signifying the decisive moment one leaves the past in its wake to begin a new and uncertain future. The open decks held as many refugees as was possible, each one staying topside until the blackness of night swallowed them whole; leaving final impressions of all that could have been; families of ancestors, lost loved ones… lost love. As long as land remained even barely in sight, the people stood on deck to the final minutes, sullenly watching their fading memories disappear into oblivion.

Within the hour, the *Marine Falcon* passed Cuxhaven, which was also cloaked in darkness, offering nothing more than the sparsely lit outline of the city. The voyage up the Elbe to the North Sea kept the attention of everyone, save for those unable to contain their growing hunger who already retired below deck for dinner.

As the ship cleared the mouth of the Elbe, its turbine engines audibly changed pitch, indicating the open throttle to the empty sea. Although it was getting late, the famished travelers remaining on the outer decks were eventually beckoned inside by the aromas from the kitchens below.

*****

Mostly standing height tables were mounted efficiently onto the floor in straight rows spanning the open dining area. It wasn't fancy or particularly inviting as a passenger cruise would have offered, but it was fully functional and never intended to impress. These passengers were nevertheless eagerly receptive to see the wholesome buffet tables replete with a variety of fresh fruits, fresh baked bread, an assortment of meats, and plenty of mashed potatoes.

As soon as their bellies were satisfied, for a random few, work assignments had been previously posted on the various bulletin boards at various locations around the dining area; generally allocating a few women to the kitchens and some men to clear tables and swab the floors. About the same time, bedsheets, blankets and stuffed pillows were distributed, and everyone busied themselves to contribute to whatever other routine tasks needed attention. Typical of these hardworking people, no one was looking for a free ride.

Within a very short time, the women and children settled in for the night, while the men congregated on the perimeter decks smoking their seemingly inexhaustible supply of cheap cigarettes, commiserating with friends from the camps, and anxious to meet anyone else seeking the company of strangers. Although it was an extraordinarily long day, the excitement to begin their journey made sleep a secondary consideration.

*****

As would be expected, Jan and Josef drew their usual gathering and met a few from other camps as well. Why would shipside be any less similar?

"Do you think Canada will be so different for us? I know we will still have to work hard. That's good for us all, but none of us speak Canadian. How will we know what to do?" asked Hermann. He was also from Wildflecken but lived in a different block than Jan.

"I expect the jobs will be simple enough. Farming and carpentry must be the same as in Poland. But I don't know anyone who speaks Canadian." Jan began to laugh and a few others joined in awkwardly, but clearly not understanding Jan's response. It had caught them by surprise. "I think we'll have a better chance to learn English there, don't you think? It's the same as the United States."

The group looked at one another and continued to mumble, but few comprehended Jan's jab at Hermann. They had the same concerns. None were the wiser. In any event it was a good laugh at Hermann's expense, but it was a moment indicating how very little they knew about the country they were about to enter. It did, however, set the tone for some light-hearted discussions.

The women were generally more timid than the men and didn't ask many questions. How many would stay together? Would they spend the rest of their lives living among strangers? They knew of many Poles and Russians who had tried to repatriate but had mysteriously disappeared and were never heard from again. Would Canada swallow them up in the same way, never to be heard from again?

These were some of the common concerns for those unafraid to ask, but for many they were simply incapable of conceiving questions, finding it difficult just to imagine what would become of them.

"Do you think Canadian women there will talk to us, or will we have to just stay together with other refugees? Other than me, few of us are any prizes," commented one of the still good-looking bucks.

"And what are your prizes, Anton?" quipped one of his friends. Whereupon Anton opened his jacket to lift his shirt, exposing his well ripped abdomen and proudly flexed his biceps for everyone to see.

"Here's a few!" A round of sarcastic whistles and hooting of encouragement followed.

"Don't be so fast, young fella. You know, there's a story about a young bull and an old bull, standing on top of a hillside looking down on the herd of cows below. The young one says, *Let's run down the hill and screw one o' them cows*. The old bull says, *No, let's walk down and screw 'em all!*"

The laughter grew louder still and as it did so, more men gathered around. Everyone enjoyed a few light-hearted laughs and had a good time. It was gratifying to leave their former worries behind them, at least temporarily.

*****

In the days ahead, routines on board became more established. Everyone was cooperative with each other and with the ship's crew, who kept busy with their usual maintenance and supervision of the ship. The crew had been increased minimally to handle and organize passenger services but relied heavily upon the refugees to provide some of the work it entailed. Despite this arrangement, the voyage still provided plenty of quiet time for most.

Meandering on the open decks helped the long days to pass, but only until the second week when heavy seas prohibited further topside gatherings. David's son, Sal, was always quick to give his point of view to almost anyone who wanted to listen. "How long do we have to stay below deck, Pa? It's been three days already and the storm is only getting stronger."

David was prompt to suggest, "None of us are enjoying this either, son. Ask me again in three more days and we might have the answer," David dismissively replied.

On the open North Atlantic, the storms in early spring often gathered strength rapidly, sucking up moisture until its fury peaked, tossing the massive ship as it drove straight into the increasingly powerful waves crashing against the bow, refusing to yield to the incredible force pounding it. Another clear demonstration of Mother Nature's astonishing power, on a scale none of the refugees had expected.

Keeping the inexperienced passengers penned up in the holds below deck was necessary for everyone's safety but became problematic during the frightening days ahead. The tables and beds, while firmly secured to the floors, allowed for routine services to continue, but the passengers found it to be anything but routine. Many among them were hurled unsuspectingly against the walls when thrown from their feet by a rogue wave.

None of them had acquired their sea legs and would likely never have cause to do so again. Severe seasickness with vomiting and diarrhea were prevalent and in the close quarters, the tolerance of those so afflicted was pushed to new heights of degradation.

By the fourth day of confinement, as the roar of the raging winds and storming seas eventually calmed, the slow rolling and more tolerable rise and fall of the groaning ship assured those on board the *Marine Falcon* that everything remained in good order. When the main doors were finally unlocked, the inevitable rush to get topside was a grateful retreat from the reeking and putrid stench below.

Throughout the war, after the scarring and indescribable losses each one had endured both physically and mentally, the refugees' painful perspectives became more deeply ingrained with each passing day. They came to expect nothing more and learned to deal with the tedium shaping each refugee's common outlook.

The usual twenty-day voyage was extended two additional days due to the delay caused by the powerful storm. Nothing ever came easy for the refugees. Not the weather, not the politicians, not world opinion of them, never mind the impersonal and dismissive treatment they received from people they encountered along the way.

Their self-confidence and self-image had slowly been eroded over time, causing them to become predictably and passively acceptive of the steady stream of frustrations and unfairness inflicted upon them. No wonder many refugees considered themselves to be almost sub-human.

As further evidence of this malignancy, the first secretary of the Canadian High Commission John Holmes, stated the DPs *"who would be permitted to come [to Canada] would be selected like good beef cattle with a preference for strong young men who could do manual labor and would not be encumbered by aging relatives."* (J. Holmes)

Regrettably, these continual denigrating experiences would continue. By so doing, the disparagement many felt would become more firmly entrenched into their own self-deprecating images of low self-worth.

*****

On the afternoon of the twenty-second day since their departure, a damp, misty shroud had enveloped Halifax Harbor. From the decks and command center, visibility was zero in every direction. To the hundreds of anxious passengers, attention to their final destination had been imperceptibly lost by the seamless string of days, very boring days.

In reality it was the dizzying effect of the grey nothingness in which they lost all frames of physical reference. There was no bright panoramic view of Canada's colorful shoreline to be indelibly etched into the memories of these people, at least not this particular day.

The ship was noticeably slowing now, and deck crews began their appointed tasks along various station posts running the starboard length of the *Falcon*. The ship sounded the horn to signal the closing distance of the silently floating behemoth, responding in kind to the sound of intermittent bells clanging from the not-too-distant shore. The refugees quickly began crowding the decks, some of them, no doubt, to seek out the unfamiliar faces of family they had never met.

Sure enough, the faint outline of Pier 21 began to separate the gloominess of the cloak of fog and sea mist. To many, the lifting fog was seen as a positive omen when the view of the Canadian harbor fought its way out of the darkness of despair from which these refugees had been delivered. Their uncertain futures here were equally undefined.

Once moorings were properly secured, the heavy steel gangplank was lowered into position on the concrete dock with a sudden, resounding *thump*, announcing with finality the voyage was successfully ended, and new lives of ambiguous direction were just beginning.

ACKNOWLEDGEMENTS

This fictional story is loosely based upon the life, times and struggles of two Polish refugees who met, fell in love, and survived the Nazi menace during WWll to eventually prevail to begin new lives in Canada in 1950. While this saga is fictitious, it is based upon true events and circumstances we can only attempt to fully grasp. The inspiring account of my mother and father in-law referred to above, graphically describes historic events, many of which were endured by them personally. Numerous disturbing anecdotes and storylines throughout this incredible saga were in fact, the reality of millions of others in their own similar desperate situations.

Although this book is a heartfelt tribute to refugees everywhere, it focuses upon those tragically displaced people throughout Nazi occupied Europe during WWll; brutal oppression to never be repeated. Yet today, the senselessness of inhumane brutality continues to violate the innocent people of Ukraine despite the valiant defense of their homeland. Has humanity learned nothing from the grievous mistakes of the past?

I must specifically recognize the tireless and heroic workers of the United Nations Relief and Rehabilitation Administration (UNRRA) who provided humanitarian, life-saving support to the millions of displaced European survivors of the war. The incredible contribution of these determined but often overlooked workers, helped ensure hundreds of thousands of families could resettle on distant shores around the civilized world to rebuild the lives so ruthlessly taken from them. It is because of these unspoken heroes, men and women, that countless millions of their descendants continue to thrive to the present day.

For me personally, their courage and perseverance made it possible for my in-laws to give birth to their infant daughter, Regina, in a German refugee camp in 1949 in *Wildflecken*, Germany; a place not appearing on any map. Only months later, the family arrived safely in Canada to begin their new lives together. Almost twenty years later, Regina became my loving wife; a mother, a grandmother, and the love of my life for almost fifty years. I will be forever grateful to her parents, Jan and Julia Szymanski, for lovingly delivering her to find me.

I must also appreciatively acknowledge the never-ending support and encouragement given me by my dear family and friends, all of whom are descendants of immigrants. They have stood by my side throughout the course of my writing journey. I am indebted to them and my friend, Adrian Pryce, who has been unwavering in his guidance and support to positively ensure this saga would be told.

About the Author

James was born in Toronto and graduated from York University in 1978. Over the next thirty-five years he was a successful Chartered Life Underwriter and financial advisor. Shortly after his beloved wife Regina passed away, after almost fifty years together, James retired to begin his career as a novelist.

Tracks of Our Tears is the second of three volumes in a trilogy by the same name, in which he brings his amazing fictional characters to life by creatively weaving them throughout actual historic events.

He now resides in Milton, Ontario close to his daughter Jennifer, her husband Mark and their three young children.

CITATIONS
Tracks of Our Tears

REFERENCES

Beevor, Antony James.
n.d. https://en.wikipedia.org/wiki/
Royal_Society_of_Literature#Fellows.

Chanel, Coco. 1941. *Chanel wrote to
the government administrator charged
with ruling on the disposition of Jewish
financial assets.* May 5.

Haushofer, L. 2010. "The "contaminating agent" UNRRA, displaced
persons, and venereal disease in
Germany, 1945-1947." *Am J Public
Health* 993-1003.

Heifetz, Jascha.
n.d. https://violinspiration.com/
inspirational-quotes-by-musicians.

Holmes, John. 1948. "European
Refugees Begin New Lives in Post-
War Canada."

Hulme, Kathryn. 1953. *The Wild Place.*

Shubert Brothers.
n.d. https://www.wikiwand.com/en/
The_Shubert_Organization.

The Times. 1942. "Air Attack on
the 'Sharnhorst" and Gneisenau."
February 14.

von Stauffenberg, Colonel, and
Larry Slawson. 2022. July 1. https://
owlcation.com/humanities/Claus-von-
Stauffenberg-The-Plot-to-Kill-Adolf-
Hitler.

von Tresckow, General. 1941. https://
quotepark.com/quotes/1810538-
henning-von-tresckow/1941.

Source Notes

1/ en.wikipedia.org/wiki/Gleiwitz_
incident - Abwehr and SS forces
including Naujocks

2/ https://en.wikipedia.org/wiki/
Oskar_Schindler

3/ https://en.wikipedia.org/wiki/
Operation_Himmler

4/ https://en.wikipedia.org/wiki/
Brandenburgers

5/ https://en.wikipedia.org/wiki/
Peking_Plan British evacuation of
Polish destroyers from Gdansk

6/ https://encyclopedia.
ushmm.org/content/en/article/
invasion-of-poland-fall-1939

7/ https://en.wikipedia.org/wiki/
Battle_of_Hel

8/ https://www.pna.gov.ph/opinion/
pieces/169-japanese-invasion-on-ph-
77-years-ago-recalled

9/ https://en.wikipedia.org/wiki/
La_Pausa

10/ https://en.wikipedia.org/wiki/
Luchino_Visconti

11/ http://www.picturequotes.com/
arturo-toscanini-quotes

12/ https://encyclopedia.ushmm.org/
content/en/map/german-conquests-
in-europe-1939-1942

13/ https://www.jewishgen.org/yizkor/
ciechanow/cie001.html28/ Found in
Wikipedia under Rzymskokatolicki
Catholic Church in Opinogora Gorna

14/ https://en.wikipedia.org/wiki/
Polish_resistance_movement_in_
World_War_II#1941

15/ https://en.wikipedia.org/wiki/
Zofia_Kossak-Szczucka

16/ https://sprawiedliwi.org.pl/en/
news/120th-anniversary-birth-zofia-
kossak-szczucka

17/ https://en.wikipedia.org/wiki/
Polish_Righteous_Among_the_
Nations

18/ https://en.wikipedia.org/wiki/
Irena_Sendler

19/ https://www.iwm.org.uk/history/
what-were-the-baedeker-raids

20/ https://www.jewishvirtuallibrary.
org/the-379-egota

21/ https://www.historylearningsite.
co.uk/world-war-two/the-bombing-
campaign-of-world-war-two/
the-thousand-bomber-raid/

22/ https://www.holocausthistoricalso-
ciety.org.uk/contents/ghettosj-r/kutno.
html

23/ https://www.jpost.com/opinion/
columnists/world-war-ii-and-the-
impossibility-of-polish-history

24/ https://en.wikipedia.org/wiki/
Catholic_Church_and_Nazi_
Germany_during_World_War_II

25/ https://en.wikipedia.org/wiki/
Rescue_of_Jews_by_Poles_during_
the_Holocaust

26/ https://en.wikipedia.org/wiki/
German_resistance_to_Nazism

27/ https://www.smithsonianmag.com/
history/raf-buzzed-germany-drown-
out-nazi-broadcasts-180974966/

28/ https://www.britannica.com/topic/
Hitler-Youth

29/ https://www.msmnyc.edu/about/
history/virtual-yearbooks-1940s/

30/ https://en.wikipedia.org/wiki/
St._James_Theatre

31/ https://en.wikipedia.org/wiki/
Carnegie_Hall

32/ https://www.pbs.org/wnet/ameri-
canmasters/jascha-heifetz-biography-
and-timeline/3731/

33/ https://www.psaudio.com/copper/
article/mozart-string-quartets/

34/ https://shubert.com/the-history/
overview

35/ https://www.wikiwand.com/en/
The_Shubert_Organization

36/ https://www.juilliard.edu/school/
brief-history

37/ https://www.iowapbs.org/
iowapathways/artifact/impact-world-
war-ii-us-economy-and-workforce

38/ https://jaschaheifetz.com/about/
biography/

39/ It was never a Nazi Orchestra: The
American Re-education of the Berlin
Philharmonic *Abby Anderton:* Volume
VII, Issue 1 Winter 2013

40/ http://www.bruceduffie.com/
rosenthal.html

41/ Symphonic music in occupied Belgium (1940-44): the Role of 'German-Friendly' Music Societies Written by Eric Derom Nd

42/ https://biblio.ugent.be/publication/8665594 (exploitation of classical music in occupied Belgium)

43/ S.O. Muller: Political Pleasures with Old Emotions? Performances of BPO in the Second World War

44/ https://en.wikipedia.org/wiki/Denmark_in_World_War_II

45/ https://en.wikipedia.org/wiki/Hans_Hinkel

46/ https://en.wikipedia.org/wiki/Reich_Ministry_of_Public_Enlightenment_and_Propaganda

47/ https://www.berliner-philharmoniker.de/en/titelgeschichten/20192020/times-of-crisis/

48/ https://en.wikipedia.org/wiki/Denmark_in_World_War_II

49/ https://www.classical-music.com/features/articles/what-happened-to-classical-musicians-during-world-war-2/

50/ https://encyclopedia.ushmm.org/content/en/article/reich-security-main-office-rsha

51/ https://www.greatsmallhotels.com/antwerp-boutique-hotels/de-witte-lelie

52/ https://en.wikipedia.org/wiki/Antwerp_Symphony_Orchestra#Vzw_De_Philharmonie_

53/ http://www.lvbeethoven.com/Oeuvres_Presentation/Presentation-Overtures-Egmont.html

54/ https://en.wikipedia.org/wiki/Christmas_in_Nazi_Germany

55/ https://www.history.com/news/the-nazis-war-on-christmas

56/ https://en.wikipedia.org/wiki/Catholic_Church_and_Nazi_Germany_during_World_War_11

57/ https://en.wikipedia.org/wiki/Claus_von_Stauffenberg#Activities_in_1939%E2%80%9319

58/ https://en.wikipedia.org/wiki/20_July_plot#Aftermath

59/ https://en.wikipedia.org/wiki/Pozna%C5%84_Cathedral

60/ https://en.wikipedia.org/wiki/Luftwaffe#Massacres

61/ https://en.wikipedia.org/wiki/Juvincourt_Airfield

62/ https://en.wikipedia.org/wiki/
Jagdgeschwader_52#Comma

63/ https://military.wikia.org/wiki/
Jagdgeschwader_52#Commanding_
officers

64/ https://military.wikia.org/wiki/
Operation_Barbarossa

65/ https://en.wikipedia.org/wiki/
Gerhard Barkhorn

66/ https://en.wikipedia.org/wiki/
Erich_Hartmann

67/ https://www.airspacemag.
com/military-aviation/
who-was-erich-hartmann-180975845/

68/ https://military.wikia.org/wiki/
Operation_Barbarossa#Germany_
plans_the_invasion

69/ https://weaponsandwarfare.
com/soviet-aircraft-of-operation-
barbarossa/

70/ https://en.wikipedia.org/
wiki/20_July_plot

71/ https://www.biography.com/news/
coco-chanel-nazi-agent

72/ https://en.wikipedia.org/wiki/
Bribery_of_senior_Wehrmacht_officers

73/ https://en.wikipedia.org/wiki/
List_of_assassination_attempts_on_
Adolf_Hitler

74/ https://en.wikipedia.org/
wiki/20_July_plot

75/ https://www.bbc.com/news/
magazine-28330605

76/ The German officer who tried to
kill Hitler by Alex Last, BBC World
Service Pub 20/07/ 2014

77/ https://en.wikipedia.org/wiki/
Friedrich_Olbricht

78/ https://en.wikipedia.org/wiki/
Erwin_von_Witzleben

79/ https://en.wikipedia.org/wiki/
Displaced_persons_camps_in_
post%E2%80%93World_War_II_
Europe

80/ https://www.history.
com/this-day-in-history/
adolf-hitler-commits-suicide

81/ https://encyclopedia.
ushmm.org/content/en/article/
world-war-ii-key-dates

82/ https://en.wikipedia.org/wiki/
Battle_of_Berlin

83/ https://en.wikipedia.org/wiki/
Rape_during_the_occupation_of_
Germany

84/ https://en.wikipedia.org/wiki/
Aleksandr_Solzhenitsyn#World_War_
II

85/ https://www.liberationroute.com/
pois/249/u-s-troops-occupying-berlin

86/ https://en.wikipedia.org/wiki/
Battle_of_Berlin#Aftermath

87/ https://www.bbc.com/news/
magazine-32529679

88/ https://www.newyorker.com/
culture/cultural-comment/the-disqui-
eting-power-of-wilhelm-furtwangler-
hitlers-court-conductor

89/ https://en.wikipedia.
org/wiki/Wilhelm_
Furtw%C3%A4ngler#World_War_II

90/ https://www.nytimes.
com/2020/08/14/books/review/
poland-1939-roger-moorhouse.html

91/ https://www.rferl.org/a/berlin-
a-city-of-rubble-after-the-war-and-
before-the-wall/30733579.html

92/ https://www.berlin.de/
berlin-im-ueberblick/en/history/
berlin-after-1945/

93/ https://www.theguardian.com/
books/2002/may/01/news.features11

94/en.wikipedia.org/wiki/
Displaced_persons_camps_in_

post%E2%80%93World_War_II_
Europe

95/ Echoes of Tattered Tongues:
Memory Unfolded by John Guzlowski

96/ In War's Wake: Europe's displaced
Persons in the Postwar Order, Gerard
Daniel Cohen

97/ The Wild Place by Kathryn
Hulme, Published 1953

98/ https://en.wikipedia.org/wiki/
Marie_Louise_Habets

99/ https://beinecke.library.
yale.edu/collections/highlights/
kathryn-hulme-papers

100/ *The Contaminating Agent,
UNRRA, Displaced Persons, and
Venereal Disease in Germany, 1945-
1947.* Lisa Hauschofer, MD

101/ https://www.britannica.com/
science/typhus

102/ https://encyclopedia.ushmm.
org/content/en/article/united-
nations-relief-and-rehabilitation-
administration

103/ https://en.wikipedia.org/wiki/
History_of_rail_transport_in_
Germany

104/ https://www.
exberliner.com/berlin/
the-women-who-raised-the-rubble/

105/ https://www.baltimoresun.
com/news/bs-xpm-1994-09-01-
1994244045-story.html

106/ https://www.bbc.com/news/
magazine-32529679

107/ https://www.ncbi.nlm.nih.gov/
pmc/articles/PMC2866594/

This untouched photograph of nature was a one in a trillion image I captured on film, when I was alone, walking near my home around the Mill Pond in Milton. It was a sunny August day when I noticed a beam of light shining through the leaves, tree branches and scattered cloud cover. I photographed the beam of light and tried to take several shots. Unknown to me, the memory of my camera was full. I could only take a single picture.

Later that day when I opened my laptop, I was shocked at the image before me. In the center of the upper third of the photo, was the distinct image of an old man's face. I could clearly distinguish his balding forehead, both eyes, his left ear, the nose, cheekbones, and white beard. The ray of light emanated directly from his right eye. For those who see the image, about half of those I've shown, they are incredulous, often emotionally overwhelmed. For others, they simply see a pleasant image of nature.

It was August 10, 2017, barely two hours after my wife's funeral; the reason I was alone at the time. I printed and framed the image and named it *The Face of God*. This implausible moment inspired me to write this trilogy. The astonishing photograph now serves as the stunning backdrop of the front and back covers of Book Two, *Tracks of Our Tears*. I hope you are among those who are deeply touched by this photograph as I was. Enjoy!